The DI Tremayne Thriller Series: Books 1-3

Death Unholy

Death and the Assassin's Blade

Death and the Lucky Man

Phillip Strang

Copyright Page

Copyright © 2017 Phillip Strang

Cover Design by Phillip Strang

All rights reserved. No part of this book may be reproduced, stored in a retrieval system, or transmitted in any form or by any means (electronic, mechanical, photocopying, recording or otherwise) without the prior written permission of the publisher, except by a reviewer who may quote brief passages in a review to be printed by a newspaper, magazine, or journal.

All characters appearing in this work are fictitious. Any resemblance to actual events, locales, or persons, living or dead, is coincidental.

All Rights Reserved.

This work is registered with the UK Copyright Service
ISBN: 9781973511335

The DI Tremayne Thriller Series: Books 1 - 3

Death Unholy

Chapter 1

'What do you know about spontaneous human combustion?' Detective Inspector Keith Tremayne asked.

'You mean when someone catches on fire for no apparent reason?' Sergeant Clare Yarwood replied. They had not been together for long as a team, the gnarled and worn-out inspector heading towards retirement and the fresh-faced twenty-six-year-old.

'That's the one.'

'Nothing. I've read about it. Who hasn't?'

'I haven't,' Tremayne replied, which did not surprise his sergeant. In the time they had been together, she had come to realise that he was a man who had little interest in the world. A cigarette in his mouth, a beer in his hand and a murder to solve was about the happiest she ever saw him, and even then he could hardly be regarded as one of life's most sociable. And as for reading? The occasional police report, an early morning newspaper, the back pages for the racing results.

'Why the interest?'

'We've got one.'

'Where?'

'Up Castle Road.'

'And who says it's spontaneous human combustion?' Clare Yarwood responded more brusquely than she would have six months previously, but that was how DI Tremayne liked his conversations.

He had made three facts clear when she had been first foisted on him: firstly, he had told Superintendent Moulton that he worked alone, secondly he did not need a wet-behind-the-ears female holding him back, and thirdly, if she had anything to say, to get to the point, no peppering the conversation with fancy words.

Regardless, she had warmed to the man behind a gruff Cornish exterior: he had grown up in St Ives, nearly two hundred miles to the west of the cathedral city of Salisbury, where he now lived. She had been naïve when she had first entered the police station on Bemerton Road, but he had soon put her straight. Clare was a tall, dark-haired woman, and most men came up to her shoulder which made it hard for her to find a boyfriend. She had taken a shine to one of the young detective sergeants, but so far he had not responded to her hints. She knew the problem: her upbringing in a wealthy family in London which had instilled the virtues of being ladylike, not imposing herself on others. She wanted to go up to the DS and tell him that he was missing out on a good thing, namely her.

'That new crime scene examiner, that's who said it was spontaneous human combustion. Another one who is wet behind the ears,' Tremayne replied.

The young sergeant knew who he was referring to. She knew it was DI Tremayne's Cornish humour, but it still carried an insult. She shrugged her shoulders before replying. 'He's been to university, got a degree.'

'What bloody use is that? We used to keep the law, sort out the villains without any fancy piece of paper. Back then, kick up the arse and a slap round the head. Now I can't even talk to them without receiving a reprimand.'

His partner smiled quietly to herself. She knew his idea of talk: pinning a hapless individual, threatening to slam him in jail and throw away the key if he did not confess. She also knew that most did, as Keith Tremayne was an imposing presence at over six feet four inches and solidly built; not fat, more like a rugby team's prop: muscular, square and intimidating.

Tremayne and Clare made the trip out to Castle Road. It wasn't far, only a few miles, but it was mid-afternoon and the traffic was building. Tremayne remembered when he had first come to Salisbury, a small country town of just over thirty thousand people, the centre overlooked by the spire of Salisbury Cathedral, the tallest in Europe. Back then everyone seemed to know everyone, but now with the high-speed rail link to London, it was full of people making the daily commute up to the capital after being forced out by the exorbitant price of property, not that Salisbury was much cheaper. Most people visiting the city back then, even today, did not know much about it other than it was only eight miles from Stonehenge, a Neolithic monument to an ancient people. Tremayne had visited it, only seen a pile of big stones, but then he had no interest in the past, other than when it related to a horse he fancied that was running.

Tremayne knew what he was and it did not bother him. The others may be there with their laptops and their smartphones SMSing each other using their disjointed language, but if you wanted to talk to him, you phoned his old Nokia. He'd read the messages, but he'd never send one back. Clare Yarwood had tried to bring him up to date, but she had given in soon enough, and she was a tenacious woman.

'Where's the body?' Tremayne asked once he had entered the house, a substantial two-storey detached building.

'Upstairs in the bedroom,' Jim Hughes, the crime scene examiner, said. He was a young man, a few years shy of forty, and although he had blended in well at the police station, Tremayne still had his reservations; anyone younger than fifty was suspect to him.

'Are you up to this, Yarwood?' Tremayne asked. She had told him to call her Clare, but that wasn't his style. She knew that he liked her in his own peculiar way, but there was no way he intended to let his guard down.

'If you are, guv.'

'It might turn your stomach,' Hughes advised.

'Not me,' Tremayne replied with his typical dismissive manner towards juniors, especially juniors who were drawing a bigger salary than him, which excluded Clare Yarwood as she was paid a pittance, barely enough to pay the rent on her one-bedroom flat and to feed two cats. Still, she had no intention of complaining. Her parents had given her the opportunity to join the family business, a hotel they owned, but she had declined. The idea of sitting behind the reservations desk, ensuring the linen was regularly changed, was anathema to her. She had avidly watched the British cop shows on TV ever since she was young, and she was where she wanted to be, even if balancing the budget could be difficult, and another dead body would give her the creeps. She remembered a body they had fished out from the river three months earlier; accidental drowning as it turned out, but it had been trapped in the reeds that lined the banks on either side. After two weeks, the once pretty female was not easy to look at, and then to add insult to injury, Tremayne had insisted that she accompany him to the parents' house to tell them that they had found their daughter.

'You can do it,' he had said on the way over.

'I'm not sure if I can.'

'I'm throwing you in the deep end on this one. It's not all fun in the police service. We've all learnt to do it.'

She remembered how she fumbled, how her legs shook and her stomach rumbled when she told the parents. The mother broke down in tears; the father remained stoic.

Outside, Tremayne gave his assessment. 'You did well. Better than me the first time. From here on it's your job.'

Clare had smiled meekly in return. 'Thanks.'

'My pleasure.'

The two police officers at Castle Road ascended the stairs, the CSE in front.

'What can you tell us about the deceased?' Tremayne asked.

'The man's name was Eric Langley. Not a lot more to tell at the present moment. Reclusive by all accounts.'

'How do you know that?'

'The man had a nurse. She found him.'

'Where is she?' Clare asked.

'She's next door.'

'Uniform with her?'

'Of course.'

At the top of the stairs, the three turned to their left. A smell of burnt flesh pervaded the air. Clare held a handkerchief to her nose.

'You're wasting your time,' Hughes said. 'Wait until you get in the room.'

Tremayne entered first. 'Jesus,' his first word. 'I've not seen anything like it before.'

'I warned you.'

'Yarwood, you'd better not come in if you're squeamish,' Tremayne advised.

Even from where she was, Clare could smell death, and it was not pleasant. She knew what her reaction would be before she entered, but she was a police sergeant, and it was her job. She intended to go in regardless of her inspector's warning. She rounded the door into the room. In front of her was a large four-poster bed. It looked antique. To one side there was a dressing table with various medicines in bottles on the top. A portable oxygen tank stood on the floor close to the bed.

'It's over here,' Tremayne said.

Clare looked around at a bay window with a view overlooking the park. She could see a comfy chair.

'You need to come around here,' Hughes said.

Clare walked around the chair, subconsciously averting her gaze, consciously unable to. 'Oh my God!' she exclaimed.

The back of the chair had looked relatively intact, although old and worn. At the front, all that remained of the man was a residue of greasy and fetid ashes.

'Have you looked down yet?' Tremayne asked.

Clare knew she had intended to be brave but was failing. 'Not yet.'

'You're here. You can't avoid it.'

The young police officer looked down. 'Oh my God. It's too horrible.'

'At least you haven't thrown up,' Hughes said.

'Did you?' Tremayne asked.

'One of the others did, and the nurse was in a frightful state.'

On the floor in front of the chair, perfectly positioned, were a pair of shoes and black socks. And in the socks and shoes were two white legs, but further up nothing except ash and an offensive odour. Clare noticed that even the shine remained on the black leather shoes.

'Spontaneous human combustion. Is that your professional opinion?' Tremayne asked.

'That's what it's described as, although I don't hold with it.'

'Why?'

'No scientific proof.'

'Can we talk somewhere else?' Clare asked.

'You called it spontaneous human combustion,' Tremayne said when they were back outside the house.

'It's the only explanation that fits,' Hughes admitted.

'What do you mean?' Clare asked.

'Firstly, it's rare. Maybe one or two cases worldwide every five to ten years, no more than two hundred in total, so there's no precedence, at least to conduct forensics.'

'Why?' Tremayne asked.

'This is what I reckon happened,' Hughes said. 'The man fell asleep with a lighted cigarette. The cigarette then dropped down and set his clothes alight.'

'That would burn the room down,' Clare said.

'It depends on the clothing.'

'Okay, he burns to death, but what we just saw?'

'What you saw was the result of the man's subcutaneous fat acting as a candle wick. Do you have any idea of how hot the temperature would be?'

'You're the scientist. You tell us,' Tremayne barked at the man.

'There was one case in America where they recorded the woman's temperature at around 3500 degrees Fahrenheit. What they believe happens is that the clothing catches on fire which triggers the release of the body's fat, and the body effectively smoulders at incredible temperatures. As you can see, there's no sign of bones, not even a head. Teeth will disintegrate at around 1800 degrees Fahrenheit.'

'Which means,' Tremayne said, 'if it were a cigarette, there wouldn't be any evidence.'

'Precisely. What do we know about the man?' Hughes asked.

Clare, who had been listening intently, attempting to forget what she had witnessed upstairs, answered. 'We're going to interview the nurse, but the little we've gathered is that the man was in his seventies, mainly bed-ridden.'

'Obese, alcoholic?' Hughes asked.

Judging by the size of the gin bottle in here, he was probably a heavy drinker,' Tremayne said.

'It's classic.'

'What is?' Tremayne asked.

'Virtually all documented cases involve someone who is either chronically alcoholic, obese or elderly. In this case, we probably have all three.'

'Fair enough. A preliminary report on my desk tonight. Is that clear?' Tremayne said.

'No problems, but I won't be able to tell you more than I've said already. We'll conduct the standard tests, but don't hold out hope for too much.'

'Is it murder?'

'Impossible to say, but I'd say no. I could be wrong there, of course, but what you saw is not easily planned. And then why? The man was old and immobile, a pillow over the face would have done the job.'

***

'I didn't like the man, so don't go offering your condolences to me,' Langley's nurse said.

'What can you tell us about him?' Tremayne asked. They had met the nurse in the front room of the house next door.

'He smelt, never took a bath, and his manners were atrocious,' Mavis Godwin, the nurse, said. Clare estimated her to be in her mid-fifties. She was matronly in appearance, her hair tied in a severe bun at the back.

'How long were you his nurse?' Tremayne asked.

'Three years.'

'Why did you stay if you did not like the man?' Clare asked.

'Someone's got to pay the bills. Every time I went near him, he wanted to start grabbing me.'

'What did you do?'

'Pushed him away, but he was strong.'

'We're told that he was obese and bed-ridden.'

'Obese like a pig and bed-ridden, I suppose he was.'

'What do you mean?'

'He could find his way to that chair, and if I had relented, he would still have managed.'

'Sexually active?'

'Not with me he wasn't.'

'With others?'

'I wouldn't know.'

'Do you live in the house?'

'Not me. I've got a cottage down in Stratford sub Castle.'

'We need to meet with anyone who he came into contact with. Do you know who visited him?'

'You don't want to meet them.'

'Why?' Tremayne asked.

'Nobody's told you?'

'Told us what?'

'I'm regular every Sunday at church. What you're asking me to talk about is evil,' Mavis Godwin said.

'We need to ascertain the cause of death.'

'It's them, that's what I reckon.'

'Them. What do you mean?'

'I'm saying no more. They could do it to me.'

'One last question. Did Eric Langley smoke?' Tremayne asked.

'The only thing we could agree on,' the nurse replied. 'He hated them as much as I did.'

Chapter 2

'You went easy on the woman,' Clare said back at Bemerton Road Police Station. It was late afternoon, and she was sitting in her senior's office. She had heard him complain about the size of it enough times, but it was better than hers; all she had was a desk in an open-plan office and a laptop.

'What did you expect me to do?' Tremayne replied. 'We questioned the woman, saw the body, or at least what remained, and spoke to the CSE. And what do we have?'

'No clear evidence of murder.'

'Precisely, and according to Hughes we're unlikely to have any either.'

'You don't believe this spontaneous human combustion theory, do you?'

'Yarwood, how long have you been with me?' Tremayne responded curtly.

'Nearly six months, guv.'

'Six months and you've gone from wet behind the ears to mildly useful.'

'Mildly?'

'Don't think you're there yet. It takes years to acquire the sixth sense.'

Clare knew what he was talking about. 'You think it's murder?' she asked.

'Bodies don't just catch on fire and burn to a cinder, I know that. How and why, I've no idea, but there are human hands behind the man's death,' Tremayne said, his gaze fixed directly on his sergeant.

'But with no proof of murder, we can't open a murder case.'

'I know that.'

'Which means?'

'We start digging. Find out what we can about this man, and what the nurse said.'

'What about Superintendent Moulton?'

'What about him? And besides he doesn't have the sixth sense, never will.'

'He could put me in another department if there are no murders to solve,' Clare said.

'I'll deal with Moulton,' Tremayne replied. 'Do you prefer to stay here?'

'Of course. You're a great mentor.' Clare smiled.

'Mentor, don't talk rubbish. I'm a cantankerous old sod who smells a rat, that's all.'

'As I said, guv. A great mentor.'

'There's still hope for you. In the meantime, before our illustrious detective superintendent deems to make his presence known, I suggest that you and I make ourselves scarce.'

'Revisiting the crime scene?'

'Not me. And besides, a pub's a good place to do some research.'

'The nurse's comment about "them"?'

'We need to know what she meant. I'll shout you a pint,' Tremayne said. It was the first time she had been invited. She knew she could not say no, although she'd only drink one beer.

'Fine, guv.'

'Okay, the Deer's Head in thirty minutes.'

'Great. It'll give me time to go home and feed the cats,' Clare said.

***

Clare Yarwood had managed to find accommodation not far from the police station. It was neither luxurious nor cheap, but it was within the constraints of her financial remuneration as a police sergeant. She had joined the police force five years previously at the age of twenty-one. The physical requirements on applying presented no problems as she had played basketball at school and had been the school record holder in the high jump, not surprising given her height. Keith Tremayne was one of the few men that she looked up to physically. Her height had always embarrassed her, and it did the first time she entered the main door at the Deer's

Head, Salisbury's oldest pub – she banged her head on a low beam as she walked in.

'Watch yourself there, luv,' the red-faced publican shouted. All the people in the small bar looked around to take in the spectacle. Clare felt her cheeks flushing.

'Over here, Yarwood,' a voice shouted.

Clare moved away from the door and the man who had had a laugh at her expense and over to where her guv was sitting. 'A pint of the best?' he asked.

'Only a half,' she replied.

'Give Yarwood a half,' Tremayne said to the man behind the bar.

'If she's a friend of yours, Tremayne, it's a pint on the house.'

'Yarwood, I'd like you to meet our genial host, Harry Holchester. Harry, this is Yarwood, sorry, Clare.'

'Pleased to meet you,' Holchester said. 'Sorry about the comment when you came in. You're not the first one to have banged their head on that beam. I've done it a few times myself, especially after a few pints.'

Clare looked up at the man as he brought the pint over to her. She could see what he meant; he was taller than her, maybe even taller than Tremayne. She noticed that he was no longer red in the face, which she had initially assumed was the result of too much drinking.

'Yarwood's working with me,' Tremayne said.

'Is he as awkward up there as he is here?' Holchester asked.

'He's winding you up,' Tremayne said. 'Take no notice.'

'He's a gentleman,' Clare replied with a smirk across her face.

'For Christ's sake, don't tell Harry that. He thinks I'm a right bastard.'

'Sorry, Harry. I was just being polite.'

'That's fine. Then I'll have no more sleepless nights over watering his beer.'

'Harry, have you got a moment?' Tremayne asked.

'I can give you a couple of minutes.'

Harry Holchester, the jovial landlord, sat down. Clare could see that he was still a young man, not much older than her. She assumed he was not the owner of the establishment as it must have been worth millions.

Harry sat down next to Clare. 'What is it you want to know?'

'You've lived here all your life, haven't you?'

'I was born not far from here. Our family history goes back generations.'

'You've heard of the death up Castle Road?'

'Langley?'

'Yes, Eric Langley. What can you tell us about him?'

'I would have thought the police would have more knowledge than me.'

'We know the normal: his age, his wealth, his military background, family.'

'What else is there?' Harry asked.

'What sort of man was he? Was he religious, friendly?'

'I haven't seen him for years, but from what I can remember, he was agreeable. He'd come in here for the occasional pint when my parents were running the pub.'

'They're not now?' Clare asked.

'Two years back, a car accident.'

'Oh, I'm sorry.'

'No need to be. Time moves on.'

'His death is suspicious,' Tremayne said, returning to the subject. He had seen Harry Holchester eyeing up Yarwood; Yarwood eyeing up Holchester. Not that he minded, as he liked them both, but there were more important matters to address.

'What do you mean?'

'We're unable to determine a cause of death.'

'He could just have died. He was not in the best of health from what I've been told.'

'That's true, but something's not right, and there was a comment from the person who found him.'

'What sort of comment?'

'That he had died as a result of foul play.'

'What did this person say?'

'The person referred to those responsible as "them". Does it mean anything to you?'

'Not to me, it doesn't. You think Langley's death is sinister?'

'It could be an accident.'

'But you think it's murder?'

'The death was unusual.'

'I can't help you anymore, and besides, I've got customers to serve. If they're not drinking, I'm not making money.'

Harry Holchester left Tremayne and Clare alone. 'What did you think of Harry's answers, guv?'

'It's still murder' Tremayne answered.

'There's not much we can do until we hear from the CSE.'

'We could still have another pint.'

'I'd still rather have a half, guv.'

'You'll not make inspector if you can't drink your pints of beer.'

'I could become the first teetotal detective inspector.'

'Now there's a depressing thought. Even worse than what we saw with that body today.'

***

The following morning, Jim Hughes, the CSE, was in Tremayne's office. He was bright-eyed, which could not be said of the two police officers he met. Tremayne had downed seven pints, Clare had kept it to three. She had intended drinking two or three half pints and leaving, but unexpectedly Harry Holchester had come into her life. She knew that the detective sergeant that she had fancied was out of the picture.

'It's not good news, I'm afraid,' Hughes said, knowing full well that Tremayne wanted a murder.

'Accident?' Tremayne said, looking at him through blood-shot eyes.

'We know that the man was obese, a body mass index of over 30.'

'How?' Clare asked, her voice still rasping from the effects of the night before. 'There wasn't much left of the man.'

'His doctor gave us all the information that we wanted.'

'What else?' Tremayne asked.

'Langley had a problem with alcohol and his liver was not in good shape. Also, his heart was weak. According to the doctor, it was a wonder he had lived so long.'

'Is there any more?'

'I can't record a cause of death, other than to offer various options.'

'And those options?' Clare asked. She was sucking a strong mint, hoping to reduce the taste of stale beer in her mouth.

'The man set himself on fire, and that a combination of alcohol and body fat contributed to the body's destruction.'

'Your conclusion?' Tremayne asked.

'The man died in mysterious circumstances. Without a body, we can't give a precise evaluation. We can only record the facts. Until I receive advice to the contrary from Forensics and Pathology, his cause of death will be recorded as accidental death by burning.'

'Not very satisfactory, is it?' Tremayne said.

'I can't make up a story to fit what you want to believe. My job is to give a professional opinion. If you want to make out a case for murder, you'll need to find a motive and a perpetrator.'

Tremayne did not appreciate the lecture.

Hughes left the office.

'What do you think?' Clare asked.

'It's still murder. I know it is,' Tremayne replied.

'But you can't prove it.'

'If I find the murderer, I can.'

'And how do you intend to do that?'

'The nurse knows something. We need her to talk.'

'If she won't?'

'We'll look somewhere else. The truth's out there, I know it is.'

'And Detective Superintendent Moulton?'

'He can go to hell,' Tremayne replied.

'I can't ignore him,' Clare said.

'Do you want to be an inspector or just someone who sits in the office filing reports?'

'An inspector.'

'Then stick with me. The world is full of self-serving, sanctimonious bastards like our superintendent. There are not so many good police inspectors. Stick with me, and I'll make you one.'

Clare Yarwood knew the choice she was going to make.

Chapter 3

Stratford sub Castle, a small village no more than thirty minutes' walk from Langley's house, was picture perfect. Clare had driven through there a few times and loved the place. Tremayne had a house in Wilton, not far from Salisbury, and it suited him fine. He had no time for more than minimal housekeeping and the only time Clare had been there she had wanted to tidy up for him. She resisted, knowing full well what the man's reaction would be. She had to admit that whereas her inspector was devoid of social graces and ambition, apart from his wish to become a detective chief inspector before he retired, he was a man comfortable in his skin. Not for him the worry of a better car, a better house, more expensive clothes, a trip overseas.

He had made it clear on one of the few occasions when he spoke about himself that all he wanted was a television, a phone to place bets, and the chance to visit the local racecourse out past Netherhampton, a twenty-minute drive. Not that Clare understood the fascination. She had ridden when younger, but the last horse had thrown her off, and she had no intention of repeating the experience. Still, if that was what he wanted, she thought, then it was not for her to change him, and she had to admit that he was an excellent detective. She knew the others at Bemerton Road Police Station would have taken Jim Hughes's report and filed theirs alongside: case closed. But that was not Tremayne's style, and she appreciated it.

In her youth watching all the cop shows on television, there was always the relentless searcher for truth, the rough diamond, and whether wearing an old raincoat or a hat skewed sideways, the detective was always a little eccentric, and she had decided that Keith Tremayne indeed qualified. If the man were house proud and cared about his appearance or what others thought of him, he would not have succeeded. Clare wondered if she was acquiring the sixth sense, that ability to sense the truth, but discounted it. She knew what she sensed: the pretence of being welcome in the nurse's small cottage when clearly they were not.

'Come in,' Mavis Godwin said as she invited them into her small thatched cottage. It was clearly old, built more than three hundred years ago when people were a lot shorter. Both she and Tremayne had to stoop to enter, and neither had been able to stand up straight since.

'I'll put the kettle on,' the nurse said. She was a lot calmer than the previous day. Tremayne could see a man out in the garden with a spade in his hand. 'Your husband?' he asked.

'That's Trevor. He doesn't hold with strangers.'

'Will he be able to help us with our enquiries?'

'And what enquiries would that be? He never met Mr Langley.'

'You called him only by his surname yesterday,' Clare said.

'I'm just showing respect for the dead, I suppose. The man's no longer here to answer for his sins. His maker will deal with him now,' Mavis Godwin said.

'Is your husband religious?' Tremayne asked.

'Trevor? He comes with me every Sunday, but I don't think he is.'

'Then why go?' Clare asked.

'If he doesn't, I'll nag him all week. One thing he doesn't like is unpleasantness.'

'Mrs Godwin, you implied that Eric Langley had not died from natural means.'

'What else could I think? You saw the man. The work of the devil, if you ask me.'

'Is that a religious view, or do you know something?' Clare asked. An old cat had jumped onto her lap.

'I did my work for that man and left. He paid me every Friday without fail. I've no complaints.'

'Langley wasn't religious, was he?' Tremayne asked. He noticed the cat on Yarwood's lap, pleased it hadn't come near him.

Mavis Godwin sat down, having forgotten to bring the two police officers a cup of tea. 'He didn't believe in the good Lord,' she said.

Tremayne noticed the religious references. He hoped his sergeant had as well. 'What did he believe in?'

'He never spoke to me about the subject. If he was in one room, I was in another, apart from the times when I had to change his bed.'

'And then?'

'He was always too ill to move. I told you he was a pervert. He wanted me, but I'm not like that. I made a vow to God to cherish my husband, to only serve him.'

'And have you?' Clare asked, remembering the woman's scathing comment about her husband the previous day.

'I have upheld my vows if that's what you mean?'

'Yesterday, you were critical of your husband.' Clare decided to remind the woman.

'Trevor's not much good for anything. Odd jobs here and there, but no more. That's why I worked for Mr Langley.'

'Even though you did not like the man.'

'It would be uncharitable for me to comment further.'

'Unfortunately, Mrs Godwin, it's necessary. Both my sergeant and I believe that Eric Langley's death is suspicious, but we can't prove it. You are the key to our enquiry,' Tremayne said.

'I've told you all I can. The good Lord will protect me if I say no more.'

'And if you do?' Clare asked.

'I'll say no more and wish you good day. I'll pray for your souls.'

'Will we need your prayers?' Tremayne asked.

'If you don't leave well alone, I don't think even the good Lord will be able to protect you.'

***

Clare had been unnerved by the small woman. Her parting statements had made her shiver as if someone was walking over her grave.

'The woman's a religious zealot. No wonder her husband kept his distance while we were there,' Tremayne said. He was in his favourite position, reclining in the corner of a pub; this time, the Bridge Inn in the Woodford Valley. Clare had secretly hoped he would have suggested the Deer's Head, another chance to meet up with Harry. He had phoned her that morning, and they had agreed to meet up that night. She was excited.

'Maybe, but she knew something. I could sense it,' Clare said, referring back to the woman's insistence on saying no more.

'You're not experienced enough for it to be the sixth sense,' Tremayne said in between sipping his pint. This time, Clare had been adamant that she was only drinking orange juice. She didn't want Harry thinking she was a lush, even if he owned a pub.

'It's a woman's intuition. Did you notice her husband watching us all the time? He gave me the creeps.'

'I'll grant you that. The man was menacing, not that he did anything.'

'So, where to from here?' Clare asked.

'For me, another pint. Are you going to stay with that orange juice?'

'Today I am. I'm going out tonight.'

'At least you'll be able to travel light,' Tremayne said.

'What do you mean?'

'You won't need to carry a brick in your handbag for him to stand on.'

'Sixth sense, is that it? Prying into my personal business.'

'A man's intuition. I saw you two making eyes at each other. I may be an old detective inspector, but I'm not blind.'

'You don't object?' Clare wasn't sure why she had asked Tremayne.

'Mind? It's none of my business. Just make sure you're in the office at 8 a.m. sharp tomorrow. We've got some digging to do.'

'Not with a spade, I hope.'

'Where we're going may be dirtier.'

'8 a.m. I'll be there,' Clare said. She could see that Tremayne had no intention of giving up even if there was no evidence, no gain to be made other than the personal satisfaction of a job well done.

***

Trevor Godwin stormed up and down the kitchen in the small thatched cottage. The man was livid. 'You know what happens to those who speak,' he said.

'It's a sin against the Lord.'

'That's as maybe according to you, but you know how they think.'

'I only worked for that man out of financial necessity.'

'Don't give me that nonsense. I pull my weight round here.'

'If you weren't so preoccupied.'

'Don't say it; don't ever say it,' Trevor Godwin said.

Mavis Godwin cowered in a corner, aware of what her disobedience would entail. She knew that she had not been so religious once, but now she could only place her trust in the Lord. She knew that he was her only saviour, not her husband, the man she now despised.

'I was upset.'

'With what?'

'With seeing that horrible man like that.'

'You were told to keep away, but what did you do? You disobeyed, and for that there is no excuse.'

'It is for you to protect me.'

'I can offer no protection. Those who disobey are destined to be judged.'

'Did that man?'

'Yes.'

'What did he do?'

'I'm not one of the elders,' Trevor Godwin said. 'I'm only a humble servant.'

'A servant to what? A malevolence that has no pity.'

'At least mine has form whereas yours is rooted in bronze age mythology.'

'Mine is benevolent; yours only controls by evil and mayhem.'

'We are a warrior race, forged in battle, not people who are subservient. We are the only true way. One day, when you have suffered enough, you will understand.'

'I'm suffering now,' Mavis Godwin said.

'Suffering comes from pain.'

The woman retreated from the room, knowing full well that the husband she had once loved, had relinquished all responsibility for her. She knew that her fate, whatever it was, would be determined by others.

The woman sat quietly for ten minutes before turning on the television. It was a programme about holidays around Britain. On the screen, it showed happy families going about their business. *If only they knew the truth*, she thought.

***

For once, Harry Holchester was not to be found behind the bar at the Deer's Head. He knew that Clare was special, which was why he had brought her to the Silver Plough in Pitton, a small village, five miles from Salisbury, along the London Road.

'I used to come here with my parents as a child,' Harry said. 'Back then, you could sit outside and have a ploughman's lunch, warm bread with a slab of cheese and pickled onions.'

'You have a restaurant at your pub,' Clare said. She had worn her best dress for the occasion and styled her hair. She knew she looked good: the intended effect.

'I'm greedy. I don't want to share you with anyone else.'

Clare felt a tingle throughout her body. She knew this was the man for her; she hoped the feeling was reciprocal. Both ate a traditional fish pie and drank a French Pinot Noir. By the end of the meal, both were over the legal limit for driving.

'If I drive, you'll have to arrest me, won't you?' Harry said.

'If I drive, I'll have to arrest myself,' Clare said in reply.

The evening was going well. Harry had told Clare that he had no one in his life; had not for several years. Clare told him that she had had a serious boyfriend when she was younger, but after two years they had drifted apart. Harry briefly touched on the night his parents had died, which brought tears to Clare's eyes. Harry had wiped them away, lingering long enough to kiss her gently on her lips.

The two left the restaurant after ten at night and strolled through the small village, aiming to sober up, attempting to prolong their time together. Harry dropped Clare off at her place at midnight. They parted with a long and intense kiss. She wanted him to come in but did not ask. She had had casual flings in the past; she did not want this relationship to be the same. She wanted this man long term.

Chapter 4

It was 8 a.m. and neither of the two police officers was in the best of shape, although Clare was the better. She had spent a sleepless night thinking about Harry; Tremayne had drunk a few too many beers the previous night and was feeling the after-effects.

Jim Hughes had filed his official report into the death of Eric Langley. Tremayne knew it was only a matter of time before Superintendent Moulton saw it. Tremayne knew he had to come up with something quick if he was to keep his sergeant with him, and himself focussed on the case.

A murder had been committed, a perfect crime with no motive, no apparent way of destroying a body, but somehow, someway, it had been achieved.

'Yarwood, you're always looking at that laptop. What do we have on Langley's death? Any other cases, any ideas on what we can do to prove this?' Tremayne said. His head throbbed, a sign of ageing, not that he was willing to admit it. In the past, he would have downed eight pints and been up the next day fresh as a daisy, but last night he had only drunk six, or maybe it was seven. It had been a good evening, he knew that. He had been sitting in the Greyhound Inn out in Wilton, not more than two hundred yards from his house. The television in the bar had been switched to the racing channel. He remembered placing a few bets, the one benefit of his phone. He had won on two races, lost on the third. Tremayne realised that with success comes celebration and he had probably drunk over his quota.

'There's not much on spontaneous human combustion. Several of the cases were found to have been caused by a naked flame catching the clothes on fire; other causes of death have been classified as unknown. None that I can see has resulted in a murder conviction,' Clare replied. She was glad to be back at work; her mind distracted from the publican at the Deer's Head. He had sent her an SMS that morning thanking her for the night, hoping to meet up soon. She hoped it wasn't the brush-off as the message had been brief and to the point; more the message of someone thanking out of politeness, not pleasure. She attempted to focus on the rasping voice of her senior. She could see he had had a hard night; yesterday's shirt testament to the fact.

'The man was murdered. Mavis Godwin knows that, and she's not talking. Any idea of what is frightening her?' Tremayne asked.

'You were there. What do you reckon?'

'No idea and that's the problem. What do we know about this woman? Any levers we can use to make her talk?'

'We could try pleading to her God,' Clare said. 'A word from him and she'd talk.'

'Get real, Yarwood. He'll not speak to me anyway.'

'Why's that?'

'Too much sinning,' Tremayne replied.

'Drinking too much and throwing your money away on horses are hardly sins.'

'Don't go lecturing. You're not my mother.'

Clare looked over at the man, knew that her outburst would cause no damage to their relationship. Tremayne, she knew, appreciated a partner who spoke back to him. The man did not like subservience. He had made that clear over the last few months when he had asked for her advice. He wanted her to question his analysis on a case, to throw in an alternative possibility

She knew one thing, that if she were his mother, she'd march him down to the barbers for a good haircut as well. She remembered how Harry Holchester had looked the night before: clean-shaven, his hair cut, a white shirt with a jacket. She looked over at Tremayne: his shirt collar skewed, his suit jacket hanging like a bag of potatoes, his two-day stubble showing.

If their detective superintendent came in, he'd have something to say. The man, Clare knew, was a stickler for punctuality and presentation, and whereas Tremayne was never immaculate, his appearance as he sat across from her was definitely seedier than usual.

'Anyway, coming back to my question before you started going on. How do we contact the woman's God?' Tremayne asked. He had enjoyed their banter, although he was not intending to give Yarwood the satisfaction of knowing that.

'We can talk to her vicar.'

'Good idea. Where is he?'

'I know she attends a church not far from where she lives.'

'Great, let's go. You're driving. Just take the long route via my house. I need to clean myself up. After an evening with the wondrous Harry, I must look to be a major disappointment.'

'You've not asked,' Clare said.

'It's none of my business. You're both over twenty-one, just. And besides, I can tell how it went by looking at you, all doe-eyed and dreamy.'

'Let's go,' Clare said. She did not want to indulge in further conversation on her love life, if indeed there was to be a love life. She knew she wanted to see Harry again, but he could not make it for another two nights. There was a publican's convention in London, and he needed to go.

***

Clare had to admit that the change in Tremayne's appearance had not been miraculous; he still looked the worse for wear, but the man smelt clean and the shirt was ironed, although the tie was still hanging at an unusual angle.

'How do I look?' he asked.

'You look great.'

'Up to Harry Holchester's standard?' Tremayne asked. Clare did not rise to the bait.

To the Reverend Jonah Harrison, a man in his sixties with greying hair combed to one side to cover a balding patch, St Lawrence's church represented sanctity, respite from a troubled world. 'What can I do for you?' he asked after the two police officers had shown their identification.

'We're investigating a death,' Tremayne said. He stood next to a bust of St Lawrence. Clare had read the plaque.

'Eric Langley?' the vicar asked.

'You knew him?'

'Not as a parishioner, but I've met him over the years.'

'What can you tell us about him?' Clare asked.

'Not a lot. I met him on various committees over the years.'

'Are you sad to hear of his death?' Tremayne asked.

'I am sorry to hear of one of God's children passing on.'

'We've been told that the man was not religious. In fact, he seems to have harboured some extreme views.'

'The Lord will forgive him for his pagan beliefs,' Harrison said. Tremayne could see where Mavis Godwin's religious zeal came from.

'Mavis Godwin said more or less the same. Where did she get this idea that telling us the truth about Langley would end in her death? From you?'

'She is a true believer in the one true God. She will be rewarded in heaven,' Harrison said. He stood close to the bust of St Lawrence and said a silent prayer.

As they stood there, Clare believed that she could feel the church walls closing in; the Reverend Harrison moved from holding the bust of the patron saint to clutching, and then grasping.

'Let's get out of here,' Clare said quietly to Tremayne; not that it mattered as the Reverend Harrison was no longer listening.

***

'I need a drink,' Clare said as soon as they were outside the church.

'Coffee?' Tremayne asked.

'Not this time. I need a stiff drink, whisky at least.'

'What is it?'

'Didn't you sense it?' she asked.

'He wasn't my idea of a parish priest. I'll grant you that.'

'The atmosphere in there. As if there was evil present.'

'There's no such thing.'

'Are you sure?' Clare asked. Fifteen minutes earlier she would have agreed with her senior, but now…

'In there, believe me, there was something, and it was evil.'

'Two stiff whiskies, Yarwood. You're scaring me now.'

***

A group of men met in another church, long since disused for its original purpose. It was night-time, and the village, no more than two hundred yards away, was shrouded in fog.

Trevor Godwin did not want to be there.

'Godwin, the police have spoken to your wife,' the senior elder said. Godwin looked up from his prostrate position to see the man who had spoken.

'She did not reveal what she knows,' Godwin said.

'What did your wife tell the police?' the third elder asked.

'I was not there.'

'Why?'

'I stayed in the garden.'

'We should make an example of both of them,' another of the elders said.

'She did not say anything. I'm certain of it.'

'The police have spoken to the priest.'

'Is he safe?' Godwin asked.

'We only kill out of necessity.'

'But you killed Eric Langley?'

'It was necessary.'

'What had he done? My wife asked.'

'You have spoken to her?' the second elder asked.

'No, but she suspects.'

'Godwin, the punishment has been decided.'

'It was decided before I came here, wasn't it?' Godwin said.

'How dare you come in here and question us.'

Trevor Godwin stood up and sat on a chair placed there by someone behind him. Godwin realised as he sat that he had not made much of his life. He knew he was trapped and that he had no option but to carry out their command.

Chapter 5

Thankfully, Keith Tremayne did not get called up to Detective Superintendent Moulton's office too often. Virtually every time it was a complaint or an ear bashing about his style of policing, or, as on the last occasion, to discuss an early retirement package.

He had dealt with all of those with his usual manner of deference coupled with a firm resolve, especially with the retirement package. Even Tremayne had been stopped in his tracks on that one, generous as it was, but as he had told his disappointed senior, what need did he have for retirement, and what was he going to do with his time.

His superintendent had suggested golf, fishing, travel. Tremayne had responded that he had no interest in walking around in the rain with a stick in his hand, and sitting by a river bank dangling a line held no allure. And as for travel, he'd been to France on a couple of occasions, and the last time he had come back with a nasty dose of food poisoning after eating some dodgy-looking frogs' legs. The superintendent had insisted with the early retirement package, but Tremayne had contacted the police union, and they had taken up his case. As far as they were concerned the retirement age for the general population was slowly moving up to seventy years of age. Tremayne thought that was a good time to retire. A time when he'd be happy to sit in the pub all day, or in front of the television at home, a beer in his hand as he watched the racing.

'Tremayne, what are you doing with this Langley case?' Moulton asked, after a perfunctory handshake.

'The CSE can't give a precise cause of death.'

'So, you assume it's murder?' Moulton was sitting behind his desk, Tremayne on the other side. Neither man liked the other, and they were not good at disguising the fact.

'I know it's murder,' Tremayne said.

'You're not going to tell me after your years of experience you can tell whether it's murder or not.'

'That's what it is.'

'But where's the evidence? You have an overweight old man with a dicky ticker and an affinity for alcohol. Why can't you accept that he died of natural causes?'

'Did you read Hughes's report?' Tremayne asked.

'I read the salient facts. The man fell asleep, his clothes caught on fire and he burnt to death.'

'With all due respect,' Tremayne said but didn't mean it, 'the man did not smoke, we found no evidence of any matches or lighters, and what about the body?'

'I read that. What does it mean?'

'I think it was evident enough.' Tremayne realised he was close to being impertinent.

'It said that the body had been consumed by the flames,' Moulton replied.

'Did you read that the body had been reduced to grease and ash?'

'That made no sense,' the Superintendent admitted.

'I saw it, along with DS Yarwood. The man wasn't there, only the bottoms of his legs with his shoes and socks still on. It wasn't natural.'

'Hughes explained that it's occurred before.'

'True, and he's right there. Yarwood checked on the internet, and there have been a few cases where no explanation was possible.'

'And this is one of these cases?'

'I believe so, sir. I need time on this one.'

'Against my better judgement stay with it, but if another murder comes in, I want you and Yarwood onto it. Is that agreed?'

'Yes, sir.' Tremayne left Moulton's office pleasantly surprised. He had expected an order to leave Langley's death to others to investigate, but the man had acquiesced to his request. He did not know why.

***

Tremayne made the trek back from his senior's office with its view of Salisbury Cathedral. For once, he would not refer to his office as the broom cupboard. He had had a win, and he was in a good mood, so much so that Clare almost made a comment.

'Yarwood, we've got work to do,' Tremayne said as he sat down behind his desk. He had brought a mug of tea with him. 'Get one for yourself,' he said.

Clare acceded to his command, although hers had no sugar, whereas his mug had two spoonfuls. 'What's the plan, guv?' she asked.

'We need to confirm Langley's death as murder.'

'But how?'

'Mavis Godwin, she's the key. She worked for the man for three years. She knows something or someone who may have had a grudge against the man.'

'There's something not right. You remember what I felt in the church.'

'I can't deal with that. Facts are facts, not the feeling that evil abounds. I don't like those places at the best of times. Okay for weddings and funerals, I suppose, but you'll never catch me in there against my will.'

'And when you die?' Clare asked.

'Take me out to sea and throw me over.'

'What do you want to do about Mavis Godwin?' Clare asked. 'You remember her husband last time.'

'We need somewhere neutral.'

'Not the church. I'm not going back there unless it's vital.'

'Yarwood, you're a police officer, been to college, have a degree, and you're still coming up with that. Seeing that body's given you these delusions.'

'I'm only saying it as it is. Maybe I'm wrong, and probably I shouldn't have told you.'

'Besides, the church is hardly neutral, not with the Reverend Harrison. I'll grant you that he was creepy.'

'What was he praying about while we were there?' Clare asked.

'Hell, how should I know? The man was a zealot, the same as Mavis Godwin. No doubt she prays to their patron saint every time she goes there. Maybe they pray together, holding hands, wrapped around each other?'

'That's a wicked thought,' Clare said.

'Why not? She can't be getting much action from her husband. The woman's frustrated, sees the church as her sanctuary, maybe the vicar as her consort. It wouldn't be the first time.'

'I know; I just don't want to believe it.'

'She's made of flesh and bone and complex emotions, the same as everyone else. If those emotions aren't being satisfied in one place, she'll get them met somewhere else. Yarwood, we're dealing with the real world here. People are people, good and bad, and we're exposed to the worst of the bad. Just get used to it.'

'I'll keep an open mind. Anyway, we still need to talk to the woman again,' Clare said.

***

'You don't understand,' Mavis Godwin protested when Clare phoned her early the next morning. A local uniform had checked that the woman's husband was out of the area.

'I don't want to do it, but I could make it official,' Clare said. She could hear the nervousness in the woman's voice at the other end of the phone.

'Come to the house, but don't bring your inspector.'

'Give me twenty-five minutes,' Clare said.

'If you must.'

'I'm sorry.'

Tremayne had been listening in on the conversation. 'Record what she says on your phone,' he said. 'I'll get some uniforms to keep a watch out for Trevor Godwin. He'll no doubt get upset if he sees you there.'

'If she's got nothing to say, what's the problem?'

'Don't be naïve, Yarwood. You know something's going on, the same as I do. The woman's involved. I don't know how and why, but she's involved, the husband as well.'

'What do we know about him, guv?'

'Not a lot. I've got some people compiling a dossier, but it appears that Mavis Godwin may be right. The man doesn't seem to do much, just a few odd jobs, helps out on some of the farms, but hardly any that qualify as a regular job. She needed Langley's money, that's plain to see. And be careful.'

***

Clare was aware that Tremayne's remark for her to be careful was out of courtesy, but she knew that danger existed. The woman who opened the front door of the thatched cottage may well prove to be innocent and harmless, but there were other forces at play. Clare had always been a sceptic, but that was being shaken now. Whenever her childhood friends had spoken of ghosts and evil spirits, she had passed them off as fanciful nonsense, but somehow the experience in the church had left her unnerved.

'My husband won't be back until late this afternoon,' Mavis Godwin said. Clare could see that the woman was more relaxed without her husband keeping watch.

Both women sat down in the kitchen of the house, each with a cup of tea. 'Mrs Godwin, we're not satisfied with the death of Eric Langley,' Clare said.

'You ask me questions I cannot answer. Believe me, if I could, I would tell you all I know.'

'Who scares you? Is it your husband?'

'There are others,' the woman said. Clare looked out the window. A storm was brewing.

'Was Eric Langley murdered?'

'You would not understand.'

'What do you mean?'

'Don't you sense it?'

'A police investigation cannot proceed to a conclusion based on hearsay and superstition.'

'It's not superstition. It's real.'

'Are you talking about biblical text?' Clare asked.

'Don't discount the good book. What it says in there is all true. I know it is.'

'How?' Clare asked, although she could sense the tension in the air. She put it down to the storm. It was almost dark outside, even though it was mid-morning.

'Evil lurks around every corner,' Mavis Godwin said. 'I cannot tell you.'

'And if you don't, I'll be going back empty-handed to an angry boss.'

'But your life will not be in danger.'

'Is yours?'

'Yes.'

'We can protect you.'

'Not from those who want me dead.'

'Who are they?'

At that moment, the storm clouds came in closer, enveloping the house. The sound of thunder could be heard.

'Go now, please. I've said too much.'

'It's only a storm.'

'Go, please go. I don't want you to suffer.'

'It's my job to ascertain the truth. Mrs Godwin, I need to know the truth about Eric Langley.'

'That's as maybe, but the needs of the living are outweighed by the vengeance of the dead.'

'Which dead?'

'You would not understand. I cannot protect you.'

'From what?'

'From that,' Mavis Godwin said, looking out of the window. At that moment, a lightning strike hit the cottage roof. 'Don't come here again,' the woman said.

Clare did not need the warning. She had no intention of returning. She phoned Tremayne. 'We'll not solve this by regular policing,' she said.

'What do you mean?' Tremayne asked. 'Where are you?'

'I'm outside the cottage.'

'I'll be there in fifteen,' Tremayne said.

'What's the weather like up there?' Clare asked.

'Clear sky. Why do you ask?'

'I'll tell you when you get here.'

***

A group of villagers convened later that night: a group that could lay claim to a lineage stretching back over the centuries. One man, who spoke with the voice of authority, stood where once there had been an altar. 'You, Trevor Godwin, have been found guilty by your peers.'

'I intended to do it, but the police were always there.'

'We know that you've lied. Your wife has spoken to the female police officer again. Do all those assembled agree with the verdict?'

Everyone shouted, 'Let the sentence be carried out.'

'No, please no,' Trevor Godwin pleaded. With no more delay, the man was bound with strong rope and dragged out of the building, his feet unable to support him. On the left-hand side of the church, the group entered a woodland. The anointed tree was chosen for its strength and its height, and not for the first time.

A rope was strung over the firmest branch. The other end was looped around Godwin's neck. 'Have you anything to say?' one of the elders asked.

'Spare my wife, please.'

'Her fate is out of our hands.'

The strongest five of the group then took hold of the rope and pulled back, the other members joining in. Trevor Godwin was drawn up high into the tree, his legs thrashing, his face distorting as the rope bit into his throat, cutting off his ability to breathe. After a few minutes, he was let down. 'They have been appeased,' the senior elder said. 'Bury him deep in the ground.'

A fine mist settled over the dead man's body. 'A good omen,' one of the group said. The others expressed their joy.

Chapter 6

Clare had never been one for sitting in a pub of a night-time, but that was before she had met Harry Holchester. He was back in Salisbury and behind the bar. He had been pleased to see her come in and made the pretence of showing her around the pub, even where the beer barrels were stored, and had taken the opportunity to grab hold of her.

'I missed you,' he said.

'Not as much as I missed you,' she said. The last few days had been rough for her and Tremayne, although more so for her as she firmly believed there was more than human involvement. Langley's death was still not confirmed as murder, and the police could not open a full-scale murder enquiry based on the aspersions of a woman who would only state that it was off the record, and then reluctantly.

Clare had phoned her up after the incident with the storm, and the woman was fine. 'The damage is only minor,' she said.

'Your husband can deal with it,' Clare said.

'He's not come back,' Mavis Godwin admitted.

'Is that unusual?'

'Sometimes he stays away for a few days. I'm not worried, glad of the peace to be honest.'

'You were frightened when the storm came,' Clare said.

'Don't you worry about anything I say. I'm just an old woman. Frightened of my own shadow sometimes.'

Clare knew the woman was lying. The woman had been terrified, the same as her.

'Are you free tomorrow night?' Harry asked.

'It depends on Eric Langley,' Clare replied.

Both were still down with the beer barrels. A voice could be heard from above. 'We could do with some service up here.'

'I'll need to deal with them,' Harry said. 'Tomorrow, is that okay?'

'Yes, of course.'

As they both emerged back into the bar, a cheer went up from the patrons.

'I didn't say a word,' Tremayne said. He was holding a pint of beer in one hand, checking a newspaper for the form of the next horse that was to lose his money. He remembered that once he had bet on a horse that never made it to the finishing line; it had keeled over halfway around, and had been removed by a front-end loader. He knew it was a foolish pastime, but he was not addicted. Only twenty pounds here and there, and on the whole he only lost a small amount each week, no more than five pints if it was equated to beer money.

'I'll take your word,' Clare said.

'All good with the young lovers, is it?' Tremayne said, barely lifting his head from his paper.

'Fine, if you must ask.'

'After you've calmed down, we can talk about the case.'

'There's nothing wrong with me.'

'If that's the case, just do up the top button of your blouse. It's a dead giveaway.'

'Is that why they cheered?' Clare asked, embarrassed that there had been more than a kiss. If it had not been for the thirsty people in the bar, she knew where their unscheduled tryst would have ended.

'No one saw. I'm trained to look for signs.'

'What signs have you seen so far in the current investigation?'

'I don't hold with this idea of the supernatural,' Tremayne said. He continued to study the horses as he spoke.

'Nor do I, or I didn't.'

'It was just a freak storm, they occur from time to time. If you check with any weather forecaster, they'll have a rational explanation for what happened at Godwin's cottage. Any sign of the missing husband yet?'

'We've got people keeping a watch out for the man.'

'Good. When they find Godwin bring him in for questioning. What do you reckon to Spooky Sue in the 2.30 at Newmarket?' Tremayne asked.

'That's the limit of your skills in picking horses? No wonder you've had such great success.'

'Don't go on, Yarwood. We're off duty. And no, that's not the limit of my horse picking skills. It's just that the name seemed to sum up the situation. You're spooked enough for the both of us.'

'I'm not spooked. I saw something that can't be explained. I saw a vicar almost comatose, a woman scared out of her wits.'

'The world is full of crazy people. Whatever happened to Langley, whatever scared Mavis Godwin and turned the vicar into a fruitcake, there's a rational explanation. There always is, and it's up to us to find it.'

'Yes, guv,' Clare said, although she wasn't so sure. She was only sure of one thing, she was falling in love with the friendly man behind the bar at the Deer's Head. She looked over at him; he smiled back.

***

In another pub, not so far away, a group of men sat in one corner. All of them were locals in the remote and lonely village, all of them well known to each other and to the community in general. They were professional men, law-abiding citizens, even church-goers when needed. They were not interested in horse racing, or world events, or whether Eric Langley had died by foul means or fair. They were only interested in the malevolence of which they had undeniable proof.

'Her fate is sealed,' the more senior of the group, a doctor, said. 'It is up to us to deal with Godwin's woman.'

Of the others in the group, one was a vet, one a butcher, and the final member of the quartet, a local farmer.

'And what of Trevor Godwin?' one of the group asked.

'His body has been given back to the soil,' the doctor said.

'We need someone to carry out the task,' the butcher said. During the day, he would be behind the counter of his butcher's shop dispensing meat to whoever came in: 'Two pounds of pork sausages, Mrs Entwhistle', 'I've got some nice beef steak put to one side for you today, Mr White'. In that small pub only frequented by locals, others discouraged by the unfriendly clientele once inside, the butcher, a dour man, did not talk about the best cut of meat or the best way to prepare a meal. He only spoke of a woman's death.

'We will let them decide,' the doctor said.

'How?'

'In the usual way.'

The word went around the pub. Silently the patrons filed out, carrying their glasses of beer. By the time they had covered the short distance to the abandoned church, their glasses were empty.

The doctor stood before the assembled group. He knew that they would support him whatever decision he made, and that dissension would not be tolerated.

'Fellow believers,' the doctor began, 'we have need of someone to deal with the nonbeliever. Who wishes to gain their favour?'

Nobody nominated themselves, most took a step back. The doctor took note of those who had seemed the most anxious to remove themselves from the task.

'We'll deal with them another time,' one of the elders said.

'Then we will decide.' The doctor pointed to a woman who had taken the first step backwards. All those close to her moved to one side.

The woman gently eased herself forward to the centre of the church. 'I'm not the best person. I'm only a woman.'

'You meet with her?'

'We are friendly.'

'You know what is required?'

'Yes.'

'And you know the punishment if you fail to complete the task?'

'Yes, I understand,' the woman said.

***

It had been six days since the storm and lightning strike at Mavis Godwin's cottage; almost seven since Trevor Godwin had been last seen. Clare Yarwood, as part of her responsibility as a detective sergeant, and also because she worried for the woman, kept in touch with Mavis Godwin, although she hadn't been near the cottage. She had been there that once, and no matter how much Tremayne told her not to worry, she did.

After the fifth day, Clare had issued an all points warning to be on the lookout for Trevor Godwin. Mavis Godwin had told her not to bother. Clare wanted to know why. She knew the woman would not tell her over the phone, and she would not talk in the presence of Tremayne. She knew what she had to do.

This time, there was no need to station a uniform outside to watch out for Trevor Godwin. If he turned up while Clare was at the cottage, so much the better. Tremayne wanted Clare wired this time so he could hear the conversation, and if the unknown occurred again, he wanted proof.

Clare agreed, knowing that Tremayne would be sitting in his car no more than two hundred yards from the cottage.

At 2 p.m. she drove from Bemerton Road Police Station to Mavis Godwin's cottage. She should have been thinking more about what was ahead, but she and Harry had met up again for a date, and that time she had not said farewell to him at her door; he had come in.

Mavis Godwin opened the door of the cottage. She was pleased to see Clare. 'Please come in,' she said. Clare saw that the woman was almost happy.

'Your husband?' Clare asked.

'He's gone,' Mavis Godwin replied.

'Where? Do you know?'

'I honoured the man while he was alive. God knows how much I suffered, but now I am free.'

'You sound as if you believe he is dead.'

'He is.'

Clare moved back in her chair, glancing outside at the sky. She had already told Tremayne that at the first sign of a cloud she was out of there.

'Do you have proof?'

'He disobeyed. That's all I know.'

'Disobeyed who?'

'Those that he had chosen to follow.'

'Are you saying they killed him?'

'Please be here as a friend, not a police officer. It is better for you to be ignorant of the truth.'

'But that's my job.'

'You are delving into something you don't understand.'

Clare took another glance through the window. It was still clear.

'What do you mean?'

'With goodness there is evil, with light there is dark. Have you not read the Bible?'

'When I was younger, but it only mentioned God as real, and Satan as a fallen angel.'

'There are others, not as powerful, but there are others.'

'Will your God protect you?' Clare asked.

'Your God as well. Remember that,' Mavis Godwin said.

'As you say.'

'My God will be there for me, for I will have stood up to the evil, looked it straight in the face.'

'Pardon my saying,' Clare said, 'but your belief in an all-powerful God is not common these days.'

'Before, I was not a believer.'

'What changed?'

'They changed me.'

'Who?'

'Please leave, Clare. I cannot tell you.'

'If I know, will I be marked?'

'If you act against them, you will be.'

'Who are they? Please tell me.'

Clare looked out of the window. Clouds were forming.

'You must go,' Mavis Godwin said.

'Tell me before I go. Are they mortal?'

'Those that carry out their work are.'

'Do you know who they are?'

'Oh, yes. Please go now. They are too powerful.'

'Your God?'

'We will need to suffer first.'

A rumble of thunder could be heard overhead. Clare's phone rang. 'Get out of there,' Tremayne said.

'Come with me,' Clare said to Mavis Godwin.

'No. This is my place. I'll not leave. My fate is sealed.'

Another rumble of thunder and Clare left through the front door. She gave the woman left behind in the cottage a hug.

Chapter 7

Two miles down the road towards the Woodford Valley, after the events at Mavis Godwin's cottage, Tremayne pulled the car over to one side. 'That was the damnedest thing,' he said.

'Now do you believe me?' Clare asked. She was still shaking.

'It'll take more than a few clouds to convince me.'

'Then why did you tell me to get out?'

'I knew you'd be frightened.'

Clare knew Tremayne was lying. He had seen the clouds, felt the tension in the air. He was more set in his ways than her, had more of an unshakeable belief that everything had a logical explanation, but what they had witnessed was not logical. She could see that Keith Tremayne, the hardened, cynical detective inspector, had been unnerved by the experience.

'What's next?' Clare asked.

'Trevor Godwin. What did you find out about him?'

'His wife is convinced he's dead.'

'There's no body.'

'Then we need to find one.'

'Around here? He could be anywhere.'

***

With little more to go on, Tremayne and Clare settled into a routine. Each morning they would meet in the office, discuss the case, receive updates from the various experts. Langley's body, or what was left of it, was released to his family. There had been a check into his visitors, but it had revealed little. All of them had been interviewed and found to be good, upright citizens.

Mavis Godwin's fears had become diluted in Clare's mind, and even the storms that had threatened the cottage had been discounted by a weather forecaster they had brought in.

It had been ten days since Clare left Mavis Godwin's cottage, and whereas she phoned every day to check on the woman, there had been no other contact. Clare was fully occupied in her spare time with Harry, either taking trips into the country or sometimes helping out behind the bar at his pub.

She was a happy woman, and thoughts of the macabre did not occupy her mind, although sometimes she would dream, only to wake when it became too frightening.

Harry had said she was foolish when she told him the story of what had happened at the cottage. 'Old wives' tales,' he had said.

Clare knew that his family had lived in the area for generations, and if he said it was nonsense, then she was inclined to grant that maybe he was correct. She had stayed over at the pub on a few occasions, he had stayed at her place on the others. Their relationship was now an acknowledged fact at the pub, and the cheering each time they brushed up against each other had declined to no more than the occasional 'Good on you, Harry' or 'She's a good sort you've got there.' Neither which worried Clare as she was the happiest she had been for a long time.

Not only was Harry the love of her life, but she also had Tremayne showing her how to be a good detective, not that his success with the horses was improving. The last time he had lost, he had jokingly asked if her mystical friends could give him a hand, although Spooky Sue had come in first at 10 to 1 at Newmarket.

Detective Superintendent Moulton was keeping his distance and Tremayne was still trying to find a logical explanation for Eric Langley's death, other than it was one or another god who had been responsible. Clare thought he was trying to make a connection when there wasn't one, but she was appreciative that he was keeping the case alive.

If Tremayne filed a report closing the enquiry into Langley's death, then Clare knew she ran a possibility of being assigned to another department. Both she and Tremayne were convinced that Trevor Godwin had come to a sticky end. Tremayne said it was his sixth sense, the ability of a policeman to know the truth without the facts. Clare knew he was dead because the man's wife had told her. They didn't have any idea where Godwin was, although his car had been found by the River Avon in

Salisbury. Tremayne thought he may have drowned, but she knew him well enough to know that he didn't really believe that. And besides, where were the man's clothes and even the body? The river did not flow that fast, and the banks were full of reeds. A dead body should have easily been spotted, and the keys were still in the car. Nothing pointed to the man having died near the car, although the cameras which should keep a watch out for vandals and thieves were not working. Forensics had been over the car and found Godwin's fingerprints as well as those of his wife and several others, but nothing suspicious.

Crime in Salisbury, apart from the possible murders of two people, was at a low. There had been a few cases of breaking and entering, a mugging in the centre of the city, a few battered wives, even a rape, which was rare, but apart from that the city maintained an air of tranquillity. Clare had to admit she liked the place, and dependent on Harry, she intended to stay, have a few children, make detective chief inspector, possibly superintendent.

***

It was around four in the afternoon when the phone call came through. Clare had been preparing to leave early and to meet up with Harry. Tremayne was planning to stay for another hour.

'You'd better forget about Harry tonight,' Tremayne shouted through the door of his office as Clare stood up ready to walk out.

'What is it?' Clare asked.

'Mavis Godwin.'

'Oh, no. Is she dead?'

'It's more than likely. The person who found the body doesn't know the woman. You can identify her.'

'Where?'

'An old water trough, not far from her cottage.'

Both of the police officers left the building soon after, Tremayne driving. Clare messaged Harry: *Sorry, can't make it.*

Tremayne and Clare arrived at the cottage. They proceeded to the back garden. At the rear, an old metal gate opened into the field. A uniform was establishing the crime scene as they arrived. A tent was being erected over the woman's body and the water trough. Jim Hughes, the crime scene examiner, was on his way. One of his assistants was taking control of the area.

'Make sure you've got foot protectors and gloves on,' he said.

Tremayne knew the man from way back. 'What have we got?'

'Woman, mid-fifties. Dressed in a black top with a wool jacket. Skirt, knee-length, tartan pattern.'

'It sounds like her,' Tremayne said to Clare.

'Let me have a look,' Clare said.

'We've not taken her out yet. I can probably turn her so you can see the face.'

'How long has she been there?' Tremayne asked.

'I'm waiting for Jim Hughes. He'll be able to give you an approximate time.'

'Your estimation will do for now.'

'Since last night, maybe fifteen to sixteen hours. If some walkers hadn't decided to take a short cut through the field, she could have been here for a week.'

'Okay, I'm ready,' Clare said.

The crime scene investigator beckoned her to come closer. Clare could see the body face down; it looked like Mavis Godwin.

'Are you ready for this?' the CSI asked.

'Not really. I knew the woman.'

Slowly the woman's body was gently lifted to one side. The right-hand side of her face became visible.

'I've seen enough,' Clare said.

'And?' Tremayne asked. He had stood back; he had seen enough dead bodies in his time.

'It's Mavis Godwin.'

'Do you have a cause of death?' Tremayne asked the CSI.

'Off the record?'

'Yes.'

'Judging by the way the woman's arms are raised as if she was grabbing on to the edge of the trough, and by the two sets of shoe prints in the mud, I'd say this woman was murdered.'

'No supernatural here, Yarwood,' Tremayne said.

'You're right, but it's a shame. I liked the woman.'

'Her husband may have been a likeable person as well, but we've no idea where he is. I reckon we've got three murders on our hands now: one confirmed, one still open to conjecture and another assumed.'

'I don't know how you can remain so calm,' Clare said.

'Professional detachment, Yarwood. It comes with time.'

Tremayne took a few minutes to phone Superintendent Moulton to let him know that it was now murder and he would be taking on the role of senior investigating officer.

Clare thought the man a bit smug, as if he was telling his senior to get out of his way. Regardless, it was murder, and the fact that she had liked the woman did not alter the facts.

The two police officers walked away from the crime scene as Jim Hughes arrived. 'Jim, I'll need it in writing by tomorrow morning,' Tremayne said.

'Not tonight?' Hughes replied.

'It's murder. We'll deal with the paperwork later. See what you can do with the shoe prints.'

Hughes looked over at Clare. 'Sergeant Yarwood, you've identified her?'

'Yes. It's who I thought it was.'

'Fine,' Hughes said. 'Another day at the office.'

Clare thought Hughes's statement was callous, but she could see that although he was not much older than her, he had already attained a professional detachment. She hoped she never would, but supposed it was inevitable with time.

**

Back in the office, Tremayne went to work. The first thing he did was to clear several desks around Clare. 'We need them for our people,' he said. 'And I need you to call in the Reverend Harrison. If he's reluctant, go and pick him up. He knows more about Mavis Godwin than we do.'

Clare could see that Tremayne was enjoying himself. She phoned the vicar to inform him of the situation. The man appeared to be upset. 'I need you in here,' she said.

'I should be with her.'

'There's not a lot you can do. Our people are in control of the crime scene. Will you formally identify her?'

'What about her family?'

'Does she have any?'

'I suppose she must. I never knew of them apart from her husband.'

'If they've seen her recently, then we'll use them. Otherwise, you'll have to do it.'

'When?' Harrison asked.

'I'll arrange it for tomorrow,' Clare said.

'Are you sure it's her?'

'Yes. I knew Mavis Godwin well enough. I could identify her if necessary, but it's best if someone independent does it.'

'Very well. I'll come in tomorrow, and we can talk then.'

'Sorry, Reverend Harrison, it's got to be today. The woman's been murdered. I need you here within the hour. Do you need a car to pick you up?'

'No, I'll be there. Where are you at the police station?'

'There'll be someone at reception. Just mention my name, and I'll come down.'

'She was a decent person.'

'That's what I thought,' Clare said.

***

Two men met in the corner of a pub. The place was empty and the night was drawing in. Outside a mist was starting to roll in, as it did most nights. A stream ran along the other side of the road from the pub. It was cold and uninviting and devoid of life, as was the village. Once the village had been a thriving settlement, but that was a long time ago in the past when they had discovered a vein of gold, English gold, in a mine that had been cut out of the rock by men with picks and shovels. They had been looking for tin, but they had found none. A small boy, one of those employed to remove the rock, had found the vein. He had not known what it was, but he had received extra rations of gruel, the only payment the boys received. The boy was illiterate and knew no better, but those who controlled the mine did. They exploited the children of the settlement through illiteracy and tyranny, taking what they wanted from the land and the people.

The two men, one descended from that small boy, the other a descendant of one of the tyrannical landowners, sat deep in conversation. Time had moved on, and no longer would a child work for food. No longer did the landed gentry ride on the backs of magnificent horses while the peasants walked half-starving back to their squalid huts. Now the workers lived in substantial houses and drove decent cars and sent their children to school in Salisbury. No longer did they doff their hats and lower their gaze for fear of receiving a swipe across the face from a horsewhip. Times had changed, but some values in the remote village, only a few miles from the normality of the twenty-first century yet holding on to values steeped in time and fear, had not.

Within that community fear and knowledge of a secret so terrible that it had remained guarded for centuries kept them bound as one. A secret so terrible, yet modern technology and the ease of communication and the inquisitiveness of the police was threatening all that they had kept hidden for so long. The two men, one a doctor, the other a farmer, talked.

'The task has been done,' the doctor said.

'Then all is well,' the farmer replied.

'She is troubled.'

'But she understands why she had to kill Mavis Godwin?'

'That she does,' the doctor replied.

***

Reverend Harrison arrived at Bemerton Road Police Station within the hour. Clare had collected him at reception and escorted him up to the second floor and the interview room.

Tremayne was to be in charge of the interrogation. Clare sat on his left side. The vicar sat on the other side, facing Tremayne.

'Sorry about this,' Tremayne said. 'It's a murder enquiry now, so we need to follow this by the book.'

'That's understood. The poor woman, a good servant of the Lord.'

Tremayne cleared his throat, hoping to distract the man from going on about the Lord and the woman's devotion to the church. As far as Tremayne was concerned, the woman had been murdered, and no amount of praying or sanctifying was going to change that fact. He didn't need a lecture on the benefits of religion, he needed what the man could tell him.

'Reverend Harrison,' Clare asked, 'when did you last see Mavis Godwin?'

'Yesterday morning. She came to put a few flowers in a vase on the altar. She often did, but in the last few days it's been for her husband.'

'We believe him to be dead,' Tremayne said.

'So did Mavis,' the vicar replied.

'And you?'

'Mavis would have known the truth. If she said he was dead, then he is.'

'But how?' Tremayne asked.

'There are forces,' Harrison said. Clare could see the man retreating into his shell.

'What forces?' Tremayne asked. He was exasperated with the talk of the supernatural.

'I've seen something,' Clare said.

'Then you need to be careful.'

'What do you mean?' Tremayne asked. 'I've had Mavis Godwin, you and now my sergeant talking about evil. What does this all mean? The woman was murdered.'

'That person would have been commanded.'

'Reverend Harrison, am I meant to believe there are forces out there that are not of the God you serve?'

'You ask me to speak of matters I cannot.'

'Will someone talk some sense here. You are the vicar of St Lawrence, a church dedicated to God and his son, Jesus Christ?'

'That is correct.'

'Are you telling me that the one God you recognise is not the only one?'

'My faith has been shaken.'

'By what?'

'By events that have occurred.'

'Detail them.'

'I cannot. I don't want to bring down their vengeance.'

'Whose vengeance, man?'

Clare felt the need to intercede. 'I was at Mavis Godwin's cottage the day of the lightning strike. Did she tell you that?'

'Yes, she did.'

'And what did you do with that knowledge?'

'We prayed to God for guidance.'

'And what did he tell you?' Tremayne asked.

'God does not answer directly.'

'You tell us that your God is not the only god and there are malevolent forces bent on destruction. But of who and what?'

'They act against those who do not heed their will.'

'What will happen?'

'They will demand an offering.'

'Okay, now we're getting somewhere,' Tremayne said. 'Reverend Harrison, I put it to you that whereas you are not guilty of any crime, you know more about this than anyone else in this room. Before you leave here today, you will tell us what you know. Is that clear?'

'If I tell you, then you will be damned.'

'Are you?'

'I cannot place you in danger. The knowledge I possess will kill you.'

'What the hell do you mean?' Tremayne said with a raised voice. Harrison was crucial to the investigation, and he was holding back. 'What is it?'

'I felt something in your church the other day,' Clare said.

'It was there.'

'What was it?'

'They watch.'

'And?' Tremayne asked.

'Your faith in the modern world will not protect you.'

'What will?'

'Ignorance will save you. Knowledge will condemn you.'

'But you know.'

'I am a servant of the Lord, a peaceful man. You are lawgivers, you will act against them.'

'Then they are mortal beings, the same as you and I?'

'Those who speak on their behalf are.'

'Clare, this is going nowhere,' Tremayne said. 'We're wasting our time.'

'Reverend Harrison,' Clare said, 'Mavis Godwin said exactly the same as you. Do you expect us to walk away from the murder of Mavis Godwin, your parishioner, my friend?'

'Yes, that's what I expect you to do.'

'Thank you, Reverend Harrison. We'll talk further tomorrow,' Tremayne said.

Chapter 8

The first night after Mavis Godwin's death, Tremayne and Clare had stayed at the police station until the early hours of the morning. Harry had phoned Clare on a couple of occasions, but she had been too busy, and eventually, at three in the morning, she collapsed into her bed, and for the first time in the last ten days there was no one at her side, except for her two cats.

Harry had an aversion to cats, and when he was there, they were in the other room behind a closed door.

At 6 a.m. Clare had awoken to a rattling of the window in her bedroom. Tales of evil, the vicar and his church, and the events at Mavis Godwin's cottage had left her on edge. She crept over to the window and peered out. It was dark outside, yet the noise persisted.

Get a grip of yourself. You're a police officer, not a silly schoolgirl, Clare said to herself.

She opened the window with gusto to show that she was brave when she did not feel it. A thin branch from a tree close to the window lashed her in the face, causing her to move back. 'Damn you,' she said. She realised that the wind, stronger than usual, had caused the branch to sway and that the supernatural did not exist, only her foolishness. She went to the bathroom and washed her face, noticing that the action of the branch had left a scratch. She applied a plaster to where there was a small amount of blood. It was still early: too early to report to work, too late to go back to sleep. She lay on her bed looking up at the ceiling. One of the cats snuggled at the bottom of the bed, the other came and shared her pillow. She phoned Harry. He answered straightaway.

'I can't sleep,' she said.

'Neither can I,' he replied, although she could tell that she had woken him up.

'I keep seeing that woman in the water.'

'Do you know who did it?'

'We're still waiting for the crime scene report.'

'No more of that evil nonsense?'

'Not with Mavis Godwin. We're certain she was killed by another woman.'

'Do women do that?' Harry asked. 'I mean, murder people.'

'In this case, it appears to be that way.'

'I could come over.'

'It's too late now. I'm expected in the office by 7.30 a.m. I just missed you, that's all.'

'I missed you as well. Tonight, then?' Harry asked.

'As long as no one else dies,' Clare replied, although further deaths seemed all too possible.

***

If Clare had phoned Reverend Harrison instead of Harry, she would have found that he was not asleep either; in fact, he had not slept for more than twenty minutes that night. Most of the night, he had knelt by the side of his bed in silent prayer.

He remembered his youth as a choir boy at his local church in the north of England. He remembered in his late teens walking through the front gate of the theological college, his proud parents accompanying him; he remembered his first parish, the first wedding he conducted. In all that time, he knew that his faith had not been challenged. His belief in the word of the Lord, his faith that his God was infinite in his wisdom and benevolence. He had studied other religions, learnt about paganism and witchcraft and how they paled in comparison to his Christian beliefs.

And yet, he had seen things, heard things. He remembered the look on the face of the police sergeant. He had seen the fear in her; she had seen it in him.

Harrison knew he was foolish, and he was wrong to worry. He knew that night, that sleepless night, that they were watching, whispering in the dark. The vicar had looked out of the window of the small rectory next to the church. There were shapes, ghostly forms, voices speaking in a language he could not understand. He prayed as he had never prayed; wished he had married, thought he was going mad.

He remembered the first time Mavis Godwin had entered his church. 'I need guidance,' she had said. It had been eight years previously when she had stood before him, a small woman approaching middle age. He saw a good Christian soul in need of his help. He had seen her before as she had walked along the path in front of his church many times; they had exchanged pleasantries, spoken about the weather and life in general, but never once had she crossed the threshold into the Lord's house, and now, here she was and she was troubled. He remembered the worry etched in her furrowed brow that first time, and now he had seen her body by the side of the water trough. He knew why she was dead, yet he did not dare to tell those who wanted to know.

The Reverend Harrison looked out of the bedroom window. The first light of a new day was dawning, and although there were a few clouds, they were benign and posed no threat.

He knew that before Mavis Godwin had told him her story he had been comfortable in his piety. But she had told him of other gods that had been summoned from the depths of hell. Gods who were not as his God; gods that demanded tributes.

He remembered his horror as she sat on one of the church pews and told him all that she knew. Both so absorbed they had not taken note of what was outside the church. It was after dark; the woman had been speaking for over two hours. The electricity had failed, and the church was plunged into darkness.

'They are here,' she had said.

'Who?' he had asked.

'The gods who fear no others.'

'Our Lord will protect us,' Harrison had replied.

As he knelt in front of his bed, his hands raised in prayer, he could feel the same indeterminable cold creeping into his bones. He drew himself up from the bed and looked out of the window again – nothing. He resumed his position, although he was not at ease. He had seen a dead woman in a field, a woman who had looked to him for protection, a woman who had died at the hand of another. He saw the devil's handiwork. He knew he was cursed. Had not Jesus been tempted in the desert for forty days and forty nights? Was this his time to be tempted, but it had been longer than forty days? It had been eight years, and he had never felt as much fear as he did now by the side of his small bed. He picked up a copy of the Bible that he always kept close at hand. He opened it at Psalm 23:4.

Yea, though I walk through the valley of the shadow of death, I will fear no evil: for thou art with me; thy rod and thy staff they comfort me.

An owl hooted outside. An omen, he thought, but of what? Was his God with him, or were there others? He did not know, and he was troubled. He had wanted to tell the two police officers all that he knew, but they would not understand fully the implications. Although maybe the young woman would, about what had happened in the past when he and Mavis Godwin held hands and silently prayed for protection.

Then they had rattled the windows and sent the wind gusting through the small church, throwing the books of prayer this way and that. It had not lasted long, but it was enough to frighten them.

'I can say no more,' the woman had said as she ran out of the church. He remembered following her to find that the night was calm with barely a breeze.

'I need to know,' he had said.

'Another time,' she had replied as she walked briskly down the road to the sanctuary of her cottage. Now she had died in a water trough close to where she had felt safest. Harrison knew he did not have long. He could choose to tell the police what he knew, or he could wait, but she had told him over a period of months what she had talked about that first night. There were gods, ancient gods, who were not recorded in a book of prayer or in a Bible, but were real nonetheless. And what of him, Harrison thought.

Each time he had spoken to the woman, they had both looked for the signs, moved apart when it looked ominous. He had written in one of his Bibles what she had told him. Would he give it to the young police officer? Or should he give it to the nonbeliever, the senior police inspector? Who would be safe? Would either of them? And what of him? Mavis Godwin had made it clear that the one thing they did not like was to be known, and he knew their names. He had checked on the internet, and whereas they were shrouded in mystery and disbelief, they were very real.

The Roman poet Lucan, writing in the first century AD, had mentioned their names. Julius Caesar was rumoured to have encountered human sacrifices dedicated to them: Taranis, the thunder-god, was appeased by fire, the victims of Esus were stabbed and hanged from a tree until they bled to death, and with Teutates, they were drowned.

The reverend knew that Mavis Godwin had been dedicated to Teutates, but what of him? Langley, who had dared to question the elder's authority, had burnt. Harrison knew that his fate was hanging, but there had been other deaths over the years. And what of Trevor Godwin, what had been his fate? Had he burnt, or been drowned, the same as his wife, or had he met his end in the branches of a tree?

The reverend only knew of one certainty; he would not tell the two innocents what he knew.

Chapter 9

Jim Hughes was in Tremayne's office early that morning. Clare had arrived late which was unusual for her, but she had had a troubled night. Tremayne was looking good and ready to crack on.

'Okay, what have you got?' Tremayne asked. He leant back in his chair. Clare was sure one of the legs would break one day, and he'd be sprawled across the floor.

'The two women spent time in the dead woman's cottage. There's a clear sign that they had a cup of tea each. We've got fingerprints,' Hughes said.

'Any chance of a match on our database?'

'Unlikely.'

'Does that mean the woman who killed her was a friend?' Clare asked.

'It's a fair assumption. Anyway, we can tell that the two women left the cottage by the back door and walked out into the field.'

'Any sign of force?' Tremayne asked.

'None that we can see. We know that the woman's murderer was a larger person.'

'How?'

'Shoe size, at least two sizes larger. Also, she was wearing boots.'

'What does that suggest?' Clare asked.

'The woman was not dressed for a night out on the town. I'd say she is a country woman. We found some wheat in the mud where she had stood to hold the woman under.'

'Wheat? Surely that would have dropped off as she walked.'

'Depends on where it was. We're assuming it wasn't on the footwear. More likely on the clothes she was wearing,' Hughes said.

'What else can you tell us?' Tremayne asked.

'The woman fought back, and there are bruises on the back of her neck where the other woman applied pressure.'

'And this woman was apparently a friend?'

'If she made her a cup of tea,' Hughes replied.

'Anything else?'

'The usual. Mavis Godwin was fifty-six, in good health, although she was troubled by arthritis.'

'How do you know that?'

'Prescription medicine in the house.'

'What else?'

'There was water in her lungs which indicates she drowned in the trough.'

'Unpleasant,' Clare, who had returned, said.

''Not as bad as Langley's,' Tremayne replied.

'Maybe, but I knew the dead woman.'

'Sorry if you're upset by all this, but we've got to find her killer and that of Langley.'

'Are you still holding on to that theory that he was murdered?' Hughes asked.

'You may not be able to prove it, but it's obvious.'

'Because his nurse has been murdered?'

'In part. But we've also the dead woman's statement, as well as the Reverend Harrison. That man could blow this case wide open.'

'And he's not talking?' Hughes asked.

'You've got it. Either the man's frightened or he's mad, and I'm not ruling out the latter,' Tremayne said.

'Mad! That's a damning condemnation of a man of the cloth.'

'Look, Hughes, you may be a hot-shot crime scene examiner, but I've got a dead woman who spouted on about evil forces, a man of the cloth, to use your terminology, who's out for the count in that church the one time I'm there with Yarwood, and there's my sergeant believing this garbage.'

'We know Langley's nurse was murdered,' Hughes said. 'Why couldn't Langley have just died of natural causes?'

'Then why don't you record that instead of a wishy-washy conclusion such as the man was obese, not in good health, a possible alcoholic, and it's not feasible for you to give a reason as to why he was only a pile of grease and ash with an offensive odour. Why? Tell me that, or are you unsure?'

Hughes, who had always respected Tremayne for his depth of experience and his age, responded. 'Langley, until someone can come up with a scientific explanation, I cannot give you an answer, but rest assured, it wasn't murder.'

'Thank you, Hughes,' Tremayne said.

'You like winding up people, don't you?' Hughes said, although he was not pleased with what had just occurred.

'I appreciate the truth. Mavis Godwin's death is very real. Langley's requires confirmation.'

'I've set up the door-to-door,' Clare said. 'I'll meet the team down there later this morning.'

'Check on Harrison while you're there.'

'You want me to go into the church?' Clare asked.

Tremayne could hear the hesitancy in her voice. 'Yarwood, get a grip of yourself. You're a serving police officer, and a good one if you stick with me, so forget this nonsense. The reverend and Mavis Godwin and whoever else can believe what they want, but we're police officers. We deal in facts, not something you read in a book or watch at the movies. You've got to get rid of this phobia.'

'I'll visit Reverend Harrison on the way,' Clare said. 'He still needs to formally identify Mavis Godwin.'

'No relatives?' Tremayne asked.

'None that we've been able to find.'

***

A meeting in what had once been a church. A congregation led by a man who wore a mask. 'Our secret is safe,' the man said. 'We give thanks to the one who has protected us.'

The assembled group turned to look at the woman who had killed Mavis Godwin, and applauded her by stamping their feet.

'Enough,' said the leader. The man, a doctor, believed as they all did. He had seen the proof: the abundant harvests, the healthy livestock, the wealth that they had all achieved. It was not important whether his belief was absolute, or whether he was a mortal representation of a god; it was only important that those assembled feared what he represented.

The doctor knew full well the history of the village from all those years ago. How in a time of strife and plague, the villagers had resorted to desperate measures, how they had embraced paganism. The story had been passed down from generation to generation, adult to child. The year had been 1351, and bubonic plague had been ravaging the country, decimating the population town by town, village by village. The people, illiterate in the main, believed that was ailed them was due to their wickedness, their lack of devotion to the church, their inability to pray enough or to pay enough to those who could save them.

It had only taken one of the villagers, at a time when the snows were at their most severe and the village had been isolated for weeks, to find the ancient texts. Texts hidden in a dark place, known to only a few. The words engraved inside that burial mound could not be pronounced, and besides, no peasant could read even their own language, let alone words that had been written in an alien tongue.

If it had not been for the son of the squire, inquisitive as all boys are, those words would never have been spoken. The doctor knew who this boy was; he was one of his ancestors. It was all recorded in the book that he kept hidden, even from his wife. She was not of the village; she would not understand. The book had detailed all that had happened. How in that village lost in misery, isolated from the outside world by the snow and by the plague, a meeting had been held in the church. The priest who led it asked the congregation to pray to God in their hour of need; to pray as they had never prayed before.

The peasants, illiterate and starving, stood at the back of the church; the squire sat with his family and son in a specially constructed pew, isolated from those that they cared little about.

The priest, an educated man, in so far as he could read and write, conducted the ceremony in his usual fashion. The peasants, understanding little, could see the Bible, yet none had ever opened it. The squire read from the good book, as did the priest. The son, just coming of age, was to be the third speaker.

He left where he had been sitting and climbed the five steps up to where the Bible was kept. He opened it to the correct page. He stood there for a moment, awed by the significance of the occasion. He started to speak. Whatever the reason, it was not the Bible text that emanated from his mouth; it was the engraved words on a wall inside a burial mound, one of many in the area.

The squire initially thought that his son was nervous, but the priest reacted with alarm. 'He is summoning the ancients. Stop him,' he shouted. He attempted to run across to where the boy stood reciting over and over again the ancient texts. The doctor remembered the story as he stood in front of the group in that very same church, separated by hundreds of years.

''I didn't want to kill her,' Mavis Godwin's murderer said.

'We honour you for what was necessary,' the senior elder said. 'And yet, there are others who still threaten.'

'Say the word, say the word,' the assembled people said.

'The time is not yet.'

***

Clare had already conducted an unofficial door-to-door of her own on the day Mavis Godwin's body was found, but Tremayne had been in such a mood with Hughes that she had not mentioned it. Not that it mattered, as she had rounded up six of Salisbury's finest police officers, namely cadets and uniforms. The weather was mild, and no one would complain too much. 'We're looking for a woman, height about five feet nine inches. She would have been wearing boots. Apart from that, there's not much to go on. Oh, just one other thing. We believe she may have been a friend of the deceased. You have an approximate time of death, and we think the woman entered Mavis Godwin's cottage about one hour before she died.'

'Sergeant,' one of the cadets said.

'Yes, what is it?' Clare replied. *At least someone's keen*, she thought.

'There was no moon. It may be possible no one saw the woman.'

'I realise that. Just knock on doors. We'll meet up in two hours down the road. There's a café there.'

'Yes, guv,' one of the cadets said.

'I've got to go and see someone local. Constable Oldfield, you can come with me.'

Clare knew why she had chosen the constable. He was the tallest and strongest person in the group.

***

It was not far from Mavis Godwin's house to the church; Clare chose to walk.

'What's the Reverend Harrison got to do with the case?' Oldfield asked.

'You know him?'

'I've seen the name on the reports, that's all.'

'You've been keeping up to date with the deaths?'

'I'm hoping to get transferred to Homicide. It's not much fun in uniform.'

'I'll have a talk to DI Tremayne if you're interested.'

'Thanks. I'd really appreciate that. What do you want to see the priest about?'

'He's holding back. He knows more than he's telling. We believe that he could bust this case wide open. He keeps giving us tales about other gods.'

'And you don't believe him?'

'Not at all,' Clare said, to calm her nerves and to gain moral support from the man who walked alongside her. 'What's your take on the supernatural?' she asked.

'I have a healthy respect for things I don't understand.'

'Which means you believe in the possibility?'

'Not really. It's a bit like believing in aliens. One part of you says it's nonsense, the other keeps an open mind.'

'If you want to join Homicide, don't tell DI Tremayne you're on the fence on this one.'

'I won't.'

The two police officers arrived at the church. 'After you,' Constable Oldfield said. He turned the large wrought iron handle to open the door and let Clare through. 'It's locked,' he said.

'Unusual,' Clare replied. 'We'll go around to the back. If he's not in the church, he'll probably be in the rectory.'

Clare looked up at the sky; there was not a cloud to be seen. No matter how much Harry and Tremayne told her that she was foolish, she could not shake her fear of the unknown. And now she was coming to meet with a man who had told both her and her DI that his knowledge would condemn them.

Oldfield tested the door at the rear; it opened. He entered first, moving through the vestry.

'Reverend Harrison. It's Sergeant Yarwood. Are you there?' There was no answer.

A mouse scurried along the floor. The vicar's robes were hanging up on a hook on the back of the door into the church. A note was on the table. Clare picked it up and opened it. She read the first line.

'Constable, he's in the church,' she shouted.

Oldfield quickened his pace and opened the door into the church. A pillar that had been erected centuries before obscured their view.

'He's here,' Clare said.

'What was in the note?'

'His suicide.'

As Oldfield rounded the pillar and reached the central area of the church, he looked up. 'Don't come in here, sergeant.'

'Why?'

'The man's hanging from a rope.'

'Good God,' Clare said as she looked upwards. 'Get him down from there.'

'It's too late,' Oldfield said. 'There's nothing we can do for him. You'd better phone DI Tremayne.'

Chapter 10

Detective Inspector Keith Tremayne was the angriest man at Bemerton Road Police Station, although not at others, only himself. He had had Reverend Harrison in the interview room and had let him walk out of there. At that time, it was evident the man was not going to talk, and Tremayne had thought that after a day to cool off the priest might open up. And now what did he have? A man swinging from a rope.

Jim Hughes had arrived at the church within the hour, to be met by Clare. Tremayne was out the back reading the suicide note.

'Another one, sergeant?' Hughes said casually.

'There's a note. It's suicide,' Clare said.

'Understood. We'll need to go through the formalities.'

Clare left the CSE and walked through to the vestry. She averted her eyes as she passed the dead vicar.

'Rum do,' Tremayne said, using a phrase long out of fashion.

'If you mean it was unexpected, then yes.'

'I thought the man was half crazy, but I didn't see this coming.'

'There were no gods involved here,' Clare said.

'As I've told you. People make out there are evil spirits and God knows what else, when it's only the wind or fog or a man dead in a chair. There's always a logical explanation. Have you read the letter?' Tremayne asked.

'Not fully.'

'Then you can read it out loud, and we'll see if we can make any sense of it.'

'What do you hope to gain? The man is hanging from a rope.'

'I'm looking for anything cryptic.'

'He was trying to protect us. That's why he never told us what he knew,' Clare said. 'You can see that the man came back from our interview and hanged himself.'

'Yarwood, you need some time off. Firstly, there's a thirteen-hour time difference between when he left Bemerton Road and when he threw a rope over that beam. I can't see that we're involved, just because the man jumps off an altar to his death.'

'But in a church?'

'I suppose that means it's no longer consecrated,' Tremayne said. Clare noticed that the man was not moved by the death. She imagined that the reverend must have suffered a great dilemma in the hours leading up to his death. She sat down on a chair close to where the note had been placed.

I, the Reverend Jonah Harrison, a man who has dedicated my life to the glory of God and his only son, Jesus, am forced to take the only option possible to save others.

'He's referring to us.' Clare temporarily stopped reading and looked at Tremayne.

'He wasn't half crazy, he was one hundred per cent certifiable,' Tremayne said.

There are those who will criticise me for my actions, others will say that I have taken the house of the Lord and turned it into a place of death, but those people will not understand. And for them, I am pleased.

The condemnation of me will save them, and my death is a small price to pay to ensure that others shall live, replete in the knowledge of the one true God.

Blessings be on you,
Jonah Harrison.

'Wordy for a suicide note,' Tremayne said.

'You've read a few?' Clare sat still, emotionally distraught.

'Normally, it's a few words: farewell cruel world, that sort of thing.'

'The man believed he was doing it for a reason.'

'Same as you.'

'Are you discounting all that you have seen?' Clare said. 'You saw the clouds over Mavis Godwin's cottage. You felt the tension in this church that time. If it can be explained away, it'd have to be damn good.'

'I've not much hope for you, Yarwood. You're too susceptible to be a good detective.'

'What do you mean? I need to be a cynical old bastard whose only joy is a few beers and a few old nags only fit for the knacker's yard.'

'Careful, Yarwood. You're looking for a reprimand.'

'I'll apologise when you accept the possibility.'

'That'll be a long time. I suggest you meet up with Harry Holchester, get yourself laid. Tomorrow, you and I will have a long talk about your attitude,' Tremayne said.

'You're a miserable old sod,' Clare replied.

'Of course I am. That's what makes me a good detective. Look, Yarwood, you're a decent person, but murder is foul and dirty. The Reverend Harrison hanging from a rope may have unnerved you, but I need you on board, focussed, and not looking to the supernatural. Real people have committed real murders and if the vicar was deranged and believed in the occult, or whatever it was, so be it, but you're a police officer, not an exorcist or someone who dances around an ancient stone at midnight with no clothes on. From here on, no more talk of gods, and no more talk of mysterious happenings. Is that clear?'

***

It had taken Clare two hours before her anger had subsided, but Harry had told her later that the man was right. 'Clare, the man's only doing it for your own good. I've known him a few years, and he doesn't rile people without reason. If he wanted you out, he would have dealt with you through Human Resources.'

As angry as she had been, she listened to reason. Tomorrow, she would apologise, but for that night, she had Harry.

'I love you,' he had said that night, the first time he had uttered the words that she felt for him. They had not known each other long, and already they were making plans for the future. He wanted to sell the pub and take up another career. She pleaded with him not to. She loved the old pub with its chequered history. She had sat where Churchill and McArthur, or was it Eisenhower, the history books weren't sure who it was, had met to discuss the D-Day invasion. She had seen the mummified hand of an eighteenth-century card player who had supposedly been caught cheating, but as with so many things about the pub, the name of the player was lost in time.

Regardless of the history, she had spent the night in Harry's arms, the confrontation with Tremayne forgotten, the death of Mavis Godwin a mere memory, and as for the Reverend Harrison, he was no longer in her mind.

Tremayne had been right about one thing, she had needed to get laid.

***

The next morning at seven Clare was in the office. 'Sorry about yesterday,' she said as Tremayne walked in the door.

'Forget it. I like someone with spirit. They're the best people to get the job done. I've no time for sycophants, and judging by your tongue yesterday, you'll not qualify. We could always kiss and make up, but I'm sure Harry dealt with that for you.'

'DI, I've said it before, you've got a foul mouth.'

Both police officers smiled at each other. Tremayne knew he had the best person for the team; Clare realised that with Tremayne her future was secured.

'Anyway, what's the agenda for today?' Tremayne asked.

'Reverend Harrison died with a secret.'

'Don't mention ancient gods again.'

'I won't, but he may have known more about the woman who visited Mavis Godwin.'

'No luck with the door-to-door?'

'Nothing. There was no moon that night, and there's a blind spot outside Godwin's cottage.'

'What's it with the moon?'

'Nothing out of the ordinary. It's just a fact.'

'Good. You had me worried there.'

'Don't worry, guv. You'll not hear a peep from me again on that subject.'

'Harrison was going to identify Mavis Godwin's body, correct?'

'I'll have to do it,' Clare said.

'No relatives?'

'None that we can find. We know she came from the West Country and that she was the only child of a shopkeeper and his wife. Apart from that, nothing. We've got the local police checking further, but her parents are dead, and there's no one else.'

'What about Trevor Godwin?'

'A neighbour two doors down said that he was a strange character in that he never acknowledged anyone else's presence other than with a nod of the head. The neighbour thought he was not all there.'

'Not all there?'

'Loose in the head, mentally deficient.'

'Was he?' Tremayne asked.

'The only time Trevor Godwin had spoken to him, he had had difficulty communicating.'

'You must have checked with other people he worked for.'

'Not really. We know Godwin used to work for other people on a casual basis; Mavis Godwin told us that.'

'But?'

'We've never found any of those people.'

'Was he bringing money into the household?'

'According the Mavis Godwin he was,' Clare said. 'How about you, guv? What about Superintendent Moulton?'

'He's keeping a watch, but I can handle him.'

'What do we know about Trevor Godwin? Are we still working on the assumption that he's dead?'

'His wife thought he was. So, did the Reverend Harrison. And now they're both dead. What do you reckon?' Tremayne asked.

'Too many coincidences,' Clare replied.

'That's how I see it.'

'The neighbour couldn't tell the constable any more, and none of the others could ever remember speaking to him.'

'A mystery man, is that it?' Tremayne asked.

'This is not over.'

'We're in full agreement there. We've four deaths, one confirmed as murder, another one as a suicide and that's suspicious.'

'Suspicious?'

'Of course it's suspicious. The man may have been certifiable with his fanciful tales, but he still committed suicide. Why not just shut up? We had nothing against him, and personally he looked harmless enough to me. We could have grilled him some more, but if he'd kept quiet, there wasn't much we could do.'

'He said he was protecting others,' Clare said.

'I know,' Tremayne said. He had stopped leaning back on his seat, the four legs of the chair firmly on the ground. 'But why? He was an educated man. At least, I assume he was.'

'He was. I saw the degree certificates up on the wall in his vestry.'

'Then why?'

'You know why,' Clare said, not willing to receive an earful if she mentioned it again.

'I've had a bellyful of that nonsense,' Tremayne said.

'Calm down, guv,' Clare said, exerting her new-found strength in dealing with the man.

'I'm calm. Keep that up, and you'll be out of here soon enough,' Tremayne said. Clare knew he did not mean it. She had come into his office that first day demure and subservient to the older man, but now she knew she was his equal, not in rank or experience or age, but as a team member. Tremayne knew it as well, but he was not going to say it.

'I'm your sounding board,' Clare said. 'What you believe is irrelevant. It's what the man believed, what Mavis Godwin believed, what...'

'Don't say it.'

'I was going to say what I had believed in. Mavis Godwin was killed by another woman and no one else threw that rope over the beam.'

'Proven?'

'Jim Hughes's team found enough fingerprints to confirm that Harrison had put the rope up there.'

'Where did it come from?'

'It was an old rope used for the bell in the past.'

'I didn't know they had a bell.'

'There's one there, but the belfry needs restoration. You must have seen the signs outside looking for donations, the thermometer showing how much they had received, how much they needed.'

'I didn't study it. How far had they got?'

'The donations?'

'Yes.'

'Just above freezing.'

'Coming back to what I was saying.' Tremayne sat down again. 'We have an educated man who feels the need to kill himself to prevent others knowing the truth. But why? Surely a religious man cannot believe Mavis Godwin's story.'

'Apparently he did. The question, as you said, is why.'

'And how.'

'You said it before: clouds in the sky, rattling doors, unexplained phenomena. It's easy for the susceptible to see those as sinister. Mavis Godwin entered his church, gave him a long story about evil.'

'Yarwood, you're missing the point.'

'Am I?'

'Yes. The priest was a man of God, not a simpleton. He must have known it was nonsense. Have you checked the Godwins' cottage?'

'With a fine-tooth comb. Nothing there apart from crucifixes, though none in Trevor Godwin's bedroom.'

'They slept in separate beds?' Tremayne asked.

'Separate rooms.'

'Are you sure that Mavis Godwin and the vicar weren't…'

'Positive. I'll bring some soap for you to wash out your mouth tomorrow.'

'Don't bother. You know I've got to ask.'

'From what we can gather, the Reverend Harrison was celibate.'

'He was Church of England. Are you sure?'

'Not certain, but it appears that way.'

'Have you checked his house?'

'We're planning to do it today, guv.'

'Okay, get on with it.'

'What about the other two?' Clare asked.

'Langley's still an unknown. I got nowhere with Hughes on that.'

'And Trevor Godwin?'

'See if you can trace his movements on the day he disappeared. In fact, find out anything you can about him.'

Chapter 11

It was evident to Clare when she entered the Reverend Harrison's house next to his church that the man led a bachelor's life. There were none of the feminine touches: no flowers in a vase, no attempt at cleaning other than a rudimentary dusting. The house was two storeys, and if it had been in good condition and not tacked on the rear of the church, very desirable.

Forensics would go over the house later, but for the moment there was nothing suspicious about Harrison's death. Clare had brought Constable Oldfield with her. She could have conducted the search on her own, but she still had some trepidation, even though the house felt calm, as had their first port of call, the vestry. Oldfield had checked in the church; the man's body had been removed, although the rope remained in place. Clare did not look.

'Constable, you know what we're looking for?'

'Call me Vic, everyone else does.'

'Fine, I'm Clare.'

'You're sure you don't want me to call you sergeant?'

'No. Clare's fine.'

'What's the deal here?' Oldfield asked.

'We know the man committed suicide because of something he did not want to tell us.'

'The supernatural, that sort of thing.'

'Precisely.'

'And we're looking for anything we can find that relates to his reasons?'

'Yes. If Harrison committed suicide, then so be it. Mavis Godwin was murdered, and we don't know by who. Also, her husband is missing, and then DI Tremayne doesn't believe the open finding on the death of Eric Langley.'

'Real can of worms, Clare.'

'As you say.'

The vestry had revealed nothing other than a few prayer books, the priest's robes, a mouse trap in one corner of the room which seemed to have achieved very little as the evidence of mouse activity was apparent. An old half-eaten sandwich in a bin to one side of the table in the room had signs that other teeth had been at it.

The house was dusty when Clare and Vic Oldfield entered. Both had put on foot protectors and gloves before entering. Clare put on a mask as well, although Oldfield did not.

'You take the kitchen and the main room. I'll start upstairs. Take a photo before and after you leave an area. And make sure everything is placed back where you found it,' Clare said.

'I'll be careful.'

Clare walked up the stairs which were close to the front door, leaving Vic in the kitchen; not that she expected much there as all that was in the refrigerator was some old bread, a tub of butter and a jar of honey. The pantry wasn't much better, and it was evident the man did not eat well.

Upstairs there were four doors. Clare looked in the first at the top of the stairs. It was the bathroom. She checked in the cabinet above the wash basin. The usual: toothbrush, toothpaste, shaving equipment, a few headache tablets. She left the room and entered the second; it was a bedroom, although the bed was not made up and apparently not slept in. An old wardrobe, with creaking hinges, revealed nothing more than an old blanket and a guitar without any strings.

The third room turned out to be a cupboard, although it contained very little other than a suitcase and an old vinyl cover for the guitar.

Entering the fourth room, the room where she thought the best opportunity would be of finding something of interest, Clare looked around. She had a sense of foreboding.

'Vic, can you come up here,' she shouted.

One minute later, the constable joined her. 'What is it? Have you found anything?' he asked.

'Not yet, but this room is giving me the creeps.'

'The whole house gives me the creeps,' Oldfield said.

'I've seen things, things that can't be explained, and this man had, as well.'

'Tremayne?'

'He was there once, but the man's too stuck in his ways. To him, everything has an explanation.'

'He's right,' Vic said.

'Is that what you think?'

'The DI wants it in black and white, not shades of grey.'

'Can you feel the cold coming from Harrison's bedroom?'

'You want me to go first?' Vic asked.

'If you would.'

***

Vic Oldfield entered the room slowly. If Clare's intuition was right, there was a good chance of finding something. Vic had completed an inspection downstairs. Apart from the dining room, which was devoid of anything other than a wooden table with four chairs and an old sideboard that contained at most ten plates and an assortment of cups and saucers, the only other room was the main sitting room. He had looked in there. The furniture was old and in poor condition. A television sat in one corner and a bookcase in the other. He had looked through the books, mostly religious in content, some on Islam and Buddhism as well. He had been preparing to look through the books in detail when he had received the call from upstairs. He had known that the sergeant was jumpy when they had arrived at the cottage, and so was he. He was a man who liked open spaces, not dark, dank and depressing places, and the Reverend Harrison's house qualified on all the negatives.

To one side of the bedroom was a single bed. It was unmade, although the sheets appeared to have been slept on. An oil-filled heater was still on, its electrical cord snaking away to a wall socket. Oldfield placed his hand on the top of the heater; it was warm, yet the room was cold.

'No insulation in these old places,' he said to Clare.

'Is it cold in there?'

Vic slowly moved around the room, almost on tiptoes. He did not know why, but he did not want to be there. 'Come in if you want to,' he said.

Clare entered with the same trepidation as Oldfield. 'Can you feel it?' she said.

'Feel what?'

'As though we're somewhere we're not wanted.'

'It's just a depressing old house, that's all,' Oldfield said.

The window rattled, a mouse scurried across the floor.

'We're not welcome,' Clare said.

'We're here to do a job. Let's wrap it up and then I'll treat you to hot coffee.'

Clare smiled, although she did not feel any contentment. She moved further into the room, felt the heater, withdrew her hand and touched the wall above the bed. The room should have been warm, but it was not.

She saw a Bible by the bed. She picked it up and ran the pages through her fingers, looking for something, anything. She wanted to leave, but could not. She was riveted to the spot. Outside the weather was calm. A tree rustled its leaves in the wind. She saw a robin sitting on the fence, cows in the field at the back, even a deer, which was rare enough at the best of times. Outside the house, she could see normality; she wanted to be there.

Oldfield continued to look on the other side of the room. He had checked out a small wardrobe, found nothing except the reverend's clothes. He had checked the man's underwear drawer: all in order.

'Are you finished?' Clare asked. She was already close to the door.

'There's something underneath the wardrobe. I need to check it.' The constable knelt down and peered underneath for a better look. 'It's a wooden box.'

Gently he eased it out. There was no lock at the front, only a metal catch. He undid the catch and opened the box. Clare had moved closer.

'There's a book in here, an old Bible,' Oldfield said.

'Check it out, and then we can leave.' A blast of freezing air gusted through the room.

'It's in there. I know it is,' Clare said.

Oldfield placed the Bible on the bed.

'Don't open it, please,' Clare said. She was shaking. She remembered back to that time in the church with Tremayne and the Reverend Harrison. She remembered back to the time with Mavis Godwin in her cottage when the daylight had turned to night, and a ferocious storm full of thunder and lightning had filled the sky.

Oldfield felt compelled to listen to her, but he knew what he had to do. He lifted the leather cover. The heater sparked and shut off.

'Get out of here before it's too late,' Clare screamed.

'It's our job. We've got to do this.'

'Look out the window.'

'The weather's changing, that all,' Oldfield said. 'We can either read it here or down at the station,' he said.

'Do it there.'

'There's some writing.'

'What does it say?' Clare, believing the worst, asked.

For those who read this be warned.

'Close it,' Clare said nervously. 'Can you hear it? The chanting outside.'

'It's the wind blowing through the trees.'

'What about the cold in here, the heater?'

'Do you expect us to tell DI Tremayne that evil lurks here?'

'Does it?' Clare asked. She was standing outside the door.

Oldfield chose not to answer. He closed the Bible, put it under his arm and left the room.

The two police officers hurried down the stairs and out of the front door.

Chapter 12

Clare had known Tremayne for almost eight months, and it was the first time she had seen him pensive.

'That's the story,' Clare said. Vic Oldfield stood beside her.

'I'm with you on this one,' Oldfield said.

'With me on what?' Tremayne said, looking up from the Bible placed in front of him. 'Are you telling me that the whole sorry saga of why a vicar hanged himself is in this?' He tapped the cover of the book. Clare eased back slightly.

'We only read the first line,' Clare said.

'And then hightailed it out of there like little children, is that it?' Tremayne said.

Clare remembered how she and Oldfield had acted after leaving Harrison's house. Both of them had not liked it there, but once distant from the area, they both agreed or maybe they'd convinced each other that what they had experienced up at the house was no more than the result of a fertile imagination.

In Tremayne's office, she knew that she could not let the man see her fear. 'Maybe it's best if you open the Bible and read what it says,' she said.

Oldfield said nothing. He was angling for a position in Homicide, a chance to get out of uniform and on with his career. Tremayne, he knew, was the best in the business, not only by reputation but because Clare had told him as well. He had to admit he liked her, would have asked her out, but he had heard her mention Harry and his pub. He knew he didn't have a chance. All he had was a constable's salary and a beat-up old Subaru, whereas the man she wanted drove a Mercedes and owned a pub. In Vic Oldfield's estimation, heaven, but he knew he was not cut out to run his own business. He needed stability and a secure job as well as the satisfaction of a job well done, but he still fancied Clare.

'And you, Oldfield?' Tremayne asked. 'What do you reckon to these stories of ancient gods?'

'Not for me, guv,' Oldfield said. Clare knew one thing, he was a more convincing liar than her.

'And you want to join the department?'

'I sure do.'

'I'll talk to your superior. See what can be done. Maybe you'll be able to convince my sergeant that whatever she believes in is nonsense.'

'I don't believe it anymore,' Clare said.

'Rubbish. You ran scared from that house, and Oldfield's covering for you.'

'That's not true.'

'It doesn't matter. What's in this Bible that's so important?' Tremayne said as he opened the front cover. Both the junior officers took one step back.

'Oldfield, you're as bad as her.'

For those who read this be warned.

'More mumbo jumbo,' Tremayne said as he read the first line. Clare looked out of the window.

'You'd better read on,' Oldfield said. Clare sat silently, uttering a prayer under her breath.

Here in the Lord's book, I have inscribed all that Mavis Godwin, one of my parishioners, has told me. Her statement of forces beyond the control of mere mortals needs to be recorded, and if what she says is true, then woe betide any who threatens them.

'I'm not reading this nonsense,' Tremayne said. 'Yarwood, you can read it.'

'If I must.'

Clare moved over to where the Bible was placed and looked at the words written by the hand of the Reverend Harrison. She imagined bolts of lightning and darkened skies, but nothing happened.

Mavis Godwin, a believer in the one true God, came to me with a dilemma. She was aware of forces that could not be explained, forces so malevolent that they require total loyalty or else they would seek retribution, they would seek death.

She has known, so she told me, of these ancient gods since an early age. There are, she said, a significant number of people, law-abiding people, respected and beyond reproach, who have given themselves over to them.

She said that she has witnessed in her youth their beneficence: the crops, the livestock, the wealth that has ensued. She also stated that she had seen their malevolence and what had happened to those who did not adhere to their strict code.

As a young woman, she had started to doubt them. For many years, she has remained separated from the others who follow these gods.

Her story was told to me over a period of several years, and finally I have summoned the courage to write it down in this Bible in the hope that the truth will be protected in the Holy Book.

Clare stopped reading from the Bible. 'That's it,' she said.

'But she's said nothing,' Oldfield said.

'I told you the man was certifiable,' Tremayne said.

'There must be more,' Clare said.

'The Bible was secured in a hidden place,' Oldfield said. 'There must be more. Clare, look further in the book.'

Clare leafed through the Bible, looking for more, hoping not to find it. All the work that Tremayne had done to convince her that it was nothing other than the imagination playing tricks, and then Harry backing up the DI's opinion, had had little effect on her. She knew something was not right.

Maybe the heater sparking and shutting down could have been an electrical wiring fault in the house. And as for the cold, yet again, poor insulation and no central heating. She could see how anyone, including the Reverend Harrison, could have started to believe in the supernatural when it was quiet and icy cold. She had been there for no more than fifty minutes and the place had left her uneasy, and the vicar had been there for ten long years. *No wonder he had started to doubt his faith*, she thought. And her doubts in Tremayne's office were doing nothing to help her career, and Harry was taking her out that night.

Clare took a deep breath and looked through the Bible. 'There's more here,' she said.

'What does it say?' Tremayne asked.

'It's next to a Bible text.'
'What text?'
'Deuteronomy 4:35.'
'What does it say?' Oldfield asked.

You were shown these things so that you might know that the Lord is God; beside him, there is no other.

'What did Harrison say?' Tremayne said.
'Sounds like he was hedging his bets,' Oldfield said.
'Whatever.' Tremayne was clearly agitated. The fingers on one hand were tapping his desk. The man looked as though he was ready to blow.
Clare looked at what Harrison had written on the blank page next to the text. She knew she had to get on with it.

Mavis Godwin had grown up with a belief in paganism, and that her family had a connection to those who practised their worship in the name of three ancient gods. She said their names were Teutates, Esus and Taranis, and whereas they were benign as long as they were honoured, they were ruthless and without mercy to those who threatened them. When she had first come to the Salisbury area, she had lived in a village where everyone believed. A village no more than ten miles from Salisbury. She said that to visit the place was to understand. There, she said, the crops were good, the livestock was healthy, and the people had an air of tranquillity.

'Why did she leave if it was so damn good?' Tremayne asked.
'There's more,' Clare replied.

She had met Trevor Godwin, a fellow believer, in the village. Their mutual belief turned to love and they married. After some years, she had become disillusioned. During a time when the weather had not been favourable, the elders determined that a sacrifice needed to be made. She was working in Salisbury at the time as a registered nurse and had seen that the conditions in the village were no better, no worse than elsewhere. Also, she had started to read the Bible, a forbidden activity.

With economic hardship about to encompass the village where she lived with her husband, a decision was made by the chief elder. On the appointed day, she and the others in the village were called to their meeting place. The senior elder made a speech, praised the gods, offered the sacrifice. The victim, suitably drugged, was then drowned in the centre of the church in an old water tank.

'That's murder,' Tremayne said.
'It's barbaric,' Clare said.
'Is there more?' Oldfield asked.
'Yes, but I'll not read it.'
'Give it to me.' Oldfield took the Bible and continued reading.

Mavis Godwin noticed that after the sacrifice, the weather changed for the better, and those with the strongest belief appeared to reap the most benefit, but outside of the village, others were also prospering. It seemed to her that it was not the gods but better farming, better land, that was more important. She read the Bible when she could. Eventually, her husband found her with it one day.

I asked her what he did. She told me that he denounced her to the elders.

'And?' Tremayne asked.
'I'm coming to it,' Oldfield replied.

A gathering of the villagers was held. There were those that wanted to show their disgust in the normal manner, but the senior elder said no. She was banished from the village on one condition: she was never to mention what she knew.

By the time of this revelation, I had had the opportunity to study the subject of paganism and ancient gods. How these beliefs had survived, I could not understand. She told me that the senior elder, a professional man, was a distant relative. She would not say his name or the name of the village.

'It's awful,' Clare said.
'Awful!' Tremayne retorted. 'It's murder.'
'They sound like a cult to me,' Oldfield said.
'I agree,' Tremayne said. 'How people can believe this is beyond me.'
'But they do,' Clare said.
'This is England, rural England.'
'They still exist, guv,' Oldfield said.

'Wherever they are we need to find them. Harrison mentioned a relative; any ideas, Yarwood?'

'None. We never asked her when she was alive, and we've found none afterwards.'

'Yarwood, you'll need to work with Oldfield on this one.'

'I'm on the team?' Oldfield asked.

'I'll deal with it. You know as much about the death of Mavis Godwin as any of us now.'

'Thanks, guv.'

Chapter 13

Clare felt the need to meet up with Harry. She had decided not to tell him about what she had read in Harrison's Bible.

She realised that Mavis Godwin's earlier life before Stratford sub Castle was vague. As part of the standard procedures, a dossier had been compiled on the woman. It was known that she had grown up in Devon, not far from Ilfracombe. Clare remembered holidaying there as a child; she also remembered that it had not stopped raining, but apart from that, there was nothing sinister about the place.

Mavis Godwin had mentioned a village close to Salisbury, but there was no reference in the Bible to its name.

Harry had organised a stand-in behind the bar at the Deer's Head that night. He picked Clare up from the office in his Mercedes. Oldfield saw him pull up for her to get in the passenger seat. *Lucky bastard*, he thought.

All he had for the night was a bottle of beer and a lasagne to heat up in the microwave. Oldfield felt dejected, although he knew he had no reason to, other than that he and Clare had shared a trip into the unknown at Harrison's house. Whatever it was at the house, it just didn't feel right to him. He could not pinpoint the reason, but the coldness went right through his bones. He had grown up close to London, a secure middle-class life, done well at school and then university, obtained the necessary qualifications for a police officer. He had breezed through training, gained top marks in virtually every exam that he had taken, and he knew that what he feared was irrational and not conducive to a secure future.

He put it to one side and opened the door to his Subaru. If he could make sergeant he would treat himself to a better car, he knew that. The car started on the first turn of the key, and he eased himself out of the station's car park and onto Bemerton Road. He turned right and headed up the road to Wilton, and the one-bedroom flat that he shared with nobody, except a girlfriend, a sweet twenty-two-year-old local, who came over occasionally.

'Where are we going?' Clare asked as Harry headed down the road from the police station.

'Your place first. I haven't seen you for a few days.'

Two hours later they left Clare's place. She had changed into a white top and a pair of denim jeans.

'Do you fancy fish and chips?' he asked.

'In Salisbury?'

'It's only thirty minutes to Bournemouth. We could drink a bottle of wine and sit on the seafront.'

'Sounds great.'

Clare had expected him to treat her to a slap-up meal, but fish and chips in a box and a bottle of wine suited her fine. She was glad just to be with him. She had to admit he was a generous man, always considering her, not withholding himself emotionally.

It had drizzled on the way down, smearing the windscreen of the car, but when they arrived, it had stopped. Harry parked the car close to the seafront. 'I often come down here,' he said.

'Who with?'

'On my own. I appreciate the solitude.'

Clare knew that men as gorgeous as Harry did not stay on their own for long. 'Who was she?'

'No one of importance,' he admitted. 'Does it worry you?'

'As long as you're not seeing her now,' Clare replied.

'Not for a long time. I've found you now.'

'And I've found you.'

'We should make this more permanent,' Harry said as he poured her wine into a glass he had brought from the pub.

'What do you mean? Is this a proposal?'

'I'll go down on one knee if you like.'

'I can't think of anywhere more romantic than a chair on the Bournemouth seafront, fish and chips and a glass of wine.'

'You accept?' Harry asked.

'Yes. You knew I would.'

***

Tremayne was a troubled man. There had been other cases over the years but none as baffling as the present one. In the past, always a clear motive, a logical path to follow; but this time, too many variables, too many unknowns. The man who could have broken the case wide open, the disturbed priest, had hanged himself from a beam in his church.

And then the husband of Mavis Godwin had disappeared without a trace. Whoever, whatever was behind the deaths was smarter than him, and he didn't like it. He knew the hand of man, not the devil or whatever Yarwood believed.

He knew she was sitting on the fence on this one, and it was not productive. Oldfield had looked more sensible, but he doubted him too.

He had heard it all before, living as he did so close to Stonehenge: tales of mysterious happenings at night, crop circles, ancient beliefs, druids.

He had arrested a few druids over the years. They had professed to be communing with nature, at one with the birds and the trees, but the ones he had come across were stoned on narcotic plants.

And as for crop circles, it wasn't aliens, it was always found to be a few locals out for a bit of a laugh and notoriety.

But in the main he knew these followers of ancient religions were, for the most part, harmless, even if a little strange. Trevor Godwin seemed to have been weird, although his wife had appeared rational. And how could a priest start to doubt his faith?

Tremayne remembered he had seen lights in the sky late one night as he was driving home from the pub. The next day he found out it was a couple of weather balloons that had been released on Salisbury Plain. And as for mythical beings, he had never seen any sign of them, but somehow, it seemed clear, some people believed in them.

Tremayne sat at his desk knowing that there was an itch he should scratch, something obvious that he was missing. Yarwood had been right, the church had been freaky, but what could you expect with Harrison's talk of the unknown, and the house was probably depressing, but that was all.

He decided he'd go out there as well. Even though it was late, he grabbed the keys. He phoned Oldfield. 'Are you up to a trip?' Tremayne asked.

'Sure, guv. Where to?'

'Harrison's house.'

'We've checked it.'

'There's something not right with this case. Maybe another visit.'

'Great night for a visit to an old church and a graveyard,' Oldfield said as they drove away from the police station.

'Old churches and graveyards and depressing old houses will make anyone feel uncomfortable, but there's nothing to them,' Tremayne said. 'They're not welcoming places at the best of times, and you and Yarwood trying to conjure up evil spirits does no credit to you both.'

'Still creepy, guv.'

The two men arrived at Harrison's house. Tremayne parked his car close to the church and next to the graveyard. Oldfield read the gravestone nearest to him: *In loving memory of Eustace Martin. Erected by his loving wife, Mabel.* The dates had worn off, and he wondered how many years it was since anyone had visited the grave.

'Come on, Oldfield. Show some backbone. They're dead. It's not as if they're going to come back,' Tremayne said.

Harrison's house was cloaked in darkness. The wind rustled through the trees, a full moon hung in the sky. Tremayne turned the key in the lock; it was tight, but it opened.

The door swung open as Tremayne entered, stooping to avoid banging his head on the beam above the door. 'Not much of a house,' he said.

Vic Oldfield could only agree. Tremayne flicked the light switch; a single bulb in the hallway lit up.

'Compared to this, my place is a palace,' Tremayne said.

'We've checked it.'

'That's as maybe, but we need to know more. What with you and Yarwood running scared, you may have missed something.'

'I don't think so, guv.'

Tremayne moved through the house, putting a light on as he entered a room, turning it off as he left. 'Nothing yet,' he said. Oldfield trailed behind, not sure what the man hoped to achieve, hoping to gain experience by observing how the man moved, methodically checking this, checking that, looking for the unusual.

'Plenty of books on early Celtic history,' Tremayne said.

'You can't avoid the Celts around here,' Oldfield replied.

'It's unusual reading for a Church of England vicar.'

'Why? You've been to Stonehenge, to the Avebury Circles, up to Old Sarum.'

'A long time ago, when I first came here. Back then you were free to walk around Stonehenge, touch the stones. Now you have to be an American President or the assorted riff raff at the summer solstice. God knows how much damage they do.'

'Not much, guv. I went up there a few years back. Most of them were harmless.'

'It's still weird,' Tremayne said.

'Not as strange as a group of villagers who commit murder, if we're to believe Harrison's Bible.'

'Sick bastards, the lot of them.'

'Have you ever come across any, guv?'

'We had one twenty years back who believed that God had commanded him to attack young girls, drag them into the bushes and rape them. Killed one of them as well.'

'What happened to him?'

'I caught the bastard.'

'And?'

'Broadmoor Psychiatric Hospital.'

'Still there?'

'Up until five years ago.'

'What happened?'

'They reclassified him as no threat to society. Put him in a regular prison.'

'One day he'll be back out on the street,' Oldfield said.

'Not a chance. The first week in his new prison, he was set on by a group of five men. They beat him to death.'

'What happened to them?'

'Nothing. No one saw anything.'

Tremayne, temporarily distracted by Oldfield, continued to look around the house.

'What are you looking for?' Oldfield asked as he pulled up the collar of his jacket. It was late, he was tired, and his girlfriend was coming over. He knew where he wanted to be.

'What did Harrison's writing tell us?'

'The man believed in the supernatural.'

'Apart from that?'

'He mentioned a village.'

'That's what we need to find. We know that Mavis Godwin married Trevor Godwin in Wilton.'

'I can't see any cults surviving there,' Oldfield said.

'A few weirdos down the pub I go to,' Tremayne said. 'Show me where you found the Bible.'

Vic Oldfield climbed the stairs first; they creaked under his weight.

'It's as quiet as a grave in here,' Tremayne said.

'You're not starting to believe, are you?' Oldfield asked, aiming to release the tension that both men felt. He had to agree with his senior that the place was spooky, typical of an unpleasant, unhomely, unloved building.

Oldfield opened the door to Harrison's bedroom. 'Someone's been in here,' he said.

Tremayne entered and looked around. The mattress on the bed was upturned, the wardrobe's contents tossed out.

'What does it mean?' Tremayne asked.

'Someone else knew about the Bible.'

Tremayne took his Nokia out of his pocket. 'Hughes, I need you down at Harrison's house tomorrow morning first light.'

'It's nearly midnight,' Hughes replied with a yawn.

'It's a murder enquiry, not a day in the kindergarten.'

'Tremayne. You're a hard man.'

'Find the miserable sods who keep murdering people, then you can have a lie in, but until then…'

'Point taken. I'll phone the team now. They'll be as excited as I am. What is it?'

'Upstairs, Harrison's bedroom. Someone's been in here. We need to know who.'

''Okay. Make sure there's a uniform outside before you leave.'

'I know how to do my job. I just hope you know how to do yours.'

'Don't worry about me,' Hughes said and hung up the phone.

Hughes's wife on the other side of the bed spoke. 'Who was it?'

'Tremayne.'

'Oh, him. Go to sleep.'

'He's right. I've got to organise for tomorrow.'

Jim Hughes's wife went back to sleep. He raised himself from the bed, put on a dressing gown and a pair of slippers and headed downstairs to his study.

'Damn you, Tremayne,' he said, his breath visible in the cold air.

***

Clare, blissfully unaware of Tremayne and Oldfield's visit to Harrison's house, slept snuggled up to Harry. They were planning to buy a ring in the morning. Her phone rang, Harry answered. 'Tell Yarwood she's to be in the office by 6 a.m.'

'We had plans,' Harry said. Clare had woken up and was looking over at her fiancé. 'It's Tremayne,' he said to her.

'The man never gives up. Tell him I'm with the man I love, and he can keep all the murders to himself.'

Tremayne, whose hearing was perfect, replied, 'Tell Yarwood it's 6 a.m. She's yours till then.'

'We've just got engaged,' Harry said.

'Congratulations. We'll have a few beers at your place after we've dealt with the recent developments.'

Clare took the phone away from Harry. 'Sorry about that, guv.'

'No need to explain. We're all young once and in love.'

'What's the problem?'

'Someone's been into Harrison's house.'

'Any idea who is it?'

'Not yet. Tell Harry he's a lucky man.'

Tremayne hung up the phone.

'What did he say?' Harry asked.

'He paid me a compliment.'

'How?'

'He said you're a lucky man.'

'He's right. Come here, you. We've still got a few hours left.'

Chapter 14

The elders met. 'It was not there,' one of them, a farmer, said. He was a well-built man in his sixties, fit as an ox, with the complexion of someone who spends a lot of time outside. He drove a Range Rover, but he was not a gentleman farmer. Besides, the car was a few years old, even carried the occasional sheep or pig, and while it was immaculate, as one of his farm hands dealt with that, it was also functional. As usual when meeting the other elders on a casual basis, he was dressed in a tweed jacket, a cravat around his neck.

His farm was five hundred acres of prime agricultural land, carefully sown with wheat and corn, the crops rotating and changing as the soil required or which produce offered the best return. He also had a herd of cattle which always won best of breed at the agricultural shows in Salisbury. He had had a suitable education, at least for farming. The farm had been in the family for six hundred years, a land grant from a king for an ancestor's services rendered. He no longer remembered the name of the king, but it did not bother him.

His wife had borne him three strapping boys, and two were anxious to stay and work the farm, one day inheriting it, which appeared as though it would be a long time off. Their grandfather had lived until one hundred and two, and their father looked as though he was good for a century. Not that it concerned them, as each had been given a house on the farm, large enough for a wife and two children. One of the sons had accomplished his task, the other was still to wed. The third son, his father despaired of him, was at university in Oxford, and he did not acknowledge the old ways. So far, he had revealed nothing, promised he never would, but the farmer knew the punishment for those who spoke against their protectors. Had that not happened to his cousin, Trevor Godwin?

'It can only be with the police,' one of the others said. His Bentley was parked outside. He was not a farmer, but a man who had travelled and obtained the necessary qualifications to allow him to practise as a doctor. He had led the group and the community for over twenty years, an honour handed down from father to son. 'If only she had married me,' he said.

The other two, a butcher and a vet, knew whom he was referring to: Mavis Godwin.

'Why did she choose him?' the farmer asked. 'She had come here with their blessing to be your wife, to ensure the bloodline continued.'

'Even then, she was unsure. She married Godwin out of spite for them. I would have treated her well,' the doctor said.

'Aye, you would have,' the others acknowledged.

'She had been promised to you,' the farmer said. He could trace his ancestry back to that fateful day in 1351 when the village had been isolated by the snow and the decimating effects of the bubonic plague.

'Mavis Godwin had told Harrison,' the vet reminded the chief elder. 'She would have told the police.'

'Our secret must be kept safe. And now, the police have it.'

'Is that confirmed?'

'It will be.'

'Then what must we do?' the butcher asked.

'We must do what is necessary.'

'Another death?'

'It is a small price to pay,' the doctor said.

***

Clare was first in the office; Harry had dropped her off. Tremayne followed her within five minutes, with Vic Oldfield a close third. Neither of the two men was in the best of moods, whereas Clare was cheerful.

'One of us looks happy,' Tremayne said. Oldfield did not reply. He knew their DI was not referring to him, and besides, by the time he had arrived home the previous night, his girlfriend was fast asleep.

'I am,' Clare replied. She had brought some chocolates with her by way of a celebration. Tremayne chose first, the one that Oldfield would have chosen.

'What's the plan?' Oldfield asked once Tremayne had finished with his chocolate.

'Hughes and his people will be out at Harrison's house by 8 a.m. I'm not sure we'll gain much though.'

'Why's that, guv?' Clare asked.

'Fingerprints. Whoever went through Harrison's bedroom is unlikely to be a criminal.'

'Why not?' Oldfield asked.

'We're dealing with strange people here, not criminals.'

'Then what do we hope to gain with checking the place?'

'More pieces of the jigsaw, that's what,' Tremayne said, tired of banal questions. He remembered when he had started out, a lowly constable. His DI back then, a dour Scotsman by the name of Campbell, would have chewed you out for constantly talking. The man had been autocratic, taught him a lot, even if his manner with those who he accosted was far from ideal. He'd have no trouble beating a confession out of a known villain down a back alley, an approach that Tremayne would still prefer to use on the occasional basis. Not that he was the man to administer the beating. In his twenties and thirties, no man could beat him in a fight, but now, though he stood six feet four and weighed nineteen stone, he was not as nimble as he once was.

That morning, the second in the last week, as he got out of bed, he had felt a twinge in his left leg. And at night he had woken up on a couple of occasions with a slight ache in the same leg. He knew it was arthritis, his father had suffered from it.

Tremayne looked over at Yarwood. 'What do we know about this village?'

'Nothing, guv.'

'We know that Mavis Godwin used a false address. What about her husband?'

'We know he was born in Salisbury Hospital to a Godfrey and Delilah Godwin.'

'How?'

'Hospital records.'

'Was there an address?'

'They gave an address in Salisbury.'

'Have you checked it out?'

'They left after two months.'

'Forwarding address?'

'It was nearly sixty years ago,' Clare replied.

'People can't just disappear. There must be records of where they went.'

'We're checking.'

'Then check harder.'

'What do you want me to do?' Oldfield asked. He noticed the bond between the older man and his young sergeant. He knew he was still very much the outsider.

'Get out to Harrison's house and let me know if Hughes finds anything.'

***

Once again, Vic Oldfield found himself outside Harrison's house. It was still dark, although the sun was attempting to make an effort to shine, not that he held out much hope.

Hughes and his team were still not there. Oldfield left the comfort of his car, a new Toyota Corolla. He still had the beat-up Subaru, but with Homicide came a police issue vehicle.

The uniform on the door appreciated the coffee that Oldfield had brought him.

'Done well for yourself, Vic,' Constable Hemmings said.

'I've worked hard, you know that.'

'You're still a jammy bastard. That Tremayne's a hard nut, though.'

'He knows what he's doing.'

'I'll grant you that. She's a looker, that sergeant of yours,' Hemmings said. Vic Oldfield had known the man since they had both reported to Bemerton Road Police Station eighteen months earlier. Hemmings had come from Liverpool, and he had a colourful turn of phrase. Oldfield also knew the man liked a drink, as they had been out on the occasional Saturday night when he had had to carry Hemmings into his flat and lay him out on the couch to sleep it off. There had been a warning in the past, and Oldfield was careful to keep his distance and not to say too much.

'She's just got engaged.'

'I would have given her one,' Hemmings said.

'Don't let anyone hear that down at Bemerton Road.'

'Bunch of wankers, the lot of them. You must have fancied her.'

Oldfield chose not to comment. Of course he had fancied her, what man wouldn't, but she was taken, and he had a job to do.

'Anything to report?' Oldfield asked as the two men stood in the front porch.

'Too damn quiet for me.'

'You've seen no one?'

'Judging by the company around here, I don't think so,' Hemmings said. Oldfield knew what he meant. There was a slight breeze, and as the men spoke, the rain started to fall.

'We can sit in my car for a while,' Oldfield said. He knew that Hemmings had been standing outside the house for hours.

'I wouldn't mind a bit of heat,' Hemmings replied, his scouse accent all too noticeable.

With both men located just eighty feet away, it was still possible to keep a watch on the house. Oldfield phoned for a replacement for Hemmings.

'Look over there,' Hemmings said.

'Where?'

'Behind that gravestone closest to the wall.'

'What can you see?'

'There's someone there.'

'Make sure the interior light doesn't show when we get out,' Oldfield said.

'I'll go down below him, you go around the back of the house and come at him from the other side,' Hemmings said.

'We'll go now,' Oldfield said. He left first, making sure not to slam the door of the car. Keeping down, he moved around the back of the house and positioned himself not more than twenty feet from the intruder. He looked for Hemmings, he could see him in position.

Oldfield crept forward, knowing that the exit points from the vicinity were limited. Where the intruder was positioned, there was a high stone wall to the rear. He knew he had the back of the graveyard covered, and Hemmings was in control of the front. Fifteen feet, ten feet. Oldfield edged forward carefully until he trod on a fallen branch; it snapped, the sound echoing off the headstones of the dear departed. The intruder, alerted, made a run for it. Vic Oldfield, a sprinter in his teens, rushed forward and grabbed the person.

'Let me go, let me go. I've done nothing wrong.'

'Then why were you here?'

'I saw the policeman. I was curious, that's all.'

'I've got him,' Oldfield shouted.

'We'll put him in the car,' Hemmings replied. 'I've got some cuffs.'

'Not me. I've done nothing wrong.' The intruder continued to squirm, attempting to get away.

Once they were in the car and with the intruder secure in the back seat, Oldfield took a closer look at him. 'You're just a kid,' he said.

'Too young for you to lock up,' the young man said. Oldfield could see that he was in his mid-teens.

'What's your name?'

'What are you going to do? Beat it out of me?'

'Have you been in trouble with the law before?' Hemmings asked.

'I'm not talking without my lawyer.'

'Another aficionado of American television,' Oldfield said.

'What's an aficionado?' the young man asked.

'Someone who likes watching make-believe on the television. You don't need a lawyer if you're not guilty. If you are, I'll organise one for you. Where do you go to school?'

'I'm not telling.'

'Suit yourself. A few days in the cells will loosen your tongue.'

'My parents will get me out.'

'Important, are they?'

'My father knows people.'

'Great. What's his name?'

'I'm not telling you.'

'If he doesn't know you've been arrested, then he can't help, can he?'

'I'm allowed a phone call.'

'Then we'll know your name. Stop being stupid and give us your name.'

'Adam Saunders.'

'Well, Adam, you'd better phone your father now. And then he can meet us at Bemerton Road Police Station.'

'I can't, not with my hands tied.'

'Release him,' Oldfield said. 'And make sure all the doors are locked.'

'No problem,' Hemmings said.

***

Jim Hughes arrived thirty minutes later. By then, young Adam Saunders was friendly.

'Check Adam Saunders' shoe and finger prints,' Oldfield said to one of Hughes's assistants.

'I've not been in there.'

'It's just a formality.'

Twenty minutes later, Oldfield arrived at Bemerton Road. Adam Saunders, no longer restrained but held firmly between the two policemen, was led into the police station and then to the interview room, after temporarily halting to let the boy visit the toilet.

The boy's father arrived shortly after. He was combative. 'How dare you arrest my son,' he said.

'He's not under arrest,' Tremayne informed the man. 'He's helping us with our enquiries.'

'What's the difference.'

'No charges have been laid against him.'

'He's free to leave?' Charles Saunders asked. Tremayne evaluated the man: educated, middle class, upright citizen.

'I wouldn't advise it. He was found in a graveyard adjoining a church where the vicar hanged himself. Coupled with that, one of the parishioners was murdered.'

'Very well, but I want to be there when you interview him.'

'That's your prerogative.'

Tremayne watched the reaction between father and son; they did not appear to be close. 'I didn't do anything, Dad,' the boy said.

'We'll talk about it at home,' the father replied.

'Adam, your story,' Tremayne said. Clare sat on his left. She felt sorry for the teenager. Apart from the fact that he was in trouble, he looked remarkably like her brother at that age. He had been rebellious, always in some trouble or other; nothing criminal, but always pushing the boundary between being adult and brave and young and stupid. Adam Saunders appeared to be on the side of young and stupid.

'I saw the policeman standing there. I was curious.

'For how long were you there?'

'One hour, no more. It was cold.'

'We know someone has been in the house. Was it you?'

'Are you accusing my son of breaking and entering?'

'Mr Saunders, you must allow me to conduct this interview. I am not accusing your son of any criminal activity. Whether your son is honest with us or not will make little difference to the police investigation. We have sufficient shoe and finger prints to make a match. If your son was in that house, we will soon know. Just be aware that if he is subsequently found to be guilty of a criminal offence, his denial here will go against him. We have no record that your son has been in trouble with the authorities before.'

Charles Saunders turned to his son. 'You'd better be honest,' he said.

Adam Saunders sat upright. 'I was just curious. I never went inside that house. I saw the policeman, that was all.'

'Adam, you're free to go,' Tremayne said.

After the father and son had left, Clare turned to Tremayne. 'You gave in easy there, guv.'

'They were a great double act. The boy was not going to talk, not with his father present.'

'You don't believe he's innocent?'

'He may not have gone into the house, but he's guilty.'

'Guilty of what?'

'We need to find out. We'll talk further in my office.'

Outside, two people walked away from the police station. 'Unfortunate that they saw you,' Charles Saunders said.

'I never got a chance. I tried, but that policeman never took a rest other than to pee on the garden.'

'We'll try another time.'

'Not with me. They know me now.'

Chapter 15

Jim Hughes and his CSI team had little to report after checking the Reverend Harrison's house. Apart from shoe prints, proven not to be Adam Saunders', they had found nothing more. There was confirmation that whoever had entered had only been in the bedroom, having broken a window at the rear of the house. The only comment of any use was that they were amateurs.

'They know the Bible's not there,' Tremayne said back in the office.

'There's one question we're not asking,' Oldfield said. He was standing close to the door. Clare was sitting down.

'What's that?'

'How did they know about the Bible?'

'You see, Yarwood. At least he's on the ball.'

'And I'm not?' Clare replied indignantly.

'You keep fiddling with your finger, wondering what kind of ring he's going to buy you. There's a jeweller next to his pub, and they're not cheap. Don't worry, Harry's got plenty of money; he'll buy you something special.'

'Sorry, guv.'

'Forget about him for now,' Tremayne said, a wry smile creeping across his face.

'Who told them about the Bible?' Oldfield asked.

'Mavis Godwin may have known but would she have told anyone?' Clare asked.

'It seems unlikely, so apart from Harrison and the woman, who else is there?'

'Maybe they assumed that Harrison had written something down,' Oldfield said. He had pulled in a seat from outside the office. Clare sat in her space, overshadowed by the two men.

'Are we assuming there might be more in the house?' Tremayne asked.

'We still don't know the name of the village,' Clare said.

'A job for you both. Recheck the house.'

'But what are we looking for?'

'Any reference to the village. Did the man have a laptop?'

'Yes, but he didn't use it much. We've checked it already.'

'Did he have a library, some books? I remember there were books in the main room. Have you checked them?'

'Not exhaustively,' Clare said.

'Then you'd better get your reading glasses on. I want every book checked. Take some help if you need it.'

'We'll manage,' Oldfield said.

***

'I suppose I'll have to get used to this,' Harry said.

'It's no worse than you down the Deer's Head every night chatting up the women, drinking with the men.'

'Alright. I'll give up the women, but I still need to drink.'

'Then that's fine. If I finish early, I'll give you a call,' Clare said. She knew their phone conversation was the banter of two people in love, two people who had just pledged themselves to each other. She wanted to be with him, especially that day, but Tremayne was fired up.

'The sooner we start, the sooner we finish,' Oldfield said as he and Clare drove to Harrison's house. He had heard one side of the conversation, imagined what the other side was. He'd been there in the past, a few years back, but the relationship had faded once he had joined the police force. She had not been able to deal with the irregular hours, and he was not willing to consider another profession.

'How do you want to do this?' Clare asked once they had arrived at the house. Neither were keen to go upstairs.

'You start at the bottom of the bookcase, I'll start at the top.'

'Fine, and remember we need to be thorough. If Tremayne finds out afterwards we've missed anything there'll be hell to pay.'

The two police officers made themselves a cup of coffee each. There was no milk, so it was black with no sugar. It suited Clare, but it was not to Oldfield's liking.

The bookcase looked as though it had been bought as a kit. It contained about sixty books: some new, some old with frayed spines.

'The man had an eclectic taste in literature,' Oldfield said.

'What do you mean?'

'I'd have thought they would be mainly religious.'

'The house is freezing. Is there any heat in here?'

'I saw a heater in the other room.'

'Then fetch it.'

Left alone in the room, Clare started to imagine things. Oldfield soon returned.

'Give it a few minutes, and it should warm up,' Oldfield said. He had plugged the heater into a wall socket behind the television.

'What did you say about his book collection?' Clare asked as she sipped her coffee, waiting to feel some warmth on her skin from the heater. She had been warm in bed with Harry, but the house was freezing. She remembered her parents telling her how cold their houses had been in their childhood, when there had been ice on the windows, and no heating after the water pipes had frozen and burst, eventually creating a flood of water throughout the house. Thankfully, her place was warm with abundant hot water, although Harry was asking her to move in with him. She had said she would think about it, but that was just being coy on her part. Once her lease was up, only two weeks, she'd be with him day and night, or given the hours they both worked, whenever possible. She knew that no icy gusts of the wind, no mouse scurrying over her shoes, no branches rustling outside giving off a melodic rhythm were going to frighten her this day.

'I met him on a couple of occasions,' Clare said. 'The Reverend Harrison always left me feeling strange.'

The heater, not the one that had shut off inexplicably with sparks on their previous visit, had warmed them sufficiently. The two police officers started to work their way through the books. Oldfield, an avid reader in his spare time, had to agree that Harrison had an excellent collection. There were thrillers, horror and reference books on various religions.

'Which ones are the most likely?' Clare asked.

'It depends on what we're looking for. I would have thought anything relating to local history. If the man was researching the area, he might have marked one of the pages.'

'We'll be here all day.'

'Fine by me,' Oldfield said.

'Not by me,' Clare said, which was true. She had wanted to take the day off, to be with the man she loved, not leafing through dusty books. At least, she had to admit, the heater was doing its job.

Oldfield took the first book, top left. It was a horror novel by an author whose name he did not recognise. He ran his fingers across the pages, upended the book and shook it.

'What are you doing?' Clare asked. She was at the bottom of the bookcase looking for books related to local history. She was keeping a note of which books she had checked.

'He could have slipped a piece of paper in any of the books. We know the man had hidden that Bible hoping no one would find it.'

'We found it. That boy you caught, do you reckon he intended to check all these books?'

'Not likely. He'd not have the attention to detail, and besides one person on their own would not have had enough time.'

'Are you suggesting he knew what he was looking for?'

'We'll never know. Once we're free of here, we should check out the boy's family,' Oldfield said.

'Agreed,' Clare said, but hoped it was another day.

Clare continued at the bottom of the bookcase. 'This looks promising,' she said.

'What is it?'

'This book. *Celts, the search for a civilisation.*'

'Let me know what you find,' Oldfield said. He had checked six books; his sergeant was on the first one.

'I'm going through it now.' Clare had taken a seat.

Oldfield despaired at how anyone could be so pedantic. He knew if he picked up a good book he'd read it within a couple of days, but his girlfriend would take weeks. He had taken her to task once. 'By the time you get to the end, you'll have forgotten what the story was about.'

'I like to savour every word,' she had replied. Oldfield had become agitated with her, so much so that she had given him the cold shoulder for a few hours afterwards.

'Not much here,' Clare said. She picked up the next book.

Oldfield was now on the second shelf, and so far nothing other than some good books to read. He'd download them onto his Kindle that night.

'It says they weren't into human sacrifice,' Clare said.

'Who said? That book you're reading?'

'I'm not reading, I'm checking.'

Oldfield sensed the terseness in her voice.

'Okay, checking. What does it say?'

'It was Julius Caesar who mentioned human sacrifices.'

'Why?'

'Propaganda. The victor writes the history. The Romans regarded everyone else as Barbarians when in reality they were as bad as the rest, often worse.'

'Christians thrown to the lions, that sort of thing.'

'Yes.'

'What else does it say?'

'The Druids did not build Stonehenge, they've only adopted it as a place of worship. There's no mention of the gods that Harrison wrote about.'

'Look for a book on the ancient gods of England,' Oldfield suggested.

'There's one here.'

'See if they're in there. Have you found any of Harrison's writing?'

'Nothing. How about you?'

'I like the man's taste in books, but nothing so far.'

'I've found something,' Clare said. She pulled herself in closer to the heater. 'It's getting cold in here.'

Oldfield put his hand on top of the heater, pulled it back quickly as he did not want to burn his hand. 'It's on,' he said as he walked over to the window, brushing aside an old curtain to get a better look. Over to one side of the graveyard he saw a woman touching one of the headstones, holding a bunch of flowers. He phoned Tremayne. 'I need someone in plain clothes to keep a watch on a woman here.'

'Can't you?' Tremayne asked.

'I don't want her to know that we're on to her.'

'Any luck at the house?' Tremayne asked. At the same time, he was calling one of the team over. 'Get down there, park far enough away. You can phone Oldfield, he'll give you the details, and whatever you do, don't let the woman see you.'

'I'm on my way, guv,' the young constable said.

'Is she suspicious?' Tremayne asked.

'It's cold outside, no one's been buried here for years, and she's saying a silent prayer, putting flowers. I'd say it's suspicious.'

'Okay, someone's on the way. He'll call you when he's nearby.'

'Thanks. She keeps looking up at the house as well, pretending not to.'

'You seem good at this,' Tremayne said.

'Misspent youth, looking for the farmer when we'd nip over the wall and raid his apple orchard.'

'Criminal record?'

'Just young children, no more than eight years old. We used to sell them on a stall at the end of our street. Even the farmer would buy from us.'

'And this woman?'

'Tell your man to hurry up. Who is it, by the way?'

'Dyer.'

'What's he driving?'

'An old Toyota. How's Yarwood?'

'She's checking out Harrison's books.'

'Remember, it's the village we need. We know about the gods. It's those who murder in their names that we want. They must be a bunch of lunatics.'

'The woman in the graveyard doesn't appear to be.'

'Describe her?'

'Late sixties, dark hair, fur coat. Not much else to say. I'm not looking at her directly, only in a reflection from a mirror in the room, and the mirror's none too clean.'

'I'll hang up to let Dyer contact you,' Tremayne said.

***

Oldfield stayed in position for another twelve minutes before his phone rang.

'I'm just down from the church,' Dyer said. 'What car is the woman driving?'

'I've no idea. She's still here, pretending to look occupied. I'm certain she's not here for the newly departed.'

'What do you suggest?'

'Position yourself so that you can see her leave. If she's in a car, follow. You can do that?'

'Not a problem. Can you give me a description?'

'You can't miss her: sixties, fur coat. I'll let you know when she moves.'

'What about the uniform. Where's he?'

'He'll come back after we leave.'

'If she's watching, she'll not move until you do.'

'Then she's in for a long wait.'

'I can see her,' Dyer said.

'How?'

'I just walked down the road.'

'Has she seen you?'

'Unlikely. You don't need to keep a watch out for her. I can take it from here.'

Oldfield went back to checking books. Clare was huddled over the heater. 'It's cold,' she said.

'That's what Dyer said.' Oldfield knew he had lied, but they still had a job to do. He knew Tremayne's response if they left the job unfinished. Also, the woman outside needed to be checked. She had been there for two hours, and regardless of her diligence, at some stage she would need to take respite from the cold.

'He's written in this book,' Clare said.

'What book?'

'*Villages of Wiltshire: a history.*'

'Go on.'

'It's a history of over two hundred villages stretching back centuries.'

'What's he written?' Oldfield had moved over close to Clare.

'He's circled one village on the map.'

'Which one?'

'Avon Hill.'

'Where's that?'

'Out past Wilton. I've never heard of it.'

'Neither have I,' Oldfield replied.

'How many more books are there to go through?' Clare asked.

'Fifteen to twenty.'

'Why don't we take them back to Bemerton Road.'

'Fine by me. We need that woman to move first.'

'She'll not move with us here.'

'Then we should look as though we're moving.'

'You pick up ten of the books, I'll take the remainder. I'll phone for the uniform to come back around the same time. Let's see what the woman does.'

***

Clare phoned up Tremayne. 'We're leaving.'

'Anything?'

'We've a village to check out.'

'We need to know where the woman goes,' Tremayne said.

'We need two more cars either end of the village. Dyer can follow first, and then another vehicle can take over. These people are not stupid. They'll smell a rat soon enough.'

'Give me twenty minutes.'

'We'll wait.'

Oldfield phoned up the uniform and Dyer to update them. The woman continued to move around the graveyard. Dyer mentioned that she occasionally looked up at the house. Oldfield reminded him and the uniform, and all those involved, that the woman was not to be restricted in her movements. It was important to know where she went.

Twenty-five minutes after the plan had been discussed, Clare opened the front door of Harrison's house. She shouted back to Oldfield. 'Let's go. I've got the books.' It was the first time that Clare had seen the woman. The woman looked up briefly and slowly ambled out of the graveyard.

'I've got her,' Dyer messaged.

Oldfield phoned back. 'Stay with her. What's the registration?'

'I'm passing it onto Bemerton Road to check. It's a light blue Hyundai. Registration: HC66 KPQ,' Dyer answered.

'No need to rush out of the house,' Oldfield said to Clare. 'The woman's taken the bait.'

'There is,' Clare said. She had not enjoyed herself in Harrison's house. She wanted out.

'If Avon Hill is correct, they won't give in easily.'

'Killing Mavis Godwin is one thing, but they won't stop there.'

'We're threatened, you know that.'

'I know. We need Tremayne to understand what we're up against.'

'We may have discovered where they are.'

'Have we?' Clare said.

'Do you believe what Harrison wrote in that Bible?'

'I'm not sure,' Clare replied.

'Neither am I, but don't tell Tremayne.'

Chapter 16

For seven hundred years the doctor and his ancestor's leadership of the believers had remained unchallenged, but now there were others who were threatening to blow it wide open.

An astute man, he realised that the modern age with its technology, its computers and mobile phones, its literate people would not be held at bay.

What fools they are, he thought. *Comfortable in their reliance on the modern age.*

The man knew that anyone who ventured to his home village would feel their wrath. He was aware of Harrison's house and young Saunders' efforts. He and his father had handled the situation well, but they were now marked, and the boy on his own and under pressure would not hold out for long. To the youth, it had been fun, a bit of a lark, hiding there in the graveyard, keeping a watch on the police, looking for an opportunity to take anything that could betray the village, and now the policewoman had found it.

The group on the conference call with the doctor knew what needed to be done.

'Tonight?'

'We will meet at the usual time,' the doctor said.

***

Constable Dyer stayed with the Hyundai as it drove through Stratford sub Castle heading in the direction of the Woodford Valley. As he exited the village, maintaining a distance of two hundred yards, another unmarked police car took over. Dyer pulled back to let it go, although he stayed within half a mile of the other vehicle.

'Take the left-hand turn over the river,' the lead police car said.

'Acknowledged,' Dyer's reply.

Clare and Oldfield were in their car and heading back to Bemerton Road Police Station, although intrigued as to where the three vehicles were heading. Dyer had his phone on hands-free to allow them to listen in. He kept in communication with the lead police car by radio.

'Turn left up Camp Hill. She's heading towards Wilton,' the lead car said.

'It must be Avon Hill,' Clare said.

Heading to the police station via Wilton was more circuitous than the usual route, but Clare and Oldfield decided to stay with the convoy. Up front, the woman was weaving through the traffic in Wilton.

'Take the A30 towards Barford St Martin.' The instruction came through loud and clear.

'Has she seen you?' Dyer asked.

'Unlikely.'

Ten minutes later. 'Take the B3089 out of Barford heading towards Dinton.'

'It's got to be Avon Hill,' Clare repeated her earlier statement.

Five minutes later, another message over the police radio. 'Our engine's blown.'

'What do you mean?' Dyer asked.

'You'll see soon enough. There's a road junction: take a left for Hindon, Chilmark and Chalfont and take a right up a small lane soon after.'

'Where did she go?'

'No idea. We can't move.'

'I want that vehicle checked out,' Clare said.

'What are you suggesting?' Oldfield asked.

'Nothing. It's just suspicious.'

'Dyer, did you hear that?'

'Yes. I'm taking the lane to the right. When you get here take a left.'

'Vic, we need to go back to the station,' Clare said.

'Why?'

'The books are more important than the woman.'

'Dyer, you're on your own,' Oldfield said.

'I've broken down now.'

'Two cars in the same place. I don't like it,' Oldfield said.

'You do realise that Dyer's only one mile from Avon Hill,' Clare said.

'What are we going to tell Tremayne?'

'Just tell him the facts.'

'These books may tell us,' Oldfield said. 'Are we picking up Dyer?'

'Not a chance. He can walk out, arrange to be picked up.'

'Is it?' Oldfield posed a rhetorical question.

'Don't even think it,' Clare replied. She was doing enough thinking for the two of them. She touched her ring finger, wished that Harry was with her.

***

'Are you two joking?' Tremayne asked once the two police officers were back at Bemerton Road Police Station.

'That's what happened. Both vehicles broke down.'

'You're not giving me that baloney again, are you, Yarwood?'

'No. I've requested a full report for later today.'

'Are you telling me that we should be concentrating on Avon Hill?'

'Yes, guv. Have you been there?'

I've passed through it on a few occasions. Not much of a place, just a church and a few houses.'

'A pub?' Oldfield asked.

'There's one, but they were a strange group. If you weren't a local, they sure knew how to make you feel unwelcome.'

'We should go there, guv.'

'I want to find out what went wrong with those cars first. I don't fancy getting stuck down there with a bunch of murderers.'

'You're not starting to believe? Clare asked.

'Careful, Yarwood. There's a rational reason for them breaking down.'

'What reason?' Oldfield asked.

'How the hell should I know?' Tremayne snapped back. The man was on his feet and angry. He was aware both of them were hedging their bets.

***

Some of the people in the village saw the end as inevitable. The doctor, with his surgery in Salisbury, his Bentley in the driveway, was not one of them.

It had been his predecessor, his namesake, Edmund Wylshere, the young boy, who had stood up in the church seven hundred years previously. The same church where they now congregated and recited the forbidden words of a language long forgotten.

Doctor Edmund Wylshere, the name passed down from generation to generation and always given to the first-born male, stood in that same church in the same pulpit. 'They will be here soon,' he said.

Those assembled knew that he had spoken the truth: some were frightened, some were unconcerned, some were thinking of leaving. The exodus from the village had started fifteen years ago with the advent of modern technology. The pagan ways had been easy when people had been uneducated, but now all the children went to school, and they were easily swayed by other ideas, even forced to attend church services. One of them had eventually embraced Christianity, but he had been dealt with. The doctor, a life giver outside the village, had death on his mind that night.

'They are looking for an offering,' Wylshere said.

'What kind of offering?' one of those assembled asked.

'A life.'

'But we have none to give.'

'The decision has been made.' Wylshere kept the name to himself. The person was unpredictable. His fate was sealed.

***

Clare, persistent as usual, had obtained the mechanic's report for the two cars that had broken down. The first vehicle had suffered a major oil leak and seized, the second, driven by Constable Dyer, an electrical fault.

'It can always be explained,' Tremayne said. 'The trucks that brought them back had no problems.'

Clare and Oldfield had been busy looking through the books they had taken from Harrison's cottage. Oldfield had found no further reference to Avon Hill. Clare had found another book referring to the bubonic plague and the history of Wiltshire, but it shed no more light on why Avon Hill was integral to Mavis Godwin's murder.

One of her neighbours had come forward to say that she had seen a car outside the Godwins' house around the time of the woman's death. She further stated that she had been away for a few days and that Mavis Godwin was a friend and they used to have a regular chat over the back fence.

'Came as quite a shock, I can tell you,' the next-door neighbour said.

'What else can you tell us?' Clare had asked when the woman had presented herself at Bemerton Road Police Station.

'I've seen the car before.'

'Any idea who the driver was?'

'She was a relative.'

'Are you sure?'

'Mavis told me she was, but she never introduced me.'

'What else?'

'I can give you the car's registration.'

'Can you?'

'Oh, yes. I always remember.'

'Good memory,' Clare said.

The two women were sitting at Clare's desk. The woman was there of her own free will, she wasn't involved, and a low-key approach seemed the best option.

'Photographic, not that it's much use. It certainly doesn't pay the bills.'

'Could I have the number please?'

'JC84 KST.'

'What make was it?'

'I never looked. It was green.'

Clare passed the number to another person to make the necessary checks. The vehicle they had tailed from Harrison's house turned out to be from the north of England. The last registered owner claimed to have no knowledge of the car, having sold it three months previously. He had the receipts to prove it, as well.

***

Tremayne was anxious to take a team to Avon Hill. Superintendent Moulton wanted proof before they went barging in. Both men were sitting in the DI's office. Tremayne, as usual, did not appreciate the visit.

'What's your proof?' Moulton asked.

'We need to conduct a door-to-door, check around,' Tremayne replied.

'And then what?'

'Everything points to this village.'

'I've read the reports: ancient gods, sacrifices. You don't believe that nonsense?'

'Not me. Whoever is behind Mavis Godwin's death and putting the fear up Reverend Harrison, they're very mortal. And then there's Langley.'

'You've no proof,' Moulton reminded his DI. He knew Tremayne was past his use-by date, and talk of ancient gods might be enough to get him out.

'We know that Mavis Godwin was murdered, Reverend Harrison hanged himself because of what she had told him, and she told Yarwood and me that there were mysterious forces behind Langley's death. There's too much there not to believe that Langley's been murdered.'

'You'll not prove it.'

'Maybe, but I'm not giving in on this one.'

'Suit yourself. If you make a fool of yourself, don't blame me.'

Tremayne looked at his senior, knew full well that the man wanted him to make a fool of himself, but he wasn't going to give him that pleasure.

'Super, we know that Avon Hill is isolated, no more than seventy to eighty inhabitants. And it's only been in the last fifty years that there's been a road through there. Before that, it was a dead end. They could have been getting up to all sorts of monkey business down there.'

'And you believe that someone will talk if you start asking questions?'

'It's a long shot.'

'I'll need more information before I approve,' Moulton said.

'It's only a reconnoitre, sir.'

'If what you are suggesting is true, they'll not give in easily; it could get violent. I propose that you do some more research on who lives down there and if they're involved.'

'I'll agree with you on that. I'll get the team on to it.'

'When do you want to go?'

'Within the next two days.'

'Make sure all your vehicles are serviced. I assume you believe the mechanic's report.'

'I do.'

'Your team?'

'They're police officers. None of them believes the two vehicles breaking down was other than circumstantial.'

'Then why didn't Yarwood and Oldfield take up the pursuit?'

'They had to get back here,' Tremayne replied.

Chapter 17

Keith Tremayne believed none of it. The most he could see was that people's wild imaginations were getting the better of them. Even Yarwood was susceptible, and he wasn't sure about Oldfield. Both of them were trained police officers, not people who believed in fairies at the bottom of the garden; at least he hoped they didn't.

There had to be a logical explanation for all that had occurred, although the first body, no more than a pair of legs, was very suspicious, and no one, not even the CSE, not even Yarwood, and she loved surfing the internet, had come up with anything to explain what had happened.

Tremayne sat back in his chair, not sure how to proceed, and not helped, he had to admit, by drinking more than he should have the previous night. And there was Yarwood in the office, full of cheer, ready to meet the day's challenge, but then she had Harry at the end of the day. No matter how taxing the day had been, there was always an outlet for her, someone to soothe away the frustrations, but what did he have? Nothing, not even a cat.

He was not a man to dwell for too long on the injustices of life, but sometimes he could become melancholy reflecting on a life wasted. He realised that the chase of a villain was more exciting than pursuing personal relationships, but now in the twilight years, possibly months, of his policing career, he had to wonder what was the point. All that he had was an adequate police pension, although there'd be no trips around the world with it, not that he wanted that either, and the house he owned was nothing special. The only companionship in the house was a square box in one corner, and he knew that apart from the sports channels, it was inane and mind-numbing.

'What's the plan, guv?' Clare asked. She had brought a cup of tea for him, one for her.

'We need to visit Avon Hill.'

'The place scares me.'

'Why? Two cars break down on the way, and you're frightened. Get a grip of yourself, Yarwood.'

'It's not that, it's just...'

'What's up?'

'I've been reading up on it.'

'On what?'

'Ancient gods.'

'You're not serious?' Tremayne said. He could not believe how many times they had had this conversation, and still his sergeant kept going back to ancient mythology.

'Not in the gods, but those who believe in them.'

'Are you telling me that people still believe in this nonsense?'

'Mavis Godwin believed in them, explains why she was so devout.'

'Hedging her bets?'

'More like she was looking for protection.'

'It didn't do her much good, did it?'

'Not in the end, but what I'm saying is that if people do believe in these malevolent forces, then whether they exist or are a figment of someone's imagination, they are very dangerous.'

'What is it with Avon Hill?' Tremayne asked. It appeared to him that Yarwood was rational. She had proven herself to be a competent police officer and the office was better for her being there. There was he with his grumpy outlook on life, and there was she, cheering the office up with her presence.

'Those who believe in these gods, or at least worship them in some pagan ritual, will do anything to protect themselves. That's why Mavis Godwin died and Reverend Harrison committed suicide.'

'But why?'

'They wanted him dead, the same as they did with Mavis Godwin.'

'Are you saying that Harrison's death is suspicious?'

'We know he committed suicide by his own hand, and that no one else was involved, but how can we be sure?'

'Hughes's crime scene team went over the place. No one else was there.'

'They must have driven him to commit suicide.'

'I'm not with you on this one,' Tremayne said.

Clare took a seat. 'What could drive a man to commit suicide? The fear of the gods, or the fear of the people who believed in them?'

'People kill, not ancient gods.'

'Precisely.'

'What are you getting at, Yarwood?' Tremayne said.

'Harrison had been with us, and we weren't going to give up on pressuring him for more information. In time, he would have broken.'

'Eventually.'

'The man was damned whatever happened. Either he committed suicide, or they would have had him killed.'

'We've agreed on that.'

'And we know the woman in the graveyard was from Avon Hill.'

'Proven?'

'Not one hundred per cent, but where else could she have been heading? There's not much else close to Avon Hill.'

'Adam Saunders was not from there.'

'We know where he lives.'

'Where?'

'No more than two miles from the village. We should interview him again.'

'If his father is there, he'll not talk.'

'Then how do you keep him away?'

'What school does he go to?'

'Bishop Wordsworth's.'

'That's where you interview him. I'll leave it up to you and Oldfield,' Tremayne said. 'You two are more his age. Just keep it informal, no heavy-handed brow-beating.'

'No roughing him up behind the toilet block, is that it, guv?'

'It's the easiest way to get the truth, but no, keep it friendly.'

'Leave it to us,' Clare said.

'And if it doesn't work, then the toilet block option. Whatever happens, find out something. We're going to Avon Hill within the next two days, regardless.'

***

Adam Saunders proved to be elusive. Where he lived, where he went to school, even his friends were known, but the young man could not be found. Enquiries at Bishop Wordsworth's Grammar School on Exeter Street revealed that he had not been seen for several days, which aligned with when he was caught at Reverend Harrison's house.

Clare, always the optimist, was confident he would be found. Oldfield, more cynical, was not so sure, and Tremayne thought the young man's disappearance was decidedly suspect.

His father, Charles, an accountant with an office in Wilton, a town close to Salisbury, was evasive when questioned. 'He's with family up north.'

Even with the police pressuring him, reminding him that his son was integral to the case, the father remained resolute. 'He had a bit of a shock after you questioned him. He's not been in trouble with the police before.'

Tremayne, when told of Charles Saunders' hostile attitude, wanted to take further action, to summons the father to produce the son, but that would have taken time.

'Give it a few days. We'll keep looking,' Yarwood said in the office.

'He's probably in Avon Hill,' Tremayne replied.

Harry, her lover and now fiancé, had warned her about going there. 'They're a strange group of people down there.'

'What do you mean?' she had asked.

Harry's explanation, not so convincing, was that the village had been isolated during the bubonic plague centuries earlier and that there had been some inbreeding.

Clare had checked up on the village's history, only to find that it had been a time of isolation for many villages, as they isolated themselves from the plague outside. Avon Hill was not the only one, but Harry seemed adamant that it was an exceptional case. She didn't know why, but she had not given it further thought. She had her man, her lover, and she was content in his arms or in his bed, which, given the demands of the case and Tremayne's driven focus to bring the investigation to a conclusion, was not often. And, Clare thought, to prove to Superintendent

Moulton that he was not ready for retirement, that he was not too long in the tooth, and that the old policing method of long hours, maintaining the pressure, pushing hard, leaving no stone unturned, was the way to solve cases.

'Charles Saunders is involved. I'm certain of it,' Tremayne said. It was late in the evening. Harry was waiting for Clare, but he would have to wait. Clare knew there was no way to leave her senior's office when he was on a roll. Oldfield was equally fired up, but then neither he nor Tremayne had a Harry to go home to. Clare knew about Oldfield's girlfriend; he had told her that much, but it did not seem to be much of a relationship, and Tremayne, she knew, lived alone. She imagined that behind the image he portrayed, self-sufficient, no need of a pet or a woman, he was a sad man, his only joy in life, policing. She could see that retirement would be the death of the man.

'You'll find Adam Saunders in Avon Hill, I'm sure of it,' Tremayne said. He was leaning back in his chair, a cup of tea in one hand, a sandwich in the other. It was past eleven at night.

'What makes you so sure?' Oldfield asked. He had not long been out of uniform, and he was revelling in working with Tremayne.

'The boy may have pretended to be an innocent bystander, but he was in that graveyard for a reason. If you find him, there's a good chance we'll have a breakthrough.'

'His father's a difficult man,' Clare reminded him.

'If we get the boy on his own, he'll break.'

'That's what you said about Harrison,' Oldfield said.

'And then the bloody fool goes and hangs himself. What is it about this case that I don't get?'

'If they're pagans, they see their beliefs are real.'

'Haven't we deduced this before?' Tremayne said.

'More or less, but they're not mad,' Clare said.

'They are to me.'

'They're not mad, guv,' Clare said. 'Deluded they may be, but they're not certifiably insane. There'll be some, the more feeble-minded, who may believe, but there will be a core person or persons who realise that it is errant nonsense, but for some reason perpetuate the belief.'

'Why?'

'Personal gain. And then some people relish the macabre, the need to prance around stone circles in the middle of the night, to engage in orgiastic rituals.'

'Mad, as I said.'

'Okay, mad, but the core group could be educated, rational, well-respected members of the community. Charles Saunders for instance.'

'And Adam Saunders is the son of one of these people?'

'Why not?' Clare said.

'Assuming you're correct, how do they keep this quiet?'

'They've kept it quiet since the middle ages, generation to generation.'

'You realise what you're saying, Yarwood?'

'Avon Hill.'

'Exactly. There's an isolated community, and before the advent of the motor car, isolated for part of the year when winter came, and then by distance, and no doubt, education.'

'As you say,' Clare acknowledged. 'And now they're threatened. Their hold on the community is starting to wither. They're becoming more desperate, more violent.'

'Are you saying that this core group will stop at nothing to remain in control?'

'Why not?'

'I suggest we call it a night,' Tremayne said. He knew that the impending visit to Avon Hill needed to happen soon.

Chapter 18

'Clare, drop this. This obsession is starting to be annoying,' Harry said. It was their first argument. Clare had been looking for moral support, and he was not providing it. She knew that Tremayne was right, as was Harry, although she could not understand the reluctance of the man she loved to even discuss the possibility.

'I saw things,' she said.

'If you keep this up, Tremayne's going to become annoyed, and then what?'

'I thought you'd be interested.'

'Well, I'm not. There are no such things as pagan gods. Can you honestly believe that people in a village not more than twenty-five minutes' drive from here are indulging in pagan rituals, worshipping gods out of ancient English history and whatever else?'

'They could still believe in the rituals.'

'It's just not possible. It may be okay for a novel or a movie, but get real, this is nonsense.'

'I was looking to you for support.'

'That's what you're getting. I love you, you know that. I can't just stand by, say nothing and allow you to continue with this. There's no such thing as the supernatural.'

'You're right, I know it. It's been a long day. I'm just exhausted.' Clare realised that she wanted Harry more than an argument, so she acquiesced and went back to her loving self. The day had been long and tense; she did not intend to allow the night to be anything other than pleasurable, and with Harry that was ensured, but there were questions unanswered, questions she felt were relevant.

***

Harriet Wylshere mourned in silence. She had believed in what she had been requested to do, but she still mourned a woman who had been a friend. She remembered how they had talked in the cottage in Stratford sub Castle; how they had reminisced about their lives. Yet their lives had turned out differently. One had stayed close to Avon Hill; the other had felt disillusionment and the need to move away. Their meetings in the years since had been fleeting: snatched moments in a café here, a shopping centre there; always hopeful they had not been seen, always aware of the consequences.

She had not visited her friend, Mavis Godwin, in her cottage for many years, but for once she had been instructed. It had not been a duty taken lightly. She remembered the fond welcome, tinged with memories of the years past and what had happened to cause her friend to isolate herself from the small community in Avon Hill. It was something she had considered, especially after witnessing the death of her friend's husband.

She, Harriet Wylshere, believed, as did the others in the village, that the gods existed. Had not their village and its inhabitants been blessed with a good life, and whereas other areas nearby had suffered from failed crops and livestock that suffered from many ailments, theirs had always prospered. There were some, no doubt, who would say it was due to the soil in the valley of Avon Hill, and the surrounding hills that sheltered them from the harsher climate not more than three miles away, but she had seen other signs that made her believe. Signs that could not be explained by rational debate. Mavis, her friend, would talk about how she had found peace with her God, but Harriet had lived with her gods since childhood, and she knew that what her parents had told her, and what their parents had told them, was true.

Even at school, when the other children were in morning assembly giving praise to their God, she would silently be giving praise to hers. One of her friends had asked her what she was saying, but she would only reply that it was of little concern. And now Harriet's grandchildren were following the same path, but although they were only young, they had iPads and laptops, and they were asking questions.

Harriet knew that the old ways would not last, as did the elders. That was why their vengeance, their offerings, had become more wicked. And why those who strayed needed to be made an example of, rather than being ostracised. That is why she had been in the kitchen of that little cottage in that small village enjoying her time there with her friend, knowing full well that she would need to kill her.

She remembered them discussing Mavis's husband, and how the woman had reacted when she had received confirmation that he was dead. After tears had been shed by both women, they had walked out through the gate at the end of the back garden and into the field.

The rest of the time there had been a dream. She remembered standing by the water trough, both women looking up at the sky, at some cows at one end of the field. She remembered her friend talking fondly of her husband, and that he had been a good man when they had first married, but with time they had drifted apart, and how they had ceased to be husband and wife for the last ten years.

Harriet vaguely remembered the details of what had occurred. One minute they were calmly talking as friends; the next she had her friend's head under the water in the trough. She knew that she had wanted to let her up, but she knew that she could not. She only knew that her dear friend was once very much alive, and then she was lifeless, her head beneath the water.

After that, she had a vague memory of walking back through the field, opening the gate, and walking through the garden and out of the front gate and to her car. The drive back to Avon Hill was a blur, although the accolades from the elders on her arrival she remembered.

'Has it been dealt with?' the senior elder, Dr Edmund Wylshere, her husband, asked.

She remembered that she had felt a great sadness, a tear rolling down her face.

'It is a time for rejoicing, not sadness,' he had said.

She could not believe what he said. She drove to her house, lay down on her bed and mourned for her friend.

***

Clare bounded into the office, Tremayne did not. The late night the previous evening had left both of them disturbed, but she had had Harry in between. Even Oldfield had had the benefit of his girlfriend, at least after she had complained for an hour about his arriving late. In the end, she had relented.

Tremayne, if he were willing to admit it, could only envy the two their luck. It was not that he believed in anything other than what was real and could be explained by logic, but the ongoing reference to paganism was disturbing. He was aware of the occasional deluded fools who believed it was the voices in their heads that made them kill and cause harm to others. But they had been individuals, and now there appeared to be a community, at least sixty to seventy persons. He knew there had to be a logical reason for their paranoia. If they were a group who wanted to dress up in robes and worship the sun and dance around Stonehenge at the summer solstice, that was one thing. Even he had been there the first year he had come to Salisbury, and all he could remember was the feeling of love in the air, not that he received any of it, and the fact that it had been blistering cold, and the heavens had opened and it had rained cats and dogs. It was his first month at Bemerton Road Police Station, and he had been a junior officer then, the same as Yarwood, and he well remembered his inspector's reaction and his comments when he went into the office the next day spreading his germs.

Yarwood and Oldfield, he knew, were both competent and hardworking, even if lacking experience. Regardless, he worried for them both, even for himself. Gods or no gods, some people killed on their behalf, and even if he thought they were mad, they were dangerous, and the three of them were possible targets.

'How's your weapons training, Yarwood?' Tremayne asked. It was just after seven in the morning, and the day had barely begun. The man was sitting upright in his chair, aiming to look alert, although Clare could see the bags under his eyes. Even with Harry at her side, she had spent a few hours awake, wondering what was going on and what to do. Harry had been adamant that she was foolish, and maybe she was, but a woman had been murdered, a woman who reminded her of her own mother.

'Are you suggesting we arm ourselves?' Clare asked.

'It could get dangerous.'

'DI Tremayne's right,' Oldfield said.

'Maybe, but I don't want one,' Clare replied. She had had the training, but had no desire to be forced into a situation of having to choose whether to shoot or not.

'I'll take a firearm,' Oldfield said.

'Fine, that's decided, but if you get into trouble, don't blame me,' Tremayne said to Clare.

'I won't.'

***

Edmund Wylshere was in his surgery. It was midday, and so far he had dealt with a couple of cases of influenza, an elderly lady with varicose veins, a man recovering after prostate cancer surgery. He had to admit that life had treated him well, but his position in Avon Hill decreed that he needed to be visibly the most prosperous. He had been married young to Harriet, the daughter of a wealthy landowner, and the union had resulted in two children.

Whereas his manner in the surgery that day had been flawless, a nagging fear ate into him. He remembered his wife when she had returned from removing the threat of Mavis Godwin, even the concern from Charles Saunders that his son was known to the law. Wylshere had tried to explain that they were invulnerable as long as they made the necessary offerings. Saunders had agreed, and even if he had not, it did not matter, he could easily be dealt with. And his son, hiding out in Avon Hill, could be addressed at the same time, but Wylshere knew his wife was wavering.

There was a time when she was as ardent as he was, yet he had seen her when they had sacrificed Trevor Godwin, and after she had killed his wife.

Godwin had remained faithful to the gods, whereas his wife had not, but if she had married him, a doctor, instead of a worthless labourer, then she would not have deviated. He could see that sacrifices would have to be made: Charles Saunders if necessary, his son a distinct possibility. It wouldn't be the first time a minor had died, although in the past it had been the child of a local, a simpleton. Wylshere, as a doctor, knew that the inbreeding of a small group of people, invariably first or second cousins, would cause the occasional problem, which is why his father had consented to bring in fresh breeding stock from outside. Mavis Godwin had been a good candidate as she had grown up outside the area. Avon Hill wasn't the only place that had kept the old ways, although it had clearly been the most successful. But there were others in the village who had not married outside, and after so many centuries, who was a cousin and who was not had become unclear.

Wylshere knew that statistically their rate of genetically-acquired defects was three times the average. He had made offerings, hoping that they would remedy the problem, but they had not.

Wylshere could see it clearly. Adam Saunders, a bright boy, and under normal circumstances a credit to the community, had been caught and interviewed by the police. If they pressured him, he would speak.

There was one certainty: Adam Saunders needed to be dealt with.

Chapter 19

The Reverend Harrison was laid to rest in the graveyard next to his cottage. Tremayne and Clare attended the service, although they kept their presence discreet. There were some that were suspicious of the police, had even been vocal the last time Clare had visited Mavis Godwin's cottage after her death. A few felt that there had been no trouble in the village except for the occasional drunk, and then with the police presence came a murder and a suicide in a matter of days.

The funeral, a moving ceremony, was attended by no more than fifteen people: a few locals, a very elderly couple who were identified as Harrison's parents, the two police officers and no one else. Tremayne was interested to see if anyone they didn't know attended, but there was no one unexpected.

Clare had been moved to tears as the coffin was lowered into the ground.

'What do we know about Avon Hill?' Tremayne asked Clare as they drove back to the police station.

'I've never been there.'

'You're always on that damn computer. Check it out, go to the council offices in the city, take a drive through the village.'

'I could be recognised.'

'What does it matter? Get Harry to take you to the local pub at the weekend.'

'I could do that, I suppose. First off, I'll need to check out who lives there.'

'I'll leave it to you. And what about Adam Saunders?'

'No sign of him.'

'We can always bring his father into the station.'

'Why not?' Clare said, although she was not sure if there was anything to be gained. The man was unlikely to say anything to inflame the situation, and the son had committed no crime.

***

Tremayne, frustrated that the investigation into the murder of Mavis Godwin was not moving forward, and his planned entry into Avon Hill was being thwarted, left early. At eight in the evening he headed off to the Deer's Head. The pub, as usual, was busy with locals, a few tourists, and Harry Holchester behind the bar.

'Yarwood's fixated on the supernatural,' Tremayne said to Harry as he was pulling a pint.

'I've told her it's nonsense, but she's susceptible,' Harry replied.

'See if you can talk some sense into her, will you. She has potential. I wouldn't want to see her career waylaid over this.'

'I'll work on her. Don't worry about Clare. She's just a little sensitive. It'll wear off.'

Tremayne picked up his pub dinner, a meat pie and chips with salad, and went back to his seat in the corner of the pub. Clare came in after forty minutes and made a beeline for her man. She gave him a kiss on the mouth, much to the amusement of the patrons who gave a cheer. Tremayne could see that she enjoyed the attention.

'What's the latest, Yarwood?' Tremayne asked after she had come over to sit next to him.

'I've been checking out Avon Hill on the internet.'

'And what did you find?'

'You remember when we checked on who Eric Langley had been friendly with, who had visited him?'

'We didn't find anything suspicious.'

'Not then, but I've been researching. One of his visitors was Dr Wylshere.'

'I know the man, even been to his surgery once or twice.'

'Wylshere is an old name for Wiltshire.'

'What are you getting at, Yarwood?'

'I checked his family history. His ancestry stretches back for centuries.'

'And?'

'They originally came from Avon Hill.'

'Do you suspect him?'

'Not in itself, but it's the first confirmed tie-in between Eric Langley and Avon Hill.'

'Any luck with Mavis Godwin, even her husband?'

'Not yet, but what is interesting is that Mavis Godwin was friends with Wylshere's wife.'

'How did you find that out?'

'It wasn't easy. We know that a woman killed Mavis Godwin.'

'Are you suggesting Wylshere's wife?'

'There's more.'

'Get to the point, Yarwood.'

'After Mavis Godwin died, we investigated her movements. She apparently had no friends, at least of any substance. Yet one of our uniforms found out that she used to meet a woman in a café in Fisherton Street, not more than a three-minute drive from here.'

'What's the significance?'

'I called into the café on the way here.'

'So who is the woman?'

'The waitress remembered Mavis Godwin and the other woman. She told me that her name was Harriet.'

'And now you're going to tell me that Wylshere's wife is also named Harriet.'

'Exactly. It's not a common name.'

'Could she have killed her?'

'I found a newspaper clipping about Wylshere and his wife. Harriet Wylshere is a tall, muscular sort of woman.'

'Strong enough to kill Mavis Godwin.'

'Exactly. We need to call her into the station.'

'Where does she live?'

'Not far from Avon Hill.'

'We'll discuss this in the morning. It's good policing on your part.'

'Shall I call her in?' Clare asked. Tremayne could see that she was pleased with herself. He knew they needed to discuss their strategy from here on in. If Harriet Wylshere murdered Mavis Godwin, her friend, then why? It made no sense for one woman to kill another. Neither of them were known to the police, and on the face of it, the murder had been committed without undue haste.

Apart from the muddy footprints next to the water trough, there was certainly no sign of anger or fighting.

**

'What about Charles Saunders?' Oldfield asked. It was early in the office again.

'If we interview him again, what do we hope to achieve?' Tremayne asked. The night before at the Deer's Head he had kept his beer consumption to a minimum. The pieces were starting to come together, and he needed a clear head.

'Not a lot,' Clare said. 'If he wants to keep quiet, there's not a lot we can do.'

'What's his background? Is he friendly with Wylshere? What about his relationship to Mavis Godwin and Eric Langley, and why can't we find a cause of death for that man?'

'You'll need to ask our crime scene examiner,' Oldfield said. He was feeling increasingly comfortable in the department, more willing to express his views. He could see that the DI was feeling the pressure and that he was starting to look old, and he had to admit that the hours they were working were starting to get to him as well. He knew that his girlfriend was complaining that he preferred sleep more than her.

Oldfield agreed with her deduction, although he was distracted by his sergeant. He was the same age as her, and he had to admit that a degree-educated police officer excited him more than a shop assistant. He knew that one day he would need to do the right thing and sever the relationship with his girlfriend, although the substitute that he wanted was not available.

Jim Hughes, the crime scene examiner, arrived in the office after Tremayne had phoned him. Tremayne still felt that the man was too young to hold the position, but then everyone was young to him, even Superintendent Moulton.

'Hughes, I need a cause of death for Eric Langley, not some mumbo jumbo,' Tremayne said. He was not in a mood for levity.

'As I've said, his case is unique. If he had been a smoker, then maybe I could offer conjecture, but as it is, I'm not able to give you a satisfactory explanation.'

'Now look here, Hughes. You're here because you're the chief scientific man in the station and you can't tell me what killed him?'

'I resent your tone,' Hughes responded. 'The man was burnt beyond recognition. You saw the body. You tell me what else I can do.'

'Check again. Someone killed this man. Don't give me this spontaneous human combustion nonsense again. We've a tie-in between one of the visitors and a village not far from here, and also a tie-in with those two to the death of Mavis Godwin. These are more than coincidences, they're fact.'

'That's maybe, but I can't give you a cause of death, other than he was burnt to a cinder. What do you want me to do? Make it up so you can pin his murder on someone.'

'Don't talk rubbish, but we're going to start questioning people soon. People who may well have killed Mavis Godwin, and I need the ammo to fire if I'm going to place the maximum pressure. Besides, what do you know about Dr Edmund Wylshere?'

'Wylshere? Is he a suspect?'

'He concerns us,' Tremayne admitted.

'I know the man,' Hughes said.

'What can you tell us about him?'

'A competent doctor.'

'No skeletons in the cupboard, scurrilous rumours?'

'Nothing,' Hughes replied. It wasn't the first time that he and Tremayne had had a heated exchange, he knew it wouldn't be the last.

'Yarwood, who else do we know?' Tremayne asked.

'Apart from Charles and Adam Saunders?'

'Yes.'

'We've not found a tie-in between Charles Saunders and Eric Langley.'

'Pressure the man. We need his son.'

Chapter 20

Adam Saunders spent the day in the isolated farm house. He missed his friends and his school, although he missed a reliable connection to the internet more. He knew why he was condemned to be in that place surrounded by fields and not much else. A more interested person would have regarded it as scenic, but he did not. He wanted out, but how? There were no guards, and it would be possible to walk out through the fields, and the wood at the top of the rise, not more than five hundred yards, but his father had told him the consequences.

'We are under suspicion,' Charles Saunders had said.

Adam, educated, computer savvy, an avid user of Facebook and Twitter, had always obeyed the rules of his father's community. But he lived closer to Salisbury, even walked through to Salisbury Cathedral for the occasional service with his school, and he could see no godly presence there, let alone in Avon Hill, which to him was devoid of any life, mortal or otherwise, apart from a dreary collection of old people.

He had spent time out at the vicar's house in Stratford sub Castle as a favour to his father: a bit of a lark, a few hours off school and the chance to rummage through the house had seemed like fun. But then the police had caught him, and apart from his grilling, another reason to brag to his friends, the rest of his time since then had been purgatory.

Firstly, the inquisition by the elders, a fossilised bunch of old cronies who only ever talked about the old ways. He had wanted to tell them to wise up, get with the modern age, instead of dwelling on the past, dressing up in strange robes and wearing masks made of paper-mâché.

He had seen them through the old church's windows on more than one occasion. He knew that his father had seen him, but he had only ever told him to be careful.

Adam, cheeky and full of bravado, as befits a teen on the verge of adulthood, could see that it was up to him to make a move. There was a sports day at the school the next day, and if he could not go to his father's house, knowing full well that his loyalty to the elders overrode his loyalty to his son, then he would go to a friend's house, not far from Avon Hill. It was only two miles away but separated by centuries of history. There, the internet worked, the television had all the channels, and the family were friendly and welcoming, not stuck in a rut, debating the ancient past and how Dr Wylshere's ancestor had saved them all from the plague and ensured their prosperity. Not that Adam Saunders could see much of it. Sure, Wylshere drove around in a nice car, had a decent house, but then his friend lived well, and his family did not creep around an old church at night and conduct rituals deep in the forest.

Grabbing his belongings, Adam left the cottage. It was past seven in the evening, and it was already dark. There was no moon in the sky, no stars. He struck out across the fields, through one that had a few cows, then through the second. Only one more to go and then he would have the protection of the wood.

He had not been into the densely-wooded area, no one had. He knew it was irrational, as did the others in Avon Hill, but they had been warned on many occasions that the place belonged to others. He remembered the tales from his childhood, when his father, as well as his mother, had scared him as he tried to sleep. His friends at Bishop Wordsworth's School would have said that he was mad to believe in such nonsense, but they had not seen the woods, not experienced the elders. He never knew why he did not speak to them about his childhood, the strange pagan beliefs, the ceremonies in the church, but he never had. That night, if his friend asked, he would tell them what he knew: that people had disappeared, some had been killed, some had had unexplained accidents, how his father had prostrated himself in that old church, purely because he, the son, had been caught by the police.

And what was it with the police? He had no issues with them, but to the elders they were akin to the devil. Those that he had met were pleasant enough, especially Sergeant Clare Yarwood.

He reached the edge of the wood, hesitated, listened to the wind rustling through the leaves. He tried to hear the voices, but he could hear none. His stomach was churning, his legs were shaking, but he put that down to the cold weather. A barbed wire fence separated him from the wood. He held the top wire down with his backpack and climbed over, one leg at a time. Once on the other side, he moved through the wood. It was only half a mile to the road leading to his friend's house, and the lights of the cars were visible in the distance. It was clear that no one had been in the wood for a long time, although there were some tracks, possibly deer.

After five minutes of pushing through the undergrowth, he paused to look around him. The lights of the cars were no longer visible, nor were the lights from the cottage where he had just spent the last few days. He took out his phone: no signal. It had an inbuilt compass, so he checked the direction and then continued walking forward. The animal tracks were no longer visible, and the meagre light from his phone was all that he had. After another ten minutes, the battery of the phone finally expired. It was now dark, the dark of the dead, and he remembered his father's warnings about not entering the wood; of how some had tried in times past, of how they had never returned. He knew it was pure superstition, at least he had until now. Regret at not listening to his father came to him; the wish that he was still back in that isolated cottage. He listened to the sounds around him: an owl in the distance, the leaves rustling, an animal scurrying somewhere near. He looked for the way out, any way out. Adam Saunders, a young man, educated, computer savvy, lover of Facebook and Twitter, was scared. He could feel the fear racing through his body; he knew it was irrational, yet somehow all that he had witnessed in that church, all that his parents had told him as bedtime stories came back to him. What if they were all true? What if the elders were correct when they spoke of ancient gods and offerings and sacrifices? Was this to be his fate, to be lost in a darkened wood, not more than a few hundred yards from civilisation?

The young man looked up; all he could see was a perpetual darkness. He listened again: nothing. Not even the sound of an owl or a scurrying animal. No longer the noise of the leaves rustling in the trees. He felt a moistness on his cheeks. He was fifteen and in mortal fear of his life. He took out his phone. For some reason, it had gained some charge and a weak signal. He dialled his father.

'Charles Saunders?' the voice answered.

'Father,' Adam Saunders said.

'Where are you?'

'I'm in the wood at the top of the rise from the cottage.'

'Get out of there now,' an alarmed voice said.

'I can't. I'm lost.'

'Stay there. I'm coming.'

'It's too late, father. They are here.'

'Who's there?'

The phone went dead. Adam Saunders realised that he was no longer in an earthly place.

Charles Saunders picked up his phone in panic; attempted to call his son, no answer.

With no success, the father called Dr Wylshere. 'Adam is in Cuthbert's Wood.'

'He was warned,' Wylshere replied.

'He needs to be rescued,' Saunders said. He was talking on the phone as he drove away from his home. He was as scared as his son.

'It is too late,' Wylshere replied. 'He had been warned. His guilt is your guilt.'

'Aren't you going to send people up there.'

'No one will enter there. It is a forbidden place.'

'But he's my son.'

'Then he is your responsibility. The consequences of his actions remain with you. You must take the burden, not us. If they deem him worthy, he will survive. Otherwise, his fate is sealed.'

***

Charles Saunders, a man whose family had for generations followed the old ways, knew that his prosperity had come, as had others', from the benevolence of the ancients, but now he was a father with a son. A son who had been given over to those forces. Charles Saunders had kept their secret safe, as had his son, and what had happened? He had been chastised by the elders for allowing his son to be caught by the police, and his son had been isolated, out of sight. He knew Wylshere and his strict code of obedience; he had even agreed to it. He had seen the need for Trevor Godwin and his wife to die, but now it was his son.

Cuthbert's Wood was so named after another person who had entered it centuries previously and had not come out. Since then, no one had entered there, no one would dare to, yet Adam Saunders had.

In desperation, the boy's father took the only action possible. 'DI Tremayne, my son is in mortal danger.' Charles Saunders knew that his life would be forfeit, but it was his son who was now threatened. If the elders decided to appease the gods with his body, then so be it, but for now it was his son that was more important.

'Where is he?' Tremayne asked.

'Cuthbert's Wood. It's less than a mile from Avon Hill.'

Tremayne called Clare and Oldfield into his office. With one hand over the phone's microphone, he spoke to them. 'Get some uniforms and get out to Cuthbert's Wood. It's near Avon Hill.'

'What is it, guv?' Clare asked.

'Adam Saunders. He's in trouble. His father is on the line.'

***

Adam Saunders, unsure of his bearings, set off in the direction that had seemed the most promising. It was as dark as a coal mine, and he could barely see his hand in front of his face. As he moved, he could feel the undergrowth thickening beneath his feet. He stumbled, he lurched, he crawled on his hands and knees. In mortal fear he tried to run and fell over a fallen branch, twisting his ankle. Instead of walking, the most he could do was stagger. Up ahead a light, the light of a car.

'I'm over here,' he shouted.

No answer. He pressed on towards the light until it disappeared. He opened his backpack, found a bar of chocolate. After a few bites, he felt better.

Get a grip of yourself, Saunders, he said to himself. The light reappeared. He shouted to it again, inched himself forward. Yet again, the light disappeared.

Frantically he screamed, hoping for a response. He could feel the cold air chilling his bones, the damp underfoot. He rechecked his phone; the battery was flat. He threw it away in frustration; wondered why he did, tried to find it again.

The darkness continued to pervade the wood; a solitary owl in the distance. He thought he glimpsed the road off to one side, and cars moving along, their beams lighting up the sides of the road. He changed direction and moved towards them. The light he had seen before reappeared. He turned towards it, it turned off. He refocussed on the road he had seen up ahead before, but it was no longer to be seen. He could feel the tears of sheer panic streaming down his cheeks. He remembered all the night-time tales that his parents had instilled in him to ensure he did not mention Avon Hill and what went on there.

He remembered that once he had followed the villagers into the wood alongside the church: seen them recite their chants, offer praise to Teutates, Esus and Taranis. He had wanted to laugh at them but did not. He had seen Dr Wylshere with the mask of a bull offer the sacrifice, and then a young child being led forward, dressed in a simple tunic.

The night had been cold, and he assumed that the young girl had been drugged as she was oblivious to what was happening.

Oh, ancient gods, our benefactors, we give you our offering in the belief that you will protect us as you always have.

Adam Saunders did not know why he had remembered that night and that verse. He had only been eleven, and for some reason it had been blocked from his mind, but there in Cuthbert's Wood it all became real again. He could see that he was to be offered to the gods where he stood.

Behind him he could hear a rustling in the undergrowth. Too afraid to look back, too frightened not to, he froze on the spot. The next second he was on the ground, feeling the force of something or someone hitting him squarely between his shoulders. He lifted his face from the mud and looked around. There was nothing there other than a broken branch on the ground. He felt relief and lifted himself up, only feeling the soreness in his body. He took stock of the situation, looked around, this time with no trepidation. He knew that he was fifteen, on the cusp of manhood, and childish stories and a belief in pagan gods were pure folly.

Ahead, in the distance, he could see clearly the main road and flashing blue lights. He knew it was the police, but he gave it no more thought other than to get to that road as soon as possible. Five minutes to the road, another five to his friend's house, and then he could relax. He attempted to stop shaking but could not. He picked up his pace; the road in the distance had given him a bearing, the flashing lights momentarily showing him the way out of Cuthbert's Wood.

Another branch hit his back; he took no notice. Then a third, heavier than the previous two, and he collapsed to the ground. It was wet to the face; he realised that it was a small pond. Another branch and his face was under the water. Two minutes later the pressure of the branch eased, although this time Adam Saunders, a smart fifteen-year-old youth, did not raise his head to look around.

***

This time, avoiding the need to enter Avon Hill, Clare and Oldfield reached Cuthbert's Wood from a different direction. Two more police cars arrived soon after. The police, including Clare and Oldfield, all holding torches, entered the wooded area after first clambering over an old wooden fence.

'You take the right-hand side,' Clare said to Oldfield. 'I'll go to the left.'

Both of the police officers took a couple of uniforms with them. Clare had seen the wood from a distance, and to her it represented evil. Oldfield, less susceptible, had to admit that it appeared to be a foreboding place, set up high above the road, but then, as children, he and his friends would have revelled in a spooky wood, and this was spooky, ominously so. Down on the road where they had parked their cars, it had been a balmy night, unseasonably so, but as they had approached the search area, Clare was sure of one fact – the temperature had progressively dropped. On the road, it had been jacket weather, but on entering the wood, it must have dropped at least ten degrees Fahrenheit.

'These places are always cold,' Oldfield said, but he had said it as much for his own benefit as Clare's.

Six people entered the wood, three went to the left, three to the right, their exhaled breath steaming in the cold air. The going was difficult, and even with the torches, it was proving hard to find their way.

'Are you sure he's in here?' one of the uniforms asked Clare.

'According to his father.'

'It doesn't look as though anyone's been in here for a long time.'

Clare had to admit it looked that way. There were no signs of human tracks, just of some animals here and there, but not much else. She looked up at the sky, could not see it. She looked forward, shining her light from side to side: nothing, apart from undergrowth and trees that seemed to be entwined with each other. She was frightened, yet not wanting to show it. The policemen with her were not helping. One was young and inexperienced, the other one older and should have known better.

'You've heard the stories about this place?' said the older one, a constable, still happy to drive a patrol car if he had been asked, not willing to take off the uniform and sit in an office.

'What stories?' Clare asked.

'Maybe it's just folklore. This close to Stonehenge, there's always somewhere or other that has some story.'

All three continued to move forward. The wooded area was not expansive, no more than three hundred yards across and five hundred yards in length. Clare realised that if Adam Saunders had entered the wood, he would not have needed to spend long there, and whichever direction he took, it could not have taken more than fifteen minutes to traverse. The reason why he was in such a place was a question for later.

'What story?' Clare asked. She was sure she did not want to hear it, unable not to ask.

'They say it's the devil's haunt.'

'How do you know this?'

'I used to ride my bicycle as a youth past here. That's what we always knew. As I said, it's just folklore, an old superstition.'

'Have you been in here before?'

'Not likely. The place scared me to death then, even does now.'

'Don't look at me,' Clare said. 'I'm scared enough for the both of us.'

'It doesn't worry me,' the younger policeman said. 'The imagination plays funny tricks on you.'

'Enough talk,' Clare said. 'What have we found so far?'

'Bugger all,' the young policeman replied. 'We'll not find anyone in here.'

***

'Vic, this is a wild goose chase,' Constable Dallimore said.

'Do you want to tell Sergeant Yarwood that you're cold and you want to get back to the car, is that it?' Oldfield replied.

'Vic, it's not that, but there's nothing here. We've covered the area as requested. What more can we do?'

'You may be right, but you know Tremayne, and Yarwood's not a person to give up so easily.'

'Okay, I'll take the left-hand side, you take the middle, and young Mike can take the right-hand side. Once we get back, that's it. Agreed?'

'And tonight the beers are on you if we find something.'

'Agreed,' Dallimore said.

Oldfield took his phone out of his pocket, attempted to call Clare: no signal. He assumed it was the trees blocking the signal.

The three, Oldfield, Bill and Mike, all constables, all drinking pals, spread out. They were no more than sixty yards from each other.

It would have been just a five-minute walk if it had been light, but in the dark, it would take ten. Bill, over on the far left-hand side, could see a cottage down below, its lights ablaze. In front of him, he could see nothing other than the light from his torch. Oldfield, in the middle, moved forward; the night was silent. Mike, the other constable, walked briskly.

The three kept in contact by calling out to each other.

Meanwhile, Clare, at the other end of the wood, was following a similar plan, and she was on her own. She could see the torches of the other policemen with her, but they were of little solace. She knew in her bones that something was wrong. She tried to rationalise it as she scoured the area, hoped her fear did not show, knew that it did.

'Vic, there's nothing here,' Bill shouted from his side of the wood.

'Nothing here,' Mike yelled.

'Yarwood, can you hear me?' Oldfield shouted. No reply.

Clare, on her side of the wood, had attempted to shout to Oldfield, but she had no voice. The fear in her was now palpable. She called to the other two flanking her, but there was no response, although she could see their torches.

The police sergeant quickened her pace, tripped over a fallen branch. She attempted to call out, with no success. With no option, she continued, moving the torch up and down and to the left and right. The torch on her right was no longer visible. She looked to the left, only darkness.

Fear gripped her; she moved towards the left, hopefully in the direction of the police cars, although she could not see them. Clare attempted to run, tripping over again. Her torch switched off when she fell over. She switched it on again: nothing. With only the light from her phone, she attempted to get out of the wood, all thought of Adam Saunders forgotten.

In the distance she could see the road, and she felt calmer. With a bearing, she could feel her strength returning. It was only two minutes to the edge of the wood, she was certain of it. She increased her pace once again, only to fall down. The ground was wet, her hands were in water. Lying there, catching her breath, she pointed her phone in the direction of the latest obstacle.

'Help!' she called out, her voice returning.

'What is it?' one of the policemen came over to her.

'Over there.' She noticed that he was using his phone as a light as well.

He helped Clare to her feet and then pointed his phone in the direction that Clare had indicated. 'That must be Adam Saunders,' he said.

'Does your phone work?' Clare asked.

'It will once we're out of this infernal place.'

'What happened?' Clare asked.

'I could ask the same of you. One minute you're there, the next you're gone. I called out, but there was no answer. I was heading out of this place, but I got lost.'

'The same with me,' Clare said.

Two minutes later, Oldfield appeared. 'We heard you shout. Is that Adam Saunders?' he asked.

'You've met him. What do you reckon?'

Vic Oldfield moved over to the body lying face down in the small pond. 'I'd reckon so,' he said.

'What happened to your torch?' Clare asked.

'It just gave up on me. It must be the cold in here.'

'Yes, that must be the reason,' Clare agreed.

Chapter 21

'You're confident it's Adam Saunders?' Tremayne asked. He had driven up to the crime scene as fast as he could after Oldfield had phoned him. He had seen the wood from a distance; it had looked depressingly ominous from back there. Now that he was closer he could understand why certain people would see something sinister and threatening. He had to admit that close to the wood it definitely felt colder. He looked at his sergeant, saw that she was not in the best condition; he could only sympathise as it had been her who had discovered the body.

'Have you told his father?' Oldfield asked.

'I phoned him on the way here,' Tremayne said. 'Not much else I could do, seeing that he called us first.'

'He'll be here soon,' Clare said.

'Just make sure he doesn't get in the way of the investigation. It is murder, I assume?'

'It doesn't appear to be an accident, unless he tripped, banged his head and fell into the water.'

'But you don't believe that, do you, Yarwood?'

'Odds on, he was murdered.'

'By who?' Tremayne tested his sergeant, looking for the correct response.

'Not by the gods, if that's what you're asking.'

'Then who?' Tremayne said.

'As you've said before, the answer lies in Avon Hill, but if he's been murdered, then it's human intervention, not godly.'

Jim Hughes arrived within the hour, but not before Charles Saunders. He had been insistent on seeing his son's body, although he hesitated before entering Cuthbert's Wood. Oldfield took him in. The two police officers who had accompanied Clare and Oldfield into the wood initially were taking control of the crime scene until a couple of uniforms from Bemerton Road Police Station arrived. Crime scene tape had been strung around a few trees, and the father had complained when told that he could not approach any closer.

'Is that your son?' Oldfield asked.

'They've killed him, haven't they?'

'Who are you referring to?'

'Not now, not in here,' Saunders said.

'Why?'

'This is their place.'

'We've two police officers here, a team of crime scene investigators on the way with floodlights and generators. That should be enough protection.'

'When will you remove my son?' Saunders asked.

'That's up to the crime scene examiner. Tomorrow, probably.'

'After I've identified him, we'll talk.'

***

'How am I meant to find anything in there?' Jim Hughes said on his arrival.

'We didn't have many options,' Clare replied. 'We were looking for a missing person, not a body, at that time.'

'That's as maybe, but it still looks as if a herd of elephants has been through there.'

Hughes and Clare stood at the entrance to the wood; Tremayne had gone back to the police station to update Moulton on the latest development. Vic Oldfield was down at the cottage identified by Charles Saunders as his son's hideout. Oldfield knew that under other circumstances the father would have been held responsible for his failure to bring his son in for questioning, although that was now irrelevant.

Oldfield and Constable Dallimore checked the cottage from top to bottom, found nothing. The constable would ask Hughes to check it later, see if they could find any fingerprints, other than of the two Saunders, which judging by the amount of dust would not be difficult.

Jim Hughes and his team set up floodlights in Cuthbert's Wood, a small generator supplying the power. Clare had to admit that it did not look nearly as spooky now that the area was bathed in light, although she remembered how she had felt in there before. She could only imagine the fear that a fifteen-year-old would have felt, and how unpleasant his death had been.

'We'll check the periphery, somewhere your lot have not marched through,' Hughes said. It was late at night, and he was not in the best of moods: on the one hand, Tremayne was criticising his lack of experience, and then, the same day, he wanted his crime scene team to work through the night in temperatures close to freezing.

'We only did what was necessary,' Clare reminded him.

'I know, but it doesn't make it any easier. You're convinced it's murder?' Both the CSE and Clare stood close to the body. Clare was no longer afraid, surrounded by another three people.

'Yes.'

'You've seen the branch?' Hughes asked.

'Not in detail. It was dark in here.'

'If that had hit his head he would have been unconscious. Have you considered that?'

'It's possible, but we know what his father told us. We're aware that the son was prowling around the Reverend Harrison's cottage, and Avon Hill is nearby.'

'Too much evidence to be circumstantial, is that what you're saying?'

'His death is too convenient. We know he would have told us more if his father had not been present that time at the police station.'

'How did the father take his death?' Hughes asked. He was bending down close to the body as he spoke.

'Badly. Supposedly he intends to tell us what the son did not.'

'Do you believe him?'

'Mavis Godwin would not tell us, nor would Harrison. There's no reason to believe that Saunders will either.'

'What's with these people?' Hughes said as he continued his examination. 'Some bruising on his back, tree bark in his hair. It's all conducive to an accident.'

'He's been killed. Don't expect me to go back and tell DI Tremayne it wasn't murder. He'll go spare if I do that. What about the branch that hit him?'

'That's next. I suggest you go and write up a report or something and leave me to it. Your constant questions are starting to annoy me.'

Clare realised that the crime scene examiner and the DI were similar in temperament. 'I'm surprised you and DI Tremayne don't get on better.'

'Tremayne's alright by me. He's a prickly character, just need to give him back what he dishes out, and Clare, I've no issue with your being here, but I need to focus, as does my team. I'll update you in two hours.'

Once outside the wood and back in a heated car, Clare phoned Tremayne. 'Two hours.'

'What's Hughes's preliminary findings?'

'He said two hours, but there's clear evidence that Adam Saunders was hit on the back of the head by a branch. That probably rendered him unconscious.'

'Accident, is that what you're saying?'

'Not yet. It's murder as far as I'm concerned,' Clare said. The fear that she had felt before, the belief in ancient gods, dissipated entirely as she spoke to her senior.

'And what about Oldfield?'

'He's checking out the cottage where Adam Saunders was hiding. He'll be back soon.'

'As soon as you two are finished there, get back to the station. We need to meet with the infamous Dr Wylshere, as well as his wife. I need you two to do some more research.'

'Are we still planning a visit to Avon Hill?' Clare asked.

'I don't want to go in there blind. The Wylsheres have some questions to answer first, and if Harriet Wylshere murdered Mavis Godwin, then we need to charge her. Any fingerprints at Mavis Godwin's cottage?'

'You've seen the report, guv,' Clare reminded him.

'I'm asking the questions here,' Tremayne replied, true to form and blunt as usual. 'Of course I've seen the bloody report. I'm talking out loud, running ideas past you.'

'Understood, guv,' Clare said, a smile creeping across her face.

'The woman who visited Mavis Godwin wore gloves, not unexpected given the weather, and the cottage was always cold. The best we have are footprints.'

'A large size for a woman, though.'

'Large, but not conclusive. The best we can hope to do is to firm up Harriet Wylshere as the killer, but we'll not be able to prove it was her.'

'And she won't confess.'

'Who will?'

'Whoever these crazy people are, they either believe this nonsense, or they're scared stiff.'

'Both, I'd say,' Clare said.

'Regardless, back in the office and then we'll deal with the Wylsheres. By the way, any car problems?'

'Not today.'

'There you are, a load of nonsense, just superstitious paranoia.'

'You're right, guv,' Clare said.

***

'It's grim,' Oldfield said as he stood in Avon Hill.

'It's hardly my idea of a fun night out sort of place,' Dallimore said.

After concluding their activities at Adam Saunders' hideout, the two men had decided to check out the place that concerned them the most. The walk from the cottage to the village had taken twenty minutes down a narrow lane. On the way, they had passed a couple of cottages, the curtains twitching in the first one, a man standing in the garden at the second. Oldfield had attempted to engage in conversation, only to receive a begrudging grunt in return before the man walked away. A dog barked inside the cottage. As they descended the lane, the temperature yet again started to get colder.

'This place interests you?' Dallimore asked.

'Whoever these people are, they're bizarre. Too many unexplained happenings, and each time the evidence leads back to here.

'Did you ever watch *Brigadoon*,' Dallimore asked.

'What about it?'

'That's what this place is like. You remember the movie when the village wakes every hundred years for a day.'

'What do you mean?'

'Look at it, Vic. It's eerily beautiful, just the sort of place that you'd see in an old painting. There's the stream running down alongside the road, a few houses, cows in the fields. Apart from the occasional TV antenna and the electricity poles, this could be a place out of time.'

'When do you get to watch movies like that?'

'It's on the television every Christmas. Scoff if you want, but that's what this place is like.'

Oldfield had to admit that Dallimore was right, the village had a strange feeling about it. It was one o'clock in the morning, and every house they passed as they walked down the main street appeared to have a curtain that moved.

'They're watching us,' Dallimore said. 'I don't like this place.'

'Don't tell me you believe that nonsense?'

'What nonsense?'

'Pagan gods, secret rituals.'

'Are you telling me that this is what these people are involved in?'

'It's possible.'

'For Christ's sake, let's get out of here.'

'You believe it!'

'I've a healthy respect for my life, that's all. There are enough lunatics in this world without coming into their front parlour.'

'Do you believe in paganism and orgiastic rituals?'

'Of course not, but looking around this place and the faces behind the curtains, they could well do. I suggest we backtrack out of here and fast. Down here, we've no protection.'

'We're police officers, we're trained to deal with these situations.'

'We're two men in a village that does not like us. When was the last time a police officer came down here? Have you checked?'

'DI Tremayne came to the pub many years ago. He said they were not friendly. Apart from that, I suppose no one's been down here, no reason to. It's not the sort of place that would have any crime.'

'Apart from orgiastic rituals and paganism.'

'We've no knowledge of those sort of rituals,' Oldfield said.

'Then what sort?'

'Human sacrifice.'

'Hell, Oldfield, don't stuff around. We're leaving.'

Oldfield, taking heed of Dallimore, turned around and headed back to the turn off to Adam Saunders' cottage and up to Cuthbert's Wood. As they reached the corner, a group of men appeared.

'What are you doing here?' one of the men asked.

'We're police officers,' Oldfield said.

'Do you have identification?'

'What's the problem?'

'It's one o'clock in the morning, and two men we don't know are prowling around.'

'Is it any of your concern?'

Oldfield tried to look at the group in front of him, only they all had torches pointing at them. He estimated that there were six men in total.

'We don't like strangers.'

'Not even police officers?'

'There's no crime here. What are you here for?'

'Are you aware of a body being discovered in Cuthbert's Wood?'

'We've seen the lights up there.'

'You've not answered my question. Do you know an Adam Saunders?'

'Maybe we do.'

'What does that mean?'

'We mind our own business. I suggest you do, as well.'

'We're police officers. We ask questions, look for answers. Once again, did you know Adam Saunders?'

'He was up at the cottage.'

'Do you know why?'

'As I said, we mind our own business. We don't ask unnecessary questions.'

'May I have your name?'

'Why? I've told you all I know. I suggest you leave and soon.'

'And if we don't?'

'I meant nothing by my comment. It's late, and I don't want you to have an accident.'

'Is that a threat?'

'It's not a threat, just advice.'

'Vic, I think we should leave,' Dallimore said.

'Your friend's right. It's best if you leave.'

The group in front of the two police officers parted, and Oldfield and Dallimore moved through it.

Once on the other side, Dallimore spoke. 'What was that all about?'

'I believe that if there were no police up at the top of the hill, we would not have left that village.'

'Are you meaning they would have prevented us?'

'Yes. I believe they would have killed us.'

'Whatever you're involved with, you and Yarwood, count me out. I'll go back to driving my patrol car.'

'Whatever it is, it has to be taken to conclusion. We can't have villagers threatening the police.'

'Are they pagan worshippers?'

'It seems likely.'

'But then we shouldn't have been walking through the village at that time of the morning.'

'I agree, but you saw their reaction when I told them we were police officers.'

'Hostile.'

'Precisely. It's hardly the reaction of law-abiding people.'

Chapter 22

The first thing Jim Hughes did after he came out of Cuthbert's Wood was to warm himself in Clare's car.

'What did you find out?' Clare asked.

'It's murder. He'd been hit by a branch across the back of the head.'

'Did that kill him?'

'He was probably unconscious, but no. He drowned.'

'Why murder?'

'Firstly, the branch did not break off a tree and smack him in the back of the head. The angles are all wrong, and we've checked the branch. It had fallen down sometime in the past. Secondly, it needed pressure to hold his head under the water. Almost certainly the branch that hit him was then used to hold his head under.'

'And the murderer?'

'We're still looking. There's another set of footprints near the body, but we'll need to eliminate all of you first, and that's going to take time.'

'The body?'

'We'll remove it in the next four to five hours. Our people will be here for some time yet, and then we need to check the cottage. I assume Oldfield has crime scene tape around the place.'

Clare thought he had, although she had not heard from him for some time. She phoned him.

'We're fine,' Oldfield replied. 'We've just met the locals.'

'Friendly?'

'Not at all. Mind you, it's hardly the time of morning for socialising.'

'They came to the cottage?' Clare asked.

'No. We've been into Avon Hill.'

'What else?'

'We've just seen the car we followed from the graveyard.'

'The mysterious woman?'

'That's the one. Did you get an address?'
'Yes. There should be a record of who owns the house.'

***

'What were the policeman looking for?' Edmund Wylshere asked in the Avon Hill pub after the body of Adam Saunders had been discovered.

'They were just walking through,' Albert Grayling, a short, red-faced man, said. He was behind the bar, his usual position as the publican of the small, quaint pub. It should have been on the list of Britain's oldest pubs, but it wasn't. Apart from the locals, and the occasional person passing through, it had not announced itself to the world: no gourmet meals, no speciality brews, no selection of wines. It was what it was, a traditional old English pub. If you wanted a pint of beer, a ploughman's lunch of freshly baked bread with a slab of cheese and pickled onions, then the place was ideal, but apart from that, the pub was barren. However, it was where the elders met when there was something to discuss, and at those times it was by invite only.

'They'll be suspicious,' Wylshere said.

'It was one in the morning. We had a right to challenge them,' Grayling said.

'We need to make plans,' another of the elders said. 'What's our approach when they come here?'

'We don't do anything to raise their suspicions.'

'But how? They know enough to arrest your wife.'

'How do you know this?' Wylshere asked.

'That's what my sources tell me.'

'But they've no proof.'

'Can you trust your wife? There are others who are losing their faith.'

'Adam Saunders did,' another elder said.

'Cuthbert's Wood has dealt with him,' Wylshere said.

'You always intended for him to die, didn't you?'

'Our secret is all that is important.'

'And his father?'

'He is ready to talk. It is time to request their help.'

***

Tremayne realised the situation was becoming critical. He had not been pleased on hearing that Oldfield had been into Avon Hill. If, as he believed, the community in that small enclave at the end of a narrow, winding road were responsible for Adam Saunders' death, then it was a foolhardy action.

Research by Yarwood had shown that cults around the world existed and that rational people could, and had been, seduced by a charismatic leader. Here, that leader appeared to be Dr Edmund Wylshere.

Tremayne had met the man on a few occasions and had not seen anything special about him. From what he remembered, the doctor had been competent and had dealt with his problems satisfactorily. Apart from that, there was no special allure, no magnetism that would have induced him to follow the man, but Tremayne knew that he was a cynical police officer who dealt in facts, not phantom spirits.

The visit to Avon Hill, Tremayne felt, should be delayed by a few days while all the facts were collated. And now, according to Yarwood and Oldfield, Charles Saunders was willing to talk. There had been others who had known the secrets but had not wanted to reveal them, and they had ended up dead. He wondered if Adam Saunders had been one of those. Sure, he had only been fifteen, but he had been bright, his academic record showed that, and Tremayne could not believe that a pupil at one of Salisbury's best schools could have been coerced by a cult to keep quiet.

After the previous night up at Cuthbert's Wood, both Yarwood and Oldfield were late arriving at the police station the next morning. Tremayne called them into his office. He was in a positive frame of mind.

'We've got them,' he said.

'Why do you think that?' Clare asked. She was still tired. It had been five in the morning before she had finally made it home.

'When is the father coming in?' Tremayne asked.

'We're not sure,' Yarwood replied. 'They've removed Adam Saunders' body from the crime scene. It's now with Pathology.'

'They'll not find any more of interest,' Tremayne said.

'You're basing that on Hughes's report?'

'This time I am. The youth was murdered. That's good enough for me. Any signs of other persons?'

'There's another set of footprints close to the cottage-side entrance to Cuthbert's Wood.'

'Do we know who it is?'

'Not yet.'

'The group you met in Avon Hill?' Tremayne asked Oldfield.

'One of them could be the murderer.'

'And you don't know who they were?'

'They weren't friendly'

'What did you expect? One o'clock in the morning wandering around a village.'

Oldfield realised that it was going to be a full day. If Charles Saunders was willing to talk, the first one to do so, then the team at Bemerton Road Police Station would be working late that night, probably into the early hours of the following morning.

'And after you showed your police ID?'

'The same as before. They didn't want us down there.'

'We still need to call in Harriet Wylshere,' Tremayne said.

'But where's the proof?' Clare asked.

'There's none, it's circumstantial, but she fits the profile.'

Jim Hughes arrived in Tremayne's office at eight-thirty in the morning. By that time, Oldfield was on his way to see Charles Saunders. None of the team placed much faith in the man opening up about what was going on in Avon Hill. As Tremayne saw it, if Charles Saunders admitted to knowledge of what happened in Avon Hill, then he was probably complicit in the murder of Mavis Godwin, the disappearance of Trevor Godwin and, by default, the murder of his son.

If Adam Saunders had died because of a fear that he might talk, then that also implied that his father was a target.

'Adam Saunders was hit a total of three times by a branch,' Hughes said.

'Why three times?' Clare asked.

'The first two could have been no more than low hanging branches, although one had knocked him over. Also, he had a sprained ankle.'

'Sprained ankle?' Tremayne asked.

151

'Yes. The first time he fell over, he caught it on the exposed root of an old tree. After that he was limping, at least for a while.'

'How long was he in that wood?'

'As far as we can tell, about twenty minutes.'

'But you can walk from one side to the other in no more than eight.'

'As I've said before, if your lot had not marched up and down like Grenadier Guards, then it may have been easier, but we found his footprints elsewhere. He was effectively walking around in circles.'

'Lost?'

'Scared witless more like,' Hughes replied.

'Not you as well?' Tremayne said.

'Are you joking?' Hughes replied.

'Then what?' Clare asked, sensing the antagonism between the two men.

'The generator failed when we were in there.'

'And?' Tremayne asked.

'Pitch black, couldn't see a hand in front of your face.'

'You had torches.'

'Of course, but for a few seconds we did not.'

'Unpleasant?' Clare asked.

'To put it mildly,' Hughes said. 'The darkness was intense, the sort of thing that gives you nightmares as a child.'

'You're not a child,' Tremayne said.

'That's what I figured. If I can finish.'

'My apologies.'

'As I was saying. It was pitch black when the lights went out. The tree canopy had blotted out the night sky, and as Clare will remember, there were no stars that evening, only clouds.'

'That's true,' Clare said.

'Adam Saunders, after being hit by the first branch, did not have a torch, only the light from his phone.'

'What happened?'

'He had broken his torch. It wasn't working when we found it, although it was only the battery that had dislodged.

'Anyway, he had no light other than from a phone, and they're only useful for finding your keys in the dark. They're hardly good enough to find your way out of a dense and overgrown wood. With no reference points, it's easy to get lost.'

'I would have just kept heading in the same direction,' Tremayne said.

'You would have, but you're an older man, not easily taken in by tales of evil spirits.'

'Was he?'

'Children are fascinated by the subject. Yarwood's younger, she'll remember.'

'Scary movies, tales under the blankets on sleepovers with friends.'

'Precisely. And if Adam Saunders had that as well as a dose of whatever goes on in Avon Hill, he would have been hearing noises that weren't there, seen shadows that were only the vegetation.'

'Are you confirming that the first two branches were accidents?' Tremayne asked.

'That appears to be the case. The third, however, is a different matter.'

'Explain what you mean.'

'The branch had been lying on the ground not more than twenty feet away from where the body was found. It is clear that someone picked it up and then hit Saunders around the back of the head with it.'

'A lot of force?'

'Sufficient for the youth to have been unconscious on hitting the ground.'

'And then?'

'The branch was used to hold his head under water.'

'Adam Saunders would not have been aware that he was drowning?'

'Probably not.'

'But wouldn't someone else in the wood have made a lot of noise?' Clare asked.

'You'd think so,' Hughes said.

'Not again,' Tremayne said.

'What I am saying is that either Adam Saunders was half-deaf or he was so scared that he imagined that the noises he heard were what he feared the most.'

153

'Pagan gods,' Clare said.

'That's what I'd reckon. He believed he was in their realm and that it was them.'

'When in reality it was a mortal again,' Tremayne said.

'No question that whoever killed him was of this world, and from Avon Hill.'

'Provable?'

'We traced the footprints down as far as the cottage.'

'Did you go down into Avon Hill?'

'Not with the crowd that was forming.'

'What does that mean?'

'From Adam Saunders' cottage to the lane leading down to Avon Hill is not far. The footprints were clear enough until then.'

'And after that?'

'As I said, a crowd was forming. Once they'd figured out what we were doing, they started marching up and down the lane with muddied boots and brooms.'

'Why?' Clare asked.

'Get real, Yarwood. They were destroying the evidence,' Tremayne said.

'Exactly,' Hughes said.

'Is there any way to identify the killer?' Clare asked.

'This is what we can tell you,' Hughes said. He had made himself comfortable on the chair in the corner of Tremayne's office. For once, the man had been civil to him. 'The murderer was left-handed.'

'Why do you say that?'

'The person was standing to the right of the youth. It's not conclusive, but I'd say there's a better than ninety per cent possibility that he was using his left hand.'

'Remember that fact, Yarwood,' Tremayne said.

'Anything else?'

'Judging by the angle that the branch hit the back of Adam Saunders' head, I'd say that you're looking someone between five feet six inches and five feet nine inches.'

'Weight?'

'Approximately one hundred and sixty pounds.'

'How do you know that?' Clare asked.

'Soil impaction close to the murder site. Forensics conducted tests and came to that conclusion.'

'As soon as we've dealt with Charles Saunders we need to start making some arrests, or Moulton will have me out of here.'

'You're joking, guv?'

'It's either him or me, and I don't fancy my chances. Besides, Hughes has given us our first concrete lead.'

'And we know the car that the woman in the graveyard used is in Avon Hill. We have to thank Oldfield for that.'

'His visit has certainly stirred them up. They'll be prepared for us when we arrive.'

'They've always been prepared,' Clare said.

'That's the truth. How and why I'd like to know,' Tremayne said.

'Harriet Wylshere?'

'We'll deal with what we have first off, and then talk to her after.'

'How long before Oldfield is here with Charles Saunders?'

'Within the hour. They've got to deal with the identification of Adam Saunders' body first,' Clare said.

Chapter 23

For seven hundred years Edmund Wylshere's family had held sway over a small and isolated, and until recent years a naïve and uneducated, community. But now the younger generation was not so easily swayed, and it had taken a combination of fear and discipline to maintain control. Those who believed were, in the main, in their fifties and older. The inner group, no more than six, were always the most devout, and then there were another twenty who could be trusted, but the membership had been declining.

Adam Saunders had not been the only one beginning to doubt. Even his own daughter, Edmund Wylshere knew, was starting to question the old ways. Whereas some still showed him the necessary respect, most did not, not even Charles Saunders, a boring accountant, the son of a subsistence farmer, whose education had come by way of the devotees' financial assistance and the Wylsheres' benevolence. And now what had happened? His son had died, a necessary act, and Charles Saunders was about to talk to the police.

Edmund Wylshere, secure in the manor house which had been in the family for centuries, contemplated the possibilities. If he stayed, the police would eventually find out the truth, and not even those that he made offerings to could hold the strength of the police at bay indefinitely.

Teutates, Esus, Taranis, our greatest challenge is ahead of us. I look to you to deal with those who threaten, Wylshere silently mouthed.

He had followed their guidance and had given orders to deal with Mavis Godwin and Adam Saunders, but now they would need to address the police.

Wylshere knew that the situation was insoluble. He could not leave, he could not stay.

'You made me kill my friend. If the police question me, I will tell them,' Wylshere's wife said. She had been close by, seen him talking to his gods.

'But why?'

'You ask me why? After all these years, you ask me that question?'

'Yes.'

'I killed my friend. I watched as her husband was sacrificed, even cheered when he was hauled up into that tree, but now, a fifteen-year-old boy. Our daughter is the same age, she has the same uncertainties. Will you kill her when the time comes, the same as you killed Eric Langley?'

'I was not responsible for Langley's death.'

'Are you still telling me that they intervened?'

'You have seen the proof. You know what I am telling you is true.'

'And the Reverend Harrison?'

'He would have told the police what they wanted to know.'

'His suicide?'

'They entered into his mind.'

'And they told you this?' Harriet Wylshere asked.

'Yes.'

'What are you? Just another lunatic masquerading as a good man.'

'I do what is necessary,' Edmund Wylshere protested.

'And kill anyone who gets in the way of you and your gods.'

'You don't believe?'

'You will kill anyone who interferes, even your own daughter when the time comes. I will not allow it. Do you hear me?'

'I hear,' Wylshere said. He had to admit that his wife was correct. For once, he did not know how it was all going to end, but one thing was sure: more people were going to die. He just hoped that it wasn't any member of his family.

'Harriet, you're right,' Wylshere said. 'Get away from here now and look after our daughter.'

'And you?'

'I will stay. Whatever happens, it is my duty to remain.'

Harriet Wylshere knew that he had spoken the truth. The safety of their daughter, fourteen and asking questions, who would not hold her tongue for very long, was her priority. It was important to get far away from her husband, but would it be far enough?

***

Vic Oldfield always knew that Charles Saunders coming clean about Avon Hill and the deaths was a long shot. Even after such a short time with DI Tremayne and Clare Yarwood, he realised that the boundless optimism which had accompanied him when he was in uniform was starting to tarnish. He could see himself in his fifties in Tremayne's seat in the corner office, full of the cynicism of having been there, seen it all.

Oldfield had to give the DI his due though; the man knew what he was talking about, and he was rarely wrong. He was adamant that Eric Langley's death was explainable, although no one, certainly not the CSE, had come up with a satisfactory cause. All the other deaths were explainable, however, and Charles Saunders was the man who had promised to bring the pieces together.

As Oldfield drew up to the Saunders' house, a substantial mock-Tudor two-storey house midway between Avon Hill and Salisbury, it was clear that something was wrong. The front door was wide open, there were suitcases in the driveway, and a car was being loaded by a woman in her late forties.

'Constable Oldfield,' he said, as he showed his identification to her. It was evident she had been crying and that she had made no attempt to make herself presentable. Oldfield assumed her to be Adam Saunders' mother.

'He killed him, that bastard,' the woman said.

'Who?'

'That son of a bitch killed our son, and all because of that stupid village.'

'Avon Hill?'

'Where else?'

'Your husband was going to reveal all that he knew,' Oldfield said. The woman continued to load her car.

'He'll not talk. The elders kill our son, yet he still protects them.'

'Where is he?'

'Indoors, feeling sorry for himself.'

'I've not heard the elders mentioned before.'

'You're the police. What are you going to do about it?'

'Once we have enough evidence, we will bring to justice those responsible.'

'You know who it is?'

'We have our suspicions.'

Charles Saunders came out of the front door, took one look at Oldfield and returned indoors, slamming the door behind him.

'They've been on the phone to him.'

'They?' Oldfield asked again.

'The elders.'

'Do you know who they are?'

'Every one of them. Pillars of society, they'd call themselves. Murdering savages who kill old women and children to protect themselves and their crazy beliefs.'

'Do you mean Mavis Godwin?'

'She's not the only one they've killed. They killed her husband as well.'

'Can you prove it?'

'I was there. I saw him die.'

'Do you know where he is buried?'

'I could take you there.'

As Oldfield and Adam Saunders' mother stood outside the house, a crashing sound could be heard from inside. Vic Oldfield rushed to the front door, attempted to break it open with his shoulder. It did not budge.

'It's double-locked,' Mrs Saunders said. 'Let me.'

With no apparent attempt to hurry, she unlocked the door and entered the house.

'Where is he?' Oldfield asked. He noticed clothes strewn in the hallway. They looked to be a man's. 'Was he leaving?'

'What do I care. He's upstairs.'

Oldfield bolted up the stairs, covering two steps at one stride. Mrs Saunders took her time. Oldfield, unsure of which way to go, waited for the woman on the upstairs' landing. 'His office is down the end of the hall, to your left,' she said.

The door was locked from the inside. This time Oldfield's attempt at shouldering the door was successful, and it gave at the first attempt. 'Don't come in,' he said.

Too late, Mrs Saunders was in. 'The coward. He took the easy way out,' she said.

Charles Saunders was hanging from a large beam, an attempt at pseudo-Tudor architecture. Around his neck was an electric cable, the other end secured to the beam. The cause of the crashing sound, a wooden chair, was lying on its side.

'Help me to get him down,' Oldfield said. He looked around, the woman was gone.

On closer inspection, it was clear the man hanging from the beam was dead. Oldfield phoned DI Tremayne and Clare. 'Charles Saunders is dead.'

Vic Oldfield realised that had he not been engaged with Mrs Saunders downstairs, the man would have still been alive. As he passed on the information to his fellow team members, he heard the sound of tyres on the gravel driveway outside. He looked out of the window to see Mrs Saunders driving away.

***

'Are you telling me you were here when he committed suicide?' Tremayne asked after he had arrived at the Saunders' residence. The man was angry, not that Oldfield blamed him. He had been responsible for seeing that the man reached Bemerton Road Police Station, not to officiate at his suicide, and that was clearly what it was.

'I was downstairs with his wife. She was leaving. I'd seen Charles Saunders briefly.'

'With you and Yarwood, I've got a pair of idiots. Not only do you believe this nonsense, but now you let people kill themselves when you're meant to be looking after them.'

'Mrs Saunders was talking. She knows what is going on. She even admitted that she had seen Trevor Godwin die, and she knew where he was buried. I couldn't leave her, and besides, how was I to know that her husband was going to kill himself?'

'How am I going to explain to our superintendent that you were distracted? He'll have my guts for garters.'

'I'll take the blame,' Oldfield said.

'It doesn't work like that. You'll get a kick up the arse, I'll be hauled over the coals. That miserable sod may even force my retirement.'

Clare stood to one side. She could see that Oldfield had acted correctly, although she was doubtful that others would see it that way. She thought Tremayne was acting harshly, although she could feel his frustration, the same as hers. And now Harry was starting to become annoyed with her extended hours away from him. The previous night when she had arrived home late, he had not been pleased, had given her the cold shoulder, not even a kiss to welcome her back home or to say goodbye when she left later. It had not concerned her at the time; it did now.

'Yarwood, find out where that damn woman's gone,' Tremayne said. 'I hope our man here has got the registration number.'

'I've got it,' Oldfield replied.

'Did he leave a note?'

'None that I could see. He only had a few minutes from when I saw him to when he was dead.'

'That'll look good on your police record. "Witnesses commit suicide when they see him",' Tremayne said.

'That's not fair, guv,' Claire said.

'Maybe,' Tremayne admitted, 'but it's a first. Don't expect to be the police officer of the month down at Bemerton Road, will you, Oldfield?'

'I know it's not good, but his wife knows what's going on. She told me more in the time I was talking to her than anyone else has.'

'Such as?'

'She admitted that Trevor Godwin had been killed, that Mavis Godwin was murdered, and she was not the first old lady according to her account. And then there are the elders she mentioned.'

'Any names?'

'None, but she said they were pillars of society.'

'Dr Wylshere?' Claire asked.

'It's probable. We still need to bring him in. First off, see if you can find the woman and her car.'

Clare left to instigate the search for Kathy Saunders. Tremayne and Oldfield entered the house after donning protective clothing. The CSE had been adamant that they followed the process, even though there had been no one else involved and it was evident what had happened.

'Nice house,' Jim Hughes said when he arrived with his team. He, like Tremayne, was unmoved by the sight of a man suspended from a beam. Oldfield fixated on the body, remembered the look of the man at the front door not more than sixty minutes previously.

Oldfield realised that the man had decided not to talk, and that suicide was preferable to a police interview. The elders, whoever they were, were dangerous, and the fear they instilled into those who followed them was extreme.

Oldfield knew they were probably being watched, and if he or Tremayne or Clare got in their way, then their well-being was at stake.

'Not much to see,' Hughes said. 'Oldfield saw the man downstairs, there's no sign of forced entry or coercion. Whatever it was, it drove the man to kill himself.'

'No one else in the room?' Tremayne asked.

'We'll check but we'll probably find nothing. If his son was murdered yesterday, and his wife was moving out, then I'd say that he committed suicide while his mind was disturbed.'

'Thanks,' Tremayne said. 'Oldfield, check on Yarwood. I want the dead man's wife today.'

'Her son and her husband have both died within fifteen hours. Shouldn't we give her some time to mourn?' Oldfield said.

'You tell me that she had witnessed the death of Trevor Godwin. Does that sound like a woman I should show some compassion to? She may well be upset, but she's been a witness to a murder, possibly a participant, and you want me to go easy. Not a chance.'

Chapter 24

Kathy Saunders drove aimlessly around the area. After her husband had told her that their only child had become a victim of Wylshere and Avon Hill, she had not been able to think straight. Her son Adam was dead, and she knew who was responsible.

Her life was over, she knew that, and what did it matter.

As she drove into Avon Hill, the woman could only feel numb. She could see Wylshere's Bentley parked outside the small pub where he and his inner circle of elders made their plans, where they drank their pints of beer and decided who was next to die.

Kathy Saunders had believed them once, but now they had killed her son. A youth who had kept the village's secret safe, yet they had not trusted him. She realised that Edmund Wylshere was not the benign and caring leader that he professed to be. The man was evil, and if others would not do it, then she would ensure that the gods could have him as well. She reached into the glove compartment of the car as she was pulling into the car park at the rear of the pub and took out a hand gun. She purposely parked behind Wylshere's car.

He's not getting away, she thought.

She switched off the car engine, calmly taking her time. Outside the car she went around to the back and opened the rear door. A shotgun lay on the floor. She took it and walked towards the back door of the pub.

Inside the group of twelve led by Wylshere discussed what to do next. Wylshere, a man used to total obedience, listened to their arguments. There had been dissent in the past, but it had been minor compared to what he experienced now. Before dissenting voices had been in private, but now, he realised, of the eleven who stood or sat around him, six were wavering.

'If you hadn't killed Mavis Godwin,' one of the group said.

'What was I to do?' Wylshere said. 'Trevor Godwin was a true believer, yet we agreed that he needed to die.'

'The man was a simpleton,' Grayling, the publican, answered. 'Don't make out that he was anything else. When he was alive, we all made fun of him and his simple ways, and he allowed his wife to control him.'

'Yet he never spoke to anyone outside of this village about what went on here.'

The back door of the pub swung wide open, its brass handle banging on the wall inside. 'You bastard,' Kathy Saunders said. Her shotgun was held up and pointing directly at Wylshere.

'Kathy, calm down,' Wylshere said as he attempted to move away from the line of fire.

'You've killed Adam, and now Charles is dead.'

'I'm not responsible.'

The others in the bar moved to one side. None appeared to be too keen to be involved. Grayling used the bar as a shield.

'I am your leader. Help me,' Wylshere pleaded. He knew then that he was a coward.

'She's right,' one of the group said. 'You killed them, the same as you killed the Godwins and the others. Kathy, do what is necessary. We will not stop you.'

Dr Edmund Wylshere, the man who had led them with almost total obedience for over twenty years, knew that his sway over the community was coming to an end. He retreated into his shell and started to mouth secret incantations, the same ones his ancestor had spoken out loud seven centuries before in the church where they held their ceremonies.

'They'll not save you,' Kathy Saunders said. The others in the bar were not so sure: the lights were flickering, their beers were frothing in their glasses, clouds were forming outside.

'Stop it, Wylshere,' Grayling said. 'We've seen enough.'

Wylshere continued to incant, the clouds growing more menacing, a streak of lightning momentarily lighting up the sky

'You've brought them here,' Kathy Saunders said. Her shotgun was loaded and still pointing at the doctor, now in a trance.'

'You'll not get any sense out of him,' one of the group said.

Kathy Saunders pulled the trigger. The recoil thrust her back against the wall. Of the twelve in that small area, two were severely wounded, another seven received minor injuries, and two were killed. Only two remained uninjured: Dr Edmund Wylshere and Kathy Saunders.

Wylshere looked around at the carnage and then up at the woman. 'You'll not survive.'

The woman took out the small gun in her jacket pocket and pointed it at Wylshere. She could see the look of horror on his face. She pulled the trigger.

The bullet hit him in the chest, and he bent over and collapsed on the floor.

Kathy Saunders, forced under extreme circumstances, had shot the man, a man she hated and had revered, a man who could summon the malignancy of pagan history. She knew she was damned.

Albert Grayling lifted his bloodied head from behind the bar. 'Kathy, go,' he said. 'Let's hope that we survive.'

'I will not,' she said.

***

Kathy Saunders was oblivious of her surroundings as she drove away from Avon Hill. She only knew one thing, Edmund Wylshere was dead. She had seen the bullet enter his body, seen the blood, seen him collapse onto the floor of the old pub. She vaguely remembered someone telling her to leave, but her recollections of the event were blurred. There had been a son and a husband, but even they were no longer clear in her mind. Unsure of where she was heading, she just drove. The narrow road leading away from the village was winding and treacherous at the best of times, but with the pelting rain and the dark clouds she had been forced to put on the car lights. Another streak of lightning, a rumble of thunder, a fox dashing across the road in front of her.

As she started to distance herself from what had happened, as she came closer to the normal world, she began to reflect. With Wylshere dead, she knew that Avon Hill would be safe, and if he could not summon the deities, so would she. A feeling of sorrow washed over her. When her husband had told her that her son had died, she remembered that she had not been conscious of what he had said, almost as if it was a dream.

She knew about the cottage where he had been ensconced, and about his hovering in a graveyard waiting for the opportunity to enter the vicar's house to look for a book. Even she had agreed with that action. Hadn't her family prospered over the centuries due to the Wylsheres?

She had witnessed Trevor Godwin's death, even chanted with the others, even stabbed him with a knife. Why, she wondered, was she so committed then, so abhorred now? She did not know, only that she needed to cleanse her spirit.

Death was what she sought, but first there was unfinished business. Wylshere had a family, and they could carry on in his place, subverting other people, committing murder, pretending it was an offering. She knew she had to stop it. She knew that the police, ineffectual as they would be against the gods, could at least deal with the mortal man.

She remembered the young police constable at her house, how he had wanted her to help him cut down her husband, how she had dashed out of the house and left. Her husband had been a weak man. She stopped the car, checked in her handbag; the card was there.

'Constable Oldfield, it's Kathy Saunders here,' she said.

'Mrs Saunders, we've been looking for you.'

'You need to send some ambulances to Avon Hill.'

'Why?' Oldfield asked. He was in the office at the police station in Salisbury, with Tremayne and Clare listening in.

'I've killed Edmund Wylshere.'

Clare was on speed dial to the ambulance service, Tremayne was immediately into action and preparing to leave for the village.

'We need to meet,' Oldfield said.

'Meet me at the Wheatsheaf Inn in Wilton, thirty minutes. I will tell you why.'

'I believe we know that already, but it's still murder.'

'You don't know the whole story, and besides, I'll never see the inside of a prison.'

Chapter 25

'Yarwood, now what do you say?' Tremayne asked. They had both arrived in Avon Hill. The first ambulance was already there, another two were on their way. Some uniforms from the nearest police station were establishing the crime scene.

'No engine problems this time,' Clare replied.

It was the second visit to the local pub for Tremayne, the first for Clare. Outside in the car park several wounded men stumbled around or sat hunched over on the ground.

'Don't go inside,' the medic said.

'Bad, is it?' Tremayne asked.

'We've removed the wounded. There's two others, but they're dead.'

'Did you come across a Doctor Edmund Wylshere?'

'Dr Wylshere, he survived. He was shot in the chest, luckily it was off centre and exited on the other side of his body.'

'Where is he?'

'In the ambulance, but don't expect too much from him. I've administered a pain killer, but he'll be as sore as hell for a few days.'

'The others?'

'Those you see out here.'

Regardless of the fact that Wylshere had been shot, Tremayne made his way over to the first ambulance. Inside, the man could be seen lying down, a medic hovering close by.

'Detective Inspector Tremayne,' he said.

'This man is not fit to be questioned.'

'That's as maybe, but this is a murder enquiry. I need two minutes.'

'Very well, but if his condition deteriorates, I'm holding you responsible.'

'Suit yourself,' Tremayne said.

Both police officers climbed into the ambulance. Tremayne took a seat opposite the wounded man, Clare sat further down, closer to the door.

'Dr Wylshere, I'm Detective Inspector Tremayne.'

'Tremayne, yes, of course. How's the prostate?'

'Fine now, thanks to you.'

'You have some questions?'

'A few.'

'It was just a misunderstanding,' Wylshere said. 'Nothing to concern yourselves with.'

'I'll grant that you've been shot, but it's hardly a misunderstanding.'

Clare could see the medic becoming agitated.

'Kathy was upset,' Wylshere said.

'It's not an everyday occurrence when your son is murdered and your husband hangs himself with electrical cable, but that's not a reason to shoot you, kill two others and injure God knows how many others.'

'I must protest,' the medic said. 'This man is under my care, and your badgering is not assisting in his recovery. I must ask you to leave now.'

'Very well,' Tremayne said. 'Tell me, Dr Wylshere, why did she want to kill you? Did you kill her son?'

'Please. I must ask you to leave now,' the medic said.

Tremayne did not move. Wylshere wasn't about to die, and Tremayne had questions that needed answers. 'What is it, Wylshere? Why you? What did you do that forced a woman to come here and to shoot you? She blamed you, didn't she?'

'What for?' Wylshere feebly attempted to lift himself from his lying position.

'We've enough on you and your bunch of deluded fools to charge you all with murder. One of those followers of yours outside will sing once I've got him in the interview room at Bemerton Road. Whatever it is that's been going on down here, I'll soon know. Yarwood, get out there and round up those with minor wounds. Arrange to transport them to Bemerton Road. If any medics protest, grab one of them and take him as well.'

'Yes, guv.'

'And don't take any nonsense from any of them. They're all guilty in my book, and this man stretched out here is the leader. I want a police guard placed on him at the hospital, twenty-four hours, day and night. And make sure it's so tight even a mouse couldn't get in and out. Do you understand, Yarwood?'

Clare nodded her head. She could see that Tremayne had his teeth into Wylshere and he wasn't going to let go until the man was locked up in a prison cell.

***

Vic Oldfield took the opportunity to have a pub lunch in the bar of the Wheatsheaf Inn while he waited for Kathy Saunders. Ten minutes after he had arrived, the woman entered.

'I have the gun in my handbag,' she said. Oldfield looked at the woman. Her appearance was disturbing: her clothes were creased and her hair was uncombed.

'Would you like a drink and something to eat?' Oldfield asked.

The woman sat opposite him, expressionless. 'I want to tell you why I shot him,' she said.

Oldfield decided not to tell her that Wylshere was still alive. The woman was clearly in shock and in need of medical assistance. He could see that some pellets from the shotgun that she had fired were lodged in her right arm, blood trickling down her sleeve. He took out his phone and requested an ambulance.

'Edmund Wylshere killed my son,' Kathy Saunders said.
'Was it him or someone else?'
'What does it matter? They do what they are told.'
'Who?'
'Those that believe.'
'Do you believe? Oldfield asked.
'It does not matter.'
'But do you believe?'
'I have seen the proof.'
'Wylshere is the leader?'
'Yes. He was the one who communicated with them.'
'Do you know who killed your son?'

'It could be anyone. They would rather kill a child than disobey Edmund Wylshere.'

'Trevor Godwin. You told me that you know where he is buried.'

'Yes.'

'How did he die?'

'They hanged him in a tree and stabbed him to death.'

'Did you take part?'

'Yes.'

'You realise I'll have to arrest you for murder.'

'It's unimportant.'

A medic arrived, administered first aid; the wounds were not severe. She left and waited outside, having been forewarned by Oldfield that the woman's questioning was to continue and that he would drive her to Bemerton Road Police Station to be charged.

'What else can you tell me?' Oldfield asked.

'They're here,' Kathy Saunders said.

Oldfield looked around the bar. It was the first time he'd been in the pub, and he had to admit that it was unlikely to become his favourite. His girlfriend came there on the occasional Friday for a girls' night out, but he'd not been invited, and often she'd arrive at his place late at night, the worse for wear.

Oldfield realised that the courts would treat Kathy Saunders leniently due to the recent deaths of her son and husband, and they'd probably convict her of the lesser charge of murder while the mind was disturbed. However, it was still a prison sentence.

'I can't see anyone,' Oldfield replied.

'Look outside. Can't you see?'

Oldfield raised himself slightly, angled his neck to look out the small window behind him. 'It looks ominous,' he said.

'The clouds, can't you see the clouds.'

'It's your imagination.'

'Haven't you experienced it before?'

'Once.'

'Where?'

'In Reverend Harrison's house.'

'When you found the Bible?'

'How did you know about the Bible?' Oldfield asked. The temperature in the bar became even chillier.

'It's getting cold in here,' the publican said. 'I'll light up the fire.'

Oldfield and Kathy Saunders moved closer to the heat. The publican looked out of the window. 'I've not seen it like this for some time,' he said.

'Have you seen this before?' Oldfield asked.

'It's the river outside. Sometimes it seems to become colder than usual, and then we feel it in here, but this has been quick. Mind you, I don't like the look of those clouds.'

'He doesn't know what he's talking about,' Kathy Saunders said.

For a woman who should be grieving, she's holding up well, Oldfield thought.

'Tell me about the Bible,' Oldfield said.

'Mavis Godwin told her friend about it once.'

'And this friend, does he or she have a name?'

'Harriet Wylshere.'

'Did she kill Mavis Godwin?'

'Yes.'

'You knew this, and still you did not tell the police.'

'They would have made an example of me if I had.'

'What sort of example?'

'They hanged Trevor Godwin, they drowned his wife, and another died of fire.'

'Who died of fire?'

'Eric Langley.'

'You knew him?'

'I knew of him.'

'How?'

'I met him once when I was younger. I remember him as rude, at least he was to me.'

'What happened to him?'

'He left the community. I don't know why, but they kept an eye on him.'

Oldfield ordered the woman some sandwiches; she nibbled at them.

'Unseasonal,' the publican said. 'It's below freezing outside. There's even ice forming on the river.'

'It's them,' Kathy Saunders said. 'They don't want me to tell you any more.'

Oldfield prodded the open fire in an attempt to induce it to give more heat. Both the police officer and the murderer, by her own admission, moved closer. Both were starting to shiver. It worried Oldfield; it did not worry the woman.

'Are you saying they killed Eric Langley?'

'Yes.'

'Why? The man had left your community years before, and he had never spoken about what went on.'

'He never spoke because if he had, he would have had to plead guilty to the murder of others.'

'So why kill him?'

'The man was dying. He wanted to make peace with God.'

'Your gods?'

'He wanted to confess to a priest before he died. He had made it clear that on his death bed he would reveal all.'

'How do you know this?'

'Mavis Godwin.'

'She told you?'

'She told Harriet Wylshere in confidence. Mavis Godwin trusted the woman.'

'And Harriet Wylshere told her husband?'

'After that Eric Langley's fate was sealed.'

'We cannot explain how he died,' Oldfield said. 'His death has been classified as cause unknown.'

'Edmund Wylshere arranged it.'

'How?'

'What do you know of our beliefs?'

'Only that there are three gods.'

'And each one requires a sacrifice.'

'I find it hard to believe that rational, sane people such as yourself can believe in such nonsense.'

'Do you believe in your God? The one that created the heaven and the earth, the one that is responsible for miracles.'

'The metaphors.'

'Many believe without proof.'

'I suppose they do.'

'Reverend Harrison did.'

The publican came over to where they were sitting. 'I've made you a couple of hot drinks. It looks as though it may snow. So much for global warming,' he said.

The man looked as though he wanted to stay and talk. Oldfield flashed his badge. The publican took one look and returned behind the bar. Oldfield yet again prodded the fire.

The flames from the fire were doing little to heat the two who huddled close to it. Oldfield was feeling uncomfortable, although he had no intention of moving.

'How did Wylshere kill Eric Langley?' Oldfield asked again, as the first answer he had received had told him nothing.

'Edmund Wylshere arranged it, the same as he arranged the death of my son.'

'Do you know who was responsible for his death?'

The woman looked down; a tear in her eye. 'Any one of them would have done it.'

'Any one of this so-called community?'

'Yes.'

'Even you?'

'Not my son, but anyone else. I've already confessed to taking part in Trevor Godwin's death.'

'Have there been others?'

'Two others, but you do not know their names.'

'Will you tell me?'

'They are not important. They're unworthy of being remembered.'

'Coming back to Eric Langley,' Oldfield said. 'The man was burnt, although there was no fuel, no flame, and yet you are telling me that Edmund Wylshere was responsible.'

'He did not kill the man personally.'

'Then who did?'

'Taranis.'

'Do you expect me to believe that a pagan god killed Eric Langley?' Oldfield was frustrated. He had spent close to an hour in the pub and still the gods that Kathy Saunders believed in were being mentioned.

'Believe what you want. It is the truth. I have seen their vengeance, as you will.'

'What do you mean?'

'Can't you feel them?'

'I can feel the cold, nothing more.'

'Then, Constable Oldfield, you're a fool. What I have told you has damned you.'

'Are you telling me that I am a target?'

'I have given my confession to you. They have not entered here, although I do not know why. Before it was only me they intended to remove, now it is you.'

'That's pure rubbish,' Oldfield said. Although a sceptic, he could not deny the sincerity in the woman's voice. He knew that he needed to get her to Bemerton Road Police Station and charged. Then they needed to find Harriet Wylshere and charge her as well.

Oldfield saw no reason to stay in the public house any longer. Outside, the weather was worsening, and the snow had started to fall.

As they left the pub, Kathy Saunders pointed to a large crucifix on the wall behind the bar. 'That's why we are still alive,' she said. Oldfield shuddered at what she said. He began to doubt his sanity, wondered if the woman was right.

'You'll need to come with me,' he said as she took the keys to her car out of her handbag.

'My car?' Kathy Saunders said.

'I'll get someone to pick it up and bring it to the police station.'

'It doesn't matter. I'll not need it anymore.'

Chapter 26

Avon Hill was in total lockdown. Clare was assigned the task of interviewing the wounded who did not require immediate hospitalisation.

Also, the car that had been seen outside the graveyard in Stratford sub Castle was around the corner, not more than a hundred yards away. Clare dispatched a couple of uniforms to check it out and impound it, and to make sure the inhabitants of the house where it was parked were detained pending an interview. It was also made clear that anyone in the village who offered any resistance or attempted to slam a door in the face of any police officer was to be arrested, slapped in handcuffs if necessary.

Tremayne knew the flak he'd receive from his senior for his actions in Avon Hill, but he was aware that the woman shooting in the pub was not only because of Edmund Wylshere but also because of the majority of the people there.

Tremayne had looked around at the wounded, decided that they were a decidedly odd crowd. He remembered when he had last visited the pub, over twenty-five years previously, and the cold welcome he and his fellow junior officers had received. They were all young, out of uniform, anxious to drink a few too many beers, chat up some local girls, but the pub had been devoid of females apart from a couple of old women, and neither of them was friendly. They had drunk one pint of the best the pub had to offer. Tremayne remembered the beer as being flat. It had been after nine in the evening when they had reached there, and any other pub would have been full of half-drunk or fully-drunk individuals making fools of themselves, playing darts, flirting with the opposite sex and generally making a raucous noise, but not the pub in Avon Hill.

Tremayne remembered everyone sitting at a table, a couple of old men propping themselves up on the bar, but there was no noise. His crowd had made plenty, as he had already downed five pints, heading to six, and the others were no better. They were out for a night of fun, but Avon Hill wasn't going to provide it. He remembered asking the publican what was going on. It's normal for around here, had been the reply.

After they had left the pub, they found another, not more than two miles away. Tremayne remembered that one well enough. The beer was good, the company congenial and the next day he had woken up in a strange bed with a throbbing headache and an obviously willing companion. They dated for three months before he proposed. It was as if it was yesterday, but after five years of wedded bliss, they grew apart.

Tremayne found that remembering his wife had left him a little nostalgic. It had been over twenty years since they had divorced, and he had not seen her since. He wondered what had become of her. For a couple of years they had kept in contact, as there was no malice on either side, but then she told him that she had met another man and they were getting married. After that, nothing. He thought that maybe he should contact her again.

'Are you alright, guv?' Clare asked. She had seen him looking wistful, an unusual condition for the man.

'I was remembering the first time I came in here. It's not changed much.'

'It's a depressing place. I don't know how the young people can take it.'

'Have you seen anyone under the age of fifty?'

'Not in the pub.'

'Leave the interviews to me. You can check out the car from the graveyard. Take a uniform in case they become awkward.'

'I've spoken to a couple of the men that were in the bar,' Clare said.

'Anything?'

'No. They just followed Wylshere's line that it was a misunderstanding. From what I gather, they want for us to leave and to let them deal with it.'

'You know what that means?'

'With this lot? The Mavis Godwin solution, I'd assume.'

'Have you spoken to Oldfield?' Tremayne asked. The survivors, or at least those with minor injuries, were in another room in the pub. Jim Hughes and his team were kitted up and in the main bar sifting through the evidence.

'Oldfield's with Kathy Saunders. She's talking,' Clare said.

'The full details?'

'It appears to be. He's taking her to Bemerton Road for a formal charging. Apparently, she's not concerned.'

'Why?'

'The usual. And besides, her family's been decimated. You can hardly expect her to be thinking straight.'

'I'm surprised she's still able to do anything. Most parents' reaction would be to collapse into total despair.'

'Ask Oldfield where Trevor Godwin is buried. We need to get the body exhumed.'

Clare left and drove to the cottage where Oldfield had seen the car. It wasn't there. She walked around to the back of the cottage after knocking on the door first. The uniform waited at the front. A face appeared through a gap in the curtain of the main room.

'There's someone here,' the uniform shouted. Clare banged loudly on the back door of the house. It opened slightly. 'What do you want?' a voice said.

'Sergeant Yarwood, I've some questions.'

'I've nothing to say.'

'Where's the car that was parked here last night?'

'I don't have a car.'

'We know there was a car here last night, and there are tyre marks on the concrete. Either you can open the door and let me in, or I'll ask the constable out front to break it down.'

'You can't do that.'

'I can and I will. This is a murder investigation. We have five deaths, and I have total authority to take whatever action is deemed necessary.'

'Very well.' The door opened to reveal a woman in her sixties. She was dressed conservatively in an ankle-length blue skirt and a matching jacket with a white blouse underneath.

'Your name?' Clare asked, once inside. The constable had been let in at the front door.

'Elizabeth Grimshaw.'

'Mrs Grimshaw.'

'It's Miss.'

'Very well, Miss Grimshaw. The car that was parked outside, where is it?'

'It wasn't mine. It belonged to a friend.'

'And where is that friend?'

'He's not here.'

'Miss Grimshaw, I was in a car following that vehicle as far as the turn off to Avon Hill. I saw the driver from a distance. There are others who were closer. I am confident you are the woman who was driving that car.'

'I had to,' the woman replied. She sat down on a hard chair in the kitchen. The air was musty, the kitchen was basic and scrupulously clean. An old dog was lying in the corner. It did not move when the two police officers entered the kitchen other than to lazily lift its head.

'That's Brutus. He's deaf and old, same as me really.'

'Are you deaf?'

'I'm old,' the woman said.

'Where is your car?'

'They took it.'

'Who?'

'Is it true about Kathy Saunders?'

'What is it that you know?'

'I heard the shots. They said it was her.'

'Do you know why she did it?'

'Is Dr Wylshere dead?'

'No.'

'Oh.'

'Does it make a difference?'

'I can tell you no more.'

'But you haven't said anything yet. Are you a pagan?'

'They killed Adam Saunders, such a sweet boy,' Elizabeth Grimshaw said.

'Do you know who killed him?'

'It doesn't matter.'

'Why?'

'They protect those who are loyal to them.'

'It is your duty to assist the police in their investigation. If the interview is not concluded to my satisfaction here, I will be forced to take you to Bemerton Road Police Station for questioning.'

'Is that where Kathy is?'

'She soon will be.'

'And Dr Tremayne? He still lives?'

'Yes.'

'Then I will go with you to your police station. I want to be near to Kathy when they come for her.'

'It's a police station. No one's coming.'

'How little you know. You sit in your police station surrounded by your laptops and your mobile phones. You go about your futile lives believing in a Christian God, indulging in promiscuity and fornication, not knowing that your existence hangs by a thread.'

Clare thought that the woman was either mad or frustrated, probably both.

'He didn't suffer,' Elizabeth Grimshaw said.

'Who didn't?'

'Adam Saunders.'

'How do you know?'

'I obeyed them.'

'Are you saying you killed him?'

'Dr Wylshere said I would not be as noisy as the others moving through Cuthbert's Wood.'

Clare took a seat. She had come looking for a car, and now she had another murderer.

'I thought everyone was frightened to go in there.'

'I had never been there before, but Dr Wylshere told me that it would be safe.'

'And you believed him?'

'Oh, yes. What he says always happens.'

Clare phoned Tremayne to update him. He said he'd be over in twenty minutes. He was occupied with those from the shooting, but as he said, he was banging his head against a wall.

Clare resumed her questioning of Elizabeth Grimshaw. 'Are you willing to make a full confession?' she asked.

'Why?'

'It may assist in your trial.'

'I am not answerable to your laws.'

179

'Miss Grimshaw, you have committed murder. Do you realise this?'

'I followed a command.'

'Were you in the graveyard in Stratford sub Castle?' Clare asked.

'Yes.'

Clare suspected insanity, but then Miss Grimshaw wasn't the only one in the case so far. Edmund Wylshere was a doctor, and if he was the leader of the disparate group in the village, then he was certifiable as well. And then there was Kathy Saunders who had shot at a pub full of patrons. Clare thought she may be able to plead mitigating circumstances, although according to Oldfield she had no intention of doing so. Whatever it was in that village, it pervaded everywhere, even that small cottage with its semblance of normality – a television in the corner, lace curtains on the windows, an old dog curled up in its basket.

Tremayne arrived later than he had said. Clare could see the frustration in the man's face. They first spoke outside the cottage, the constable staying with Elizabeth Grimshaw.

'What do you have?' Tremayne asked.

'She admits to killing Adam Saunders.'

'A written confession?'

'She'll write it down, even sign it, but it's not a confession.'

'Then what is it?' Tremayne asked.

'A statement of fact.'

'She's the same as the rest.'

'No luck down at the pub?' Clare asked.

'I've spent the last hour wasting my time. All I got was that it was a misunderstanding.'

'What is it with these people? The woman shows no emotion, no concept of right or wrong.'

'Living down here would make anyone slightly mad. Can't you feel it?' Tremayne said.

'Are you starting to believe, guv?'

'Don't talk rubbish. What I'm saying is that it's an isolated village at the end of the road, and it wouldn't take much for some of them to believe in any nonsense.'

'Some? It appears to be all of them.'

'Kathy Saunders is willing to talk.'

'So is the woman inside, but neither of them expresses any guilt for their actions.'

'Okay, let's wrap this up and head back to the police station.'

Tremayne and Clare entered the house. Elizabeth Grimshaw was watching the television. 'It's my favourite,' she said.

'I'm Detective Inspector Tremayne. Can we talk?'

'Yes, if you like. Would you like a cup of tea?'

'No, that's fine.'

'I've told your sergeant all there is to know.'

'You've admitted to killing Adam Saunders.'

'I had to, you know that.'

'I'm afraid that to us it's murder.'

'They'll not let you leave here.'

'Who?'

'They.'

'Do they have a name?'

'Dr Wylshere knows who they are. They talk to him.'

Clare looked over at Tremayne. The man lifted his brow, a clear indication that he thought the woman was crazy.

'Dr Wylshere is on his way to the hospital. At the present moment, he's not able to talk.'

'Then you have time.'

'To do what?'

'To leave Avon Hill. They are at their strongest here. If Dr Wylshere wants them to deal with you, they will.'

'Are you saying that he controls these forces?'

'He knows how to summon them.'

'Miss Grimshaw, you're sitting here watching the television, and you're telling us that you believe in paganism, ancient gods and sacrifices?'

'Oh, yes, and I've got the internet. I like to keep myself informed.'

'The night of Adam Saunders' death. Can you please tell us what happened?' Tremayne asked.

'I saw him leave the cottage. It's not far from here, and I'd been told to keep a watch out for him.'

'By who?'

'Dr Wylshere.'

'Did he explain why?'

'I did not need an explanation.'

'Carry on,' Clare said.

'I saw him walking up from the cottage towards Cuthbert's Wood. I phoned Dr Wylshere, and he gave me instructions.'

'Instructions to do what?'

'To kill him.'

'And you did not refuse?'

'Why should I? I've killed others.'

Clare sat back, stunned by the indifference.

'Who else?' Tremayne asked. Clare felt sick to her stomach.

'I was there when Trevor Godwin died.'

'Kathy Saunders has admitted to having been there as well.'

'We were all there.'

'Two people have died in the pub.'

'They have served their purpose.'

'What purpose?'

'Dr Wylshere is still alive.'

'When I first came here, you asked me if he was alive,' Clare reminded the woman.

'The Wylsheres have controlled our lives for centuries. Why should I want it to stop?'

'Because you commit murder in his name,' Clare said. She realised that she was becoming emotional, not an admirable trait for someone in Homicide.

'We'll continue this interview at Bemerton Road Police Station,' Tremayne said. 'I'll return to the pub. I need to check with the CSE and see if anyone in this place is sane enough to talk.'

'I can assure you that I am sane,' Elizabeth Grimshaw said.

Tremayne said nothing as he left by the front door. Clare could see him muttering to himself as he walked across the frozen lawn at the front of the cottage.

Chapter 27

Vic Oldfield, with Kathy Saunders in the passenger seat, pulled out from the car park at the Wheatsheaf Inn in Wilton. The roads were icy, more suited to the woman's four-wheel drive than the car he drove, but he was taking a murderer to the police station, and it would have been inappropriate for him to take her vehicle. Besides, it was evidence in the shooting in Avon Hill.

'What will happen?' Kathy Saunders asked as Oldfield drove along King Street.

'You'll be asked to make a formal statement.'

'I'll need to arrange my son's funeral.'

'That may not be possible.'

'You cannot stop me. It's a mother's right.'

'I'll see what can be done,' Oldfield said, although he realised that it was unlikely that she would be given the necessary permission.

The weather was bleak, the snow was starting to intensify, and visibility was being hampered. Oldfield put the windscreen wipers on full and blasted the hot air in the car up at the screen from the inside.

He passed over the Minster Street roundabout and headed down Salisbury Road. He had less than two miles to go. The road cleared of traffic, and with the snow easing up, he increased his speed. The woman at his side started to cry.

Delayed shock, Oldfield thought.

Oldfield looked at the speedometer, realised he was travelling at over fifty miles an hour. He eased his foot off the accelerator: no effect. The vehicle continued to accelerate. He passed the turn off to Netherhampton, narrowly avoiding a motorcycle.

'You're going too fast,' Kathy Saunders said.

'I can't slow down.'

The vehicle continued to move at speed. Oldfield pumped the brakes, wedged his foot under the accelerator pedal in case it was jammed; it was not. Realising the urgency of the situation, he pressed the call button on his police radio.

He outlined his current predicament. A police car set out from Bemerton Road Police Station, but Oldfield was already travelling at over seventy miles an hour on a road that was covered in ice. He pumped the brakes, flashed his lights, pressed the horn on the steering wheel. Vehicles up ahead moved to one side; he missed a slow-moving truck, caught the rear of another car, smashing its right-hand tail light.

Kathy Saunders crossed her arms and closed her eyes. She took a deep breath and relaxed in her seat.

Oldfield continued to control the car, thankful that the road was at least straight, but he remembered that it bent to the left not more than two hundred yards ahead as it crossed over a railway bridge. He knew that at the speed it was travelling the car would not make it round the bend. He had to stop the vehicle, but his options were limited. There was a mobile crane up ahead. He decided to allow his car to hit it at the rear.

The crane was looming closer, closer – impact. The car shuddered as it hit.

He looked at his passenger. She was still alive, the airbag having cushioned her as she was thrown forward.

The mobile crane slowed down, its red stop lights visible inside Oldfield's car. The woman alongside him looked over at him. 'We're not going to survive,' she said.

Oldfield focussed on the road ahead; he offered no comment.

The mobile crane, now only travelling slowly, turned to its left to negotiate the railway bridge. Dislodged from its place of protection, Oldfield's vehicle separated from it and veered over to the other side of the road. He saw the brick wall of the bridge. His vehicle was heading towards it, he could not stop it. There was a roadworks sign on the bridge: the wall was unstable and in the process of being repaired. He did not have time to look at the sign, only to see the wall, to hear the noise as the car impacted it. He remembered the car in mid-air.

***

The mood at Bemerton Road Police Station was sombre when the news came through of the deaths of Constable Vic Oldfield and his passenger. The accident, no more than a four-minute drive from the police station, had hit Tremayne hard, Clare even more so.

'We've got to continue,' Tremayne said. He had experienced death too often to allow it to affect his determination to bring the case to a conclusion. Clare had not been able to continue at Elizabeth Grimshaw's cottage, and it had been the woman who had consoled her.

'I'm sorry, but I warned you,' she said.

'But why?' Clare's response.

'I told you what would happen. I have lived with this all my life.'

Harry Holchester phoned soon after the news had circulated throughout Salisbury. He had liked Vic Oldfield, knew that he fancied Clare. 'I'm coming out to Avon Hill,' he said.

Under normal circumstances Clare would not have appreciated his coming, but she was not in a fit state to continue.

Tremayne was busy on the phone, firstly enquiring about Oldfield, secondly talking to Jim Hughes, the CSE. 'Any more?' he asked.

'Nobody wants to continue,' Hughes said. Tremayne could hear the sadness in his voice.

'We're professionals. We do our job,' Tremayne said.

'We realise that. We'll keep working, but apart from the obvious, there's not much more to tell you. There's a shotgun in our possession. It's covered in fingerprints. I've had someone down to the Wheatsheaf in Wilton to check out Kathy Saunders' car, and the prints match. Apart from that, there's two dead, four that need hospitalisation, although they'll live, and the others are minor.'

'Wylshere?'

'He's in the hospital now. Apart from some internal bleeding, he'll pull through. What about the woman you're with?'

'Elizabeth Grimshaw. She's admitted to killing Adam Saunders. Unrepentant, as they all are. What is it with these people?'

'You'll need a psychologist to understand how the minds of such people operate.'

'How's Yarwood?'

'She's not taking it well.'

'You can't blame her. She was closer to Oldfield than any of us. What's happening with him?'

'I'm on my way over there.'

'And Yarwood?'

'Harry Holchester's coming to pick her up.'

Clare sat in the corner of the kitchen; Brutus the dog had come and sat down next to her. She was patting it.

'She'll be fine,' Elizabeth Grimshaw said.

'I don't get it,' Tremayne said. 'You seem to be a kind person, yet you can kill a fifteen-year-old youth.'

'Death does not concern us.'

'What are we going to do with Vic?' Clare asked.

'We need to get back to the station. There's not much we can do here.'

'And Miss Grimshaw?'

'She'll have to come with us.'

'I'll get my coat,' Elizabeth Grimshaw said. 'I'll need to pop next door to ask them to look after Brutus.'

'I'll come with you,' Clare said.

The two women left by the back door and walked through a small gate in the adjoining fence. Tremayne sat down and patted the dog. He remembered his first partner and how he had felt when he had died in a motorcycle accident. It had upset him at the time, but with Oldfield he did not feel the same degree of sadness. He wondered if he had become jaundiced by too many deaths over the years.

Tremayne spoke to the dog. 'You're right. It's not time yet for me to retire. A few more years in me yet.'

The dog went back to sleep.

Clare and Elizabeth Grimshaw returned. 'I've phoned Harry, told him that I'm going back with you,' Clare said.

'And next door?'

'They said they'd look after Brutus. Can you believe it, nobody locks their doors here?'

'The old ways are the best,' Elizabeth Grimshaw said. Clare found it difficult to remember who she was talking to. For some inexplicable reason, she liked the woman, even after what she had done.

Chapter 28

Tremayne drove, with Clare and Elizabeth Grimshaw in the back seat. The two women said little. He could see Clare with a handkerchief in her hand, occasionally dabbing her eyes. Elizabeth Grimshaw just sat calmly, her face expressionless.

Even he, cynical and seen-it-all, had been shaken by the suddenness of Oldfield's death. Before leaving Avon Hill, Tremayne had obtained the phone number of Oldfield's parents and had made the phone call, offering his condolences. Clare had called Oldfield's girlfriend; she was coming down to Bemerton Road Police Station. Clare had told her that there was no reason to, but the woman had been adamant. 'I want to be near him,' she had said.

It was clear that the most direct route from Wilton to Salisbury and Bemerton Road Police Station would be heavily delayed due to the accident. Tremayne decided to take the longer route up to Devizes Road and then down Highbury Avenue and right into Bemerton Road, down from the crash site. The trip took thirty-five minutes. Clare escorted Elizabeth Grimshaw into the police station for formal charging; Tremayne headed up to the accident scene. He needed his siren and flashing light to extricate himself from the traffic build-up. The police were attempting to redirect traffic around the area, but it was late afternoon, and it was at its heaviest. He parked his car fifty yards from the railway bridge and walked up.

'It's not a pretty sight,' a uniform said on seeing the detective inspector. Tremayne continued walking. Oldfield's car could be seen down below on the railway tracks.

'They've stopped the trains running,' Moulton said. He was last person that Tremayne had expected to see out of the office.

'Oldfield?' Tremayne asked.

'Dead on impact, the woman as well.'

'How long have you been here?'

'Ten minutes after word came through. I've phoned his parents.'

'So did I. They'll be here in the next few hours. How long before the bodies are removed?'

'I've been told within the hour. Where does this place the investigation?' Moulton asked.

'We have the person who murdered Adam Saunders.'

'Can you prove that the woman with Oldfield killed two people in Avon Hill?'

'That's conclusive. The witnesses will confirm, not that I'd give them much credence.'

'What do you mean?'

'The same as the woman with Yarwood. They always went on about how it was a misunderstanding, or it was a command or some such other nonsense.'

'No sense of guilt?'

'None at all. If Wylshere commanded, they obeyed.'

'These gods, what's the truth?' Moulton asked. Down below on the railway tracks the two men could see the first body being removed from the vehicle. Heavy-duty cutting tools had sliced open a section of the roof.

'I'll admit that Avon Hill is a place to believe in such things, but it's nonsense. Wylshere for some reason was able to control these people.'

'I've met him,' Moulton said. 'He never struck me as anything special.'

As the two men spoke, for once in a cordial manner, the second body was removed from the vehicle. A crane was waiting to lift the car from the rail tracks once it had been given the all-clear. The bodies would be taken to Pathology, the vehicle would be subject to further checks.

'Do you know what happened?' Moulton asked.

'No. Yarwood spoke to Oldfield a few minutes before the accident. He told her that he was driving the woman to the police station.'

'It's not a dangerous road, yet he smashes into the back of a mobile crane, sideswipes a couple of cars, almost runs a motorcycle off the road. What speed was he doing?'

'No idea, sir,' Tremayne said. The first body passed by the two men. Tremayne checked; it was Oldfield.

***

One hour later and Elizabeth Grimshaw was in the cells. Clare wanted to go home and be with Harry, but first there was another pressing matter: Edmund Wylshere.

Clare, realising that a police officer needed to rise above the sadness she felt, accompanied Tremayne to the hospital. They found the man sitting up in bed. He was surrounded by well-wishers. Tremayne recognised a few from the pub in Avon Hill; the others he did not.

'Detective Inspector Tremayne, I'm pleased to see you,' Wylshere said. The well-wishers left the room.

'They're looking after you?' Tremayne asked.

'I know everyone up here. It's almost a second home to me.'

Tremayne could not agree with the home analogy. The hospital was too clinical for him, too clean and too full of the ill. He had not been sick, apart from a brief prostate scare, in the last twelve years. He hoped it would continue. To him, the worst thing in life would be to be incapacitated, being fed through a tube, wheeled from one place to the next.

'You look well enough,' Clare said.

'Pain killers. A couple of days and I'll be out of here.'

'Dr Wylshere, we're not here for a social visit,' Tremayne said. He could see the smugness in the man, almost as if he was thumbing his nose at the two of them. He could only feel contemptuous of the man.

'It was a misunderstanding. Kathy would never have done that normally.'

'Then why?'

'The woman was upset,' Wylshere said. 'Her son's been killed. She needs to blame someone.'

'Adam Saunders was murdered. We have the proof,' Clare said. 'And now Kathy Saunders is dead as well. That's three in one family, all within the space of sixteen hours. Doesn't it concern you?'

'I'm sorry. What do you want me to say?'

'Adam Saunders was murdered by Elizabeth Grimshaw,' Tremayne said.

'And you believe her?' Wylshere said.

'We have proof.'

'She's always been a little crazy.'

Tremayne could see Wylshere attempting to divert them by pre-empting their questions. He had seen the trick used before; he wasn't going to fall for it.

'Dr Wylshere, we are aware that within Avon Hill there are ceremonies where the ancients are summoned. Is that correct?'

'Is that any crazier than the Druids at Stonehenge for the summer solstice, children believing in Father Christmas, Morris dancing with men dressed in costume, bells on their knees?'

'It is when people die.'

'What people?' Wylshere asked.

'There were two in the pub with you.'

'As I said, it was a misunderstanding.'

'You've said that. The woman may have been stricken with grief at the deaths of her son and husband, but it's not normal to go out and shoot people straight after. She blamed you for their deaths. The question is why?'

'You'd need to ask her.'

'We would have.'

'Dr Wylshere, did you kill Kathy Saunders?' Clare asked. Tremayne winced at the question.

'From an ambulance? You've been listening to Elizabeth Grimshaw. She's full of such rubbish.'

'You've not denied the ceremonies to summon the ancients,' Tremayne said.

'Why should I? It's a tight-knit community. We keep ourselves entertained. It's just harmless fun, that's all.'

Tremayne and Clare knew there was nothing harmless about what went on in Avon Hill.

They both knew that Wylshere was going to block every question they threw at him. They left him to the nursing staff at the hospital and returned to the police station.

***

Tremayne phoned Jim Hughes on his return to Bemerton Road Police Station. 'Elizabeth Grimshaw?'

'It's a possibility. The woman would have been physically strong enough to have killed Adam Saunders, and the shoe prints we found at the murder scene are the same size as hers. Neither is conclusive, and there are no fingerprints. If she says that she killed him, then she probably did.'

Elizabeth Grimshaw was escorted into the interview room. She had a lawyer with her.

'Miss Grimshaw,' Tremayne said after he had completed the formalities, 'you have admitted to the death of Adam Saunders.'

'It was for the good of the village, don't you see?' The woman sat calmly.

'Miss Grimshaw, the taking of life is a crime,' Tremayne said.

'It depends on the reason.'

'And you believe this?' Clare asked.

'I have seen what they can do.'

'Miss Grimshaw, can we go through the night that you killed Adam Saunders?' Tremayne asked.

'Very well. I had been keeping a watch on him for some time. I even took him an apple pie earlier in the evening. He thanked me for it. Such a sweet boy.'

'And then?'

'I went back to my cottage. I can see his cottage from my upstairs window. I saw him leave. I made a phone call to Dr Wylshere, he told me what to do.'

'Don't you have any guilt with this?' Clare asked.

'Why should I?'

Tremayne knew that if she held to her testimony, she'd never see the inside of a prison. Her confinement would be in a secured psychiatric hospital.

'After Dr Wylshere told you what to do?'

'I followed Adam up the hill towards Cuthbert's Wood.'

'Did he see you?'

'It was dark.'

'Then what?'

'He climbed over the fence and walked into the wood. I was frightened to go, but Dr Wylshere had told me that I would be safe.'

'Now you're in the wood. What next?'

'I followed Adam's light until he fell over. After that, I asked for help.'

'What sort of help?'

'I could hear them talking to me.'

'What did they say?'

'Kill, kill, kill.'

'Are you sure it wasn't the wind in the trees?

'It was them.' Elizabeth Grimshaw's lawyer did not speak. Tremayne thought the man was speechless after hearing such drivel.

'Adam Saunders was hit three times by a branch. Was that you?'

'The first time, it was an accident. I hit him the second time, but he just stumbled.'

'And he never saw you?'

'I told you. It was dark.'

'Then how could you follow him?'

'I could see him silhouetted.'

'Yet he couldn't see you.'

'He was frightened. He never looked around.'

'Please continue.'

'The second time that I hit him, he fell over. I thought he was dead.'

'Why did you hold his head under water?'

'It was the chosen way.'

'Kathy Saunders has been killed,' Clare said.

'I'm sorry to hear that.'

'Was it your gods again?' Clare asked.

'She tried to kill their conduit to the mortal world.'

'Is that a yes?' Tremayne asked.

'Yes.'

The interview concluded, the lawyer left, and Elizabeth Grimshaw was taken back to her cell.

'She's mad,' Tremayne said.

'The whole village of Avon Hill is,' Clare said.

***

Moulton made an impromptu speech, attended by everyone in the police station, where he praised Vic Oldfield as a credit to the police force, a man who had had a great career in front of him, and said that he'd be sorely missed.

Tremayne also spoke. Clare was surprised that a man who was usually direct in his speech could be so eloquent. She realised, perhaps for the first time, that her DI was an emotional man, not given to showing it, but on that stage in that assembly hall he had shown his vulnerability.

Clare, who had not wanted to speak, felt the need to join her DI on the stage when he mentioned his team. 'I am proud to have worked with Vic,' she said. They were the only words she said, interspersed as they were with tears. Tremayne put his arm around her. 'It'll be fine, Clare. We still have a case to solve.' It was the first time he had addressed her by her first name.

After the speeches had concluded, Harry came to pick Clare up and to take her out of the station, at least for a few hours. 'I'm sorry, Clare,' he said. 'I liked the man, but accidents happen.'

'It wasn't an accident,' Clare said. 'You weren't in Avon Hill. I know these people, what they're capable of.'

'Clare, you've got to stop this. The man was driving too fast, he had an accident.'

'Not Oldfield. I'd been in that car enough times to know he was not a fast driver, and he was safe.'

'Maybe the woman in the car started acting irrationally, lashing out, grabbing the steering wheel, putting her foot on the accelerator?'

The two were sitting in a café not more than two hundred yards from the police station. It was the first time they had met for some time, their unusual working hours impacting on their relationship. Clare realised that no matter how much grief she felt over Oldfield's death, she loved the man sitting opposite with an immense passion. She also realised that they had not made love for some time. She knew that she wanted him, but Tremayne's messaging to come back to the police station would not allow them.

'Yarwood, they've recovered Oldfield's phone,' Tremayne said.

'Does it matter?' Clare asked.

'He recorded his conversation with Kathy Saunders. We need to hear it.'

Clare did not like the idea of hearing the voices of the recently dead, but it was important. She and Tremayne made themselves a cup of tea and locked themselves in his office.

Tremayne switched the iPhone to play, the voice of Oldfield loud and clear. Clare looked for a handkerchief, found it in her handbag. She held it close to her face, although the numbness from what had happened had stopped her tears. Tremayne sat close to his desk, listening intently.

So far Tremayne had not spoken about their former colleague's death, other than at the meeting where they had both spoken. 'The woman's admitted the shooting,' he said.

The two listened as Kathy Saunders spoke about the pub at Avon Hill, her belief in the pagan gods, her sorrow at the death of her son. 'She sounds sane to me,' Clare said.

'They all do, that's the trouble.'

'Do you believe it was an accident, guv?'

'I don't know what to think,' Tremayne admitted. 'We've a woman in the cells who's admitted to killing Adam Saunders, another one with Pathology who admitted to the shooting at Avon Hill, and a doctor in the hospital who's treating us as if we're damn fools.'

'We are, guv,' Clare said.

'What do you mean?'

'People kill for a reason; there's always a motive, whether it's anger, hate, revenge. With these people, we assume that it's one or the other, but it's not.'

'What are you saying?'

'They don't see that they've done anything wrong. If that's the case, then there's no motive. Or, at least, no reason that we'd understand.'

'But these people are apparently sane,' Tremayne said.

'They are. If we had Elizabeth Grimshaw checked out by a psychologist, the result would be exactly that.'

'And if she starts telling the psychiatrist that a pagan god through his mouthpiece had commanded her to kill someone?'

'Apart from that, but on all the other tests she'd check out.'

'As would Kathy Saunders. What are you getting at, Yarwood?'

'We should try to empathise.'

'How?'

'Elizabeth Grimshaw. Let's bring her back up here to the interview room.'

'I'll leave it up to you, but we need to follow this by the book.'

***

'Before we start with Elizabeth Grimshaw,' Tremayne said, 'I've had a preliminary report on Oldfield's car. Apart from the weather conditions, they've found no explanation as to why his vehicle was going so fast, attempting to overtake, smashing into the rear of the mobile crane.'

'Kathy Saunders?' Clare asked.

'There's no sign that she attempted to interfere with the vehicle.'

The two police officers moved from Tremayne's office to the interview room. Elizabeth Grimshaw sat opposite Tremayne. The woman's lawyer sat opposite Clare. Tremayne dealt with the formalities. 'It up to you,' Tremayne said, giving Clare the first question.'

'Miss Grimshaw, we need to understand why perfectly reasonable people commit what to us is a crime,' Clare said.

'I've protected the community.'

'That's hardly a reason for killing someone.'

'It is for me.'

'Miss Grimshaw,' Tremayne said, 'I've asked Sergeant Yarwood to lead the questioning with you. She feels that an understanding of Avon Hill and its beliefs will help to wrap up this case. I've had one of our team killed; I don't want another.'

'What you want is not important,' Elizabeth Grimshaw said.

'Are you telling us that the police have no authority?' Clare asked.

'You'd need to understand our history.'

'Will you tell us?'

'It would be better to talk to Dr Wylshere.'

'Why?' Tremayne asked.

'It was his ancestor who found the ancient words.'

'Miss Grimshaw, you must understand that this sounds bizarre to us,' Clare said.

'That's why we keep it secret.'

'The whole community in Avon Hill?'

'Those who dissent know the penalty.'

'Death?' Tremayne said.

'Mavis Godwin lived for a while.'

'Why did she live?'

'Dr Wylshere protected her.'

'Why?'

'You'd need to ask him.'

'But we're asking you. Why did he protect her?'

'She was promised to him, but then she went and married that Trevor Godwin.'

'You did not like Trevor Godwin?' Clare asked.

'He was a lazy man, good for nothing, but we protected him, even ensured that his woman was safe.'

'Did she live in Avon Hill?'

'A long time ago, but after she had rejected Dr Wylshere and chosen Trevor Godwin, she left.'

'There was a relationship between Edmund Wylshere and Mavis Godwin?'

'A long time ago.'

'Did Harriet Wylshere kill Mavis Godwin?'

'Yes.'

'Why are you telling us?' Clare asked.

'Dr Wylshere will deal with those deemed unworthy.'

'Are you unworthy?'

'It is you that needs to worry.'

'What do you mean?' Tremayne asked.

'They will deal with you.'

'Yarwood and myself?' Tremayne asked.

'You have interfered.'
'We responded to a shooting at the pub.'
'It did not need the police.'
'It was a crime scene.'
'It was a misunderstanding.'
'Kathy Saunders?'
'They killed her, two birds with one stone.'
'They killed Constable Oldfield as well.'
'An officer of the law and Kathy Saunders, the two birds,' Elizabeth Grimshaw said.
'Wylshere was sedated,' Tremayne said.
'Check with the hospital, the medic in the ambulance.'
'What will we find?'
'At the exact time your constable and Kathy Saunders were killed, Dr Wylshere was awake and coherent. Check, you'll find that I'm correct.'

***

Clare left the police station late that night. After the strange interview with Elizabeth Grimshaw, she had phoned the hospital to check on Wylshere's condition and also to check his times of consciousness. They tallied with what had been said in the interview room.

Vic Oldfield's parents had arrived earlier in the day, and Clare had spent time with them, organised for them to see the body. Oldfield's girlfriend had also been present, and she had bonded with his parents. Clare had ensured that the parents had a hotel room in Salisbury for the night.

Harry was at home when she arrived. He had prepared a meal and a bottle of wine for her. She spoke about her day, Vic Oldfield, the investigation, but not for long. In the end, they drank two bottles of wine, the majority consumed by Clare, before retiring to bed. They made love, and she had cuddled up into his arms and fallen asleep. It was five in the morning when she woke.

Harry told her to be careful and not to revisit Avon Hill.

Tremayne was in the office when she arrived. He did not look well 'What is it, guv?' she asked.

'I've been checking Avon Hill on the computer.'

'Not like you, guv.'

'Did you know that statistically Avon Hill has on average more sunshine and less rain than anywhere else in Wiltshire?'

'Is that relevant?'

'Here's another fact. There have been no reported sales of property in the village for over eighty years.'

'Which means?'

'I don't know, unless the properties are passed from father to son.'

'Or mother to daughter,' Clare reminded him, in the interests of political correctness.

'It's unusual. Also, the pub has been in the same family for three hundred years.'

'Any information about births and deaths?'

'Sketchy. There are six distinct family names spread amongst a population of fifty-six, and then there are others who have lived there in the past: the Saunders, Edmund Wylshere and his wife, and Trevor and Mavis Godwin. There are probably others, but I've not been able to trace them.'

'Are you saying there's a lot of intermarrying between the families?'

'We've looked into this before. I think we agree that the answer is yes.'

'What's the significance of the church in Avon Hill? Supposedly they conducted their ceremonies there and then sacrificed around the back,' Tremayne said.

'I've no idea. We've never checked the church,' Clare said. She was sitting in Tremayne's office. The man was fired up, always a dangerous sign as it meant he had his teeth into something and he wasn't going to let up until he got a result.

'We need to check with Wylshere. Push him, see if he'll tell us more. Miss Grimshaw opened up here away from the village, maybe he will.'

'Don't count on it,' Clare said. 'Elizabeth Grimshaw placed her fate in the hands of Dr Wylshere. He's not likely to tell us much.'

'Regardless, that's where we'll head first.'

'And secondly?'

'I need to check that church and get a full team into the wood around the back. If Trevor Godwin's in there, I want him,' Tremayne said. Clare shuddered at the thought.

Chapter 29

'He left thirty minutes ago. I'm surprised you didn't see him on the way here.' Not the words that Tremayne wanted to hear from the nurse outside Wylshere's hospital room.

'I thought he was here for a few days,' Tremayne replied. He was leaning with his back against the wall, dismayed at the nurse's statement.

'It was against advice, but he's a doctor.'

'Any idea who picked him up?'

'Not really.'

'Do you just let patients walk out of here of their own free will all the time?'

'I didn't. You should ask the doctor who was responsible for him. I'm just the nurse.'

'Sorry,' Tremayne said, 'it's been a tough week.'

'I know that. I knew Vic Oldfield.'

'How?'

'We went out together a few times, nothing serious.'

'Yarwood is taking it badly.'

'And you, Detective Inspector?'

'Ask me after we've arrested whoever was responsible.'

'Yarwood, you know where he's gone?' Tremayne said after they had left the hospital.

'Avon Hill.'

'Exactly. We need to find him. Have you tried his number?'

'I'm trying now, guv.'

The two police officers left the hospital on Odstock Road and headed back to Bemerton Road and the police station. Tremayne called the CSE on his mobile phone. 'Any more?' he asked.

'No more to tell you about Vic Oldfield and Kathy Saunders. They were both killed on impact with the railway line below. Their deaths would have been instantaneous.'

'Avon Hill?'

'We're preparing to check out the area to the rear of the church. No one's keen to go back.'

'Not your people as well.'

'You have to admit that it's a strange place, almost medieval.'

'I'd agree with that,' Tremayne said. 'Mind you, if you find Godwin's body, then we'll all be spending a lot more time down there, even Yarwood, who doesn't look too keen on a return either.'

'When will you be in Avon Hill?' Hughes asked.

'We're looking for Dr Wylshere first. After that, we'll be there.'

Tremayne ended the phone conversation. The police station was nearby. He was anxious to press on, although a return visit to Avon Hill needed backup. Oldfield had told Clare and him about the reaction that night when he had ventured there with Constable Dallimore. Even though they had been wrong to walk around a village in the early hours of the morning, the men they had encountered had possibly been violent, and no doubt were the same people as at the pub after the shooting.

Moulton was in the office when Tremayne and Clare arrived. 'What's this with Wylshere? How did he get away?'

'He's a free man. There's no charge against him,' Tremayne replied. He wasn't in the mood for debating with a man who was out of touch with the reality of the case. He'd not been to the village; he'd not seen a dead fifteen-year old youth or a man whose legs were the only part of his body that remained, and he'd certainly not seen a woman face down in a water trough.

'I would have thought you'd have stationed a uniform outside his room,' Moulton said.

Tremayne could see the CSI was dangling the bait, waiting for him to bite, and then he could add insubordination to the list of reasons to retire him. He wasn't going to fall for that trick. 'There was. I'll deal with what happened later,' he said.

Clare called Oldfield's parents to see how they were. They were fine, although they had not slept the previous night. As Clare was due to go back out to Avon Hill, she asked if they could go with someone else to deal with the formal identification of their son. They agreed and told her that their son's girlfriend would be going too. Clare had always thought that the relationship of Vic

Oldfield and his girlfriend was not intense, although she may have misread the signals. Clare knew that he had always shown an interest in her, and it was more than professional, but he had never said anything, never intimated that he wanted more. She knew that she had liked him very much as a person and as a fellow professional, but apart from that, she had never felt the need or the desire to reciprocate with any more than the cordiality required, and besides she had Harry, although their periods of not talking to each other were increasing. It was evident that the current case was impacting on their relationship, and she hoped it would be over soon. And as for a visit to Avon Hill, she did not look forward to it. It was a place that caused people to commit acts, violent acts, that they would not normally consider. She went to visit Elizabeth Grimshaw in her cell.

'I'm worried about Brutus,' the woman said. She was sitting in her cell, oblivious to the surroundings.

'I'll check on him,' Clare said.

'Are you going out there?'

'We need to find Trevor Godwin.'

The woman raised herself from where she had been sitting and rushed up to Clare. She threw her arms around her. 'Please don't.'

Clare was not sure how to react. Never before had a prisoner in the cells, charged with murder, shown affection for the person who had put them there.

'Why?' Clare asked. After the embrace, the two women had sat down on the bed in the cell.

'They will kill anyone who goes there.'

'Why are you telling me?'

'They frighten me, they always have. I don't like them, any more than the others, but they control our lives.'

'It's centuries since the lord of the manor held sway over the people. Back then, the peasants were illiterate, easily led, but now…'

'Dr Wylshere is their voice. Others have tried to go against them, but none have survived, you will not survive.'

'Are you saying that I'll be killed if I go into the wood behind the church?'

'Some will die, probably you.'

'Why me?'

'Because of what I have told you.'

'You never answered my earlier question. Why are you telling me this now?'

'I don't want you to die.'

'But you are going to prison for what you have done.'

'Brutus is innocent. Promise me that if anything happens to me, if you survive, that you will look after him.'

'I promise,' Clare said.

***

Eventually, at two in the afternoon, Jim Hughes and his crime examiners relocated to Avon Hill. The welcome as they drove through the village and past the pub was distinctly chilly. Hughes had offered a wave, received none in reply.

There was an old wooden garage next to the church. Hughes decided that it would be suitable as a base. He could see that they would need to spend two days, possibly more, in the village. The area to the back of the church was extensive, and even more overgrown than Cuthbert's Wood. The uniforms rolled out the crime scene tape around the entrances to the church and to the wood.

'A bit gloomy,' one of Hughes's team said.

'Don't start. Half the people here are scared as it is.'

Hughes knew those who showed the most bravado would be the first to freak out. He had noticed no wildlife near the church, no birds. 'Two of you can check the church,' he said.

'What about the vicar?' someone asked.

'There's no vicar, and whatever goes on down here, it's got nothing to do with Christianity.'

Hughes and his team, it was decided, would conduct the initial check in the wood behind the church. After they had concluded, there would be a more detailed search by two CSEs, who would conduct a methodical check looking for signs of recent soil disturbance. Hughes thought that may not prove to be so easy, and he had a ground penetrating radar coming down from London. It was due to arrive within twenty-four hours.

Clare and Tremayne arrived two hours later. The day was drawing to a close. Clare left Tremayne with Hughes and went to check on Brutus. The dog was pleased to see her and gave her a big lick on her face. Its tail was wagging as well.

'She's not coming back, is she?' the next-door neighbour, an elderly man in his eighties, asked.

'That's not for me to say,' Clare replied.

'You can't put her in prison.'

'She's admitted to the crime.'

'You don't understand.'

'What don't I understand?' Clare asked. The man, initially friendly, had changed. His appearance was menacing, and he was standing too close to her. She did not feel comfortable with the situation. He grabbed her wrist, his grip firm.

'I'm telling you. Leave this village.'

Clare removed the man's hand from her wrist and moved closer to the door out into the garden. 'Why? A young man is killed, and you act as though it doesn't matter.'

'You must understand, even if it's only for your well-being, that you cannot stay here. Once it's dark, then…'

'Then what?'

'Things happen.'

'Are you trying to scare me?'

'I'm only telling you what you must know. Elizabeth liked you, so does the dog. I don't want to see you hurt, even killed.'

'Is that possible?'

'Not all of you will leave this village, believe me. Please, I beg you. I'll even ask your God to tell you if it helps but go now. Do not even go back to the church. Just take your car and drive out of here and don't stop until you can drive no more. Don't stay.'

'I'm a police officer. I can't disregard my responsibilities.'

'You have only one responsibility.'

'And that is?' Clare asked.

The man looked at her, this time in a friendly manner. 'To yourself and those you love. For the sake of Elizabeth and her dog, please leave.'

'And Dr Wylshere?'

'He is here.'

Clare left the small cottage, unsure of her feelings. One side of her wanted to run and never stop, the other regarded what the man had said as superstitious nonsense. She remembered the intensity with which he had gripped her, the imprint of his fingers still on her wrist. If she had phoned Harry, she knew what he would say, but she was a police sergeant, not a little girl afraid of the dark, looking under beds.

Once in her car, she locked the doors just in case, she took a deep breath, turned the ignition switch, tightened her seat belt and headed down to the church. She passed the pub on the way; a group of people were still standing around outside it. She recognised some from the shooting less than twenty-four hours earlier. She could see the look of seething hatred aimed at her. If it wasn't for Tremayne and the full team of crime scene examiners and uniforms, she knew what she would have done: she would have turned the car around and driven out of that awful place at maximum speed, but she knew she couldn't.

Tremayne depended on her, Vic Oldfield needed the truth. She reflected on Oldfield, a man who had been with her in the Reverend Harrison's house next to the church where Harrison had thrown a rope over a wooden beam.

She phoned Harry. His phone did not answer. Back at the Avon Hill church, she left her car, put on a coat against the cold and went to join Tremayne. The man was busy and anxious.

'They've found Trevor Godwin,' Tremayne said. He was kitted up in overalls, foot protectors and gloves. Uniforms were standing around the church and the entrance to the woods at the rear; crime scene tape was everywhere.

'Proven?' Clare asked.

'There's freshly disturbed soil.'

'A grave?'

'It's about the right size.'

'I'm scared,' Clare admitted.

'We're all on edge. I've asked for backup. That mob back at the pub look dangerous to me.'

'I've checked on the dog.'

'And?'

'The dog's fine.'

'That's not what I meant, you know that.'

'I know.'

'What else. There's something, isn't there?'

Clare took a seat. 'The next-door neighbour told me to leave, for us all to leave.'

'One of those from the pub shooting?'

'He wasn't at the pub.'

'What then?'

'I'm not sure if he was trying to save us, or threatening us.'

'What did he say? We've got another body to add to the list now. I don't have all day. And besides, it's freezing.'

'It's not freezing in Salisbury,' Clare said.

'We're not in Salisbury. We're in the arsehole of the world, down a narrow road at the back of beyond. Don't talk about your pagan gods again, please.'

Clare realised that the man rarely swore, at least not in front of her, though she had seen him blast out the occasional dumb motorist with a few choice words. She knew that even he, Detective Inspector Keith Tremayne, was sensing the tension in the air, the hatred that emanated from the pub not more than two hundred yards away.

'He told me, us to leave immediately.'

'You've just said that. Why? Did he give a reason?'

'He said that Dr Wylshere is here, and they will return. After he had scared me, his attitude changed. He may have been one of the group, but down here, I don't know.'

'Nor do I, but Wylshere's behind all this. We need to find him. Do you think he's up at the pub?' Tremayne asked.

'We've uncovered another body,' Hughes said as he entered the temporary crime scene headquarters. 'I'm bringing up an ambulance to transport the body back to Pathology.'

'That's two bodies,' Tremayne replied.

'It's a woman, probably in her seventies.'

'But who?'

'I've no idea.'

'I do,' Clare said.

'Who?'

'The next-door neighbour's wife. That's what he was trying to tell me.'

'Then why didn't he mention it?'

207

'How would I know?'

'The cause of death?' Tremayne asked.

'I'd say she was suffocated, but I can't be certain.'

'That's murder, Yarwood. Nothing unnatural about that.'

'Any sign of Trevor Godwin?' Tremayne asked.

'The first grave, but not confirmed yet. You've got enough to be going on with.'

'You'll be here all night.'

'I've phoned a catering company in Salisbury. They're bringing food and drinks.'

***

Tremayne and Clare left the crime scene at the church and drove up to Elizabeth Grimshaw's cottage. Tremayne stopped at the pub to buy some food. He returned within two minutes. 'No food,' he said.

'There's food there,' Clare said.

'That's not what I meant.'

'Unpleasant?'

'Very. Mind you, it's very quiet. No one said a word, other than the publican.'

'And what did he say?'

'He made it clear that I was not welcome. He must be a relative of Superintendent Moulton.'

Clare laughed, the first laugh since the death of Oldfield. One minute later, they were outside Elizabeth Grimshaw's cottage. Another police car stood outside. Tremayne had dispatched it the same time they had left the church. If there was another murderer next door, he wanted him arrested and in the cells at the police station. Tremayne knew that it was to be a busy night whatever happened.

'How did he seem, this neighbour?' Tremayne asked as they walked to the next-door cottage. Brutus barked from inside it.

'Quiet, Brutus,' Clare said.

'Do you like dogs?' Tremayne asked.

'I like Brutus.'

'He'll be looking for a new owner soon.'

Tremayne knocked on the neighbour's front door. It opened. 'I told you to leave,' the man said on seeing Clare.

'I'm a police officer. This is Detective Inspector Tremayne.'

The door opened wider to let the two police officers in. The man showed them to the front room.

'You know Sergeant Yarwood,' Tremayne said.

'I told her to leave.'

'We found a body,' Clare said.

'She wanted to tell you.'

'Tell us what?'

'The truth.'

'The body we found. Was it your wife?'

'I told those down the pub that my wife wanted to give evidence, to protect Elizabeth.'

'Who killed your wife?' Tremayne asked.

'I did what I was told.'

'Are you saying that you killed her in this cottage?'

'Yes.'

'And who buried her behind the church?'

'I did.'

Tremayne looked at the man. He was in his eighties and walked with a stick. There was no way that he could have dug a hole sufficiently big to bury a body. Regardless, he had admitted to murder.

'You've killed your wife, someone I assume you've been married to for forty, fifty years, yet you show no remorse,' Clare said.

'My wife was not well. I will be with her soon.'

'How?'

'Dr Wylshere gave me some poison to take. I can feel its effects now.'

'Yarwood, call an ambulance,' Tremayne said. 'This man needs to be in the hospital.'

'It is too late for that,' the neighbour said. He sat down in a chair by the fire and closed his eyes.

***

As Tremayne and Clare arrived back at the church, an ambulance arrived. 'There's another body up the road,' Tremayne said.

A uniform had remained at the scene of the latest death. 'It's murder,' Tremayne said.

'More like an assisted suicide,' Clare said.

''What is it with these people? They kill, allow themselves to be poisoned, talk rubbish.'

'According to what he had told us, we're about to find out. We need more people down here.'

'I've already asked.'

'They're not here.'

Tremayne made a phone call. 'They'll be here soon,' he said after ending the call.

'Are they armed?' Hughes asked.

'They'll be armed. Why do you ask?'

'Have you seen the locals?'

'Only at the pub.'

'They're congregating outside on the street. They don't look friendly.'

'We know that already.'

'My people want to wrap up, come back tomorrow. There are more bodies in there,' Hughes said, pointing to the trees at the back of the church.

'Many?'

'Three that we know of. We need to take soil samples, check compaction rates, attempt to ascertain for how long, and then conduct a full exhumation.'

'How many more?'

'Hard to tell, but if this has been going on down here for generations, then there could be dozens.'

'Focus on the more recent,' Tremayne said. 'Whoever killed them is here somewhere.'

'You talk in the singular,' Clare said.

'In this village? They're all as guilty as each other. No wonder they were so unfriendly when I came down here in my twenties. They were up to all sorts of monkey business even then.'

'If you had stayed, it might have been you, guv,' Clare said.

'It could have been, but judging by the mob Hughes has just pointed out, they may be attempting to make up for lost opportunities,' Tremayne said.

Chapter 30

To Edmund Wylshere, it resembled a monarch's court with its courtiers, its sycophants, its fools assembled below. Unbeknown to those down at the church, he had been in the pub all the time. He knew that the time had come for a showdown. His belief in his own importance, his ability to sway the descendants of former serfs to do what was necessary, was inviolate.

Hadn't that foolish boy, Adam Saunders done what he was told, hadn't Elizabeth Grimshaw, with her funny ways and her old dog, done what was needed, and as for his wife, she was putty in his hands, believing in him, even loving him, Wylshere thought.

Wylshere knew that whatever happened to Avon Hill, it would be that night when its fate would be determined.

The doctor could see from his vantage point in an upstairs room at the pub the activity down at the church. He could see them in the woods behind the church, and there, distinctly visible, the outlines of DI Tremayne and his sergeant. He felt a particular venom for them. If the older of the two had not interfered, then there would have been no problem, but he had, and he would continue to do so until the truth was revealed.

And then the young sergeant, pretty at any other time, too dangerous to live at another. Wasn't it her who had befriended Mavis Godwin, almost to the point where the woman was ready to reveal their darkest secrets? He had enjoyed watching her death, using a pair of binoculars. His wife did not know that he had seen her hold the woman's head under water, the tears rolling down her cheeks, but she had done her duty. She would be spared. And now there was Grimshaw's neighbour, the interfering old fool who had told the sergeant to leave the village. *Oh, yes,* Wylshere thought, *he could be the court jester, every royal court needed one.*

He was pleased that his wife, Harriet, and their daughter were over two hundred miles away. Whatever was to happen in the village, they would at least be safe. In the years since he had taken over the leadership of the community, there had never been such a challenge as what they faced now. He knew there were some down below in the pub, congregating on the street, who would be willing to walk down to the church, caps in hand, and confess to their sins. There were some who had always stood back when the knife needed to be thrust in as part of the sacrifice. They would be the first to go after those who represented law and order had been dealt with.

He looked upwards at the night sky. Darkness was starting to envelop the village already. *They know what's coming*, he said silently to himself. He looked down at the church again. He could see the lights inside the church, his church, the place where they were at their strongest, apart from the woods behind. How many would they find buried in there that night? How many more would be added to the total of those who had died already?

Wylshere knew that it had been easier in past centuries when infant mortality had been higher, education had been limited or non-existent, and there was no dissension in the village, but now there were those even more educated than him, and they questioned. He had dealt with them all too easily, and the gods he would summon would deal with the rest. In the village, those that had bred offspring had been confined to areas outside the village, but not so far as to not be under his influence.

It had been good that Adam Saunders had died at the hand of Elizabeth Grimshaw. Even he, Dr Edmund Wylshere, respected in the city of Salisbury, was suspect. His daughter, Wylshere realised, was questioning. If the gods would accept her, would she be willing to accept them?

He mulled over the situation, the consequences, and more importantly what the future would hold. Once the secret was revealed, then the place would be overrun with scientists and sceptics and officers of the law and tourists. The tourists he could deal with, at least the most curious who decided to stay after nightfall.

The crowd on the street outside the pub were becoming restless. They were preparing their ceremonial costumes, their ceremonial finery, their knives. Wylshere knew it was premature; he had to call them back into the bar where the less resolute would be drinking beer. He left the room and proceeded downstairs.

'Edmund, what do you want?' Albert Grayling asked from behind the bar.

'I want discipline,' Wylshere's reply. 'They will be here soon.'

'They'll want a pint then,' the publican's reply.

'You mock them.'

'Just making light of the situation.'

Wylshere could see that Grayling was not a true believer, although he did not know why. The publican had seen their power on many occasions, but yet he preferred financial gain over his devotion to them, and tonight the pub was busy. Grayling had even wanted to open up to the police and to supply them with food.

Grayling had protested when told that he could not, but he had obeyed, as he would that night, but Wylshere knew that the pub would need a new publican come the morning.

'Bring them all in here,' Wylshere said. Grayling followed the instruction and went out into the street. Within a few minutes, all those that were to be involved were in the bar at the pub. Grayling was pulling pints for whoever wanted, ensuring to take their money at the same time.

'Close the bar,' Wylshere said. Grayling obeyed.

'What are we to do?' one of the assembled asked.

'Avon Hill will never be the same again,' Wylshere said.

'What do you mean?'

'We can no longer keep it a secret.'

'Why?'

'You don't understand,' Wylshere said. He was tired of dealing with fools.

'Even if we deal with those that are here, others will follow.'

'Why don't we let them conduct their investigation and leave?' Grayling asked.

'Grayling, you're a fool.'

'I resent that.'

'Shut up and listen.'

'He's got a point,' another of the people in the bar said.

'Very well,' Wylshere said. 'If I must explain this to you. We can deal with those at the church, we can deal with any who subsequently come, but we cannot isolate ourselves indefinitely. All of us at some stage need to live in the outside world, and once we leave here, we will be subject to their rules and conventions. Even if we let them remove those in the woods, then what?'

'You're our senior elder. You tell us,' Grayling said. Wylshere ignored his sarcasm.

'If they have bodies, they will want explanations and those responsible. How many here have not been involved? I'll tell you, none. We're all guilty of murder according to their law.'

'We were commanded,' someone shouted.

'They will not accept our law. They will enforce the law that exists outside of this village. They will find evidence and make arrests. How many of you want to spend time in their prisons?'

No one in the room offered a comment; some shook their heads.

'Very well, then we must resist.'

'And after tonight?' Grayling asked.

'After tonight, our future lies with the gods. We must place our future in their hands as we have so many times in the past. If we do not survive, either as individuals or as a community, then it will be up to them. I can do no more.'

'Dr Wylshere, you have served us well, as have your ancestors. We are behind you.'

Outside the pub, a catering van drove by.

'They'll have full bellies,' Wylshere said.

'I could have supplied them with food,' Grayling said, smarting that his profits were being given to someone else.

'Grayling, stop your complaining. Neither the caterers nor the police will be leaving the village this night.'

'And us?'

'It is time to prepare.'

***

Tremayne was impatient. Hughes and his team were working hard, even he would admit to that, but now they were all out of the wood and the church and helping themselves to seconds at the catering van. He realised the excuse of a pint of beer would not be unreasonable. The pub was not far away, only an eight-minute walk, two if he drove.

He chose to drive. Besides, he had seen the people milling around outside of the pub on the road, and now they were no longer visible. He knew something was going on and he wanted to know what it was. 'Yarwood, I'll buy you a drink,' he said.

'I'm fine with a cup of coffee,' she replied.

'It's not a request.'

'Very well.'

The two drove up in Tremayne's car. There wasn't enough time for the heater to warm up the interior. Clare felt uncomfortable as they drew close to the pub. A lone drinker stood in the doorway. As he saw the police car approaching, he slipped back inside.

'They've been keeping a watch out for us,' Tremayne said.

'It could be dangerous, guv,' Clare said.

'That's as maybe, but we're here to uphold the law, not to pussy foot around with this bunch of country yokels. Besides, I'm armed.'

'These people are murderers.'

'I want to see the face of the enemy when we walk into that bar and order a couple of drinks.'

'Is that how you see them?' Clare asked.

'You've not seen them rushing to help us.'

'No.'

'Then they're the enemy, and from what I can see, very dangerous.'

***

Clare, reluctant to join Tremayne at the pub, had no option. The two arrived at the front door to find a burly man blocking the way.

'We'd like a drink,' Tremayne said. The man stood to one side, making sure to brush up against Clare as she pushed by. At any other time, she would have seen his action as sexual intimidation, but in Avon Hill she knew it was not, more a case of this is our place and you're not welcome.

Tremayne had missed the man's response at the door, or maybe he hadn't. Clare wasn't sure, but her DI acted as if nothing had happened. She looked around the bar for familiar faces, but there were none she recognised immediately, and besides, the majority of the patrons were out the back in the car park.

'Check them out,' Tremayne said. He had a pint of beer in his hand, orange juice for her.

'No cost,' the publican said. The pub was warm, the smell of sweating men still noticeable, even the traces of cigarettes: both were anathema to Clare. Once Harry had come near her after a night in the Deer's Head reeking of stale beer and body odour coupled with the lingering smell of cigarettes. She had wanted him, but not in that condition, and it had taken a couple of showers and thorough brushing of his teeth before he was deemed worthy. She took her glass of orange juice and looked out of the window to the rear of the pub; she could not see very much. It was clear that whoever was out there had no intention of coming back into the warm bar with its open wood fire, at least not while there were two police officers there.

Tremayne brought his pint over to the window. Clare noticed that he had not drunk any.

'Anything?' Tremayne asked.

'Too dark for me.'

'Then we'd better go out there and have a look,' Tremayne said. He made a phone call to Hughes first. 'Any more bodies?' he asked.

'It's perishing cold down here,' Hughes's reply. 'What's it like where you are?'

'The locals are cold, as is the beer, but the pub's warm enough.'

'Then I'll come up there with some of the team.'

'Don't expect the traditional country pub welcome.'

'We won't.'

'Come on, Yarwood. Let's go and stir the pot,' Tremayne said.

Clare could see it was dangerous. She knew out in that car park were murderers who had killed, would kill, for some malignant reason that made no sense.

The two walked through the door at the rear, Tremayne almost knocking his head on the lintel above the door. The assembled group outside turned towards them and glared.

Someone shone a light in Tremayne's face. 'DI Tremayne and DS Yarwood,' he said.

The person holding the light lowered its beam.

'Thank you,' Tremayne said. 'We're looking for Dr Wylshere,' he said.

'He's not here,' two men said, almost in unison.

'Then who is?'

'This is our village. You've no right coming here with all your people disturbing the peace,' a voice at the rear of the group said.

'Come forward, identify yourself,' Clare said. Nobody moved.

'You're wasting your time, Yarwood,' Tremayne said quietly to her, ensuring that the group did not hear.

'We've every right to be here,' Clare said. She was nervous, desperate not to show it, but her voice was quavering. She remembered the man as she had entered the pub, imagined that those in front of them would be of the same ilk: capable of intimidating, capable of violence, capable of murder.

'We've found a body down behind the church,' Tremayne shouted.

'It's a church. What did you expect?' one of the men said.

'In the woods, not the graveyard,' Tremayne replied. Clare studied those opposite, almost silhouettes from where she was positioned. She looked for a reaction, saw none. She moved to one side, aiming to use the light from the pub window to her advantage; it helped.

Clare did a rough count. There appeared to be more than twenty individuals: some were dressed in suits, others in work clothes. She scanned for Edmund Wylshere.

'The body's not been there for more than a day,' Tremayne said. 'We need someone to conduct an identification.'

'You know who it is,' Clare said, mindful to keep her voice down. She had moved back closer to Tremayne. She almost felt like grabbing his arm for emotional support. She was shivering from the intensifying cold. Tremayne, she noticed, was cold as well, but he was still standing firm, unwilling to move from where he was until someone said something or even made a move. He knew he should not be there baiting these people, and he should have brought armed backup, but he was desperate for answers.

'We don't know who it is,' the man at the front said.

'And your name?' Tremayne asked.

'It would be best if you leave.'

'Is that a threat or a request?' Tremayne answered back. Clare could feel the tension in the air; it was electric. It reminded her of a movie where the opposing sides faced each other across open land, brandishing spears, hurling insults, but this was not fiction, this was real, and the odds were stacked against the side of right over wrong by at least ten to one.

'We need to back off,' Clare said.

'You're right. They're not going to budge,' Tremayne said. He had the measure of what they were up against. He picked up his phone and made a call.

'It'll not work,' the spokesman for the opposing force said.

'Why's that?' Tremayne asked. He had tried to phone for a dozen men, armed and ready for whatever the night brought.

'We've isolated the village.'

'Let's get away from here. We can get one of the uniforms to drive out to Wilton,' Clare said.

'You're right. Drink your orange juice, and we'll be off.'

'How about your beer?'

'I only used it as an excuse, I don't intend to drink it. I'll have a hot drink with you when we get back to the church.'

Tremayne and Clare walked away and around the side of the pub. Two minutes later they were back at the church.

'What was it like?' Hughes asked, his team still at the crime scene.

'Dangerous. They're as mad as hatters up there. Keep your men away if you don't want trouble.'

***

'I expect you to play your part this night,' Edmund Wylshere said. He had seen the events in the car park from an upstairs window. He had seen Tremayne attempting to bait those outside into an inappropriate response. The idea to remove the power from the mobile communication towers within a radius around the village

219

had been his, although it had not been wise to tell the two police officers.

'I will play my part,' Gerald Saxby, a local farmer and one of the elders, said.

'And the others?'

'What is to become of us?' Saxby asked. He had lived close to the village all his life. He did not want to leave, knew that the current situation could not continue.

'Have you made provision for your future?' Wylshere asked. He was aware that he did not intend to leave, and if he were to die in that village, then that would be his fate. As for the others, he had only a mild interest in them, although Saxby had been a loyal servant.

'I will not leave, whatever happens. My wife is no longer well and able to travel, and why should we? We have placed our trust in you. We expect you to protect us.'

Edmund Wylshere sat on the small bed in the room. He looked at the man in front of him and knew he had gone soft.

The door to the small room opened and two men entered. 'It is beyond our control,' Wylshere said.

The two men, one tall and overweight, the other a runt of a man, not even up to the shoulders of the other, nodded their heads in agreement.

'Good. Then sit down here while we discuss what will happen.'

'Is there no other way?' Michael Carter, the local butcher, asked. Of the four assembled, Wylshere was the only one convinced that their village had reached a turning point in history and there was no way going back.

'There is no other way,' Wylshere said. 'If we hadn't dealt with Eric Langley, he would have told all; led them to the village and shown them where the offerings are buried.'

'But now they are here, and they are finding the bodies,' Slater, the vet, said. He could trace his ancestry back hundreds of years, good and bad, and he had enjoyed the ceremony, the dressing up in ancient robes, the masks, the pretence that something alien existed. But now it was all to come to an end, and he wasn't sure what to do. The outside world was there for him, but he would be tainted. Slater wondered, in that small room, what had happened. Even as a young man, when he had first been invited to partake in the ceremonies, he had revelled in their crassness, their cruelty, their camaraderie. And Wylshere had found him a wife from another community, something that he would not have achieved on his own due to his profound stutter and his stunted build, the result of inbreeding. And now his wife was causing trouble, threatening to leave, threatening to talk. He knew he should tell Wylshere about her, but in the small room surrounded by the other elders was not the right time.

If they survived, he would tell him, or maybe he wouldn't. His wife, he knew, deserved better than him, but she had stood by him even when he had failed to provide her with children. Regardless of her nagging, her constant fastidiousness about cleanliness, and her coldness towards him for the last few years, she was still the best thing in his life.

Michael Carter, an unsociable man, did not like the other men in the room. A willing particpant, he had arrived in the village eighteen years previously. He remembered the intimidation at first, the veiled and not so veiled threats, but he had legal title to the butcher's shop and to the small house at the rear, thanks to his distant relative.

Wylshere had confided years later, once Carter had established his credentials and his willingness to serve, that the arrangement had been that the relative was to have ceded his property and his business to him and that he would hold it in perpetuity for the community.

Carter, a cruel man used to the slaughter of animals in the farmyard, wringing their necks, slitting their throats, had known then, as he did now, that Wylshere's interest was not beneficial; it was solely financial. As for the gods, the verdict was out on them, although he had seen things that defied logic. And now, Wylshere, through his need to maintain discipline, had brought the police to their village. Even at the time, he had thought that such an intricate death as Eric Langley's had been unnecessary. It would have been so much easier to give him a slow-absorption and undetectable poison. The man had been old and physically weak as it was, and Wylshere was a doctor: easy for him to arrange, and then no police enquiry, no Mavis Godwin, and indeed no Reverend Harrison.

Carter knew he was trapped. He'd have to go ahead with Wylshere, hoping there was a resolution that would protect his life, although there were still the bodies behind the church. Someone would have to pay for their deaths, and he was as guilty as the others.

Chapter 31

Tremayne realised the situation was dangerous. Not only were the mobile phones not working, neither were the police radios. In fact, nothing seemed to be working correctly. The generators used to power the floodlights around the crime scene were starting to have problems, and some of the lights had failed already.

Clare had found a hot drink for her and Tremayne on returning from the pub. She knew she had been frightened up there, as had Tremayne, but in his usual manner he had shrugged it off.

Tremayne had told her before about his visit there when he as a junior officer at Bemerton Road Police Station, and now she could see what he meant, although then they had not been violent.

One of the police cars was dispatched to Wilton, the nearest police station, to organise more police officers to come immediately to Avon Hill.

Tremayne wasn't sure how long they would take to arrive, and, if they did, there'd still be the debate, especially with Moulton, about the need for a heavy-handed approach.

Moulton had been updated about the rumours, and he, like Tremayne, had been sceptical.

Regardless, Constable Dallimore, still upset over the death of his former drinking pal, Vic Oldfield, left Avon Hill and headed up to the main road, and then into Wilton.

'Whatever you do, don't let them browbeat you into submission. We need help, and we need it now,' Tremayne had told him.

Dallimore had seen that Tremayne had not been lying as he drove past the pub. His car misfired as it passed, but did not stop. The main road was no more than two miles, although the road could be treacherous, especially in winter.

The police constable picked up his phone and speed dialled: nothing. He keyed the speech on his radio: nothing. The vehicle continued to move forward. *What the …?* he said to himself.

Dallimore looked in his rear-view mirror; the village was no longer visible. In front of him, visibility had reduced almost to zero. He had briefly seen the lights of the cars on the main road at the top of the rise, almost within walking distance, but now he could see nothing except for the snow that was falling. He remembered that he had liked snow as a youth: throwing snowballs at his friends, sliding down a hill on a homemade sleigh, diving head first into a snow mound, only to receive a telling off from his mother.

The snow that confronted the young constable now was neither fun nor slushy; it was heavy and getting heavier. The windscreen of the vehicle was being pounded by the relentless snow coming at it horizontally. He knew he had no option but to stop the car and attempt to walk to the main road. There, he would be in his police uniform and flagging a car down should not present any difficulties.

Dallimore switched off the car engine, put on the jacket that had been lying on the back seat of the vehicle, and opened the door. The cold was intense, too cold for snow, but yet it was still coming at him, stinging him as it hit. It was not like the snow that he remembered; this was laden with ice, and it was sharp and it was painful. He swore loudly, although no one could hear.

Dallimore realised that he would not make it to the main road. He peered in front of him through squinting eyes. He briefly glimpsed the lights of the main road, even saw a moon hovering beyond it. The snow continued to pound him. He grabbed hold of the car door handle.

I'll be warm in there, he thought, but the door would not open. The cold was getting worse, and his joints were starting to ache. Dallimore, realising the desperation of the situation, attempted to open the car boot. It opened without difficulty. He took out the jack handle and used it to smash a rear door window. He leant forward and put his arm through the broken glass; he opened the door from the inside. Once back inside the car, he reached over the front seat and inserted the key in the ignition and turned it. The ignition light momentarily flickered before dying. Dallimore climbed out of the car, a snow bank was already starting to form where it had previously been clear.

He struck out on foot for Avon Hill. Soon he was sinking into the snow, almost to his waist at times. Twenty minutes later, or was it two, or was it five, Dallimore could see the light of the pub.

'You'll not leave this village.' A man stood in Dallimore's way.

'I need help,' Dallimore said.

'You'll not find any help here.'

'I'm Police Constable Dallimore.'

'I don't care who you are. I'm not here to help you.'

Dallimore, approaching hypothermia and shivering uncontrollably, looked at the man. He could not distinguish him from any other, and he did not remember him from those who had stood outside the pub.

The man raised his arm and hit the constable across the head. Dallimore fell down, unconscious.

'Nobody leaves here tonight,' the man said, as he turned around and walked back to the village. After fifty yards, the snow that had determined the fate of an honest and decent man had subsided. Back in the pub, on his arrival, Edmund Wylshere approached the man.

'It is done,' the man said.

'Good. Then let's begin,' Wylshere replied, an evil smile creeping across his face.

***

Jim Hughes returned to the temporary crime scene headquarters next to the church. Tremayne and Clare were inside, waiting for an update. 'We can't carry on for much longer,' Hughes said.

'The weather?' Tremayne replied. Since leaving the confines of the warm pub, even if its inhabitants were anything but warm, the temperature had continued to plummet.

'It's them,' Clare said.

Tremayne chose to ignore his sergeant's sombre analysis. He had asked Harry Holchester enough times to make her see sense that the supernatural only existed in the mind of the believer, not in fact, but even her lover had not been able to stop this fascination with the unnatural. Tremayne realised that he, as the crusty old detective inspector, wasn't likely to have much success, but it was a distraction. It was true, though, that it was perishing cold, the heater in the garage no longer worked, and even the tea urn, previously piping hot, was no more than tepid and getting colder.

Tremayne had to agree that the situation was unnatural, but unholy he couldn't swallow. It was clear that a cult existed in Avon Hill, and that it was led by Dr Edmund Wylshere, but why and how Tremayne did not know.

Clare had feared going back to Avon Hill, but she had as it was her job to do so. Harry, her fiancé, had been adamant that going back there would serve no useful purpose and her place was at his side. She had seen the last time they had spoken about their wedding, now planned for next year, February or March, that he wanted the traditional housewife: at home, looking after the children, pampering to his needs. The romanticism appealed, and she wanted Harry and his children, even the house with the wooden fence out front and the dog, but she also needed mental stimulation. The sort of stimulus that the police force, especially Homicide, offered, and to be confined to the house on a full-time basis did not appeal. She was confident that his demands were fuelled by an old-fashioned sensibility instilled by his parents, but her parents, both of them, had always worked and cared for her and the house as well. That's what she saw for her future. She was sure that Harry would come around in time.

'Yarwood, come and look at this,' Tremayne said.

Clare left the tea urn that she had been using to alleviate the cold in her hands and walked to the front of the garage where Tremayne was standing. 'What is it?' she asked.

'The weather, it's getting worse.'

'Maybe it's because we're in a valley.'

'I suppose so,' Tremayne replied. As a crime scene, it was too cold to continue, too important not to, and up the road, the lights of the pub still shone. Clare was certain that something was going on, something they would be aware of all too soon. Tremayne would have told her to wise up, she knew that, so she kept quiet.

'Have you exhumed anyone else?' Tremayne asked Hughes.

'The soil's too heavily compacted, and in some areas it's frozen. We'll do it tomorrow.'

One of the investigators came back from the church. 'There's no blood in there,' she said.

'What else can you report?' Hughes asked. Both Clare and Tremayne stood nearby.

'They've been conducting some sort of ritual,' the CSI said. 'There are circles on the ground, and the altar's been removed and a platform put in its place. Some robes are hanging in the vestry, or what would have been the vestry.'

'What do you mean?'

'There are masks made out of paper-mâché.'

'What sort?'

'Animals. It's all a bit primitive, disturbing.'

'Did you leave them there?' Tremayne asked.

'We're conducting an investigation. We've not removed anything. Apart from what I've told you, there's no sign of overt violence in there, but it's been a long time since there's been a church service.'

'We know that already,' Clare said. 'How did you deduce that?'

'The pews have all been removed, and there's enough dust in there to know that a lot of people have been standing in there, although within the central circle, it was clean.'

Tremayne, a man who needed action, even if only to keep warm, lifted himself from his chair and moved over to the door leading out of the temporary respite from the cold. 'Yarwood, we can't stay here waiting. Let's check out this church.'

Clare, still with her hands around the tea urn, knew that when Tremayne had something to do, it was best just to acquiesce and go with the flow. This time, however, she wasn't so keen. Her subconscious told her that something about the church did not bode well. Never overtly religious, not even as a child at Sunday School, she still maintained a respectful belief in the God that the church represented, had represented, but if it had been turned over to pagan worship, she was not sure it was the place to go.

'Come on, Yarwood.' Tremayne repeated his previous command.

The two police officers walked across the frozen ground towards the church; the gravestones, none more recent than two hundred years ago, loomed ahead of her as if they were sentinels warning her to progress no further. If she had been on her own, she would not have ventured in the graveyard.

'Have you had a look inside here?' Clare said once they were inside.

'After you let go of me, I will,' Tremayne replied. Clare released her grip, embarrassed that she had allowed herself to be so frightened.

The two walked up through the centre of the church, where once an anxious bride had been escorted on the arm of her father, where a coffin had been borne by six men. But now there were no weddings, just plenty of funerals, although not with the Lord's prayer being recited, but with a chant like the one that could now be clearly heard coming from the pub.

'They're summoning their gods,' Clare said.

'Those damn fools. Don't they know the repercussions of what will happen?'

'If they're right, there'll be no repercussions.'

'Not much to see in here,' Tremayne said.

Clare could see the signs of their worship, the marks on the walls, the altar upturned, but she had to agree with her senior, and besides, she wanted out of there.

Clare kept close to Tremayne as they walked through the graveyard and back to the crime scene headquarters. Hughes was there on their return. 'We can't do much more tonight,' he said.

'What are you suggesting?' Tremayne asked.

'We secure the site and come back tomorrow.'

'With those up at the pub?'

'We place the uniforms here. It's the best we can do.'

'Until we have armed support, you'll need to stay,' Tremayne said. 'Yarwood, we need to send another vehicle to Wilton.'

Clare left the relative warmth of the garage where they had been talking to Hughes and walked over to one of the police cars. 'Any word from Constable Dallimore?' she asked.

'How? The radio doesn't work,' the patrol car driver said.

'We need you to go to Wilton and bring help.'

'Those idiots at the pub?'

'Those idiots,' Clare replied. The chanting from the pub echoed throughout the valley.

'It's almost musical,' the driver said.

'There's nothing musical there; it's evil.'

'What are they doing?'

'You know about this place, don't you?' Clare asked.

'Vic Oldfield told me before his accident.'

'It was not an accident. You need to go now, and if any of those fools stand in your way, run them down. Do not stop until you reach the police station in Wilton, and if you can, head on to Salisbury and update Superintendent Moulton.'

'Run them down?' The driver looked perplexed.

'Run them down. If Vic Oldfield told you the full story, those chanting up at the pub have killed four confirmed, another three possible, and dozens more once we exhume all the bodies in the woods.'

'He said there were some mysterious deaths.'

'Hopefully, it's enough to convince you of the urgency.'

Chapter 32

At the pub, a group of men stood outside and chanted; inside, Edmund Wylshere considered the situation. He only hoped those he worshipped would see him as worthy. They had never spoken to him directly, only actions in response to his requests, but tonight they would need to intervene.

Before, their actions had been subtle; that night they would need to act overtly. Edmund Wylshere knew the chant that was required: a chant so dangerous that it had only been used once before when the outside forces in the sixteenth century had wanted to destroy their community. It had been a time of ignorance and religious fervour; a time when they were at their most vulnerable.

Edmund Wylshere knew all this because it had been recorded in the history of the family through the ages. The book was well hidden, unknown to any other, even his wife. He had shown his daughter once, but she had not been interested, only laughed at him for believing in nonsense, but he had seen them with his own eyes up there in Cuthbert's Wood, behind the church, and their appearance had been menacing, with their black robes and their piercing eyes. Wylshere knew they were real enough; real enough to bring the snows early and isolate the village.

'We wait,' Wylshere said. Those in the bar knew that his word would be obeyed. The publican remained behind the bar, the others sat wherever they could. The chanting continued outside, its melodious tone echoing through the village. A rolling mist could be seen coming down the valley. Some saw it as a good omen, Wylshere saw it as validation.

A car could be seen at the church, its headlights on full beam. 'Stop it,' Wylshere shouted from inside the bar.

The men outside moved across the road, forming a human barrier. The car continued to accelerate, in part driven by fear, in part by the last words of Sergeant Yarwood. 'If they get in your way, mow them down.'

Constable Hopwood, a friend of Vic Oldfield, could see in his main beam the men across the road. Every one of them glared at the approaching car, not blinking, not averting their eyes.

Hopwood was panicking. If he stopped the vehicle close to them they would attack; that was evident from the knives they were carrying; if he reversed, then the whole team would be under threat. A police officer, he was forced to make a decision that he should never have to make. He had been conditioned to uphold the law, protect the people, but now…

With no option, Hopwood pressed hard on the accelerator. The vehicle, its engine still cold, was sluggish in responding. He hit the group that were hindering his path at fifty-five miles per hour, the thuds clearly heard inside the car. Hopwood drove on, not looking back at the carnage. The road ahead was clear, even though there was a thick mist. He glanced down at the speedometer; it was over sixty-five. Not caring about the fate of those he had hit, oblivious of all around him, other than the need to bring help to those trapped in the village, he kept up the speed. The first sign of snow came after one mile. Up until then, the roads had been clear, but then it had started to show on the road sides and up ahead. Two hundred yards ahead, he could see the other police car, its roof just visible above the snow.

Hopwood, confused between the need to stop to help a fellow officer and the command of Sergeant Yarwood, chose the latter. Dallimore, the driver, was not visible, but it was clear to Hopwood that the man was not in the vehicle, and that he must have been dead as the temperature outside was ten degrees below freezing.

Hopwood continued to drive forward, although the road was covered in snow. His vehicle was sliding across the road, and the tyres, designed for standard conditions, were not making traction. The car was revving, but his progress was slowing. Up ahead he could see the main road, the lights of the cars clearly visible. He could not see snow up there, but where he was, it was snowing heavily. He checked the inbuilt thermometer in the car; it showed fourteen degrees below zero. The engine stopped; the heating as well.

The young constable, trained to maintain the law, not to deal with an Arctic climate, opened the door of the car and headed back towards Avon Hill. He did not consider those at the pub. He glanced over his shoulder. The main road was still visible, but the snow was heavier up the road. He knew he could not make it to there, but getting back to Avon Hill was a possibility. He checked the temperature. He continued down the road, hopeful of finding somewhere warm.

After eight minutes, he was exhausted and delirious. He sat down at the foot of a tree.

***

The events at the pub had been witnessed at the crime scene. Tremayne was up on his feet and heading over to his vehicle. Clare caught up to him soon enough.

'DI, it's Hopwood.'

'He's driven through them,' Tremayne said.

'That was his instruction,' Clare reminded him.

'This is serious. We've got to help.'

'Hughes, we need to get people up to the pub,' Tremayne said.

'We're not doctors,' Hughes's reply.

'That's as maybe, but you'll be able to help.'

'I suppose so. I'll get a few people together and head up there.'

***

Edmund Wylshere cared little for those who had died, only for what was going to happen that night. Outside the pub, the seriously injured were lying on the ground, the dead had been hastily covered with a blanket or someone's coat, and those who had only received minor injuries were inside the bar. Wylshere may not have been interested, but the others in the community were. To them, they were husbands, sons and brothers, and loved.

The man alternated between a trancelike state and normalcy. 'They had completed their task,' he had said when told that two had died.

'This is folly,' Gerald Saxby said.

'The gods will protect us,' Wylshere replied.

'Wylshere, you're mad.' Saxby, a man who had loyally served the community for over forty years, could see the madness in his leader. For Saxby, as for some others in the small bar, it had gone on long enough. Sure, there had been pleasant times over the years, but at what cost? Until Edmund Wylshere had ascended to the leadership of the group, the deaths had been few, but now it was anyone who opposed his will.

Saxby had never believed in the gods, and only saw them as a figment of the imagination, an outlet for the frustration of living in an isolated village. He did not want to continue with the charade, he wanted to place himself in the hands of the law.

Mike Carter, the village butcher, remonstrated with Wylshere for the callous manner in which he had disregarded the deaths as no more than a minor nuisance.

'They did their part,' Wylshere's reply.

Outside, the weather continued to worsen, and now the snow had started to fall in the village. 'They are with us,' Wylshere said. Across the other side of the room, a number of the men gathered. They watched the doctor's behaviour, wondered what to do. Another group hovered close to their leader, the only person who could control the portal to the other world.

Wylshere, the only trained medical practitioner, took no notice of those receiving medical assistance from Slater, the vet. 'It will be soon,' he said.

'Soon for what?' Saxby asked.

'He intends to attack the police,' a lone voice said from the other side of the room. The others, wavering about the way forward, moved away from the lone voice.

Wylshere put his hand down and mumbled almost inaudibly. He spoke words they had heard before but did not understand. For five minutes, he continued to mutter. Eventually, he lifted his head. 'They have spoken,' he said.

'And?' Saxby asked.

'They will deal with all those who doubt.'

Saxby, along with Mike Carter, two of the community elders, realised that the man they had for so long admired was a fanatic only driven by self. Saxby regretted that he had been swayed, although he had prospered through his alliance with Wylshere, as had Carter. If Wylshere did not kill him, Saxby knew, then the police would arrest him, as they would everyone else in the pub, and then what? All that he had worked for would be gone in an instance.

Outside, those injured lay in the snow, their moaning heard in the bar.

One of the dead had been dragged under the police car for twenty feet, the other had taken the full force of the front of the car and been thrown over its roof and head first into a stone post outside the pub, his head cracking open on impact. The injured men, one a labourer, the second an accountant, the third a local shop keeper, moaned as the vet attempted to help. Even he could see that the prognosis for the three men was not good. Slater looked down the road, saw the lights of two cars approaching. He returned inside the pub.

***

Jim Hughes was the first to reach the bodies lying in the snow.

'Dead?' Tremayne asked.

'Two are. The others are in need of immediate medical treatment. We'll need to get them into the pub.'

Two of Hughes's people picked up the stretcher that they always carried when at a crime scene. They loaded one of the injured men onto it, and carried it towards the pub; the door would not open. Tremayne came over and flashed his badge through one of the windows. 'Police,' he said.

Still, the door would not open. One of the uniforms walked around to the back of the pub; the same response.

'Men are dying out here,' Tremayne shouted.

'There's only one now,' Hughes corrected him. 'He may pull through if we can get him to a hospital in time.'

'That's not likely,' Tremayne said. Clare stayed inside one of the cars. Tremayne had told her to stay where she was and to record all that happened. If there was violence, he wanted her out of it, and when the men in the village were tried for murder, she would be able to give an accurate account of why a police car had driven through a group of people, killing some, wounding others.

Tremayne continued to bang on the door. The lights were on inside the pub, and he could clearly see some of the men sitting down. 'If this man dies, it will be on your consciences.'

'It will be because of you and your police,' a voice said from inside.

'Dr Wylshere, do you know what you are doing?'

'I am protecting this community. Something you are not able to do.'

'What do you mean?'

'The driver of the police car has been dealt with.'

'You've killed him?' Tremayne asked. Clare had wound down the window of her car and was listening to the conversation.

'He is dead.'

'That's murder,' Tremayne said.

'You will not find the hand of man.'

'Then whose?'

'They.'

'Not this nonsense about the gods again,' Tremayne replied.

'They dealt with him, the same as they did with your colleague and Kathy Saunders.'

'That was a car accident.'

'How little you know. You sit in your police station, believing in right and wrong, the laws of the land, a Christian God, but you are all wrong.'

'Is that a threat?' Tremayne asked.

'There is no threat, only fact. You and your people will not leave this village.'

'Tomorrow, this place will be swarming with police.'

'Tomorrow is a long time away. I suggest you return to your supposed crime scene. Take the man who was critically injured when your police car hit him.'

'And then?'

'Prepare yourself for the inevitable.'

'And that is?'

'Your death and that of your sergeant, Sergeant Clare Yarwood.'

Chapter 33

'You've heard Wylshere,' Tremayne said. He, along with Clare and Jim Hughes, was back at the crime scene. The critically injured man they had brought back with them was in one corner of the garage.

'He might live,' Hughes said, glancing over at the man.

'Constable Hopwood's dead though,' Clare said. She sat glumly, unsure what to feel. After so many deaths, including the murders of Vic Oldfield and Kathy Saunders, she could see that their remaining time in Avon Hill would be short.

With Hughes's team no longer working in the woods, most were huddled in the church vestry in an attempt to keep warm. The crime scene resembled a horror movie. There was the church, its spire looming high in the sky, the headstones in the graveyard standing to attention. Clare imagined she could hear noises other than the chanting. She wanted Harry, she knew that, but he was not contactable, and he'd be behind the bar at the Deer's Head dispensing beers, sharing a joke and generally being his usual affable self.

Clare knew one thing: if they ever left that village, Harry could have his wife at home looking after the children, ensuring there was a meal when he arrived, her loving arms around his neck. If policing meant that she had to endure another Avon Hill then she did not want it. If it meant that she had to suffer the deaths of people who she had worked with, attached some fondness to, then the cost of policing was too much, and Tremayne, her mentor and a person she greatly admired, could have his Homicide department to himself.

'Yarwood, what are you doing there?' Tremayne shouted. Clare lifted her head and looked at him.'

'Yes, guv.'

'No use sitting there feeling sad for yourself. We've got to do something. We still need help.'

'But how? We'll never get out by road.'

'How far are we from civilisation as the crow flies?' Tremayne asked.

'Not far if you cut across the fields.'

'Then that's what we'll do.'

'We?'

'Not us, but someone's got to go. Any ideas?'

'I'll ask,' Clare said, 'but everyone's just waiting for the morning now.'

'Too late.'

'What do you mean, guv?'

'You never saw inside that bar.'

'What did you see?' Clare asked. She had only heard the voices of Tremayne and Wylshere through the open window of the car.

'They were getting dressed up in their robes. Some had masks on as well.'

'The same as in the church?'

'The same.'

'What does it mean?'

'It's clear what it means. You heard Wylshere. What do you think he was saying?'

'He was threatening, talking big when there was nothing else to say. The classic standoff.'

'Yarwood, you're sitting there hoping it will all go away. Well, let me tell you, it won't. They were arming themselves in that pub. They are going to fight, and it won't be an immortal or phantom spirit or eerie sounds from the woods; it will be twenty to thirty men armed and willing to kill.'

'What are you suggesting, guv?'

'I'm not suggesting, I'm saying. We need help, and within the next hour, otherwise that bunch of lunatics will be down here.'

'They'll kill us?' Clare asked.

'Why not? What have they to lose? They know, or at least Wylshere does, that after tonight no one in this village will be free of suspicion. Once we start diving into the underbelly of this community, we'll find at least those in the bar guilty of murder, and then there'll be an explanation of how Eric Langley died. Wylshere's going down for a long time, as is his wife, and we've seen all those up at the pub.'

'What about the other people in the village, the women and the children?'

'Have you seen any of them?'

'None, other than Elizabeth Grimshaw and her neighbour.'

'I don't get it with these people, but it doesn't matter now,' Tremayne said. 'We need help, armed help, and it needs someone to cut out across those fields.'

Eventually one of Hughes's CSIs agreed to go. Tremayne had rejected an offer from one of the uniforms as they were trained in unarmed combat and they had also had weapons training, and he needed them.

Two hours later, it was into the early hours of the morning, and Clare was hopeful that the night would pass uneventfully. Tremayne had posted one of the uniforms on guard duty to keep a watch on the pub. Most of the CSIs were sleeping or attempting to. Clare was dozing, dreaming of Harry, trying to think pleasant thoughts. Tremayne could not rest, and his eyes were focussed on the pub and the village of Avon Hill; only the pub had lights, everywhere else were ghostly outlines. He wondered how anyone could live in such a place, even when there was no threat of mayhem and evil. He was, he knew, a man who needed movement, whether it was people or cars, and some noise, but in that village, there was nothing. He could see why Clare felt scared there. He had to admit to himself that the place scared him as well and that anyone susceptible to a fertile imagination could see things that weren't there, believe in things that had no foundation in reality.

The one certainty in the whole sorry saga of Avon Hill was that Dr Edmund Wylshere was certifiable, and those that followed him were misled or equally mad.

'Yarwood, wake up,' Tremayne said, shaking Clare's shoulder. 'Something's up.'

***

Edmund Wylshere could see there was dissension and conflict, so much so that some in the pub were openly defying him.

Disregarding those dissenters, Wylshere made his plan. The first stage was to deal with those down at the church. He knew that would not be difficult.

'Wylshere, you've condemned us,' one of the elders said, his face covered in a mask.

'The gods are always stronger after we have made a sacrifice.'

'The police?'

'Tomorrow those that come will find nothing.'

'And us?'

'We will not exist.'

'What do you mean?' The elder was confused. He had agreed with the death of the others, necessary in his estimation, but now their leader was plotting wholesale carnage.

With Wylshere not willing to give an answer, the elder moved away. He, even as one of the most fervent, did not understand the logic of the man. He would support Wylshere, but he had a feeling the night was not going to end well. He wished it could be different, but decent people who had meant no harm to anyone were to die for something they did not understand. He knew that was how it had always been – the weak destroyed by the strong.

He looked out of the window at the church. *So near, yet so far*, he thought. He regretted that he had not dealt with Wylshere before. But they would all be condemned for their murderous activities, those condemning not knowing the truth of the matter. He had seen their power when they had brought the heavy snow down on the road out of the village, and then the cold that had frozen the one who had mown down the people outside the pub. He remembered the first of the police officers, Constable Dallimore, and how he had looked when he had struck him across the face, the sight of his blood as he lay dying, and then the look of the second officer as he lay freezing, his back against a tree.

The elder knew he was damned, as were the others, equally as guilty as Wylshere. The decision had been made, he would comply.

Chapter 34

Tremayne's initial concerns about the tenuous situation in Avon Hill proved to be ill-founded. Not only did the anticipated assault on the crime scene not eventuate, but they received a visit from one of its inhabitants.

'Who are you?' Tremayne asked.

'They will come for you tonight. You must leave.'

'We're police officers, sworn to uphold the law, not people who will scurry away at the slightest provocation.'

'You don't understand. Their strength comes from the quality of the offering.'

'If they're looking for a virgin to sacrifice, they're too late,' Tremayne said in a moment of rashness.

'You will all make ideal offerings, especially your partner.'

'What do you mean?' Clare asked. The man in front of her was making her scared, not that he needed to try very hard. He had a menacing tone in his voice, the voice that she would expect death to use.

'They're too late for the virgin,' Clare said.

'What are you here for?' Tremayne asked.

'You must leave now.'

'There is no way to leave. The road is blocked.'

'Then you must walk out.'

'We've already sent someone to go for help,' Clare said.

'He did not make it.'

'There are some at the pub who do not want this to continue. They have asked me to tell you to leave.'

'Are there many of you who feel the same way in this village?' Clare asked.

'There are others.'

'Elizabeth Grimshaw?'

'She followed their orders.'

'Why didn't you go to the police with this knowledge?' Tremayne asked.

'Would you have believed us?'

'That there were pagan worshippers in the village of Avon Hill; regular people by day, murdering heathens by night? Probably not.'

'That is why no one came forward. We live in fear here.'

'You could always leave.'

'No one leaves without their permission.'

'Whose permission?'

'Edmund Wylshere and the other elders.'

'If, as you say, they are coming for us, will you and the others in this village give us assistance?' Clare asked.

'No one will help. We have only come to warn you. Leave this place.'

'This is a crime scene. We cannot.'

'Then you have been warned. Tomorrow, when it comes, we will see what remains.'

'What do you expect to see?' Clare asked.

'Unless the two of you leave immediately, you will both be dead.'

***

Tremayne, left confused by the unexpected visit, did not know what to say. He checked the gun in his pocket; it was still there, although it would not be enough to hold off a mob intent on mayhem and murder, and he wasn't sure if he would be able to shoot someone.

Clare, suitably frightened by the ominous villager, wondered what they should do. The villager had recommended that they all bolt for it: the crime scene investigators, the patrol car drivers, the uniforms, as well as her and Tremayne. She knew that would never happen, and besides, how could they explain it back at the police station. They'd be laughed out of the police station, her and Tremayne, as two people who had allowed their fantasies to get out of hand. And she knew that her DI would never back off.

'The situation's grim,' Tremayne said.

'What do you suggest?' Clare asked.

'There's not much we can do. We can't get the people out, and besides reducing the numbers would make our situation more precarious.'

'Have you ever come across a situation like this before?' Clare asked.

'In Wiltshire, never. In London, when I was starting out, there was a riot. That was violent, some people were hurt, but there we had tear gas and backup; here we've nothing. He mentioned the last person we sent out to get help is dead as well, which means these people have killed two police officers and one crime scene investigator since we've been here. They're not going to stop now.'

'They've no reason to,' Clare said.

'I suggest we prepare our line of defence.'

'With what?'

'We'll block the entrance with the vehicles.'

'They'll be on foot. They'll just walk around them.'

'Then what do you suggest?'

'We barricade ourselves in the church until daylight. Then we can reassess the situation. They're bound to come looking for us in due course.'

'That could be twenty-four hours.'

'They're not as strong during the day.'

'Not that ancient gods nonsense again, Yarwood.'

'Maybe, maybe not, but the people up at the pub believe it.'

They positioned the five remaining vehicles as best they could to obstruct any unwelcome visitors.

Tremayne, unable to relax, positioned himself outside the main entrance to the church, his eyes focussed on the pub. Clare, not wishing to be outside, knowing that it was her responsibility to be with Tremayne, could see occasional flickering lights in some of the houses.

'There's no one asleep up there,' she said to Tremayne. He had a cigarette in his mouth, the red when he inhaled giving an eerie glow. Clare, not a smoker, could only watch as he found solace in the nicotine.

A hush fell over the crime scene area, only disturbed by the muffled sound of a generator inside the church. 'I don't like it, Yarwood,' Tremayne said.

Clare knew what he meant. The mist was swirling, the temperature was still dropping, and up the road a malignant group of individuals waited to carry out their master's bidding. She imagined herself as the sacrifice, tied to a cross in the woods while they stoked the fire beneath her. She could imagine herself screaming in sheer agony while those watching relished the moment.

Tremayne broke the silence. 'There's movement up at the pub.' Clare looked and could see the men milling around the front door, its light casting a shadow over some of them.

'They're dressed up,' Clare said. Even though it was some distance, she could still make out the shapes.

'How long to daylight?' Tremayne asked.

'Long enough for them to do what they want.'

'Hours, not verbiage.'

'Three hours.'

'Long enough for them to cause trouble. How are we placed to defend ourselves?'

'You know the answer.'

'We're not. I've got a loaded gun, but it's only good to take down six.'

'You'd use it, guv?'

'For warning them to back off.'

'And then?'

'Then I've no gun. And I'm not about to shoot them dead the moment they cross the line.'

'But they would kill us.'

'They've already killed tonight. A few more won't make any difference.'

'Then you know the answer,' Clare said.

'I can just imagine Moulton's reaction if we get this wrong.'

'He's not here facing a bunch of murdering imbeciles, is he?'

'If they cross the line, I shoot to kill, is that it?'

'What option do you have? Everyone here will back up your story.'

'No one will believe us. They'll put it down to mass hysteria. Even if they believe us, do you think they'll want to admit that there is a bunch of paganists worshipping ancient gods, committing murder in their midst?' Tremayne said.

'It's not the first time?' Clare asked.

'Not that I know around here, but these cults occur from time to time.'

The activities near the pub began to intensify, the chanting became more audible. Jim Hughes came out from the church, took a deep breath as he felt the blast of cold air. 'There's some that want to make a run for it,' he said.

'Are you one of them?' Tremayne asked.

'It's better than sitting here. My people have been in the woods. We've seen the graves, two of the bodies. That group coming down here are not the local Boy Scouts.'

'It's your decision, but it leaves us exposed.'

'I'll stay, the others can go if they want to,' Hughes said.

'Then tell them to go now and to send help for us.'

'How long?' Hughes said, referring to the chanting mob walking towards the church.

'Five minutes before they're here, another ten while I remonstrate with them, fire my gun in the air a couple of times.'

'That's a waste of two bullets,' Clare said. She looked up towards the mob, their bizarre uniforms and masks now more visible. Some, she could see, were carrying staves, others were brandishing knives. 'They're going to cut us up,' she said in a sheer panic.

Hughes took one further look at those approaching and moved back inside the church. Two minutes later, six of the crime scene examiners left from the rear of the church. Tremayne and Clare looked up at the mob. 'They've seen them,' Tremayne said. 'Two of the mob are going after them. I hope our people can run faster than the locals.'

'Can they?' Clare asked.

Tremayne did not answer her question. 'How many in that mob now?'

'Seventeen or eighteen.'

'We can't hold them off. It might be better if you make a run for it.'

'And leave you defenceless?' Clare replied.

Up the road, the mob continued to move forward, their chanting more rhythmic, louder. They did not appear to be in a hurry. A sound of anguish came from behind the church. 'They've got one of ours,' Tremayne said.

'We should help,' Clare said.

'How? And what would it achieve? We need to make a stand against this lot here.'

Jim Hughes returned to join Tremayne and Clare. 'Did you hear it?'

'We heard.'

'What are you going to do about it?' the crime scene examiner asked. Clare could sense his fear. It was clear that all three, as well as the others remaining, would not see the morning sunrise, and she, for one, would not feel Harry's arms around her. She started to cry. Tremayne handed her a handkerchief.

Chapter 35

A lonely road, a group of men clothed in their ceremonial robes, an opposing force at the church. Edmund Wylshere had always known that this day would come. He relished the fact that he, as the chief elder, the only man entrusted with reciting the words that his ancestor had spoken seven hundred years previously, would wake them from their slumber.

It was not often that he did so. Most times the mention of their names would be sufficient to ensure the total obedience of the narrow-minded, simple folk in Avon Hill. Enough to scare those that doubted, to ensure the deaths of those who reasoned or debated or questioned.

Wylshere was aware of the old, the infirm, the women and the children hidden behind the twitching curtains, their only safety lying in their compliance, their obedience and their ability to keep all that had occurred a secret.

Once the decision had been made in the pub to retake the church, those who had gathered on the other side of the bar had been given an ultimatum: you're with us or else.

Not one of those who had doubted Wylshere's authority refused to join the mob as they commenced their march towards the church. Wylshere had seen them hanging back, hoping to be spared any involvement in the fight that was to come, although when the cannon fodder was required, they would be thrust forward.

Only the elders, five in total, wore the masks of office: Edmund Wylshere, the bull, the other four a ram, a goat, a stag, a bear. 'Maintain the chant,' Wylshere cried out as they marched slowly, keeping a rhythmic beat that disturbed the still night.

Saxby, the farmer, walked alongside Wylshere, his robes scarlet, as befitted an elder. Those who were not elders wore ankle-length robes of blue.

Saxby was not comfortable with the situation. He had managed to live a decent life, free of worry, with plenty of wealth to sustain him and his family. If that came as a result of the occasional sacrifice, it was a small cost, but with Wylshere over the last few years it had become more malevolent, more sinister, and he did not like it. He knew that Wylshere directed their activities and his need for more controversial deaths had become obsessive: Mavis Godwin had not deserved to die, nor had her husband, a man of few words and little intellect. Trevor Godwin, Saxby well knew, was one of the most devout, second only to Wylshere. And then Adam Saunders, a child. What was the worst he could do? Talk to his friends in the schoolyard?

Saxby knew that the night would end badly. There were another three hours before daylight, and even they could not hold that off.

The third elder, Mike Carter, the only one who could not claim ancestry in the village, and now its sole butcher, walked alongside Saxby.

James Slater, the vet, had been born in the village, as had his parents and their parents before them. No such doubts flowed through his veins. One of his predecessors had been in the church when Wylshere's ancestor had climbed into the pulpit and uttered the words. Slater knew there were others who would protect them, as did Wylshere. He had been the most vehement in his opposition to allowing Mike Carter, the butcher, into their group, but Wylshere had opposed him. Slater, a man steeped in the old-fashioned ways, still believed that what they had in the village was unique and no one else should have been invited into their community.

The fifth elder, a man who did not say much, his secret not known to many, walked down the road with the others, his chanting muffled. He was a man who had seen the world, and he knew that whatever happened, the night would irrevocably change the future of all those present, villagers and police. He, more than the others, could see a nexus where the forces of modernity and civilisation would confront the forces of the middle ages and paganism. He did not know which of the two was the greater, but he did not concern himself with that, other than to maintain a detachment.

He knew that for that one night, Wylshere was going to bring all the forces he could rally to bear, and that Edmund

Wylshere was mad. The fifth elder, confronted with such realities, knew that as a fact.

Behind the five elders, the men in blue marched. Of the nineteen, six were unsure and wanting to leave, but they were well aware that so far that night three had died already, and one word from the chief elder and they would be dead as well. The six were frightened, as was everyone else that marched, that is, apart from Wylshere.

The man could be seen striding forward, occasionally stopping to raise the level of the chanting even higher. 'We need them to hear us. To come when they are needed,' he said.

The mob, disparate in their enthusiasm, unwilling individually to show dissension, chanted ever louder, each louder than the other. In the night air, their voices echoed. Up at the village, there were twitching curtains and shaking heads. The uncertainty about who would be alive in the morning was thought, but not spoken.

Of the elders, Saxby wanted to pull out. He could see the vehicles angled across their route in a vain attempt to stop their movement. Outside the front of the church were a man in police uniform and two others, one a woman. He knew that this had gone too far. 'Wylshere, enough is enough,' he shouted. The mob halted in their tracks; those outside the church strained their eyes to see.

'This must continue,' Wylshere said from behind his bull mask.

'You cannot go killing the police,' Saxby said. He was aware that he had committed the unpardonable sin in criticising the chief elder.

'There is no place for cowards amongst us.'

'I am not the only one. Speak out all those who are with me,' Saxby said, turning to face the mob. A shaking of heads.

'Saxby, you're on your own.'

'Nonsense, there are some who want to speak.'

'They are sensible. They know the punishment.'

'I am leaving,' Saxby said.

'It cannot be allowed. What do you say?' Wylshere said, addressing the mob.

'Sacrifice, sacrifice.' With that, they moved forward, those with staves hitting Saxby, those with knives stabbing him. The man collapsed to the ground.

'We continue,' Wylshere said. The chanting recommenced, the mob stepping over the bloodied body of the man who had once been a farmer in Avon Hill.

***

The sight of a man dying at the hands of the mob sent a wave of panic through those at the church. Even though their visibility had been restricted, it had still been enough.

Tremayne, the most resolute of those at the crime scene, was taken aback by the brutality. He had always maintained a modicum of hope that sense would prevail, and that what had apparently transpired in the village since their arrival was no more than hearsay, and that the two police officers and the crime scene investigator, declared dead by Wylshere himself, were in fact still alive.

However, the brutal slaying of one of the mob convinced the policeman that Wylshere had been telling the truth. Clare, who stood alongside him, had never had such illusions, and she knew that those now moving around the vehicular blockade had only one intent: their deaths. Jim Hughes, a man whose function was to investigate the crime scene, not become a crime statistic, was back inside the church with his remaining people. 'We're going to make a run for it,' one of his team said. Hughes could offer no constructive reason as to why they should not.

'We'll all leave now,' Hughes said.

He went back outside the church, to Tremayne and Clare. 'You cannot stop this,' he said, looking at Tremayne.

'We need to go, guv,' Clare said.

'There's not enough time,' Tremayne replied. The mob was within one hundred feet of the church. They were standing still, their robes and their masks more visible in the light from the blazing fire torches they carried.

'You were warned,' the man with the bull mask shouted.

'Wylshere, why the pretence. I recognise your voice,' Tremayne shouted back. Clare stood at his side. Hughes had left and was striking out for the safety that lay not more than thirty minutes away.

'The mask is not for you; the mask is for them. It's what they demand.'

'You're certifiable,' Tremayne said.

'You will never understand,' Wylshere said, removing his mask. 'That is why you and your sergeant are suitable.'

'We need to get out of here,' Clare said. She was shaking with fear. Her DI may not have believed, but she did.

The mob continued to chant.

'It's too late for that now. Where are the other police officers? We had two before,' Tremayne asked.

'They're in one of the cars.'

'Can they get it out of here?'

'That's why it's there.'

'Right. We'll make a run for it and drive out of here.'

Clare, for once, could see some hope for their predicament. She shouted to the police officers sitting in the car. 'Okay?'

'Okay,' the reply that came back.

'Yarwood, make a run for it. I'll hold them off for as long as I can.'

'I'm not leaving you, guv,' Clare replied.

'Don't worry. I'm right behind you.'

The two police officers dashed towards the patrol car and jumped into the rear seat. 'Go,' Yarwood shouted to the driver. The car moved forward, the mob attempting to impede its movement.

'Let them go,' Wylshere instructed the mob. 'They cannot go far.'

'Where to?' the driver asked.

'The road out of here.'

'The road that Dallimore and Hopwood took?'

'It's bound to be blocked, and there's snow up there,' Clare said.

'Okay. Head up through the village and then take a left.'

'What are you thinking, guv?'

'You know Cuthbert's Wood and the area around it.'

'Well enough to know I don't want to go there again.'

'Any better ideas?' Tremayne asked.

'No.'

Once free of the mob, the four police officers headed up through the village. They passed the pub, its lights on inside. 'We could make a phone call,' Clare said. 'They may have a landline.'

'Too risky,' Tremayne said. 'We need to protect ourselves first, and besides, no one is coming to rescue us, not before daylight at the earliest. We can't stall them for that long.'

'Is this the turn?' the driver asked.

'Yes,' Clare replied. The road they turned into, more a lane, narrowed dramatically until it was barely wide enough for the car to pass through. 'That's Elizabeth Grimshaw's cottage,' she said.

Two houses up, a man emerged from behind the hedgerow. Clare wound down the window on her side of the car.

'Drive up past Adam Saunders' cottage for as far as you can and then leave the vehicle. Elizabeth is a friend of mine,' the man said. Tremayne held a gun in his hand.

'That's not necessary. I can be trusted.'

'In Avon Hill!'

'Some of us can.'

'It's not safe for you here,' Clare said.

'If they see me talking to you, then no, it will not be, but it does not matter. This curse that has lasted for centuries must end. The events of tonight will sever the Wylshere family's control. If they're not summoned, then they will cause no more trouble.'

'Yarwood, we don't have time,' Tremayne said. The lights of the mob could be seen back at the pub.

'Come with us,' Clare said.

'It is too late for me. You will need to move fast. I'll attempt to get a message out of the village to summon help.'

'Can you?'

'I will try.'

'Very well. Thank you,' Clare said.

'Don't thank me. You're not free yet, and your chances are slim. There is still Cuthbert's Wood to negotiate.'

Tremayne realised they had lost precious time, and help, even if it were forthcoming, would not extricate them from their current predicament. The mob was still in pursuit, and some could be seen running up the road past the pub. 'Drive, for God's sake, drive,' Tremayne said.

The driver put his foot to the floor, the wheels slid on the icy road. He eased his foot off the throttle hoping to gain grip. The vehicle moved forward, its speed limited.

'Through that gate,' Clare said.

The cottage where Adam Saunders had hidden out before his untimely death lay in front of them. It was in total darkness. The driveway, gravel turning to frozen mud, ended at the front door. To the left and the right of the cottage, there was only frozen grass.

'Take the left,' Tremayne said.

'The right's better,' the driver said.

'Whatever you do, do it quickly.'

Clare craned her neck to look out of the rear window; it was iced over. She opened the side window, the cold was intense. She angled herself out of the window, lifting herself out of her seat to get a better look. The mob, she could see, were close to Elizabeth Grimshaw's cottage, not more than five minutes from where they were. 'Drive,' she shouted at the driver. The man looked stunned, unsure what to do.

Tremayne jumped out of the car and opened the driver's door. 'Get in the back with Yarwood. I'm driving.' He slammed the car into gear and drove off the driveway and to the left of the cottage. Unable to get the car out of first gear, he kept his foot firmly welded to the accelerator. The left-hand route around the cottage appeared to have been the best choice. Up ahead, silhouetted at the top of the hill, they could see Cuthbert's Wood. To Clare, it looked menacing, but it was their only hope, she knew that. She had walked around it that time when Adam Saunders had been discovered there. She went through in her mind the layout inside the wood. She knew that evil lurked there, but evil lurked everywhere, and those who had entered the cottage's land were evil in physical form.

The vehicle lurched across the land at the rear of the cottage and then through an open gate into the field at the back. It was clear that it was used for grazing. A few cows could be seen in one corner. They took no notice of the vehicle and its occupants. All they did was huddle together to keep warm, their hot breath visible.

Although the frozen field was smooth, the vehicle could not move very fast. Gradually, though, Cuthbert's Wood drew nearer, the mob behind losing ground.

'Keep driving,' Clare urged Tremayne.

'Another one hundred yards and we have to get out and make a run for it,' Tremayne's reply.

Clare could see the trees in front of her looming nearer. She felt fear, even more than she had felt before, as she remembered her last time there. Tremayne stopped the car. 'That's it,' he said.

The four police officers left the car and stumbled, walked, ran towards the trees. A barbed wire fence blocked their way. Tremayne held the top wire with his coat, ripping it in the process, to allow Clare to step over the fence. The other police officers had taken hold of one of the wooden uprights and vaulted across the fence, one of them twisting his ankle on landing.

The four entered the wood using the same path that the young Saunders boy had used, a marker left by the crime scene investigators still visible. The officer with the twisted ankle struggled to keep up, the others offering assistance as best they could. After five minutes inside the wood, the lights of vehicles on the main road could be seen. It was no more than three hundred yards across the open field on the other side once they had cleared the wood.

Behind them, the sound of the mob could be heard. Tremayne knew they were not safe yet. 'Keep going,' he said.

'We're nearly there,' Clare said. She could see the other side of the wood, the open field beyond clearly visible.

'Wait until tomorrow,' Tremayne said. He knew that once he was back in Bemerton Road Police Station, once all the events had been recounted, confirmed by all those who had been present at the crime scene, there would be a massive clean-up operation. He would need to bring in additional police teams from other cities.

Clare, in her enthusiasm to leave the woods, surged forward. She did not see the fallen branch; she tripped and fell, face down. Tremayne picked her up and sat her against a tree. 'Yarwood, are you alright?' he said, shaking her shoulders gently.

The mob could be heard entering the wood, their chanting frenzied.

'Yarwood, Yarwood, we've got to go.'

Clare dazed, but still conscious, got to her feet. The four police officers continued forward, the lights on the highway even more visible. A police car could be seen, its flashing light visible, an ambulance in hot pursuit. Tremayne hoped it was for them; it wasn't.

'Grab them.' The last words that any of them heard before they were trussed up with rope and tied to nearby trees.

Chapter 36

Tremayne realised that in the struggle he had been knocked unconscious. Over to one side of the small clearing, not more than six feet away, Clare was tied to another tree. 'Are you okay, Yarwood?' he whispered. The mob was at least twenty feet away. Tremayne could hear them chanting again, Wylshere with his ridiculous mask the most visible.

'They intend to kill us,' Clare mumbled.

Tremayne did not reply directly to the obvious. 'Let's hope our people got the message out,' he said. He could see that the other two officers, Constable Bradshaw and Sergeant Stanforth, were both conscious. The detective inspector, a man who never gave in and always had a plan, realised that for once he could not think of anything useful to say or do. His ability to do anything was severely hampered by his current predicament, the ropes across his upper body holding him firm, a protruding branch pushing hard into his back. The ropes around his legs had already cut circulation to his lower left leg and were about to cut it to the other one as well. He realised that he was getting too old for this, but then, he observed, the other three weren't faring much better. Still, he knew it was up to him to provide leadership.

'Yarwood, can you loosen your ropes? Bradshaw, Stanforth, any luck?'

'I'm held firm,' Clare said. The other two police officers shook their heads weakly.

In the distance, the lights of the main road could be seen; in the woods were only the men in their blue and scarlet robes. 'It is time,' Wylshere said, standing on a rise in the ground. Tremayne looked over at the man, his robes and his mask lit by the glow from a blazing fire torch held by one of his followers.

'You're mad, the lot of you,' Tremayne shouted.

One of the group came over to where he was tied and struck him hard in the face with a clenched fist. 'Shut up, your time will come.'

'Leave him alone,' Clare screamed, so loudly that it interrupted Wylshere's flow of speech to the devoted.

'If she speaks again, gag her,' Wylshere said.

Tremayne, his face bloodied, looked over at Clare. 'Stay quiet. Try and loosen the ropes; it's our only hope.'

'What about your gun?' Clare asked.

'They never checked. It's still in my trouser pocket.'

'We can't shoot our way out of this.'

'If we're free, you and the others can make a run for it. I can hold them off for long enough.'

'I'll not leave you.'

'I'll not be far behind.'

On the other side of the small clearing, Wylshere continued to lift his followers to a crescendo with a combination of rabble rousing speeches and foreign tongues. The man was in his element. Even Mike Carter, concealed behind his stag's mask, could see that the situation was out of hand. He knew that it could not continue, but how could he stop it. He, like all the others, was guilty of heinous crimes, and he knew that there was not one of those dressed in robes who would not be convicted of murder. Slater, with the mask of the ram, stood resolute to one side of Wylshere. The man knew that what was coming was stronger than any police force, and he was convinced that theirs was the right course. His ancestors had longed for it, as did he, when those that he believed in would reassert their authority over the country that he held so dear. The fifth elder said little, other than to regret that it had come to this, a turning point in his life when he would have to make a decision. He readjusted the bear mask that covered his face, realised how silly he looked, and what fools they all were to be there in that wood intent on killing. He knew that he was as guilty as the others, but his dedication was wavering between allowing what was going to happen to continue or making the ultimate sacrifice, knowing full well that the anger of the mob would be vented on him. It was either the four police officers' lives or his.

He was not sure which way to go. He leant over to Mike Carter, identifiable by his stag's mask. 'Are you willing to let this continue?' he said.

'It is the way,' Carter replied. A cautious man, he was being asked to make a decision with a man whose loyalty he could not trust. The fifth elder could be laying a trap for him, willing him to falter, and then denouncing him to the mob.

The fifth elder realised it was up to him. He moved to distance himself from Wylshere's side. The man observed, said nothing.

Clare attempted to move her arms, firmly bound as they were. The cold was starting to freeze her hands, her feet had lost all feeling. The other three attempted to move as well, with Stanforth, a muscular man, flexing his muscles, aiming to weaken the knots on the ropes. 'I've some movement,' he said, as he managed to free one arm. With one arm free, he focussed on the other, and soon it was also free. Bradshaw struggled with his bindings. Clare also continued to struggle, but Tremayne, weakened after the punch in the face, did not have the strength.

'It is time,' Wylshere shouted to those assembled. He uttered the forbidden words, the mob following as best they could, encouraging him on. He repeated the words, the night sky darkened, the main road in the distance faded from view.

Clare knew what she was seeing, even if Tremayne remained a sceptic.

'They are here,' Wylshere proclaimed. The mob acknowledged their presence. 'We are ready with our offering,' he said. The wind rustled through the leaves, emitting an ominous sound, and the mist swirled around their feet.

'The woman, the woman,' the men in blue shouted. Tremayne could see their frenzied attitude, the glances towards Clare.

'Stanforth, are you free?' Tremayne shouted.

'Almost.'

'Get Yarwood out of here and run like hell for the road.'

'I'll not leave you,' Clare said. She had seen the robed men brandishing knives.

'What is her fate?' the mob shouted.

'Esus demands to be honoured,' Wylshere said.

'They intend to hang me,' Clare said. She had read up on the subject; she knew what they were talking about, and Jim Hughes had explained what had happened to Trevor Godwin: the stabbing wounds, the burns on his neck where he had been hanged. Clare longed for Harry to be there to rescue her, the knight in shining armour, but she knew that would not happen. A woman on the cusp of marriage, a career she loved, a boss she respected, and yet, no more than five hundred yards from civilisation, she was to die in a pagan ritual.

Tremayne wanted to rush over and comfort her, but he could not move.

On the main road were flashing lights, the sound of sirens. 'We do not have long,' Wylshere proclaimed. 'Bring the woman. Her death will strengthen those who protect us.

'There is no protection,' Mike Carter said, removing his mask. 'This has gone on for long enough. You cannot kill a police officer, let alone a woman.'

'Grab him,' Wylshere screamed. 'Teutates, we honour you first.' With that, the mob grabbed hold of Avon Hill's butcher and dragged him screaming towards the water where Adam Saunders had died.

'Get free and get out of here,' Carter yelled at the top of his voice to the four police officers.

Tremayne was frantic, attempting to use the last strength in his body to save Clare, to save the man whose face was already in the water. Some of the mob, those who had wavered in the pub, fought with the men holding the butcher under the water. They managed to bring his head up to allow him to take a breath, while the others, wresting control again, pushed it under. Wylshere stood remote, almost in a trancelike state, reciting the forbidden words.

'I'm free,' Stanforth shouted.

'Get Yarwood out of here,' Tremayne repeated his earlier order.

The mob, distracted by Stanforth's shouting, focussed on the four police officers.

'Stop them leaving,' Slater, the resolute elder, said.

Mike Carter, the pressure on his head relieved, drew another breath. This time, there was no one holding him down again. He pulled himself clear of the pond and lay on the frozen ground. He looked up to find three of Wylshere's most loyal supporters fighting with some of the others. He could see Slater coming for him. He grabbed a knife from one of the mob and rammed it hard into the vet's stomach. Slater fell forward, holding the knife in his two hands in an attempt to remove it. He hit the water face down; he did not come up.

Carter pulled himself to his feet and moved over to where the other battle raged. He could see the mob fighting close to the police officers, the fifth elder attempting to remove the bindings that held them.'

'Get Clare out of here,' the fifth elder said.

'Harry?' Clare let out a gasp.

'I'm sorry. I can't explain, it goes back too many years. I tried to warn you not to come here.' Harry Holchester looked over at Tremayne. 'Get her out of here.'

'Why?' Clare asked.

'There's no time for explanations. My family have been part of this for centuries. I love you, but please go. I must stop this madness.'

'How?' Tremayne asked.

'I must kill Edmund Wylshere.'

'That's murder.'

'Don't you understand? He is the conduit, he and his family.'

'Please come, Harry,' Clare said, tears streaming down her face.

'It's too late. Nothing can be done to stop this. Tremayne, get Clare out of here.' In the distance, the sound of sirens could be heard coming closer.

Wylshere, his work completed, came out of his trance. He saw what was happening in front of him. He saw the four police officers leaving the woods, the female being dragged reluctantly. He did not see the knife enter his heart, or the hand of Harry Holchester as he held it firm.

With Wylshere dead, Harry focussed on the ongoing affrays. 'It is over. Edmund Wylshere is dead. Go back to your homes. Tomorrow we will be answerable for our sins.'

The fighting ceased within minutes, and those who could walk did so, back to Avon Hill and away from the police cars on the other side of Cuthbert's Wood. Those who could not walk were either helped or left where they were.

Harry knew there was no hope for him and resigned himself to his fate. His family had prospered under the curse that had held the community in bondage for so long. His parents had grown up there, although he had not, yet he believed in the old ways, as had they, and now it had cost him the one woman he had loved. His life he knew was at an end.

Clare was out of the wood and sitting in a warm police car, Tremayne at her side. 'Why?' she asked.

'I'm sorry, Clare. This madness has destroyed so many, including Harry.'

'What will happen?'

'The police will cordon off Avon Hill. All those involved will be arrested.'

'And Harry?'

'We can't make an exception.'

'But he tried to help us,' Clare pleaded.

'He helped you, and you know it. I, and the two others, were secondary.'

'There's no snow up here.'

'I can't explain it. Down there in the village and in Cuthbert's Wood, the climate is different to up here.'

'I'm going back for Harry,' Clare said.

'Officers are preparing to go in for him now. If the road is still blocked, we can get enough men down there on foot, and we'll bring up some motorcycles and four-wheel drives. Avon Hill will be swarming with police today.'

Clare looked up at the sky; daylight was almost upon them. She left the car and headed back to the woods. Tremayne kept close to her. He could see that she was not rational, although he could understand. They found Harry sitting against a tree near the body of Edmund Wylshere.

'Why, Harry?' Clare asked. She had thrown her arms around him.

'Others will have to tell you. I am as guilty as all the others. In time, you will forget me.'

'I won't,' Clare said.

'Did you kill Wylshere?' Tremayne asked.

'I've stopped it,' Harry replied.

'I'll need to arrest you for murder.'

'I understand.'

Harry stood up, freeing himself of Clare's embrace. He walked over to the pond where Mike Carter had nearly died, where Adam Saunders had.

Clare was the first to sense it, although Tremayne did soon after. A wind blew through the wood and in the direction of Harry. It was bitterly cold. Clare knew what it was; Tremayne did not speak.

'They are still here,' Harry said. He looked up to see a large branch falling from a tree. It hit him firmly in the chest, its secondary branches piercing his chest in several places. The branch continued its trajectory, holding Harry firmly in its embrace, and lodged itself against another tree.

'Help him,' Clare shouted.

Two police officers came running over. One climbed the tree, the other assisting him.

'How is he?' Tremayne asked.

'He's dead,' the officer who had reached him said.

'Esus has his offering,' Clare said. Tremayne led her out of the wood and to an ambulance which had just arrived.

'She'll need a sedative,' he said.

Chapter 37

To Clare, the days following Harry's death were a blur. Her ability to remain focussed and a member of the Homicide team was compromised. Tremayne understood that, and that eventually she would return home to her parents' house to distance herself from what had happened in Cuthbert's Wood.

Tremayne went to see her, as did Superintendent Moulton. Moulton offered his and the police station's condolences; not that it helped much, Tremayne could see that. The genial host of his favourite pub, the man his sergeant was going to marry, had turned out to be one of the pagan worshippers, and not only that, one of their leaders.

'Why?' Yarwood had asked Tremayne after Moulton had left.

'Who knows what goes through people's minds? Why are some people good, some people bad? What makes a person believe in ancient gods from antiquity, and others total sceptics?'

'Are you still a sceptic?' Clare asked.

'Always. All that occurred, tragic as it was, was engineered by the hand of man. Maybe I don't have all the answers, maybe I never will, but there's no way that I will ever accede to the belief that there was something else. No one died for any reason other than a man or a woman was responsible. You know that.'

'I know it, apart from Eric Langley, but even so, we saw things that defy explanation.'

'And what for you now, Yarwood?'

'It will take time,' Clare replied.

'There's a job here for you when you return.'

'I'm not sure. I'm not thinking straight. What about Harry?'

'His body is in the local mortuary.'

'When will it be released?'

'It depends. It's part of a murder investigation.'

'You were there. You saw what happened. Do you believe that was an accident?'

'Yarwood, I must. I can only deal with facts, not someone who sees things that aren't there, and I certainly can't believe in the supernatural, nor can you.'

'But I do. I know what I saw, what I felt in that church in Stratford sub Castle and what I experienced in Mavis Godwin's cottage.'

'It doesn't help to dwell on those things, does it?' Tremayne said.

'Maybe it doesn't, but those events occurred, you know that,' Clare said.

Tremayne left his sergeant, his colleague, his friend, resting. She had been given a sedative and would sleep for twenty-four hours, the doctor said. He knew that he did not have that luxury.

He had only left Avon Hill out of concern for his sergeant. He had to be back there as soon as possible to lead the investigation.

The snow that had held the body of Constable Dallimore had melted with the early morning sun, and it was only slush as he drove down the road towards Avon Hill. The area around the village within a two-mile radius had been established as a crime scene, and those in the community who had tried to leave had been stopped. This time the crime scene headquarters would not be an old wooden garage next to the church; this time it would be the pub.

Tremayne stopped twice on the drive down to the village, to check on Constables Dallimore and Hopwood. Both were dead, as stated by Edmund Wylshere, as well as the first crime scene investigator who had attempted to bring help. Eventually, it had been Jim Hughes and those who had left with him who had been able to raise the alarm. It had been smart thinking on his part to alert the police that if the road was blocked, then Cuthbert's Wood offered the best possibility of getting through.

Tremayne stopped at the church first to check on proceedings. The equipment from London had arrived, and the CSIs were combing the ground for additional bodies buried amongst the trees behind the church.

'We've found forty at least, although some go back a long time,' Hughes said.

'The recent ones interest us.'

'There's six those up at the pub are answerable for.'

Tremayne left the Avon Hill church and drove the short distance to the pub, diverting around the body of Gerald Saxby, the elder slain the previous night. An ambulance was there, as were two crime scene investigators.

'Nasty way to go,' one of the CSIs said to Tremayne.

'We saw it.'

'I'm told it was pretty rough down here after we left.'

'It was.' Tremayne did not feel the need to elaborate. He knew what he and Yarwood had seen and experienced. As a detective inspector of long standing, he had investigated many murders, but never once had he been so integrally involved, had almost become a victim. He shifted in his seat, the bruising left by the ropes and the branch pushing into his back still hurting. He knew he needed a complete rest, but he had to conclude the investigation. He owed that much to Yarwood, although there was nothing that he could do or say that would alleviate her suffering.

Tremayne commandeered a room upstairs at the pub; the publican did not comment. He had been one of those that had pursued them the previous night, the blue robe hanging behind his bedroom door testament to the fact. He, along with all the other men in the village, had been held pending charges. In total, there were thirty-six men in the village, although it had been possible to eliminate all of them except for twenty-three.

Outside, in the pub car park, there were six police cars and two ambulances. Due to the severity of the situation, Tremayne had commandeered virtually every additional police officer at Bemerton Road Police Station. He realised that for once his star was flying high, but it was small compensation for all that had happened.

The first person he interviewed was the publican, Albert Grayling. 'What's the story?' Tremayne asked.

'What's to say? You were here.'

Tremayne did not like the man's attitude, but it was not important. He wanted those who had killed Saxby, those who had attempted to kill him and Yarwood and the other two constables who were already back on duty in the village, almost certainly due for a medal for bravery beyond the call of duty. Tremayne assumed he and Yarwood would receive one each as well. He realised as he sat there looking at the pagan worshipper that he was more shaken than he had thought initially. He knew he should not be there, but there was no one else with the intimate knowledge of the night before. Bradshaw and Stanforth were both too young and inexperienced, and neither had the qualifications to run a homicide investigation.

'We intend to prove that you were a member of the group that killed Gerald Saxby,' Tremayne said, 'attempted to kill Michael Carter, the local butcher, and intended to kill Sergeant Yarwood, myself and two of the police officers that were with us. Do you deny this?'

'I was one of those who tried to stop it,' Grayling said. Tremayne did not believe him.

'We will prove this one way or the other.'

'How?'

'Fingerprints, DNA. There are plenty of ways to find the truth. If you're lying, it will be discovered.'

'What will happen to us?'

'There is still the murder of Trevor Godwin. If any of you were in that mob last night, then you are all guilty of murder.'

'You'll not be able to prove it,' Grayling said. Tremayne knew the man was well experienced in lying.

'Are you willing to admit that you were in the mob that attempted to attack the church, and then was up at Cuthbert's Wood?'

'I was there, but I did not take part.'

'I and my sergeant saw Saxby die. Everyone in that mob was involved.'

'Are you going to arrest us all?'

'After preliminary interviews here, you will all be charged with the lesser offence of causing an affray with an attempt to cause physical harm. Once at the police station, and after detailed forensics and further interviews, you, along with the others, will be charged with murder and attempted murder.'

'This village is finished,' Grayling said.

'It was finished centuries ago.'

'I will tell you what I know.'

'In writing?'

'Yes.'

Tremayne left the room, a sergeant taking his place while Grayling wrote.

Weary as he was, the adrenaline was keeping him focussed. He entered the bar, where a group of local men sat quietly. Four police officers were keeping watch over them. Tremayne walked out of the bar and phoned Hughes, the mobile phone network functional again. 'Any updates?' he asked.

'We're exhuming two more bodies. The same.'

'Stabbing, hanging?'

'It's too early to be more precise, but the method of their deaths varies. Pathology will be able to tell you more.'

'Your report is good enough for me,' Tremayne said.

Hughes realised that he had broken through Tremayne's reluctance to accept him as an equal. 'Yarwood?' he asked.

'She's an excellent police officer. In time, she'll be back.'

'Not easy to take, something like that.'

'That's what being a police officer is about.'

'Seeing someone you love strung up in a tree, dead?'

'Not that, I suppose.' Tremayne had seen death, anticipated his own death, but he had not felt revulsion at what had happened, only a jaundiced indifference as if he had seen all the misery that life could offer, and there was nothing more that could shock him. He was aware that he was devoid of any feeling, good and bad. He knew it was unhealthy. He knew he needed to get away from Salisbury for a while.

Tremayne ended the call. He returned inside the pub and climbed the stairs to the room where Grayling sat.

'You've finished?' Tremayne asked.

'I'm damned whatever I say and do,' Grayling said. He noticed that the man had organised a cup of tea. He asked the sergeant who had sat in for him to get him one as well. He felt like a pint of beer, the type they served in Harry Holchester's pub, but he knew that it would be a long time before it opened again, and even if it did, Tremayne knew that he would never go back there.

Tremayne read what Grayling had written. 'You've been careful to avoid implicating yourself in any of the deaths.'

'I did not kill anyone. Okay, I was foolish, led astray by Wylshere, but I've killed no one. It was good for business, surely you understand that.'

'People died, most of them violently, and you say it was good for business.'

'You can't lock me up for being a callous bastard.'

'Maybe not, but we'll be going over this place with a fine-tooth comb. If we find one piece of evidence that ties you into any of the deaths, then I'll personally make sure that you receive the maximum sentence for murder.'

'You'll not find anything.'

'The five elders: Edmund Wylshere, Gerald Saxby, James Slater, Mike Carter and Harry Holchester. Is that correct?'

'Yes.'

'Harry Holchester came as a surprise,' Tremayne said.

'He hid it well.'

'The same as you?'

'Yes, but they'll not be coming back.'

'Who?'

'The secret on how to summon the gods died with Wylshere.'

'That nonsense again,' Tremayne said.

'If they were still here, we wouldn't be having this conversation.'

'Why?'

'If Holchester hadn't killed Wylshere, you'd be dead.'

'Are you seriously trying to tell me that you were there, but not involved.'

'Yes. I was one of those attempting to stop the drowning of Mike Carter.'

'He's the only one of the elders still alive.'

'How is he?'

'He's in hospital, under police guard.'

Tremayne realised that he had not slept since the events of the previous night, almost twenty-four hours. He left Grayling with one of the constables and walked out to his car. He started the engine, put the heater on maximum and fell fast asleep.

***

Mike Carter was not pleased to see Tremayne. The man was confined to a secure area of the hospital out on Odstock Road, less than two miles from the centre of Salisbury. He was sitting up in bed when Tremayne arrived after a two-hour sleep in his car.

'You're only here as a precaution,' Tremayne said.

'Then why the guards? I tried to help you.'

'That will go in your favour at your trial.'

'For what?'

'You were one of the elders?'

'I'll not deny it.'

'And a believer?'

'In the rubbish that Wylshere spouted?'

'Yes.'

'Not me.'

'Then why did you take part in the ceremonies?'

'I wasn't born there. I inherited the butcher's shop and a house in Avon Hill from a relative. I never knew what they were up to when I moved there.'

'And when you did?'

'At first, I resisted, but Wylshere made it clear that I could not stay unless I joined with him and his group.'

'Did he threaten you?'

'Not in so many words, but the man could be persuasive.'

'Yet you became an elder.'

'It was good for business.'

'How can killing people be good for business?'

'I didn't kill anyone.'

'Mr Carter, your defence is feeble. The reality is that you saw people killed, yet you did nothing.'

'If I had come to the police and told them about what went on in Avon Hill, what do you think would have happened?'

'We would have conducted an investigation.'

'That's the problem. How long would that take?'

'It would not be immediate, although it would have been if you had told us there were bodies behind the church.'

'How long do you think it would have been before I was dead, strung up in a tree or burnt?'

'Burnt, have there been any of those?'

'Only one that I know of.'

'Will you give a full statement of the history of Avon Hill and all that has been going on there?' Tremayne asked.

'It'll not do me any good,' Carter said.

'It will help.'

'I'll still be convicted of murder, whether I'm guilty or not.'

'You'll be given a fair trial.'

Tremayne left Carter to reflect on his future. The man was to be discharged from hospital that day and would be transferred in handcuffs to the cells at the police station. There he would be formally charged. Tremayne knew that for all the man's posturing Mike Carter, the local butcher, was a mass murderer.

Harriet Wylshere, Edmund Wylshere's widow, still remained at large. A police hunt was under way for her. Tremayne was confident that she would be found in due course, and charged with the murder of Mavis Godwin, the kindly woman that Yarwood had liked.

Tremayne decided to visit Yarwood again. She was staying at the Red Lion Hotel in the centre of Salisbury, and her parents were with her.

'I want to see Harry before I leave,' she said when she saw Tremayne. Her parents had smiled weakly at him as they left him and his sergeant alone.

'Later today, if you're up to it.'

'I'm not. I need to see him one more time, that's all. He tried to help in the end. That's how I'll remember him.' She stood up and threw her arms around Tremayne's neck.

Tremayne could see that she was appreciative of his visit. Her parents had been there for her in that hotel, but only one other person understood how she felt, had experienced all that she had, and that was the lovable bear of a man, Detective Inspector Keith Tremayne.

She saw, in the close embrace, the small crucifix around his neck. She knew then that he believed in the forces that had held Avon Hill in its grip for seven hundred years.

Tremayne noticed that she had seen what was around his neck. He smiled at her and gave her a kiss on the cheek. 'Come back when you're ready, Clare. There's always a job here with me,' he said. She noticed a tear in his eye.

The End

Phillip Strang

Death and the Assassin's Blade

Chapter 1

Detective Inspector Keith Tremayne knew one thing: his idea of fun was not sitting on the grass on a balmy summer's night watching a rendition of Shakespeare's *Julius Caesar* acted out by the local dramatic society. He had to admit, though, that choosing the Anglo-Saxon fort of Old Sarum was as good a location as anywhere; not that much of it remained, just a few old stones here and there.

It had been six months since the events at nearby Avon Hill, and the village was supposedly half empty after ten of the men arrested were sent to prison for murder. The media had invaded the place for a few weeks after the revelations of pagan rituals and human sacrifices, but they had soon tired of it. Tremayne knew full well that what they really wanted was orgiastic rituals with a naked woman writhing in the centre of the old church while lecherous men ogled and took advantage. However, for worshippers of ancient gods, they had been a dreary group of people. There they were, a captive group of believers, and their idea of enjoyment was sacrificing some hapless individual whose only crime was believing in such nonsense.

Sitting there at Old Sarum, being bitten by mosquitoes and listening to amateur dramatics, was not the time to dwell on that case, especially as it was his sergeant's first week back at Bemerton Road Police Station, and he had agreed to accompany her to the play.

Personally, he would have preferred a quiet pint or two of beer, but Clare Yarwood, his sergeant, was definitely teetotal after the love of her life and her fiancé, Harry Holchester, the publican of the Deer's Head, his favourite pub, had turned out to be one of the elders of the pagan sect.

Tremayne could see that Yarwood was still not happy, even after several months of compassionate leave. He had never imagined that she would return, but there she had been several days earlier, standing in front of his desk on a Monday morning. 'Reporting for duty,' she had said.

It surprised him so much so that he had rushed round to her side of the desk and given her a big hug. The department had not been the same since she had left, and the only murder in the time she had been away, a wife of a butcher who had caught her husband in bed with her best friend. By the time she had finished with the two of them, they could have been served up in the man's shop, skilled as she was in preparing a cow or pig carcass for sale.

Tremayne looked up at the stage, looked at Yarwood. She looked fine, he thought, but he was still concerned. After all, she had seen the man she loved plucked from the ground and pinned in a tree, branches stabbing his body, even heard his last gasping breath. On the way to Old Sarum, she had asked him not to drive down Minster Street, so as not to see Harry's pub, closed since he had died.

For someone uncommonly disaffectionate, he had grown fond of her; she was almost like the daughter he had never had. And now, she was back in Salisbury, and there was no way that she could avoid painful memories being reactivated as they moved around the city.

On the stage, or in this case a rise in the ground, a man dressed in a Roman tunic made his speech:

Cowards die many times before their deaths; The valiant never taste of death but once. Of all the wonders that I yet have heard, it seems to me most strange that men should fear; Seeing that death, a necessary end, will come when it will come.

Tremayne wondered why the man didn't speak plain English, but then he was a blunt man, not used to beating around the bush, which was what the man was doing up on the stage. It was the last place that he'd ever visit of a night time, but he owed it to his sergeant to at least show interest in what she liked. It had been the two of them who had been intimately involved with the pagans, although others had come and gone in the Homicide department during the investigation, especially Vic Oldfield, the young and keen constable who fancied Clare but who had never had a chance while Harry was alive. And Oldfield had then died, along with a self-confessed murderer, in a crash on the Wilton Road.

Tremayne touched the crucifix around his neck at the thought of it. It was nonsense, this talk of ancient gods, and being able to summon them from the depths of wherever, but he had seen things he couldn't explain, the same as Yarwood. He would never admit it to her, nor even to himself, but it was weird at the time. The memory still remained of that night up in Cuthbert's Wood where the two of them, along with a couple of uniforms, had nearly been sacrificed in a pagan ritual.

If it hadn't been for Harry Holchester freeing Clare first, and then the others, all four would have died. Tremayne noticed that Yarwood still touched her ring finger. He knew that idling her time in the office would do her no good, but then idling her time back at her parent's hotel in Norfolk had got to her in the end; she'd admitted that to him.

What she needed, what they both needed, was a good juicy murder to take their minds off the past, not a group of actors prancing around in Roman attire. The only problem was that there weren't any murders on the boil at the present time, although after the medals had been dished out for bravery above and beyond the call of duty that night in Avon Hill, any talk by Superintendent Moulton of his forced retirement was definitely off the agenda.

He'd accepted the award on Yarwood's behalf, said a few words for her, but she had not wanted to come. It would have inevitably led to further discussion about her dead fiancé and Avon Hill, and she wasn't up to that, not even now.

***

Tremayne fidgeted where he sat, and cramp was starting to affect one leg. Any other time he would have run a mile from such an event, but he could see that Yarwood was engrossed. 'The good part is coming soon,' she said.

'Act 3, scene 1,' Tremayne said, which surprised him considering the violence in it. He had thought that after the events in Avon Hill and Harry's violent death, she'd not want to see any more.

'You've seen it before?'

'I went to school, you know. The English teacher was mad for Shakespeare. He made us read it through, and then a test to check that we had.'

'And had you?'

'Only to save one of his detentions, writing out one hundred times:

There is a tide in the affairs of men,
Which, taken at the flood, leads on to fortune;
Omitted, all the voyage of their life
Is bound in shallows and in miseries.
On such a full sea are we now afloat;
And we must take the current when it serves,
Or lose our ventures.

It made no more sense then than it does now.'

'It's beautiful,' Yarwood replied.

'At least one of us is enjoying the night out.'

'The production and watching you squirm are poetic. Thanks for coming anyway. I knew it wasn't your kind of entertainment, but I didn't want to come on my own.'

'Don't expect me to come the next time, will you?'

'I'll be okay in a few days. It's just that coming back to Salisbury is not easy.'

'I'm pleased you're here.'

'You've missed me?' Yarwood asked.

'No one else could make a cup of tea like you,' Tremayne said. The friendliness between the two was making him uncomfortable. He had preferred it when he had snarled at her, and she had given him the occasional smart comment.

'You can make your own from now on. And besides, I prefer you grumpy.'

'Tomorrow, I promise. For tonight we'll labour through this.'

Tremayne had to admit that the production was professional, even if it was only the local dramatic society. He looked around: a full crowd. Amongst those watching were some in their teens, who seemed more engrossed than him. Also a fair smattering of retirees. He looked back at Yarwood.

'Don't worry about me. I'm made of stronger stuff,' Clare said. 'Harry's gone, life moves on, and I'm here.'

'I had you down as the whimpering type.'

'I was, but I've seen too much. I'd prefer him to be here, but he's not. It's no use dwelling on the past, is it?'

Tremayne had, that was the problem. The events in Avon Hill, the memories of his former wife, had made him phone her up. It had taken a few phone calls, a search on Facebook before he had traced her, and then it had been difficult.

They had met up: he, the set-in-his-ways detective inspector; she, the widowed mother of two.

'You look well,' she had said.

'So do you,' he had said, having to admit that she had fared better than him, but then, she hadn't spent nights in a pub drinking beer or working exhausting hours on murder investigations.

For a couple who had once been so close, it had been an uncomfortable night, too much water under the bridge. They had parted, a kiss on the cheek, not sure that they would meet up again, and Tremayne had to admit, he did like being on his own.

***

Tremayne was surprised that Yarwood would want to watch a production where there was to be a frenzied attack on the play's namesake, but for some reason it did not seem to affect her. As if the deaths of Harry, impaled by tree branches, and of an actor stabbed with fake retractable daggers and spilling red paint, were not similar.

He looked over at her as one of the major scenes in the play continued towards its crescendo. Up there on the stage were Caesar and the soothsayer.

CAESAR. *The ides of March are come.*

> SOOTHSAYER. *Ay, Caesar; but not gone.*

Caesar, ignoring the advice, moving into the Senate and taking his seat. The plotting of Brutus and Cassius, the pleading of Metellus for his brother's banishment to end.

> *Is there no voice more worthy than my own*
> *To sound more sweetly in great Caesar's ear*
> *For the repealing of my banish'd brother?*

Casca stabbing first, then the others, Cassius, Cinna, Ligarius, Metellus, Decius Brutus, and finally *'Et tu, Brute!'* as Brutus thrusts the final dagger in. Thirty-three times in total until the body lay at their feet.

Tremayne had to admit that it had been dramatic. The body of the actor covered in his robes, the blood oozing through, the conspirators with their bloodied hands, and then Brutus in the forum defending his and the conspirators' actions:

> *Be patient till the last.*
> *Romans, countrymen, and lovers! hear me for my cause; and be silent, that you may hear: believe me for mine honour, and have respect to mine honour, that you may believe: censure me in your wisdom, and awake your senses, that you may the better judge. If there be any in this assembly, any dear friend of Caesar's, to him I say, that Brutus' love to Caesar was no less than his. If then that friend demand why Brutus rose against Caesar, this is my answer. Not that I loved Caesar less, but that I loved Rome more.*

And then, the arrival of Caesar's body and the rebuke by Mark Antony:

> *Friends, Romans, countrymen, lend me your ears;*
> *I come to bury Caesar, not to praise him.*
> *The evil that men do lives after them;*
> *The good is oft interred with their bones;*
> *So let it be with Caesar. The noble Brutus*
> *Hath told you Caesar was ambitious:*

If it were so, it was a grievous fault, …

Finally, the body was taken away, to a hearty round of applause from the audience, even Tremayne. Yarwood was moved to tears.

'Are you alright?' Tremayne asked.

'The realism. I thought I could deal with it, but it made me remember.'

'Do you want to go?'

'No. I'll be fine. It's an intermission. I'll treat you to orange juice.'

'I could do with a beer.'

'After it's finished, we'll go to the Old Castle pub across the road,' Yarwood said. She had wanted to say the Deer's Head but corrected herself. That had been Harry's pub, the memory still painful of how he had saved her, how he had renounced the pagans up in Cuthbert's Wood and had come to her protection. She wanted to forget, but she could not.

***

'Tremayne, have you got a minute?'

Tremayne looked up from where he and Yarwood were sitting. 'Freestone, how are you? This is Sergeant Yarwood, Clare.'

'Pleased to meet you,' Clare said. She realised that he had been one of the actors on the stage, still dressed in his Roman tunic.

'It's around the back. We've called an ambulance and the police. I didn't realise you were here.'

'It's Yarwood. She's into this sort of thing.'

'At least one of you is not a philistine. Please come, it's serious.'

The two police officers got up from the grass and made their way around to the back of the stage, behind a cloth used as a backdrop.

'It's Gordon, he's dead.'

'Julius Caesar?' Clare said.

'They were meant to be fake knives. We'd purchased them especially.'

Tremayne knelt down, steadying himself on a chair to one side. He lifted the robe covering the man's face. 'You'll need to make an announcement.'

'That's what I was preparing to do. It has to be an accident, doesn't it?' Freestone said.

'That's not for me to say. Yarwood, make sure no one leaves until we've got their details and a brief statement.'

'The audience?'

'They may have seen something.'

Chapter 2

Peter Freestone handled the announcement reasonably well, Clare reinforcing his statement that the actor portraying Julius Caesar had unfortunately passed away.

There were one or two in the crowd who took the news badly, expecting a refund of their admission fee. They were more upset when told that no one was to leave until statements had been taken.

Tremayne didn't care whether they liked it or not. This was a murder, he was sure of it. He had been around long enough to know the difference between blood and red paint.

Clare was out front, trying to control the crowd, only one hundred and fifty or thereabouts. The sound of an ambulance could be heard as it hurtled up Castle Road towards the ancient site of Salisbury. Tremayne was around the back of the stage dealing with the cast. Freestone had returned to where the body was, leaving it to Clare and an employee of the Old Sarum Heritage Society to line up the people.

Already Clare had had to warn some of the more inebriated that leaving the scene of a crime was a criminal offence, even if they were not guilty of any wrongdoing.

The ambulance arrived, the medic rushing to examine the body of Gordon Mason, the actor who'd played Julius Caesar. 'I thought they used fake knives,' the medic, a petite woman, barely up to Tremayne's shoulder, said.

'I noticed the knife wounds. I'm assuming they killed him,' Tremayne said.

'That's not my area. I came here to save the man's life and to transport him to the hospital out on Odstock Road.'

'He'll need to go via Pathology first.'

'I take it you want me to leave the body where it is for your crime scene people.'

'You know the routine?'

'Once or twice. And besides, the man is dead. There's not much I can do.'

Jim Hughes, the crime scene examiner, the man that Tremayne begrudgingly had to admit was competent, even if he was still on the young side, arrived. As Yarwood had told him on more than one occasion, Hughes was degree educated, as if that somehow helped. Tremayne knew that he was a cantankerous sod, always pushing those who did not push back, and Hughes had given as much as he'd taken.

As far as Tremayne was concerned, strong-willed, competent, willing to challenge him with rational argument and a little sarcasm were plus points, and Yarwood was fast becoming the master, or should it be mistress, he wasn't sure which of the two was politically correct. Not that he had a lot of time for those who expounded the virtues of talking nicely to one another, showing due deference. If the person was a villain, enquiring after their health wasn't going to help, but a kick up the rear end and a few firm words, expletives included, would do more good.

'What do you reckon?' Tremayne asked one minute after Hughes had commenced his examination of Gordon Mason.

'He wouldn't have lasted long as King anyway.'

'You've lost me there.'

'Didn't you read the synopsis?'

'Yarwood did. She gave me the gist,' Tremayne said. He knew the plot as well as any of them, having had it drummed into him at school, but playing the uncouth policeman, ignorant of anything other than the racing results and a police report, maintained the image he wanted to portray.

'Cassius convinced Brutus that Caesar was attempting to be the King of Rome, do away with the Senate. That's why they killed him.'

'As you were saying about Mason?'

'Heavy smoker, overweight, and certainly no exercise judging by the tone of his muscles.'

'You can tell all that by looking at him lying there?'

'Not at all. Mason dealt with the purchase of our house. He was a solicitor, competent as far as we're concerned.'

'How many knife wounds?'

'Daggers.'

'Daggers, knives, what's the difference?'

'In this case, not a lot. I can see that the body's been pierced in several places.'

'They stabbed him at least thirty times on the stage.'

'Did you count?'

'No, but it's thirty-three according to Shakespeare.'

'You read that in the programme?'

'Yes, that's it,' Tremayne said. He had almost slipped up; almost revealed a hitherto hidden area of his knowledge.

'There's not that many stab wounds, maybe four or five. There's a couple in the area of the heart, two or three on the body. Pathology will be more precise, but I'd say that just one or two of them were fatal. The daggers? Are they here?'

'I have them.'

'How many?'

'Seven.'

'Okay, that's the right number. Any chance of fingerprints?'

'It's possible, but they've got lacquered rope on the handles, wooden pommels.'

'Are the daggers safe?'

'They're all in the same area,' Tremayne said. 'I've already shown one of your team where they are.'

'And the actors from the scene?'

'They're out the front.'

'We'll get their fingerprints first, and then see if we can get a match.'

Hughes concluded his preliminary examination of the body. He and Tremayne walked around the area. 'He was there when he was stabbed,' Tremayne said, pointing to a rise in the ground.

'Where Caesar was assassinated,' Hughes corrected him.

'He doesn't look much of a Caesar back there, does he?'

'You're right. What else do we have?'

'The other actors, although your people are dealing with them,' Tremayne said. 'The only thing that confuses me is how they came to be using real daggers. I thought they always used fake knives, plastic blades, blades that retracted inside the handles when they were pressed against a hard surface.'

'That's what we'll need to find out. One other thing, whoever killed Gordon Mason would have known that his dagger was entering the body.'

'Are you certain?'

'I'll confirm it once Forensics has checked the daggers, but yes, I'm certain. It's one thing to push a blade into a body, another to jab, the blade retracting.'

'One of the actors?'

'I found four to five wounds. It's one, maybe two actors.'

'And the other actors? Wouldn't they have realised that something was amiss?'

'You'd think so, but they may have been focussing on their part, their lines.'

'In that case, the murderer or murderers must have known which daggers to pick up. I never saw any markings to separate them.'

'There'll be something. I'll get them checked, let you know.'

Tremayne, an admirable man in many ways, had difficulty in accepting people unproven, but Hughes had won the blunt DI's respect in their previous case in Avon Hill, as had his sergeant, Clare Yarwood. Tremayne walked over to her. 'Okay, Yarwood?' he said.

'I'm just getting the details of the actors. Some of them are upset.'

'Not all of them,' Tremayne replied.

'It's not an accident, a faulty prop?'

'One, maybe two, of our thespians here is a murderer, and he or they know it.'

'They'll not admit to it, not up here tonight.'

'If they can pretend to be someone else on a stage, I'm sure they can maintain the pretence of being innocent.'

'The uniforms are taking the names and addresses of the audience, taking brief statements, but they're unlikely to have seen anything.'

'The same as us. We were out front, and we didn't see it, and we're trained to observe,' Tremayne said.

'Can I tell the actors that Julius Caesar was murdered? Most of them think it was an accident. They keep telling me what a great guy Gordon Mason was.'

'And a good solicitor no doubt.'

'They didn't mention that.'

'Hughes did. I'll tell them the truth. You watch for their reactions.'

'Ladies and gentlemen, I'm Detective Inspector Tremayne. I'll be leading this investigation.'

'We're all upset. We'd like to go home,' a woman said.

'And you are?' Tremayne said.

'Fiona Dowling. I played Calpurnia.'

Clare leaned over towards her boss and whispered, 'Caesar's wife.'

'Yarwood, I don't need a lesson on Shakespeare. I'm not the fool you take me for.'

'Sorry, guv.'

'Miss Dowling?'

'Mrs.'

'Mrs Dowling, I'm afraid it's not that simple. Gordon Mason was murdered.'

'But why? How?' one of the men asked.

'And you are?'

'Trevor Winston. I played Casca,' a slightly built, effeminate man said.

'The first assassin,' Tremayne said.

Clare looked at her DI in bewilderment. A man with no interest in anything outside of the police station, save for horse racing and pints of beer, and yet here was a man who knew his Shakespeare.

'One or two of the daggers were either tampered with or exchanged for real daggers. Forensics will tell us in due course. In the meantime, all of the conspirators must remain suspects.'

'But how would we know that the dagger was real? I'm Geoff Pearson, Cassius.'

'Mr Pearson, the difference between stabbing a man with a fake dagger and a real one is noticeable. Unfortunately, one or two of you here, or should I say of the men, is a murderer.'

'It can't be,' another woman said.

'Your name?'

'Cheryl Milledge. I played Portia.'

'Brutus's wife,' Tremayne said.

'You know your Shakespeare.'

'I know what they drummed into me at school.'

Clare realised that Tremayne may pretend that he was a simple man with few interests, but he was, in fact, more knowledgeable that he was willing to admit. She also realised that it was the first time that she had not thought about the events at Avon Hill when Harry had died.

'As I was saying,' Tremayne repeated, 'one, possibly two, of the seven men who stabbed Gordon Mason here tonight is a murderer. We don't know which of you it is, but we will in due course.'

Clare spent another forty minutes dealing with the actors before returning to the other side of the makeshift stage.

'Any reaction?' Tremayne asked.

'Apart from them all profusely protesting their innocence?'

'*Methinks thou dost protest too much*,' Tremayne said. 'Hamlet, by the way. It's not the correct quotation, but it's the one people remember.'

'You've been studying while I've been away,' Clare said.

'Don't get ahead of yourself, Yarwood. Just because I remember a few lines of Shakespeare, it doesn't mean I'm not the same cranky bastard that you know.'

'I won't, guv.'

'After I told them that one or two of them was a murderer?'

'A look of shock from all of them, nothing more.'

'You'd never know with them, trained to cover their true feelings.'

'They're the local drama society, they're hardly the Royal Shakespeare Company. I doubt if they're that good.'

'Maybe, but it's not important. We'll wait for Hughes's report before our next move.'

'You're not holding the seven?'

'We know where they are. Let them go. And besides, I could do with a beer.'

'Too late, guv. The pubs are all closed.'

Tremayne looked at his watch; it was close to midnight. 'Hell, Yarwood. Shakespeare, murder, and not even a pint. What a way to spend an evening.'

Tomorrow, I'll treat you,' Clare said.

'You know what will happen?'

'Another murder, more evidence, longer hours in the office and on the road.'

'And less time for a beer. I was hoping to go to the races this Saturday. I can guarantee I won't be.'

'For me, I'd rather be busy.'

'At least one of us is pleased,' Tremayne said.

Clare knew that, regardless of his protestations, the man was pleased as well, and this case had intrigue, the sort of case that her DI, even she, liked.

Chapter 3

Clare hadn't slept that first few nights back in Salisbury. She had leased a small cottage in Stratford sub Castle, not far from where Mavis Godwin, another victim of the pagan murderer, had lived. Her return to the city with its unpleasant memories had not been easy, but being back home with her parents, well-meaning but always trying to organise her life, convince her to take over as the manager of their hotel, had not been easy either. And besides, Salisbury had been where she had felt some contentment until that awful night when she had nearly died, and Harry, her fiancé, had. She had hoped to avoid the memories of him, the places they had visited together, but she knew that would not be possible, and now she wasn't sure if she wanted to.

He had turned out to be bad, but in the end he had saved her life at the expense of his. Tremayne would not agree, but he had not loved the man, she had, and her memories of Harry Holchester would only be good ones. He had been buried in the graveyard at Avon Hill, the church re-consecrated with a new vicar. Clare knew that she wanted to go out there, place some flowers on the grave, but she was not ready yet.

At seven in the morning after the play, she was in the office at Bemerton Road Police Station. She could see that Tremayne was all the better for a night without beer, but then, the man always looked better when he had a murder case.

'You're looking smart, guv,' Clare said.

'Don't think it's because of you,' the standard gruff reply. Clare had missed his abrasive manner, his self-deprecating comments, even their repartee. With her parents, sticklers for good manners, dressing for dinner, it had become boring, but with Tremayne, his shirt sometimes unironed, his tie off to one side, his attempts at picking the horses, she felt a homeliness in his company.

'I didn't think it was, guv.'

'And besides, you look smart enough for the two of us.'

'What's the plan for today?' Clare asked.

'Unless Jim Hughes comes up with something, which I don't think he will, you and I are out on the road interviewing the seven assassins.'

'You don't have much hope with Forensics?'

'I hope we get something, but all the daggers were identical, visually that is.'

'But there must have been a difference.'

'There has to be, but they had been thrown on a table at the rear after the scene. I'm certain that other people came along afterwards and moved them. There's bound to be plenty of fingerprints, but it'll be difficult to find one set that identifies the murderer.'

'Who do you believe is the most likely assassin?' Clare asked.

'Murderer, you mean.'

'Yes, murderer.'

'What do we know about Act 3, Scene 1?'

'The assassination?'

'Yes.'

'Seven assassins, the first stab from Casca, then the others join in. The final stab from Brutus.'

'Et tu, Brute.'

'Brutus only stabs Caesar once, but Jim Hughes said there were four or five stab wounds,' Clare said.

'In that case, Peter Freestone, he played Brutus, is not guilty on his own.'

***

'No luck,' Hughes said, in Tremayne's office.

'What do you mean?' Tremayne asked. It was apparent that Hughes and his team, together with Forensics, had worked all night, as it was only eight thirty in the morning, and they had a report prepared.

'Two of the daggers had been tampered with.'

'What do you mean?'

'It was clever. The retracting mechanism would work, but someone had drilled a small hole through the handle on each one.

It's not easy to see, but once we examined them under a bright light, we could see it.'

'Are you saying that they were all dangerous?'

'Only the two.'

'Someone had taken them and fitted metal blades?'

'It's very clever. Those that retracted did no harm; the murder weapons when pressed hard did.'

'So afterwards, it would have been possible to identify which blade killed the man.'

'They were covered in blood or red paint up at Old Sarum. There was no way to tell up there.'

'Fingerprints?'

'Inconclusive.'

'How many of the daggers had real blood on them?'

'Most of them, as they had all stabbed the body a few times. They would have picked up at least some blood on the outside of the man's robe. What I can tell you is that you have two murderers. Those daggers that had entered the body had substantially more blood than the others, consistent with entry through the flesh.'

'Anything more?'

'Pathology will conduct the autopsy. They'll be able to tell you the extent of the wounds, and which of the daggers killed the man, but you've still got two potential murderers.'

***

'Dreadful business, Tremayne,' Peter Freestone said. The man, someone that Tremayne occasionally drank with, was in his office in Salisbury, perilously close to Minster Street and Harry Holchester's pub. Tremayne, sensitive to his sergeant's fragile nature, had attempted to deviate around the area, distracting her as they drove past the end of the road. It had not been successful as she had looked, seen the pub sign hanging over the door, not that there would be much of a welcome, closed as it had been for some months. There had been a couple of offers since to buy the place, but none had come to anything.

Freestone sat in his office at the far end of Guildhall Square. Tremayne thought the room had a warm and cosy feel;

Clare did not like it. Freestone, an accountant, was successful by all accounts, in that he lived well, had a big house not far from Salisbury, drove a late model Mercedes, and smoked a pipe in the office.

Tremayne liked the idea of the pipe, Clare did not, the smell permeating the office. 'Sorry about the smell,' Freestone said as he opened the window.

'It's fine by me,' Tremayne said. 'Okay by you, Yarwood?'

'Fine,' Clare replied, which it was not, but they were there to discuss a murder, not to debate the offensive smell.

'None of us slept last night,' Freestone said.

'Did anyone admit to killing the man?'

'I can't believe that one of us killed him.'

'Someone did,' Clare said.

'But why? We act for the love of theatre, not for an opportunity to commit murder.'

'That's as maybe,' Tremayne said, 'but some of your group killed the man.'

'Some?'

'There were seven in that assassination scene, seven who stabbed Gordon Mason. Two of you had lethal weapons.'

'But how?'

'We know how. We still don't know who. What can you tell us about the other six?'

'I was Brutus. Then there's Casca, Cassius, Cinna, Ligarius, Metellus, and Decius Brutus.'

'Maybe you can start with Casca?' Clare asked.

'Trevor Winston. He has a hairdressing salon. He would like to act professionally, but he's not good enough. He knows that, so I'm not talking out of turn.'

'Anything else?'

'He's effeminate.'

'Gay?'

'He tries to downplay it, but yes, he probably is. He wouldn't harm a fly.'

'We're not dealing with flies here,' Tremayne said.

'You know what I mean.'

'Of course. I'm sure they are all fine, upstanding people, but two wanted Gordon Mason dead. Any ideas as to why?'

'Not that I know of. The man was competent, active in the dramatic society. He could be blunt sometimes, especially with Trevor Winston.'

'Any reason why?'

'Mason was a strict Baptist. He didn't hold with homosexuals.'

'Reason enough for Winston to bear a grudge?' Tremayne asked.

'I wouldn't have thought so. They tolerated each other, worked well together on stage, and besides, Winston's harmless.'

'You've already said that.'

'Apologies. Who else do you want to know about?'

'The assassins.'

'Cassius, the villain of the piece.'

'Why do you say that?' Clare asked.

'I thought you knew your Shakespeare,' Tremayne said.

Clare ignored his barbed comment. She much preferred the philistine to the educated man that her DI had temporarily become.

'Cassius was the one who convinced Brutus that Caesar wanted to wrest control from the Senate and to pronounce himself King,' Freestone said.

'Who played that part?' Tremayne asked.

'Geoff Pearson, an archaeology student, very bright, talented actor.'

'Local, is he?'

'Born and bred. He's studying at the university in Southampton, drives there and back every day.'

'Any aggravation with anyone else in the cast?' Clare asked.

'Not Geoff. He gets on well with everyone.'

'Cinna, what about him?' Tremayne asked.

'Gary Barker.'

'Profession, age?'

'He's an easy-going person, mid-thirties, not very ambitious. He's a good actor though. Cheryl Milledge, his girlfriend, played Portia, Brutus's wife. She likes to drink, so does Gary.'

'Decius Brutus?'

'Len Dowling. You must have seen his signs around the city.'

'The estate agent?'

'I thought I recognised him,' Tremayne said. 'He gave me a lousy valuation on my house a couple of years back. He was desperate to sell it for me.'

'Did you?'

'No way. He showed me what I could buy instead. I was better off where I am, and besides, I like it where I live. Apart from him being a sharp operator, what more can you tell us about him?'

'He's very keen on the theatrical. He's a competent actor, agreeable with everyone, although he can be overbearing. His wife, Fiona, played Calpurnia, the wife of Caesar.'

'Is Dowling capable of murder?' Tremayne asked.

'How would I know?' Freestone replied. 'How does anyone know if someone else is capable of murder?'

'Metellus, what about him?'

'Bill Ford. He's a funeral director. He's not an affable man, but yet again, enthusiastic. Always puts in a good performance. He keeps to himself, lives on his own.'

'Gay?'

'Unlikely. I can't see him being close to anyone, male or female. He comes to our rehearsals, knows his lines, and he'll always be here on the night. Apart from that, I can't tell you much more about him.'

'Apart from you, that only leaves Ligarius,' Tremayne said.

'Jimmy Francombe. He's only young, no more than eighteen. He's exceptionally keen, impetuous, always wanting to hog the limelight, reckons he's better than the parts we give him.'

'Is he?'

'Probably, but he needs to mature. Sometimes, he'll turn up with a throbbing headache and a hangover after a night on the town. We can't trust him with the major parts until he grows out of it.'

'What about Mark Antony?'

'Phillip Dennison.'

'Friends, Romans and countrymen,' Tremayne said.

'Yes, that's it. Dennison, wealthy, thinks he's superior to all of us, but he's reliable, and he enjoys acting. His wife's a handful.'

'Any reason why you say that?'

'You'll judge for yourself when you meet them. Phillip's in his late fifties, his wife's twenty to twenty-five years younger, trophy wife.'

'Is she?' Clare asked.

'I might be wrong, but that's how I see it. Mind you, she's beautiful. I can't blame the man. That's the cast for the scene, apart from me. I played Brutus. I only stabbed Gordon once.'

'A clear target to the heart, though,' Tremayne said.

'Not me. I had nothing against Mason. He could be a killjoy, orange juice at the pub, but apart from that he was a good solicitor, used him myself on more than a few occasions.'

***

Tremayne and Clare left Freestone to his pipe and his spreadsheets. They walked across Guildhall Square, Tremayne aiming to walk in one direction, Clare walking in the other.

'Are you ready for this?' Tremayne asked.

'I doubt if I'll ever be ready, but I can't be in Salisbury and do my job if you keep driving down other streets, trying to avoid Harry's pub.'

'It's still raw?'

'It's better here, and now we've got another murder to deal with. I'll be better, believe me.'

Tremayne was not sure; his sergeant still looked emotionally disturbed to him, although he could not blame her. He had liked Harry Holchester, always thought him to be a decent person, and he had been equally surprised when he had turned out to be one of the pagan worshippers.

The two police officers rounded the corner. There, in front of them, the Deer's Head, the pub where Tremayne had often enjoyed a pint, where Clare had first met Harry. Tremayne, a man who rarely showed emotion, let alone felt it, looked at Clare.

'I shouldn't have come,' she said.

Tremayne felt sad for her. 'We've got work to do,' he said.

'Give me a few minutes on my own.'

Tremayne walked away, took out a cigarette and lit up. He kept a watch on his sergeant, saw that she was just standing there, not moving, not crying. She reminded him of a porcelain statue. He didn't know why he had made that analogy; he wasn't a man who delved too deeply into the romanticism of a moment, but for some reason, he did that day.

Clare looked over at him. 'I'm fine now. I just had to deal with the rush of emotions. In future, if driving down past Harry's pub is the quickest way, then we drive down there. No more diverting up this road and down that. Clear?'

'And from here on, no more inviting me to watch boring plays. Clear?'

'There's still a murder to deal with,' Clare said.

'We need to interview the others.'

Chapter 4

Tremayne did not like Len Dowling, having met him before. To him, the man was too brash, too pushy, and above all, intent on distorting the truth, telling a vendor their house was worth more than it was, telling a purchaser that it was a bargain.

That was what had happened to him when he had let the man show him a few houses. On the one hand, he was there attempting to convince him that it was a steal, the owner desperate, and with a little bit of TLC he'd clean up financially on this one, and then with the vendor, singing another tune.

Tremayne remembered when he had allowed Dowling to show a young couple around his house in Wilton. The estate agent was priming him to expect an imminent offer, and then Tremayne had overheard him telling the young couple that the owner was desperate to sell: financial difficulties. As far as he was concerned, the man they were going to talk to was guilty of crimes against decency. It was not the ideal situation, Tremayne realised, to harbour prejudices.

'Sorry, busy day,' Dowling said. For a man with so much energy, he did not look healthy. His skin was pallid, his weight was on the heavy side. He wore a suit with a red tie, although even Tremayne had to admit he wore it well, handmade probably, whereas Tremayne was strictly an off-the-rack sort of man.

'We've some questions,' Clare said.

'In my office,' Dowling said.

Inside were the pictures of houses sold, the advertising leaflets on the floor, the awards on his desk. 'Business good?' Tremayne asked.

'Booming market, interest rates are low. It's never been a better time to buy.'

'Or sell?'

'I remember your place. I could get you a good price.'

'We're here to discuss a murder, not my house.'

'Understood. I get wound up sometimes. We never slept last night, Fiona and I.'

'Calpurnia.'

Tremayne knew that Dowling was not a man who would have any trouble sleeping.

'You played Decius Brutus?' Clare said.

'I wanted to play Caesar.'

'Any reason?'

'Fiona was playing his wife. I thought it would be fun, great for the business.'

'Why?'

'I'd ensure an article in the paper. Local estate agent and his wife take leading roles in Shakespeare's *Julius Caesar*.'

'Instead of a local estate agent takes a minor role, while his wife gets the plum female part.'

'You've got it,' Dowling said. Clare thought the man was awful, the same as her DI, judging by the way he looked at the estate agent.

'Caesar died,' Tremayne said.

'In the play.'

'Outside of the play as well.'

'Yes, but that was Mason, not Caesar.'

'Was it? What if someone wanted to make a statement, or they were jealous that they did not get the part?'

'Whoa. Are you accusing me of murder just because I didn't get to play the lead?'

'People murder each other for the strangest of reasons, jealousy is as good as any.'

'It wasn't that important. Granted that Gordon Mason wasn't the most jovial of men, but a part in the local dramatic society's production is hardly a reason to kill him.'

'What would be?'

'He was a good solicitor.'

'Don't tell me that you use him as well.'

Clare could see that Tremayne was baiting the man, attempting to get past his supercilious grin.'

'I've never used him. My brother is a solicitor in Salisbury.'

'What would be a good enough reason to kill Mason?' Tremayne asked.

'Can there be any?'

'You've got your finger on the pulse of what goes on in this city. Any rumours of suspect property transactions, criminal activities?'

'There's always rumours, but nothing specific, and besides, Gordon Mason was a strict Bible-bashing Baptist. He's hardly likely to be the type of person to be involved in anything criminal.'

'Dodgy property transactions, rezoning industrial into residential, may not be illegal, only fraudulent. Are there any such activities?'

'Not that I know of.'

'You'd tell us if you knew?'

'Inspector, I gild the lily, portray myself as Jack the lad, everyone's friend, but basically, I'm a decent person. Mason may have been involved in shady deals, he may have been obstructing some, but I don't know any more than you do. I can't say that I'll miss the man. I didn't know him that well, and maybe I'll get a crack at Caesar next time, but I didn't kill him, and I don't know who did.'

'Thanks. You've answered our questions,' Tremayne said.

'Have I?'

'You gave an honest reply. Murderers invariably defend themselves by effusing excessively about the victim, a great loss to society, loved his wife, loved animals.'

'He'll not be missed much,' Dowling said. 'Now can I get back to what I do best?'

'Of course.'

Tremayne and Clare left Dowling's agency, the man back into ingratiating mode – it's a bargain, we'll get you a good price – with an elderly couple who had walked in the door.

'They'll see through him soon enough,' Tremayne said.

'Will they?' Clare said.

'Not really my concern.'

***

'Yarwood, you can deal with Jimmy Francombe. He'll open up more with you,' Tremayne said.

The two had just had a break, discussed Len Dowling. Both agreed that the man was a typical salesman, but it was hardly a reason to become a murderer.

'Why me?' Clare said.

'You're more his age. He'll clam up with me.'

'What do you mean? He'll see me as a bit of fluff, attempt to chat me up.'

'Yarwood, you know I didn't say that. You're getting touchy. What I meant to say is that he'll see me as an old man, more like a father figure. With you, he'll see you as his age. No doubt he'll fancy you, what young hot-blooded male wouldn't, but that's not the reason.'

'Thanks,' Clare said. 'You know how to compliment people.'

'That wasn't a compliment.'

'It was to me.'

'Anyway, you deal with Francombe.'

Clare found Jimmy Francombe at his school. As it was a murder investigation, she had contacted their administration department, who had pulled him out of his class.

'I've a few questions,' Clare said, once they were sitting in a small office at the school.

'I saw you up at Old Sarum. Did you see me?'

'On the stage and when I took your statement.'

'I'm better than them.'

Clare could see that the young man, who looked older than eighteen, more like twenty-two to twenty-four, had the arrogance of youth, the infallibility of the young, and the raging hormones of an adolescent teenager.

'You played Ligarius?'

'I didn't kill him.'

'Caesar or Gordon Mason.'

'Both.'

'What can you tell me about the death scene?'

'It was as we had rehearsed it. Casca, that's Trevor Winston, he stabbed Caesar first.'

'Do you like Trevor Winston?'

'He's not a bad person; he's gay.'

'Has he tried it on with you?'

'He knows I'd give him a thump if he tried it.'

'Are you violent?'

'Not me. With Trevor, it's a few laughs, make a few gay jokes, but the man likes a drink occasionally. I see him around the city with his gay friends sometimes, that's all.'

'After Casca?'

'Do you know the story?' Francombe asked. Clare could see that he was looking her up and down. She was not much older than him, and with her fresh-faced look and his mature, slightly-lined face, complete with a two-day stubble, they looked as if they could have made a couple, not that she was interested in younger men, or men in general, at the present time. And she resented his piercing eyes. She regretted that she had worn a white blouse that day, see-through if the sun was shining in the right direction.

'Jimmy, do me a favour.'

'What is it?'

'Stop eyeing me up and down. I'm here as a police sergeant investigating a murder.'

'You should have sent the old man.'

'The old man, as you refer to him, is a detective inspector, a very experienced police officer.'

'I'm sorry,' Francombe said,' I'll be on my best behaviour from now on.'

Clare's impression of the youth changed. He seemed to be a pleasant person, even if a little immature. She understood the reluctance of the dramatic society to rely on him for more significant roles.

'According to Peter Freestone, you're a good actor.'

'I know, I know. When I grow up.'

'Something like that. Jimmy, swap seats.'

'Sorry.'

'You've said that already.'

'You're a good sort. Has anyone told you that before?'

'No, you're the first,' Clare said with a smile.

The two of them changed seats. Clare was now in shadow.

'As I was saying, do you know the plot?'

'Yes.'

'After Casca, the other conspirators come forward and start stabbing Caesar. And finally, the 'Et tu, Brute' where Brutus plunges the final dagger in.'

'When you used your dagger, did it feel unusual?'

'Do you mean if it felt as if I was using a real dagger?'

'Yes.'

'It felt the same as we had practised.'

'How many times did you stab?'

'Three, maybe four.'

'You can't be sure?'

'I'm fairly certain it was three, but there's not a lot of room up on the stage with six of us attempting to stab Caesar, and I wasn't counting.'

'Are you certain your knife was retracting?'

'I thought it was. I'm not certain if I'd know.'

'Thank you. I've no further questions for now.'

Francombe stood up. 'My mates are going to ask questions. They saw me come in here with you.'

'Tell them you've set up a hot date for the weekend.'

'Have I?'

'Not a chance.'

'I thought not. I'm sorry about what happened.'

'At Old Sarum?'

'No. Before.'

'Avon Hill?'

'I was friends with Adam Saunders.'

'He didn't deserve to die.'

'Nor did the other man, the one you were keen on.'

'No, I suppose he didn't, but that's life. It's not all a bed of roses.'

'Are you sure the hot date is off?'

'Certain. Thanks for your assistance.'

'I'm going to brag about this, you know that?'

'Brag on, that's all you've got.'

'Holchester was a lucky man.'

'It's in the past.'

'Sorry, I've brought up unpleasant memories.'

'Please leave. You've plenty of bragging to do.'

Jimmy Francombe left. Clare took out a handkerchief and cried. After five minutes, she left, remembering to wave at Jimmy as he bragged to his mates.

***

Clare returned to Bemerton Road. She found Tremayne in his office, in deep thought. 'What's up, guv?' she asked.

'I'm just thinking through what we saw on the stage. Apart from the melee of the actors stabbing Mason, was there anything else?'

'Such as?'

'Is it possible to make any assumptions as to which of the assassins was stabbing harder. I'm assuming that someone with a fake knife is going for effect, not intending to hurt the man.'

'You're right. Even a fake knife would hurt if pushed hard against a body, whereas the murderer would not be concerned.'

'There'd be bruising. Fancy a trip to Pathology. They're conducting the autopsy today. Have you ever seen one?'

'Not me.'

'Come on. It's good experience,' Tremayne said.

Clare was well aware of the procedure, the slicing open of the body, the removal of all the vital organs, the extraction of the brain, the attempt afterwards to make it palatable for the family to see their loved one.

Tremayne and Yarwood found the pathologist in his office, the examination of Gordon Mason completed. Tremayne appeared to be disappointed, Clare was not.

'What do you want to know, Tremayne?' Dr Stuart Collins, the forensic pathologist, asked. Clare had met him before.

'Gordon Mason. Do you have a report?'

'I'm typing it up.'

Clare knew the pathologist to be a precise man, not willing to give much away until the report was complete. Tremayne, she knew, was the opposite: wanting to get on with the investigation, not appreciative of delays.

'We've a few questions,' Tremayne said.

'You'll not go away until I've given you something, will you?'

'You know how it is.'

'With you, Tremayne, I do. What is it?'

Clare could see that the two men had a good relationship.

'The man was stabbed thirty-three times,' Tremayne said.

'Thirty-four,' Collins replied.

'One extra,' Clare said.

'Shakespeare may be rolling over in his grave that someone deviated from the script, but it was thirty-four.'

'How many penetrated the skin?'

'Five. One in the liver, another in a kidney, one a minor wound, and two to the heart.'

'The heart wound's fatal?'

'I'll detail it in my report, but yes, both of the wounds in the heart would have been fatal. The other wounds in the body would have caused severe bleeding, but the man would have been conscious long enough for an ambulance to arrive and administer emergency treatment.'

'After the wounds to the heart, how long would he have lived?'

'He'd have been in shock within a minute, possibly less. He would have died soon after. There's still some final analysis on the heart as to whether it was the left or right ventricle. I'll be more precise in the final report.'

'One other question,' Tremayne said.

'I'm a busy man.'

'We all are.'

'What is it?'

'Can you tell how many times the area around the man's heart was impacted by a dagger, retractable or not.'

'There's slight bruising from the retractable daggers. The man should have been wearing a specially-designed padded vest, but apparently he was wearing a camping jacket under his robe.'

'How many daggers to the heart?'

'Four. Two pierced the skin, two did not. Any more questions?'

'Of the daggers that pierced the heart and the body, can you tell how many there were?'

'We found irregularities in the wounds which would indicate two different blades.'

'Thanks. That agrees with Jim Hughes's analysis.'

***

'You look as though you could do with your roots being dealt with,' Tremayne said outside the pathologist's office.

'Is that a criticism or your way of saying that we should visit Trevor Winston?'

'Just my attempt at humour.'

'A feeble attempt.'

Trevor Winston was not difficult to spot in his hairdressing salon on New Canal Street. At Old Sarum, he had been dressed in a Roman tunic, the same as all the other assassins, but in his shop the man wore bright yellow trousers, a white shirt open almost to the waist. He was welcoming to the two police officers as they came in.

'They're going to arrest me for your hairstyles,' Winston joked with his customers.

In the backroom, Winston apologised. 'Sorry about that. They expect me to be over the top, a younger version of Kenneth Williams. You remember him, I'm sure.'

'I do,' Tremayne said.

'Vaguely,' Clare said.

'Are you? Tremayne asked. 'Gay, that is?'

'If you mean homosexual, then yes, I am. We're not all over the top though. Outside of the salon, you'd not pick me from any other man in the street.'

'Gordon Mason did.'

'The man was a bore. He didn't like anyone who wasn't like him.'

'Baptist, teetotal?'

'Repressed,' Winston said.

'Was he?'

'I'd say so. Gordon was friendly with Peter Freestone and Bill Ford. Both of them had boring professions.'

'An accountant and a funeral director,' Clare said.

'I like Bill Ford,' Winston said. 'He takes himself seriously, the profession I suppose, but he's easy enough to get on with.'

'Peter Freestone?' Tremayne asked.

'He likes to take control, he was the director of this production, but he's okay. At least he'll have a pint with you at the end of the day.'

'What about the other cast members?'

'Jimmy Francombe, he's only young, but he's a good actor. Len Dowling and his wife, Fiona. I don't mind them, although Len is up himself.'

'Up himself?' Tremayne asked.

'Thinks he's better than he is,' Clare said.

'We'd agree with you on that,' Tremayne said.

'Who else?' Winston thought out loud. 'Gary Barker, he's keen. Not much of a conversationalist. And then there's his girlfriend, Cheryl Milledge.'

'What about her?' Clare asked.

'I've known her a few years, the town bike back then.'

'You don't want that explaining, do you, guv?' Clare asked.

'I know what he means.'

'They've both settled down now, but she can drink like a fish. Gary tries to stop her, but he's wasting his time.'

'Tough woman?'

'With Gary. They're both keen on acting.'

'You didn't like Gordon Mason?' Tremayne asked.

'He didn't like me, but I had no real problem with him. We both enjoyed acting, and we could work together. Outside of acting, he'd ignore me in the street.'

'Peter Freestone said that you had regarded acting as a vocation.'

'I would have loved to do it, but I'm not up to the leading man status, and the money's dreadful if you're not on top. I make a lot more here, and I'm content with that.'

'Anyone you would suspect of wanting Gordon Mason dead?'

'He was a gruff man, but dead? I don't think so, but then I didn't know him very well.'

'Anyone who would have?'

'As I said, Peter Freestone and Bill Ford.'

Chapter 5

After the flamboyant Trevor Winston, Bill Ford came as something of a revelation. One had looked like an advert for high-definition television with his vivid colours, the other like a flashback to the days of black and white.

Clare half-expected the man to put on a top hat, as she had seen in English horror movies from the sixties. However, apart from his sombre appearance, he was polite, even if rather direct.

'What can you tell us about the events of last night?' Tremayne asked. The three of them were standing in a back room of the funeral director's premises, where several coffins were lined up ready for use.

'Excuse the surroundings. It's a busy day.'

'Gordon Mason?'

'I've been contracted to deal with him.'

'His body's not been released yet.'

'That's understood,' Ford said. Clare thought he smelt of formaldehyde.

'You took the part of Metellus?' Tremayne asked.

'I was the one pleading with Caesar:

Is there no voice more worthy than my own?
To sound more sweetly in great Caesar's ear
For the repealing of my banish'd brother?

Tremayne did not need another recital. Clare thought it attractive to see a funeral director dressed in black reciting his lines.

'You were there when Gordon Mason was stabbed?'

'I was integral to the scene. I must have stabbed him at least twice.'

'Nobody seems firm on the numbers,' Tremayne said.

'It's always frenetic. There's six of us crowded around Caesar, lunging forward, pulling back, aiming to get out of the way of the others.'

'Is that all?'

'Not really. We're all trying to make it look realistic, attempting not to let the audience see the daggers retracting.'

'Did yours?'

'No question on that.'

'According to our reports, it's not so easy to tell if the dagger is entering the body or not.' Tremayne knew that he had made up the statement to judge the man's response.

'I'm a funeral director. I know what it feels like to insert a knife into sinew and gut. My dagger retracted, I'm sure of it.'

'Is there anyone who may have had a grudge against Gordon Mason?'

'Not me, that's for certain. I knew the man, I acted with him, and I'm going to bury him, but apart from that, there's not a lot I can tell you about him.'

'Did you socialise with him?'

'Mason was not much of a socialiser, neither am I.'

'What do you like to do, Mr Ford?' Tremayne asked.

'I like acting. It gets me away from here. You'd understand if I told you that this job sometimes gets you down.'

'I'd understand,' Tremayne said.

'So would I,' Clare said.

'Apart from acting, what else do you do?'

'I go up to London most weeks. There's always a play on somewhere up there. If I stay here, I only work.'

'Are you married?' Tremayne asked.

'My wife died a few years back.'

'Sorry about that. I was indelicate.'

'Don't worry about it. In our professions, we become only too familiar with the deceased. It's best to maintain a detachment.'

'You never answered my previous question. Is there anyone who may have had a grudge against Mason?'

'I don't think so. We were all united by a love for acting. Apart from that, some socialised with each other, others didn't.'

'Which group did you belong to?'

'A drink of a night after rehearsals, the occasional night out with Freestone and his wife, but apart from that, you'd find me at home.'

'It's not much of a life,' Tremayne said.

'I'm not a gregarious man. The simple pleasures suffice.'
'We're told that Mason did not like Trevor Winston.'
'I can't say that I approve of his behaviour.'
'A religious view?'
'Not at all. It just seems wrong to me. I'd never say that to Winston, though. I get on well enough with him, and I would have thought Winston would have brushed off Mason's occasional jibes.'
'Were there many?'
'Once or twice, but only when Winston messed up his lines.'
'Did he do that often?'
'Not often, but Mason would get annoyed.'
'Would he get annoyed with anyone else if they messed up?'
'No, only with Winston.'

***

Clare, glad to be busy, had found that since the murder at Old Sarum she had slept better. The nights were still restless, but with exhaustion came sleep, and Tremayne, if nothing else, was a determined man.

So far the case had revealed nothing that could indicate a reason for Gordon Mason's murder, no obvious suspect either. The fact that Trevor Winston was gay and Mason did not approve seemed inconsequential.

'What do we know about the murder weapons?' Tremayne asked. It was early in the office, the usual procedure when there was a murder to be solved.

'It would have needed someone with a degree of skill to modify them,' Clare said, not that she had a great deal of knowledge on the subject.

'We've not interviewed all the possible suspects yet.'

'It could still be someone who didn't know that their dagger was more than a toy.'

'According to Hughes, that was unlikely. The pressure of the fake compared to a blade entering a body would have been obvious.'

'To him, it may have been, but Jimmy Francombe said he wouldn't have known.'

'It's a possibility. Does that mean that it could have been someone other than the seven conspirators?'

'It's always possible.'

'If a small metal rod was inserted then that dagger could have become lethal, but how did the person ensure who was going to pick up the correct daggers?' Tremayne asked.

'Does it matter?'

'I think it does.'

'What do you mean?'

'According to Shakespeare, Casca stabs Caesar first, a non-fatal stab in the back, and then Brutus is the final of the assassins.'

'And Brutus only has one stab to the heart.'

'Which means,' Tremayne said, 'that Julius Caesar was not dead when Brutus stabbed him.'

'Does it, guv?'

'Isn't Brutus meant to be separated from Caesar, and Caesar staggers over to his friend after the others have finished and utters the immortal lines? YouTube last night. Marlon Brando as Mark Antony, John Gielgud as Cassius, before you comment.'

'Did Mason stagger over to Peter Freestone at Old Sarum?'

'I'm not sure. I was bored by then,' Tremayne said.

'It may suit your image, guv, but you were enjoying it up there.'

'Don't get ahead of yourself, Yarwood.'

'Anyway, I've no idea,' Clare said. 'I didn't look either.'

'Which means, if he didn't, he could have been dead, held up by the others.'

'You're not accusing all of them of being involved.'

'That's highly unlikely. If Mason's death was the intended result, it's a bit hit and miss.'

'With all that was going on, it was unlikely that the two murderers would have been able to accurately insert their blades in the right places, which means that Mason could have lived.'

'For a while, but he had five wounds.'

'So we can assume that the end result would be death. When he finally collapsed he didn't move again.'

'Which means that someone was certain that he would be dead.'

'Only Freestone had the opportunity to place the blade precisely.'

'It's still speculation, guv.'

'It's good policing, that's what it is.'

'A visit to Freestone?'

'Not yet. Who else have we got to interview?'

'Geoff Pearson, and then Gary Barker and Cheryl Milledge.'

'The town bike.'

'Don't let Superintendent Moulton hear you saying that,' Clare said.

'Why? We're looking for motives here, not Sunday School teachers. If she's got a background, then she's got skeletons.'

'We'll interview Pearson first. He's in Southampton at the university there.'

'Yarwood, you can drive.'

Clare noticed Tremayne pick up his newspaper. 'You'll not get to the races this weekend.'

'That's why you're driving. I need to check the form. I can place my bets online.'

'Bets?'

'Okay, some lose, some win. A man has got to have a hobby. What do you expect me to do, take up stamp collecting?'

'An interesting thought, but you don't look like a stamp collector.'

'I look like your senior, be careful with the lip.'

As they left the office, Clare was glad to be back. She had missed the curmudgeon with his inability to pick a winning horse, his questionable attempts at ironing his shirt with its frayed collar, and his drive to solve a murder.

***

Southampton, the largest city in the area, was only twenty miles away. Clare phoned ahead to ensure that Pearson would be available. Thirty-five minutes after leaving Salisbury, they were seated in the cafeteria at the university.

'I'm studying archaeology and anthropology. It's a three-year course, I'm hopeful of finishing in two.'

'Is there much money in that?' Tremayne asked.

'There's enough. It's a vocation, at least to me. The same as policing, I assume.'

'A lifetime of poverty then.'

'You're probably right,' Pearson said.

'We need to understand what happened,' Clare said. In the daylight, she could see that Pearson was an attractive man in his late twenties. Apart from a scar on his face, she would have described him as handsome. He was also well-dressed.

'Mason could be a tyrant, but I couldn't wish him dead.'

'That's the first time we've heard him called a tyrant,' Tremayne said. He was sipping a cup of tea that Clare had purchased for him. It tasted of cardboard, but Tremayne had thanked her. She was still at the sensitive stage, he could see that, and his acerbic comments were moderated, but her observation about his betting skills had struck a tender spot, the reason he had told her to be careful. Not that he meant it, he knew that, but everyone wanted to offer a comment as to how he was wasting his money, but what did it matter. He didn't throw his money away on trivialities, such as clothing, and he could see that Yarwood spent plenty. Even Geoff Pearson, judging by his clothes and the expensive laptop he had placed on the table, spent more than his fair share, and he was at university, supposedly studying hard with no income.

Betting on the horses, to Tremayne, was his hobby; the fact that he was not very good at it did not change the fact that it kept him occupied when there was no case, a healthy distraction when there was.

'Tyrant may be a little extreme,' Pearson said. 'Did you know the man, when he was alive, that is?'

'I don't remember him. I know Peter Freestone though.'

'It's not surprising you didn't know Gordon Mason. The man was one of life's morose people.'

'What do you mean?' Clare asked.

'A negative personality, the sort of person that after five minutes in their company, you'd end up leaving sadder than when you had first met.'

'Elaborate on that statement,' Tremayne said.

'Okay. The man did not like alcohol, gays, lesbians, anyone not like him.'

'How would you describe him?' Clare asked.

'A killjoy. The type of person you'd not invite to a party.'

'Would he have come?'

'Not to one of mine anyway.'

'Why's that?'

'I'm twenty-six. What sort of parties would you think they are?'

'A lot of alcohol, a lot of sex, a lot of people having a good time,' Tremayne said.

'I'll agree with your first and last analysis, not so sure about the sex,' Pearson replied. He looked over at Clare and smiled.

'Did Mason approve of you?'

'He thought I was brash, a little too sure of myself.'

'Are you?'

'I'm always confident, never let anything get me down. Mason used to get angry in rehearsals. I'd see the positives, he'd be looking for the negatives. I'm a cup half full, he was a cup half empty.'

'His dislike for you, a reason to wish him harm?'

'Not me. I always used to have a laugh at him.'

'To his face?'

'In the pub afterwards with Gary and Cheryl.'

'Gary Barker and Cheryl Milledge?'

'I'm friendly with them.'

'We're told that Gary Barker is not an ambitious person,' Clare said.

'That's true, but I choose my friends based on whether I like them or not. I'm not their judge. If Gary wants to drift that's up to him. Personally, I don't.'

'And Cheryl Milledge?'

'What have you heard?' Pearson asked.

'We're asking the questions,' Tremayne said.

'I've known Cheryl for a few years, a heart of gold. She's a drinker, more than Gary, more than me. She's been around.'

'Been around?' Clare said.

'She had a reputation as being easy when she was younger.'

'Was she?'

'Since she's latched on to Gary, she's changed.'

'For the better?'

'I'd say so. She still drinks too much, and she's got a raucous laugh, but as I've said, a good person. She'd give you the last coin in her pocket if she had to.'

'Does she have money?'

'Enough for a beat-up old car, and a half share of the rent on a bedsit up Devizes Road she shares with Gary.'

'Is that sufficient for her?'

'They don't want much out of life.'

'As compared to you.'

'I want to do archaeology. It's not the way to a fortune unless you can get a programme on television, old ruins of England, that sort of thing.'

'Is that part of your plan?'

'It's in the back of my mind. You need to be pushy, presentable. I think I've got it.'

'You've got plenty of brass, I'll give you that,' Tremayne said. Clare could tell that the DI liked the young man.

'Who would want Gordon Mason dead?' Clare asked.

'I'm not sure. Not many of us liked the man, but he was easy to ignore. Why would anyone want to kill someone else? It makes no sense to me.'

'Gary Barker, Cheryl Milledge?'

'Not a chance. They're harmless, even if a little rough around the edges.'

'Are they?' Tremayne said.

'You know about Cheryl. Gary just goes with the flow. His language can be a bit colourful.'

'Swears a lot?'

'Not when he's sober, but after a few drinks, he will. You've probably seen him around.'

'I don't recollect him.'

'You will, once he's had a few.'

Chapter 6

The last time that Clare had had fish and chips out of a cardboard box was in Bournemouth, not more than a forty-minute drive from Southampton. Then it had been accompanied by a bottle of wine and a wedding proposal from Harry Holchester, but now it was with Tremayne. He had insisted on stopping to eat before they carried on; she would have preferred a sandwich.

She enjoyed being with the man, watching his technique, observing his mannerisms, his foibles. For a man who pretended not to be intellectual, not personable, not caring, he was letting his guard slip, at least with her.

Behind that rough exterior there was a man who cared, an intelligent man who could collate all the evidence they were gathering, all the information about the people they were interviewing, and come up with a reasoned chain of events, a motive, a culprit.

'Come on, Yarwood, the day's young,' Tremayne said. He was out of his chair, his oily chips gone, the fish, if it was indeed fish, gone as well.

Clare took her box with its half-eaten contents and dumped it in the bin at the door. She made a note to not come back to the greasy shop, its disinterested staff behind the counter slapping the fish in batter and then in the boiling oil.

She looked at her watch. It was two in the afternoon.

'We'll find Gary Barker at his work. You've got the number?'

'I'll phone him.'

'Good. You've got the keys,' Tremayne said. It was good that she enjoyed driving, Clare thought. If she was there, she was in the driving seat, while he took the opportunity to catch up on a little shut-eye, the horses, or just to lie back, close his eyes and consider the case.

They found Gary Barker working at a garden centre close to the river in Harnham, a pretty part of the city. Apart from the weather, which was wet, and the mud underfoot where Barker was busy with a spade, it would have been pleasant.

'Sorry, I've got to get the plants in the ground today. If I leave them, they may not take.'

'You know a lot about gardening?' Tremayne asked.

'Green thumb. You're here about Mason?'

'I wouldn't be standing here if it wasn't important.'

'Five minutes, and I'll be with you.'

Ten minutes later, instead of the five, Gary Barker graced them with his presence. The three were sitting in a greenhouse to one side of the office. 'They don't like me slacking,' he said.

'We're here investigating a murder. Surely they'll understand.'

'Not them, a miserable pair.'

'I could square it with them,' Tremayne said.

'They don't hold with acting either, and they positively hate Cheryl.'

'Why are you concerned with what they think?' Clare asked.

'They're my parents, not that I let too many people know that.'

'Why do they hate Cheryl?'

'My parents, old school.'

'What do you mean?'

'Seeing the young lady's here, I'm not sure I want to say.'

'I'm a police officer,' Clare said. 'Say what you need to.'

'I'm the only son, and those two, my parents, have some dated ideas.'

'I'm not sure we understand.'

'Back when they were married, it was one man, one woman, virgin on the wedding night, total fidelity, a glass of wine at Christmas.'

'They must have liked Gordon Mason.'

'He was their sort of man.'

'Was he yours?'

'What do you think? It wasn't as if I hated him. I just ignored him, laughed it off, had a few jokes in the pub at his expense.'

'Your parents part of the joke as well?'

'I don't tell anyone about them unless it's important.'

'It's important now.'

'That's why I'm telling you. Anyway, back to Cheryl. I love the woman.'

'We're aware that she has a chequered past,' Clare said.

'Chequered, that's a good word. Cheryl, God bless her, has had a chequered past: married once, engaged to another, lived with a couple of other men.'

'And your parents disapprove?'

'To them, she's the devil's spawn.'

'To you?' Clare asked.

'We're kindred spirits. I've got a few things that I regret. I deal with the present and Cheryl's with me. What she may have done in the past is none of my concern, and it's certainly not my parents' either.'

'Have they met her?'

'Once. They didn't like her. It ended badly.'

'Are you the only son?'

'That's what they don't like. My father's not well, another few months, no more, and my mother's starting to forget.'

'You'll inherit?'

'Yes. Don't tell anyone if you don't have to. Everyone sees me as a loser, but I'm not. I could make something of this place.'

'And they don't want Cheryl involved?' Clare said.

'They don't want anyone involved, not even me, but with Cheryl, it's venomous.'

'You played Cinna?' Tremayne asked.

'That's where we met, at the dramatic society, Cheryl and me.'

'You're both keen?'

'We love dressing up, and we take it very seriously.'

'Did you have any problems with Gordon Mason?'

'Not me. He'd sometimes go on to Cheryl about her being a fallen woman.'

'How did you take it? How did she?'

'She'd give him the sharp edge of her tongue.'

'And you?'

'He'd not talk to me unless it was necessary.'

'Because of your parents?'

'He got on well enough with them. I know they've tried to stitch me up, negate my inheritance. They took advice from Mason.'

'Were they successful?'

'I keep my eyes peeled. I saw the correspondence.'

'What did you do?'

'I took legal advice.'

'Does Cheryl know about this?'

'Not in detail. She'd be the classic bull in the China shop.'

'And you need a subtle approach?' Clare said.

'They could always run down the garden centre, sell it for a pittance.'

'Would they do that?'

'They're total bastards, so was Mason. The three of them, Bible-bashing hypocrites.'

'It's a motive to kill Mason.'

'That's why I've told you. If you'd found it out from someone else, it would reflect badly on Cheryl and me. I only need to wait a few more months, and this place is mine. We've got great plans for here. Cheryl's a smart woman, she'll look after the administration and the financial; I'll look after the plants.'

'We need to talk to Cheryl,' Clare said.

'Seven this evening, 156 Devizes Road. Is that fine by you?'

'That's fine,' Tremayne said.

***

It was late afternoon before the two police officers left Gary Barker, not long enough to interview anyone else before meeting Barker's girlfriend. Instead, they returned to the police station on Bemerton Road. Superintendent Moulton was in the reception area as they entered. 'Good to see you back, Sergeant Yarwood,' he said.

'Thank you, sir,' Clare replied.

'How's the case going, DI?' Moulton asked.

'We're interviewing the suspects. There are a few that have motives.'

'An arrest soon?'

'We're working on it.'

'Keep up the good work,' Moulton said as he left the building.

'A changed man,' Clare said.

'Another few weeks and he'll be on about my retirement again,' Tremayne said.

'You don't like him much, do you?'

'What gave you that idea?'

'Your curtness with him.'

'Why pretend? He doesn't think much of me, I don't think much of him. You'll learn, Yarwood. You don't need to be friendly to everyone. Do your job, take no nonsense, get results; they're more important.'

'Office politics?'

'If you're Moulton, but you're not. You're shaping up to be a good officer.'

'Shaping up?'

'You're not there yet. Stick with me, and you will be.'

'That's what I intend to do. What do you reckon to those we've interviewed so far?'

The two had settled themselves back in Tremayne's office. The man was leaning back on his chair again, the front two legs off the ground.

'Barker had a reason to dislike the man; I'd say it was sufficient as a motive.'

'Could Barker's solicitor put on a caveat to prevent a sale?' Clare said.

'That seems weak to me. Check it out, see what you can find. If his parents own the business, then how can its sale be stopped? I know there are laws about divesting assets to the children to save on inheritance tax, but that doesn't apply here. It's strange that Gary Barker was so affable, yet, according to him, his parents are total bastards.'

'Maybe they aren't. We need to talk to them.'

'Not today. We've got an appointment.'

'Do you want me to drive?' Clare asked.

'What do you think?'

***

For someone who was hopeful of taking over his parent's garden centre and the house that came with it, Gary Barker and Cheryl Milledge's bedsit did not impress either of the two police officers. The first-floor apartment with a fold-down bed secured to the wall was not a place that Clare warmed to, nor did Tremayne. Clare knew his style of living, having been to his house on a couple of occasions. It was nothing special, he'd admit to that, singularly lacking in any of the touches that convert a house into a home. Cheryl Milledge was a busty individual; Clare could not describe her as beautiful, or even attractive. However, the woman was welcoming on their arrival.

'Take a seat,' she said. Clare looked around in dismay. Every possible space was covered with magazines or old newspapers. 'Here, that'll do,' Cheryl said, as she pushed a pile of papers to one side.

'Sorry about the mess,' Barker said. 'We're normally tidier.' Clare doubted the man.

'You're here about Gordon Mason,' Cheryl said. 'Do you fancy a beer?'

Tremayne certainly did; it had been a long day. 'No, thanks,' he said. Beer and policing did not mix. He'd buy one later at the pub. For now, they had to find out from Cheryl Milledge what she knew.

'You played Brutus's wife?' Clare said.

'Portia.'

'A good part?'

'I'd have preferred Calpurnia, but I'm not married to one of Salisbury's leading estate agents.'

'Is that important?'

'It is with the Salisbury Amateur Dramatic Society.'

'What does Fiona Dowling have that you don't?'

'It's not acting ability. She couldn't act her way out of a paper bag, although she's managed to convince her husband that she's faithful.'

'You shouldn't say that,' Barker said.

'They're the police. They'll find out later, and we'll be suspect if we hold back. That's how it works, isn't it, Detective Inspector?'

'The truth is always best. We will corroborate any information received, careful not to reveal our source.'

'It may be best if you tell us the full story,' Clare said.

'Hang on while I get another beer. Are you sure you don't want one?' Cheryl said.

One minute later she returned, handing her boyfriend a can as well. 'You've met Geoff Pearson?'

'Today, in Southampton.'

'He's a friend of ours, or at least we drink together.'

'What about him?'

'He's screwing Fiona Dowling.'

'He's younger than her,' Clare said.

'Has Pearson told you this?'

'Not him, he's smart. We've teased him a few times after a few beers, but he'll not talk.'

'Then where's your proof?'

'I caught them at it hammer and tongs once.'

'Where?'

'We sometimes meet at the Dowlings' house to rehearse. One time, Len's not there. No idea where he is, but we carried on anyway. Fiona, she put on a spread of food, drinks. I drank more than I should, but I do that all too often. I'm trying to cut back, but you know?'

Clare didn't know, but she did not intend to comment.

'Mason's there casting accusing looks at me, but he's got no right to complain.'

'What does that mean?' Tremayne asked.

'I'll come back to it.'

'Cheryl, it's not right to tell them,' Barker said.

'Wise up, Gary. They're police officers, they'll find this out eventually. I'm just helping them.'

'Carry on, please,' Clare said.

'We've all left, or I thought we all had. I'm outside the house, desperate to go to the toilet. I would have gone on the flowers, but Mason's still hanging around, as is Bill Ford.'

'Peter Freestone, Jimmy Francombe, Phillip Dennison?'

'I don't know about them. If they had been there, I'd have still gone on the flowers. Mason freaked me out. Anyway, I'm there bursting, the front door's still open. I go in and dash for the toilet.

There's one downstairs. I forget to pull the flush. As I'm coming out, still pulling up my jeans, I can hear a sound in the other room. I'm feeling better by this time. There are two people, their voices are low.'

'Who was it?'

'I'm coming to that. I'm careful, and I take off my shoes and creep along the hallway. The door to the dining room is open. There on the floor, Fiona, flat on her back, Geoff Pearson on top of her going for his life.'

'Sexual intercourse?' Clare asked.

'What do you think they were doing, playing monopoly? It was full on, let me tell you.'

'Did they see you?'

'Geoff did.'

'What did he do?'

'He pushed the door shut with one of his feet.'

'Did Fiona Dowling see you?'

'Not a chance. She was in second heaven by then.'

'Afterwards, did he confirm it?'

'He'd only smile if I asked.'

'Are they still involved?'

'We've both seen her looking over at him at rehearsals. They're still into it. Apparently, Len Dowling, the full of himself, hotshot estate agent, is a lousy lover.'

'How do you know that?' Clare asked.

'That's what I've been told,' Cheryl Milledge said. Clare knew where that information had come from, from Cheryl Milledge herself. Clare could see why she had such a dreadful reputation.

'You mentioned Gordon Mason before,' Tremayne reminded the woman.

'We put on a play at a church hall. I forget the production, but there's a kissing scene with Mason and me.'

'You agreed?'

'We're acting. I didn't need to like the man.'

'How about him? Was he comfortable with it?'

'He seemed to be. In rehearsals, we just pretended, held each other, made the motions, no contact.'

'I assume that was not the case when you presented it to the public,' Clare said.

'There's an audience, about eighty people, some children. It's time for our scene. We're there professing our love for each other, sealing it with a kiss. It's a darkened room on the stage. I come over to him, act the part, put my arms around his shoulders, he puts his arms around my waist. That's when it went astray.'

'Overly amorous?' Clare said.

'The man pulls me in close. I can feel the erection, and then he rams his tongue down my throat.'

"What did you do?'

'What could I do? I acted out the scene, quicker than I should have, and pulled away. The audience never realised what was going on.'

'And afterwards?'

'I put my fist into his face once we were backstage. Nothing more was said after that.'

'You could have reported him.'

'What's the point? No one will listen to me, and it wasn't the first time a man has thrust his unwanted affections on to me. And besides, I wanted to continue to act.'

Chapter 7

Phillip Dennison adopted a haughty tone when Tremayne and Clare arrived at his house. It was clear the man was loaded. In the driveway, an Aston Martin.

'Beautiful car,' Tremayne said, in an attempt to break the ice.

'Paid cash for it,' Dennison said. Tremayne sighed, realising that the man liked to flaunt his wealth.

Tremayne had no interest in the Aston Martin, although Clare liked it. Once inside the house, more a mansion, they were ushered into the main room. The walls were lined with oil paintings, a grand piano stood in one corner, its lid raised.

'I like to play it every day,' Dennison said. For a man in his fifties, he had a healthy tan, not the result of an English climate. He was dressed in a pair of beige-coloured trousers and a polo shirt, the type that Harry had liked.

'Gordon Mason?' Tremayne said.

'Tragic, tragic,' Dennison said. Clare could hear the insincerity in his voice.

'You were playing Mark Antony?'

'That's correct.'

'If you don't mind me being blunt,' Tremayne said out of courtesy, not out of concern for the man.

'Not at all.'

'Why were you involved with the local dramatic society? You're obviously wealthy, well connected. Surely you must have better opportunities elsewhere.'

'If you mean, could I afford to sign on for acting classes in London, use my contacts to attend workshops with some of the best actors, then, yes, I could.'

'Why don't you?'

'The Salisbury Amateur Dramatic Society is a diversion from the normal stresses. I go there, enjoy myself, mingle with them, rich and poor. I enjoy it greatly.'

'What do you do for a living?'

'I play the financial markets, very successful actually. Each day, I'll trade on the price of one commodity going up or down against another. Some days, I'll make a small fortune, other days I'll lose it. It's high stress, high reward, high risk. I could ease the stress with alcohol, with a mistress, or with golf. Acting is my outlet, and if it's a local production where I get to stand up on stage and say a few lines, then that's fine by me.'

'I understand,' Clare said.

'I'm sorry about your loss. I truly am.'

'You knew Harry?'

'We went to school together. We stayed in touch on an occasional basis.'

'I'll be fine. Thank you for your concern.'

A woman came breezing into the room; Clare was taken aback by the look of her.

'I'm Samantha,' she said, as she made a beeline for Tremayne, warmly shaking his hand.

You're wasting your time there, the man's got no money, Clare thought.

'Pleased to meet you,' Tremayne replied, sucking in his stomach at the same time.

The woman dressed expensively, her hair was blonde and out of a bottle, her jewellery designed to order from what Clare could tell. She was the sort of woman that men lusted after, and she knew it. 'What's Phillip been up to? Cheating the old ladies out of their savings?' she asked.

'We're investigating the death of Gordon Mason.'

'Oh, him.'

'Did you know him?'

'Phillip dragged me along one night to one of their productions. For the life of me, I can't see why he bothers.'

'It's an outlet for me, you know that.'

Clare could see, she assumed that Tremayne did as well, that the trophy wife and her older husband did not get on. The arrangement was financial, in that he had the money and she wanted it. Apart from that, there was the appearance of love, the reality of disdain.

'Gordon Mason was murdered.'

'Phillip mentioned it.'

'Did it concern you?'

'Why? Should it?'

'The man was a fellow actor of your husband.'

'Acting, is that what you call it? A bunch of locals pretending that they have talent, and as for Mason, the man was a pig.'

Clare could understand her contempt for Mason, in that if he had not liked Winston with his effeminate manner or Cheryl Milledge with her promiscuous past, he was probably not going to like the woman standing in front of them, even if she was exquisite. Clare had to admit she was an attractive woman until she opened her mouth. From there on, it was constant abuse against her husband. She didn't understand why he put up with it, or she with him, but then Clare knew that her family had money, as did Harry, and what she had wanted was love, nothing more. Her parents were cold, Harry was not.

'My wife's not a fan of my nights out. I've asked her to accompany me, but she'll not come.'

'You're right there. I've got better things to do.'

'If you'd excuse us, Mrs Dennison,' Tremayne said, 'we need to talk to your husband alone.'

'I'm off anyway. I'm going to hit the shops again.'

The woman left, jumped into the driver's seat of the Aston Martin and accelerated out of the driveway.

'She's not normally like that,' Dennison said.

'That's fine,' Tremayne said, knowing full well that she was. His wife had been a person who had loved him, showed encouragement, even tolerated his funny ways. He still missed her after all these years of being on his own. He could see that Dennison, for all his wealth, his younger wife, no doubt very physical in keeping the man young in her bed, was not a contented person.

'Did you like Gordon Mason?' Clare asked.

'Honestly, not very much. It doesn't qualify as a motive.'

'We're not accusing you or anyone else at this time. We're just interviewing everyone who was up at Old Sarum. Can we come back to the previous question? Did you like Gordon Mason?'

'I despised him.'

'Yet you acted with him.'

'It was my outlet.'

'From the stresses here?' Clare said.

'It's not only work-related.'

'Your wife? My apologies if it seems as if I'm prying, but we need to know all the facts, no matter how irrelevant they may seem.'

'I'm not sure if my wife is relevant, but yes, there are difficulties.'

'Are you able to elaborate?' Tremayne said.

'I've told you. Some days I'm flush with money, others I'm not. My wife does not moderate her behaviour.'

'She continues to spend,' Clare said.

'Don't judge her for what she is. I knew that when we married, and she knew that I saw her as a reward.'

'Was she?' Tremayne asked.

'At first. Holidays overseas, expensive nights out, but now it doesn't have the same interest. If it weren't for my wife, I'd cash in, take a small place in Salisbury and enjoy myself. It's the ageing process unfortunately. I want a quieter life, she does not.'

'And the dramatic society is part of that quieter life?'

'I know it's only a group of locals having fun, but we enjoy ourselves, and believe me, we put on a good play.'

'We were told that you have a superior bearing, as if you see yourself as better than them.'

'It's not that. I arrive in an Aston Martin, I speak with a refined accent, but I don't aim to put anyone down.'

'Cheryl Milledge for example.'

'Earthy woman, I like her. She's not out to bleed some silly old fool out of his money. She's there with Gary, not the smartest guy, but they seem happy. You've heard the saying "if I only had money". Well, I do, and it's not all it's cracked up to be.'

'Coming back to the night of Gordon Mason's death,' Tremayne said.

'I wasn't involved in the assassination. I wasn't even there.'

'You weren't on the stage.'

'I was around the back, waiting for my cue.'

'Where was Caesar's body when Brutus was addressing the crowd?'

'To one side of the stage.'

'In the play, it is Mark Antony that comes out from the Senate with Caesar's body.'

'That's true. There's a period when the conspirators are outside with Brutus, attempting to justify their actions to the crowd.'

'And you're alone with Caesar's body.'

'In the play, but up at Old Sarum, he's off to one side, lying down with his tunic over his body and face.'

'Did you speak to him when he was lying there?'

'No.'

'Any reason?'

'I act with the man. I don't talk to him.'

'That much animosity?'

'I've told you. I did not like the man.'

'Did he criticise you because of your wife?'

'He called her a tart, selling herself to an old man.'

'How did you take that?'

'What do you think?'

'When was this?'

'The only time I took her to one of our productions. Six months ago.'

'And you still continued to act with him?'

'It was my outlet, and besides, he wasn't far off the mark.'

'That's a damning comment about your wife,' Tremayne said.

'Is it? You're here investigating a murder. There's no point in trying to pretend. My wife is here because I'm rich. I married her because she's young and she made me feel young. There's no pretence on either side of the marriage.'

'Did you kill Mason?' Tremayne asked.

'How? I wasn't one of the assassins.'

***

Of all the key players that night in Old Sarum, only one remained to be interviewed, the notorious Fiona Dowling, if Chery Milledge's statement about the woman and Geoff Pearson was correct. They found her at home.

'I played Calpurnia,' Fiona Dowling said. She was smartly dressed, in her mid to late thirties, and, as could be seen, a woman comfortable with herself.

'We know that Gordon Mason was stabbed thirty-four times.'

'Thirty-three in the play. Act 5, Scene 1: *Never, until Caesar's thirty-three wounds are well avenged, or until I too have been killed by you,*' Fiona Dowling said.

'That's the play. Mason was stabbed thirty-four times at Old Sarum; five of those stabs entered his body.'

'Poor Gordon,' Fiona Dowling said.

'You've expressed concern for the man,' Clare said.

'It's a figure of speech.'

'Did you like him?'

'He was a strange character, almost out of time.'

'What do you mean?'

'His prudish views, his intolerance.'

'Were you like him?'

'Not in my views, but I represented the values he admired.'

'What values were those?' Clare asked.

'Loyal wife, faithful to my husband, good mother.'

Clare wasn't sure what to say next. If it weren't a police investigation, she would have commented on the accusation that she was having an affair with Geoff Pearson, but that wasn't proven yet. If it was, then Cheryl Milledge with her past, Samantha Dennison with her older husband were better people, in that they were honest about what they were.

Fiona Dowling may have looked saintly, but if she was involved with Pearson, her husband oblivious to the fact, then there was intrigue, possible motives for murder.

'Let us go back to that night at Old Sarum,' Tremayne said. The three of them were sitting in the dining room, the room where Fiona Dowling and Geoff Pearson had writhed in passion on the floor. Tremayne could see Clare looking for the spot, nodding his head for her to focus on the woman.

'I was waiting backstage for my cue.'

'Did you see anything suspicious?'

'No. It was fairly dark back there, as you know. We have a backdrop on the stage, and our changing rooms were there and behind some ruins. Apart from that, I just sat and waited.'

'Cheryl Milledge would have liked to play Calpurnia.'

'Cheryl's always pushing for the lead female role.'

'Is there any reason why you were given the role of Caesar's wife?'

'Has Cheryl said anything?'

'Not at all. We're trying to find out the relationships between the actors and Gordon Mason, that's all.'

'Cheryl may tell you different, but I'm a better actor than her. The fact that Len sponsors our productions is not important. Peter Freestone would not allow the production to be affected due to nepotism.'

'Ancient Rome was full of nepotism,' Clare said.

'Maybe it was, but we aren't.'

'Tell us about the other actors and your relationship with them.'

'Is this relevant? I've got to pick up the children from school. I wasn't on the stage, I didn't thrust a dagger into Gordon. What else is there?'

'You were backstage with the daggers.'

'So were Cheryl and Phillip Dennison.'

'Did they touch the daggers at any time?'

'Not that I saw. They were in a box, anyone could have touched them. We used the daggers in rehearsals. They were fakes, okay for spreading butter, not for killing someone.'

'Were they?'

'At rehearsals they were. I ran my finger along the blade of one.'

'Blunt?'

'It would open a letter, I suppose, but nothing more.'

'And how long ago was that?'

'Our last full-dress rehearsal. Two days before Old Sarum.'

'The other actors?' Tremayne said.

'Peter Freestone likes to take charge. Cheryl Milledge, competent, keen, well known around Salisbury.'

'Well known?' Clare said.

'We were in the same class at school. We were both a bit free with it back then, but I settled down, Cheryl discovered alcohol.'

'Free?' Clare said.

'Men, really boys back then. I met Len, decided he was the man for me. Cheryl continued playing the field, still is, or at least she was until she met Gary.'

'Faithful to him?'

'I've no idea. She's got no money, neither has Gary, although that never meant much to her.'

'And it did to you?'

'When I met Len, he had nothing, the son of a postman. We made the business together.'

'The others?' Tremayne said.

'Trevor Winston, good hairdresser. I go there myself. He's gay, but that doesn't concern me. Bill Ford, decent. Jimmy Francombe, full of hormones, always eyeing Cheryl and me.'

'Visually undressing you,' Clare said.

'He's given you the treatment?'

'Yes.'

'Phillip Dennison?'

'Bitch of a wife.'

'You've met her?'

'He brought her along once. She bothered Gordon, but I took no notice. I've seen her type before, a tart trying to sell herself off as something better. Take off the war paint and she'd be nothing special.'

'Does her husband know this?'

'He should after Gordon insulted her. I thought the two men were going to come to blows. If Phillip loses his money, she'll be off soon enough.'

'Gary Barker?'

'He's keen on Cheryl. She seems keen on him. They're a matched pair. Whether it will last is anyone's guess.'

'Cheryl's had a few relationships,' Clare said.

'A few, that's as good a way of saying it.'

'Many?' Tremayne said.

'We go back a long way, Cheryl and me.'

'Geoff Pearson?'

Clare looked for a reaction, couldn't see any.

'Smart man, he'll go far. He's charismatic, good with the ladies. No doubt he's got plenty of girlfriends, although he's never brought any along.'

'Your husband?'

'Len, you know. Brash, ambitious, hard-working, good provider. What else is there to say about him.'

'He's full on,' Tremayne said.

'I know he can rub people up the wrong way, but we're close.'

Chapter 8

It was dark by the time Tremayne and Clare arrived back at Bemerton Road Police Station. The two of them had eaten at a Chinese restaurant in Fisherton Street on the way there. For the first time, Clare realised, she had not thought of Harry all day. The preoccupation with the murder enquiry was doing her good.

Back in the office, the two of them drank cups of tea, Clare having made them, regardless of Tremayne's earlier comment that he had only missed her tea making when she had been away for several months.

'What do you think, guv?' Clare asked.

'There's plenty of motives, but are any strong enough to stand up?'

'Not really. There's plenty of petty politics, a few that don't like the others, but it's hardly enough for murder.'

'Don't believe it, Yarwood. People kill for less.'

'Fiona Dowling?'

'Strange, she's the one I trust the least, especially if Cheryl Milledge's story is correct.'

'Any way to prove it?'

'Jim Hughes could check the rug on the floor.'

'Get real, guv. If those two were on it, there's hardly likely to be any proof now.'

'We've focussed on seven assassins, two murderers.'

'They were the only ones who stabbed the man.'

'Were they? Mason's lying on the floor. Is it possible someone else came up and stabbed him again, dealt the fatal blow.'

'It doesn't make sense. Why would the man be lying there if he wasn't dead already?'

'Then why didn't anyone investigate? It couldn't have been comfortable with his face covered.'

'Maybe they did, saw he was dead and left him.'

'If he wasn't dead, then who else could have stabbed him?'

'Mark Antony.'

'Phillip Dennison?'

'He had the motive to want the man dead.'

'The daggers all had blood on them, and Mason had been stabbed with a sharp blade on the stage. If it's Dennison, then his was not the first fatal blow. That would have had to have been one of the assassin's blades.'

'It's plausible, I suppose, but you'll need a better motive than Mason insulted Dennison's wife.'

'The lovely Samantha.'

'Did you think that?' Clare said.

'What do you think, Yarwood?'

'You'd prefer Cheryl Milledge.'

'At least she'll drink a pint of beer with me.'

'If you're paying, you'll need to improve your win rate on the horses.'

'Insults aside, Cheryl Milledge, apart from her atrocious housekeeping, was the only one who opened up with us.'

'I think Samantha Dennison did.'

'How?'

'The way she treated her husband. She knows she's controlling him, and she's taking advantage. She didn't pretend to be anything other than what she is.'

'A gold digger?'

'Mason was more direct, but that's what she is.'

'What's her history? We should check her out.'

'Is she relevant?'

'It's possible. Did Mason have any money? Was he insulting her as a diversion?'

'You're stretching it there.'

'We're clutching at straws, and you know it. We know there are two daggers, five wounds. Do we know which dagger entered where and how many times?'

'We've not asked.'

'It's important. We need to know whether he died on that stage, and if there were any wounds inflicted afterwards.'

***

The dramatic society's performance for the following night at Old Sarum had been cancelled. Peter Freestone had called all the main suspects to his office to discuss what had happened, and what their future held.

'I'd like to express my sorrow at the death of a fellow thespian,' Freestone said.

'We should dedicate our next production to him,' Bill Ford said.

Cheryl Milledge said little. It was eight o'clock in the evening, and she and Gary had had their fair share of alcohol by that time.

'You're a drunk, Cheryl,' Fiona Dowling said. The extraordinary meeting was not going well, Freestone could see that plainly enough.

'Fiona, Cheryl, all of us,' Freestone said, 'the situation is more serious than you believe. We've all been visited by Detective Inspector Tremayne and Detective Sergeant Yarwood. We're all aware of their investigation into how Gordon was killed, and by whom.'

'They're saying that two of us are murderers,' Jimmy Francombe said.

'They have scientific proof to make that statement.'

'Well, I didn't kill him.'

'Jimmy, if you could suppress your boyish enthusiasm for a minute, we need to discuss what we know, and how to proceed.'

Francombe sat still, fuming and glaring over at Freestone.

'Freestone's right,' Bill Ford said. 'If one or two of us are murderers, and I can't believe that, how do we continue?'

'A murder mystery night, is that what you are suggesting?' Phillip Dennison said.

'I'm good at those,' Gary Barker said, temporarily reviving from his alcohol-fuelled stupor.

'I don't think so,' Freestone said. 'The police will do the investigating. We just need to coordinate our approach to them, if that's possible.'

'How? They have forensic and pathology evidence. We'll not be able to outthink them and why should we? Fiona and I have done nothing wrong,' Len Dowling said.

The two Dowlings were sitting close to each other, Geoff Pearson was on the other side of the room. Cheryl Milledge looked across between the three of them, looking for the tell-tale signs of recognition; she couldn't see any, but then she knew the woman from their schooldays, knew her to have been the more promiscuous back then.

'The police said that two of the daggers entered Gordon's body,' Freestone said. 'I only stabbed him the one time, and my knife retracted.'

'How do you know? You had the clearest target,' Len Dowling said. 'And it wasn't me.'

'I'll vouch for my husband,' Fiona Dowling said.

'How can you do that, Fiona?' Gary Barker said.

'I know my husband better than you.'

'And how well does your husband know you?' Cheryl said.

The atmosphere was electric. Everyone knew that within that office were two men who had committed murder. Freestone realised that convening the meeting had been a mistake.

'Maybe none of us killed him,' Pearson said. Fiona looked at him, so did Cheryl.

'How?' Ford said. For once he was not dressed in black, but casual in a pair of jeans and an open-necked shirt.

'Could anyone else have stabbed him before or after?'

'I thought you were smart,' Freestone said. 'That sounds crazy. The man collapses on the ground. Mark Antony comes in, and he's placed on the stretcher. He was dead then.'

'Was he? What if he was only unconscious? Those daggers can hurt, even the fake ones.'

'What are you trying to do? Make out that it was an innocent mistake.'

'Hold on, Freestone. You're getting carried away here,' Dennison said. 'Don't forget that a man died.'

'You despised the man, the same as Trevor did, don't deny it.'

'I didn't despise him,' Trevor Winston said. 'I've had a lifetime of abuse. One bitter old man wasn't going to affect me. I just used to laugh it off.'

'Rubbish, the man used to utter derisory comments in your direction,' Fiona said. 'I used to see the expression on your face.'

'I'm not saying that I liked it, but I had no intention of killing him. If I'd killed everyone who's baited me, beaten me up for what I am, then there'd be a lot of dead bodies, and besides, killing the man because he's a bigot doesn't make sense. Look at Len, look at Mason. One's an estate agent, the other's a solicitor, and you, Peter Freestone, are a councillor here in Salisbury. A dodgy deal, cheating someone out of their property, would make more sense, and then there's Phillip with an expensive lifestyle, an expensive wife. If there was a financial gain, Phillip, would you consider killing him?'

'You little bastard,' Dennison said as he lurched towards Winston.

'Hold back,' Bill Ford said as he grabbed hold of Dennison, Barker grabbing hold of Winston.

'I'm with Freestone,' Ford said. 'We need to be united. Our animosities and prejudices will not help here. Whatever the outcome, two of us wanted the man dead, maybe more, but two that we know of.'

'My apologies to Dennison,' Trevor Winston said'

'Accepted. I understand the tension here,' Dennison replied, although he did not look as if he meant it.

'Ladies, gentlemen, this is getting us nowhere,' Freestone said, attempting to bring the group to order.

'Will you let me speak?' Fiona Dowling said.

'Carry on,' Freestone replied. The man was exasperated, and he had taken his seat, leaning back in dismay. 'I tried,' he said.

'You were right to bring us here tonight,' Fiona said. 'Our lives are in turmoil because of what has happened. Let us not pretend that we liked the man. He had his faults, the same as all of us, so let's not dwell on his unless it's relevant. The police will not give in until they've found whoever was responsible. It's clearly not an accident, in that the daggers had been tampered with.'

'What are you trying to achieve?' Cheryl asked.

'In this room are two people who are capable of violence. We are a disparate group, and whereas some of us will distort the truth if it is to our benefit, the majority of us would not consider murder.'

'What are you getting at?' Len, Fiona's husband, asked.

'Gordon was a good solicitor. He understood the law better than anyone else in this room.'

'Are you suggesting he may have been crooked?' Dennison said.

'What are the options? One, he has dirt on somebody, or two, they have the dirt on him.'

'There are two people.'

'Agreed, but let us consider the possibilities first. Gordon was blackmailing, or he was being blackmailed. That's two options.'

'And the others?'

'He knew something that other people did not want to be revealed. Or he was about to do something that would have been injurious to others.'

'Such as?'

'I don't know. I'm only putting forward theories. Two people in this room know the answer, but which two? Is anyone willing to stand up and tell us why they're innocent?'

'Don't look at me. I'm still at school,' Jimmy Francombe said.

'Any inappropriate gestures from Gordon?' Dennison asked.

'If he had tried anything, I'd have hit him.'

'I did once,' Cheryl said.

'Do you want to elaborate?' Fiona asked. She knew the story. She just wanted her former school friend to feel the heat.

'Last year when we put on that modern play, the one we'd all rather forget.'

'The one where two of us forgot our lines, and the backdrop fell down.'

'Don't mention the name.'

'I won't. Is that when you hit him?' Fiona asked. She was enjoying Cheryl's squirming. After the heated exchanges of five minutes before, she was feeling relaxed again. She had seen Cheryl looking at her, looking at Geoff. Fiona was sure she couldn't know, as they'd always been careful, and Len had no idea. Poor Len, the man of action, barely able to perform in bed, yet always attempting to soothe the men, charm their wives, into parting with their hard-earned cash for an overpriced renovator's delight, most times succeeding.

'The kissing scene, where we had a passionate embrace.'

Everyone in the room was quiet, even Jimmy Francombe, hoping for some titillation, something to tell his friends.

'What happened?' Fiona egged Cheryl on.

'We're meant to lock lips, but he's there forcing his tongue down my throat, pushing his groin into me.'

'What did you do?' Freestone asked.

'I would have kneed him in the groin if it wasn't on stage. Instead, I hurried the scene. Later backstage, I confronted him.'

'What did he say?'

'There wasn't much he could say with my fist in his mouth.'

'Why didn't you tell us?'

'He's not the first man that's tried it on. I dealt with him in the only language that he understood.'

'Did he try it again?'

'Not him. Others have fancied their chances.'

'Who?' Fiona asked.

'It's not important unless they want to be bent over grabbing their balls the next time.'

'I had no issue with the man,' Pearson said. 'He was polite with me, acted his part. We were always civil, but we had nothing in common.'

'Apart from a love of ancient monuments,' Dennison said.

'Are you referring to that monstrosity of a house that he lived in?'

'What style is it?'

'I agree it's a grim looking place, overgrown, almost Gothic, but it's only seventy years old. My interest goes back further than that. Medieval and earlier is what I'm interested in.'

'You could still have killed him.'

'What for? I'm at university, my life before me. I don't want to spend time in prison for the murder of a bigot.'

'Is that how you see him?' Fiona said.

'What do you want us to say? Do you want us to defend him? Who liked him? Is there anyone willing to put up their hand and say that?'

'You've made your point,' Freestone said. The atmosphere in the room was improved. Dennison looked as if he was ready to leave, Gary and Cheryl looked as though they needed another drink, and Fiona was looking at Pearson. Len Dowling was surveying the room, focussing on his wife and Pearson. He said nothing.

'I suggest that we cancel next week's meeting,' Freestone said.

'I'll second that. We'll not be able to work together until whoever killed Mason is arrested. Whatever happens, we'll be short of a couple of actors,' Ford said.

Nobody said anything, apart from a shaking of the heads, a denial of involvement.

Chapter 9

Clare never enjoyed the visits to Pathology, and there she was, twice in the one week.

'Tremayne, I thought I'd seen the last of you,' Collins, the pathologist, said.

'I couldn't keep away. We need five minutes of your time,' Tremayne said.

'Which means ten. Carry on, what do you want to know?'

'Is it possible that Gordon Mason did not die on the stage?'

'It's possible, but he had been knifed five times, two of the wounds were fatal.'

'I'll accept that, but is it possible that one or two of the wounds could have been inflicted at the time the body was not visible.'

'After the assassination and when Mark Antony comes out from the Senate with the body?'

'That's it.'

'It's possible, I suppose. It's not a situation I've considered.'

'But it's still possible.'

'I'd be willing to consider it, although I have difficulty with all of the wounds being inflicted off the stage.'

'That's not what concerns me.'

'What then?'

'We've seven assassins, as well as Mark Antony. I just want to know if Mark Antony, or at least the actor, could have stabbed Mason as well.'

'Anyone could have if it was out of sight.'

'Even a woman?'

'Why not? Do you have any suspects?'

'There are others that I would consider.'

'What about the stretcher bearers, the crowd outside, the servants?'

'They changed their clothes, depending on their part. We're working with the ten, possibly eleven.'

'It's not possible to give you an exact time of death, other than within a one-hour period. That will allow the stabbing to have occurred on the stage, or behind the scenes. Whatever happened, he would have been dead when he was brought out for Mark Antony's denouncement of Brutus.'

'Any reason?'

'Yet again, it seems illogical. The man was stabbed on the stage; he's in agony and dying, and you expect him to remain motionless for another thirty to sixty minutes. It just doesn't make sense, that's all. I'll still hold to my opinion that he died on that stage and that neither Mark Antony nor Calpurnia and Portia were involved.'

'I'll still keep my options open. One more thing, you've been able to ascertain that two different blades were used.'

'Yes.'

'How?'

'Imperfections in the blades.'

'The two blades in the heart, were they different or the one dagger?'

'Two. I believe I've told you this before.'

'I just needed to double-check.'

'Mark Antony, sorry, Phillip Dennison, could be one of those involved or totally innocent,' Clare said.

'We need to check him further. Maybe we can dismiss some of the others, the young man for instance.'

'Why?'

'Where's the motive?' Tremayne said.

'I can't see it at this point in time, but murdering someone just because they called you young or gay or drunk hardly seems to be a reason.'

'It may do to the person being called it. We don't know the mental state of these people. They're an unusual bunch, that's for sure.'

'You're getting the hang of it now, Yarwood.'

'Are you putting me on the spot, testing me out?'

'Not totally. I'm throwing up ideas, seeing where they fall. We can't cover everyone with the same intensity, we need to prioritise, and we need a damn good motive.'

'We'll not find it here in Dr Collins' office,' Clare said.

'Thank you, Sergeant. Please take Tremayne out of here and let me get on with my work.'

***

Tremayne, a perceptive man, able to separate the circumstantial from the relevant, had to admit confusion as to who the murderer was. There were plenty of reasons to dislike Gordon Mason, none sufficient to kill him. 'Yarwood, what's your take on this?' he asked.

'Why kill the man? He's the sort of person that you meet from time to time but learn to ignore. If all the negatives against him are correct, it only shows the man to be a bigoted misogynist,' Clare said.

'Misogynist? Do you think he was?'

'If what Cheryl Milledge said is true, his attempting to take advantage on a stage in front of an audience, then I'd say he was.'

'You're sure that he wasn't a closet deviant, and she represented an object of lust.'

'Trevor Winston called him repressed. Maybe Mason was unable to make it with a woman and was relegated to prostitutes.'

'There's no record of her selling herself,' Tremayne said.

'I'm aware of that.'

'And we know that Fiona Dowling is probably no better.'

'But she's married, refined. Considering the two women went to school together, it's hard to see two more dissimilar women.'

'It still doesn't solve the reason why Mason was murdered, and it needed two people or one person and two daggers.'

'Or if he visited prostitutes.'

'It's possible he didn't, and if he did, he'd want to keep it secret.'

'Someone was blackmailing him?'

'If they were, it would be him killing them, not the other way around,' Tremayne said. 'We need to find out the truth about Pearson and the lovely Fiona Dowling.'

'Is that how you see her?'

'Not really. I prefer Cheryl Milledge. Earthy, that's what Dennison called her, an apt description. She's an open book. What you see is what you get, no airs and graces,' Tremayne said.

'You wouldn't want her cleaning your house.'

'I can do that badly enough without her assistance, thank you very much. If I gave you half a chance, Yarwood, you'd be there making me run around with a mop and a bucket of water.'

'You're right there, guv.'

'Not a chance. Let's go and find out about this affair.'

'Southampton?'

'No. Let's make Fiona Dowling sweat.'

'It's probably the only motive so far that's strong enough to justify murder.'

'It's good enough, that's for sure.'

***

As assumed, Fiona Dowling was busy, ready to go out. To Clare, it seemed that the woman always wanted to portray activity and importance. Clare was sure that she was addicted to the smartphone she clutched in her hand, its gold case clearly visible.

'I can't give you long. I'm meeting up with some friends. We're organising a charity drive for the school.'

'Are you involved with lots of worthwhile causes, Mrs Dowling?' Tremayne asked. Clare could see that the man was not going to let her get out of giving him a straight answer.

'I see it as my civic duty.'

'Don't you help your husband with his business?'

'I've done my fair share. We set it up together, not a penny between us. I've told you that.'

'Commendable, I'm sure,' Tremayne said. 'I suggest you cancel your meeting. Some questions need answering.'

'Why me?'

'You were at Old Sarum, you saw the man stabbed.'

'I was around the back. I didn't see it. I heard it, that's all.'

'We have one important question for which we need an answer.'

'Give me two minutes. I'll delay my meeting for an hour.' Fiona Dowling took out her phone and made several phone calls. 'One hour, is that sufficient?'

'It should be,' Clare said.

'What do you want to know?'

'We don't have a reason for the man's murder. We're certain that two people are responsible. There may be some conjecture there, but at least one person wanted him dead,' Tremayne said.

'Why on a stage?'

'The sense of the theatrical?' Clare said. She realised that it was a valid point that the woman had raised.

'Sergeant Yarwood is probably right. The ultimate accolade – to commit murder in front of a live audience,' Tremayne said.

'But no one knows who it was,' Fiona Dowling said.

'That's as maybe, so why do it if there is no acknowledgement? Do actors suffer from self-doubt, the inability to believe in themselves, the need to convince themselves that they are the best, even if others don't think so?'

'You don't know actors, Detective Inspector. They're full of self-doubt and neuroses. Gordon Mason barely said two civil words off stage, but up there, he's extrovert, pawing the females, projecting his voice.'

'Pawing?'

'Yes. He tried it with me, but I made it clear enough that if he got too close, I'd scream blue murder and have him up in front of the local magistrate. And yes, I know about Cheryl and Mason.'

'What do you mean?' Clare asked.

'On the stage when he became excited.'

'Outside of there?'

'I wouldn't put it past her. She'd be game for anything.'

'That's a damning indictment.'

'I've nothing against the woman personally. We were the best of friends once, but now we have little in common.'

'Is she an intelligent woman?'

'Cheryl, very. She was certainly smarter than me, but she didn't have the drive. It's not the best who make it, it's the most determined. You must know that.'

'I'm determined to crack this case wide open,' Tremayne said.

'What is it you want to know?'

'We are led to believe that you are having an affair with Geoff Pearson,' Clare said.

'What, are you joking? Who made such a scurrilous statement? I'll take legal action.'

Clare could see that the woman was taken aback. Her protestations were a clear sign of guilt.

'We have a strong belief that this is correct,' Tremayne said.

'It can't be. I'm faithful to my husband, a good mother.'

'We're not here to judge, and this is confidential if it does not pertain to the murder enquiry.'

'My position? What if people find out about this lie?'

'If it's a lie, what does it matter?'

'You know it matters. The people I associate with thrive on gossip.'

'You do as well, would that be correct, Mrs Dowling?' Clare said.

'I suppose so. It's harmless.'

'You also had a past in your youth that you'd prefer no one to know about.'

'I admitted that to you before. I was young and into one-night stands, but that was a long time ago.'

'Would your friends understand, your committees?'

'Most of them have a past. That wouldn't be an issue.'

'But an affair would?' Tremayne said.

'An affair, yes. Some of them would shun me, tell Len. My life would be hell.'

'Is it true? We will find out.'

'Who told you?'

'Does it matter?'

'Was it Geoff?'

'Our source does not matter. The truth is important.'

Fiona Dowling sat down and closed her eyes. Clare could see that the woman who had portrayed herself as one of the doyennes of the social set was in turmoil.

'Sometimes, I feel the need. You don't understand how hard it is pretending all the time, always making sure that I'm dressed correctly, the hair and the makeup are perfect.'

'Then why do you do it?' Clare asked.

'Why, you ask me why I put up with some of those stuck-up bitches on their church committees? I'll tell you why. Because I can. I grew up with Cheryl, spoke like her, screwed around like her, but I wanted more. I fought for what I have, dragged Len along

343

with me. And, believe me, back then he was a whimpering fool, ambitious but clueless. I made him what he is today.'

'Why the affair?'

'You don't understand, do you?'

'Not really,' Clare said.

'You're still young and pretty. I'm getting old. I need to be loved.'

'You have a husband.'

'He's getting old as well. I need more. I need a young man, virile and strong. I need Geoff Pearson. Is that enough for you?'

'That's fine,' Clare said. 'We'll leave you alone now.'

'Are you satisfied?' Fiona Dowling asked.

'Satisfied? We're police officers, not arbiters of morality. We deal in facts only. Unless it is vital, what you have told us here today will remain confidential.'

'I hope it does. You don't know how it feels to get old, to not turn a man's head.'

Outside the house, Tremayne turned to Clare. 'That woman has got enough neuroses for all of the Salisbury Amateur Dramatic Society.'

'And some. She's not much older than me.'

'She's a woman who could hate.'

'Murder?'

'She'd be capable if it was to protect her perfect life.'

'Do you call that perfect?'

'Give me Cheryl Milledge any time. At least she's good for a pint and a laugh. With Fiona Dowling, I'd be forever treading on eggshells.'

'Len Dowling must know what he's got. He can't be that naïve.'

'We'll need to interview him again. We'll not bring up the affair, of course.'

'It's bound to come out sometime.'

'It may have already. I wouldn't have thought that Cheryl, for all her good points, is the sort of person to keep a secret indefinitely.'

'A motive for murder?'

'Without a doubt. The woman would murder to keep it quiet.'

'Or Gordon Mason may have found out about it, threatened her.'

'Money?'

'Not money. The man was desperate. He would have enjoyed forcing Fiona Dowling to have sex with him to protect her secret, the ultimate misogynist's degradation.'

'What happened to a good old husband beats wife, wife kills husband murder?' Clare said.

'You'd be bored within a day. This case has legs. We just need to wind up the suspects.'

'All ten?'

'All of them. Who's next?' Tremayne said.

Clare could see why Tremayne liked Cheryl Milledge, they were both open books. What you see is what you get.

Chapter 10

Tremayne and Clare waited outside the Dowlings' house for twenty minutes. Fiona Dowling came out of the front door, slamming it shut. She then opened the driver's seat of her Range Rover and drove off.

'The woman doesn't give up, does she?' Tremayne said.

'She's even fixed her makeup. She intends to continue relentlessly, no matter what was just said,' Clare said.

'I always thought that Len Dowling was the driven one, but apparently it's her.'

'It could be both. She's not the sort of woman to give credit to others.'

'It's strange that everyone is willing to offer a comment about Cheryl Milledge, yet it's her friend who is much worse.'

'How do we find out if Mason was pressuring her?'

'Bank account records.'

'The woman doesn't look short of cash, judging by the house and the car.'

'Can an estate agency make that much?'

'It probably does well enough, but they may have investments.'

'Dodgy deals?'

'Some of those. We can ask Fraud to check out Dowling.'

'What's for us?'

'Samantha Dennison,' Clare said.

'Why her?'

'She's a mercenary woman and a hater.'

'She's not the murderer.'

'She'd know the dirt, especially if her husband had told her. I doubt if she's discreet either. She can fill us in on the background of the others. It may help.'

'You know the address.'

'I'm driving, is that it?'

'Yarwood, you'll make a great detective inspector. I can see the sixth sense there.'

'Just because I figured out that you're too lazy to drive.'

'That's it, and besides, I need to check the form for tomorrow.'

'You mean which horse should win, and the day after, why it lost.'

'Just drive, no potholes either.'

'Yes, Detective Inspector.'

Samantha Dennison was at home when they arrived. Clare had taken the precaution to phone ahead.

'Where's your husband?' Clare asked once they were inside the house.

'He's got a place at the end of the garden; his den, as he calls it.'

'What does he do there?'

'That's where he conducts his business. Unless it's vital, I'm not allowed there.'

'Harsh,' Tremayne said.

'It doesn't concern me. Let him have his little secrets if that's what he wants.'

'Mrs Dennison, we need to know about your secrets.'

'Why? I wasn't there when that man died.'

'We're aware that you're not involved. It's just that you were there once, your husband had a run-in with Mason, and you've probably got a good eye for people.'

'If you mean I'm nosy?'

'Not at all. You're an impartial observer. Everyone we've interviewed so far could have a vested interest, could even be the murderer.'

'Including Phillip?'

'It's possible,' Tremayne said.

'What do you want to know?'

'The one time you went to one of their productions. What can you tell us?'

'It was a rehearsal. It was Phillip, he was keen to show me what he got up to, or to convince me that he wasn't playing up with one of the women.'

'Was that likely?'

'You've seen me, you've seen Phillip.'

'What are you getting at?'

'I'm not under any illusions, are you?'

'He's an older man,' Clare said.

'As you're the police and you can check me out, it's better if I tell you. Phillip plays the financial markets in a big way. The man has an ego that allows him to take risks. I have to admire him for that. That ego needs feeding.'

'And?'

'I'm part of the ego. Don't get me wrong. I know what I am, what other people see me as, especially that Mason. He looked me up and down, had me stripped naked there in front of his beady eyes, trying to look down my cleavage.'

'You must have come across that before. You're not a shrinking violet,' Clare said.

'I don't make a pretence. I set out to snare Phillip, I don't intend to let him go.'

'And the women at the dramatic society?'

'There was one, a bit rough around the edges. I didn't mind her nor her layabout boyfriend. The man in charge, what was his name?'

'Peter Freestone,' Clare said.

'Yes, that's him. He was polite, as was the funeral director, although he wasn't a cheerful person, the job I suppose, looking at dead bodies every day. The young kid fancied his chances, and Trevor Winston, he's a good hairdresser and certainly not interested in me. He would have fancied the young kid, given half a chance.'

'Jimmy Francombe's not homosexual,' Clare said.

'He's tried to chat you up?'

'He's tried.'

'He's got plenty of nerve, I'll give him that. I couldn't get rid of him.'

'Was that an issue?' Tremayne asked.

'Not really. The boy was harmless, and he behaved himself, not like some others.'

'Mason?'

'He sees me walk in the door, pretending to turn up his nose, made some disparaging comments about me to the others.'

'What sorts of comments?'

'I couldn't hear, but I can tell you what they were: old man's fancy, gold digger, tart, hawking herself for an old man's money. I've heard it all before.'

'Does it upset you?'

'Sometimes. It's not all true. I'm fond of Phillip, the same he is of me. He's a few years older than me and lonely, I was poor and attractive. Please, that's not false modesty. I'm honest as to what I am, how men see me, especially men like Phillip who've spent a lifetime chasing money, failing to settle down, bring up a family. I'm the substitute reward, although what he really wants is to relive his life, the same as everyone else, but it's too late for him.'

'Too late for you?' Clare asked.

'I'm not wired that way. I'm not into domesticity and children. If it's not Phillip, I'll find someone else, until I'm old and no longer desirable.'

'And then?'

'Retire to a convent,' Samantha Dennison said.

'Would you?' Tremayne asked.

'Not likely. I've got a small house in the Caribbean. I'll move there and surround myself with animals, the eccentric old woman in the house up the end of the road.'

'What were you doing before you met your husband?'

'I was working in an office, being ogled by the manager, pawed by the office boy if he got half a chance, squeezing me against the photocopier. One day, Phillip comes in, we get talking. Three months later we were married on a beach in Antigua.'

'You've been honest with us,' Tremayne said.

'I've no reason not to be. I've done nothing wrong. I've made Phillip happy; he's made me happy. Is there anything else in life?'

Clare wanted to say the unconditional love between two people but decided not to.

'What can you tell us about Geoff Pearson. You've met him, I suppose.'

'The university student?'

'That's him,' Clare said.

'He was polite, but he wasn't interested in me.'

'Why not?'

'He's screwing the estate agent's wife. Sorry about the language, but that's the truth.'

'How do you know this?'

'I've got two eyes. I could see them making sure to avoid eye contact, and in the rehearsal, when he has to hold her, he's not holding her tight, pretending to be impassive.'

'Did anyone see this?'

'If they did, they never mentioned it.'

'You deduced that they were involved purely by observation.'

'I was the impartial observer. I picked it up straight away.'

'You've told your husband.'

'I've told no one, only you.'

'What did you make of Len Dowling, the estate agent?'

'Not much. He sounds off a lot, but there's not much substance. Geoff Pearson doesn't say much, but he's certainly getting on with it, at least with that woman.'

'You didn't like her?'

'I saw through her. The affected accent, the mannerisms.'

'You saw that?'

'A kindred spirit, competition under different circumstances.'

'You were hard on your husband the last time we were here,' Tremayne said.

'He thrives on it. I act like a bitch, but that's what he wants. He wants to be dominated.'

Clare did not believe the woman. Samantha Dennison was, by her own admission, a gold digger. By Clare's definition, a bitch.

'We've not discussed Gordon Mason in detail,' Tremayne said.

'He told Phillip what he thought of me, not that it stopped him undressing me. Phillip reacted, pushed Mason to one side, causing the man to fall over.'

'What did the others say or do?'

'It was outside. I don't think anyone saw it.'

'And your reaction?'

'I kicked the man on the ground.'

'What did Mason do?'

'He swore, called me a whore. Phillip didn't see that. We left soon after. Phillip was upset for a while, but I calmed him down.'

'How?' Clare asked.

'You're a smart woman, you figure it out.'

'Thank you for your time, Mrs Dennison. If your husband asks, we were just following up on our enquiries.'

'I'll not tell him. He's in his own little world down there.'

***

Fiona Dowling attended the all-important meeting with her social friends, even conducted herself in her typical effusive manner. Once free of them, she was on the road.

Geoff Pearson was surprised to see her outside in the street when his last lecture for the day concluded. 'Fiona, what are you doing here?'

'The police. They know about us.'

'How?'

'I never told them. Who else knows about us?'

'We were always discreet, careful where we met, and you being here doesn't help. You could be seen.'

'In Southampton? Get real, Geoff, I can't afford to lose Len, nor you. I need you both.'

'One to provide you with the money, the other to satisfy you,' Pearson said.

'I made Len what he is, you know that.'

'Yes, and you'd have me jumping through the same hoop if you had half a chance.'

'You've never loved me, it's true, isn't it?'

'Fiona, you've always known what it was. I'm a struggling student, you're a bored housewife. It's been fun, still is, but don't get carried away.'

'I trusted you, and you told the police.'

'I never told them, that's the honest truth. Others have suspected, but I've never admitted to anything,' Pearson said, knowing full well that Cheryl had seen them that one time and Gary Barker knew as well.

'You've got to do something.'

'What do you want me to do? The police suspect that we're having an affair. There's no proof.'

'I admitted it to them. I was flustered, they were determined, and I needed to get out of the house.'

'You stupid, stupid woman. Don't you know anything? Always deny. What do you think Len will say when he hears about this? He'll divorce you, take away your car and your house, even claim custody of the children.'

'I love you, Geoff. I want to be with you. He can't take the house and the car, they're in my name.'

'Why?'

'Tax avoidance. It's legitimate, sort of, and besides, he'll not divorce me. The man's weak without me, but I need you, I love you.'

Geoff Pearson could see difficulties, difficulties he did not want. He was a man destined for greatness; he did not need a clingy and neurotic woman. He needed to get rid of her. 'Fiona, this can't continue. You need to go back to Len, beg his forgiveness if it comes out, but you can't rely on me.'

'What was I, just another screw? I was better than all those young girls you take out, more mature, more able to guide your career, your life.'

Pearson was panicking, he knew it. It had been fun, the older woman, the meetings at the out-of-town hotels, the back of the Range Rover with the seats folded down, but now the situation was serious. He had exams coming up, a potential new girlfriend in his year at university. He no longer needed the distraction, although when they had first made love, one night after rehearsals when she had given him a ride home in her car, it had been fun, and Fiona, he had known, was lacking the attention that she needed.

Then it had been a bit on the side for her, a substantial boost to his male prowess, but now she was in love, desperate love, and he did not want it. 'Sorry, Fiona, it was fun, but it's over. I wish you well, but that's it.'

Pearson left the car and walked, almost ran, away from the scene. Fiona, heartbroken but still resolute, spoke to herself: *You bastard, you'll pay for this.*

She then turned the ignition key of her car and pulled out from where she had been parked. She wiped her tears away with the sleeve of her blouse.

Chapter 11

Clare, feeling better than she had for a long time, joined Tremayne for a drink. This time, the Bridge Inn in the Woodford Valley. It wasn't the first time they had been there; the last time she had been drinking whisky.

Tremayne remembered that night well, the clouds, the roar of thunder, the lightning over Mavis Godwin's cottage, but neither of the police officers wanted to discuss that case: too many unpleasant memories, especially for Clare.

Tremayne had a pint of beer in his hand, Clare was sticking to orange juice.

'What do you reckon, Yarwood?' Tremayne asked.

'The motives to kill the man are not strong. I can understand their dislike, but murder hardly seems justified. For sure, Fiona Dowling's a case, what with her airs and graces, butter wouldn't melt in her mouth attitude, but she's more concerned with her place in society. Languishing behind bars wouldn't suit her image.'

'Samantha Dennison?'

'The woman was refreshingly honest. She made no attempt to conceal what she was, what her husband was. She might fleece a man for his money, but there's no percentage in murder, and besides, she wasn't at Old Sarum.'

'The perfect alibi.'

'But why would the others have wanted Mason dead?'

'This angle on him blackmailing Fiona Dowling? Do you give it any credence?'

'It's a possibility.'

'Geoff Pearson, her accomplice?'

'Only if she had had a chance to knife Mason, and then that's hit and miss. What if Pearson had missed the heart on stage? Mason would still be conscious, and he wouldn't have lain down still.'

'And remember Mark Antony had time on the stage, the Senate scene where Brutus and his fellow conspirators leave to address the mob. Mason wasn't moving then, and Mark Antony, or should I say Phillip Dennison, did not have a chance to stab him. The man was dead on that stage after the conspirators had stabbed him. I'm discounting Dennison, the same as I'm discounting the women.'

'Then you believe it's two of the conspirators,' Clare said.

'Peter Freestone is an accountant, serves as a city councillor, and Len Dowling's an estate agent.'

'Too predictable: a rezoning, privileged information, buying up land for a steal, selling it on afterwards.'

'We're not looking for the obscure here, just the murderers.'

'Freestone and Dowling were both on stage, both had a clear target. It could be them, but we never checked how far Mason staggered after the main assault. If there were thirty-three stabs before the final stab of Freestone's, then four would have penetrated his body, one of them at least in his heart.'

'How do we find out?'

'We can't ask the actors in case of collusion.'

'Yarwood, you interviewed the audience, took names and addresses. We'll need to talk to them.'

'I'll set it up.'

'In the meantime, I'll have another pint. Are you sticking to that orange juice?'

'Someone needs a clear head.'

***

'We often go to one of their productions. They're not bad for amateurs.' Tremayne and Clare were standing in a warehouse on the outskirts of the city. Derek Wilkinson, the manager of the wholesale electrical supplier, was a man with similar tastes in clothing to Tremayne, judging by his tie off to one side, his shirt marked with a felt pen. To Clare, the two men were similar in looks as well, apart from the fact that Tremayne was well over six feet and Wilkinson was a short man, almost dwarfish.

'We were there, but there's one crucial scene that we're unsure of,' Clare said.

'Ask away. It was a shame that it ended suddenly. Poetic, I suppose.'

'What do you mean?'

'No disrespect for the dead, but it was meant to be a play, fake daggers, fake blood, a fake death, and there is Gordon Mason dead on the floor.'

'Did you know the man?'

'In passing. I can't say I liked him, but he was competent, honest as well.'

'And some are not?'

'Not really, but you always hear stories about solicitors and estate agents, city councillors.'

'Have you heard about any of those recently?' Tremayne asked.

'Not recently.'

'In the past?'

'There was a subdivision, about a dozen blocks of land that had been zoned industrial.'

'What happened?'

'I was looking for somewhere to build this warehouse, and the price was reasonable. At the rear, there was a floodplain.'

'What happened?'

'It was rezoned residential, the price shot up. Not that it did any good for those who built their houses there.'

'What do you mean?'

'You remember when it rained solidly for two weeks, a few years back?'

'I remember,' Tremayne said.

'Half of the houses were flooded out, the insurance companies rejected their claims, said it was an act of God. Serves them right.'

'Why do you say that?'

'A good solicitor, a few checks, would have found out about the potential of flooding.'

'Who was the solicitor?'

'For the vendor, or for the purchaser?'

'Either.'

'Len Dowling sold the land. Joint ownership with his brother, he's a solicitor.'

Tremayne looked at Clare: a motive.

'Let's get back to the play,' Tremayne said.

'What do you want to know?' Wilkinson asked.

'When Caesar staggered over to Brutus.'

'I remember it.'

'Did he stagger?'

'It wasn't far, but yes, he staggered.'

'How far?'

'Six feet, maybe eight.'

'And then, did he utter *Et tu, Brute*?'

'It was weak, but yes, I heard him say it.'

'Thanks. That's all we need to know.'

'A motive that holds up,' Tremayne said to Clare once they were outside the warehouse.

'It still raises more questions,' Clare said.

'Such as?'

'If someone is stabbed in the heart, or in the body, it can't be guaranteed that they will still be able to stagger. The man could easily have collapsed on the spot.'

'The dramatic effect would have been lost, but the man would still have been dead.'

'And if he were, then Peter Freestone would never have had a chance to stick his dagger in, no immortal line from Caesar.'

'Are you saying that Freestone's not guilty?'

'He could still be guilty, but it's illogical. You have two lethal weapons, why would you leave it to chance to use the second one?'

'Are we discounting Freestone as one of the murderers?'

'I think we are,' Clare said. 'We're assuming that he was involved in a possible fraudulent rezoning, and maybe he was, but he's not one of the murderers.'

'I'll make a good police officer out of you yet, Yarwood,' Tremayne said. 'I thought we had the case sewn up in there, but now it's obvious that it's still wide open.'

***

With the preliminary interviews concluded, the most potent motive was that Peter Freestone, Len Dowling, and Dowling's brother had been involved in a fraudulent land deal. And that Gordon Mason had knowledge of the fraud, either through involvement or through investigation, and the man was about to reveal what he knew. The weakest motive was that Trevor Winston had objected to the treatment meted out in rehearsals, and Mason's continuing bias against him because of his sexual orientation. The other motives, the blackmailing of Fiona Dowling for sexual favours or for money, seemed a long shot, but yet again the two police officers were clutching at straws.

Tremayne was sure there was more depth to the motives. Clare was not sure how to proceed. The one interview she did not want her and Tremayne to conduct was with Len Dowling's brother, Chris. She knew the day would come when she'd have to confront a return to Harry's old pub, or next door, which was where Chris Dowling had an office, on the first floor.

'If you'd rather not,' Tremayne said, but Clare knew that was not possible. She was a police officer, not a schoolgirl crying over being dumped by her boyfriend; she was a mature woman, rapidly becoming an experienced homicide detective, not that Tremayne said so, but then she knew the man gave compliments sparingly.

She was aware that he was looking to her, not only as a sounding board for his analysis of the case, the direction to move forward, but also to bring new ideas into the discussion, and she had. She had been the one who had seen the possibility that Peter Freestone, the last assassin up at Old Sarum, could not have been one of the murderers, and if that was the case, then the motive of the suspected rezoning fraud may not be correct. Regardless, it wouldn't be the first time that murder had been committed over money.

If Clare's preliminary checks were accurate then the change from industrial to rezoning had increased the value of the land from half a million pounds sterling to two million pounds sterling, and the owner before and after, Len Dowling. The necessary legal ownership had been dealt by Chris Dowling, and the city council meeting where the decision had been made for the rezoning chaired by Peter Freestone. Gordon Mason's involvement was not so clear, as the council had their own legal team, and the change from industrial to residential was an internal matter.

Minster Street was busy as Tremayne and Clare walked down it. They had parked their car in the Guildhall Square and walked past the Poultry Cross, another ancient building, before turning right towards Chris Dowling's office.

Clare looked at the pub, Harry's pub, their pub, as she had loved it as much as he had. She saw the first-floor window of the room where they had made love. Even imagined the cellar where the beer barrels were stored, and where they had almost made love that first time, only to be interrupted by the anxious patrons upstairs, and then the gentle rebuke from Tremayne about the buttons on her blouse being undone.

'Doesn't do to dwell on the past, Yarwood,' Tremayne said in his typically blunt manner.

Clare knew that the man cared, even if he wouldn't admit to it, and since the events in Avon Hill his choice of favoured pub varied from night to night; sometimes he had even spent a quiet evening at home.

They were ushered into Chris Dowling's office by an efficient woman who asked them to sign a book on her desk recording times in and out before she opened the door to the solicitor's office to let him know that they had arrived.

'Come in, please,' Chris Dowling said. Clare could see that he bore no similarity to his brother.

'We're here investigating the death of Gordon Mason.'

'Tea, coffee, Detective Inspector, Sergeant?'

'I'll have tea, milk, two sugars,' Tremayne said.

'No sugar for me, thank you,' Clare said.

'What can I do for you? Gwyneth will only be a minute with the tea.'

'Your brother, Len, said that you handle all his legal work.'

'Step-brother, but yes, that's true.'

'Not far from here, off Churchfields Road, there was some land that was rezoned from industrial to residential.'

'It happens from time to time.'

'Only this time, the guidelines relating to the floodplain were ignored. Subsequently, some houses were flooded.'

'Are you saying this was a possible motive for Mason's murder?'

'If there was fraud, then your brother, and possibly Peter Freestone, stood to gain.'

'And me. I've a twenty per cent interest in Len's business.'

Clare could see that the two brothers were not alike in mannerisms either: one was loud and extrovert, the other was careful in what he said, not wishing to incriminate, not wanting to make a firm denial of anything untoward. She was not sure which of the two she preferred, or even if she liked either. Len Dowling was a salesman, his brother was possibly devious, and if there had been something underhand, the man would have covered their tracks well.

'You are aware of the land in question?' Tremayne said.

'It may be best if you do your research before you come here, Detective Inspector.'

'Why?' Tremayne said. Clare could sense the atmosphere becoming frosty.

'At the time of the flooding, some of the residents contacted the local newspaper. There was an article in there, a subsequent special meeting held in the council chambers. In the end, the council agreed to put in place measures to prevent another flood, and compensated all of the affected houses with a rates reduction.'

'That doesn't alter the fact that the rezoning may have been fraudulent.'

'Heavy words, legally prejudicial against my brother and myself, not to mention Peter Freestone and the other members of the Salisbury City Council,' Dowling said. Tremayne sat quietly, taking in the man who had gone from pleasant to aggressive in no more than a few minutes.

'Mr Dowling, I believe that your attitude is counter-productive,' Tremayne said. 'We did not come here to be confrontational, we never accused anyone of any wrongdoing. A man has been murdered. It is for us to follow up on any innuendo regardless. If, as I infer by your attitude, you are threatening us with legal action if we persist, then you should think again.'

'Very well, but I should warn you that I team up with Superintendent Moulton at the golf club out on Netherhampton Road every Saturday afternoon.'

Clare visibly sat back at Dowling's oblique threat.

'Mr Dowling, with all due respect, you could be teaming up with the Almighty, it does not impact on the fact that Sergeant Yarwood and I are conducting a murder enquiry. Our visit here today, our questioning of you, is within our rights as police officers. I suspect that you have not been involved in a murder enquiry before, I have, and Superintendent Moulton will not interfere with how I run this investigation. Now, getting back to our previous questioning. What do you know about the rezoning of this land? Did anyone benefit financially?'

Dowling did not speak for several minutes. Tremayne knew the man wasn't used to being put in his place. 'Len benefited,' Dowling finally said.

'Who else?'

'Apart from the additional revenue to the city council, no one.'

'The rezoning application, did you prepare the submission?'

'Yes, but it was all above board. We brought in an expert, well-respected in his field, who said the chance of flooding was a once in a one-hundred-year event.'

'What happened?'

'Three years after the last house there had been completed, we had the one-hundred-year flood. It probably won't happen again, at least not in our lifetimes.'

'Any payments to Peter Freestone?'

'None. I ensured the necessary council fees were paid, that was all.'

'And Gordon Mason?'

'He acted on behalf of some of the purchasers, nothing more.'

'Thank you, Mr Dowling. We've no further questions.'

Tremayne and Clare left the office without their cups of tea.

'What do you reckon, Yarwood?' Tremayne asked.

'I didn't like him.'

'A slimy individual, worse than the brother.'

'Was there any illegal activity?'

'With the rezoning, almost certainly. It still doesn't tie in Mason.'

'We don't know if he was involved, or just became aware of it, threatened to take action, or was blackmailing them for other reasons.'

'The motive is strong, even if unproven. We'll need to keep a watch on Solicitor Dowling. Estate agent Dowling's not as sharp as that man.'

Chapter 12

Jim Hughes was in the office on Tremayne and Clare's return to the office. 'I've been working with Forensics on the daggers.'

'Any luck?'

'Some. The retractable daggers are an exact copy of an original that was discovered fifty years ago in an archaeological dig in Rome.'

'Does that help us?'

'It does. Up till then, the exact specifications were well known, but the look and feel were vague. Once this dagger had been found, some companies in the USA started making exact replicas. There's demand for knives, daggers, and swords around the world.'

'Here in England?' Tremayne asked.

'There are collectors here, although our laws are strict on the importation, unless they've been blunted or you're a registered collector.'

'Are there many collectors?'

'Not a lot.'

'In America?'

'They're easy to obtain there.'

'What are you telling us?'

'It would be possible to obtain metal blades in the USA and to change them with the plastic blades on the fakes.'

'Dimension, fitting into the retracting mechanism?' Tremayne asked.

'If an example was sent. Not too many questions would have been asked. We'll keep checking, but as I see it,' Hughes said, 'the person who purchased the fakes is probably not the person who purchased the metal blades.'

'How do we find out?' Clare asked.

'That's up to you. You're the investigators, but don't go looking for names. It's almost certainly an online transaction,

PayPal, maybe a bank transfer, but if someone were intent on murder, they'd have covered their tracks. Anyone smart enough?'

'There are several who spring to mind,' Tremayne said.

***

It was known that Peter Freestone, as the dramatic society's current president, had purchased the fake Roman daggers. The man had proof, and he had already stated that they had remained in his possession up until the staging of the play at Old Sarum.

Tremayne was willing to give Freestone the benefit of the doubt concerning his placing the fakes on a makeshift table at Old Sarum. If that was correct, then how were they changed, and by whom? It was Clare who suggested it first: a re-enactment.

Clare realised afterwards that getting everyone up there at the same time as the previous performance was not going to be that easy. For one thing, she needed the cooperation of the heritage society, then there was Len Dowling who was busy, Fiona, his wife, who was socialising, and Trevor Winston who was involved with the ladies in his salon.

Gary Barker and Cheryl Milledge were keen. 'Can we come in costume?' Cheryl asked.

'It's up to you,' Clare replied. She thought that it would have helped, but getting all the people there was one thing, getting the others in costume would have been nigh on impossible.

Geoff Pearson was reluctant, what with exams coming up, but Clare had leant on his good nature, not on an official summons. 'I'll be there,' he said. 'I wanted to avoid Fiona.'

'Lover's tiff?'

'You could say that. She's a vengeful woman. She could even tell Len out of spite.'

'Would she?' Clare said.

'With Fiona, who knows?'

'We'll be there. If there's an issue, we'll deal with it. We know about you and her.'

'She accused me of telling you.'

'She'd not believe you,' Clare said. 'You were playing with fire there.'

'It was fun for a while.'

'No guilt about her husband?'

'None. The man is not the type of person who'd garner respect from me.'

'Any reason?'

'No substance, no backbone. His wife screws around. Maybe he doesn't know about me, but there would have been others.'

'Would there?'

'What's your honest opinion of her?' Pearson asked.

Clare wasn't sure if she should divulge too much, but the man was talking, and he seemed to have his ear to the ground. 'Someone said that Cheryl Milledge is what you see, what you get.'

'It may have been me, not sure, but yes, with Cheryl, she's transparent. With Fiona, she's deep. I never knew when she was pretending or when she was honest.'

'You've broken up with her?'

'She came to Southampton; it got very nasty. Never trust her.'

'Could Mason have had some dirt on her?'

'She'd do anything to protect her reputation.'

'Murder?'

'I wasn't thinking of that, but she could be violent. I got out of her car fast before she started hitting me.'

'The scar on your face?'

'Not a woman. An accident as a child, that's all. I'm not a bastard, just a young guy indulging a fantasy.'

'The married, more mature woman?'

'Sergeant Yarwood, if you must know, she's a passionate woman.'

'Nymphomaniac?' Clare asked.

'Not far off. I've got a girlfriend down in Southampton. I hadn't intended to return to Salisbury for some time.'

'You need to be at Old Sarum.'

'I'll be there, maybe I'll bring the girlfriend.'

'If you want a catfight.'

'I'll take a chance.'

Clare realised that it had been an illuminating phone call, in that Geoff Pearson had revealed more about Fiona Dowling's nature. She knew that they needed to talk to Cheryl Milledge at some stage to see if there was more in her previous friend's background than they were aware of.

Phillip Dennison was willing to attend the re-enactment. Clare could hear his wife in the background, complaining. The woman had said that her husband needed to be bossed around, a defect in his personality. Clare thought that she was playing a dangerous game, and unless she had a sharp solicitor, she could find herself back in an office being pressed up against the photocopier by every young lothario.

Bill Ford was willing, although it was inconvenient, needed some rescheduling, but, as he said, the dead don't keep to any timetable, and he would be there.

Jimmy Francombe was excited to hear from Clare, wanting to know if the hot date was still on, maybe after the re-enactment. Clare had to admit that she liked the young man, good-natured, willing to have a joke at himself. He took her put-down in good heart. 'I'm still working on you,' he said.

'Goodbye, Jimmy, not a chance,' Clare said.

***

Gordon Mason's body was eventually released and sent to Bill Ford for burial. The funeral was held in a Baptist church close to Salisbury. A pastor conducted the ceremony, Peter Freestone made a speech praising the man's commitment to the dramatic society, another woman, identified as an older sister, spoke on behalf of the family. Everyone in the dramatic society attended. Cheryl Milledge was for once dressed sombrely, Gary Barker in a suit. Clare noticed that his hands were clean, and there was no dirt under his fingernails. Len Dowling had appeared agitated, wanting to message on his phone, only to have Fiona, dressed to the hilt with a large black hat, chastise him to put it away.

Trevor Winston sat with Jimmy Francombe and Geoff Pearson. Pearson was keeping a low profile, hoping to avoid a face-to-face confrontation with Fiona Dowling. Clare could see her furtive glances as she looked for him. He had positioned himself behind a pillar, arriving late, hoping to leave early. All seemed suitably sad at the passing of the man that no one had liked.

Tremayne remembered the last funeral he had attended: a detective inspector colleague of his, younger than him by a few years, who had suddenly keeled over when he had been at a crime scene. The diagnosis was a massive heart attack brought on by too many drinks, often with him, too many cigarettes, and too many hours. Tremayne had recollected, in the church watching the congregation, the pastor conducting the funeral, strict Baptist, that he was as guilty of all the offences that his colleague had indulged in. For a few minutes, in the tranquillity of the moment, he had promised to himself to turn over a new leaf: no more getting drunk, cigarettes down to ten a day, and a stiff walk around the block every morning. Once the service concluded, and they were out in the fresh air, he had taken out a packet of cigarettes and lit up. *To hell with it*, he'd thought.

Clare, observing her senior indulging his favourite pastime, apart from beer and horse racing, left him and walked around the churchyard. Mason was not to be cremated but buried in the graveyard next to the church. She looked back at the church, its similarities to the church in Avon Hill undeniable. She thought that within a few weeks, once the current case was wrapped up, she would visit Harry's grave in the church where the pagans had conducted their rituals.

Harry had never mentioned other relatives, but it appeared that there was an uncle who had surfaced in Salisbury two days after his death. Apparently, his solicitor had known about him and his family but had not been authorised to reveal the details unless Harry was dead.

The uncle had turned out to be a Christian, dismissive of Harry and his parents' foolish ways, fully cognisant of who and what they were. Clare had spoken to the uncle briefly. At least the man had had the civility to ask her opinion of a Christian burial; she had agreed, but she had not attended the funeral, the grief had been too raw, although now she wished she had.

A graveyard outside a church was too much for her; she walked away and out to the road. 'Sergeant Yarwood,' Geoff Pearson said.

'I'm surprised to see you here,' Clare said.

'I had to do the right thing. The man was not easy to get on with, but he was genuine enough.'

'And the dramatic society?'

'It's hard to say. Once we've completed the re-enactment, I'll move to Southampton on a longer-term basis.'

'Fiona Dowling?'

'I was wrong, no need to lecture me.'

'I'm a police officer. I only want to solve this case.'

'Look around. There's the murderer.'

Clare turned her head, could only see the dramatic society members, the pastor, and Mason's sister. 'It doesn't help. Has she seen you?'

'Fiona, she sees everything.'

'And her husband?'

'Who knows. I'll honour Mason here today, attend your re-enactment and then make myself scarce. Hopefully, Fiona will find someone else.'

'Young and virile.'

'Young, at least. If you'll excuse me, Fiona's heading this way. You can deal with her.' Pearson jumped into his car, a female in the passenger seat, and left at speed.

'He's a miserable bastard. Don't go falling for him,' Fiona Dowling said, the brim of her hat attempting to fall down over her face in the wind. She took hold of it and held it high with one hand.

'He's a witness to a murder. I've no need of him, and even if I did, he's too young.'

'He was a great lay, I'll give him that.'

'Was that all it was? Nothing else?'

'Why should it be? I need some excitement in my life.'

'And he was the excitement?'

'It was better than playing tennis.'

'Do you?'

'Play tennis? Of course I do. I'm on their committee.'

'Your husband's here. Aren't you concerned that he'll find out about Pearson?'

'I'll deal with it if it happens.'

'You're a hard woman, Mrs Dowling.'

'I'm determined, never let anything get in my way. If Len is not up to it, I'll find someone else.'

'What are you referring to?'

'Business, screwing, whatever.'

'Would you kill for your lifestyle?'

'I'd kill for my children, not for that. If I want the lifestyle, I just have to wiggle my arse, flash some cleavage.'

'The other day you were complaining about your age.'

'Some days down, some days up.'

'Any reason?'

'Self-doubt. We all suffer from it. It's not always easy maintaining the pretence.'

Clare wondered if there was something more, something medical, that could change a vain and driven woman into a killer.

***

Tremayne had not gained much from the funeral, apart from how easy it was for the dramatic society to pretend to have liked the man when apparently none of them did. Peter Freestone had admitted to a grudging respect for him as a solicitor, and as an actor, and Cheryl Milledge had said some kind words about him at the wake. The last wake, Tremayne remembered, had been awash with alcohol, but this was Baptist, and it was teetotal, not that it stopped Bill Ford reaching for a small flask hidden in the inside pocket of his suit.

'I need to keep myself warm while they're in the church,' he said to Tremayne when he had been spotted. 'Most times at a funeral, I'm out in the cold.'

Tremayne had no issues with the man imbibing; he wished he'd brought a stiff drink as well. He was not a churchgoer, he knew that, though he'd attended enough funerals in his time. If it weren't for the murder, he'd not be there at all. He had to admit to feeling a little out of it, almost the relative who receives an invite out of kindness but isn't expected to come. However, this was the first opportunity to see all the suspects gathered in one place; to see the interactions, endeavour to pick up the nuances, the gestures, differentiate between genuine and feigned friendship.

As he stood to one side, observing, he could see that Cheryl Milledge and Fiona Dowling had acted correctly: a warm hug on meeting, a complimenting of each other's attire, a willingness to sit next to each other on the church pew. Tremayne wasn't sure what to make of the two women. Len Dowling, once he had stopped fiddling with his phone, had spoken to the pastor, as well as to Mason's sister. His wife had circulated, even pausing to have a chat with Jimmy Francombe.

Phillip Dennison was there, the Aston Martin parked in a prominent position for everyone to admire, but his wife not present. 'She's out shopping again,' he said with a sigh of exasperation. Tremayne felt for the man, though he wasn't sure why he did. He remembered that his wife had been the opposite, excessively frugal, always looking for the bargain. He had tried to explain that even though he was a humble police officer, they weren't destitute, and it's not a bargain if you didn't want it in the first place.

'You'll never understand,' she had said, as if there was something that he didn't get. He wondered what it was with the disparate group in that church and its graveyard that he didn't get with them.

'Tremayne, have you figured out which one of us is the murderer?' Freestone said as he came over to him.

'You purchased the daggers?' Tremayne said.

'A company online, remarkably cheap.'

'Realistic?'

'Considering the price, they are.'

'Who took responsibility for them?'

'I did initially, although the others would take them home occasionally if they wanted. The ones I purchased were harmless. No doubt Dowling's children had fun with them.'

'You'd trust a child with them?'

'I wouldn't. I don't know about Dowling, he may have.'

'His wife?'

'Not sure about her. I'm not always sure what she's thinking.'

'What do you mean?'

'Nothing in itself. I'm not judging anyone.'

'We still think it's two murderers. Just a question, off the record.'

'With you, Tremayne?'

'With me.'

'You're never off duty.'

'The land on the floodplain. We've people checking whether it was above board.'

'Are you insinuating that there may have been graft and corruption?'

'It's been mentioned.'

'Mason thought there was.'

'Did he say anything, do anything?'

'He would have, but there was nothing to find. There was an expert opinion, a rezoning unanimously agreed to by a quorum of councillors, a sign-off from our building inspector.'

'Dowling would have made plenty of money.'

'No doubt he did, but that's down to his good judgement in buying the land overpriced and then changing the zoning. He was close to the wind financially on that one, but it set him up.'

'The submission was backed up by experts?'

'And our building inspector. He's not a man to be easily swayed.'

'And the councillors?'

'We make our decisions based on advice received.'

'And if the advice is incorrect?'

'That's why we have people working for the council, people who check these things. I'm an accountant. I can tell you if it's financially viable, the tax implications, but don't ask me about floodplains, how to put one brick on top of another.'

'You're not handy?'

'I can barely fix anything.'

'Is there anyone that can?'

'In the dramatic society?' Freestone asked.

'Yes.'

'No idea. Geoff Pearson is good with tools. He fixed up our backdrop once, started one of the cars after rehearsals when it had a flat battery. Apart from that, I wouldn't know. Any reason to ask?'

'Someone modified the two daggers.'

'Is that what you think happened?'

'Would you have known if they had been changed?'

'On the night? Up at Old Sarum? Probably not. I don't think any of us would have been looking too closely. We were all tense, worrying about our lines, listening to our cue.'

'Cheryl Milledge works for the council, doesn't she?' Tremayne said.

'In our building approvals department. You don't think…'

'I don't think anything. I just observe, ask questions, look for answers.'

Chapter 13

Tremayne organised a team to check into the land rezoning that appeared to be flawed. He liked Cheryl Milledge, earthy as she had been described by Phillip Dennison, and now she was possibly the one person who could have changed the documents that were presented to council, and as they had been approved, then the building inspector would have been in on the fraud too. He had no time for Dennison's wife, the gold digger as he saw her, but she was honest about what she was, her purpose in the marital arrangements with her husband. And besides, she had not been up at Old Sarum that night when Mason had died, a plus in her favour, Tremayne had to admit.

Apart from a couple of wins on the horses in the last couple of days, Tremayne realised not a lot was going his way. Superintendent Moulton, the honeymoon period over following the success of the previous murder enquiry, was back into his attempts to retire Tremayne. He knew what it was, an effort to bring the average age of the police force in Salisbury down; most of them already looked to him as though they were just out of school, but they weren't, he knew that. Moulton saw a modern computer-driven procedural force, always smiling, or at least that's what was shown on the posters erected on Bemerton Road, the latest public relations exercise to instil confidence in the force, to encourage others to join.

Tremayne's gut instinct told him that the death of Mason was only the calm before the storm, a hornets' nest prodded, its occupants restless, waiting for the opportunity to strike and inflict their wrath on their victims. Yarwood, he could see, was coming over to his style of policing, but she was still young, susceptible to Moulton and his ideas. He hoped he could convince her in the long term to stay strong, but he wouldn't be around forever, and she was still vulnerable. He could see in her face at times the fragility after her fiancé's death. He assumed that once she left work and was back in the cottage that she was renting, the memories would return to her. He wanted to help but knew he could not. The best he could do was to keep her busy.

Tremayne realised that he had been sitting in his office for forty-five minutes, reminiscing, thinking. Too long for him, he realised, and there was a time when he would not have been able to do that. He envied Yarwood her ability to be in the office first thing in the morning, wide-awake and bushy-tailed, ready for the day ahead, yet as he pulled himself up from his chair, he could feel a twinge in his hips, tenderness in both of his knees. He cast a glance at his reflection in the glass partitioning that separated his office from the larger office beyond. He looked for the tell-tale signs, the signs that stared back at him every day as he stood in front of his bathroom mirror: the thinning hair, the lines in his face that weren't there before, the marks of ageing. The glass partition, an imperfect surface, showed what his mirror did, and he did not like it. He had been willing to accept the ageing process as inevitable, and now it was on him and he was not sure how much longer it would be before health problems started to set in.

Some of his work colleagues had passed on, his brother had gone, as had a cousin, a couple of drinking pals, even the bookmaker at Salisbury Races, and that man had had every reason to live, seeing that he had taken enough of his money.

Tremayne sat down. He made a phone call. 'Jean, let's meet in the next couple of weeks, go away for the weekend.'

'If you like,' his ex-wife replied.

Tremayne put the phone down and walked out of the office, the pains in his body temporarily forgotten.

***

Clare had not expected to run into Samantha Dennison, and if she had known that she would be in Trevor Winston's hairdressing salon, she would not have gone in.

'Sergeant Yarwood,' said Samantha's voice from under a hairdryer.

'Mrs Dennison,' Clare said.

'Call me Samantha. Us girls have got to stick together.'

Clare was not sure what the 'us girls' referred to, but let it pass.

'I thought I'd see how good Trevor Winston is,' Clare said.

'Sergeant Yarwood.' The unmistakable voice of Trevor Winston, the flamboyant clothing, the effeminate walk in the salon, although not outside in the street. Which was as well, Clare thought, as there was a rough element in the city, the legacy of the army bases in the area, the large number of men from more deprived parts of the country who saw violence as a solution, prejudice as a way of life. An effeminate man would have suited them fine to exercise their frustrations.

'I could do with a quick wash, style. Can you fit me in?'

Clare realised that she may be placing herself in the hands of a murderer, but she did not believe that he was, and it was unlikely that he'd inflict injury in his salon.

'No worries, just sit down next to Samantha, and I'll be right over.'

Clare turned to Samantha Dennison. 'How long have you known Trevor?'

'Ever since that time Phillip dragged me along to the dramatic society's rehearsal. Trevor gave me a card, the only good thing to come out of that evening.'

'Is Trevor a murderer?' Clare asked, knowing full well that she was using Tremayne's technique of baiting, hoping to elicit a response.

'He's skilled with a pair of scissors, but killing someone, I don't think so, and why?'

'Everyone has reasons, even you.'

'Don't look at me, I wasn't there that night.'

'You don't go along, support your husband?'

'Why should I? I'm an open book, a rich man's trophy. I'm under no illusion, neither is he. I admitted this before to you and your detective inspector.'

Clare knew she had an unexpected opportunity to see if the woman would open up, though she wasn't sure if there was anything more to be gleaned from her. Clare had to admit as she sat alongside the woman that she was attractive, the object of many men's fancy, in that she wore her skirts high, her blouses tight, her lipstick red and applied with care.

Trevor Winston was in the background, discussing with his assistant, another gay man, what style they should give Clare. She had wanted to spend no more than thirty minutes in there, a quick wash and blow dry, and then out to follow up on the team checking out the land deal. She messaged the team to tell them she would be late; she then messaged Tremayne to let him know that she had inadvertently run into Dennison's wife, and she'd take the opportunity for some gentle prying.

Tremayne had smiled on reading the message. *She's learning*, he thought. It was a technique he had often used over a pint of beer. The formal interview resulted in considered answers, carefully thought out, but no scurrilous rumours, innuendos, no dirt. Tremayne knew that Dennison's wife would be into all three. He was pleased that Yarwood was with the woman. He was interested to hear the results.

'Who else did you speak to that night when Trevor gave you his card?' Clare asked Samantha.

'The men were friendly, apart from that bastard.'

'Gordon Mason?'

'Yes, him.'

'Were you upset when your husband told you that he'd been murdered?'

'Phillip, he came in at four in the morning, babbling about it.'

'What was your reaction?'

'At that time? Nothing, I wasn't interested.'

'Someone is murdered, and you show no interest?' Clare said.

'Why? Phillip's always threatening to do me in.'

'To kill you?'

'He's all mouth and trousers.'

'What does that mean?'

'All talk, no substance. You've not heard that saying before? Where have you been living?'

'Norfolk.'

The two women laughed. Clare warmed to the woman.

'They used it all the time where I grew up. Phillip's all boast, no substance. He can threaten, but he'll do nothing.'

'Can you be sure?' Clare asked.

'He's had plenty of provocation, and all he does is rant and rave, pace up and down, occasionally throw something down hard on the floor, but he's never touched me.'

'We've always seen your husband as benign.'

'He is, but he's got a temper. He hit Gordon Mason that time.

'Would your husband be capable of murder?'

'Of Mason?'

'Of anyone.'

'I don't see it, but who knows what anyone is capable of. I grew up as the child of a devout family. I even took the pledge to remain a virgin until married.'

'Did you?'

'Hell, no. The young man was just on sixteen, I was fifteen. He never knew what hit him, nor did I.'

'After that?'

'I could have screwed for England.'

'And with your husband?'

'I'm faithful to him, not that he wants me much.'

'Why's that? You're a beautiful woman.'

'With Phillip, the same as other men, the pursuit is what they want, not the ownership. Before he made it rich, he drove an old bomb, now he drives an Aston Martin, or at least I do. And what do I hear? How much fun he had with the old bomb. He owns an Aston Martin, he wants a Roll Royce.'

'He's got you. Does he want to trade up?'

'Trade me in for a younger version, is that what you think? Of course he does, but I've got a sharp lawyer. If he tries it, I'll sue him for half his assets, and I'll win, mark my words. And I'll take his precious Aston Martin, even the Rolls Royce, and he knows it.'

'A good enough reason for murder,' Clare said.

'Of me, yes.'

'Would he?'

'Phillip, I'm not worried about him. All mouth and trousers, I told you that.'

'But he laid out Gordon Mason.'

'He hit him, but not that hard. I had my leg out behind him. The man fell hard, banged his head on the road, nothing more. Don't tell Phillip, he thinks he was the macho man defending his wife's honour.'

'You're not all mouth and trousers,' Clare said.

'I'm a mean bitch who says it as it is. I neither liked nor disliked Gordon Mason. I love my husband conditionally because he treats me well, let's me buy lots of trinkets.'

'And if he didn't?'

'I'd find another man. I've told you all this before. Think what you want of me. Phillip knows this.'

'Would you be capable of murder?'

'I wasn't at Old Sarum when the man died.'

'Hypothetically?'

'If my life was being threatened. If my children, assuming I had any, then yes, I could kill, and I'd have no guilt.'

'Would you have killed Gordon Mason if he had persisted with his derision?'

'That night he insulted me? Not a chance. If Phillip hadn't pushed him, and if Mason had come too close, I'd have kneed him in the groin, slapped him across the face.'

Trevor Winston came over, too early for Clare. 'How are you, ladies? A glass of champagne?'

'I'll have one,' Samantha said.'

'So will I,' Clare said. The woman was talking, she did not want her to stop.

'Sergeant, you're an attractive woman, why do you mess around playing cops and robbers? You could snare a man, enjoy life.'

'I had a man.'

'What happened?'

'He died.' Clare did not want to elaborate.

'Then get another one.'

'It doesn't work that way with me.'

'Idealistic, is that it? I was once, thought I'd get married, have a few children, and live the sweet life in the country.'

'What happened?'

'I wised up. In another ten years, the looks will have faded, and then it'll be hard.'

'That will happen to you.'

'I know that. That's why I've got a sharp lawyer and a place in the Caribbean.'

'Are you content, living the life that you do?' Clare asked.

'Are you?' Samantha Dennison asked.

'Not totally.'

'Neither am I, but with me, I'll be able to make the best of it. With you, it's work until you're in your sixties, then retirement in a place that you can barely afford, looking for the bargains in the supermarket. If my life is not perfect, it's better than yours.'

'We'll agree to disagree,' Clare said. She had to admit that although life was not good at the present time, it had been with Harry. She was sure that there would not be another man in her life. For the first time in several days, she felt sad.

'All done, Sergeant Yarwood,' Trevor Winston said.

Clare looked in the mirror; it was a vast improvement on when she had come in, but no one would appreciate it. Samantha Dennison had someone, even if it was not love, but Clare knew she did not envy the woman her superficial life.

Clare left the woman still being pampered and continued with her police work.

Chapter 14

Tremayne met Peter Freestone at the Pheasant Inn on the corner of Salt Lane and Rolleston Street. It was only a ten-minute walk for Freestone, and there was parking opposite for Tremayne. The pub was five hundred years old and wearing its age well. The half-timbered inn, a reminder of the time of Shakespeare and Elizabeth the first. Tremayne liked the pub, thought that it may become his favourite now the Deer's Head had closed.

Freestone was already seated in the corner closest to the fire on Tremayne's arrival. He had purchased two pints of beer: one for him, one for Tremayne.

'I've ordered a steak for both of us,' Freestone said.

'Fine,' Tremayne said. 'I thought we should get together before the re-enactment, run through some of the finer points.'

'Is there any suspicion that I'm involved?'

'It's a murder enquiry. I can't exonerate you just on the basis that we have the occasional pint together.'

'I understand,' Freestone said.

'Will the dramatic society survive?'

'Unlikely. I intend to leave anyway.'

'Because of Mason?'

'That's the catalyst, but the whole affair has brought out the worst in the people. Before, the members would meet, enjoy the moment, and then we'd go our separate ways, but now there is suspicion and doubt. There are unpleasant truths about all of us that we would prefer not to confront.'

'Such as?' Tremayne asked as he drank his beer.

'That two of us are murderers seems as good as any.'

'You realise that this land deal we're investigating is a strong motive.'

'I'll give you my word that I was not involved,' Freestone said.

'I'll accept your word, but we've got professionals checking it out.'

'Sure, I've made certain that the roads near where I live are in good condition, the local park is well looked after, but I've not taken money. My conscience is clear on this one.'

'The re-enactment,' Tremayne said, changing the subject.

'It's all arranged. Everyone will be there. How do you want to do this? And remember, we have no Julius Caesar.'

'Can you arrange a stand-in?'

'It's possible, but if we can't, you'll have to take part.'

'We need the full production. I can't learn the lines, and besides, I can't act.'

'Fine. I'll find someone.'

'If anyone feels like chickening out, let me know, and I'll organise a police car to pick them up.'

'And for the daggers? The ones up at Old Sarum are with you as evidence.'

'That's where they'll stay.'

'Fine. I'll organise some more. You can check them before we start.'

The two men ordered another pint. It was still early in the afternoon, and Tremayne knew he'd be working for a few more hours yet, at least until nine or ten in the evening. By that time, he'd arrive home, a quick brush of his teeth, or maybe not, before he collapsed into his bed. He thought about his ex-wife as he ate his meal and drank his beer. He remembered when they had first met, how he had woken up next to her the following morning, not remembering if they had made love, the months they had spent together before they had married, the drifting apart over the next few years, as he became a detective inspector.

The final straw had been when he came home in the early hours of the morning to find her sitting on the corner of the bed, dressed, two suitcases in the hallway downstairs.

'Sorry, Keith. I want a normal life, children, a dog in the garden.'

Tremayne remembered that day vividly. It wasn't as if the love between the two had waned; it was his devotion to his police work that had come between them. He could have said there and then that she was more important than his career, but he hadn't, couldn't, and then she was gone.

For over twenty-five years they had not spoken apart from the occasional phone call for the first couple of years after she had walked out, but she had met someone else, and then nothing.

He had contacted her after their previous case, and found she was widowed with two adult children. Their first meeting after so many years had been awkward and it had not been successful, but now there was a weekend away, and he was hopeful of a reconciliation. He realised that would impact on his policing. He knew he may have to make a decision: the ex-wife he still felt strongly about, but not sure if it was love, as that seemed more for Yarwood's age group.

There had been a few women over the years, but they had only been dalliances, no more than a passing attraction. One had moved in, wanted to change him, moved out within two months after realising that the man was an immovable object and it was either her or him. Apart from that, there had been very little love in his life. He regretted that as he sat with Freestone, a man who had been married to the same woman for nearly forty years, a man he may have to charge with murder within the next week.

He hoped it wasn't the accountant that he regarded as a friend. If it were, Tremayne would do his duty, he knew that.

'Who do you suspect?' Freestone asked.

'You've got a motive if we find anything underhanded,' Tremayne said. Peter Freestone was an intelligent man, so there was no point in telling him otherwise.

'Apart from me?'

'Who would you suspect?' Tremayne asked. 'Who do you think would have a violent streak? Who would have a reason to want the man dead?'

'Have you checked Mason's records?'

'Not in detail. The man was methodical, we know that. We've found no illegal dealings, nothing untoward.'

'He was tough as a solicitor. He must have ruffled a few feathers, put a few noses out of joint.'

'Enough to kill for?'

'Check with Len Dowling's brother.'

'Do you know anything?'

'Have you met Chris Dowling?'

'Yes. I met him with Sergeant Yarwood.'

'Aggressive?'

'He wanted to be.'

'I like Len,' Freestone said. 'Not his brother.'

'Any reason?'

'I don't trust him. He's too smart for me.'

'Any dirt on him?'

'Nothing specific.'

'Fiona Dowling?'

'My daughter went to school with Cheryl Milledge and Fiona Dowling. They used to come over to the house at weekends.'

'And?'

'Fiona was pretty, Cheryl was not. My daughter was friendly with them for a couple of years, and then they stopped coming.'

'Any reason why?'

'Nothing special. It's not the sort of conversation you have with your children. I was aware that Cheryl had changed, as had Fiona. Our daughter, thankfully, got through her adolescence without too much trouble. She came home a few times drunk, no doubt experimented with the boys, but not too much.'

'Your daughter told you that?'

'She'd speak to her mother, who'd tell me, not that I wanted to hear that our daughter was not the vestal virgin, no father wants to hear that.'

'What else can you tell me about Cheryl and Fiona?'

'Only titbits from our daughter. Cheryl started sleeping around, an unwanted pregnancy at one stage.'

'What happened to the child?'

'I've no idea. She may have aborted it or had the child adopted. I don't know the answer. I certainly didn't ask questions.'

'Fiona Dowling?'

'I used to see her around with Len Dowling. They were both no more than children then, and I was friends with Dowling's father.'

'Where is he now?'

'He went overseas, chasing the sun. I've lost contact with him.'

'What did the father say about Len and Fiona?'

'He was very fond of her, saw her as a good influence.'

'Is she?' Tremayne asked.

'She can be bossy, always wanting the lead female role. There's only two in *Julius Caesar*: Calpurnia, Caesar's wife and Portia, Brutus's wife.'

'Does she justify the lead role?'

'Most times, but Cheryl doesn't see it that way. To be honest, Cheryl is keen, but she's heavy on her feet. Calpurnia is assumed to be attractive, vivacious, not that anyone knows for sure.'

'Why do you mean?'

'We always assume that successful and powerful men have beautiful wives, that's all. Calpurnia could have been ugly for all we know, but she lived two thousand years ago.'

'Dennison qualifies on the successful and the beautiful wife.'

'The lovely Samantha.'

'Sarcasm or a genuine reflection of the woman?'

'Sarcasm, I suppose. She's a knockout, no doubt keeps Dennison happy, but she's not my type.'

'Why do you say that?'

'She's high-maintenance.'

'A driven woman?'

'Fiona is. Samantha Dennison would be as well. Fiona portrays herself as a socialite, into charitable causes, always there supporting her husband. Samantha makes no pretence of what she is.'

'Are you saying that Fiona is tarred with the same brush.'

'As I said, a driven woman.'

'Capable of murder?'

'How would I know? It may be something you're used to, Tremayne, but the majority of us live our lives oblivious to the harsh realities. I've seen death, who hasn't at our age, but I've not experienced murder before. All I've said is that Fiona and Samantha are determined.'

'And Cheryl Milledge?'

'She's latched on to Gary Barker. That man's not going far.'

As far as a profitable garden centre on the outskirts of Salisbury, Tremayne thought but did not mention it to Freestone.

***

Tremayne and Clare met back in the office. It was dark outside, and it was close to eight in the evening. Tremayne wanted an early finish, Clare did not. In the office and during the day, she was fine, but the nights still remained difficult. It was hard not to think of Harry.

She had to agree that Trevor Winston and his team had done a great job on her hair, but who was it for? Harry would have complimented her on how lovely she looked; Tremayne wouldn't even notice. Still, she was better in Salisbury, in that the tears were slowly drying up. Back with her parents, her father had wanted to distract her from her recollection of Harry; her mother had told her to get out into the dating market again, find a good man, a good Christian, an every Sunday at the church man. The only every Sunday at the church man she knew in the current case had been Gordon Mason, a misogynist bigot. No thanks, she thought.

If another man came into her life – and she felt almost guilty that she even considered it, so soon after Harry's death – she wouldn't care what he was as long as he was kind to her. Harry had been, but love was not about choosing the perfect mate based on a set of criteria. Samantha Dennison had done that, and hers was a pretend happiness. Fiona Dowling had evaluated her mate and then moulded him into what she wanted. No, Clare knew it would be love, the only criterion that mattered, and she would not try to change the man.

She knew it served no purpose to think of the past when the present was all around her, and when there was an active murder case about to be burst open. The motives, the skeletons, the rumours, were all coming together.

'Yarwood, what do we have?' Tremayne said. He had seen his sergeant drifting off into memory land. He had given her a few minutes while he collected his own thoughts.

'We've not found any wrongdoing at the council offices so far. Cheryl Milledge was there, helping us.'

'She's the one who could have made the changes, you do realise that?'

'She's an administrator. She may have been involved, but I'm not so sure.'

'Why?'

'If the documents were altered, it would need someone to prepare them, the building inspector to see them, and then someone to register the change.'

'And?'

'I think we may be chasing a red herring here.'

'I still don't trust Len Dowling, nor his brother,' Tremayne said.

'Neither do I. If I'm buying a property in Salisbury, I know where I'm not going.'

'If you can find an agent who's any better, let me know.'

'You've met Peter Freestone,' Clare said. 'What did he have to say?'

'He knew Fiona Dowling and Cheryl Milledge as schoolgirls.'

'Any observations?'

'Fiona, he reckoned, is driven; Cheryl rolls with the punches.'

'Cheryl's a smart woman, don't underestimate her.'

'Capable of murder?'

'I've no idea. She's smart, devoted to Gary Barker from what I could make out.'

'Her records at the council?'

'Considering the condition of that awful bedsit they share, her files were correctly labelled, and her work area was spotless.'

'If we're discounting the land deal, then what is the motive?'

'It has to be blackmail.'

'There's Fiona Dowling's affair. Did the man have some dirt on Dennison or his wife? He'd acted inappropriately towards Cheryl Milledge.'

'Dennison's wife may have a history. According to her, she had a background.'

'Background of what? By the way, your hair looks nice.'

'I didn't think you'd noticed.'

'I'm not good with compliments.'

'Thanks, it's appreciated.'

'Can we get back to the case instead of going on about your hair?'

Clare could see that the man was embarrassed at showing kindness. She liked him even more for his saying the right thing.

Tremayne leant back on his chair; Clare rested her back against the office wall. The day had been long; both were tired.

'Samantha Dennison said that I should find myself a rich man,' Clare said.

'That's not your style.'

'I know that, but if Dennison's wealth was threatened, he knows that Samantha would be off very quickly.'

'Are you suggesting that Mason could have impacted Dennison's wealth?'

'It's possible, although I'm not sure how. Gordon Mason was financially comfortable, lived frugally. Why would he care about Dennison?'

'He had insulted Samantha, had an altercation with Dennison. Maybe Mason bore a grudge.'

'That's possible, but how could he have an impact on Dennison?'

'Check it out,' Tremayne said. 'Dennison's playing the financial markets, no doubt using offshore bank accounts to hide his money from the tax man. There's also the possibility of insider trading. That's a criminal offence, time in jail. That's a motive, even better than a fraudulent land deal.'

'I'll look into it tomorrow,' Clare said.

'I'm off home, fancy a pint on the way?'

'I'll drink orange juice.'

'Yarwood, there's no hope for you. A police officer who can't drink a pint.'

'I had a glass of champagne with Samantha Dennison.'

'You don't want my definition of champagne, do you?'

'Not tonight I don't.'

Chapter 15

Bill Ford seemed to be the only one of the dramatic society who had no skeletons, no axe to grind. According to Freestone, the man attended rehearsals and the performances, put in a solid effort, and would have a drink afterwards at a local pub, but apart from that he did not socialise, abuse the women, threaten the men.

Freestone acknowledged that he and his wife would take the man out for the occasional meal, more out of sorrow for him after the death of his wife. But even then, he couldn't say that he knew Bill Ford in that he said little about his life.

Years of experience had told Tremayne that no one is without some misdemeanours, something they regretted, a wrong turn in life. He knew that he needed to find out, see if the man had an Achilles heel that would turn him from passive to active, something that could be construed as a motive.

It was cold in the back room of the funeral home where Ford was preparing an old man for his funeral, the coffin open for his nearest and dearest to say their fond farewells. Tremayne knew the deceased, having run him in on a couple of occasions for grievous bodily harm. He thought that he'd have no one crying over him, but according to Ford, the man's family were paying for the full treatment.

'Mr Ford,' Tremayne said, oblivious to the man continuing to work. Clare thought it disrespectful, but said nothing. 'We've interviewed everyone so far in depth apart from you.'

'I've spoken to you on a couple of occasions.'

'That we understand, but so far we know very little about you.'

'What's to tell? I do my job, go home, go to London on a regular basis.'

'Our problem still remains with a motive.'

'Mason wasn't the easiest man to get along with.'

'But murder?'

'Who knows what goes through the minds of people.'

'Which people, anyone in particular?' Tremayne asked.

Bill Ford continued to prepare the dead man. 'Sorry, but I'm working to a schedule here. The relatives will be here within the next two hours.'

Tremayne knew that some of those coming would not be pleased to see him. They were a family of villains, but apparently with money, judging by the meticulous care that the funeral director was taking with the body.

'You mentioned people. Anyone in mind?'

'I joined the dramatic society to get out of the house after my wife died. I didn't join to pry into anyone else's business.'

'But you're an astute man, you must have seen something.'

'The one thing about my regular friends is that they say very little, they mind their own business, and they don't become involved,' Ford said, nodding his head in the direction of the dead man.

'We're very much alive, we're police officers, and we do become involved. It's unfortunate, but I must continue to probe. Gordon Mason died for a reason, a reason that still remains unclear.'

'The man wasn't popular.'

'It's not a reason for murder. Did you like him, Mr Ford?'

'I neither like nor dislike anyone. I'm friendly with Peter Freestone and his wife. Gordon Mason was a fellow actor. We'd meet with the group, discuss the script, assign the roles, practise our lines. Apart from that, I rarely spoke to the man.'

Tremayne could see that the conversation was going nowhere. He looked over at Clare. She knew that he wanted her to become involved.

'Mr Ford, we are aware of reasons for your fellow actors to dislike Gordon Mason, but none seems strong enough to want him dead,' Clare said.

'Look at this man,' Ford said, pointing to the dead man. 'He was loved.'

'What's your point?'

'I've met his family, I know some of his past, yet he was loved. Gordon Mason was not loved, certainly by nobody that I knew of. Why do you think that is?'

'I've no idea. What do you think?'

'I don't think. It's just strange that a person can have a life devoid of any affection, that's all.'

'It's hardly a reason for murder. Tell us about your fellow actors.'

'As long as I don't miss my deadline. My client isn't concerned as to time, but his family is.'

'Okay, brief, single sentence answers.'

'Fire away.'

'Peter Freestone?'

'Decent and honest.'

'Phillip Dennison?'

'Wealthy, likes to show it off, attractive wife.'

'Any more to say about Samantha Dennison?'

'No. It's not my concern that she's a lot younger than her husband. That's between her and him.'

'Jimmy Francombe?'

'Young, keen, always cheerful.'

'Geoff Pearson?'

'Ambitious man. The women like him.'

'Anyone in particular?'

'I don't become involved.'

'It's a murder enquiry, Mr Ford,' Tremayne said. 'If you know anything, it's your civic responsibility to tell us.'

'Fiona Dowling liked him.'

'Anything more?'

'Mason suspected something.'

'I thought you didn't speak to him.'

'Once or twice he'd want to talk. He assumed I was a religious man, the same as him.'

'Are you?'

'I believe, but that's all. I've not seen anything to make me a fervent believer like Mason. My religion is private, moderate, and above all else non-critical. If Pearson and Dowling's wife were involved, it's between them and her husband. Mason didn't see it that way.'

'How did he see it?'

'He saw it as a sin against the Lord.'

'Did he tell Len Dowling?'

'He didn't like him.'

'But did he tell him?'

'You'll need to ask Len Dowling.'

Clare pressed on, aware that the man was non-committal with all his answers. It appeared to her that was how the man lived his life: a cold fish who neither loved nor hated, expressed anger or joy. Clare assumed it was as a result of spending too much time with the dead, being soulful and understanding with the relatives. Whatever it was, she didn't like it. To her, life was for the living, not standing for hours in a windowless room with only a corpse for company. She wanted out of that foreboding place and some fresh air.

'Gary Barker?'

'Easy-going, drinks more than he should.'

'I thought you weren't concerned about other people.'

'Drink himself under a table as far as I'm concerned, but he drinks and drives, that's all. One day, he'll have an accident, and then it'll be him in here or someone he hit.'

'Cheryl Barker?'

'Strong-willed. Keeps Gary under control.'

'Capable of losing her temper, capable of hate?'

'I'm not sure about hate, but she has a temper.'

'Any examples?'

'Her and Fiona Dowling don't get on.'

'They went to school together.'

'I know that.'

'How?'

'I took Fiona out once or twice before she met Len.'

'You're a few years older?'

'Only five or six.'

'It's eight actually.'

'Anyway, we went out together.'

'And what happened?'

'We were in our teens, or at least she was. I was in my early twenties. It was fun for a while.'

It was the first time that Ford had even referred to the possibility of fun. His countenance all the times they had encountered the funeral director rarely showed emotion and never a smile.

'Does Len Dowling know this?'

'I've never told him, and I doubt if Fiona has.'

'Why's that?'

'Dowling knows of his wife's wild behaviour in her teens. I doubt if she wanted to elaborate on it. She'd rather forget, no doubt.'

'But you're a remembrance.'

'I was just one of many. I don't intend to denigrate Fiona. I've some fond memories, one of the few times in my life when I felt free.'

'You don't feel free now?'

'What do you think?'

'I couldn't do what you do,' Clare said.

'Family tradition. Someone had to carry on with the business.'

'Coming back to Fiona. Did Cheryl know about you two?'

'There was one night when she came out with us.'

'And what happened?'

'The three of us ended up in my bed,' Ford said. Tremayne looked up in shock, Clare felt like sitting down. The man with no apparent vices, no joy, had a past.

'Why have you told us?' Clare asked.

'I don't know. Maybe I just wanted to relive another time when I wasn't a funeral director.'

'Did Gordon Mason know about this?'

'I may have told him.'

'But why?'

'I don't know. Sometimes I get melancholy, feel like standing up on the roof and shouting.'

'You've spent too long in here with these bodies,' Tremayne said.

'It's a family tradition. The Fords have been funeral directors in Salisbury for the last one hundred and ten years.'

'You need to get out of here more often,' Tremayne said.

'I can't end the tradition.'

Tremayne and Clare left the man to his work. As they left the building, Tremayne could see some villains coming their way. He took hold of Yarwood's arm and steered her into a café nearby.

'What do you reckon?' Tremayne asked.

'The man has a macabre personality. Too long with those bodies has affected him.'

'Capable of murder?'

'Capable of anything. The only spark in him was when he spoke about Fiona and Cheryl.'

'That came as a shock.'

'It's a motive, especially if Mason knew. Fiona's not his murderer, though.'

'She wouldn't want it bandied around that she had indulged in a threesome. Her social set would accept that she had been wild in her youth, but a threesome has connotations of perversion. She would do anything to protect that information.'

'What about Cheryl?'

'Would she care what people think of her? Her past is an open book.'

***

Tremayne and Clare returned to Bemerton Road Police Station. On Tremayne's desk, an official letter marked private and confidential.

'Important, guv?' Clare asked. She had seen Tremayne looking at it with contempt.

'It's Moulton again, trying to intimidate me into retiring.'

'He can't do that.'

'He can intimidate, keep up the heat in the hope that I'll cave in.'

'Will you?'

'What do you reckon, Yarwood?'

'Can he force you?'

'No.'

'Then why ask me? Just ignore him. We've got a murder enquiry to deal with.'

'Yarwood, you're becoming pushy.'

'I've had a good teacher.'

'I suppose so,' Tremayne replied, a smile on his face.

'Bill Ford, what do you reckon?' Clare asked.

'How did he become like that?'

'Life takes turns you least expect. It's certainly had some effect on him, and he'd be inured to the sight of death.'

'A potential murderer?'

'They all are.'

'As I told you, Yarwood, everyone has skeletons in the cupboard. Everyone is capable of causing harm to another if their life or their families are threatened.'

Tremayne looked around his office, realised that he had paperwork to do, but not today. Yarwood, he could see, was all the better for being busy. The man wanted out of the office and soon.

As the two prepared to leave a familiar if not welcome face appeared at the door. 'A moment of your time, Detective Inspector.'

Clare could see the look on her senior's face, the look of determination on Superintendent Moulton's.

'What can I do for you?' Tremayne asked. Clare thought Tremayne was brusque in his reply.

'You've seen my letter?'

'It's not the first one.'

'And not the last, either.'

'I thought we'd resolved this.'

'The Police Federation have, I realise that, but there's a directive from senior management to bring in fresh blood,' Moulton said. Tremayne knew that the directive was a recommendation, not an order. He had contacts in other police stations within the region that were going through the same exercise. Some of his contemporaries had accepted, some hadn't.

'It's a generous package,' Moulton said.

'I never said it wasn't, but I'm comfortable. The house is paid off, I've no debts.'

'Put your feet up, enjoy yourself.'

Clare, who should not have been listening, but was only eight feet away at her desk, realised that Moulton did not understand. The man was career-driven, Tremayne was results-driven, and he was enjoying himself. She had to admit that she was, as well. She hoped the feeling of a job well done, the satisfaction of a result, would not leave her. If it did, she knew that she may as well be back at her parents' hotel as manager.

She had considered it for a time while she was consumed with grief, but it had not helped. There were too many times to reflect back to Harry, too many hours between the guests leaving and their replacements arriving. She knew that with Tremayne and a murder enquiry it was full on from morning to night, and then exhaustion once she made it back to her cottage. The cats that Harry had had an issue with would be waiting for her, a warm bed that she would share with them. She had heard the rustling of the branches, their scraping against the roof, an owl hooting in the distance, even deer in the field behind, but she had felt no fear.

In fact, the place was coming up for sale. She needed Tremayne and his Homicide department, the security of the police force, for the finance. Her parents, she knew, would have lent her the money, but she did not want their input; it would come with conditions, and her mother would be down at the cottage advising on what colour to paint the walls, the style of furniture, the need to find another man.

Tremayne, the cantankerous detective inspector, would never offer advice, would always be there for her. Clare realised that she appreciated his company more than that of her parents. She thought it was wrong somehow, but she could not alter the facts.

'Yarwood, are you ready or are you going to sit there all day?'

'Superintendent Moulton?'

'He'll leave us alone. The man's a pain, always worrying about his key performance indicators, whatever they are.'

'You don't know?'

'I know what they are. I just don't understand the relevance. He talks about lowering the average age of the people in the station, reducing expenditure, and only hiring degree-educated people.'

'They're important. Maybe not the age issue.'

'The man means well, I suppose, and we always need people in Administration.'

'Administration? He's a police officer.'

'Administration. He doesn't understand villains. Probably never met one.'

'He was out on the street once,' Clare said.

'If he was, he's forgotten what it was like. He wanted to give me a lecture on how to conduct a murder investigation. The man's probably never seen a murder victim.'

'I'm sure he has, guv.'

'Yarwood, let me have my two minutes. The man irritates me, and I've got to call him sir. I know what I'd call him if I had half a chance.'

'He can't make you retire, correct?'

'Not for another couple of years.'

'Then why worry about him?'

'You're right, Yarwood. What's next? Who haven't we interviewed?'

'We've interviewed everyone. They've all got reasons to not like Mason, but none has admitted to killing him.'

'Do they ever?'

'The re-enactment's this weekend.'

'We'll go and see Freestone, check that it's all organised.'

Chapter 16

Phillip Dennison had gone short on the exchange rate between the American dollar and the English pound when he should have gone long. Most days he read it right, but it had been three in a row now, and he was worried. His wife was continuing to spend as if there was no tomorrow, which in her case, he thought may be possible.

He didn't know why she was that way. When they had met, she had been beautiful and genuinely desirable, but since he had joined the dramatic society as a way of reducing his stress, she had become difficult, unable to listen to criticism, unwilling to curb her spending when the finances were precarious. He knew it could not continue. He needed out.

Dennison made a phone call.

'What can I do for you?' Chris Dowling asked on picking up his phone.

'We need to meet.'

'My office, forty-five minutes.'

Dennison left his laptop on, the negatives in his account visible on the screen. He left the house and drove to Salisbury. The Aston Martin was with his wife; he took a BMW. It was her car really and when he had bought it for her, she had been delighted, but now it was a never-ending cycle of increased spending on cars and holidays and clothes that remained in the bags that she had brought them home in. His situation was desperate; Chris Dowling was his way out.

He found Dowling in his office. He'd seen the Aston Martin parked next to one of the most expensive shops in the city on his way there. He remembered her in that office when they had first met. How he had lusted after her. He had seen the young men with their eyes peering at her, taking every opportunity to be close to her, but it had been him with his wealth who had won her.

She wasn't the first that had succumbed, she wouldn't be the last, although the next time he'd be more careful. Or maybe he wouldn't, he knew that. When the market was running, and he was on a winning streak, the money would flow in. He needed an outlet. The dramatic society had provided it for the last couple of years; before that, it had been expensive cars and expensive women. Now, one woman was causing him aggravation. That day, as he entered Chris Dowling's office, he was down over one hundred thousand pounds, and that was likely to increase by at least another two thousand by the time his wife had finished exercising her gold credit card.

'Look, Dowling, I'm desperate. The woman's bleeding me dry.'

'I said at the time that she was going to cause you trouble.'

'I know. I didn't listen.'

'I told you to put an agreement in place, but what did you do?'

'I loved her.'

'Dennison, you may be a hotshot money man, but you're clueless with women. It's one thing to seduce women like Samantha, it's another to keep them. What do you think she finds attractive in you: your good looks, your good manners?'

'I know. Don't lecture.'

'You can divorce her, but she'll take half your assets.'

'She's welcome to them today.'

'That bad?'

'Tomorrow I'll make it up.'

'No doubt you will, but Samantha's not going away. As long as you indulge her, she'll stay.'

'I'll talk to her tonight. Tell her what's happening,' Dennison said.

'She'll not be responsive to your charms afterwards.'

'She hasn't been for some time.'

'Women like her need a man in their bed. Any suspicions?'

'None that I know of. Do you believe that's possible?'

'We've known each other for a long time, what do you think?'

'With who?'

'How the hell would I know? She's your wife, you ask her. And take the keys of the Aston Martin. You don't want her fancy man driving it, do you?'

***

'It's all arranged,' Peter Freestone said. This time Clare had asked him not to smoke his pipe.

'A stand-in for Caesar?' Tremayne asked.

'I've got someone.'

'Another actor?'

'He doesn't often come, but he will as a special favour to me.'

'He owes you one?'

'I've offered to help him out with a business plan. It's costing me to help you.'

'You're still a suspect,' Tremayne said.

'Hopefully, you'll deduce who is the guilty party at the re-enactment. It's not much fun sitting in a pub with a man who thinks you might be a murderer.'

'It's not much fun for me either,' Tremayne said. 'At least you'll drink a beer. Yarwood's on orange juice, champagne even.'

'Just the once,' Clare said.

'We've drawn a blank on your rezoning. It appears that it was above board.'

'Len Dowling took the risk, reaped the reward,' Freestone said.

'He's still a suspect.'

'Who isn't?'

'Until this is wrapped up, everyone is. Do you deal with Dennison's tax returns?'

'I have in the past, not recently.'

'Anything unusual?'

'The man understands his tax liabilities, structures his dealings accordingly.'

'Any suggestion of tax avoidance?'

'If there were, I'd be required to notify the authorities.'

'Would you?'

'Don't use Dennison as a way of getting at me again. I've been honest with you.'

'You've seen where he lives, the car his wife drives. Do his tax returns reflect his income?'

'I prepare his tax returns based on the information received from him.'

'That's not what I asked.'

'I know that. I would have prepared Dennison's tax returns based on the information received. He, as with any other client, will sign that they are declaring the truth. I will then sign that I've prepared the return based on the client's input. Legally, I've acted in accordance with the law.'

'You've still not answered my question,' Tremayne said.

'I have.'

***

The last person that was expected at the re-enactment was Samantha Dennison, but there she was, sitting in the front row. The cast were all there, although Fiona Dowling had been late arriving, and Len Dowling was complaining about a potential lost sale.

Phillip Dennison did not appear to be in a good mood, casting glances at his wife, for once dressed sensibly. Nobody seemed to be in the best of humour, apart from Gary Barker and Cheryl Milledge, both of whom had come in costume.

Tremayne took centre stage at the old fort. 'Ladies and gentlemen, thanks for coming tonight. I've asked Jim Hughes, our crime scene examiner, to be present. It's not usual for him to attend a re-enactment. I've asked him as a special favour as we still have the issue of how Gordon Mason died.'

'I thought that was clear,' Bill Ford said.

'You're correct in that we know that he died from two stab wounds to the heart, as well as three others. Four of the five would have ultimately been fatal. The question is, how did those who committed the murder know which dagger would kill him, and how were the fake daggers swapped?'

'Was every dagger we carried on that stage modified?' Geoff Pearson asked. Clare noticed that he was standing at some distance from Fiona Dowling, his latest girlfriend sitting to one side of Samantha Dennison.

'Two were.'

'And you don't know who held those two?' Cheryl Milledge asked.

'No. We're assuming that whoever had the lethal daggers knew. Jim is certain that a retractable dagger punching the man's body and one that entered would have distinctly different feels. There is some conjecture on this, as in the scene, frenetic as it was, an adrenaline rush may have confused those taking part. Regardless, we need to see if that was the case. There is also the additional factor of how the daggers were swapped. Peter Freestone brought the fakes here, two of you have testified that they were indeed plastic bladed and harmless. That means the swap occurred here.'

'Someone would have seen,' Fiona Dowling said.

'Not necessarily. It was dark.'

'It can't be Cheryl or me.'

'We know there were two daggers, which would suggest two men,' Tremayne said. 'Can we be certain that Mason was not stabbed off the stage? It would not have to be a man then. We have, more than likely, two murderers here tonight, possibly three, maybe only one. We need to know how many and who.'

'It makes no sense,' Gary Barker said. 'The man was not liked, but three people. What's the motive?'

'There are motives, but none seem sufficient for murder, and if they were, how do those responsible expect to maintain their innocence. We will find out who did it and they will be arrested. I've also arranged for two police cars, five uniforms to be present.'

'That's intimidation,' Dennison said.

'It's policing. Someone here is a murderer. They can either admit to their guilt now, save us all a cold night up here, or we'll carry on. Any takers?'

Clare looked around to see innocent looks on all the faces. Samantha Dennison, not present on the night of Mason's murder, scowled. Clare could see that the situation between her and her husband was not good. She walked over to her. 'Samantha, I'm surprised to see you here,' Clare said.

'Phillip's threatened me.'

'How?'

'He's had his solicitor on to me.'

'Why?'

'He's a bastard, that's why. Phillip wants to clip my wings, take the Aston Martin away from me.'

'You do spend a lot.'

'He knew the deal.'

'Is he trading up?'

'The younger model? No. I think he's lost the edge. He can't afford me.'

'You'll take off?'

'Once I've secured my share of the deal.'

'And what's that?'

'Half the assets.'

'For four years of marriage?'

'Phillip did say he'd see me right when the time came.'

'In writing?'

'He's pleading poverty.'

'Maybe he is.'

'Not him. He's stashing it somewhere, and he's got someone making sure I can't get my hands on it.'

'Any idea who?'

'He's using Chris Dowling as his solicitor.'

'You know the man?'

'We've met.'

Clare left the woman and went back over to where Tremayne and Freestone were setting up the re-enactment. 'She's a bitter woman,' Clare said to Tremayne.

'You've seen Phillip Dennison. He's not in the best of humour either.'

Jim Hughes was with Freestone, discussing the daggers. 'These are the ones I've purchased for tonight,' Freestone said. Hughes ran his fingers over the blades, checked the retracting mechanism. He declared them harmless.

***

Tremayne and Clare had focussed on the assassination scene, not the entire production, up to now. The idea that three people could have been involved seemed illogical. And even if it was three, the question remained as to why kill the man on a stage in front of a group of people. If Mason had deserved to die, at least in the minds of the murderers, then why at Old Sarum? The man, it was known, lived in a depressingly drab house not far from Salisbury. Tremayne and Clare had been out there after his death, found nothing of interest, just an unkempt garden, a house that smelt of disinfectant, and not much else, not even a television. There was a library, complete with books, but most were legal or thrillers, neither of which interested Tremayne.

Peter Freestone, directing as well as playing the part of Brutus, was a busy man. The scene where Mason was killed was some way into the production. Firstly, there were three scenes in Act 1, four scenes in Act 2, not that most people knew the full play, only Mark Antony's speech to the crowd inciting them against the conspirators, and little else.

Friends, Romans and countrymen, lend me your ears,
I come to bury Caesar, not to praise him…

What concerned Tremayne was how the daggers had been changed and when, and what could have occurred before the assassination. The crowd scenes involved some of Jimmy Francombe's school friends. Clare had spoken to them, received the Francombe chat-up lines, been asked about the hot date.

She had brushed them off with a smile, realising that they were just the same as Jimmy: polite, full of testosterone, and desperate to show their friends that they were better than them.

Act 1, Scene 1, and Bill Ford and Gary Barker were on stage, playing the parts of Flavius and Marullus respectively. Two of Jimmy's friends were playing the two commoners, one a carpenter, the other a cobbler. Clare sat out the front with Samantha Dennison. Tremayne was around the back. The problem with the re-enactment, Tremayne could see, was that the people taking part were not taking it seriously; there was no sense of urgency. The first act had concluded and Act 1, Scene 2 should have commenced promptly, but it was five minutes, and no one was on the stage. It was the first scene for Caesar, as well as for Casca, Calpurnia, Mark Antony, the soothsayer, Brutus, Cassius, and Trebonius. Caesar was being played by William Bradshaw, an actor who had come down from Swindon, a city about forty miles north of Salisbury. As Freestone had said, the man was familiar with the part, having played it in another production. Tremayne knew that the man was not involved, as he had not been present on the night of Mason's death.

The soothsayer, eight lines in total, a minor part, although with the immortal line *Beware the ides of March,* was played by Robert Hemsworth, a local schoolteacher. Freestone had told Tremayne earlier that the man rarely attended their meetings, never came to the pub, and was not friendly. He was, however, dependable, punctual, and a decent actor. Tremayne had discounted him from being involved. He knew that whoever had swapped the daggers had to have a tie-in with the conspirators. Trebonius, one of the conspirators, played by Hemsworth's brother, James, had not been present at the stabbing, as his part required that he had to take Mark Antony out of the Senate when Caesar was assassinated.

Ten minutes later, instead of one, the actors filed onto the stage for Act 1, Scene 2. Trevor Winston was in costume, as was Jimmy Francombe; the others were not.

Clare looked at Samantha Dennison as her husband came onto the stage; she could see the contempt in the woman's face. 'What are you going to do, Samantha?'

'I've told you.'

'He's brought you tonight. He must care.'

'He wants to keep an eye on me.'

'Why?'

'In case I do something foolish.'

'Is that likely?'

'It's always possible.'

'What sort of thing?'

'Cut his clothes with a pair of scissors, run the edge of a coin down his Aston Martin.'

'That seems extreme.'

'Not for that bastard, it isn't. He's taken my credit cards.'

'Samantha, someone murdered Gordon Mason. If it's your husband, he could murder you.'

'Not him.'

'Are you certain? I don't want to be the one who has to identify you.'

'Do you think he could do something?'
'I don't know. I suggest you don't provoke him.'
'I already have.'
'How?'
'I told him I had a lover.'
'Is it true?'
'I told him it was Geoff Pearson.'
'Is it true?'
'If he had money it could be, but no.'
'And your husband's reaction?'
'He slapped me across the face, called me a shameless tart, no better than a common prostitute.'
'What did you do?'
'I came here tonight.'
'And Geoff Pearson?'
'Phillip will do nothing.'
'Are you sure?'
'I hope I am.'

Chapter 17

Act 1, Scene 3, and Len Dowling was playing the additional role of Cicero, the only scene in the play where the character appears. Dowling had used a wig to change his appearance on the night of the production. The parts of Casca, Cassius, and Cinna were again played by Trevor Winston, Geoff Pearson, and Gary Barker respectively. Cicero came on with Casca, said his lines and departed, and Cassius walked on.

Tremayne occupied himself around the back looking for an opportunity to change the daggers, realising that the two lethal weapons could have been hidden under the Roman robes the actors wore. He also realised that all he was going to get that night was cold and wet. It had started to drizzle, and those who had been standing outside or sitting on the grass had moved to somewhere under cover. Tremayne looked for Yarwood; he could see her talking to Samantha Dennison. He did not want to disturb her.

'Do you want to carry on?' Freestone asked. 'They're starting to complain about the weather.'

'Would you have cancelled on the night because of a little rain?'

'No.'

'Then that's what we'll do. So far, I've not seen how the daggers were changed.'

'Don't ask me. I only put on the production, take a leading role on stage.'

The weather improved, the production continued: Act 2, Scenes 1 to 4 passed by. Tremayne focussed on the daggers, aiming to get an angle on how it was done, and on why the man was murdered during a production of Shakespeare's *Julius Caesar*, and for what reason.

The most crucial scene, at least for Tremayne, was Act 3, Scene 1: a crowd of people, Jimmy Francombe's friends, amongst them the soothsayer and Artemidorus.

Caesar speaks to the soothsayer: *The ides of March are come.*

The soothsayer responds: *Ay, Caesar; but not gone.*

Artemidorus, played by another friend of Jimmy Francombe, attempts to warn Caesar about those who plot against him.

Then Caesar's entry into the Senate, Metellus pleading for Caesar to end the banishment of his brother, the casting aside of his request.

The daggers plunging into Caesar: the first by Casca, and then the others, Cassius, Cinna, Metellus, Decius Brutus, Ligarius, and, finally, Brutus.

Tremayne could see it clearly. The two murderers on the stage had the daggers that had killed Mason hidden inside their robes. Whoever they were, they had brought them with them.

Tremayne went over to where Clare was sitting. 'I've seen enough,' he said.

Clare excused herself to Samantha Dennison and walked away with Tremayne. 'You know who did it?'

'I know how the daggers were brought in.'

'How?'

'The two who killed Mason had them hidden under their clothes when they came to Old Sarum, and after they changed into costume, they hid them under their robes. It's easy once you see it,' Tremayne said.

'No idea on who, though?'

'None. What's the deal with Dennison's wife?'

'He's clipped her wings.'

'Why?'

'According to her, he's taken away her credit cards, the key to the Aston Martin.'

'She'll not like that. She'll be off soon.'

'She wants her money first.'

'How much?'

'Half of everything that the husband has.'

'She'll be lucky. What security does she have?'

'Only his word. She may have genuinely loved him at first,' Clare said.

'And now?'

'I don't think there's much love left. He threatened her; she told him that Geoff Pearson was her lover.'

'Is he?'

'According to her, he's not.'

'If Dennison's a murderer, then Pearson's compromised.'

'We need to talk to Dennison,' Clare said. 'The man's threatened his wife, and now he believes she's cheating on him.'

Tremayne left Clare and went back to Peter Freestone. 'You can wrap it up. I've seen enough.'

'We were just about to go anyway. Did you get what you wanted?'

'I think so.'

'The murderer or murderers?'

'Not yet, but the pieces are coming together.'

'Don't ask for another re-enactment,' Freestone said.

'Why?'

'We're disbanding, too much has happened. It was fun, but now we don't feel comfortable in each other's company. Maybe after this is all over, but for now, we'll not meet, at least not as a dramatic society.'

'Sorry to hear that,' Tremayne said.

***

The body was found ninety minutes later. By that time, virtually everyone had gone, apart from Tremayne, Clare, and Peter Freestone. The first they knew that something was wrong was when Geoff Pearson's new girlfriend from Southampton came running over to them. 'I can't find Geoff,' she said.

Up till that time Clare had taken little notice of her, apart from saying hello to her when she arrived.

'We'd thought you'd gone.'

'We were leaving and then we decided to take a walk around outside, where the old cathedral was.'

'What happened?'

'We were fooling around, seeing who could get to the car first. I'm up ahead, Geoff's behind me, and then all of a sudden, nothing. I thought he was just playing a game. I went back, but I couldn't see him.'

'We'll find him,' Tremayne said.

Two uniforms, who had hoped for an early night, took out their torches and headed in the direction of the cathedral ruins. They came back within ten minutes. 'We've phoned for an ambulance,' one of them said.

'Is he hurt?' the girlfriend asked.

'I'm sorry.'

'Serious?' Clare asked.

'He's gone off the side of one of the ruined walls. There's a significant drop. He's landed heavily by the look of it.'

Tremayne and Clare, as well as the uniforms, the girlfriend, and Freestone, headed over to the area as fast as they could. It was dark, and the only torches were being held by the uniforms. 'He's down there,' one of the uniforms said.

Clare walked further along to some wooden steps. She descended, one of the uniforms with her, Geoff Pearson visible on the ground twenty feet in front of them. Clare approached the body, careful not to disturb the surrounding area, while the uniform shone the torch. She shouted up to Tremayne. 'We need Jim Hughes up here,' she said.

'Dead?'

'He's fallen heavily, broken his neck probably.'

The girlfriend collapsed into Tremayne's arms. He led her away.

Clare came back up the steps. The uniform shone his light at the area above where the body lay, the signs all too clear. 'It's murder. The man was pushed.'

She then phoned Hughes to confirm that the man's death was no longer suspicious as the signs of his being pushed were visible on the grass above where he fell.

Tremayne, once Clare had updated him, took control. The uniforms were establishing a crime scene, ensuring that no one else was in the area. Freestone confirmed that all the cars belonging to the dramatic society members had gone, except for Pearson's. The girlfriend sat in Clare's car, keeping warm with the heater on. Tremayne knew she would have to be interviewed and then taken home. Once again, as he'd expected, the one murder had become two; he was sure that Pearson would not be the last.

Clare came back from the crime scene, visibly upset.

'You need to detach yourself, Yarwood.'

'It's still sad.'

'Maybe it is, but we've got a job to do, and remember, he may have been one of the murderers.'

'Is that likely?'

'Why not? If he was, then the other one has dealt with him, destroying anyone who may have had a guilty conscience. What do you reckon?'

'Fiona Dowling, Phillip Dennison.'

'The spurned lover, the cheated husband. Anyone else?'

'Fiona Dowling won't be able to keep the affair secret from her husband.'

'Maybe he knew. He's a suspect as well. That's three. Any more?'

'It's enough to be going on with.'

'We're in for a long night.'

'Jim Hughes may be able to tell us if it was male or female.'

The crime scene team arrived at Old Sarum. They came equipped with a truck with a generator on the back. Within two hours, the site was ablaze with floodlights. A statement had been taken from the girlfriend, a blossoming romance in that she and Pearson had only been together for two weeks. Clare organised one of the police cars to take her home.

Tremayne was anxious for a definite suspect; Hughes was trying to do his job. 'Give me time, Tremayne,' Hughes said.

'Male or female?'

'The grass is damp underfoot. The man could have just slipped.'

'I don't believe it, neither does Yarwood.'

'And when did you two become experienced crime scene investigators?'

'It's murder, I know it is.'

'You may know it, but I need to prove it. They're not the same,' Hughes said.

Jim Hughes checked the man's body. It was clear that he had a broken neck, as Clare had ascertained, and that he had hit his head hard on the exposed wall of the cathedral as he fell, the blood visible in the grass beside the body. Hughes's team of investigators were up above, tracing the movements of three people: Geoff Pearson, his girlfriend, and the person responsible for pushing him over the wall. It was clear to Hughes that the fall, whereas a long drop, would not have automatically killed him. It would have caused broken bones and severe bruising, but the body would have been relaxed, not able to see where it was falling.

The verdict for him was either an unfortunate accident or attempted murder, as death was by no means certain. He knew Tremayne wanted clear proof of murder, but he was not going to get it.

'Okay, what is it?' Tremayne asked. He had moved away from the immediate area to smoke a cigarette, but now he was back.

'Yarwood was correct. The man's neck has been broken.'

'Male or female?'

'If you are referring to who he had an altercation with, then it's a female.'

'Are you certain?'

'We'll need to do further analysis, but the size of the shoe print is only small, the shape is feminine. Anyone you suspect?'

'A jilted lover.'

'Not the young girl that was here before?'

'She's not involved.'

'It's going to get nasty.'

'When hasn't it been. I'm afraid the Salisbury Amateur Dramatic Society is the same as everyone else, full of love and hatred.'

'A Shakespearean tragedy,' Hughes said.

'That's what it is,' Tremayne said. 'It's not over yet.'

***

Fiona Dowling arrived at Bemerton Road Police Station at two in the morning with her husband, Len. His brother, Chris, came five minutes later.

'You can't be in the interview, Mr Dowling,' Tremayne said to Len Dowling.

'Chris?'

'If he's Mrs Dowling's legal representative.'

'He will be.'

Tremayne commenced the interview, followed the procedure. At 2.38 a.m. the first question: 'Mrs Dowling, you are aware that Geoff Pearson has died at Old Sarum?'

'That was explained on the phone to me.'

'Do you wish to make a statement?'

'I was not involved. Why am I here?'

'Mrs Dowling, we have proof that Geoff Pearson was firmly pushed off the ruins of the old cathedral. We know from our crime scene team that a woman was close to him when he was pushed.'

'He was there with a young woman.'

'We've discounted her. And besides, she had no motive.'

'Neither do I.'

'Mrs Dowling, we know that you had a reason to hate the man,' Clare said.

'Does Chris need to be here?' Fiona Dowling asked.

'He is here at your request. I would suggest that he stays. The charge for Pearson's death will be murder, and at this time, all the evidence points towards you.'

'What proof do you have?' Chris Dowling said.

'We have a shoe print which will be subjected to further analysis. We also have a motive.'

'What motive?' Chris Dowling asked.

'Do I have to tell him?' Fiona Dowling asked Tremayne.

'We have sufficient proof to place a charge. It cannot be avoided.'

'It will destroy my marriage, my life.'

'I'm afraid that you should have considered that before.'

'Very well, but I did not push the man. It was an argument, that's all.'

'With his girlfriend nearby.'

'She wasn't his girlfriend. He had no right to be with her.'

'Why?'

'Because he was mine.'

'Fiona, what are you talking about?' Chris Dowling asked.

'We were lovers.'

'You and this man?'

'Why not? Your brother couldn't keep it up. I needed a man, a real man.'

Chris Dowling sat back, shocked by his sister-in-law's revelation.

'Mrs Dowling, you will be held in custody. Pending confirmation from the crime scene examiner, you will be charged with murder. Is there anything else that you wish to say in your defence?' Tremayne asked.

'Nothing. I was angry. I didn't know there was a drop. He belonged to me, not to that young girl.'

'It can be used in your defence,' Tremayne said. 'Are you able to assist in the murder of Gordon Mason? Was he blackmailing you over your affair? Did he know?'

'He knew. He wanted something in return to keep quiet.'

'What was that?'

'What do you think?'

'Sexual intercourse?' Clare said.

'With that awful man, no way. I've got my standards.'

'Instead of agreeing to his demand, you murdered the man.'

'I didn't kill him. You should have asked Geoff.'

'He denied it.'

'You believed him?'

'We had no reason to doubt him. He kept your secret.'

'He told Gordon Mason.'

'To our knowledge he did not. On the contrary, he was always discreet.'

'If he didn't, then who did?'

'We have no idea. Do you want to talk to your husband?'

'Not tonight. Chris can tell him.'

Chapter 18

Superintendent Moulton was pleased to have one murder solved; Tremayne was not. The killing of Gordon Mason remained predominant in his mind. The death of Geoff Pearson, caused by a possessive woman who had pushed him, was probably not premeditated. It seemed to Tremayne that pushing someone in anger in a grassy area, not knowing about the drop to one side, would not necessarily be construed as murder, and that manslaughter may well be the eventual verdict. Even so, to Fiona Dowling, a woman whose public persona was all important, her time in jail would be a death blow to her social aspirations.

'Yarwood, was Pearson involved in Gordon Mason's murder?' Tremayne asked.

'Fiona Dowling revealed that Mason knew about her affair. It could be a motive for Pearson.'

'I can see Pearson hitting the man, but not murder.'

'It's four in the morning, can we go home, guv?' Clare asked.

'I thought we were having fun.'

'Tomorrow, early, as much fun as you like. For now, I need to sleep.'

***

The news of Geoff Pearson's death and the subsequent arrest of Fiona Dowling sent shock waves throughout the dramatic society. Peter Freestone had wanted to disband the group, but now they had a common cause; the defence of Fiona, the shock and abhorrence at Pearson's death. Cheryl Milledge took it particularly badly, but then it was known that she was an emotional person, able to fall in love with ease, to fall out at the same rate, the reason that her love life had been so varied.

Cheryl was the first to react on hearing the news. She arrived at the police station at seven in the morning after a phone call from Peter Freestone, who had been kept updated as to the situation. 'I'd like to see Fiona Dowling,' Cheryl said to the police constable on duty in reception.

'Are you a relative?'

'I'm a friend.'

'I can't let you see her without the permission of Detective Inspector Tremayne.'

'Please ask. I'm sure he will allow me to see her. How is she?'

'I'm not sure I know. She was remanded last night; she's in the cells.'

Cheryl helped herself to coffee from the machine nearby and took a seat. Gary Barker was coming in later for moral support. After a ninety-minute wait, Clare walked in.

'Sergeant Yarwood, how is Fiona?' Cheryl stood upon her arrival to make sure that she was seen.

'As well as can be expected.'

'This has come as a complete shock.'

'You've known her longer than anyone else.'

The two women moved to Clare's desk in Homicide.

'Our story is known,' Cheryl said.

'We know that Gordon Mason knew about the affair.'

'Not from me.'

'Would Gary have said anything?'

'Gary wouldn't have wasted his time telling Gordon. He knows about my past, and he never mentions it. As far as Gary would be concerned, if Geoff was playing around with Fiona, then good luck to Geoff. Gary rolls with the punches; he doesn't take life too seriously.'

'The garden centre, he seemed keen on taking that over.'

'Only because he gets to play with the plants. He's not got a head for business.'

'Whereas you have?'

'It's a good business apart from his parents.'

'We're told that you don't get on with them.'

'Gary told you this?'

'Yes. Is it true?'

'They go to the same church that Mason did. If you think he was bad, you should meet Gary's parents.'

'He doesn't seem affected by them.'

'He left home in his teens, roamed around, got into trouble, nothing serious, before going back there.'

'That must have been hard.'

'It's best if you ask Gary.'

'You're here. I'm asking you.'

'Gary wasn't into drugs, not in a big way, but one day, after a severe reaction, he ends up on their doorstep. They take him in, get him detoxed. As long as he's got his plants, he's okay.'

'And his parents' fervent hatred of you?'

'They know about my past. They see me as a bad influence.'

'Have you been involved with drugs?'

'Not me, or at least not seriously. I smoked, still do. I tried marijuana when I was younger, snorted cocaine once or twice, but nothing more.'

'Alcohol?'

'More than I should. It doesn't control my life.'

'Who could have told Gordon Mason about Fiona Dowling and Geoff Pearson?'

'I'm not sure. I could see them looking at each other, not sure if her husband did, but then he was always a bit thick.'

'Salisbury's premier estate agent?'

'Fiona was the driving force, you must have known that. Sure, he can stand up, talk the talk, make you believe in Father Christmas, but he needed pointing in the general direction. Why do you think Fiona stayed with him?'

'I don't know,' Clare said. 'You tell me.'

'Fiona needs to control, and with Len, he was a prime candidate. He was someone she could mould.'

'Did she love her husband, does she?'

'She loved that she could mould him to what she wanted.'

'Bill Ford mentioned that you and he went out together in the past.'

'A long time ago, before he took over the funeral business from his father.'

'What can you tell me?'

'Is it relevant?'

'Probably not, but you're here. It's a question that begs an answer.'

'So did Fiona. What's he been telling you?'

'He said that you two had been wild, so had he.'

'He was fun back then. Now he's a boring man. It's hard to believe that they are one and the same.'

'Is that it?'

'If you want me to mention the threesome, then yes.'

'Fiona was possessive of Geoff Pearson. Have you seen that side of her personality before?'

'She likes to control, I've told you that.'

'Did she try to control you?'

'She always wanted to organise where we were going when we went out for the night. There's nothing strange with that. She was driven, I was not. We went our separate ways. She married Len, I moved from man to man.'

'Is she jealous of you now?'

'Fiona? I don't think so. She wouldn't fancy Gary.'

'Why not?'

'You've met Gary. He's not a person you can drive. He lets life pass him by, takes what it gives, asks no more.'

'Apart from the garden centre.'

'I gave him that idea.'

'Do you stay with him because of it?'

'Not a chance. It's there, I'm getting older. I want children, a home, a husband, someone to care for. Gary will always treat me well, and I've no intention of changing him. That's what Fiona likes doing, not me.'

'Would you like to see Mrs Dowling?'

'Yes, please.'

'I'll arrange it for you. You'd better get yourself another cup of coffee.'

***

Chris Dowling had the unenviable task of telling his brother, Len, what had transpired at the police interview, and the fact that his wife was being held in the cells at Bemerton Road Police Station.

'I didn't know,' Len said.

'Len, you can be stupid sometimes. Your wife is screwing Pearson, and you didn't suspect?'

'It's the truth. She's been a bit cold lately. I assumed it was because she was busy.'

'Do you believe that Fiona has spent all those years waiting at home for you?'

'I've always been faithful. I assumed she had.'

'Even Mason knew about it.'

'How?'

'He kept his eyes open, I suppose. Maybe he wasn't as naïve as you. He was attempting to blackmail Fiona.'

'She never said anything.'

'What did you expect her to say? I'm sorry, but I've been screwing Geoff Pearson, and now Gordon Mason is trying to blackmail me into having sex with him.'

'Did she?'

'She said she did not.'

'Did she murder Gordon Mason?'

'According to the police, it seems unlikely. Whoever put the daggers into Mason would have had to have been on the stage. She could have been an accomplice.'

'With Pearson?'

'Len, how the hell do I know? I'm your brother, not your keeper. Do you think Fiona would be capable?'

'To protect her perfect life? She'd be capable of anything.'

'Even the murder of Gordon Mason, of Geoff Pearson?'

'Yes.'

'Whatever you do, don't tell the police of your suspicions. They've got enough to convict her.'

'For what? Pearson fell to his death.'

'A long way. He may not have died; she may not have known the wall was there.'

'It's not murder then?'

'The police will make sure the case is tight. If they can tie her in with Mason's death, then it will not look good for her.'

'I need to see her,' Len Dowling said.

'Are you capable of murder, Len?'

'Why me? I'm the wronged party here. I'm the one with the cheating wife.'

'If you had known, what would you have done?'
'I would have forgiven her.'
'Why?'
'Because I love her.'
'After what she's done?'
'I can forgive, I can't replace.'
'Len, you're a weak excuse for a man.'
'What would you have done?'
'I'd have beaten the living daylights out of her, and made sure that Pearson never walked again.'
'And Gordon Mason?'
'That bastard. He would have had an accident.'
'Maybe you killed him.'
'Why? He had nothing on me, only you. And besides, I want my money from your business within forty-eight hours.'
'Will you defend Fiona?'
'I'll do that once you've paid me the money.'
'I need longer.'
'Forty-eight hours.'
'You're a bastard, Chris.'
'I know it, and I'm proud of it. Just because I have a snivelling weasel of a brother doesn't mean I have to be like him.'

Chapter 19

Tremayne came into the office later in the morning. Clare could see that he was not well. 'What is it, guv?'

'I had trouble sleeping, nothing more.'

The man did look tired, not surprising given the long night that they had just endured. She said no more on the subject.

'Pearson's family?' Tremayne asked.

'His father will conduct a formal identification today.'

'Fiona Dowling?'

'Cheryl Pearson is with her.'

'Is that wise?'

'I've ensured a constable is present.'

'Fair enough. And the husband?'

'He's not been here yet.'

'Was Pearson one of the murderers?'

'It seems possible, although Mason's blackmailing of Fiona Dowling was none of his concern. He was a young man with a married woman. Nobody is going to criticise him; his friends will probably buy him a drink. If Mason knew, it was not a motive.'

'Fiona couldn't have killed the man, but someone could on her behalf.'

'There'd still need to be two.'

'We've always assumed that.'

'Could it be only one?'

'Not in the assassination scene.'

'It's bizarre,' Clare said.

'But why the stage? And then why does Fiona Dowling confront Pearson when we're not far away?'

'Pearson's death could still have been an unfortunate accident. Fiona's angry, the man has turned her over for a young and innocent girl. She's feeling her age, realising that her life is not as perfect as she likes to portray. She stalks Pearson, hoping to confront him with his girlfriend, to intimidate him and to scare her off, to convince Pearson that she needs him and that she can care for him.'

'That wasn't the story we got from Fiona Dowling,' Tremayne said.

'No woman wants to admit that she's getting old, that she can't turn a man's head.'

'And that would be important to her?'

'Critical, I'd say. It would be a motive for a confrontation, for violence if she lashed out. I don't believe that she intended to kill him. She had no issue with hitting him or the girlfriend, but it wasn't murder. The charge won't stick.'

'Are you saying that we should release her?'

'What can you charge her with, assault occasioning actual bodily harm?'

'Not really. If she had hit Pearson or the girlfriend out of anger or jealousy, it's not a custodial sentence. She'd be bound over by a magistrate to keep her distance, maintain the peace, probably some community service and anger management.'

***

Fiona Dowling and Cheryl Pearson sat across from each other in a small room. A policewoman stood to one side at a discreet distance. It was not the first time in a police station for Cheryl, as she'd spent the occasional night in the cells for committing an affray, the result of too much alcohol. For Fiona, it was a new experience. The two women held hands across the table.

'You should have told me that Gordon knew,' Cheryl said.

'You knew about Geoff and me?' Fiona said. She was still wearing the same clothes from the night before.

'I saw you with him.'

'Where?'

'In your house. Both of you were on the floor.'

'And you didn't tell me?'

'What was there to tell? You're my oldest friend. I wasn't passing judgement, and I wasn't about to tell anyone.'

'Gary?'

'He knows, but he'll never tell anyone.'

'And Geoff?'

'He saw me when you two were on the floor. Believe me, you weren't focussing by then.'

'You must think me an awful tart,' Fiona Dowling said.

'We've both been tarts in our day. I've worked it out of my system, you haven't.'

'I didn't mean to kill Geoff. I was angry, hurt.'

'How did Gordon find out?'

'I've no idea. Geoff wouldn't have told anyone.'

'I couldn't get him to talk about it afterwards,' Cheryl said.

'You tried?'

'We used to tease him. Sorry, it was at your expense, but he never said anything, and he wouldn't have told Gordon.'

'Then who else would have known?'

'Did Len ever suspect?'

'Never. It's not been good between us for some years, but Len is not the jealous type. He wouldn't have known about Geoff.'

'Were there others?'

'Geoff was the only one. It's not always been easy. Len is not the great lover.'

'I remember that.'

'You've slept with him?'

'You know I did. The week before you latched on to him.'

'We were terrible,' Fiona said. The first smile since Old Sarum crept across her face.

'It was fun, though,' Cheryl said. The women squeezed each other's hands. The policewoman looked, said nothing.

'I miss it sometimes.'

'You've chosen your life, I've chosen mine. I may have a unambitious man, a lousy job, and a disgusting place to live, but I'm happier than you.'

'If I get out of here, I'll follow your example,' Fiona said.

'Don't make promises you won't keep. If you walk away from here, you'll either stay in Salisbury or you won't, you'll stay with Len, or you won't, but in a couple of years, you'll have your social set and your perfect life. For me, I'll marry Gary and keep him happy. He can stay just the way he is.'

'You're a true friend,' Fiona said.

'Not good enough to introduce to your social set.'

'None of them will be down here to visit me. I'll be a parasite once the news of Geoff's death becomes public knowledge.'

'What are you going to do about Len?'

'I'll fix it up with him somehow. He's the one constant, even if he can be a pain sometimes.'

'And lousy in bed,' Cheryl added. 'You can always take another lover.'

'Not again. I've learnt my lesson there.'

The two women parted. Len, Fiona's husband, was outside and wanting to talk to his wife.

Cheryl left the room, smiled at Len as she walked past him. He glanced over at her and gave a weak smile, the only recognition he was capable of. Cheryl knew of two certainties: Fiona, her friend, would survive regardless, and that she'd find another man if it were necessary.

***

Jimmy Francombe had skipped school, and Trevor Winston had left his salon for his assistant to run. Gary Barker was not present, as he already knew the news. Phillip Dennison was due shortly. Peter Freestone, a busy man that day, had put his work to one side. The situation was grim.

The men sat in Freestone's office. It was still early, and the news had not permeated through the city. 'Geoff Pearson died last night,' Freestone said.

'What!' Jimmy Francombe said.

'After you left, his body was found near the old cathedral. If you know it, there's some of the original building and a drop to one side.'

'I know it,' Dennison said, as he came in the door.

'So do I,' Francombe said.

'Not me, but carry on,' Winston said. 'What were you saying about Geoff?'

'Geoff Pearson fell over the drop and was killed.'

'Are you certain?' Dennison asked.

'I was there. I saw his body. Fiona Dowling has been arrested.'

'On what charge?'

'Murder.'

'But why?'

'She's admitted to an altercation with him.'

'Why would Fiona fight with Geoff? I always thought they were friendly,' Winston said. 'She used to come into my salon. She only had good words to say about him, about all of us.'

'The police will probably want to interview us again.'

'Why?'

'We were there at their re-enactment and went home,' Dennison said.

'There's still the matter of Gordon Mason.'

'Did Geoff kill him? Is that the reason Fiona argued with him?' Winston asked.

'Are you kidding?' Francombe said. 'She hated Mason, more than any of us.'

'Hate. That's a strong word.'

'Dislike, not hate.'

'Did you hate Mason?' Freestone asked.

'Okay,' Francombe admitted, 'I hated the man with his snide remarks.'

'Enough to kill him?' Dennison asked.

'Why me? He fancied your wife. I saw you and Mason outside. I saw you hit him.'

'Is that correct?' Winston asked.

'He made an inappropriate comment about Samantha,' Dennison said.

'He made inappropriate comments about everyone, especially me,' Winston said.

'I may have hit him, but I didn't kill him.'

'How do we know?' Freestone asked.

'You've not answered why Fiona was arguing with Geoff,' Dennison said.

'They were involved.'

'An affair?' Winston said.

'Good old Geoff,' Francombe said.

'He may have been good old Geoff to you, but the man's dead as a result,' Freestone said. 'Did anyone else know about this?'

'She always had eyes for him, but Len was always there. I assumed that was all it was,' Winston said.

'Apparently not. I don't know the full story, only snippets from what I gleaned up at Old Sarum. No doubt the police will know a lot more.'

'If Geoff was one of the murderers, that still means that one of us is guilty,' Winston said. 'Who is it? And why are we meeting here? One of you could take out a knife now and stab us.'

'Get real, Trevor,' Dennison said. 'I don't know how it was done, but it wasn't any of us.'

'Can you be sure?' Freestone said.

'I am.'

'Why?'

'None of you have the nerve.'

'Gary Barker and Bill Ford are not here.'

'Maybe Gary, maybe Bill.'

'I don't believe it,' Freestone said.

'I'm leaving, important issues to deal with,' Dennison said.

'Was Geoff messing around with your wife as well?' Winston asked.

Dennison, a man angered by his financial losses and by his wife's behaviour, lunged forward at the hairdresser, striking him across the face.

'Back off, Dennison. Trevor's winding you up. You know he's a mincing little queer,' Freestone said.

'I'll not have anyone making comments about my wife,' Dennison said.

'If you don't want comments, then don't let her parade herself in public half-undressed. She's got a reputation as it is,' Winston said, cowering in a corner of the room.

'I've heard the rumours,' Jimmy Francombe said.

'You little bastard. I'll get you for that,' Dennison said, freeing himself from Freestone's grip. He grabbed the young man and smashed his head against the wall. He then stormed out of the room.

Winston moved over to Francombe, took a handkerchief out of his pocket and attempted to wipe away the blood. 'You'll need some stitches there.'

'That man could kill,' Freestone said. 'We need to tell the police.'

'You can deal with it,' Winston said. 'I'm taking Jimmy to the doctor's.'

***

Len Dowling sat across from his wife in the small room at the police station. Fiona Dowling avoided his gaze, her head held low. 'It was an accident,' she said.

'You were screwing him,' Len Dowling said.

'I made a mistake.'

'You've made me look a fool. How am I going to continue in this city?'

'Is that all you're concerned about, your precious reputation? What about the fact that I was having an affair? Doesn't that upset you?'

Both of them were on their feet. 'I'm sorry, you'll both have to sit down or I'll terminate this meeting,' the policewoman said.

'It won't happen again,' Fiona said, resuming her seat. Her husband sat down at the same time.

'I knew that you fancied him,' Len said.

'Why didn't you say something?'

'Such as?'

'That you loved me and that you didn't want me making a fool of myself.'

'Why? It's you who wears the trousers in our house.'

'That's a terrible comment. I've always supported you, driven you on to better things.'

'And screwed around in the meantime, while pretending to your friends. You're no better than Cheryl. Just a pair of tarts.'

'She has been here. She came as a friend, wanting to help. She didn't come here as judge and jury, ready to condemn without a trial.'

'What trial? Chris was here when you told the police about getting together with Pearson, your little trysts in our house, the back of the Range Rover.'

'I've never told them that. How do you know the details?'

'I'm not a total fool,' Len Dowling admitted.

'You knew all along? What kind of man are you? What kind of husband? You could have stopped it, given Geoff a good thumping, but what did you do? Nothing, that's what.'

'At least you left me alone.'

'To do what? Sell more houses? Screw the women in the office?'

'Would you have cared?'

'Of course I would have cared. I want a man, not an excuse. I want a man to love me, to protect me, to care for me.'

'Don't give me that crap, Fiona. You're in here feeling sorry for yourself, looking at spending a few years in jail for murdering your lover.'

'He wasn't my lover. He'd ended the relationship.'

'You couldn't keep him satisfied. That's why he had the young woman with him. He needed someone younger, firmer, not sagging around the edges. Admit it, Fiona, you're past it.'

'You bastard.' The two of them were on their feet. Fiona slapped her husband across the face; Len Dowling punched his wife. The policewoman pressed a bell; two police officers came in and separated the warring couple. The policewoman took hold of Fiona Dowling and escorted her back to her cell, arranging for a doctor to visit and check her condition after the punch. Len Dowling was led out to another room to cool down.

Chapter 20

Cheryl, oblivious to the events at Bemerton Road Police Station, headed out to the garden centre to see Gary. She realised that it was against her better judgement and she should have phoned, although when Gary was working he always left his phone in his other clothes, having changed into more suitable gardening wear.

'You shouldn't be here,' Gary said. 'If they see you…'

'They can go to hell for once. I've met Fiona.'

'How is she?'

'As you'd expect. I've also spoken to Sergeant Yarwood.'

'Is there any reason that you're telling me this now?'

'Gordon Mason knew about Fiona and Geoff. He was attempting to blackmail her.'

'Money?'

'No. He wanted to sleep with her.'

'Did he?'

'Fiona said no. I believe her.'

'How did Mason find out?'

'I never told him, and I trust you, Gary.'

'Then he either saw them together, or Geoff told him.'

'Unless someone else knew.'

'This is all too complicated for me,' Gary said. 'Just give me my plants and the soil, and I don't want any more.'

'That's why I love you,' Cheryl said. 'Fiona can have her action man; I'll take you.'

'I can be all action.'

'In that bedsit, I know you can.'

Gary looked up, could see his father coming over. 'You'd better make yourself scarce.'

'Not today, I'm not. I've had to see my oldest friend arrested, a friend of ours killed. Your parents can go to hell.'

'You're not welcome here. This is private property,' Gary's father said. Cheryl could see that he was puffing, even after walking the short distance from the office to where she stood with Gary.

'The sign out the front says open 9 a.m. to 5 p.m. I'm here as a member of the general public.'

'Not to us, you're not. You're just a shameless hussy aiming to take our Gary from us.'

'From what I can see, it'll be your maker taking you first.'

Gary Barker stood to one side, observing the spectacle. He'd taken enough abuse from them over the years. It was good to see them getting some back.

'How dare you mock the Lord.'

'I could tell you more about your religion than you'll ever know. You're a hypocritical bastard, you and that fool Mason.'

'Gordon Mason was a God-fearing man.'

'He was a misogynist bigot. I assume you know what a misogynist is?'

'Don't get smart with me. Get off my property.'

'It'll be Gary's soon.'

'You can't wait, can you, to get your hands on his money?'

'I can get my hands on him anytime. His money's not important, although we'll gladly accept it.'

'Over my dead body, it'll be.'

'Not long to go then,' Cheryl said.

'You'd better go, Cheryl,' Gary said.

'I'm off. See you later, lover.'

The two lovers shared a passionate kiss and embrace in front of the father. The man seethed. For once, Gary was not concerned.

***

Phillip Dennison arrived home to find his wife sitting quietly in one corner of the sitting room; she was reading a book. 'You're not going out?' he said.

'Looking like this?'

'No one will notice.'

'A black eye and a cut lip, they will.'

Dennison was in a good mood. He had checked his latest trades on the drive back from Freestone's office to the house: his luck had changed and he had recouped his losses. Also, his wife had received what was long overdue: a good beating.

It had been the same with his previous women. At first, they were grateful they had been lifted from the mediocrity of an office or a shop, the mediocrity of men with no money, the mediocrity of suburbia. With them, as with Samantha, their gratitude had lasted for a few months, a few years, and then came the demand for a better life, the ability to forget where they had come from, and then they were off and spending, not willing to give him the time he required.

With Samantha, he felt an affinity, a desire to keep her, but they had come at a cost. He had had to threaten her with a letter from Chris Dowling, a couple of smacks across the face, and the separation from her beloved Aston Martin. He hoped it was sufficient.

'We're going out tonight,' he said.

'What for?' the woman replied, without much enthusiasm.

'To celebrate. Our troubles are over.'

'What do you mean?'

'It doesn't matter. I want you to stay, that's all.'

'I'll try to be more careful in future,' Samantha said.

Phillip Dennison knew she would not, but it did not matter. A solution had been found, not of his own doing. From now on, he'd keep a watch on his wife. If she stepped out of line, then he knew the answer. If she considered being unfaithful in future, then he would know how to stop it. He thanked Fiona Dowling for inadvertently providing the solution.

**

Peter Freestone visited Bill Ford at his place of work. The man, as usual, was busy. 'You didn't meet with us,' Freestone said.

'Geoff Pearson's dead,' Ford said.

'Len Dowling must have known about him and Fiona.'

'Did you?'

'I've known Fiona a long time. The woman has needs. Len's a braggart, not much substance,' Ford said.

'You know Fiona better than I do.'

'I do. And Cheryl.'

'Did Geoff Pearson kill Mason?'

'For what reason? Geoff may have been playing with fire, but I don't see him killing the man.'

'Mason may have known about him and Fiona.'

'He may have, but Geoff was a young guy making out with an older woman. It's not something for him to worry about. Fiona would have been more concerned to keep the relationship secret, but as I said, I've known her a long time. She's smart, weighs up the pros and cons.'

'The police said that Pearson's death may have been an accident,' Freestone said.

'She'd be capable of anything to protect her life. Back when she was younger, she enticed Cheryl into our bed.'

'Why are you telling me this?'

'I know you'll keep it confidential. What Fiona wants, she gets.'

'You think she'll get off a murder charge?'

'We've walked around the old cathedral in the past, you and I. Maybe she pushed him, a gentle shove, slap around the face, or maybe she pushed him hard.'

'We'll never know, nor will the police.'

'She couldn't have killed Gordon Mason.'

'I agree with you on that. If there were two men on that stage, then two had a reason. I wouldn't discount Fiona having some involvement, even if it was in the background.'

'Len?'

'It's possible.'

'Jimmy Francombe, Gary Barker, Trevor Winston?'

'Even us two,' Bill Ford said.

'It's not one of us,' Freestone said.

'Why?'

'I've no reason to kill him.'

'Would you know if you had stabbed him with a real dagger?'

'I'm certain I would have. And besides, he was still alive when he staggered over to me.'

'I know that, so do the police.'

'But he spoke?'

'Did he? You could have uttered the line. Would anyone have known?'

'Bill, you've spent too long in here with these bodies. That's just fanciful nonsense. I had no reason to kill him, and I was not after Fiona or Dennison's wife. I've been happily married for too long.'

'So you keep telling us. Are you trying to convince yourself, or did you fancy Fiona? She's a good-looking woman, and Dennison's wife is a knockout. I fancied her, I know that.'

'I thought you were a one-woman man?'

'I was,' Ford said, 'but the nights get lonely sometimes.'

'Get out of this place,' Freestone said. 'It's making you crazy.'

'Maybe it is, but I have my suspicions.'

'What are they?'

'I'll keep them to myself for now.'

***

Fiona Dowling, finally released on her own surety, retreated to her house. Tremayne still had his suspicions that she had known what she was doing, and there had been some moonlight that night.

Superintendent Moulton was suitably displeased at what had happened, as one murderer had been better than none. It was clear that Pearson's death, unfortunate as it was, was not related to the primary death of Gordon Mason. Pearson, whereas he may have been involved in the murder of Gordon Mason, had not died as a result of that, although knowledge of his affair may well have been the catalyst for Mason's death.

Clare was willing to give Fiona Dowling the benefit of the doubt, as in her teens she had experienced the anguish of being discarded by a young man at her school. She had not contemplated either hitting him or pushing him to his death, but she remembered the hurt she had felt. Fiona Dowling was married, supposedly happily, but then, Clare wondered, what was happiness: an illusion or was it tangible? She had felt happiness with Harry, but would it have been eternal, or was that just a fleeting fancy?

She realised that she had been in mourning for long enough. It was time to embrace the world again; hopefully to find love.

Fiona Dowling, keeping a low profile after her release, was quiet for a few days. The local newspaper had recorded Pearson's death as an accident, and it was likely that the coroner would as well, the altercation mentioned but not deemed relevant. There'd be an inquest, but it would not last long. Jim Hughes, in his role as the crime scene examiner, would be required to give evidence. His report had shown that there was clear evidence of two people standing on the lip of the drop and that the shoe prints indicated that one was facing towards the other in a stance that was suspicious. Apart from that, there was no proof. The woman, her shoe prints checked and found to match those at the scene, would be required to give evidence. Clare wondered how she'd be able to square that with her friends, although she assumed she would.

After an absence of a few days, Len Dowling was back in his office, his agency signs visible around the city. Clare had received a price for the cottage she had been leasing in Stratford sub Castle. The purchase would not need Dowling, and she was anxious to keep his grubby hands away from the deal.

The Deer's Head, Harry's pub, reopened with the appropriate fanfare. Neither Tremayne nor Clare attended the ceremony, although Clare realised that she could drive past the place without feeling the tears welling up in her eyes.

Eventually, Fiona Dowling reappeared in the city. Clare first saw her in Guildhall Square parking her car, and then she was at Winston's getting her hair done. From what Clare could see, the woman was without shame. The dramatic society knew about her affair, as did her husband, and no doubt there were others.

Clare decided a visit to the woman's house was in order. 'I've just a few questions,' she said, after being invited in.

'I've moved on from Old Sarum.'

'You've admitted to an altercation.'

'Yes.'

'How have you explained that to your friends?'

'They understand.'

'Understand what? That you had an argument with your ex-lover?'

'It gives me a sense of mystique.'

'If they accept that, then they're not worth your time.'

'You'll not understand. I need them, even if they are vacuous and empty-headed.'

'And loaded with money.'

'As you say, loaded with money. Cheryl may be willing to live like a pauper, I'm not.'

'Your husband's business?'

'It's doing well.'

'And your husband?'

'He understands.'

'Is he willing to accept that you were having sexual relations with another man?'

'He was angry, but I've fixed it with him.'

'How?'

'I've promised to devote myself to him.'

'Will you?'

'He's a weak man. He needs a strong woman. Whatever I say, he will agree.'

'Even if it's not true.'

'Even then.'

'Did Geoff Pearson kill Gordon Mason to protect you?'

'I didn't need his help.'

'Did he know that Mason was trying to blackmail you?'

'I never told him. I don't need a man to do my dirty work. If Mason had persisted, I would have dealt with him.'

'Murder?'

'Not murder. The man may have convinced other people that he was honest, but I knew him for the charlatan that he was.'

'Will it implicate your husband? Is it to do with the land deal?'

'It cannot be proved.'

'We've found no evidence.'

'You won't. And besides, I've no intention of telling you any more.'

'Why did you tell me?'

'I don't know. Maybe I'm upset by recent events. Maybe I needed to clear my conscience.'

'Or maybe you want to pre-empt my questioning, knowing full well that you knew about the drop over the side of the old cathedral at Old Sarum, that you wanted Geoff Pearson dead for the hurt he had caused you. Is this talk of Mason's blackmail just a red herring, aiming to divert the blame from you? To make you look like the victim instead of the villain? Mrs Dowling, I put it to you, that you murdered Geoff Pearson for no other reason than anger at the man who had spurned you.'

'That's a scurrilous lie. I invite you into my house, show you cordiality, and then you accuse me of murder.'

'Why not? You're a devious woman. You could have been the instigator of Mason's death, if not the person holding the dagger.'

'Leave, leave this house immediately. I will need to talk to my solicitor about this. I'm a private citizen being subjected to police brutality.'

'Mrs Dowling, this is not police brutality. And if you feel the need to take action, and we subsequently find you guilty of the murder of Geoff Pearson, and an accomplice in the murder of Gordon Mason, it will reflect badly on you.'

'It wasn't me.'

'What do you mean?'

'I didn't kill Gordon Mason. I wasn't involved.'

'Then who was?'

'I don't know.'

Chapter 21

Clare found Tremayne sitting at his desk on her return to the station. The man for once was quiet. 'What is it, guv?'

'This weekend. I'm meeting up with my ex-wife.'

'What's the problem?'

'I've been on my own for a long time. I'm used to doing as I please.'

'Too long being selfish. If you're both free, both lonely, then there's no harm done?'

'I'm not lonely.'

'Of course you are. What have you got in your life? A television, a pint of beer, a few old horses that can barely run, and me.'

'You?'

'This department then. You're getting on. It'll be good to have company.'

'For when I become old and senile, is that how you see it, Yarwood? You and Moulton, both of you see me as past it.'

'A little bit of fire there, guv.'

'Are you winding me up?'

'You know I am. Anyway, we need to talk.'

'About what?'

'Fiona Dowling, the death of two members of the Salisbury Amateur Dramatic Society.'

'What about Fiona Dowling?'

'I've been to see her.'

'What does she have to say for herself.'

'She's a tough woman. If she had been on that stage, she could have killed him.'

'But she wasn't.'

Tremayne raised himself from his seat. Clare's comments had struck home. He was the person who created the action, not her. 'What's first, Yarwood?'

'Len Dowling. We need to understand the man. His wife has spent time in custody, has been accused of murder, and he must know that she had been sleeping with Pearson.'

'He'd be an odd individual if he accepted his wife sleeping around. Where is he?'

'We'll find him back at work.'

The two police officers left the police station, Tremayne driving for once.

They found the estate agent in his office. 'Mr Dowling, a few questions,' Tremayne said.

'Don't you ever give up? I've got a busy schedule,' Dowling said.

'So do we. We need to talk to you about your wife.'

'She's at home. You can talk to her there.'

'It's your views that are important.'

'Okay, twenty minutes.'

The three retreated to an office at the rear of the agency. Out front, three agents were on the phone or talking to anyone who walked through the door.

'Mr Dowling, your wife was arrested on suspicion of murder.'

'Yes, I know this.'

'Do you know why she was suspected?'

'If you want me to say that she was involved with Pearson, then I will.'

'Was she?'

'I know about it.'

'How do you feel that your wife is unfaithful?'

'What do you want me to say?'

'It's not what we want you to say. We want to know your reaction.'

'Angry, bloody angry. Does that satisfy you?'

'You're not very convincing,' Clare said. 'Did you know or did you suspect?'

'I know Fiona. I've always been hopeful that she'd stay faithful, but I've never been certain.'

'When it was confirmed, it did not come as a big shock.'

'It was a shock, but I was not surprised, or not much. No man wants to know that his wife is cheating, it's a blow to the ego, but I will tell you one thing, I will not give up on my wife.'

'Why?'

'Because I love her. We built this business up together, and she was here in the early days working horrendous hours. Our history runs deep, and if the cost is the occasional infatuation, then I must accept.'

'That's a magnanimous attitude,' Clare said.

'It's not magnanimous. It's the reality.'

'Were you aware that Gordon Mason was attempting to blackmail your wife?'

'No.'

'What would you have done if you had known?'

'Are you asking if I would have killed him?'

'Would you?'

'I would have threatened the man. I'd have asked my brother to pressure him.'

'And what does your brother think of your forgiving your wife?'

'I've not forgiven her; I've been forced to accept it.'

'Your brother?'

'He thinks I'm a fool and that I should get a backbone.'

'Do you agree with him?'

'He's right, no doubt, but I'm not going to give up on Fiona.'

'If you had known that Gordon Mason was pressuring your wife, that would be a motive for murder.'

'I didn't know, and I didn't kill Mason.'

Tremayne and Clare left the office, walking past Harry's old pub. They could see the patrons inside, a new publican behind the bar. Neither made a comment.

'Why would the woman continue to go to the rehearsals, take part in the play, if one of the men was blackmailing her? It makes no sense,' Tremayne said.

'You'd think she would have kept away,' Clare said.

'And even then, she was maintaining cordial relations with him.'

'Do you think she had given in to his demands?'

'With Fiona Dowling, who knows?'

***

Tremayne and Yarwood continued working the case, re-interviewing the main suspects, checking out Old Sarum, looking for an angle. Clare had to admit that the reduced pace in the department did not suit her. For a few weeks, she had been busy, close to exhaustion, which was how she had managed to handle the return to Salisbury, but now she had time to remember. Even driving down Minster Street and passing Harry's pub had proved to be painful. She wanted to visit his grave, but not yet.

Tremayne had met up with Jean, his former wife, and they had spent the weekend at a hotel not far from Salisbury. They had discussed getting together on a more regular basis, even a holiday overseas, anathema to Tremayne, but he had agreed. It would have to wait, though, until they had dealt with the murder of Gordon Mason.

Fiona Dowling almost revelled in her notoriety, of how she had risen from a foolish and then promiscuous schoolgirl to being the wife of Salisbury's leading estate agent. She had even agreed to make a speech on the subject at the next meeting of her group.

Len Dowling continued to sell residential property, even calling up Tremayne one Saturday morning with a firm buyer, and could he show them around his house. Tremayne made short work of his request, vowed to check out the man more intensely for his nerve in disturbing him after a few too many drinks the previous night.

Clare had managed to secure the finance for the cottage that she was leasing and the purchase was going through, no thanks to Dowling who had tried to scupper the deal by telling the vendor that he had a better offer. As it turned out the vendor had been a friend of Mavis Godwin, and she remembered Clare fondly. There was no way that she was going to let a slug of a man take the house from the police sergeant, the vendor's words not Clare's, although she had to agree with the woman.

Samantha Dennison had been seen around the town, back to driving the Aston Martin. Clare had seen her on a couple of occasions, had a coffee with her once. The woman was calmer than before, not as extravagant, judging by the reduced number of shopping bags.

Although a sense of normality reigned amongst those who had been up at Old Sarum that night, Tremayne was still biting at the bit. The man wasn't calm, far from it, and he was subject to the occasional bout of frustration, sometimes losing his cool with Clare.

Geoff Pearson had been laid to rest, the entire dramatic society present, apart from the Dowlings, and a verdict of death by misadventure recorded. Tremayne didn't hold with it, convinced that there was malice on Fiona Dowling's part, but he couldn't prove it.

Superintendent Moulton, continued with his attempts to retire Tremayne. The last time that it had been mentioned, Tremayne had told him what to do with it. The end result – an internal hearing as to why a detective inspector had instructed his superior what to do with his badgering. The Police Federation would deal with it on his behalf, although he knew he'd receive a warning. Tremayne knew his time was coming to an end, but not before he wrapped up the murder of Gordon Mason. For several days, he had mulled over what to do. He still had suspicions about Fiona Dowling and her husband, supposedly reconciled and openly affectionate. Gary Barker and Cheryl Milledge seemed to be innocent bystanders, and Bill Ford was a grave man, although Tremayne did not believe that his sedentary lifestyle and his bland countenance were all there was to the funeral director. He had admitted to being a passionate man in his youth, the threesome with Fiona and Cheryl testament to that fact, but now the man seemed to have little interest in life, other than spending time with the dead of the city and taking off to London every week or two.

Both Trevor Winston, a man who minced in his salon but not outside, and Jimmy Francombe, an enthusiastic thespian who had been drunk more than a few times around the city and suspended once from his school, seemed harmless to Tremayne.

Freestone seemed a more straightforward man to read, more Tremayne's age group, and the men shared similar tastes, similar vices. Freestone was not into horses, but he enjoyed a good smoke and a few too many beers on occasion.

***

Time had moved on, too slowly for Tremayne. The man liked being busy, Clare could see that, and for weeks there had been no progress. Sure, the paperwork was up to date, but with no clear direction on how to move the investigation forward. Even interviewing those who had been present that night in Old Sarum had run its course. There still remained the fact that seven men alive and one dead included two murderers, but a tie-in between any two of them was tenuous. Apart from a possible rezoning that was not above board, none of the other conspirators was visibly linked.

Bill Ford and Peter Freestone were friendly, but Freestone only had one stab at the man, whereas Ford would have had plenty. Even that, Tremayne felt, was not sufficient grounds to murder Mason, and besides, Ford was a funeral director, he was financially sound, and was only interested in maintaining the family business.

And why, Tremayne wondered, did anyone want to risk being caught, spending time in prison? And again, why on a stage? It seemed ghoulish to him, as if the persons responsible not only wanted the man dead, they also wanted the notoriety of the unsolved murder, being the unknown assailant. It seemed strange to Tremayne, but then he had dealt with worshippers of ancient gods and human sacrifices in his time, and nothing would surprise him now.

The death of Bill Ford did, though. It was four in the afternoon when the call came through. Clare was in the office. 'Yarwood, get your coat,' Tremayne said.

'What's happened?'

'Another murder.'

'Someone we know?'

'Bill Ford.'

Upon their arrival, they found a distraught man standing outside in the reception area of the funeral home. 'I found him,' he said.

Clare assumed he was there for a loved one. He would need to be interviewed later.

In the room at the back, the same place where they had spoken with Ford before, they found the man lying in a coffin, his arms folded across his front.

'Someone needs psychiatric help,' Tremayne said.

Clare could see what he meant. In the man's chest was a Roman dagger. 'It's more than blackmail,' she said.

'We've been looking for a motive, but it's been the wrong motive.'

Around them, the crime scene team were filing in. Outside, in the reception area and on the street, the uniforms were following procedure. Inside, Clare and Tremayne moved closer to the body. 'It's a crime scene,' Jim Hughes said. 'Where's your protective gear?'

'Sorry, we've just arrived, the same as you,' Tremayne said.

'I understand that, but from here on, it's my show. I'll let you know what I find.'

'It's clear what happened here.'

'There's no sign of a struggle, a dagger in the heart. It's murder,' Hughes said.

'We'd figured that out.'

Tremayne and Clare sat down next to the man in reception. 'I came to organise the burial of my wife,' he said.

Clare could see that the man was elderly, and grieving. 'I'm sorry for your loss. Can you tell us what happened here?'

'I came here to check with Mr Ford that all was in order. There wasn't anyone at the front, so I walked around to the back. I knew where my wife was as I had been here before. I found Mr Ford lying in one of the coffins. That's all I can tell you.'

Tremayne realised that the man had nothing to do with the crime. 'We'll need a written statement. Apart from that, you're free to leave.'

'What for? My wife is here. The burial is tomorrow.'

'It's a crime scene. I suggest you contact another funeral director, and I'll see if your wife's body can be released to you.'

'Thank you. Can I see my wife before I leave?'

'I'll get you a set of crime scene protective gear.'

***

With little more to be achieved, and pending Jim Hughes's report, Tremayne and Clare returned to the police station. Tremayne phoned Peter Freestone, made sure that he was available for further questioning.

'You place a lot of reliance on that man,' Clare said.

'Not totally, but the man is observant. Bill Ford has been killed for a reason. We assume it's related to what happened at Old Sarum.'

'It's a Roman dagger.'

'Precisely, which means there are more than the two with metal blades that we originally assumed.'

'It's three now. How many more are there?'

'It's impossible to say. We weren't able to trace where the blades came from, nor the extra daggers.'

Freestone arrived at Bemerton Road Police Station within the hour; the man was distraught. 'This means something else, doesn't it?' he said to Tremayne. They were sitting in Tremayne's office, Clare as well.

'We've assumed that the motive was tangible,' Tremayne said.

'What do you mean?'

'Gordon Mason was as a result of blackmail, or he knew something, threatened to talk. The latter of those two being the land deal.'

'The first?' Freestone asked.

'Fiona Dowling and her relationship with Geoff Pearson.'

'Why did Geoff Pearson die? Was it murder?'

'Fiona Dowling admitted to the altercation, although she didn't stay around at the site after Pearson's death, suspicious in itself but not conclusive.'

'Then why Bill Ford?' Freestone asked.

'Our investigations have shown nothing against the man. He led a solitary life, he'd admitted to knowing Fiona and Cheryl when they were younger. He's not been involved in any criminal or dubious activities to our knowledge, and if he had known about Fiona Dowling and Pearson, he did not seem to be a man who'd use it to his advantage.'

'So why is he murdered?'

'And why is he placed in a coffin, his arms folded?' Tremayne said.

'Someone with a sense of the macabre,' Clare said.

'Or someone who enjoys murder,' Tremayne said.

'Whoever it is, he could be after me,' Freestone said.

'Even us,' Clare said. 'This person is obviously unhinged, and he's probably one of those on the stage that night.'

'That only leaves Jimmy, Gary, Trevor, Phillip and me,' Freestone said.

'Who else would know where to buy the retractable daggers?' Clare asked.

'It was no secret. I sent out a monthly report on the finances of the dramatic society. The information is all there,' Freestone said.

'If we discount you for the moment,' Tremayne said.

'For the moment? Am I still a suspect?'

'I can't negate the possibility.'

'We've been through this before,' Freestone said.

Clare could see that the man was not comfortable in the police station. She left and went to get him a cup of tea in an attempt to calm his nerves.

'It could be me next,' Freestone said.

'As well as Yarwood and myself.'

'What causes people to commit such acts?'

'You'd need someone other than me to answer that, but now I'm willing to concede that Bill Ford's murder is as a result of a disturbed personality, not as a result of a tangible motive.'

'You mean that this person is avenging the death of Caesar?'

'Why not?'

'Then it could be any of us five,' Freestone said.

Clare returned and gave a cup of tea to Freestone, another to Tremayne. 'What's the plan, guv?' she asked.

'Interview the main suspects again.'

'And the two women?'

'Would they have had the strength to place Ford's body in the coffin?'

'Cheryl Milledge may have.'

Chapter 22

A few days after Bill Ford's death, the primary suspects met in Len Dowling's office. It was after seven in the evening when all those involved arrived. First at the office was Phillip Dennison, this time with Samantha. Soon after came Jimmy Francombe and Trevor Winston, and ten minutes later Peter Freestone, Gary Barker, and Cheryl Milledge. Fiona Dowling was already there with her husband.

'What is it, Freestone?' Len Dowling asked.

'I thought that was obvious.'

'One of us is a murderer, is that it?'

'Precisely. Bill Ford was an innocent bystander. The man wasn't having an affair with your wife or insulting Dennison's. On the contrary, the man always behaved impeccably.'

'How dare you disrespect my wife,' Dowling said.

Dennison could see the evening getting out of control. 'It doesn't help, trading insults,' he said.

'I'm not insulting anyone,' Freestone said. Everyone was sitting down, all a little nervous as to what was happening to the group that had once met out of love for acting, but was now meeting to discuss a murderer.

'It sounded that way to me,' Dowling said.

'Sit down, Len,' Fiona Dowling said. 'Let Peter talk.'

'Thank you, Fiona. As I was saying, there were a number of motives for Mason's murder. Maybe they weren't sufficient to justify the taking of a life, but they were there.'

'Get to the point,' Dowling said.

'The point is that one of us seems to enjoy murder. None of us is safe.'

'Did you see Ford's body?'

'No, but I've seen a photo. It was one of the daggers.'

'If someone killed Bill Ford, it must be because they had a reason,' Cheryl said.

'That's an assumption. What I am saying is that someone is killing us off. Even if Geoff Pearson was one of those on the stage with a lethal weapon, there is still the fact that someone else is still alive. There are nine people here. One of this nine murdered Bill Ford.'

'Are you suggesting that this person intends to kill us all?' Dennison asked.

'Why am I here?' Samantha Dennison asked.

'I'm sorry to say it, but your husband had a reason to dislike Gordon Mason, and you've become involved in our group by default. If your husband is not the murderer—'

'I'm not.' Dennison defended his position.

'—if your husband is not the murderer,' Freestone continued after the interruption, 'then it is still feasible that someone else killed him on your behalf, or maybe it was someone defending Fiona's honour.'

'I don't get what you're trying to say,' Dowling said. 'You insult my wife, accuse Dennison of murder. Is that all this is tonight, a chance to vent your spleen, to take control of us the way you did the dramatic society?'

'Len, listen to what I'm saying. There are nine here, and one of us is a murderer. That leaves eight people still alive. What if this person is determined to keep murdering? We are all potential victims.'

'It can't be Cheryl or me,' Fiona said.

'Why?'

'We weren't on the stage, we didn't plunge a dagger into him.'

'It doesn't need to be one of those on the stage, does it?' Samantha said. 'Any one of us could have killed Bill Ford.'

'At last the words of wisdom,' Freestone said. 'Samantha's right. We've always assumed that Bill Ford was innocent, in that he had no motive for Mason's death, but what if he did?'

'And someone else wanted to remove the only remaining link to him and the crime,' Gary Barker said.

'It's conjecture, but it's possible.'

'So who is it?' Jimmy Francombe asked.

'Let's analyse it.'

'That person could have a dagger with them now,' Winston said.

'He could,' Freestone replied.

'He?' Francombe said.

'Gordon Mason died at the hands of a man. Who killed Bill Ford is unclear. It could be a woman.'

'It's not me,' Fiona said.

'Nor me,' Cheryl added.

'Fiona and Cheryl, everyone in this room will declare their innocence,' Freestone said. 'The police cannot protect us, and they've no idea. It is up to us to protect ourselves.'

'What do you suggest?' Trevor Winston said.

'If everyone leaves Salisbury, then we're all safe.'

'I can't leave,' Dowling said.

'What do you suggest?' Winston said again.

'We could hold a murder mystery night.'

'When?'

'This week. We can meet at my house or Len and Fiona's.'

'We'll use my house,' Dennison said. 'Do we need a script?'

'We'll replay the events to date.'

'Are we involving the police?'

'I would suggest that DI Tremayne and Sergeant Yarwood are there.'

'Very well, this Friday at 8 p.m.'

***

Jim Hughes's report on Bill Ford's death had revealed little more of value. The man had died after being stabbed in the heart with a dagger. There was no sign of a struggle, and the one stab had resulted in a rapid blood loss.

'Whoever killed him cleaned up afterwards. The victim was a meticulous man, and he had sufficient cleaning materials,' Hughes said in Tremayne's office, a place that no longer held any fear for him since the CSE had gained the DI's hard-won respect.

'Male or female?'

'We're unable to tell you. Whoever it is, he's becoming smart.'

'He?'

'A figure of speech. It could be a female. Mind you, it would have been difficult for a woman to lift the victim into the coffin, but not impossible.'

'It's possible, though?'

'As I've said, I believe so. Who do you think is the murderer?'

'It's no clearer. Bill Ford was always seen as a neutral character: mild-mannered, polite, did not make scurrilous comments about the women, never attempted to force himself on them.'

'Not a bad word against him, is that it?' Hughes asked.

'That appears to be the consensus.'

'You believe the killer is deranged?'

'Or enjoying the notoriety.'

'There's no notoriety if you're not known.'

'Maybe they enjoy the fact that they committed the perfect crime.'

'In that they've stayed free.'

'That's it,' Tremayne said.

***

Tremayne always appreciated a working lunch at the Pheasant Inn in Salisbury. For once, Clare had accompanied him, even agreed to a glass of wine.

Peter Freestone was already there. He was a busy man, the same as the two police officers, and he needed to be back in his office within the hour.

'Do you have it?' Tremayne asked.

Freestone handed over the recording that he had taken at the meeting in his office with the remaining members of the dramatic society. 'Does that mean I'm no longer a suspect?' he asked.

'You're not high on my radar,' Tremayne replied as he drank his beer, almost downing the full pint in one gulp. 'I needed that,' he said.

Clare had no intention of drinking more than the one glass of wine, and she was drinking it slowly.

'It's all arranged. This Friday night, eight in the evening, Dennison's house.'

'They've agreed to my idea?' Tremayne said.

'Whoever this person is they certainly have some nerve,' Freestone said.

'He's enjoying it, or maybe it's a she.'

'And you've no idea?'

'Motives, but no proof.'

'Did Fiona kill Geoff Pearson?'

'Unless she admits her guilt, there's no way we can prove it. You've been up there at night.'

'I still think it was intentional to push him over,' Clare said.

'Death was never certain,' Freestone said as he ate his steak. Tremayne had ordered a steak, as well; Clare, a salad.

'Agreed. It depends on how hard she pushed him. Maybe she just wanted to hurt him, but she's out and about, somewhat of a heroine with her friends.'

'Not my kind of friends,' Clare said.

Tremayne ordered another pint, as did Freestone. Clare could see that the two men were firm friends, although one may have to arrest the other before the week was out. She continued to eat her salad, listening to the two men as they talked.

Clare had to acknowledge the similarities in the two men: both were in their fifties, both dressed in a similar manner, almost could have passed as brothers, although Freestone was at least six inches shorter than Tremayne.

'We'll run through the chain of events, the motives of each, the truth.'

'Geoff Pearson and Dowling's wife?'

'Everything. Even Cheryl Milledge and her past, Gary Barker and the garden centre.'

'What about Winston's homosexuality, Jimmy Francombe's drunkenness of late?'

'Everything, warts and all. It's a murder enquiry, and I intend to wrap it up. If there is to be anger and embarrassment, then so be it.'

'Dennison and Samantha, and what Mason called her?'

'Everything. It's going to be a wild night. We're not going to leave there without an arrest,' Tremayne said. He ordered another beer; he was in no hurry to leave.

***

Tremayne was confident that a confrontation with all the possible suspects was the only solution. The case had dragged on too long, and as far as he could see, if the people remained in their comfort zones, there'd be no resolution, and it was a resolution that he needed. And then there was his ex-wife, Jean; they regularly spoke, almost as if they were in their twenties and newly in love, although Tremayne knew it wasn't love. However, the idea of companionship appealed, even if only on an occasional basis.

Jean had booked a trip to southern Spain in three weeks' time. He had looked it up on the internet. It looked hot, too hot for him, but they served beer there, and he had agreed. He never let on that he was pleased to be going, not to his wife who knew it would be out of character to show too much emotion, and not to Yarwood who would have a smart comment.

Tremayne knew he could only go if the current case were concluded, and he hoped the event scheduled for that Friday evening would give him a result. Clare, pleased to be busy, occupied herself with the preparations, compiling a scenario of how the night should unfold. She had struggled to reconcile herself with being back in Salisbury, but was finding it easier to deal with Harry's death, even considering a date with another police officer. She would not see it as anything other than a night out, and she wasn't sure about it, but she wanted to stay in the city with its history and its quaintness.

Her parents, especially her mother, continued to ask her to return to their hotel and Norfolk, but she knew she would not. Besides, it was only two weeks before she moved into her cottage, and she needed some time off to check out the local shops for furnishings.

Samantha Dennison was also occupied preparing for the evening, treating it as a social event rather than a police investigation. Clare hoped she wasn't involved, as she had grown to like the woman, a person who had been blunt in her evaluation of what she was. Her openness was refreshing compared to Fiona Dowling, who had complained about the way Clare had confronted her in her house. Police intimidation, verging on brutality, was how it was described in the letter from her brother-in-law, the solicitor Chris Dowling.

Clare had to credit Superintendent Moulton in his support for her. He had worded a reply to Chris Dowling, and ultimately to his client, that Sergeant Yarwood was well within her rights to question a suspect, to apply pressure if required, and that it was murder, not a minor misdemeanour. No more was heard on the matter and the next time that Clare had run into Fiona Dowling in the city centre, not difficult in a small city, the woman had been polite and friendly.

Tremayne called Clare into his office. The investigative team consisted of just the two of them, as since the death of Vic Oldfield, their previous constable, there had been no replacement. Just the two of them, supported by a group of diligent professionals in the office, suited Tremayne and Clare, but they knew it would not be long before they'd be asked to take on additional investigative staff if there were any new murder cases.

'Yarwood, are we ready?'

'For the Friday night?' Clare said. She could see that Tremayne was champing at the bit to get on.

'What else?'

'We'll be ready. Are we taking uniforms?'

'We'll have a police car outside in the driveway.'

'What are our chances of an arrest?' Clare asked.

'There'll be an arrest.'

'It could be the Dennisons.'

'No one is safe from our questioning, not even them. The fact that it's their house is inconsequential.'

Chapter 23

Phillip Dennison's house, large and expensively decorated, was welcoming on the Friday night. Clare had arrived early, Tremayne was due within twenty minutes. On the dining room table, a buffet was laid out.

Clare had to admit that if the night were purely social, then it would have been enjoyable. She wasn't sure if the dramatic society members understood the seriousness of the situation, as if they thought that Tremayne often took part in murder mystery nights, where amateur detectives dress up in Sherlock Holmes' deerstalkers and period costumes, and act out the murder and then attempt to solve it.

It was strange, she thought, that all those invited were excited to come, but then, she realised, they were imbued with the love of acting, and the murderer was apparently the most accomplished in avoiding detection. And as for those genuinely innocent, they had nothing to fear, only the joy of being present at the event.

Even Clare had to admit to some excitement in that she would be required to play a part: the good police officer to Tremayne's bad. One would be raising the heat, the other would be soothing, consoling, and gently pressuring to let the person confess.

Peter Freestone was the first member of the dramatic society to arrive, closely followed by Gary Barker and Cheryl Milledge. The others came soon after.

The main room of the house was to be the setting. Everyone helped themselves to the buffet, and the alcohol. Clare noticed that Tremayne kept to a soft drink.

'Ladies and gentlemen, I would like to offer our appreciation to Phillip and Samantha for making us all very welcome, but let me remind you that this is a police investigation, not a social gathering, and not something that anyone here should regard as frivolous. Sitting here in this room are two murderers.'

'What do you reckon, DI Tremayne?' Phillip Dennison asked. He was sitting on a sofa, his wife at his side.

'We assumed initially that Gordon Mason was killed as a result of something he knew. In truth, we were looking for a motive.'

'And now?'

'There is an unknown factor. The possibility that the murderer or murderers kill for pleasure, or for the gratification that they are able to commit the perfect crime in front of an audience, surrounded by fellow actors.'

'A sick individual,' Len Dowling said. He was sitting on the other side of the room to Dennison. His wife sat nearby, holding his hand.

'If I look around this room,' Tremayne said, 'I see no one that fits the description of sick or psychotic, quite the contrary, but believe me, someone here is in need of medical treatment.'

'Then why would they be here tonight?' Fiona Dowling asked.

'The perfect crime requires it to remain hidden under the most intense scrutiny. The person responsible is laughing at us, sneeringly hiding behind a look of innocence,' Tremayne said.

'How will you find this person?' Samantha Dennison asked.

'I won't. It's your murder mystery night. You will identify the culprit. We will conduct this along the lines of a fictitious murder mystery, except this time there are real murders, those of Gordon Mason and Bill Ford.'

'What about Geoff Pearson?' Jimmy Francombe asked. Fiona Dowling said nothing, just stared at the young man. Her husband sat impassively.

'Tonight, all facts relating to our murder enquiry will be revealed. Geoff Pearson's death has been evaluated. The reason for his being pushed is known to most of you here, probably all, as you have no doubt discussed the matter.'

'I object to you accusing my wife,' Len Dowling said.

'Let it go,' Dowling's wife said. 'If they don't know, then I'll tell them. I was having an affair with Geoff. He had dumped me, I was angry. I confronted him at Old Sarum, pushed him, wanted to hit him, but he fell to his death. I panicked and left the area. I'm guilty of stupidity, not murder.'

'Thank you, Mrs Dowling,' Tremayne said. 'There are others with facts that they would prefer not be revealed, but tonight no one will be spared.'

'Why do we have to endure this?' Phillip Dennison said.

'You know the answer to your question.'

'Do I?'

'I'll explain so we are all clear where this night is heading. Gordon Mason has been murdered, so has Bill Ford. Geoff Pearson has died. We have possible motives for Mason's death, none for Bill Ford. Our investigation of Ford indicates no negative marks against his character, no dislike of the man, no behaviour on his part that could be regarded as offensive. If that is the case, then Bill Ford was innocent of any crime other than that he was a member of the Salisbury Amateur Dramatic Society and that he was one of the conspirators who stabbed Caesar. If that is the motive, then you all know what will happen next.'

'He intends to kill the remaining conspirators,' Freestone said.

'Exactly. Which one of you sitting here tonight will be the next to be stabbed in the heart? Does anyone want to question what we are trying to achieve here?'

No one spoke. All looked ready for the murder mystery to begin.

Clare stood up. 'This is a summary of the mystery. A Shakespearean tragedy, *Julius Caesar*, was being acted out by an amateur dramatic society. The crucial scene acted in front of an audience was where Julius Caesar is stabbed to death by the conspirators, seven in total. A fictional slaying in that the knives were meant to be retractable and plastic bladed, only two weren't. Of the seven conspirators, and the thirty-four stabs at the body on that stage, five stabs entered his body from two modified daggers.

'Gordon Mason who played Julius Caesar died on that night. Since then two of his assassins have also died, Geoff Pearson and Bill Ford. That only leaves Trevor Winston, Gary Barker, Jimmy Francombe, and Len Dowling alive.'

'Are you suggesting that those five are possible victims?' Cheryl Milledge asked.

'Or potential murderers,' Tremayne said.

'This is ludicrous,' Winston said. 'Why would anyone want to kill me?'

'Why is it ludicrous?' Clare asked. 'You're homosexual by your own admission, you were one of the conspirators.'

'But I'm harmless.'

'So was Bill Ford, unless anyone can tell us to the contrary.'

No one said anything. Tremayne looked around the room; he could see no facial expressions of someone trying to hide something. Cheryl Milledge excused herself and went and got some more food, as well as two cans of beer, one for her, one for Gary Barker.

'We need to discuss the motives for Gordon Mason's murder,' Clare said.

'Do we need to reveal everyone's dirty laundry?' Fiona Dowling asked.

'Unfortunately we must, unless you want to go home tonight wondering if your husband is next, or whether he's a murderer.'

'That's slanderous,' Len Dowling said.

'Dowling, shut up,' Dennison said. 'Tremayne and Yarwood are attempting to save us. Your bellyaching, your promiscuous wife, your lousy reputation are of little consequence.'

Dowling was up on his feet, heading over towards Dennison, ready to land a punch. Gary Barker interceded and pushed him back in his seat.

'Sit down,' Fiona whispered to her husband. 'The police are baiting us all, seeing who will react.'

'I'll not have you insulted,' Dowling said.

'Very chivalrous, no doubt, but it's a bit late in the day to defend my honour.'

'I could hardly do it while you were screwing Pearson, could I?'

'You bastard.'

'If you two have finished talking,' Freestone said, 'I'd like to hear what Sergeant Yarwood has in store for us tonight.'

Clare continued. 'There are some possible motives for wanting Mason dead. I will detail them, hopeful that no one will react vocally or violently. This is no time for false modesty or downright denials. The police work on facts, and I will reveal what we know, what we've investigated, and possibly what we conjecture.

'We became aware of a possible fraudulent land deal which pointed to Peter Freestone, Len Dowling, and Gordon Mason working in collusion.'

Freestone rose from his chair to comment. Clare ignored him. 'We have found no proof that fraud was committed. We know that Mason had often insulted Trevor Winston, made reference to his homosexuality. Also, Mason insulted Samantha Dennison, called her a tart.'

'He called me a prostitute, selling myself to a rich man,' Samantha said.

'As I was saying, Mason called Samantha Dennison a prostitute. Phillip Dennison confronted the man and hit him. And finally, we also know that Mason was attempting to blackmail Fiona Dowling over her affair with Geoff Pearson.'

'My bastard husband knew all along. It would have saved me screwing the odious man.'

Tremayne stood up, the others in the room focussed their attention on the woman's remarkable admission. 'Are you saying that you had sexual intercourse with Gordon Mason?'

'It's a night of truths, isn't it? I don't want to be the next victim of whoever killed Mason, although I wish it had been me. Of course I screwed him. The man was going to tell Len. That wasn't such a big deal, but Mason could have spread the gossip around the city.'

'And now everyone here will tell,' Cheryl said.

'What does it matter? And besides, the reaction has been exactly the opposite of what I expected. DI Tremayne, or was it Sergeant Yarwood, said it correctly when they called my friends vacuous and empty-headed. To them, I'm the fallen woman redeemed, the woman who stands by her man, the woman who will not fail.'

'It's a good enough motive for murder,' Cheryl said. 'You would have had no issue with killing Gordon Mason, nor Bill Ford if he found out. Were you screwing him as well?'

'Cheryl, please. I'm frightened of whoever this killer is, the same as everyone else here.'

Cheryl said nothing, nor did anyone else. Tremayne studied Fiona Dowling. He knew that she could have killed Mason and Ford, could have killed Pearson too, but that would require a confession.

'We cannot rule out either Geoff Pearson's or Bill Ford's involvement in the death of Gordon Mason, nor can we prove that whoever killed Ford was also one of Mason's murderers, but the connection is indisputable.'

But why Bill Ford?' Winston asked. 'He was a decent man.'

'There's one more motive that we need to mention,' Clare said. 'It may not be known that Gary Barker is to inherit his parents' garden centre. It may be that most of you do not know that where he works is his family's business. The bad relationship between parents and son is exacerbated by his relationship with Cheryl. They see their son as incapable, and Cheryl as manipulative, only using Gary as a means to get their property.'

'Their view of me is worse than that. They hate me with a passion,' Gary Barker said. 'My father is in the hospital now; he's unlikely to last the night.'

'You should be there,' Samantha said.

'If he was a decent father, then maybe, but he's not. He's a vindictive, evil-minded hypocrite, the same as Mason. It was Mason they were using to prevent my inheriting.'

'Did he succeed?' Francombe asked.

'No. It'll be mine within the week, and then I'll move in with Cheryl.'

'What about your mother?' Clare asked.

'You've never met her. The doctor wants to put her in a nursing home. She needs constant supervision for dementia. There's a place ready for her. She'll barely notice the change in surroundings.'

'That's callous,' Samantha said.

'After the way they treated me, the way they treated Cheryl?'

'It's a motive for wanting Gordon Mason dead,' Tremayne said.

'It's an excellent motive, but I'd not have killed him on that stage. And why? He'd lost, my parents had lost. Why would I destroy all that I have out of anger and hatred? The man's dead and good riddance to him. Tonight, after we find the murderer, I'll shake his hand and thank him.'

Clare looked over at Tremayne, who cocked his head slightly upwards in acknowledgement of what they had both seen and heard: a man who could have killed both Mason and Ford.

***

Tremayne knew he had emotions running high, exactly where he wanted them. 'Mr Dowling, it is time to evaluate you.'

'Why me? Just because I've got a slut of a wife doesn't mean I killed Mason.'

'I know about you and the woman in the office, the extended meetings,' Fiona Dowling said.

'That's lies. You may screw around, I don't.'

'Not up to it, is that it? Not from what I know. If you weren't so busy with her, then maybe I wouldn't have needed to screw Pearson and whoever else.'

'Whoever else?'

Tremayne knew that this was precisely what he wanted, the heated passion, the anger, the contradictory statements, and now he had the Dowlings opening up. He could see the others watching and enjoying the spectacle, but their time was coming.

'What does it matter? I'll screw around, you'll screw your secretary, but don't worry, I'll not leave you. We need each other, we're a great team.'

Clare listened, not sure what to make of the conversation. With Harry, it had been one man, one woman, and fidelity, but here were the Dowlings, two people who were married and wanted to stay that way, yet they regarded fidelity as a dispensable commodity.

'Who else in this room have you slept with? You're the one with your night of truths. Then come out with it, tell all,' Len Dowling said. 'Who else have you screwed: Dennison, Jimmy, although he may be a little too young, even for you. I assume you draw the line somewhere, although Freestone could just about manage it. Certainly not Winston; he's only able to make it with men. Come on, who is it?'

Fiona realised that she was enjoying the argument, appreciative of an audience, oblivious of whether they approved of her or not. 'Okay, if you must know, I was sleeping with Bill Ford.'

Tremayne sat up at the revelation. 'Mrs Dowling, is that true?' he asked.

'It's true. The man was lonely, in need of a woman. He told me one night after rehearsals.'

'Not the night I found you screwing Geoff on the dining room floor,' Cheryl said.

'Not that night. I hope you had a good look,' Fiona said.

'There wasn't that much to see, other than Geoff's lily-white arse between your two legs, and your moaning. And besides, it's not the first time I've seen a man on top of you.'

Jimmy Francombe loved the spectacle; he knew he'd have plenty to tell his friends. The conversation, the visual images in his mind, were causing him to get an erection. He grabbed a magazine from a table close to where he was sitting and placed it over his lap.

'That night with Bill Ford, the three of us, is that it? You weren't looking so good that night either.'

'At least I don't pretend to be holier than thou. My past is an open book; I'm neither proud nor dismissive of it, and Gary knows all about it. And believe me, with Gary it will only be him and his children. I suppose it's because Len's such a lousy lay.'

'And you'd know, wouldn't you?'

'A long time ago, but yes, I know. I suppose the woman in his office, the dark-haired one, she'd be able to corroborate Len's lovemaking ability.'

The two women came at each other, or Fiona did, Cheryl responding. Clare stepped in and separated them. Jimmy Francombe was beside himself with excitement, Trevor Winston took in all that was occurring. Peter Freestone sat quietly, pleased that his daughter had severed her friendship with the women in her early teens. The Dennisons sat to one side, saying nothing.

Tremayne re-entered the fray, and Clare sat on a seat equidistant from the two women.

'Mrs Dowling, we were led to believe that you were fond of Geoff Pearson. If, as you have professed previously, you love your husband and were fond of Pearson, then why were you involved with Bill Ford?' Tremayne asked.

'He was a good man, a man that I loved in my rebellious teenage years.'

'Is that the reason?'

'The man was lonely, and in need of affection. We'd meet occasionally, that's all.'

'That's all?' Len Dowling said.

'Shut up, Len, you're becoming a bore,' Fiona said. 'You knew what I was when I married you. We're a team, but for tonight, this one night, I intend to reveal everything, the same as everyone else. I didn't kill Geoff, although I was angry with him, and I didn't kill Bill Ford for the one reason that I couldn't: the man was more important to me than that. And I didn't kill Gordon Mason.'

'But I could have killed Bill, and you've given them a motive,' Dowling said.

'Not you, you couldn't harm a fly,' Fiona said. 'You may be able to sell them a house, but that's as far as it goes.'

'Mr and Mrs Dowling, can we come back to Bill Ford. We know about your past relationship with the man, we know that you and Cheryl had a threesome.'

Jimmy Francombe excused himself and dashed to the bathroom. He looked at Cheryl as he left and smiled. She did not return the smile but continued to look at the woman who had angered her, although she knew it was not anger that would last. The woman, for all her faults, was still her friend.

'Mr Dowling, Len, your wife has given multiple motives for wanting Gordon Mason and Bill Ford dead,' Tremayne said. 'Are you willing to confess to their murders?'

'Why me? What about the others? Cheryl's been around, the same as Fiona. Why don't you ask her if she was screwing Ford as well? Or maybe Gary was jealous of a previous lover, wanted him dead. What if Cheryl was screwing Mason? Maybe he had something on her, something he didn't want Gary to know.'

Cheryl Milledge sat still, outwardly portraying calmness, inwardly seething. 'I was not involved with either of the two men. Gordon Mason was an awful man, Bill was not,' she said.

'Let me put this to you,' Tremayne said. 'If Bill Ford had approached you to admit that he was lonely, would you have slept with him?'

'Before I met Gary, I would have, but now, not a chance. As much as I liked Bill, there's no way that I would cheat on Gary, or him on me. Fiona, for all her airs and graces, has not changed; I have.'

Chapter 24

Clare had not said much so far. She felt the need to remind Tremayne of the structure of the evening. 'Guv, we should ask the others here to offer their opinions of what has happened so far. Did Fiona kill Geoff Pearson out of passion and anger? Did Len kill Mason and Ford? Or did someone else kill Ford?'

'I did not kill Geoff,' Fiona said. Clare noticed that she was no longer holding her husband's hand and that they had separated by at least a foot on the sofa they sat on.

'This is a murder mystery,' Clare said. 'All possibilities are open to conjecture. We do not have fictitious deaths here, only real ones with real killers.'

'Very well, carry on. Have your entertainment at my cost.'

'There is no entertainment here tonight,' Tremayne said to the assembled participants. This is a murder enquiry, and tonight, I can assure you, someone is going to be arrested for murder. I don't know who, but I have my suspicions. It will be up to all those present to assist Yarwood and myself in this matter.'

'And if we don't?' Phillip Dennison asked.

'Your non-compliance is an indication that you are hiding something. There is a hidden component in this enquiry. We need to find it.'

'Not with me there isn't,' Samantha Dennison said. 'I married Phillip for his money, he married me as a reward. It's a good arrangement, and we prefer to be together, not apart. As for me, I've slept with enough men in my time. I do not need an old and angry man who insulted me or someone who spent his time with the dead.'

'What about Geoff Pearson?' Fiona asked. 'Were you screwing him?'

'Not a chance. He tried it on, but I know which side my bread is buttered. I have no intention of cheating on Phillip; count me out as a potential murderer.'

'Before we move on to the others in this room, let us have everyone's opinion of Fiona and Len Dowling. A show of hands will be sufficient. As for the Dowlings, I would remind you that this is a police enquiry,' Tremayne said.

'I'll not stay here to be judged,' Len Dowling said.

'Listen to the detective inspector, Len. Inspector Tremayne is right. We're only guilty of offending public morality, not of killing someone. If the others in this room want to pass judgement, then so be it. I'll not object,' Fiona said.

'Did Fiona push Geoff Pearson,' Tremayne said, 'knowing full well that the drop was sufficient to cause him injury? Remember, death was not certain from the fall, in that the grass below was wet from the recent rain. It was soft underfoot. That does not obviate her intention to murder, just the fact that death could not be guaranteed. If he had not hit his head on the ruins' protruding stones on the way down, he might have broken some bones, but possibly nothing more.'

The hands went up around the room. Clare counted them. 'Mrs Dowling, it appears that the majority believe that you acted out of anger.'

'What about Cheryl? She didn't put her hand up,' Fiona said.

'I've known you longer than anyone else. You were angry, but you did not mean him any harm. You're innocent of that crime,' Cheryl said.

The two women stood up and hugged each other. 'You're a bitch, but you're still my friend,' Cheryl said.

Tremayne needed to wind up the heat; a tender moment between the two women had brought a sense of calm to the room. 'Let us come to Len Dowling, a man who has every right to dislike Mason and Ford. One was forcing his wife into sex, the other she has voluntarily admitted to sleeping with. What man would not be driven to murder?'

'If Len did kill Mason,' Freestone said, 'then he has my acceptance for what he did. I liked Bill Ford, even met up with him on occasions, yet the man is party to adultery. He was a man who had great respect in the community, yet the chance to sleep with Fiona and he took it.'

'He did not take it, I offered. He was my friend, and I cared for him.'

'It doesn't excuse him.'

'What man could resist? Bill was guilty of no crime, and he does not deserve your condemnation. I know all about you,' Fiona said.

'What do you know?' Clare asked.

'I know that he has used his influence as a city councillor to his advantage.'

'Is this about the land deal that we were investigating?'

'No, but he's used his influence elsewhere, the same as everyone on the council.'

'Cheryl, she works in the building department,' Tremayne said.

'She's not involved.'

'Can you prove what you've said against Peter Freestone?'

'It's not a crime, just unethical, that's all.'

'That's slanderous,' Freestone said. 'I've always acted in the best interests of the community.'

'Fiona, you've got a big mouth,' Len Dowling said. 'This is going to cause trouble.'

'Why? It's in here, not outside. The next question is whether you killed Mason and Bill. Is that correct, Detective Inspector?'

'Yes.'

'Thank you. What do you want, Len? Do you want Peter Freestone sitting there voting against you? I know he's a friend of the detective inspector. If you killed Mason, then admit it, even if you killed Bill, but don't allow yourself to be judged by anyone else in this room. They've all got things they'd rather keep hidden.'

'I don't,' Jimmy Francombe said.

'Too young, is that it?'

'I didn't kill anyone.'

'What about you and Trevor? Are you his playmate? You're always friendly.'

'That's scurrilous, and you know it,' Winston said. He had been enjoying the spectacle of the Dowlings sounding off at each other.

'Maybe it is, but what have you got to hide, Trevor?' Fiona said. 'What's hidden in your cupboard? You must be sleeping with someone, and if it's not Jimmy, then who is it? What is the dirt on you?'

'There is no dirt on me. I have some friends, but they're not here. I hated Gordon Mason, liked Bill, but I did not kill either of them.'

'And what about you two, Mr and Mrs Perfect?' Fiona said, focussing her interest on the Dennisons.

'You've got a foul mouth, Fiona,' Phillip Dennison said. 'What have we done to you? I've always been polite, never tried it on with you, not that I ever fancied you.'

'What do you mean? You prefer a painted tart to me, is that it? Does a mature woman intimidate you, or do you get your kicks with adolescent females?'

'I'm not an adolescent,' Samantha Dennison said. 'I'm over the age of consent and Phillip treats me well, more than can be said for your husband.'

'I've no complaints with Len, but look at you. Do you dress up in a school uniform for him: frilly knickers, a short skirt, tight blouse, pretend that he's your teacher about to give you a spanking. Is that how he gets his kicks?'

'You bitch,' Phillip Dennison said. 'Don't talk to my wife like that.'

'I know about you and your offshore companies, you fiddling the tax man.'

'How?'

'Chris has the dirt on you, the same as Freestone does. Is Peter Freestone to be the next man you kill? Did Gordon Mason know what you were?'

Tremayne felt the need to interject. 'Mr Dennison, you're obviously very successful. This raises the question as to whether your financial dealings, your business structure, are fully legal.'

'They are. Fiona and Len are just fishing, aiming to direct the blame away from Len. I have not broken any laws.'

Clare thought that Phillip Dennison had probably done nothing wrong, but she could not be sure. What was sure was that any group of people would have something they did not want to be revealed, even her, but she was not defending herself; the others were, and so far, no one had cracked, although some were wounded. Fiona was, as was her husband, but she was sure they would rise above it. For Freestone, the mere suggestion that he had not conducted his city councillor's duties in accordance with the guidelines would lead to him being ejected from the position. It was a motive for murder, and Mason was the sort of man who would reveal the wrongdoing, but what about Bill Ford? The man had no black marks against him, other than he had been sleeping with another man's wife.

Jimmy Francombe, apart from his overactive teenage hormones, seemed harmless, as did Trevor Winston. Both seemed the least likely, in that one was young, the other older and homosexual. Killing Mason may have had some validity for Winston, but not Bill Ford, who was known not to be gay.

'This is going nowhere,' Gary Barker said.

'The night's young,' Tremayne said.

'You can't hold us here against our will.'

'Outside there is a police car. Anyone who feels inclined to leave will be taken down to the police station for questioning. It's either here or down there, you can decide.'

'In that case, get on with it,' Freestone said.

'Let us examine the Dennisons,' Tremayne said.

'Why us?' Phillip Dennison asked. 'We're an open book.'

Clare decided it was time for her to speak. 'Not so long ago, Samantha was placed under control. I believe that you slapped her, took away her credit cards and the key to the Aston Martin. Is that correct?'

'Phillip was under a lot of strain,' Samantha said. She had her arm through her husband's.

'DI Tremayne and I have spoken to you on several occasions. I don't remember you defending your husband at those times.'

'I was wrong.'

'You said that you were the trophy, he was the older man, and if he could not keep you in the manner that you required, then you would leave, take your share of the assets, and find someone else.'

'That's what I said.'

'What has changed?'

'I don't want to leave Phillip. He's a good man, always treated me well.'

'Is it because you will not get your share of his money? What if he's found guilty of murder? How will that affect your wealth? You're the legal wife, and you'll have access to his money. I put it to you that you know he is guilty of murder and that you are waiting for him to be arrested. That is why we are so welcome here tonight. You just need one more night of pretence, and then this is all yours. Am I right?' Clare said. She realised that what she had just said was plausible.

'That's rubbish. Phillip knows that I want him here, not in prison.'

'How does he know? Did you twist him around your finger, flaunt the assets? Samantha, compared to you, Fiona Dowling is a paragon of virtue.'

'Don't compare me to that woman. She screws who she wants, I don't. I've got Phillip, I don't need anyone else. Her husband may be lousy in bed, but Phillip is not.'

'How did you know about my husband's lovemaking?' Fiona asked.

'You told me.'

'No, I didn't. Who have you been talking to? Bill Ford? Have you been screwing Len?'

'Why would I do that? I've no need of another man.'

***

The evening was going well; Tremayne sat back to let the fireworks continue. So far, he kept coming back to Fiona Dowling. Her husband, Len, had not acquitted himself any better either, but loose morals, a lack of backbone, were not confessions of guilt. The constant haranguing across the room had not, so far, produced any indication of who he would be placing in handcuffs before the end of the evening.

The tension between Samantha Dennison and Fiona Dowling was palpable. Both women had dressed for the occasion. Cheryl Milledge had arrived wearing a tee-shirt and a pair of jeans. Clare could see that Cheryl and Gary Barker were hitting the beer and were becoming drunk. She let them continue, knowing that both could drink a lot, and tongues loosen with alcohol. Fiona Dowling was steering clear of alcohol, as was Samantha Dennison. Clare did not like Fiona any more than her senior did, but Samantha had acquitted herself well. For a woman who had had no involvement with the dramatic society except on infrequent occasions, she seemed to know a lot about them, especially Len Dowling and his inability to keep his wife from straying.

'Samantha,' Clare said, 'you told me about your past once. Are you willing to reveal it here?'

'What's there to tell. I was working in an office, being accosted by every rampant male. One day in comes Phillip, we start talking and then soon after we are married.'

'This is a night for warts and all. Why Phillip? Was it love or his money?'

'His money initially, but after that love. Phillip treats me well, I am content.'

'The need for a younger man must remain. My apologies to your husband, but you're young and full of vitality, your husband is at the age of slowing down.'

'I look as though I need a man constantly in my bed, but that's not the case. I've enjoyed the ability to spend, to live well, but there are times when I could stay at home and read a book.'

'Are you well read?'

'Yes, and well-educated.'

'Then you, as the only bystander here tonight, let us have your opinion as to who the murderer is.'

Samantha focussed on those assembled in that elegant room with its paintings on the wall, the flat-screen TV, the expensive furniture. 'There are three deaths,' Samantha commenced. 'Gordon Mason, Geoff Pearson, and Bill Ford.'

'I did not murder Geoff,' Fiona shouted. Clare looked over at her, holding a finger to her mouth in a gesture to be quiet and sit down.

'Let me deal with Gordon Mason,' Samantha continued. 'The man was an obnoxious bore. I did not like him, but his comments meant little to me. I know that is how most of you see me, a cheap slut selling herself to an older man, but you're too polite, or not committed enough, to say anything. Mason was, as you say, killed at Old Sarum, probably by two men. Neither Fiona nor Cheryl are involved. Those who killed him must have had a close relationship to consider such an option. Alternatively, there was one man with two daggers.'

'Impossible to swap in a frenzy,' Clare said.

'Then it was one man on the stage, another off the stage. Was the body visible at all times?'

'Yes, and he was dead by the time he was placed on the stretcher by Mark Antony.'

'Then it's two of the men on the stage, but which two? Phillip tends to be a loner, and not involved with the other men in the dramatic society. Len could be involved with Peter Freestone, complementary professions, and Gordon Mason would have been able to see through any crooked deals they had hatched together.'

Freestone made a move to open his mouth. Tremayne looked over at him, a clear sign to keep quiet and to let the woman talk.

'Geoff Pearson, from what I can see, had no reason to kill Mason, no collusion, no special relationship with anyone else in the group,' Samantha continued. 'The man was attracted to women, not men, and as we can see with Fiona, he was not averse to seducing Len's wife. He was a young man full of libido, and he must have had a great deal of satisfaction acting on that stage with Len, the unknowing husband. Geoff, for all his virtues, was a shallow man, bereft of true emotions, other than for self. He is not a murderer, but not a person of true substance either. Len, for all his faults, is. He's a man who stands by his wife, the most devious of all of us here tonight. The woman has not handled herself well, and those that she calls her friends, are not. They're fair weather, not visible when times are tough.'

'Not like me,' Cheryl said.

'Cheryl is a decent person, and, as she says, she is a true friend. The only one who was with Fiona when she was arrested after Geoff's death. However, I don't believe that Fiona wanted the man dead, although she would not have been upset to have seen him in the hospital. Regardless of what I've said, I don't see Fiona as a murderer.'

'Everyone will have their say after Mrs Dennison has finished,' Tremayne said.

'Gary Barker is a man who lets life pass him by, not interfering with its flow,' Samantha said. 'He's now got Cheryl to look after him. The two of them complement each other, and Gary could not kill anyone; it's not in his nature to take himself or life too seriously. Cheryl has a kind heart and the anger to kill Mason, but not the opportunity, and she would not have been capable of killing Bill Ford, a former lover, and still a friend of hers and Fiona.'

'What about the relationship between Peter Freestone and Len Dowling?' Tremayne asked. He had changed his opinion of Dennison's wife. Regardless of why she had married her husband, she was an articulate woman. He was willing to let her continue, although he had a shrewd idea where she was heading.

Samantha, emboldened by her new-found importance, stood up and moved to one corner of the room. 'Len would not be capable. He's able to run a successful business due to Fiona's support and pushing him on, but he could not kill anyone. Maybe if Fiona had pushed him hard enough, but she wouldn't. Not that she would have any issues with doing that, a good woman on your side in a fight, but her social prestige is all important to her. She's admitted to sleeping with Mason, and whereas she may say he's an odious man, it would have only been a case of lying on her back, opening her legs, and thinking of England, or whatever she thinks off. Probably her social standing, as that is more important. Apart from that, she'd have no reason to kill Mason. She is not a likeable person. Sorry, but there it is.'

Fiona Dowling sat in her chair, saying nothing. Tremayne looked over at her, could see the anger directed at Samantha Dennison. 'Mrs Dowling, I suggest you digest what Samantha has just said,' Tremayne said. 'Harsh words, but she's just given you the best alibi possible.'

'I don't like what she said,' Fiona replied.

'Maybe you don't, but we're here to solve a murder, not to make friends. After tonight, you can all go your separate ways, but for now, Mrs Dennison has the floor.'

Samantha continued. 'Len could not kill Mason without his wife's direction, and even if he had known about her and Bill Ford, he would have done nothing, or maybe remonstrated with the man, attempted to push him around, but that's all. The man does not have the backbone, I believe we're all agreed on that.'

Len and Fiona Dowling sat close to each other again, holding hands.

'And if Len and Peter were involved in something illegal and they wanted Mason dead, there's no way that Len would act without his wife's encouragement, which would then mean that Peter Freestone knew of Fiona in the background, and besides, Peter did not kill Mason.'

'That's correct,' Tremayne said. 'He had only one stab at Mason. If it was to be a murder, it has to be those who stabbed him more than once.'

'There are only two left,' Samantha said. 'Does anyone want to take over or shall I wrap up this night?'

'Carry on,' Clare said.

'You're doing a fine job,' Tremayne said. No one else said anything. Phillip Dennison looked at his wife in admiration. Cheryl and Gary were no longer drinking. Trevor Winston and Jimmy Francombe sat motionlessly.

'Doesn't anyone else see it?' Samantha said.

'What do you mean?' Clare said.

'Jimmy, he's gay.'

'I'm not,' Jimmy protested.

'Let Mrs Dennison continue,' Tremayne said. 'Everyone else sat quietly while she was denouncing or exonerating them. You will do the same,' he said, directing his gaze at the young man.

'The over-attentiveness to women, the need to chat them up, to show off how manly he is in front of his friends. I've seen it before. I'm sure he's tried it on with Clare and Fiona.'

'He has with me,' Clare said.

'He got a smack from me for trying to look down my blouse,' Fiona said.

'Trevor Winston is gay. The two of them are lovers.'

'That's not fair. I'm straight,' Jimmy said.

'Let me put it to everyone here,' Samantha said. 'When has anyone here seen Jimmy with a woman? He's eighteen, the city of Salisbury is awash with teenage girls looking to be taken out. He's an attractive young man, and he'd have no trouble seducing a few, but where are they? Has he ever brought any to your rehearsals?

He's a show-off, but he never shows a woman. The man is gay, and so is Trevor.'

'We've not seen him with a girlfriend,' Fiona said.

'Nor have I,' Cheryl said.

'Mrs Dennison, Samantha, please continue,' Tremayne said. 'And Trevor and Jimmy, please be quiet. Samantha has the floor, and we intend to hear her out.'

'But–' Jimmy started to say.

'You've heard the police officer,' Trevor said. 'Let Samantha have her say. You'll get a chance afterwards.'

'Trevor is openly gay and proud of it,' Samantha said, 'but he's a mature man in a liberated society. Jimmy is still concerned about how his friends see him, not willing to tell his parents either. There is only one conclusion.'

'Which is?' Tremayne asked. Everyone in the room was listening with bated breath. No one was eating or drinking.

'Trevor and Jimmy killed Gordon Mason.'

'And Bill Ford?' Clare asked.

'Mason knew about them. The man was vindictive enough, bigoted, willing to tell Jimmy's school friends that he was gay, as well as his parents. Neither he nor Trevor could allow that to occur.'

'It's a lie,' Trevor Winston said, jumping to his feet.

'Mr Winston, please sit down. You'll have a chance to offer a defence. Mrs Dennison, please continue,' Tremayne said.

'Bill Ford would not have been interested, and the man's discretion was well known. He knew about Fiona's and Cheryl's past histories, the fact that he had slept with both of them. The fact that Jimmy was gay and sleeping with Trevor would not have concerned him. He may have had a word in Jimmy's ear to tell him to be more careful, but he would have done no more. They killed Bill Ford, but not because he threatened their cosy love nest; they killed him because they enjoyed it.'

'Only one of them killed him,' Clare said.

'One dagger and the place was cleaned afterwards.'

'Spotlessly.'

'You've been to Trevor's hairdressing salon. How would you describe it?'

'Spotless.'

'Precisely. One of the two stabbed the man, the other was present, and may or may not have taken an active part.'

'It was Trevor's idea,' Jimmy Francombe said as he stood up and moved to the other side of the room.'

'Shut up, just shut up. They can't prove anything,' Trevor Winston shouted at him.

'I didn't want to kill Bill Ford. It was Trevor's idea.'

Clare went over and stood next to the young man. 'Why did you kill Bill Ford?' she asked.

'It was Trevor; he stabbed him. I wasn't in the room. Bill was a good man, my friend.'

'Yet you let the man be murdered. Why?'

'Trevor thought it would be fun, but I didn't.'

'Why Mason?' Clare asked. She looked over at Tremayne, saw him signalling out of the window for a couple of uniforms to come in.

'Gordon was going to tell my parents. I couldn't let him do that.'

'But why murder?'

'You don't understand. You're young and pretty. I hate being what I am, but I can't help it. Trevor knew what I was six months ago. He put pressure on me, I reacted.'

'Reacted?'

'Okay. I slept with him.'

'And how did that feel?'

'Dirty, but I couldn't stop. And then Gordon Mason was threatening to tell my parents if I didn't stop sleeping with Trevor.'

'How did he know?'

'He saw us once in Trevor's car after rehearsals. The man was nosy, that's how he knew about Geoff and Fiona. He observed, prowled around, probably a peeping tom as well, getting his kicks watching others screw.'

'Did he enjoy watching you and Trevor?'

'Maybe, maybe not. I don't know. Trevor said we had to kill him, make it look as if it was an accident.'

'And you agreed?'

'What could I do? I want to finish school, go to university, and now what?'

The others in the room said nothing. Fiona sat close to Len, Samantha near to her husband. Peter Freestone relaxed back in his chair. Tremayne was on his feet, as were the two uniforms who had entered through a door at the rear.

'You damn fool,' Trevor Winston said. 'If you had only kept quiet.'

'Mr Winston, why did you kill Bill Ford?'

'Jimmy did, not me.'

'You liar, you bloody liar. You enjoyed every moment up there at Old Sarum.'

'Mr Francombe, are you willing to confess to the murder of Gordon Mason?' Tremayne asked.

'Yes, but I did not kill Bill Ford. I liked the man.'

'You've said that already,' Tremayne said. 'You will be taken from here and formally charged with murder.'

'What will happen?'

'That depends on a judge and jury, not me. Yarwood, can you accompany Francombe to the police station, let his parents know?'

'I'll do it,' Clare said.

Tremayne turned to Trevor Winston. 'You will be charged with the murders of Gordon Mason and Bill Ford. Do you have anything to say?'

'You can't prove it.'

'Jimmy Francombe is young. He'll get off with a shortened sentence due to his youth. As long as he maintains his story, he'll be out in a few years. You, Mr Winston, will not. The only hope you will have is to plead guilty, hopeful of a reduced sentence due to insanity.'

'They'll not believe me,' Winston said.

'Killing a man just because you enjoy the thrill of it is hardly the act of a sane man.'

'You may be right. I'll take legal advice first.'

'That's your prerogative. Mine is to arrest you for the murders of Gordon Mason and Bill Ford,' Tremayne said. 'Take him away,' he said to one of the uniforms.

Clare left with Jimmy Francombe, Tremayne returned to his seat. 'A successful evening,' he said.

'Successful, is that how you'd describe it?' Peter Freestone said.

'I'm sorry for what has been said here tonight, but it was necessary. Murder is a crime that brings out the worst in people, that makes emotions raw. Hopefully, you can all forgive what was said, what was revealed.'

'I can,' Fiona Dowling said. 'Trevor would not have stopped. He'd have chosen another target, any one of us.'

'Thank you,' Cheryl Milledge said. Samantha Dennison came over and gave Tremayne a kiss on the cheek. The DI sat back, complacent, knowing full well that it would take a week to wrap up the paperwork, and then it was a holiday in Spain with Jean, his former wife. He had to admit that he was looking forward to it.

The End

Phillip Strang

Death and the Lucky Man

Chapter 1

Someone had once told Detective Inspector Keith Tremayne that some people were lucky and some weren't. Tremayne knew only one thing: the man lying dead in a pool of blood had qualified on the lucky after winning sixty-eight million pounds on a lottery ticket, but now his luck had run out.

Tremayne knew the victim, Alan Winters; even knew his family.

The man with all his new wealth had not hidden behind closed doors, fending off the scrounging relatives, the newly-found friends. That wasn't Winters' style. He had been out and about, driving expensive cars, living well.

It had been big news at the time in Salisbury, a small city to the south-west of London with its imposing cathedral, the spire at four hundred and four feet the highest in the United Kingdom. Tremayne remembered the day Winters had won his prize: the front page of the local newspaper, interviewed on the radio and the television. He recalled the next week when Winters, drunk after treating all of the patrons of his local pub to copious rounds of drink, wrapped a Ferrari that he had purchased the previous day around a lamppost. The car had been written off, yet the alcohol-sodden multi-millionaire had staggered away with no more than a scratch. He had lost his driving licence as a result of the escapade, not that it stopped him from driving, often with a chauffeur, one of his numerous relatives.

Tremayne knew how many relatives he had, no more than could be counted on one hand, but Winters had hundreds. He was going through the money at a rapid rate, but still had plenty to go, and the man, not the most attractive in that he was in his forties, balding and overweight, had plenty of friends as well, plenty of female companions.

And now he was dead. Tremayne knew the questions would start to roll. And why was he lying on the Altar Stone at Stonehenge, naked, with his throat cut? Clare Yarwood had seen the body as well, turned away initially at the sight of it, but had taken a deep breath and stood alongside Tremayne. 'Nasty one, guv,' she said.

Time had moved on since Harry Holchester, her fiancé, had died the night he had saved her from the pagan worshippers in Cuthbert's Wood, not more than five miles from where they were now standing.

'It can't be the Druids,' Tremayne said. 'They're into communing with nature, smelling the flowers and whatever.'

Clare Yarwood knew that her DI would, as usual, affect ignorance, yet she knew the man well enough. They had been working together almost two years; she, the young officer in her late twenties, he, the curmudgeon going on sixty. Apart from the few months that she had been on compassionate leave after the death of her fiancé, she had stayed in the Homicide department at Bemerton Road Police Station in Salisbury.

Tremayne knew that the national media would soon be on the scene and the gossip mill would be working overtime in Salisbury and the surrounding area: local boy makes good, comes to a sticky end. Not that Tremayne was surprised about the man's demise, having seen his behaviour in the time since he had been feted locally and nationally as the man who had beaten the odds. How he had been struggling to make ends meet, how his mother, ailing and infirm, was going to have that long-overdue holiday in Europe, and so on.

Tremayne had heard it all before, read about it enough times, and he knew the problem with Alan Winters' life before he had bought that one ticket in a newsagent on the way home from the pub of a Saturday lunchtime. The man, a labourer for Salisbury City Council, was bone idle, did nothing much as far as Tremayne could see except for getting drunk once too often.

And as for Winters' mother, ailing and infirm, Tremayne knew her story well enough. The Winters, Tremayne knew, were not battlers, struggling to make ends meet; they were the flotsam of society who drifted along from one disaster to another, one fractious relationship to the next. The ailing and infirm mother had seven children, including the lucky man. Two were in prison, one was selling herself around the area, another was married and living in Southampton, and as for the other children, Tremayne knew their stories as well.

At Stonehenge on a cold morning, the wind rattling across Salisbury Plain, he realised that it was not going to be a straightforward murder investigation. There was a story here, he could see that, as could his sergeant, Clare Yarwood.

Tremayne knew that he could not bring himself to call her Clare; it was always Yarwood, although he had relented when he had gone with her to Avon Hill to visit the grave of her fiancé, who had been publican of his favourite pub. She had proved herself to be resilient on her return to Salisbury after compassionate leave, even attempting to enter the dating scene again: disastrous, according to her. All they wanted was a few drinks, a decent meal, and then back to the man's place. These were facts that Tremayne did not want to hear, but for whatever reason, he had become the one person that she could open up with.

Tremayne remembered the visit to Harry's grave, the almost pleasant look of the village as they passed through it. After the paganists had been dealt with, the church authorities had been quick to re-consecrate the old church and had soon installed a new vicar. He had hovered around the two of them in the graveyard until Tremayne had taken him to one side to allow his sergeant time to reflect over the man who was buried there.

'I shouldn't have come,' Clare had said.

Tremayne had understood and had put his arm around her. He had watched her standing next to the grave, cleaning the weeds growing around the edge, touching the headstone, even seeing her name as the beloved – she had to thank Harry's relatives in Salisbury for that. Clare knew that if he had lived, he would not have been free. The evidence against him was overwhelming, and he had been party to multiple murders, including the deaths of two police officers, who had attempted to leave Avon Hill that night to bring help.

Tremayne remembered the only words she had spoken when they had driven back to Salisbury: 'Now's my time to get on with my life,' she had said.

Not that he believed her. He knew that she was an emotional woman, and it would be a long time before she detached from Harry, a long time before she was emotionally stable. One thing he knew above all else: he'd always be there for her.

For once, Stonehenge was closed to the general public, not that the visitors were allowed to get too close anymore, and the tourist couches were lined up in the park across the road. Tremayne realised that if they enclosed the crime scene, the tourists would have something else to send home on their smartphones – an actual murder at the ancient moment. And Stonehenge had never been a place of death, although even after thousands of years the history of the site, the people who had built it, what they had worshipped, even its significance, were still hotly debated by academics, and the archaeologists were conducting another dig not more than three hundred yards away.

Jim Hughes, the crime scene examiner, and his team were at the scene, busy as usual, impervious to the dead body, conducting their investigation. 'His throat's been slit,' he said.

'Stating the obvious,' Tremayne replied.

'Is this a sacrificial slaying?'

'I hope not. Did you know the man?'

'I've seen him around the city, showing off, flashing his money. I was not impressed by what I saw.'

'I knew him even before he won all that money. If there was anyone less deserving, it was Alan Winters. I can't say I liked him. Some of the villains, ne'er do wells, and the plain useless can be charming, but he wasn't.'

'It didn't stop him having plenty of friends.'

'That wouldn't have lasted long the way he was burning money. He would have been back in a council house before long, pleading for a handout.'

'Instead of that place he bought.'

'Instead of that. It hasn't pleased the police too much. Every weekend the parties, the drunkenness, the abuse of the neighbours if they dare to complain.'

'Any ideas as to who might have killed him?' Hughes asked as he continued with his investigation, oblivious of the tourists in the distance.

'There's no shortage of suspects this time.'

'Relatives?'

'More than you and I ever had, but that's not surprising the way the Winters spread their seed around the area.'

'And Winters didn't care that some were bleeding him.'

'With over sixty million pounds, what do you think?'

'I'd certainly care,' Hughes said. 'Mind you, I'd not agree with any publicity.'

'That's because you've had money, know how to handle yourself. Alan Winters never had any, just enough to get drunk and cause trouble. I'm surprised he lasted long enough to be murdered.'

'Regardless, he was, but what's the significance? I'd say there were at least two people up here, possibly three.'

'That many?'

'Whoever brought him up here, even if he were unconscious, would have had to carry or drag him. We'll try to be more specific, but two to three people.'

'Any chance of fingerprints?'

'We'll try, but don't hold out too much hope. The murderers, are they likely to have a criminal record?'

'Judging by the company the man kept, a few suspects would. We'll work our way through his known associates. It may take some time. It'll keep Yarwood busy. She's been taking it easy lately, decorating her cottage, wanting to decorate my house as well.'

'I've given up on yours,' Clare said.

***

On Tremayne and Clare's return to Bemerton Road Police Station, the welcoming presence of Detective Superintendent Moulton, the last man that Tremayne wanted to see. They had been at a freezing murder site, and now the one man who never gave up on trying to retire the detective inspector was in his office.

'What's the situation?' Moulton asked. Tremayne knew it was the opening salvo leading up to the inevitable.

'Alan Winters, forty-eight, a council worker, or he was until he won the lottery.'

'The fancy cars, the raucous parties?'

'That's the one. He's been murdered up at Stonehenge, spread-eagled across the Altar Stone, his throat cut.'

'Is there a religious significance?'

'Not that we know, and besides, although the Altar Stone is the name given to it, there's no history that it was ever used for any religious purpose, pagan or Christian.'

Tremayne could see the superintendent was lingering, waiting for an opportunity to offer a comment. He did not intend to give him a chance. 'If you've got no more questions, Yarwood and myself have got a busy day ahead.'

'Are you sure you're up to it?' Moulton asked.

'I've still a few more years in me if that's what you mean,' Tremayne said with a brusqueness verging on insubordination. He'd already received a rap over the knuckles for talking disrespectfully to his senior. 'Apologies, sir, but this case has legs, and plenty wanted the man alive, not so many who would want him dead.' Tremayne hoped his last sentence had defused the tension that was building between the two men, and if it hadn't, then the man could go to hell. He had a murder to deal with, and even after so many years, so many deaths, the freshness of a new one always excited him.

'Don't be reluctant to take on help. You and Yarwood make a good team, but this man had a lot of acquaintances. It may take you some time to get around to them all.'

'I may be on this case until my retirement, is that it?'

'I hope not. Tremayne, you're a fine detective, but I've got a job to do, you know that.'

'So have I, sir.'

'You're a hard man, Tremayne, I'll grant you that.'

'You know what happens with one murder.'

'At least with yours.'

'The man died for a reason. He was likely to kill himself within the next year with his drunken driving, not to mention his alcoholism, the greasy food that he consumed, and the women he went around with.'

'Okay, I relent. I'm off, but don't take too long with this case. A prompt conviction always looks good.'

'The man never gives up,' Tremayne said to Clare after Moulton had left.

'You two were almost friendly there.'

'Never,' Tremayne said, not wanting to be seen as anything other than difficult to deal with.

'Regardless of your new-found friend,' Clare said, aiming to rustle Tremayne's feathers, 'Alan Winters must have a lot of relatives. Where do we start on this?'

'His wife, has she been notified?'

'Probably, but we should go there first. I didn't know he had a wife, or one that was still with him.'

'She's the first person we'll talk to. When we get back, start compiling a dossier of all his relatives, all of his friends, where he drank and ate, who he gave money to.'

'We've got a department of people who can do that.'

'Then delegate. Regardless, before anyone goes home tonight, we need a board up on the wall with a list of all the salient facts.'

'It'll be there. Let's go and see the grieving widow,' Clare said.

'Grieving? The Winters? I doubt it.'

Chapter 2

Alan Winters, it was known, had, before his big win, lived with his wife in an area to the west of the city, in an enclave populated by the least motivated, the least educated, the most likely to be in trouble with the forces of law and order.

'I've spent too much time up there,' Tremayne said.

Clare, who had only driven through the area on the occasional basis, could not see what he was referring to. Sure, the old cars jacked up on wooden blocks in some of the driveways, the abundance of graffiti, the children aimlessly wandering around the streets were all a little disconcerting, but at least the weather was pleasant, and even the worst day always looked the better for the sun's rays. 'Have there been many murders up here?' she said.

'It's normally wanton violence, the husband beating the wife, that sort of thing, or the local hooligans vandalising the toilet block in the park.'

'So why were you up here?'

'It's where I first lived when I came to Salisbury. A group of us from the police station clubbed together to pay the rent. Back then vacant accommodation was hard to come by. Alan Winters was in his teens then, but he was starting to become a nuisance.'

'Did he cause you any trouble?'

'A houseful of four junior police officers? I don't think so. Everyone gave us a wide berth, and we were all fit back then, not averse to giving anyone a smack if they played up.'

The Winters had moved on from the small terraced house that Tremayne had shown Clare, and after his win, Alan Winters had purchased a substantial six-bedroom home in Quidhampton, a small village between Salisbury and Wilton.

Tremayne and Clare drew up at the entrance to the house. Two men were standing in front of the secured gate. 'Who are you?' Tremayne asked as he flashed his ID.

'Security.'

'Is that necessary?'

'With the money here, what do you think?' the tougher-looking of the two said.

'We've come to see Mavis Winters,' Tremayne said.

'She's already been told. You're not welcome here.'

'Don't give me any of your nonsense. I know you well enough.'

'And we know you, Tremayne. Unless you've got a warrant, you're not going in.'

'Now look here, Gerry, your brother's been murdered, and I'm in charge of the case. Unless you want to put yourself down as a suspect, or I haul your sorry arse into the police station, in handcuffs if you resist, you'll open that gate and let us through.'

Gerry Winters moved away and made a phone call.

'You know this man?' Clare asked.

'The man's vermin, but don't let Superintendent Moulton know that was how I referred to his villains.'

'Okay, you're free to progress,' Gerry Winters said. 'And don't go upsetting Mavis. Her husband has just died. You know what will happen if she's upset?'

'And what's that? You'll be making a complaint down at Bemerton Road, is that it?'

'Not me, but I'll come into the house and deal with the situation.'

'Lay one hand on either my sergeant or me, and you'll be in the cells.'

'Don't threaten me, Tremayne. You've got nothing on me.'

'Petty crime verging on stupidity is not my area of responsibility.'

'I'm not involved in any crime.'

Clare could see the heavily-tattooed man getting agitated. She could also see that Tremayne was doing nothing to calm the situation. The gate swung open, and she drove in, parking behind a Bentley.

'Why did you bait the man?' Clare asked.

'Gerry Winters, the prime suspect.'

'Is he?'

'Alan Winters was a braggart, argumentative, drunk, worthless. So's his brother, except with Gerry, he can be violent,' Tremayne said.

'Mrs Winter's husband has just been murdered, she's hardly likely to be in a mood to talk to us.'

'She'll be interested in the money.'

'It would belong to the wife surely?'

'That's what we would assume, but they were independent most of the time; she'd go her way, he'd go his. The money has to be the motive, but who has first claim to it? It's important, you know that.'

'If he was killed for his money, then those who killed him must be certain of not being caught.'

'That's what doesn't make sense. Why kill the man at Stonehenge? Maybe it's nothing to do with his money? Maybe it's something to do with the belief that the man's luck is transferred by his death, not that I'd believe in such nonsense. Anyway, there's another problem up ahead,' Tremayne said.

Clare could see what Tremayne was on about. From out the front door of the house, a woman was approaching and fast. 'You bastard, Tremayne. In my hour of sorrow, and you're here raking over the coals. Can't a woman mourn in peace?'

'If I believed in your sadness for one minute, I'd leave you alone, but I don't, so don't try to get me on the sympathy vote. This is Sergeant Yarwood, by the way.'

'She's just a child. What are you doing? Training them young or is she there to look pretty, make you feel important?'

'You've got a foul mouth, Mavis, so let's just cut out this nonsense. Your husband's been murdered. I don't believe that you did it, but someone did, and if it was for his money, then you could be next on the list.'

'Okay, Tremayne, come on into the house and bring your sergeant. If you drink a beer with me, then we can talk. However, it doesn't stop you being a bastard.'

'Thanks, Mavis.'

Clare leant over to Tremayne. 'You were rough there, guv,' she said.

'If you want respect from these kind of people, you've got to talk in a language they understand. Your fancy educated Norfolk accent, your polite manners, are not going to cut much mustard with this these people. I've known them long enough, and I can tell you one thing about Mavis Winters, she isn't grieving.'

'Involved in the murder of her husband?'

'It's possible, but I'd discount it for now, and besides, we need her cooperation. She's the key to the motive for her husband's death, and remember, the woman can be coarse, so you'll need to be.'

***

To Clare, the house was staggering in its beauty, although the interior, no doubt initially resplendent when the current occupants had moved in, was showing the signs of wear and tear. In the first room to the left, apparently the main room of the house, a stereo blasted gangster rap and a couple of drunken men gyrated to the music, a female lying sprawled across the couch. 'That's Bertie and some of his friends,' Mavis Winters said.

'Aren't they upset that your husband is dead?' Clare said.

'Why should they be? With him gone, Bertie believes he's in for a share of his money.'

'Even so, it seems sad that your husband has died.'

'Why? The man was going to kill himself anyway, and he was burning through the money. Whoever killed him has saved us all a lot of aggravation.'

Tremayne looked over at Clare with an 'I told you' look.

At the rear of the house, the kitchen had marble-tiled work areas, an air of opulence. An older woman slaved over the hot stove. 'That's his mother,' Mavis Winters said.

Clare could see that the woman had been crying.

'How long before our lunch is ready?' Mavis shouted to the woman. Clare was upset by the scene; Tremayne remained impassive.

'Soon, very soon. I was just upset by Alan's death, that's all,' the older woman said.

'Why? You bred the mongrel. What did you expect to happen to him, that he'd live into his nineties? He was going to go soon anyway, and as far as I'm concerned, good riddance to bad rubbish.'

Clare found the situation intolerable. Tremayne glanced her way, nodded his head, a sign to keep calm; it was a murder investigation, not a social outing. Clare could only imagine the hell the neighbours were going through. She considered herself blessed that her neighbours in Stratford sub Castle were caring people, and if she were working late, one or the other of them would ensure that her cats were fed. And they were always quiet, not like the house she was in now. If this was what sixty-eight million pounds did to a family, then she was glad that she was struggling with a police sergeant's salary. Not that it had been enough to buy her cottage and furnish it entirely. The inevitable result of the five-thousand-pound temporary loan from her parents was a visit for four days by her mother, and the constant redecorating that she wanted to force on her daughter. Clare had put up with the negativity of the woman, and once she was gone, cancelled all of her ideas and bought what she wanted. One thing she knew, that five thousand had to be paid back as soon as possible.

'Mavis, what can you tell us about your husband's death?'

'Tremayne, I'll be honest with you,' the woman said. She was holding a can of beer, as was Tremayne. Clare, to be agreeable, had consented to a glass of wine, cheap and nasty though it turned out to be. 'Alan was a bastard, but somehow we'd stuck together through good and bad for over twenty years.'

'You don't seem upset,' Clare said.

'You look like a gentle soul, not like your boss,' Mavis said to Clare. 'Tremayne knows where I'm coming from. Alan, for once in his miserable life, struck it lucky. He'd go his way, I'd go mine. I didn't ask about what mischief he got up to.'

'Did you get up to mischief?'

'A lot less than Alan.'

'And your husband said nothing?'

'What could he say? And now that he's Lord of the Manor, he expects to bring them around here.'

'And you agreed?'

'He had made it clear that if I left the house, then I wouldn't receive any money, and I'd be out on the street.'

'Would he have done that?' Tremayne said.

'Alan was easy to handle when he had no money, and I'd be out cleaning houses to help out with the bills, but now, there he is, driving around in a fancy car, screwing fancy women, buying them expensive gifts. I could control him back then, but now he's receiving bedroom advice from these tarts. Of course he'd follow through and cut me off with nothing.'

'You would have been legally entitled,' Clare said.

'Legally, yes, but he could afford the best legal advice. I've checked, and he could tie up my money for years.'

'It's not much of a relationship if after twenty years he's willing to do that,' Clare said.

'Alan was a weak man. In some ways I loved him once, but since the lottery I've grown to loathe him. Maybe when it's quiet, and I reflect back to when we first married, then maybe I'll be sad, but for now, I'm not.'

'Do you know who killed him, Mavis?' Tremayne asked.

'Not me, but I've told you the truth from my side. No doubt we'll have a get-together after the funeral, say lovely words about what a good man he was and how he had looked after the relatives.'

'Had he?' Clare asked.

'If they came asking, he'd help.'

'Did they come?'

'How long have you been in Salisbury? Haven't you heard about the Winters?'

'Nearly two years, but apart from being aware that your husband had won a lot of money, I hadn't.'

'Tremayne has; he'll tell you how many have been around. You tell her,' Mavis said, looking over at Tremayne.

'Everyone of them, plus a few more.'

'Tremayne's right. There was a queue halfway around the block the day the news of his win became public. How we celebrated that night.'

'The queues?' Clare reminded the woman.

'Not only that. The bags of begging letters, the onslaught of Facebook messages once they knew our eldest's name. In the end, we moved here and made sure there was security. Not that it hasn't stopped people trying to get in, but Gerry, he deals with them.'

'How?'

'He scares them, and gives them a good belting.'

'He's got a bad reputation around Salisbury. Do you trust him?'

'I'm the next of kin, and I'm not stupid with money.'

'You've given us the motive for your husband's murder, Mrs Winters,' Clare said.

'I didn't kill him; I wished him dead. Why do you think I'm telling you all this?'

'To pre-empt our suspicions.'

'There are those who wanted him dead because he was a bastard; there are others, the women, the parasites, those where he frittered away our fortune, who wanted him very much alive.'

'And what about those who had benefited by his generosity?'

'The women, Gerry has already dealt with them, nothing violent.'

'What did he do?'

'Whatever Alan gave them, he's taken back.'

'Such as?'

'Cars, clothing, accommodation.'

'They've been thrown out on the street?'

'That's up to them. I'm not supporting them.'

'Your children, his relatives?'

'It depends, but I'll support those that deserve assistance; the others can go to hell.'

Tremayne took another beer from the woman who was now friendly after her earlier outburst. Clare was not sure who the real Mavis Winters was, although she was sure that she did not like either. The woman looked tired for someone in her late forties, the effects of a lifetime of smoking reflected in her voice, the sagginess in the body indicative of a fast food diet, the discarded KFC and Big Mac containers still visible in a rubbish bin in the kitchen. The old woman, the mother of the dead man, continued to slave away. Clare could tell that she had led a hard life.

In the other room, the stereo played loudly, the singing of the occupants all too clear. Clare did not like the house and its occupants; Tremayne took no notice and continued with his questioning.

'Now that your husband's dead, what are your plans for the future?'

'We'll bury him first, give him a good send-off, Winters' style.'

'A lot of drinking?' Tremayne said.

'Of course.'

'And then?' Clare said.

'I've already started. Those who deserve help will receive it, the others won't. It's as simple as that.'

'Then whoever killed your husband will target you,' Tremayne said.

'Alan was weak, I'm not.'

'Are you strong enough to have dragged him up to Stonehenge and killed him, Mavis?'

'Tremayne, don't try your tricks with me. I remember when you lived two doors down from us. You weren't so high and mighty then, always trying to look up my skirt, mentally undressing me.'

'A long time ago.'

'That didn't stop you grabbing me at that Christmas party and dragging me off into the other room, did it?'

'We were both over the age of consent.'

'Am I shocking your sergeant?'

'Nothing shocks me, Mrs Winters,' Clare said.

'You're prim and proper. I'm surprised you can put up with Tremayne.'

'He's a good man, but that doesn't alter the fact that your husband has been murdered, and you act as if it's not important.'

'Sergeant, Alan was going to kill himself anyway. The man continued to drive when he was drunk, even though he had no licence, the women he fooled around with would have given him a heart attack, and his friends, if you could call them friends, were determined to fleece him. He put two hundred thousand pounds into the lame-brained idea of a friend to open a used car dealership not far from your police station, and what did the man do?'

'It's your story, Mrs Winters.'

'I'll tell you what he did. The bastard took off to the South of France with the money. Gerry found him shacked up in a fancy hotel with a couple of tarts.'

'He took the money back?'

'What was left off it.'

'And the man who took the money?'

'He's not shown his face in Salisbury since.'

'Does he still have a face?'

'Gerry didn't kill him, if that's what you're asking. He just won't be so pretty now, that's all.'

'I'll need to conduct interviews with all those close to Alan,' Tremayne said.

'Start with my family first.'

'Are you confident that they're all innocent.'

'Of killing Alan? I'd say so. Some of them are villains, not averse to violence, but none are that stupid to kill the golden goose.'

'You're the golden goose now,' Clare said.

'Maybe I am, and if anyone thinks otherwise, they'll find my foot in their arse.'

'Who's living in this house?'

'I am, plus our two children – Rachel, she's the eldest at twenty-four, and then there's Bertie, he's twenty-two – and Alan's mother.'

'Good children?' Clare asked.

'Rachel's sensible, takes after me, although it didn't stop her getting pregnant at sixteen, and landing me with her son to look after.'

'And where is the child now?'

'He died. He was a nice boy, but that's how it is.'

'And your daughter, how did she take it?'

'She was upset for a while, but now she's fine. Even with all our money, she still goes to work every day. According to her, she likes her job, although I made sure that she had a decent car to drive.'

'Bertie?'

'That's him next door, celebrating. He's as useless as his father. He thinks I'm going to be a soft touch, the same as his father, although his father wouldn't let him have an expensive car, just gave him a Toyota to drive.'

'Could he handle an expensive, no doubt powerful, car?' Tremayne asked.

'He's the same as his father. He'll be dead in a week.'

'And you intend to indulge him?' Clare said, appalled by the wife's callousness towards her dead husband, uncaring that her son was likely to commit involuntary suicide due to her generosity.

'Not a chance, Sergeant. He's still my son. He'll be lucky to keep the Toyota, and as for lying around the house snorting cocaine with his so-called friends, that'll stop once I've secured legal control of all of the money.'

'Any dispute over that?'

'None that I can see. It was Alan who bought the ticket in the first place, and he only spent two pounds. Not a bad return on his investment, don't you think? Although he must have spent plenty over the years on lottery tickets. It was about time for our luck to change.'

'Any idea how much money is left?' Tremayne asked.

'Of the sixty-eight million. I reckon there's still thirty, maybe thirty-two. Not bad for two years, is it? Between us, we've spent over thirty million pounds, or mainly squandered it.'

'Have you, Mavis?'

'Not me. I have always worked. I know the value of money. This house is in my name, for one thing, and there are a few other properties that I've bought. Regardless of how much is left, there's still money. Alan never had a clue with money. What he brought home from his council job, half was gone at the end of payday on alcohol and gambling. Financially, we're sound.'

'Who would want him dead?'

'I would, but then you know that. As for others, I've no idea. There were some he refused to help: relatives, friends. They won't be sad that he has died.'

'Will they receive any assistance from you now?'

'Some will, but I'll want security. I've no intention of handing out vast sums of money with no surety, that's for sure.'

'Would they know that?'

'Probably not.'

'We'll need their names.'

'I'll help you,' Mavis Winters said.

'Why?' Clare asked.

'I want you to find his murderer as soon as possible. No doubt the transfer of full financial control will be delayed until the murder investigation is concluded, and I don't want any doubts over my involvement remaining.'

'And Alan's mother?'

'She'll be looked after. I can't say I like her, but she'll have a place to stay.'

'She works hard.'

'She can go and sit in her room for all I care, but if she wants to look after the place, I'll not stop her.'

'And your son?'

'His day of reckoning is coming.'

'He has a motive,' Tremayne said.

'Bertie? Too bone idle to commit murder. He can find his way to the fridge for a beer, but Stonehenge, I don't think so.'

'Why the change of attitude? You were belligerent when we arrived.'

'Tremayne, we go back a long way. I'm still angry with you from that party all those years ago.'

'Why?' Clare asked.

'A woman doesn't forget her first man, and there he is, the next day, pretending that nothing happened. Mind you, he'd have been in trouble. I'd only just turned sixteen, and he was a police officer. No doubt seducing the neighbour's daughter after she had drunk a few too many would not have looked good up at Bemerton Road. Sergeant Yarwood, your DI is not the saint he pretends to be.'

'Saint Tremayne, I don't think so,' Clare said. The two women looked over at Tremayne. He shrugged his shoulders and turned away. 'Come on, Yarwood, we've got work to do,' he said.

Chapter 3

Back at the station, Tremayne focussed on the board set up in the Homicide department. He had purposely avoided talking to Clare on the drive back from Mavis Winters' house, knowing full well that she'd attempt to wind him up. Not that he had anything to regret, he knew that, and back then Mavis has been a pretty young thing, mature for her age, and he'd been in his twenties, starting to make his mark at Bemerton Road. The most that he would have received, if it had become known, would have been a rap on the knuckles from his senior and a pat on the back with a 'we're only young once' comment.

And now Yarwood wanting to make a sarcastic comment was not what he needed. It also brought in another complication, Tremayne knew, that he had some involvement with one of the suspects, even though it was almost thirty years ago. Superintendent Moulton may have some issues with it, but Tremayne didn't.

'Yarwood.' Tremayne decided to speak to her in the office. 'Mavis and me, it was a long time ago. Do you have any issue with it?'

'Not me, guv.'

'But it amuses you.'

'I might remind you occasionally.'

'A joke at my expense, is that it?'

'You've got to admit it's not what an innocent young sergeant expects to hear.'

'What? That her senior was young and foolish once.'

'It must have been a hell of a party.'

'It was. Now drop the subject. Where do we go from here?' Tremayne said, noticing the smile on Yarwood's face.

'We need Jim Hughes's report, see if he can give us the number of persons up at Stonehenge.'

'And why Stonehenge? That just doesn't tie in. If we accept that he was murdered for his money, then why up there, and why was his throat cut?'

'Mavis Winters, could she be involved?'

'She has the strongest motive, but it's unlikely that she murdered him.'

'Why? She's the one who'd gain most from it.'

'We'll check of course, but you've met the woman. What do you think of her?'

'She's not stupid.'

'Exactly, and she knows that we'll find the murderer eventually.'

'Involved?'

'If she is, she'll have covered her tracks well. We'll not find a link back to her, or, at least, not easily. For now, she's our best means of uncovering the truth. You'll need to go back to the house and interview her again, get a list of all known relatives, all friends, all the women that Alan Winters was messing around with.'

'And Mavis?'

'Check on who she was involved with. She seems to place a lot of reliance on her brother-in-law, Gerry. Check him out and see if they were up to something.'

'A bit close to home,' Clare said.

'It's a big home, and if Alan was bringing his women there, then Mavis could have been fooling around with Gerry.'

'Does she have a history of other men?'

'Not that I know of. Apart from running into Alan and Mavis on an occasional basis, I've not seen much of them for more than twenty years. I know that she latched on to Alan when she was eighteen, going on nineteen, but apart from that, I can't help much.'

'Was she attractive?' Clare asked.

'As a teenager.'

'What do you know about Alan Winters?'

'I never really knew him. I remember him as a skinny kid, always getting into trouble, but I'm not sure if I spoke to him more than once or twice as a youth. I arrested him a few times when he became older, but we didn't dwell on his childhood, and Mavis was never mentioned.'

'Did he know about you and Mavis?'

'It's unlikely, and besides, it was just the one time at a party. After that, I'd see her on the street with her friends, but we never went out together. It was our secret, that's all. And even if he knew, what did it matter? It was the start of the age of sexual freedom; nobody, not even Alan, would have been concerned. And besides, my private life is past history.'

'It's a murder investigation, and you know two of the main players. I don't think it is. What about Gerry, Alan Winter's brother?'

'He was a few years younger. I knew him vaguely.'

'Capable of murder?'

'It's possible.'

'Any other brothers?'

'Alan Winters was one of seven; I knew Stan and Fred, the older brothers.'

'What about them?'

'They were closer to my age. Back then they were starting down the slippery slope. They're both in jail now: one for extortion, the other for attempting to pull out an ATM from a bank building with a truck and chain.'

'What happened to the ATM?'

'It didn't budge, ripped off the back of the truck. Fred Winters is serving time courtesy of Her Majesty. The other brother, Stan, attempted to heavy the boss of a construction company in Salisbury.'

'What happened?'

'He offered to protect the man's equipment on site, to ensure that no damage occurred to any of his construction projects. The only problem was that Stan had failed to do his homework.'

'What do you mean?'

'The boss of the construction company had wrestled professionally a few years earlier. One night, after the man had refused Stan's generous offer, Stan and some of his colleagues decided to visit one of the construction sites.'

'And?'

'They found the boss there with three of his former wrestling friends. They beat the hell out of Stan and his people, put one in hospital.'

'Did anything happen after that?'

'Stan and his friends were arrested; there was verifiable proof.'

'The other siblings?'

'Cyril, waste of space, Dean made good and left the area, no idea what he's doing now, and then there's Margie.'

'What about her?'

'She's the worst of the lot: heroin addiction, pretty as a child, but now she's in her early forties. I see her occasionally late at night as I leave the pub. She's attempting to feed an addiction, and there's only one way to get sufficient money.'

'What about Alan? He had money.'

'You'll need to ask Mavis, but Margie's still out there selling herself.'

'And the children?'

'Not much I can tell you there. Neither has been in trouble with the law, although the son looks as though he's heading that way. That's about it for now. It's up to you, Yarwood, to find out more.'

'The women who he wanted to move into the house?'

'Mavis may not know who they are, not totally, and if they're not there now, we need to find them. I'll make some enquiries. I know where Alan Winters liked to drink. As for you, there's the less immediate family, and what about Mavis's siblings? I can't say I knew if there were any, although I think she was an only child. It's worth checking, anyway.'

Tremayne picked up his phone and called Jim Hughes. 'Any updates?'

'We've moved the body to Pathology. What I can tell you is the following: one, the man was unconscious when he was laid out on the Altar Stone.'

'Drugged, drunk, bashed?'

'Bashed. There's a clear sign that he had been hit on the back of the head with a blunt instrument.'

'Any idea what type.'

'Not at the present moment. Pathology may be able to help.'

'What else?'

'Two sets of footprints, slightly off-centre to the direction they were walking.'

'What does that mean?'

'They were carrying something between them.'

'Alan Winters?'

'Almost certainly. It would have required two men of sufficient strength.'

'What else?'

'Apart from his throat being cut, there's not much more I can tell you.'

'How would they have got the body to the site unseen?'

'You're the detective. I would have thought it would have been difficult. Even at night, there's always cars driving by, and no doubt everyone takes a look. It's hard to ignore. The death seems symbolic, although there were no signs of a ceremony, just the man's body and a slit throat.'

'Weapon?'

'We never found one. It's probably just a sharp knife, but we can't be sure.'

'Okay, thanks. Send me the full report when it's ready. In the meantime, we'll continue our investigation.'

'Tremayne, how do you do it? Every time you become involved, the deaths multiply.'

'Just lucky, I suppose,' Tremayne said, which to him seemed a flippant comment, seeing that the luckiest man in England at the time of his win was dead and about to be carved up by the pathologist.

***

Tremayne left the office soon after. It was six in the evening, and whereas there was plenty to do, paperwork included, they still needed to find out about any friends, as well as the women that Winters had wasted his money on. Clare had an appointment to meet up with Winters' widow again.

The Old Mill Hotel in Harnham, twelfth century originally, although modernised since then, had been one of Winters' favourites. The publican knew Tremayne on sight, pulled a pint of beer for him as he entered the pub. 'What'll it be, Tremayne? We've salad or sirloin steak.'

'Are you joking?'

'The steak then.'

'Correct, well done, not half cooked as you normally serve it up to the trendies.'

'The trendies are into the salads. What is the reason for you gracing our premises so early?'

'Alan Winters.'

'Salisbury's richest inhabitant.'

'I never thought about that,' Tremayne said, 'although he must have been.'

'Couldn't have happened to a more deserving person.'

'Mike, you may serve the best beer in Salisbury, but you're full of hot air. What's your genuine opinion on Alan Winters?'

The publican drew a pint for himself and sat on his side of the bar, Tremayne on the other. An open fire burnt in one corner. It was still early, and apart from Tremayne, there was only a couple in one corner snuggled up close to each other, which caused the detective inspector to reflect back to his recent trip to Spain with Jean, his former wife.

He had to admit the trip had been a success, in that they had both enjoyed it, but both were set in their ways, although they were meeting up again next month, which seemed an ideal relationship to both of them. The occasional getting together, the romantic weekends, and then back to their regular lives.

'Winters, quite frankly, was a pain in the rear end. All that money and he's still an ignoramus,' the publican, a red-faced man, said. He downed his pint, drew another for himself and Tremayne. 'On the house,' he said.

'We need to know who he was friendly with, the people bleeding him for money, the ones who didn't get close, the women.'

'The who's who of the city's ratbags, is that it?'

'Are they?'

'I'd say so. He used to bring me plenty of business, but I've tried to go upmarket here. Anyone not into drunkenness and whores wouldn't stay in the bar for very long when Winters was here.'

'Were the women whores?'

'They weren't here for Winters' charm, were they?'

'I suppose not. What else can you tell me about his friends?'

Another pint appeared in front of Tremayne, along with his steak. As he commenced to eat his meal, the publican continued to talk. The Old Mill had not been his favourite pub, Tremayne knew that, but since the Deer's Head had lost his patronage, he'd been looking for somewhere to visit on a regular basis, although he assumed the pints on the house would not occur every time he visited.

'Three to four nights a week, Winters would breeze into here, his retinue in hot pursuit.'

'Describe them,' Tremayne said between mouthfuls of food.

'His brother, Gerry, as well as Cyril.'

'Any sign of the sister?'

'Margie?'

'The only one that I know of.'

'No. I've never seen her in here.'

'You know her?'

'Professionally, yes.'

'Is she still heavily into heroin?'

'She's still injecting herself. I hope I haven't shocked you.'

'You'd be surprised what people will tell a police officer. If I were charging for confessions, I'd be a rich man by now. And besides, I'm interested in solving a murder before there's another.'

'Will there be?'

'More often than not, although this case is unique.'

'The Altar Stone?'

'That's it. Does it mean anything to you?'

'Not really. It's odd though. People always want to attach significance to Stonehenge that's not there.'

'Tell me about the men who came in with Winters?'

'Apart from the brothers, there were a few others from where he lived before he won the money. I don't know their names, although they looked as though they were bad news, and then there's a loose group of drunks looking to con Winters out of a drink.'

'Did they?'

'Not always. He could be a moody bugger. Some days he'd only buy for his inner group, other days he'd buy for everyone. He splashed the money around like there was no tomorrow, which in the case of last night, there wasn't.'

'What does that mean?'

'He was in here. In a good mood as well. He must have spent a thousand pounds in here, fed everyone as well. I had to call in extra staff at short notice, cost me plenty due to penalty rates. Not that I'm complaining as it was profitable.'

'Any reason for the good mood?'

'Not that I could see. I know he was shouting off at one stage that he had dealt with a major problem.'

'Any idea what he was talking about?'

'With the workload behind the bar? You've got to be joking. I was exhausted, glad when he left.'

'What time did he leave?'

'About ten in the evening. The man had had a few drinks by then, hardly seemed up to the task.'

'What do you mean?'

'He had a couple of women draped around him. They got into the back seat of the Bentley, the three of them. His brother Gerry was driving. I assumed his idea of a celebration was a threesome with the two women, not that I can blame him.'

'Why?'

'Both of them were very tasty.'

'Do you know who they are?'

'Neither of them is on the game, I know that.'

'How?'

'If they were, I would have found them and treated myself.'

'Who were they? They're important. We believe that Winters died between the hours of three and four this morning. It may be that they were the last two people to see him alive.'

'Or passed out on a bed.'

'As you say, but I need to find these women.'

'They're not the only women I've seen him with. Bees round a honeypot, they were. Mind you, he looked after them well.'

'Let's focus on these two women. Who were they?'

'The blonde, she goes by the name of Polly Bennett. You'll find her working during the day at a furniture store out on Devizes Road.'

'I know it. If they're not on the game, then what were they doing cheapening themselves with Winters?' Tremayne asked, realising that he was on his fifth pint.

'As I said, bees round a honeypot, hoping he'd spend it on them.'

'Would he?'

'The man had won sixty-eight million pounds. There were plenty more women ready and willing after he had tired of Polly and her friend.'

'The friend's name?'

'Liz worked at the same place, a double act.'

'What do you mean?'

'Both of them were attractive. One was blonde, the other brunette. Winters wouldn't know what had hit him.'

'And you never will.'

'Not unless I win the lottery,' the publican said. 'Mind you, I'm not complaining, but it's always good to dream.'

'Winters had the dream, and now he's dead and on a slab.'

Tremayne phoned Clare on leaving the pub, the fresh air making him realise that he had drunk more than he should: six pints eventually, a good steak, and it was nine thirty in the evening. It was a murder investigation, and he should have continued, but he knew it would have to wait for tomorrow, early. 'Where are you, Yarwood?'

'I'm just wrapping up in the office. I've been to see Mavis Winters again. She was friendly, tried to set me up with her brother.'

'Gerry?'

'Not a chance.'

'You can do better, Yarwood.'

'Another compliment. You'll have to watch yourself, guv.'

'None of your lip. I've just had to spend a tough three hours in the pub at Harnham interviewing the publican.'

'What did he have to say?'

'We've got to meet a couple of Winters' women in the morning. Meet me in the office at six, and we'll go over what we've got.'

'At 6 a.m. I'll be there bright and breezy. And you, guv?'

'I'll be neither. How I suffer for the police force,' Tremayne said.

Clare knew his kind of suffering.

Chapter 4

Polly Bennett was not pleased to see two police officers at the door of the furniture store.

'Detective Inspector Tremayne and this is Sergeant Yarwood,' Tremayne said to her, the first of the women to arrive. Clare couldn't see what Winters would have found attractive in her, as the woman was showing dark roots in her hair and her fashion sense was woeful in that her skirt rode too high, her blouse was too tight.

'What can I do for you?' Polly said as she grabbed herself a cup of coffee. 'Do you want one?' she said.

'White, two sugars,' Tremayne said.

'I'll pass,' Clare said, noticing the dirty cups in the sink.

'Alan Winters,' Clare said after the other two were settled. Tremayne, she could see, liked the look of the woman. A man thing, Clare thought.

'When was the last time you saw him?'

'Yesterday morning, early.'

'What time?'

'He gave us a lift home. Just after midnight.'

'Us?'

'Liz and I.'

'Did he often do that?'

'Sometimes. It's nice to be driven home in a Bentley.'

'And after he dropped you home?'

'I went to bed.'

'Where is Liz Maybury?'

'She'll be here soon. She's not an early morning person.'

'Alan Winters was found dead. Are you aware of this?'

'He was alright when I last saw him.'

'You don't seem concerned,' Clare said.

'He was a generous man, plenty of money.'

'You and Liz Maybury spent a lot of time with the man. If he was so generous, why are you working here? And what time did you last see him? The truth this time. We are well aware that you and Liz were involved with Winters.'

'Okay, what if we were? He had plenty of money; we had what he wanted. There's nothing wrong with what we were doing.'

'We're not your mother. We're police officers, we only want the truth,' Clare said. Tremayne could tell that she did not like the woman, did not approve of her behaviour.

Polly Bennett shifted in her seat and went and made herself another cup of coffee. She returned and sat facing Clare, giving a sideways smile to Tremayne. 'Sometimes Alan likes to come in.'

'And?'

'You know.'

'No, I don't,' Clare said. 'He comes in for what? To play games, watch the television?'

'Games – I suppose you could call it that. Liz and I, we've got an agreement with him. He pays for our accommodation, and we look after him.'

'Sex, is that it?'

'We're not prostitutes. It's just an agreement we have with him.'

'This place?' Tremayne asked.

'Alan owns the business. He promised to put it in our names.'

'We were not aware that the man had any business sense.'

'Alan, not a clue, but Liz and I have. We dealt with the purchase; he supplied the money.'

'But not as a gift to you?'

'If he's dead, I suppose it won't happen. That cow will see us out on the street soon enough.'

Clare thought that was where Polly Bennett belonged anyway but said nothing.

The door to the store's kitchen burst open. 'I slept in again,' a woman said. The two police officers had just had an abrupt introduction to Liz Maybury. 'Oh, sorry. I thought Polly was here on her own.'

'I'm DI Tremayne, this is Sergeant Yarwood,' Tremayne said, eying the woman who had barged in.

'Oh, okay.'

'Alan's died,' Polly said to her friend.

'Not Alan. I don't believe it,' Liz said. Clare took stock of the woman: early thirties, shoulder length hair, brunette, seemed natural, firm figure, medium height, attractive even if the makeup was laid on too thick. She judged the woman to be the more attractive of the two.

'Why don't you believe it?' Clare asked.

'He was very much alive the last time we saw him.'

'When you two had a threesome with him, is that it?'

'What's with you two? Are you here to judge us? The man looked after us; we looked after him,' Polly Bennett said.

'What you ladies did with Alan Winters does not concern us. What we are interested in is when you last saw him.'

'He left at one o'clock in the morning.'

'Was there anyone waiting for him outside?'

'Only Gerry.'

'He doesn't come in.'

'Alan's the one with the money. And besides, Gerry's rough with his women,' Liz said.

'How would you know?'

'Before Alan struck it rich, when we were younger, we'd sometimes mess around with him.'

'Are you upset that Alan Winters is dead?'

'Should I be?'

'We're asking the questions. Are you sad that Alan is dead?'

'His bitch wife will want everything back.'

'Alan's wife has instructed Gerry to deal with it.'

'We've not seen him.'

Tremayne took note. According to Mavis Winters, Gerry Winters, her brother-in-law, was dealing with the reclaiming of all assets from Alan Winters' mistresses, yet he had not got around to Polly Bennett and Liz Maybury. If that was the case, then there were other women, or he was intending to maintain the relationship with the two women, substituting himself in their affections.

'When did Alan die?' Polly asked.

'You've taken a long time getting around to asking,' Clare said.

'We believe that Alan Winters died between the hours of two and four on the morning that you last saw him. Are you certain of the time he left you?'

'One o'clock. Gerry was waiting for him.'

'Can you confirm it was Gerry?'

'It was the Bentley. I assume it was.'

'And you've not heard about the death at Stonehenge?'

'Why? Did he die there?'

'Are you telling us that since the news of the death at Stonehenge, you've heard nothing?'

'We don't listen to the news,' Liz said. 'And we were at home last night, drank a few too many bottles of wine.'

'Yet you are smart enough to run this place?'

'That's as maybe, but we don't concern ourselves with local gossip.'

'The murder of a man is hardly gossip.'

'Alan was murdered?'

'His throat was cut. It took two people to carry him up to the site, two people with a reason to want him dead. Had he told you that he was not going to sign over the deeds to this business? Is his wife taking control? Did Gerry pick him up, or have you hatched a deal with him once he transfers Alan's wife's affections to him? It seems that you women had a strong motive for his death, and this nonsense about not knowing he was dead, I can't believe you,' Clare said.

Tremayne sat back, taking in how his sergeant was dealing with the women. He had to admit that his mentoring was paying off.

The two women sat still, not sure what to say. Polly was the first to speak. 'We did not kill him. A person has got to use whatever to get ahead. Alan, maybe we're sad to some extent, but our arrangement with him was business, not emotional. The thought of someone slitting his throat sounds gruesome, but it wasn't us.'

'Mavis Winters?' Tremayne asked.

'The woman hated us.'

'Have you been to the Winters' house?'

'Sometimes.'

'When Mavis was there?'

'Yes.'

'And what did she say?'

'Not a lot. She called us tarts, hit Alan once, but we took no notice, and besides, she had someone there.'

'Who?'

'No idea, but Alan said she had another man.'

'And you believed him?'

'Believe, not believe, what did it matter?'

'As long as you two were fine, is that it? What about the children, Rachel and Bertie? Were they there?'

'Bertie's a space cadet, and Rachel, we never saw her.'

***

Tremayne was a man who did not judge people, not even Polly Bennett and Liz Maybury, and if the two women wanted to screw Alan Winters, he had no issues either way.

Yarwood, Tremayne knew, was more uptight, a believer in common decency, the distinction between right and wrong, and she had not approved of the two women. Tremayne thought it was her upbringing, her parents, especially her mother, whom he had met when she was fussing over Yarwood's cottage. He had to admit he had not warmed to the woman, even if she was ingratiatingly pleasant. He understood why Yarwood preferred to be in Salisbury with him. Even so, the mother had subjected him to the third degree: how is Clare coming along? What are her promotion prospects? Is she cut out to be a police officer, so much unpleasantness, so much crime?

He had left the woman feeling as though he was Yarwood's school teacher giving an end of year evaluation at a parent's evening instead of a work colleague. Clare had apologised for her mother afterwards, although it wasn't important.

'What do you reckon? Tremayne said as the two officers drove to Pathology.

'They'd do anything if it was to their advantage.'

'Most people will, but we're looking for two people who committed a murder. Would they have been capable?'

'Liz Maybury, maybe,' Clare said.

'Polly Bennett?'

'I'm not so sure about her. She seems more responsible, although she didn't care that the man was dead.'

'As if they already knew. But why pretend to us? It can't be a great secret in Salisbury. Even customers in their business must have been talking about it. It's been on the television, another case of the downfall of an average man who strikes it lucky.'

'They knew,' Clare said. 'As to why they said they didn't needs to be added to the board in the office, and why's Gerry sitting in the car while Alan's with the women?'

'The man must not have liked that, and Gerry Winters would be capable of murder.'

The two officers arrived at Pathology and entered the depressingly cold and austere premises. They found Stuart Collins, the pathologist, washing up after completing his investigation. He was pleased to see Clare, not as much to see Tremayne standing next to her.

'Alan Winters, I assume?' Collins said.

'What can you tell us?' Tremayne asked.

'Considering that I've just concluded my examination, you're a little premature.'

'You've had the body for a day.'

'We're not here for you. We have other responsibilities. And besides, I needed to send some samples away for analysis.'

Clare, sensing the tension, entered the conversation. 'What can you tell us before you file your report?' she said.

Collins mellowed. 'As you know, a male aged forty-eight, in reasonable health considering.'

'Considering what?' Tremayne said.

'Tremayne, just hang on and let me speak. Winters was carrying about twenty pounds too much weight, his liver was showing the early signs of cirrhosis.'

'The heavy drinking?' Clare said.

'As you say, but it wasn't advanced; he probably hadn't noticed any of the signs such as fatigue, fluid build-up in the legs, yellowing of the skin, itching. There are other symptoms; I'll not go into them now.'

'You'd sent off some samples?'

'The man was taking high dosages of Viagra.'

'He needed it,' Tremayne said.

'He also had pancreatic cancer, although it was in the early stages. Yet again, he would not have known about it until it was too late. The man was a smoker, tending to obesity. Over time, it would have claimed his life.'

'If he had known?' Clare asked.

'Assuming he did, then moderating his lifestyle: no smoking, healthy weight, salads, low red meat diet.'

'That would have been anathema to Alan Winters,' Tremayne said.

'Then the man would not have made fifty-five years of age.'

'What can you tell us about the wound to the back of the head?'

'It was probably inflicted with a metal object, flat, and used with a degree of force.'

'Could a woman have inflicted the wound?'

'I don't see why not,' Collins said. 'Also, his throat had been cut with a sharp knife. A kitchen knife would have sufficed.'

'Type, brand?'

'I'm a pathologist, not a clairvoyant. It's a kitchen knife, approximately six inches long, small serrations, and very sharp.'

***

Clare left Tremayne at Bemerton Road; he had some paperwork to deal with, a few phone calls to make.

Mavis Winters was welcoming on Clare's arrival, a pre-arranged meeting. The front room where the son had wasted his time on the previous visit was empty. 'Bertie?' Clare asked.

'He's in a clinic. He's not coming back until they've sorted him out.'

Outside in the driveway were two vans belonging to a professional cleaning company. Inside, a team of workers in overalls, the sound of vacuum cleaners pervading the house. 'I couldn't stand the mess anymore,' Mavis said.

'You could have done it when your husband was alive.'

'Maybe I could, but it wasn't my house then, not with him and his women, and then Bertie making a nuisance of himself.'

'We've interviewed the women.'

'Which ones?'

Clare did not feel it was wise to mention their names. 'Are there many?'

'Two that I've seen here. He set them up in a furniture store.'

'That's who were interviewed.'

'That Polly's sharp. The other one, Liz, she's not so much.'

'You knew them from before?'

'Polly, she's the youngest daughter of one of my mother's friends. Liz, she's the extra. That Polly would have had me out of here in an instant if she could.'

'She'll not be able to do it now.'

'Not a chance, and I've sent Gerry up there to deal with them.'

'When?'

'Today. He was taking his time, probably anxious to grab them for himself, or maybe they laid on the charm, bedded the man.'

'He'd disobey you?'

'For a chance to get his leg over? What man wouldn't? They're all the same, you must know that.'

'I suppose I do,' Clare said, although she was sure that was not a suitable analogy to apply to all men.

Once the cleaner had moved out of the room, the two women sat down. Clare looked around her. 'We paid for an interior decorator to furnish the house. I couldn't have done it, nor could Alan, although as soon as it was finished he was spoiling it,' Mavis said.

'Was he?'

'It's his mother. She never brought him up correctly, neglected him. Out every night on the town, bringing home stray men, even when he was a child. You can't blame Alan for turning out the way he did.'

'And you?'

'My father was strong on discipline, and my mother was always at home. I had a good childhood, Alan didn't.'

'You still don't seem upset that he's dead.'

'Stoic, a family tradition. I'm sorry that he's dead, although I don't miss him, never will. I had tried to make something of him, but he wouldn't bend, and besides, I wasn't much of a role model.'

'What do you mean?'

'You saw how I treated Tremayne, what I said about him and me.'

'It came as a bit of a surprise.'

'Why? He was a good-looking man back then, fit and strong. It was me who grabbed him, and he'd had a few beers by then. After that, he didn't come back for seconds. He's a decent man, better than Alan was. I should have taken your detective inspector instead, but then he went and met someone else.'

'Jean.'

'That's her. I used to see her sometimes, occasionally have a chat.'

'Did she know about you and Tremayne?'

'Not from me.'

'You said that you weren't much of a role model before.'

'I'm common. Don't say anything or try to deny it. You went to the best schools, elocution lessons probably. Me, I had the local secondary school, always in trouble. Not boy trouble, just a general disinterest in school really. I regret it now, but it's too late.'

'It's never too late.'

'I suppose you're right, but my father was a strict disciplinarian, easy to anger. School and outside of the house was my chance to rebel. It's a wonder I stayed a virgin until Tremayne.'

'Why did you?'

'I don't know. I always think that I wanted my own place, my own house, the loving husband, the ideal children.'

'And now?'

'Rachel's turned out fine. Bertie will once I've dealt with him. Alan was a major disappointment, and now I've got this house.'

'Another man?'

'In time, maybe. Who knows?'

'Your mother-in-law?'

'She took off upstairs to her room when the cleaners came in.'

'What will you do about her?'

'I'll do the right thing. I'll buy her a flat in town, make sure she's got money. Apart from that, I don't want to see her.'

'Do you have access to all the money now?' Clare asked.

'Sufficient. Until you solve Alan's death, the full amount will probably be held up.'

'But you know where it is?'

'I know exactly where it is and how much is remaining. I'll need a death certificate before I can access all of it.'

'There'll be no death certificate yet.'

'It doesn't matter. I still have access to a few million, and no one's going to get any of it unless I agree.'

'Gerry, Alan's brother?'

'He's an employee, would like to be more.'

'Is that possible?'

'After he took advantage of those two women, and them not kicking him out of their house? He's tarred with the same brush as Alan, and he's violent.'

'Your claim on the money, is it indisputable?'

'It should be. Apart from some money for Rachel and Bertie, then the rest is mine, and besides, I intend to contest Bertie's share. He'll only fall into bad company again.'

'Let us come back to who would have benefited from your husband's death?' Clare said, her initial negative impressions of Mavis Winters moderated.

A woman came in with tea and biscuits. Mavis said, 'I've hired some help for the house. I'm not much of a cook, chicken and rice is about my limit, and I eat too much fast food. I intend to get myself into shape now.'

'You look fine,' Clare said.

'Next to you with your perfect body? You're too kind. Anyway, who would benefit from his death? I'm the only one. No one else has a clear claim. I know a few have their noses out of joint because Alan wouldn't give them anything.'

'Names?'

'Cyril, his useless brother, but the man's too lazy to tie his own shoelaces. He'd not be capable. There's his brother, Dean. The only one of the brothers who's amounted to anything. I've seen him once since Alan bought that ticket, but he's never asked for a handout. There are the two brothers, Stan and Fred, but they're both in jail. No doubt they'd appreciate some money, no doubt they'll be a nuisance when they're released.'

'What will you do when that time comes?'

'I'll give them a cash settlement, legally tied up on the condition that they ask for no more.'

'Bad men?'

'Not really, just weak. Fred concerns me; Stan doesn't.'

'What about your side of the family?'

'I'm an only child. I've a few cousins, but I've not seen them in years. Nothing there.'

'You realise that if there are no more suspects, then the suspicion will fall on you and Gerry. There were two people at Stonehenge, and the link will be made.'

'But no proof.'

'No proof, but guilt by association will remain. It may delay your inheritance.'

'Where was he the night he died? After the pub, I mean,' Mavis asked.

'Is it important?'

'If he was with his two women, then I'd be looking to them. What does Gerry say? He's normally the driver.'

'We've not spoken to him about that night yet.'

'Why not? He's more integral to the investigation than I am. I'm just the wronged woman sitting at home waiting for her man to come back.'

'You don't qualify for that description.'

'You mean the bitch with the rolling pin, ready to bash him over the head for his misbehaving.'

'That's more like it,' Clare said.

'I've already told you that I'm useless in the kitchen. I wouldn't know one end of a rolling pin from the other.'

'They're the same,' Clare said.

'As you say, but I didn't kill Alan. Whoever it was did me a favour. I know that sounds callous, but that's how I feel.'

'Did you know that his health was suffering?'

'He was putting on weight, but apart from that, no.'

'There was Viagra in his system,' Clare said.

'Not because of me,' Mavis said. 'We were sleeping in separate beds, almost from the day we moved in here. No doubt Polly and her friend reaped the benefit, not that I envy them.'

'Why's that?'

'Alan was not one of the world's great romantics. I can't say I miss that side of our marriage.'

'With someone else?'

'Once I'm fit. Give me three months, and I'll be giving you a run for your money.'

'More of a saunter,' Clare said.

'A pretty woman like you? You must have plenty of men.'

Clare did not respond, only smiled.

Chapter 5

'The golden boy,' was Dean Winter's reply after Tremayne and Clare had introduced themselves at the man's house in Southampton.

Tremayne had noticed a late-model car in the driveway, the neat and tidy house, the same as all the others in the street. It was middle-class, middle management territory, mow the lawn on a Saturday, trip to the sea on a Sunday with their two or three children, and it did not excite him.

'We've a few questions about your brother.'

'What do you want me to tell you? That he had spent a lifetime on his backside, and the most he had ever done was to walk into the pub or the local newsagent to buy a lottery ticket.'

'You're bitter about his good fortune?' Clare asked. The two police officers and Dean Winters were sitting in the front room of the house.

'Bitter, not really, but it's ironic, isn't it? I get out of that awful area, educate myself, put myself through university, and put in the hours, and there he is or was, sitting on sixty-eight million pounds.'

'It was fairly won,' Tremayne said.

'I'm not saying it wasn't, but there wasn't a more undeserving person.'

'Have you been up to his house since he died?'

'I've phoned Mavis. That'll do.'

'Will it?' Clare said.

'It will for me. I'm not about to profess friendship and brotherly love now, not for you or anyone.'

A woman busied herself in the kitchen. 'Your wife?' Clare asked.

'Tell us about your childhood,' Tremayne said.

'Our father was a bastard, never there, and by the time I was seven, he'd disappeared.'

'Where to?'

'I've no idea, none of us does.'

'Your mother?'

'She didn't care. You've met her?'

'We have,' Clare said.

'What did you think?'

'She seemed sad that your brother had died.'

'She probably was, but it's too little, too late for her to care.'

'What do you mean?'

'She was always out and about. There was a succession of men pretending to be our father, some hitting us, one abusing Margie. That's why she's on drugs and prostituting herself. Did anyone tell you that?'

'No. What happened to him?'

'I've no idea. When Stan and Fred found out about it, they took him out of the house. He never came back.'

'How old was Margie?'

'Twelve, going on thirteen.'

'What did Margie say?'

'Nothing. She'd sit quietly after that, barely said a word to anyone. She could have done with some professional help, but we had no money, no idea where to go, and our mother just brushed it away as a foolish child's make-believe.'

'Was it?'

'Hell, no. I was two years older. I tried to pull him off of her, but he punched me in the face, broke two of my teeth. By the time I came around, the man was out of the house and down the pub. That's when I phoned Stan. When the man returned, Stan and Fred confronted him; Stan had an old car, and they bundled him into the back seat and took off.'

'You have your suspicions as to what happened to him?'

'I was fourteen at the time. I hoped that they had killed him.'

'But they never said.'

'I never asked, but to them, I was just a kid. And now, they're both in jail.'

'Do you go to see them?'

'Sometimes, more for Margie than for me. I like Stan, not so much Fred, but both of them were violent, and they'd been in trouble with the law in their youth. We're not a good family, mongrel DNA, probably some inbreeding in the past. I don't want to associate with any of them, only I feel guilt over Margie.'

'Do you ever see her?'

'Not for a long time. I know where she is, or which part of Salisbury she hangs out, but it's painful to see what has become of her. Pretty when she was young, but now? I suppose she's still pretty, but the years must have taken their toll on her, and there's our bitch mother living with Alan. Do you think they did anything to help her? Nothing, I'll tell you, nothing.'

'You're an angry man, Mr Winters,' Clare said.

'That's why I keep away. I'd prefer Alan to be alive and well, and then you wouldn't be here making me revisit the past.'

'Angry enough to wish your brother dead?'

'Angry, yes. But I didn't kill him. Stan and Fred are violent, I'm not. If they weren't in jail, I wouldn't put it past them.'

'After what they did to the man who'd raped your sister?'

'I don't know about him. And besides, it a long time ago. Don't go raking up the past. It's only Margie who will suffer.'

'Why did you tell us?' Clare asked.

'Outside of the family, no one knows. You're bound to want to question Margie at some time. I told you in the hope that you'll be sensitive to her past, not too judgemental.'

'We'll not mention it to her, but, yes, you're right. We will speak to her in the next day or so.'

Outside Dean Winter's house, Clare made a phone call. 'Mavis, what do you know about Margie?'

'We offered her help, even paid for a month in the same place that Bertie is.'

'What happened?'

'She walked out after two days. There's no hope for her. The offer of a place to live, treatment for her addiction, is always there. She's a strange one.'

Clare ended the phone call and turned to Tremayne who had lit a cigarette. 'Someone's not telling the truth. We'd better talk to Margie Winters as soon as possible,' she said.

***

Mavis Winters' description of her sister-in-law, Margie, that she was a strange one, was correct. Clare could see that on meeting the woman. This time she had left Tremayne back in the office, knowing full well he wouldn't be there long before he was out interviewing someone else. And in this case, there wasn't a shortage of people to interview. Apart from the immediate family, there was a group who attempted to stay close to the money, as well as those who had begged: former work colleagues of Alan's, childhood friends, the usual types that hang around money – the reason that Alan Winters, as well as Mavis, always had security.

As Clare sat in the small room at the top of a terraced house in Wyndham Road, she could see someone who definitely needed help. Surrounded by cats, a woman bizarrely dressed in leopard-patterned stretch pants and a white blouse sat leaning back, a cigarette in a holder hanging out of her mouth.

Clare knew her to be forty years of age, although she looked older.

'You're aware of what's happened?'

'Dead, up at Stonehenge, is that it?'

'You don't seem concerned,' Clare said. To her, the woman seemed out of it, and if she was on the game, then she was a poor representative of her profession. Apart from the cats which smelt, the room was in a general state of disarray. Over to one side of the room there was a double bed, its sheets pulled back and clearly unchanged for some time.

Clare prided herself that in the short time she had been in her new cottage, the restricted hours that she had to devote to such matters, it was always clean, and the bed was changed regularly, not that anyone else saw it apart from her two cats.

'Mavis tried to get me to leave here and go and live with them.'

'Why didn't you?'

'I've got my gentlemen friends, they'd not want to go there. And what about my cats? Mavis would only let me take one of them, and I can't part with any of them, not now, not after what we've been through.'

'And what have you been through?'

'You'd not understand,' Margie said. As she spoke, she drank from a small glass, constantly stopping to top it up from a bottle of gin. 'Do you want one?' she asked.

'Not for me,' Clare said.

'They wanted to put me in a home first to clean me up.'

'Mavis told me that. What happened?'

'They wouldn't let me take my cats.'

'So you left?'

'I'm comfortable the way I am. And they wanted me to wear their clothes. I've got plenty of my own.'

At least that was true, Clare realised, as she looked inside a wardrobe to one side of the bed. It was full of clothing equally odd to what the woman was wearing, some on hangers, some just stuffed in the bottom, a cat sleeping on the pile.

'Your brother has died. Were you close?'

'Alan, when we were younger, but not now, not since he left home and left me on my own.'

'He won a lot of money, you do know that?'

'I know it, but what's it to me? I've got all that I want.'

'Tell me about yourself,' Clare said. 'What do you do for a living.'

'A whore, is that what they tell you?'

'Yes.'

'They're right. I'm nothing but a dirty whore.'

'You don't seem concerned.'

'Why should I be? Men, they're all bastards, only after one thing. At least I make them pay these days.'

'You've had a lifetime of abuse?'

'Abuse? Men pawing me, sleeping with me, forcing their tongues down my throat.'

'According to Mavis, one of your mother's boyfriends raped you.'

'Him and others.'

Clare could tell that the woman was embittered, psychologically disturbed. She knew that may have been the alcohol and the drugs, although there was no sign of a syringe or the tell-tale signs of shooting up.

'Is there anyone who would want Alan dead?'

'Dead, Alan?'

'I thought you understood.'

'Maybe I did, maybe I didn't. Sometimes I'm not sure…'

'Of what?'

'Not sure of what's real or what's not. Mavis wanted to lock me up, did I tell you that?'

Clare realised that Margie Winters was not capable of murder, not even capable of looking after herself. The woman may not want to take advantage of her brother's good fortune, but she needed help, voluntary or otherwise.

'Alan, your brother? Anyone who'd want to kill him?' Clare repeated the question.

'Not him. He was everyone's friend.'

'And you?'

'He looked after me once, a long time ago, but now he doesn't care.'

Clare left the woman to her cats and her bottle of gin.

***

Tremayne, as Clare had suspected, had been unable to stay in his office for more than forty-five minutes. He knew where the Winters had grown up, a council house identical to the one he had shared all those years before. He drove past the old place, smiled as he remembered Mavis and that night.

Tremayne pulled up outside Cyril Winters' house. A car in the driveway, a late-model BMW, a clear sign that the man had gained something from his brother's wealth. Tremayne walked up the driveway, knocked on the door twice before there was any movement from inside. 'What do you want?' a voice shouted upstairs.

'Detective Inspector Tremayne. I've got a few questions.'

'Okay, hang on while I put on my trousers.'

Five minutes later the door opened. In front of Tremayne stood a slovenly man dressed in a pair of navy tracksuit bottoms and a string vest. 'I was having a nap,' he said.

'Cyril Winters?'

'That's me. You're here about Alan?'

'If you've got thirty minutes.'

'Me? I've got all the time in the world.'

'Why's that?'

'I've retired.'

'At forty-nine?'

'Why not? No law that says a man has got to work until he keels over.'

'I suppose not. Alan's money?'

'He gave me some, enough to live on.'

'Enough to live here?'

'Tremayne, I remember you from when you lived here. I was only young, but you were a snob then, thought you were better than us, and there's your sucking up to Mavis.'

'Mavis?'

'She fancied you. You could have had her, and then she'd have not married Alan.'

'Are you saying she's not been a good wife to him?'

'Alan was tired of her. He wanted fresh meat.'

'Polly Bennett and Liz Maybury?'

'Them and others.'

'Who were the others?'

'Whoever he wanted. There's plenty out there wanting a man with money.'

'How about you?'

'I've got no money.'

'But you were close to it. Attraction by association.'

'I took advantage, sometimes I told them that I could get them close to Alan, get them a car, a holiday in the sun.'

'And did you?'

'Sometimes.'

Tremayne had recognised the man when he opened the door, having seen him with Alan Winters a few times. The similarities between the two men had been striking. Both men were unambitious, in poor condition, and less than ideal specimens of manhood. If the situation had been reversed, and it had been Cyril who had purchased that lottery ticket, it would be Alan living in the council house, Cyril in the mansion with the fancy cars. Tremayne realised that if he had struck lucky, unlikely given his poor record of picking the winning horses, he'd be content, although he couldn't imagine a future without the police station on Bemerton Road. Sometimes, late at night while lying in bed, he regretted that no one was there beside him. He considered whether he and Jean should attempt to move in together again, instead of the occasional weekend, although he realised that would be doomed to failure. He was, he knew, a solitary man, comfortable in his own skin, content with his life.

'Cyril, your wife?'

'Don't you remember? I married Mavis's friend, the pretty one.'

Tremayne cast his mind back. He recollected Mavis and a friend: the same age, dark hair, thin with a pleasant face. 'Vaguely,' he said.

'She took off a few years back.'

'Sorry about that. Any children?'

'Not us. I wasn't keen, and she wasn't able. After growing up in a family of seven children, the last thing you want is to bring any more into the world.'

'A tough childhood?'

'You know it was. You know about Margie?'

'My sergeant's gone to see her. What's the relationship with your mother?'

'Alan was easier with her, more on account of Mavis.'

'What do you mean?'

'Alan hated her. He'd have thrown her out on the street, but Mavis wouldn't hear of it. Kept telling him that she's his mother, and regardless of what has happened in the past, she still deserves respect.'

'She didn't look happy in his house.'

'No more than a drudge, there to serve them hand and foot. Still, it's no more than she deserves.'

'Your enmity, is it as intense as your brother's?'

'If you mean that I hated her, then yes. She'd come back here, but I'll not take her, not after what she subjected us to.'

'Apart from Margie?'

'Some of the men she brought home were perverts; some wanted to hit us, make us squeal, some wanted to touch us.'

'Sexual abuse?'

'A fancy police term, but yes.'

'And what happened to these men?'

'When Stan and Fred were not in jail, we'd tell them, and they'd sort it out.'

'The same as the man who abused Margie?'

'We never saw them again.'

'Murdered?'

'We were only young, but I don't think so. Not that I cared.'

'Cyril, you're not an ambitious man, are you? Why is that?'

'It's not a crime.'

'I never said it was. You've retired to do what? And what about Mavis? Is she going to support you? She could even send your mother back here.'

'I'll not let her in the door. And Mavis, she'll look after me.'

'Are you sure? She's not a stupid woman. The car in your driveway, she could take it back.'

'She wouldn't dare.'

'Why not?'

'I'll stop her.'

'How? You can barely get out of bed, yet you think you can hold off a woman with that much money? Did you kill Alan? Was he starting to tighten up on you? Thought you'd have a better chance with Mavis, maybe take her out, get her drunk, get her into your bed, and then you could move into her house, is that it?' Tremayne knew he was pushing the man to see if there was any emotion in him.

'Tremayne, you're a bastard. You were back then when you screwed Mavis in your house.'

'How do you know about that?'

'Mavis told my wife; she told me. You're lucky Stan and Fred didn't know about it. They'd have sorted you out.'

'The same as the other men?'

'Maybe.'

'What do you know? Are Stan and Fred capable of murder? What will happen when they're released? Will they want their share of Alan's money?'

'They're bad men, especially Fred, I'll grant you that. None of us is looking forward to the day when he is released.'

'How long before they're out?'

'Stan's out in thirteen, maybe fourteen months; Fred's got another three years. Alan wasn't concerned.'

'Alan's dead, Mavis is alive, the same as you. Will they be around here looking for accommodation, looking for you to help them?'

'With Stan, I've no idea.'

Tremayne could see that Cyril was typical Winters stock in that he contributed little to society. The man seemed incapable of anything other than a general apathy, and if the mother were foisted on him, his complaints would be muted. He could not see the man as a murderer. Stan and Fred were possible, although their dealings with the mother's previous lovers were in the past; if there was a case to be answered, it was for others to investigate, a cold case, but Tremayne assumed it wouldn't be. The men who had died, if that had indeed happened, were possibly low achievers, probably criminals, and their disappearances would not have registered significantly in any database.

'And you're worried?'

'I'll deal with it when it happens.'

'Your philosophy on life?'

'You'll be the one dying of an ulcer, not me,' Cyril Winters said. Tremayne thought the man's comments banal as he, DI Keith Tremayne, was still active and motivated.

Tremayne left the man to his rest and walked down the driveway. As he closed the gate, he could see Cyril Winters turn on the television, a reality show, set on a tropical island. In the man's hand, a can of beer. Tremayne knew that later that night he'd have a few beers himself in the pub, and woe betide anyone who flicked the channel on the television high in one corner of the room from horseracing to a reality show or a quiz with insipid contestants answering insipid questions, revelling in their stupidity. He'd had enough of that with one of the Winters brothers. He still had three more to see. Although two could not have committed the murder, the third was a distinct possibility.

Chapter 6

'I'm giving you two whores thirty minutes to vacate this shop and to hand over the keys to that fancy place Alan rented for you, and no showing your assets, the same as you did to Gerry. I'm not interested,' Mavis Winters said as she stood in the furniture store. On one side of her stood Gerry Winters, on the other a couple of customers with a young child.

The customers moved away and quickly left the shop, Gerry bolting the door after them, turning the sign to closed.

'You've no right to come in here demanding anything,' Polly Bennett said. Liz Maybury, the third member of Alan's threesome, also Gerry's the first time he had tried to evict them, stood slightly behind Polly.

'I've every right. I put up with you when Alan was alive, had no option, but now you're out, and if that means you're back on the street, letting any drunk screw you, that's up to you.'

'We were running this place for Alan, making a good job of it as well, turning a profit. Don't you want us to continue?'

'A lousy thousand pounds a week. Do you think I care about that?'

'Just because you married money, what makes you think you can order us around?'

'It's ours,' Liz Maybury said.

'Gerry, grab hold of them and kick them out. You know where they live?'

'I do.'

'I want the keys now. You've organised some men to deal with their belongings?'

'Are you sure you want to do this?'

'Gerry, watch what you're saying. I've got control of the money. Any trouble with you and you'll be on the street with these women, or keeping Cyril company in that hovel he calls home.'

'For your information,' Mavis said, addressing Polly Bennett, 'I didn't marry money. I married a weak and lazy man who happened to buy a lottery ticket and was rapidly throwing it away on whores like you. You've got thirty-five minutes now before I call the police.'

'We've not broken the law. Alan gave us this place, the cars, the flat.'

'Legally, or just when you and your friend were screwing him?'

'Legally,' Polly said.

'Where's the proof?'

'It's with my solicitor.'

'Where is he?'

'He's out of town.'

'Gerry, grab hold of these women and their bags. I want the keys.'

'Did you kill Alan?' Liz Maybury blurted out.

'You bitch,' Mavis said as she lunged at the woman, grabbing her by the hair, forcing her to the ground. Polly joined in, pushing Mavis's head to the floor. Gerry stood back, not sure what to do. If it had been three men, he would have grabbed the first one, hit him across the head, before starting on the second, but three women? Gerry had to admit that he was enjoying the spectacle: two women that he had slept with, another one that he wanted to if he played his cards right, although if he helped Polly and Liz out of their current predicament, they'd see him right later that day. If he helped Mavis, she'd see that his current employment lasted, and he'd be able to drive the Bentley, an ideal machine for picking up women.

He chose Mavis as the more in need of his attention. He leant down, took hold of Polly's arm and yanked her up. 'You bastard, we screwed you, not that we enjoyed it, and now you're taking her side,' she said.

'Gerry, take hold of this other tart. I don't pay you to screw the women.' Mavis said. 'I pay you to do your job, to protect me from the parasites with their bleeding-heart letters, their lives that have gone wrong, and the first time there's something for you to do, you stand there gawping.'

Mavis pulled herself up from the ground, steadying herself on Gerry's spare arm. In the other Polly Bennett wrestled, trying to free herself from his grip. 'I'll have the law on you,' she said. 'This is assault. There are laws in this country.'

'What chance do you think you'll have? The only money you'll have is from spreading your legs, and not much judging from what I've seen here today. I don't know what Alan saw in you two, both skinny with barely an arse between you. Your breasts, a bicycle pump every night, is that it?'

'You'd know his taste in women,' Liz said, standing at some distance away. 'A worn-out old prune for a wife.'

Mavis took her hand from the table she'd been using for support and launched herself at the woman again, almost a flying leap. Both of them hit the wall behind, Liz collapsing to the ground unconscious.

'You've killed her. It's murder. I'm a witness,' Polly screamed. Gerry, stunned by what had happened, released the woman.

'Check her out,' Mavis said.

Polly had hold of Liz's head. 'Can you hear me?' A weak murmur from the woman on the floor.

'She's alright,' Mavis said.

'It's assault. We'll sue.'

'Join the queue. You'll not be the first, not the last either.'

'She'll need a doctor,' Gerry said.

'Rubbish. The woman's feigning injury, hoping that I'll relent, give them some money.'

'I don't think so. She's genuinely hurt.'

'Okay, take her to the hospital, get her fixed up.'

'In the Bentley?'

'Not a chance. Take one of their cars. And when you've finished, bring both of the cars to the house.'

'You'll pay for this,' Polly said, her friend slowly coming around.

'Pay? I've paid enough for you two already, screwing my husband, disturbing my life. Once she's better, you're out of your flat, two days maximum. At least she's gained some experience of being flat on her back. All she needs is a man on top of her, and she's got it made.'

'It wasn't like that, us and Alan,' Polly said.

'Rubbish. You thought he was an easy touch, plenty of money. How you two got past the other tarts is beyond me, but you did. You've had your fun, but now it's over. Forty-eight hours and you're out, and next time I'll send someone other than Gerry. If he comes, he's more likely to screw you than do his job. And let me be clear, if he stuffs up one more time, brother-in-law or no brother-in-law, he's out on the street with you two. Maybe he can pimp for you.'

Gerry said nothing, realising that his chances of getting into Mavis's bed were looking very remote indeed.

***

After dealing with Margie, Clare found Rachel Winters, the eldest child of Alan Winters, to be a breath of fresh air. She was hard at work at Salisbury Hospital on Odstock Road. 'I'm interested in hospital administration,' she said. Clare could see the resemblance to the mother, although the young woman looked after herself, the mother did not.

The two women sat in the cafeteria; Clare bought herself a latte, another one for Rachel. 'You seem to be handling the situation well enough,' Clare said.

'Not really. I just need to keep busy.'
'What can you tell me about your father?'
'He was a weak man, I suppose you know that.'
'We do. What about his behaviour after the lottery win?'
'It destroyed him, Mum as well.'
'All that money?'
'Before, my dad didn't do much, but he'd go to work, come home, get drunk, and my mother was there for him. The pair didn't have the greatest of marriages, not many do, but at least they were together, and most times they were content.'
'And you?'
'I had a child when I was young, but you know that.'
'An accident?'
'Young and silly, I thought it was love. Never considered that I'd end up pregnant. Anyway, he died.'
'Sad about that?'
'What do you think?'

'Devastated.'

'At the time, but I'm okay now. I'm still young, there's still time to find another man, have a few children.'

'You're not like your parents,' Clare said.

'Bertie's like my dad; I'm the spitting image of my mother.'

'I can't see it.'

'Mum never had the opportunities or the education. She's a hard worker, always there for Bertie and me, and then with Dad, well, he was another child as well, even before we had money, and then after the win.'

'You'd prefer that it hadn't happened?'

'I suppose so, but how can anyone resist that much money? It would drive anyone mad. The fact that you never have to worry again about paying the bills, the ability to indulge every obsession, every fantasy.'

'The women?'

'Dad never looked at another woman before, except in his mind, but then, there they were, so many.'

'He had two specials.'

'Polly and Liz.'

'You knew them?

'Vaguely, before they latched on to Dad. Polly, I liked, not so much Liz, but they were decent enough, but then the money and the clothes, and being squired around in a Bentley. Any woman would be seduced.'

'I wouldn't,' Clare said. 'You weren't.'

'Don't get me wrong. I love the money, the fact that I can drive a nice car, live well, but I need the mental satisfaction that I'm contributing, not just hanging like a leech on the fortune. It's good to know that I can attend all the courses, buy all the books I want, but I refuse to let the money dictate my life.'

'The people here? Do they hassle you?'

'Not the people I work with, although if someone in one of the wards finds out, they can sometimes be a nuisance.'

'Your brother?'

'Same as Dad, but with money. My father could only drink so much with no money, Bertie has no such restraint.'

'Your father could have stopped him having the money to buy drugs.'

'My mother will deal with Bertie.'

'Will she?'

'As long as she controls the money.'

'And now, will you stay at the house?'

'I'm not sure. I've got a boyfriend, or I think he's my boyfriend.'

'You're not sure?'

'There's been a few who've fancied their chances, but I've never been sure if it's the money or me.'

'You're an attractive woman,' Clare said.

'Maybe I am, but I can't be sure if it's me they want. You won't tell Mum, will you?'

'Your secret is safe with me.'

***

Clare was preparing to leave the hospital and to drive back to Bemerton Road Police Station when her phone rang. 'Stay where you are,' Tremayne said.

'What's up?'

'Liz Maybury. She's in the Intensive Care Unit.'

'How? Why?'

'I've just had a phone call from Polly Bennett. Apparently, there was an altercation with Mavis Winters. It'd be best if you get over to her as soon as possible, find out what's going on.'

Clare locked her car and walked the hundred yards from Administration to the Intensive Care Unit. She found Gerry Winters soon enough. 'What's going on?'

'Liz, she hit her head hard on a wall. There's internal bleeding in the brain.'

'Polly Bennett?'

'She's nearby. It was an accident.'

'After we've found out her condition, we need to talk.'

'Mavis blew it, took her anger out on the women.'

'Where?'

'At the furniture store. Mavis wanted them out, the cars back, and then to evict them from the flat Alan had set them up with.'

'She's within her rights.'

'I know, but Mavis is acting unreasonably. Alan was the one with the money. Polly and Liz were just taking advantage, trying to survive.'

'Are you defending their behaviour?'

'Not me, but I've known what it is to be poor, the same as them. And besides, Liz could die. It's an accident, but you'll distort the evidence, make it out to be manslaughter.'

'Mr Winters, we do not distort evidence.'

'Sorry. I'm just angry that this has happened.'

'Do you like the two women?'

'I've nothing against them. It's alright if you win the lottery, but others have to survive, kowtow to those who've had the luck, even if they did not deserve it.'

'We're not here to discuss the injustices of life,' Clare said, realising that if life were just, then Harry Holchester, her fiancé, would still be alive, but he wasn't, and that was fate, nothing to do with luck.

Tremayne arrived to find Clare and Gerry Winters sitting in the waiting area. 'What's happened? he asked.

'There's been an altercation between Liz Maybury and Mavis Winters,' Clare said. 'If the woman dies, it's manslaughter.'

'It's an accident,' Winters said.

'We'll take the statements later. We'll decide then,' Tremayne said.

Clare could see that he was reluctant to consider laying charges against Mavis Winters; she realised it was understandable under the circumstances.

Polly Bennett came through the doors that separated the waiting room from Intensive Care. 'She's under sedation. They think she'll pull through,' she said.

'Her parents?' Clare said.

'I've phoned them. They're on their way. I want to press charges against Mavis Winters.'

'That's up to us,' Tremayne said. 'We'll take statements from everyone before we decide on a course of action.'

'She did it on purpose. Gerry was there, he'll tell you.'

'Miss Bennett, Polly, we've got to consider your friend first. Standing here debating what we're going to do does not help her. We'll need to talk to her first,' Clare said.

'You're right, I suppose, but I need somewhere to stay tonight. The bitch has kicked us out.'

'That's not true,' Gerry said. 'She's given you forty-eight hours. Under the circumstances, she'll reconsider, give you longer. She was angry; you know she had every right.'

'You'll not take our side?' Polly asked, miffed that the man was hedging his bets.

'I'll tell the truth. An accident, unfortunate maybe, but she only wanted you and Liz out of her life.'

'Was she angry enough to hurt the woman?' Tremayne asked.

'Angry, but she had been provoked. Liz was hurling insults. Apart from that wall, it would have ended there and then, and I would have evicted them that day. As it is, they can stay until Liz is better.'

'You bastard. After the way we treated you,' Polly said.

'What does that mean?' Clare said, looking at Gerry Winters.

'The Alan Winters treatment, what else?'

'What else indeed,' Clare replied, knowing full well what the treatment entailed. She realised that Mavis Winters' summation of the two women was spot on: they were a couple of whores.

Chapter 7

Bertie Winters: dissolute, reprobate, of little worth. As good a definition of the man as any, Clare thought. He had not been hard to find after checking out of the facility where his mother had placed him in a last-ditch attempt to save him.

'What do you want?' the young man said after he had opened the door at Cyril Winters' house.

'Sergeant Yarwood, I've a few questions.'

'You'd better come in,' the twenty-two year old replied, his straggly hair touching on his collar, his three-day stubble clearly seen. Clare had to admit that behind the unkempt appearance there was probably an attractive man. The smell of marijuana pervaded the air.

'No cocaine?' Clare said.

'That costs money.'

'You've got plenty.'

'Not anymore. That bitch of a mother has cut me off, told me to get a job.'

'Your sister wants to work.'

'Why should I? My father had plenty, and he did nothing for it. I'm entitled to do what I want.'

'Your father had been lucky. Are you expecting to win the lottery anytime soon?'

'I've got my legal rights. I'm entitled to some of the money.'

'Legally, you're probably entitled to nothing.'

Clare could see the man looking her up and down. It made her feel uncomfortable. She had sometimes seen it at Bemerton Road. There they were careful not to be too obvious and smart enough to keep their comments in check, but she knew that Bertie Winters would get around to it soon enough.

'What do you want anyway? I saw you round at my house the other day.'

'Your father's been murdered. Aren't you concerned?'

'Should I be? The man had a good time, plenty of good-looking women, and what did I get? Nothing, that's what. Just an old Toyota to drive and an allowance. I'm not a child doing chores to receive pocket money, I'm a man. I need my own place, my own money, a few women. Dad, he wasn't much, but he respected me, gave me money.'

'He wouldn't buy you a fancy car.'

'He would have in time. I knew about him and those women. He'd have paid for me to keep quiet.'

'If you're referring to Polly Bennett and Liz Maybury, your mother knows.'

'Not that.'

'What then?'

'There were others.'

'And why are they so important? Your father is dead, your mother needs your support. You should be with her.'

'Why? She doesn't care if my father's dead,' Bertie said as he puffed on his joint. 'Do you want some?'

'No thanks,' Clare said. She'd tried it at boarding school once, everyone had, but she had not enjoyed the experience, and besides drugs were not her thing, and sitting down with Bertie Winters did not appeal. It was clear that the lottery win had helped some people, Mavis and Rachel Winters, in particular, but it had destroyed or was about to destroy others. Alan Winters had died because of his money, and Bertie, the son, was a sure-fire candidate for premature death in the next few years, even if he went back to drug rehabilitation, moved back into the mansion in Quidhampton. The man was lazy, as had been the father, as was Cyril, and even with an old Toyota, he was bound to have an accident at some stage.

'Your uncle? Where is he?'

'Down the pub, I suppose. He likes to drink.'

'The same as your father.'

'Maybe, not that he'll be able to impress any of the women.'

'Mr Winters, did you kill your father? Would you kill your mother if she does not give you what you want?'

'Are you mad? Why would I do that?'

'For the money. Without your parents, the money would be yours and Rachel's.'

'Would it? It's a good idea.'

'I'm a police officer, yet you continue to smoke an illegal substance.'

'You're uptight, and besides, you want to find out who killed my father. Arresting me for a minor misdemeanour won't help your investigation.'

'Why?'

'I've seen things, know things.'

'It's a maximum of five years in jail if I arrest you.'

'What's the point. Mum, even if she won't give me what I want, she'll ensure that I have the best lawyers.'

'It's clear that you are not without some intelligence. Was your father intelligent?'

'He could be. He was lazy, the same as I am, and then he was rich. I'll be rich one day.'

'How?'

'You've just told me. If my mother dies, then I get half of what's left. It'll be enough for me.'

'Your mother could disinherit you, give it all to your sister.'

'She can't do that.'

'Yes, she can.'

'Then I'd take her to court.'

'With what? You'll have no money. You'll not win. Mr Winters. I'll put it to you again, did you kill your father because he would not buy you a better car? Are you planning to do the same with your mother? Are you aware of any will?' Clare knew that she was using a trick of Tremayne's in throwing rapid-fire accusations at the person, knowing full well that it would test their resolve to deflect the answers, and would confuse and divert them.

Bertie Winters stood up, made for Clare, attempted to grab her. She took one swipe at him, causing the man to fall back onto his bean bag. 'You bitch, I did not kill my father. He was a lovely man, the only one that cared. That Rachel, with her stuck-up manner, her ambition. That bitch can go to hell. If my mother dies, then I'll take it all for myself, I'm telling you that.'

'Thank you, Mr Winters, you've told me all I need to know.'

'What's that?'

'That you are a weak excuse for a man and that you have not killed your father.'

'How dare you insult me.'

'I'll do what I want. What are you going to do? Complain to the police?'

'I'll remember, that's what I'll do.'

'And that's all. You should be grateful that I'm not arresting you today. Another day I might not be so generous. You did not kill your father, you'll not kill your mother.'

'What makes you so sure?'

'Because you're like your father, like your uncle. They are, were, both lazy, boring and fat men, full of bravado with a few pints in them, but up at Stonehenge on a cold night, a knife in their hand, they'd be running home to their mother, the same as you will eventually once the money runs out. Cocaine, marijuana, beer, they all cost money, and you don't have enough, or do you?'

'I've got some.'

'Enough to register the car? Enough for drugs? Enough to keep you here in this depressing little council house when there's a beautiful house not far from here? I don't think so.'

'If you weren't a woman…'

'Then what? You'd take me outside and kick my arse, is that it?'

'That's it. I'll not let any man talk to me like that.'

'But you'll let a woman, you'll let your mother. I suggest you get yourself back into rehab before your brain is totally addled.'

Clare left the house, phoned Tremayne. 'Bertie Winters did not kill his father,' she said. 'He's a drugged-out reprobate of no consequence, but not a murderer.'

'Can you be sure?'

'We can never be one hundred per cent certain, but I pushed him hard, rapid-fire questions. He'd have let slip something if he was guilty, and besides, he'd still need an accomplice. Alan Winters' death needed forethought and planning, and Bertie Winters is capable of neither.

***

Liz Maybury, under mild sedation for ten days, was slowly brought back to full consciousness. The private ward, the specialist treatment, were paid for by Mavis Winters on legal advice. The woman's death or incapacity would reflect poorly on her if Mavis had not ensured the best medical care.

Liz Maybury's parents had taken turns to be at her bedside since the injury; Polly, her friend, visited every day. Liz's parents had not been pleased when interviewed by Tremayne and Clare, upset when told the reason for the altercation.

Polly was still living in the flat supplied by Alan, a possible payoff from Mavis if necessary. As for the furniture store, it was closed and up for sale, at a bargain price if anyone was willing to pay.

On the eleventh day, Clare was let into the ward, as long as she was willing to keep her questioning low key, no loud voices, no anger, and nothing that would disturb the fragile condition of the patient. Tremayne was not given permission; his presence was deemed not agreeable.

'Liz, Sergeant Yarwood. How are you feeling?'

'Fine, I think. They told me I've been here for nearly two weeks.'

On a chair in the far corner sat Liz Maybury's father.

'Do you remember what happened?'

'The woman went crazy, accusing Polly and me of seducing her husband, telling us to get out and on the street. We're not like that, really.'

Clare looked over at the father; he seemed uncomfortable about his daughter's revelations, although he had already been told, as had his wife, of Polly and Liz's relationship with Alan Winters. Clare could only feel compassion for them, as they seemed to be good people with a good daughter who had been swayed by the lure of an inordinate amount of money and luxury and a bad influence, namely Polly Bennett.

Clare had had to agree with them, it seemed to be the only right thing to do, but her investigations pointed to the woman in the hospital bed as the worst influence.

'Did she slam you into the wall intentionally?'

'It was an accident. She was angry, we all were, and Gerry, he stood there and did nothing, only held Polly's arm. Alan's wife, she was crazy, crazy angry. I suppose I can't blame her, but he didn't love her.'

'Did he love you?'

'Not us, but he was going to see us right.'

'Did you like him?'

'Not really. He was okay, but he was not an attractive man.'

'Only rich.'

'As you say. I've no regrets, neither has Polly.'

'And your relationship with Polly?'

'We're friends, that's all.'

'Lesbian?'

'Not me, not Polly. We like men.'

'Richer the better?'

'Maybe, and now Alan's dead.'

'We've spoken about this before. Are you sorry that he's dead?'

'Not really. When can I leave here?'

'That's not up to me. You need rest.'

'There's a place at home with us,' the father said.

'Not there. I want to be with Polly.'

'She's still at the place that Alan gave you.'

'That's what Polly said. Why? I thought his wife wanted us out.'

'You would be if you weren't here. Mavis Winters is paying for your treatment, did you know that?'

'Why?'

'Guilty conscience, legal advice. Whatever the reason, be thankful.'

'And after I'm out of here?'

'You'll need to talk to Mavis, not me.'

Outside the ward, the father spoke to Clare. 'Is it true? Liz and her friend were trading sexual favours for the place where they live, the cars they drive, the furniture store?'

'You've been told this before.'

'I know we have, but I need to check again.'

'I'm sorry, Mr Maybury, but yes, Polly Bennett and your daughter were doing just that.'

'It's not something you expect to hear about your children. A daughter who is no more than a prostitute.'

'I can't offer you any words of consolation, I'm afraid. We're conducting a murder investigation. I can't ignore certain facts which are relevant to the case in an attempt to hide the truth, protect the feelings of loved ones.'

'I understand,' Maybury said. Clare left a sad man talking to his wife.

***

Tremayne and Yarwood met in the office at Bemerton Road. The Homicide department was not busy, a sure sign that Superintendent Moulton would be on the warpath soon. There was another letter from Human Resources with an improved retirement package on the desk. Tremayne pushed it to one side.

'It's worth considering,' Clare said, although she didn't know the amount specified, only noted her senior's look when he had seen the figures.

'And leave you here on your own. Not a chance.'

'We need to talk about this case. What do we have so far?'

'A motive.'

'The money. Can there be anything else?' Clare said.

'It's this Stonehenge connection that I don't get. A death up there must be symbolic, but what is it?'

'Who are we discounting as the murderers?'

'Cyril Winters, too lazy, and nothing to gain. He's received some money; no doubt would have received more from Alan if he had asked. Mavis won't be so easy.'

'I'm discounting Bertie Winters, the son, for the same reason, although with the mother dead, he'd inherit. But he's still lazy, not enough energy to cross the road let alone drive up to Stonehenge,' Clare said.

'Mavis Winters has the strongest motive, but she's smart enough to know she'd be a primary suspect. And she'd still need an accomplice.'

'No one has an immediate motive; no one was going to gain in the short term.'

'Dean Winters. He says he's not interested in the money, but he's angry enough to want their lives destroyed.'

'He'd still need an accomplice.'

'If it's Dean, then who could be his accomplice? His wife maybe. We didn't interview her, saw no point at the time. If Stan and Fred, the two brothers, were not in prison, I'd consider them as potential murderers.'

'What about the man who raped Margie? The other live-ins of the mother? Did they kill them or frighten them off?'

'Raping their sister? I'd say they killed that man, not that you can blame them.'

'It's still murder.'

'I know it is, and I'd arrest them if there were a case, but it's not part of the current investigation. Could either of the two brothers have been capable of organising Alan Winters' death from behind bars?'

'What would they have to gain? Assuming Alan Winters is dead, then the money goes to his wife, then his children.'

'And what about Alan Winters' father? What happened to him?'

'The mother may know.'

'We'll interview the mother today. I'll arrange to meet up with Stan and Fred later in the week.'

Chapter 8

The house in Quidhampton was abuzz with decorators on Tremayne and Clare's arrival. They had phoned ahead, spoken to Mavis Winters, told her the reason for coming.

'You'll not get much out of Alan's mother,' Mavis Winters said.

'Why?'

'Inconsolable grief, although it's too little, too late. She should have thought about her children when they were young.'

'She'll talk to us?'

'She'll talk, not that she'll make much sense.'

Tremayne could see an angry woman, remembered a girl of sixteen. It was as if she was two separate people, but then he had changed too. Back then, when they had made love, or more accurately fumbled around in the dark, somehow consummating the relationship, he had been young and dark-haired, with a sideways profile that was as flat as a board. She, he remembered, had been firm and tender, and compliant in his arms. And now she was rich when she had been poor. He was not rich, never wanted to be, although the offer from Human Resources was indeed generous, certainly more than enough to redecorate his house to allow Jean to move in, even if it was only on an occasional basis. He kept thinking of her, knowing that she was a good woman, loyal to a fault, comparing her to the Winters. They may be as rich as Croesus, but they had nothing that he wanted. The lottery win, all sixty-eight million pounds, had transformed their lives, not enhanced them. Alan had died, Mavis was in despair over her son and worrying about who was after their money. The only one who was immune appeared to be the daughter, Rachel. Yarwood had admitted to liking the woman, believing her not to be involved, but she, it was assumed, was in for a half-share of a fortune when her mother died; enough to turn a saint into a sinner, and Rachel Winters was no saint, only a woman of flesh and bone.

Alan Winters' mother was upstairs in her room. Clare could see that it was large enough, although its condition was far from ideal. The woman did not look after herself. In the bathroom, clothes were hanging from the shower curtain rail. 'I'm not going down there,' the woman said.

'Your name is Betty Winters?' Tremayne said. The three were sitting on some chairs close to the window. Clare wanted to open the window to let in some fresh air, but did not. Betty Winters sat on the edge of her chair, her feet barely touching the ground. Tremayne remembered her vaguely from years ago, had seen her in the house since her son's death, but he had not realised how haggard she was. Before, downstairs in the kitchen when she had been preparing a meal, with Mavis Winters abusing her, the woman had seemed upright and hard-working. Now she was bent over, wearing just a pink-coloured dressing gown. On her feet, she wore a pair of slippers.

'She killed him, the bitch.'

'Who?'

'Who do you think?'

'Mavis?' Tremayne said.

'Yes, her. She never liked him, always screwing around she was.'

'We've found no evidence of that,' Clare said.

'I know her type. String a man along, milk him for all he's worth and then dump him.'

Clare thought it sounded like an apt description of the woman they were talking to.

'Tell us about Alan,' Clare said.

'He treated me well. He was my favourite.'

'Why? Because he let you live here? Because he had money?'

'She wants me to go and live with Cyril.'

'Will you go?'

'What option do I have? Cyril hates me, they all do, a poor old woman.'

Clare could not feel any sympathy for the woman if what they had been told was true. 'We've been told that your husband moved out of the house.'

'After he'd given me seven mongrel children.'

'We've spoken to all of them, except for Stan and Fred. Have you seen them?'

'Not them. They're ashamed of their own mother, and there they are, in prison. They've no right to stick their noses up at me.'

'We've been told that after your husband left, you had a number of men.'

'I was still young.'

'We're not criticising; we just need to ascertain the background to this investigation. To see if your children's upbringing has any bearing on the investigation.'

'I was on my own. I did the best I could.'

'What about the men who abused your children? What about the man who raped Margie?'

'Margie was a tart, even back then.'

'Margie was an adolescent. It was up to her mother to protect her,' Clare said. Tremayne could see that his sergeant was becoming upset, imagining the horror that the woman's daughter had gone through.

'Mrs Winters, Margie was a child in the eyes of the law. It was your responsibility to have her checked out by a doctor and for charges to be laid against the man. Why didn't you?' Tremayne said.

'I used to see her, short skirts, stuffing toilet paper down her bra. What man can resist?'

'Were you abused as a child?' Clare asked.

'Who wasn't, but we didn't end up on the street as a prostitute. Margie was always weak.'

'You knew, yet you did nothing. Was the man more important than your daughter?'

'I hated them all. I only cared for Alan. He was the only one who looked after me.'

'What happened to the man who attacked Margie?'

'He disappeared. I don't know. They never lasted anyway, too many children for them to care about.'

'You neglected the children, blaming them instead of your husband. What happened to him? Where can we find him?'

'I've no idea. Ask Dean, he may know.'

'Why Dean?'

'He's the smart one, not that he cares about me, never a birthday card, never a phone call.'

'Mrs Winters, I'm afraid you don't deserve anything from your children. You knew that your daughter had been raped, yet you did nothing. What were you planning to do? Sell her off to the local perverts? What sort of mother are you? Did you kill Alan, arrange for someone to take him up to Stonehenge and cut his throat?'

'Why would I do that? He was my son, I loved him.'

'Mrs Winters, you love no one. You are beneath contempt. If Mavis wants you out and with Cyril, then she is within her rights.'

Downstairs Tremayne and Clare found Mavis Winters involved in the redecorations. 'What do you reckon? Mavis asked.

'She's a hard woman,' Clare said. 'She knew about Margie.'

'Poor Margie, she's beyond hope.'

'Bertie?'

'He said you had given him an earful. Thanks for that.'

'Will it help?'

'He's back in rehab, but no. He'll try if pushed and I'll maintain a firm hand, but he's an adult. Apart from keeping him out of trouble, it's up to him, and I'm afraid he just doesn't have it in him.'

'Rachel?' Clare asked.

'She'll do well. Maybe she'll be able to look after Bertie when I'm gone.'

'You're only young,' Tremayne said.

'I suppose so. I'm just hoping that Bertie will outlive me.'

'Will he?'

'He's entitled to some of the money. There's not much I can do to stop it. Our solicitor set it up. When he reaches twenty-five, he's entitled to ten per cent, so is Rachel. It's a shame Alan died.'

'Why?'

'If he had lived, it would have been ten per cent of nothing. I've limited the losses; there'll be over thirty million, and with some investments, it should be more. I'm learning economics, money management on the internet.'

'Polly Bennett and Liz Maybury?'

'I was angry that day, but I didn't intend for one of them to end up in hospital. I've spoken to Polly, told her that the two of them can keep the flat and the cars. They'll still belong to me, though.'

'The furniture store?'

'Maybe they can manage it for me, as long as Gerry keeps away.'

'Will he?'

'They'll not give him the time of day if he doesn't have any money.'

'You'll ensure that?'

'He's got a job here. I'll pay him twice what he's worth, but it's nothing like the money that Alan had. They'll not waste their time on him.'

'And Alan's mother?'

'There's Cyril's place. She doesn't deserve any better.'

Clare could only agree. She knew she needed a drink. The time with the mother had left her feeling upset and down. The lot of a police officer is what Tremayne would say, but it still didn't alter the fact that she had spent time upstairs in that house with an evil woman.

***

Gerry Winters was not the most pleasant of men, in that he had a history of low-level violence in the city: drunken brawls, arguments with the neighbours, roughing up one of his girlfriends.

The first time they had visited the house in Quidhampton, he had been at the entrance keeping away the media and the general public after the death of Alan had become known. And whereas the media interest had waned, the beaming face of Alan Winters holding the cheque for sixty-eight million pounds still graced some magazine covers, the story inside plotting the fall of the luckiest man in England from infinite wealth to eternal death, the murder described in as much detail as possible. Stonehenge, the location of his death, was open to the general public again, although as always, the inner circle was restricted to just a few visitors, apart from during the summer solstice when the Druids and the other lovers of nature made a pilgrimage to the site.

'What do you want, Tremayne? Haven't you caused enough damage as it is?' Gerry Winters said. He was propping up the bar at the Old Mill in Harnham, the Bentley not visible outside.

'It's a murder investigation. A few eggs will be cracked on the way, and besides, what do you mean? Nothing's happened to you.'

'She's put me on wages, her own brother-in-law. What right does she have?'

'It's her money.'

'It's not. I drove him to that newsagent. I lent him the money to buy the damn ticket and then what happens? He goes and wins.'

'He repaid your loan?'

'We always joked that if either of us won, we'd share it with the other.'

'And he reneged on the deal?'

'It was her. She wouldn't let him.'

'Are you sure? Or is it just a few pints of anger and bitterness?'

'I've only had two.'

Tremayne looked over at the barman. He shook his head, raised one hand, palm forward, all five fingers.

'How about you and the two women?' Tremayne asked.

'Not a chance there. I liked Polly, but she only wants rich money.'

'You could borrow the money from Mavis, set up your own business,' Clare said. She was sipping from a glass of wine, Tremayne was on his second pint of beer. If Gerry Winters was feeling sorry for himself, drinking more than he should, then an otherwise hidden fact might be revealed.

'What skills do I have?'

'You must be good at something.'

'Hard work is for mugs. Alan didn't do anything with his life, and he ended up rich.'

'Rich and dead,' Tremayne said.

'What can you tell us about the night? Where were you? And what's the truth with you and Mavis?'

'I thought I could take her off Alan's hands after he died.'

'And before?'

'What do you mean?'

'According to Polly Bennett and Liz Maybury, on one of the occasions he took them back to his house, Mavis was occupied in another room. Any truth to that and was it you?'

'Not me. And I don't believe it. Mavis was a decent woman, still is, and whereas Alan was a waste of space, she was the one who kept the house together.'

'Apart from Bertie?'

'It runs in the family.'

'What? General apathy and disinterest in anything other than screwing and getting drunk. And what about Margie? She's in a terrible state. Don't you care about her?'

'What are you, Tremayne, a bleeding social worker or a police officer? How we run our lives is none of your concern, nor your sergeant's, granted that she's prettier than you. How about it, luv? Fancy a man down on his luck?'

'I've spent an unpleasant forty-five minutes with your mother. You don't want my answer and don't treat me as one of your tarts. We know about your arrangement with the two women. How you'd look after their interests, how they'd look after you.'

'I told you that.'

'They'll not be interested now. You've got nothing to offer, not even a ride in the Bentley.'

'Mavis has me trapped. She knows I'll keep working for her. I'm no better than a lap dog.'

'It's better than the alternative. There's always a spare bed at Cyril's house, or maybe you can lodge with Dean, although his wife would have you jumping through hoops.'

'Another bitch.'

'What do you mean?'

'She wears the trousers in that house. If it weren't for her, we'd be able to go down there, Dean would come up here. As it is, he keeps his distance.'

'He's never asked for money.'

'Dean, he knows the value of money, but she's extreme, believes that hard work, not charity, is the solution. She'd rather sleep on the street than come up here and ask for help.'

'She sounds a decent woman, a person who believes that it is the individual who determines their future, not a lottery ticket.'

'Lovely words, no doubt, but do you believe that rubbish? Dean's wife is a bitch; the one time we saw her, she launched into a tirade about how she was going to make one of the Winters into someone respectable, and as far as she was concerned, the rest could go to hell, especially the mother.'

'What did you do?'

'I hit her, right across the face.'

'And then what?'

'She hit me back, harder than I hit her. Dean stood there, his mouth wide open. She grabbed him by the arm and shot out of the house. None of us has seen her or Dean since, apart from Alan that one time.'

'How long ago since you've seen Dean?'

'It must be fifteen years.'

'Not even your mother?'

'She doesn't care anyway.'

'You dislike your mother the same as the others?'

'Dislike? That's probably right. She wasn't there for us when we were young.'

Chapter 9

Tremayne, back in the office, sat at his desk. He was leaning back, eyes closed, the front two legs of the chair off the ground. Clare could see that he was mentally going over the case so far; she decided to give him a few minutes until he'd concluded, or until the chair collapsed under his weight. The man was neither small nor light, and the chair was not heavy-duty.

Clare continued with her paperwork, an unfortunate result of the computer age, where the administrators enjoyed thinking up new ways to keep people confined to their desks. Superintendent Moulton relished reports. Tremayne was dismissive of their superintendent, but she was not. To her, he was trying to keep the police station efficient without being overly authoritative.

Clare typed away, pleased that she was capable with a keyboard, and a couple of hours every few days was enough for her to get through the bulk of the administrative tasks. Not that it helped Tremayne, who'd labour over every report he had to prepare, cursing under his breath as he pressed each key one after the other. It was painful to watch, and if he had wanted, she would have helped, but she knew him to be a proud man.

Her boss, she knew, was a stereotype of the archetypical policeman: dedicated, terse in manner, economical in compliments, determined to leave no stone unturned, no matter how small it was. She saw him as an excellent character for a television series; he fitted the mould perfectly, though he would not have appreciated her analysis of him.

Clare looked again. The man was now sitting on his chair, the four legs firmly on the ground again. It seemed the time for her to approach. 'What's the verdict, guv,' she said.

'What verdict? We've got nothing.'

'We've got a lot of people. There's a few in there who could have killed him.'

'Mavis is the most likely, but she would have needed help. The man, we know, had some medical issues, even if he did not know about them, or didn't care. Who would think that Stonehenge would be the ideal place? And the only people who would gain from his death are the immediate family. There's no question that it was Alan Winters who purchased the ticket, or is there?'

'I've checked. The man won the prize fair and square. The newsagent said he was a regular in the shop, always bought a ticket every week, before heading over to the pub. He placed a sign outside the shop after Winters had won. You know the sort of thing, buy your ticket here, you could have the same luck.'

'And they fell for it as if the shop was blessed by the god of good fortune.'

'Why not? People believe that if they see a four-leafed clover, it somehow foretells their future. Even you hold up your betting slip and say a few words as the horse lumbers around the track.'

'That's just fun, at least for me.'

'For you, but some people believe in the rituals. We've spoken about this before, but there are some who would see Winters' death as a rite of passage, the transference of his good fortune onto the murderer.'

'Dean Winters said there was mongrel DNA. Maybe he knew something.'

'He'll not appreciate another visit, or his wife won't.'

'And you care, Yarwood?'

'Not at all. If there's a screw loose somewhere, we need to know. Maybe all of them, although some are just too lazy to do anything about it.'

'Gerry Winters would, and he's angry enough, believes that he was cheated out of his fair share of the money.'

'Why was he? Legally he didn't have a leg to stand on, but Alan was his brother. According to him, it was Mavis who did not honour the agreement, and if she had so much sway over her husband, why did she allow him to play around with other women?'

'A visit to Mavis first, then on to Dean, is that it?'

'I reckon so. I'll make the phone calls.'

'Don't bother. We'll just knock on the doors, judge the reaction,' Tremayne said.

***

Compared to their previous visits to the Winters' house, it was quiet. The cleaners, the interior decorators, the general hubbub of family visiting to offer their sympathies no longer apparent.

'She's gone,' Mavis Winters said as she opened the door.

'Who?' Clare asked.

'His damn mother.'

'Gone where?'

'Back to that depressing council house. She came down from her room, a stinking mess by the way, cost me plenty to get it fumigated and cleaned out, and she was in the kitchen accusing me of killing her beloved son. She's one to speak, the old trollop. She didn't care when he was alive, not even as a child, and there she is, lecturing me for all her worth.'

'She went voluntarily?' Tremayne said.

'Not a chance. I grabbed her suitcase, stuffed a few of her belongings in it, and shuffled her out the door. Gerry dropped her off at Cyril's house. It must have been some homecoming.'

'And you don't feel a little sad at what you've done?' Clare said.

'She was a wicked old woman, not deserving of any kindness. We reap what we sow, that's something I remember from Sunday school, and she sowed plenty of weeds.'

'It's still sad,' Clare said, remembering her grandmother who had passed away not long before her initial move to Salisbury. The grandmother had been loved, even though as she aged she became progressively more cantankerous, and here was a woman who professed no compassion for an old woman. Maybe it was right, in that the woman was demanding and embittered and had led a fruitless life, full of malignancy, but she was still an old woman, not more than a few years left in her. It just didn't seem right to Clare.

'Anyway, what are you here for? Not to talk about Polly Bennett and Liz Maybury?'

'What's happened to them?' Clare said.

'I've met up with Polly. I don't mind the woman, apart from what she did. She's smart enough, a bit of a tart, but then most of them are these days. No sooner are they out of their school uniform and they're down behind the bike shed with the local stud.'

Or in the other room with a young police officer, Clare thought but did not say it out aloud.

'What have you agreed with her?' Tremayne said, noticing the smirk on his sergeant's face. He knew what she was thinking.

'The two women can run the furniture store, keep the flat and cars. It's a purely financial agreement. I need to consider the future, make some investments. They know that if they don't make a go of it, they're out on the street.'

'You've forgiven them?' Clare said.

'It takes two to tango, or in their case, three. Men, they're all the same, a tight arse, a wiggle, a heaving bosom pressed against them in the pub.'

Clare, who had warmed to the woman since their initial meeting, could see a hardness developing. She wasn't sure that she liked Mavis's attitude. For the first time, she felt that Mavis could indeed be capable of murder.

'We had come here to talk to you about two issues that give us concern, although I believe that you've answered the first one.'

'Why I let him play around?'

'That's the first.'

'What else could I do? The man's flush with money; he's driving a Ferrari until he prangs it, then it's a Bentley. The man was not a saint, and besides, I was busy enjoying myself as well.'

'Other men?'

'Not me, although there were opportunities. I was into expensive clothes, beauty treatments, eating at expensive restaurants, no longer looking in my purse wondering if I could afford to buy the brand-name food rather than the generic. We were both mad for a few months, and by then, Alan's well entrenched into his lifestyle and I'm into mine. And then this house came along, and I'm busy indulging myself. Having unlimited money is seductive. It's a mistress you can't refuse, you know you should, but it's impossible. It destroyed us in many ways, enriched us in others. Unless you've experienced it, you'll never know.'

'You could have given it away,' Clare said.

'That's never an option. As much as you believe it's the right thing, you will never do it.'

'Did Gerry ever stake a claim on the money?' Tremayne said.

'That old chestnut, the belief that he was entitled to a half-share because he had driven Alan to the newsagent.'

'Something like that.'

'How many times have you heard it? When I win the lottery, we'll share the proceeds.'

'Plenty, but no one ever does.'

'We all used to joke about being rich, everyone does. It's harmless make-believe, a fantasy.'

'Your fantasy came true,' Clare said.

'It did. And then the people came. All of the relatives, Gerry at the front of the queue, even his mother, who somehow believed that giving birth to the winner gave her some rights.'

'Did it?'

'Nothing, although she's been looked after, we even paid for a hip replacement, fixed up a few health problems. Apart from the relatives, there are the friends we never knew we had, even the newsagent where Alan bought the ticket. He thought he was entitled to at least fifty thousand.'

'What did he get?'

'Nothing. He had the ticket, could have purchased it for himself, instead of allowing the suckers to spend their wages on a frivolity.'

'Not a frivolity in your case.'

'Good luck, nothing else. Anyway, the newsagent got nothing. The brothers each received a cash payment of one hundred thousand and a solicitor's letter to sign.'

'Even Stan and Fred?'

'Even them.'

'And Dean?'

'It was offered.'

'What happened?'

'That stupid wife of his. Have you met her?'

'Not yet.'

'Don't bother. She's a venomous toad of a woman. I've no idea what Dean sees in her, although he's a weak man, the same as the others.'

'He's been successful.'

'I'll grant you that. Dean was the only one who did well at school, and he can be academic. Then he meets up with her, and she's pushing him forward. Heaven to him, hell to anyone else.'

'You never answered the question about Gerry. Was he entitled to a half-share?'

'Just because he drove Alan to the newsagents? Get real. The man was entitled to nothing, the same as the other bloodsuckers. He got his hundred thousand, even Alan's women, Polly Bennett and Liz Maybury. What else does he need?'

'He's fond of you,' Clare said.

'He's not a bad man, but I've no need of him. I've just got rid of his brother. What makes you think I'd go back for seconds?'

'Got rid of!' Tremayne said.

'A figure of speech, and you know it. It was luck on my part that he died, my lottery ticket if you like, and now the money will all be mine in another week.'

'Why's that?'

'You're releasing his body. We'll have a get-together here after the funeral. You'll come?'

'We will.'

'Come and enjoy yourself. Don't come here as a police officer.'

'But that's what we are. You realise that his murderers could be among the mourners?'

'I'm aware of it, but do you honestly believe this is related to the money?'

'It's the only motive that makes any sense, and now you're the person with the money.'

'I'll make sure I have security.'

'So did Alan and he ended up dead.'

Chapter 10

In one house, a woman, even if she could be hard with her relatives, had been friendly. In another, that of Dean Winters and his wife, there was no friendliness, and the hardness was like a brick wall.

'Why do you keep bothering us?' Dean Winters' wife said. Tremayne and Clare were in the house, just. Further entry into somewhere more conducive was being prevented by a woman with a scowl on her face. In the background, peering through a slightly open door, the husband's countenance.

'Mrs Winters, a man has been murdered. If we need to come here a dozen times, we will, or else we can meet at the police station,' Tremayne said.

'Are you threatening us?'

Clare could see that she was an unpleasant person, venomous as described. 'Mrs Winters, DI Tremayne is correct. We can summons you to the police station, even arrange a police car with flashing lights and a siren to pick the two of you up, or you can show us civility and invite us in. The decision is yours, but we will question your husband, even you, if it is necessary.'

'Very well, come in. And watch where you put your feet. I've just vacuumed the place; I don't want you dirtying it again, or I'll send the police a bill.'

'Mrs Winters, they'll not pay. I suggest you stop your bellyaching and let us in.'

'You can't talk to me like that. It's police brutality. Dean, take a note of what they've just said. In my own house.'

Tremayne turned to Clare. 'How long before you can get a marked police car here?'

'Ten minutes. I've got a friend at the local police station. Do we need handcuffs?'

'Tell them to bring them just in case. And remember, we want the siren as well.'

'The kitchen,' Mrs Winters said.

'I'll put on the kettle,' the husband said.

'Don't you bother. They're not staying long.'

'I'll have mine with two sugars, milk. No sugar for Sergeant Yarwood,' Tremayne said. He'd met enough awkward people over the years. He had no intention of letting this woman get the better of him.

In the kitchen, not one thing was out of place, there was not a dish in the sink nor an animal in the corner. A table stood in one corner, and four chairs, each lined up in perfect symmetry. Tremayne pulled his chair back so he could sit down, making sure to drag the chair's feet across the tiled floor. Clare looked at Mrs Winters, could see she was angry.

Clare took her seat, careful not to aggravate the situation. The husband came over with the tea: four cups and saucers, a sugar bowl, and the milk in a jug. All the cutlery matched. 'Make sure you use the table mats,' Mrs Winters said.

'I'm sorry,' Dean said. 'Barbara likes a tidy house.'

'And no interruptions.'

'Mrs Winters, do you want it recorded that you are a hostile witness?' Tremayne said.

'I'm not hostile. We have no dealings with those people. Why should we be subjected to questioning as if we are common criminals?'

'You are assisting the police,' Clare said. The woman opposite was clearly a tyrant who controlled her husband, even though she was significantly shorter than him, even slight in stature. One puff of wind and she'd blow over. She was no doubt keen on eating sensibly, dragging her husband along for the ride whether he liked it or not.

'Mr Winters, you say that you've not been to see Mavis Winters since Alan died,' Tremayne said.

'That is correct,' Dean Winters said. He was sitting next to his wife, ensuring that he did not put his elbows on the table.

'Yet your wife, who is clearly hostile to your family, is upset that you have not offered your condolences in person. Why is that?'

'I'll answer that,' Winters' wife said. 'It's the Christian thing to do, that's why. We're strong believers in the Lord.'

'Yet you do not want your husband to associate with them?'

'A family of criminals, that's what they are.'

'Mrs Winters, what is your background?'

'I'm from Southampton. I met Dean at the place where he works.'

'The boss's daughter,' Dean Winters said.

'My father was a hard-working, God-fearing man. He's worked hard all his life, never cheated on his taxes or my mother.'

'When did you first meet your husband's family?' Clare asked.

'He took me up there after we were engaged.'

'And you disapproved?'

'Of course. They were living in a slum. The place was dirty, there were bottles of alcohol everywhere. And do you know where they took us for a meal?'

'You tell us.'

'A pub lunch: mushy peas, soggy chips, and a limp piece of undercooked fish. It was an insult, and then they expected Dean to pay.'

'You did?' Tremayne asked, looking over at the husband visibly shrinking in his seat.

'Yes. They had no money. Alan had spent his salary the night before getting drunk, Cyril was penniless, as was Stan.'

'And Fred?'

'He was in jail.'

'Mrs Winters, did you know about your husband's family before you went there?'

'Dean had warned me, but I didn't believe him. No family could be that bad, I was certain of that.'

'And were they?'

'Worse, and then his mother sits there and tells me about their father and the men she had been with. I'm still cringing to this day.'

'You still married your husband.'

'I made a commitment to God to look after him. I wasn't going to let him down. I have made it my life's work to raise Dean from that cesspool to become someone worthy of my family's name.'

Tremayne pitied the man.

'You've not mentioned Margie, your husband's sister.'

'She wasn't there. I never knew about her until after we were married.'

'How did you find out?'

'She ended up here on our doorstep after we had been married for two years,' Barbara Winters said.

'She had your address?'

'Dean, he'd kept in contact with her. Even been helping her with money.'

'She's my sister. I can't ignore her, the same as the others,' Winters said. Clare thought that he was a compassionate man.

'She was dead, is dead. How many times have I told you? She's given herself over to the devil. Let him look after her.'

'We've seen her recently,' Clare said.

'How was she?' Dean Winters asked.

'She was living in a terraced house near to Wyndham Road. Her condition was not good, although she seemed safe. There were a lot of cats.'

'That's where I last saw her.'

'Is she?'

'Say it out loud, will you. Is she still selling herself?' Barbara Winters said. 'If you're willing to bring your family's shame into this house, you may as well tell the police, tell the neighbourhood. Why I put up with you and your family, I'll never know. If it weren't for the Lord, I'd turn you over for someone else.'

'I apologise for my wife. The strain of Alan's death has affected us badly.'

'Talk for yourself. One less mongrel on this planet.'

'That's a cruel thing to say,' Clare said.

'The world is full of the deserving, and then that mongrel goes and wins a fortune. Where's the justice in that?'

'All of the brothers were offered a substantial cash payment. Did you accept yours, Mr Winters?'

'Dean did not,' his wife said.

'Why not? Surely you could do with the money?' Clare said.

'It is the result of gambling. It would be a sin to accept it.'

'You'd rather hold to your beliefs than accept the money?'

'God will remember us on the day of judgement.'

'Mrs Winters, you hated the Winters, especially Alan for his wealth,' Tremayne said. 'Was it enough to want the man dead? Not that you would have benefited financially, but spiritually you may have believed that you were doing God's work, and Stonehenge may have been another blow to those who hold different beliefs.'

Barbara Winters was up on her feet; Dean Winters stayed seated. Clare could see that he was enjoying the spectacle. 'That's slanderous. I'll sue you for everything you've got. I've no doubt your superiors will take action once I contact them.'

'Mrs Winters, my superiors will do nothing. You've shown your hatred for the Winters, your abhorrence of the money they have, ill-gotten according to you. Someone murdered Alan Winters, and all those who may be suspect will be subjected to rigorous questioning. I repeat yet again – did you murder Alan Winters?'

'Leave my house this instant.'

'We are leaving, but we will intensify our checks into you. A person who refuses to accept a substantial cash payment with no obligations must have some issues. You must now be a prime suspect. Mr Winters, did you assist your wife?'

'Not with Alan.'

'Why not?'

'He was my family. I cared for him, the same as the others. We all suffered as children in that house. It's a bond that cannot be broken. My wife doesn't understand.'

'You bastard,' Barbara Winters said.

'For once in your goddamn life, woman, just shut up.' It was the first time that Dean Winters had spoken to his wife in such a manner. He had to admit it felt good.

***

'You were tough in there,' Clare said on the drive back to Salisbury. As usual, she was in the driver's seat.

'We need to break through these people, push them to the limit. Barbara Winters is a clever woman, careful in what she says, how she says it. The only way she'll speak the truth is when she's angered,' Tremayne said.

'Did you break through?'

'Not totally. The woman shows her hatred well enough, her prejudices as well, but this not accepting the money still seems bizarre. Who could resist that much money?'

'Some people believe strongly in the concept of right and wrong. Let's accept her at face value.'

'And then what? Are you saying that she's innocent of all crimes?'

'Not at all. You were on the right track there. A lingering hatred, the confusion between how the meek shall inherit the earth, better a sinner repented, that sort of thing, and then one of the fallen had hit the jackpot, while she, no doubt devout, has won nothing, apart from a subservient husband. Mind you, he cheered up at the end, told her to shut up.'

'It'll be fun in that house for a while. What do you think happened after we left?'

'Fireworks. I'm not sure who would have got the better of the situation.'

'My money is on the wife.'

'Where are we heading?' Clare asked as they crested the hill on the A36, the sight of Salisbury Cathedral spire in the distance.

'Liz Maybury.'

'Why?'

'We've not spoken to her since her time in the hospital, apart from a gentle questioning. We know Polly Bennett's account as to what happened, but not hers.'

'She said it was an accident, so did Liz Maybury. And now Mavis Winters is letting them stay where they are. They'll not be truthful.'

'I know that, but let's see.'

The furniture store was again open, some cars parked outside. Inside, Polly Bennett was near the cash register, making phone calls. On the floor, Liz Maybury was attempting to entice a couple into buying a coffee table.

'Inspector Tremayne, we never expected to see you in here,' Polly said as the two police officers entered.

'How's Miss Maybury?'

'Liz, she's fine. Her memory of that day is a little hazy, but apart from that, there she is, selling away. She's a good talker.'

'You and Mavis Winters?'

'There's a legal agreement in place. It's not as good as what Alan promised us, but we'll go along with it. And besides, we both like to work.'

'You could have done that all along, instead of sleeping with Winters,' Clare said.

'We're not perfect, none of us is.'

'Why run this place when you could find another man?'

'Sergeant Yarwood, I'm a pragmatist, so is Liz. If a man is there, we'll take advantage. In the interim, we'll survive.'

'You're still looking?'

'Always.'

'Anyone else in Salisbury that interests you?'

'Gerry Winters would if he had the money.'

'That's unlikely.'

'It depends on whether he latches onto Mavis or not.'

'Why are you telling us this?'

'I'm testing you. You still don't trust Liz and me. You see us as lesbians, witches practising satanic rituals, breaking the golden egg on a golden altar at Stonehenge.'

'It's plausible,' Tremayne said.

'That's why I said it. I'm not a dummy, neither is Liz. If I can come up with it, so can you.'

'Tell me,' Clare said. 'Now that you don't have Alan Winters, what are you doing for a man. Surely you need someone in your bed.'

'The same as you without Harry Holchester, lots of cold showers.'

Clare realised that she had not thought about him for several weeks, even after driving past his old pub. She knew that she would visit his grave in the next few days; this time she would not go with Tremayne.

Tremayne and Clare moved away from the cash register; the interested couple had been swayed by Liz Maybury's eloquent sales pitch. Clare did not like the coffee table, could not see it fitting in with her decor at her cottage, although there was a bookcase that she liked, the price was reasonable, and she knew they'd give her a discount. She couldn't see any conflict of interest; she'd check with Tremayne first, register that she had had financial dealings with the two women in case it came up in a subsequent trial.

'Inspector Tremayne, Sergeant Yarwood, pleased to see you. It's worked out fine as you can see,' Liz Maybury said as she approached them.

'Unexpected,' Clare said.

'It wasn't what we expected, but we're pleased.'

'How are you?' Tremayne asked.

'I'm fine, the occasional dizzy spell, but apart from that I just carry on as normal. You've been speaking to Polly.'

'She says that Mavis Winters has been pleasant.'

'She has. We like the woman. She knows the way of the world.'

'It was her husband you were sleeping with.'

'We've done nothing wrong except being foolish. It's not so easy when there is that much money around. Mavis said that she had known Inspector Tremayne for many years.'

'We've known each other since she was in her teens.'

'Boyfriend, girlfriend,' Liz said.

Clare could see Tremayne blushing. 'Not at all,' he said. 'We lived not far from each other. We used to talk occasionally. I understand that Polly's mum was friendly with Mavis Winters.'

'She was. I'm not sure if they still are.'

'How about you?'

'I came here from Bristol, following a boyfriend.'

'And what happened to him?'

'He fell by the wayside.'

'Not enough money?'

'He had some, enough for me, but he wasn't ambitious, I am. He's still around. I see him occasionally, but he's pushing a buggy with two children in it, a pregnant wife at his side, and no doubt a mortgage. I could have had that, didn't want it.'

'And now, what does the future hold for you and Polly?'

'We'll run the shop, find ourselves a couple of men. Nothing firm, just ideas.'

'Alan Winters is being buried this weekend. Will you be going?'

'Not us. I don't think we'll be welcome. We may watch from a distance. Will you be going?'

'We'll both be there.'

'Ex-boyfriends of the deceased's wife excepted.'

'As I said, Miss Maybury, we were friends. I also knew Alan from back then, as well.'

Outside the shop, Tremayne lit a cigarette. 'What did you reckon, Yarwood?'

'There's no question in my mind as to their relationship.'

'Lesbian?'

'Probably bisexual, but yes, the two of them are not lonely in their beds; they've got each other.'

'Capable of murder?'

'Without a doubt. They could have engineered all of this, but it seems unlikely.'

'What do you mean? Forcing Mavis Winters to hand over the shop to them?'

'Only if they have some dirt on her.'

'Would they?'

'Who knows? Alan Winters in bed with those two would talk. Who knows what he could have said.'

'It's an angle worth exploring, Check it out, Yarwood. Let's go back to the station,' Tremayne said. 'You're driving.'

Chapter 11

Clare had not been inside a prison before, a situation for which she was thankful. She felt that Pentonville, C Wing, was not conducive to the rehabilitation of a criminal, only a means of removing a man from society for the allotted period of time deemed necessary by judge and jury.

Clare had driven. They had had an early start, and she had picked up Tremayne from Bemerton Road Police Station at seven in the morning.

'We'll see Stan today, Fred tomorrow,' he said. Tremayne had a newspaper with him, as well as a form guide.

'Stan and Fred Winters, character witnesses?'

'We need some background on the suspects.'

'Do we have any? None of them has any record of violence.'

'Gerry Winters does. That's why we're seeing Stan and Fred, to see if any of the others are capable. They can't have been involved, the perfect alibi.'

'In prison courtesy of Her Majesty.'

'That's it, although I suppose she doesn't come to visit them too often.'

Stan Winters, forty-one years of age, and a man whom Tremayne had known for over thirty years. 'Tremayne, what are you doing here?' Winters said when they met.

'They told you we were coming?'

'They did. You can't pin Alan's death on me.'

Separated by a table, Clare and Tremayne sat on one side, Stan Winters on the other. The man was not deemed violent, the reason they were allowed to be in such close proximity. In one corner, a prison officer. Both Clare and Tremayne had shaken the man's hand on entering, Clare noticing that he held onto her hand for longer than Tremayne's, even pulling her in closer. She realised that it must be hard for a man in his forties to be denied female company. It had made her uncomfortable, but she said nothing.

'We realise you're not involved, but we still need to find a murderer. Whoever killed Alan could kill again.'

'He was harmless. Apart from the money, that is. Not that it did me much good, and he refused to fund my appeal.'

'I've read your case file. You and two others were caught red-handed, and you've only got just over a year to go.'

Clare could see that the man was not pleased to be in prison, but that was understandable. She knew she would not have lasted there for long, as the place was functional but austere. As they had walked through the prison gates, and through the intervening secured doors, she had not seen any warmth in the surroundings. The building was spotless, she'd accede to that. It reminded her of a public toilet, the old-fashioned type with its porcelain implements, the brass pipes, the white tiles on the floors and the walls.

Stan Winters, a similar height to Gerry Winters, was physically impressive. It was apparent that he worked out in the prison gym. The tattoos on his arms and neck looked crude, prison style. Even so, he retained some politeness, especially towards her. With Tremayne, he was blunt. Tremayne had told her that it had been necessary to be tough, or seen to be tough, in the area where Winters had grown up, or else you were likely to find yourself face down in the mud.

'One of your police officers lied at the trial, that's all I'm saying. The man they claimed that one of us had hit, it wasn't true. He slipped and fell.'

'Stan, let it go. You can plead your innocence with me all you like, but I'll not buy it. Yarwood may, but she's willing to listen to any hard luck story. You were a hooligan as a child; you've not changed.'

Winters sat still, looking at Tremayne, glancing at Clare. She was pleased that she had worn a heavy jacket, buttoned up to the neck.

'Tremayne, you're a bastard, always were,' Winters said. 'What do you want to know?'

'Alan's murdered at Stonehenge. If anyone's after his money, then why there? And what's the point? The money goes to Mavis and then her children.'

'You're the police officer, not me.'

'It's their backgrounds we need to understand. We know that Mavis can be tough, Bertie, the son, is incapable, and Rachel, the daughter, does not appear to be interested.'

'What about Cyril and Gerry?'

'They're your brothers.'

'I'll tell you what you want to know. Not because I need to, but I'm glad of someone to talk to, other than the prison officers and the other prisoners.'

Tremayne knew that what he meant was that he was glad that Yarwood was with him.

'Give us a rundown of your family.'

'Cyril, lazy, Gerry, could be violent, not ambitious though. Dean, you've met?'

'And his wife.'

'I was there that day we went down the pub with her.'

'She mentioned it.'

'And what was her recollection?'

'Mushy peas, soggy chips, and a limp piece of undercooked fish.'

'The woman had us saying prayers, holding hands, before we ate. And it wasn't what she described. It was good pub food.' Tremayne knew what the man meant, having enjoyed a meal in a pub on many occasions.

'So why did she lie to us?'

'She didn't lie. That's how she sees us, the trash of society. If it were up to her, she'd have us all sterilised, let us die out. Poor old Dean, all that education, and what happens to him: henpecked, doing what he's told.'

'Instead of being in Pentonville,' Clare said.

Stan Winters laughed. 'You've got a sense of humour,' he said. 'At least I'll be free at some stage, he won't be.'

'Completely under the thumb?' Tremayne said.

'Completely. If she tells him to jump, he jumps.'

'If she tells him to kill Alan for whatever reason?'

'Hold on, Tremayne, don't go putting words in my mouth. Murder, that's serious. Just because Dean does what he's told, doesn't mean he'd be capable of murder.'

'Anyone in your family capable?'

'Fred can be violent, but killing someone is different, and why Alan? The man had the money, and he was generous.'

'But he wouldn't fund your appeal.'

'He still made sure I had a hundred thousand pounds.'

'You've still got it?'

'Yes. It's invested with the bank, not that they pay much in the way of interest. They lock you up for robbing a building society of a few thousand pounds, and they're ripping us off for billions. There's no justice in the world.'

'Life isn't fair. If it were, I'd be a superintendent, and you wouldn't have been caught.'

'Mr Winters, does anyone visit you here?' Clare said.

'Dean comes occasionally.'

'His wife?'

'Not her; she probably sits in the car, but she'd not come in here.'

'Anyone else?'

'Alan used to come occasionally, as did Gerry. Even Mavis.'

'Why did Mavis come?' Tremayne said.

'She's a decent person, you know that. You were friendly with her once. She's single now, maybe you two could get together again?'

'Everyone seems to know about us,' Tremayne said.

'I was just a kid, peering through cracks in windows. Don't worry, your secret is safe with me. And you were a decent man back then. You could have rounded us up. Why didn't you?'

'I'd grown up in a similar neighbourhood, played up the same as you had.'

'What happened?'

'I grew up, became a police officer.'

'And I became a criminal.'

'The dice rolls in the direction you want,' Tremayne said. 'And besides, you've not answered my question: why Stonehenge?'

'No one in my family would have done it. Dean's wife, she's crazy enough, but she'd not get Dean to do that. Anything else, but not murdering his own brother.'

'He refused to accept the one hundred thousand pounds.'

'He told me on one of his visits. I told him that he was mad. It got quite heated.'

'What happened after that?'

'He must have told her. I didn't see him for a few months after that.'

'She told him not to come?'

'Dean's a good brother, straight as they come, no petty crime with him. And yes, it was her. If you want someone mad, she's the person.'

'These women that Alan was messing around with?'

'I told him not to upset Mavis, but what's a man to do? These women are throwing themselves at him. How could he refuse?'

'Would you have?' Clare asked.

'Sergeant, we're not perfect, the flesh is weak. If I had won that lottery, I'd have been into the women and the good life, the same as everyone else.'

'If Dean had won?'

'She'd have given it to charity or refused to accept it.'

'Would she?'

'Ask her. Everyone's got a price, what's hers? Focus on that stupid woman, not my family.'

'We've seen Margie,' Clare said.

'Still the same?'

'Yes.'

'Even Alan with his money couldn't help her.'

'I can remember her as a child,' Tremayne said.

'Pretty little thing back then, not so pretty now.'

'Has she been here to visit?'

'Never. Mind you, I'd prefer her not to come.'

'Why?' Clare asked.

'You've seen this place. It's hardly a resort. I stay afloat, we all do, by focussing on when we get out, our first beer, our first woman. Sorry, Sergeant.'

'No need to apologise.'

'I maintain positive thoughts in here. I deal with the daydream, not the reality.'

'And Margie is the reality?' Tremayne said.

'You'll go away from here, distracted by other things. For me, I'll be thinking about her for days.'

'Sorry about that,' Clare said.

'It's fine. It's good to see friendly faces, even you, Tremayne.'

'The funeral is this weekend.'

'I've made a special request to attend.'

'Will it be granted?'

'They'll only agree to the church service, not the wake afterwards, and then I'll be with a police officer, probably handcuffs.'

'I'll see what I can do,' Tremayne said.

'No handcuffs, the prison officer in civilian clothes.'

'We'll deal with it.'

'I trust you, Tremayne. And find out who killed Alan.'

***

Some things can't be predicted in every murder investigation, even Clare knew that. On the drive back from London and Pentonville, a phone call to Tremayne.

'Put your foot down, Yarwood,' Tremayne said on ending the call.

'Another death?'

'Not this time.'

'Who?'

'Rachel Winters.'

'Why her?'

'How the hell should I know? Supposedly, she's been in a car accident. She's in the hospital.'

'Serious?'

'According to Mavis, it's not.'

Clare accelerated up past the speed limit, even for the motorway they took to get back to Salisbury. Tremayne leant over and switched on the grille mounted flashing lights. The just over two-hour trip reduced to one hour and forty minutes. At the hospital, out on Odstock Road, Clare parked next to the A & E. Inside they found Mavis with Gerry.

Mavis gave Tremayne a warm hug. 'Thanks for coming,' she said.

'How's Rachel?'

'She'll be fine. She's suffering shock, a bad concussion, but apart from that, nothing.'

'Do you know any of the details?'

'You saw the car as you drove up here?' Mavis said.

'By the side of the road. It looks totalled.'

'She was hit on the side by another car.'

'The driver?'

'The vehicle took off. That's all we know. Rachel's resting now. We can talk to her in a couple of hours' time.'

'We'll wait,' Clare said.

The four of them walked to a cafeteria and sat down. Mavis excused herself and went and organised a coffee for everyone. After driving faster than usual for an extended period, Clare would have appreciated a few minutes to close her eyes, but that was not going to be possible.

'What has Rachel said?' Tremayne asked as he sipped his coffee.

'According to her, she was driving home, only slowly, when a car pulled out to overtake and slammed into her on the driver's side.'

'Have you experienced this sort of thing before?'

'When Alan first won the money. Everyone thought they were entitled to a handout, some became aggressive. We had to hire a security firm to protect us for a few months. After that, Gerry has dealt with security, hired a few casuals as we needed them.'

'Is there any question that this was anything other than an accident?' Clare said.

'It's suspicious, but we've had no trouble for some time. And why Rachel? I'm the one controlling the money.'

'We've been to see Stan,' Tremayne said.

'How is he?'

'He's fine. Upset to be in prison.'

'He did the crime,' Gerry Winters said.

'It's still tough.'

'He'll be out soon, good behaviour.'

'How about Fred?' Tremayne said. 'We've not seen him yet.'

'We're not looking forward to his release,' Mavis said.

'Why?'

'You knew Fred. He's more aggressive. He'll cause trouble unless I pay him off.'

'Will you?'

'If it's necessary. I don't want him around the house all the time, or around the city, bad-mouthing us.'

'Would he? I thought you were a close-knit family. Stan said you were.'

'Close-knit if we're threatened, but there's bickering behind the scenes, you know that.'

Tremayne could see Gerry causing trouble. He had just heard Mavis offering to pay off his brother, Fred, and all he had was a salary and a hundred thousand pounds.

Two cups of coffee later, all four were back at A&E. A doctor came over, spoke to Mavis. 'It's okay. We can go in.'

'I'll go in with Yarwood later. We'll need a statement,' Tremayne said.

'Then you can go first. I'll be staying the night here, as will Gerry.'

'Very well.'

The two police officers found Rachel propped up in bed, a bandage around her head, another around her right wrist. 'I'm fine, just a little dazed,' she said.

Clare compared it to where they had met Rachel's uncle. There it had been cold and austere, here it was warm and inviting. In one corner of the room stood a vase containing flowers. Upon the wall, a flat-screen television. There was even a view out of the window. Stan's view, even in the prison yard, was of a brick wall.

'Do you remember the accident?' Clare asked.

'I think it was intentional.'

'Why?'

'I've driven down that road many times. There's plenty of room to overtake, and it was a clear day.'

'Did you see the car?'

'It was blue.'

'Any idea as to the make?'

'It was so quick, and no. I'm not interested in cars, not like Dad who was out buying anything he could. I'd know a Bentley, we've got one of those, but apart from that, it was large and blue.'

'If we showed you some pictures?'

'Maybe, but don't hold out much hope.'

'If it was intentional, any reason why?'

'Not with me. There are some crazy people out there, I know that. Maybe it was someone who was jealous of our good fortune.'

'Do you sometimes experience that?'

'Sometimes, but they are mostly harmless.'

'Did you see the driver?'

'Nothing. The car was bigger than mine, maybe it was a four-wheel drive. Apart from that nothing, sorry. Is Mum here?'

'She's outside with your uncle.'

'Could you ask her to come in. She'll only worry.'

Chapter 12

Dean Winters sat at the table in the kitchen of his and his wife's perfect house in Southampton. His wife was standing up. 'You've let that malignant family of yours rule your life. What did they ever give you?' she said.

Dean Winters knew he was hen-pecked; he didn't know why he tolerated the situation. He knew that his situation was intolerable. If he could speak to Mavis, instruct her to give him the hundred thousand pounds, then he could plot his way out to freedom.

'And then you want to visit your brothers in prison. What have I been doing all these years? I've been making a better man of you, haven't I?' No reply from her husband. '*Haven't I?*' she said with emphasis.

'Yes, dear.'

'And what thanks do I get? I'll tell you, nothing. And then all you can talk about is that whore of a sister.'

'She's my family. We stuck together as children, we'll stick together now.'

'Don't give me that story about how you were neglected, how you starved, what a bitch your mother was. I've met her; she is a bitch, but you're a man now. Stand up and be counted.'

'You'll never understand. You with your perfect childhood, your perfect family. Didn't your father ever make a fool of himself, chase your mother's friends after a few drinks?'

'He never drank in his life. It would be a sin against the Lord.'

'It's Alan's funeral this weekend. I expect you to attend.'

'I'll be there. I will do my duty. And don't expect to get drunk afterwards.'

Winters sat silently; there was no more to be said, no more that would serve any purpose. He knew why he had married her. He was a weak man who needed a strong woman. For the first few years of their marriage, it had been gentle encouragement coupled with love; now it was with force, and her approach was of anger and hatred towards him. They had started sleeping in separate beds a year before, her idea, and whereas he had agreed, he was still a young man. If only it had been him who had purchased that lottery ticket instead of Alan. What fun he could have had. But then Alan had died, and he was still alive. He wasn't sure if he was the lucky one, or his brother.

'Are you going to sit there all day? There's work to do.' A jolt of reality from the other side of the room. Dean Winters raised himself from his chair, taking care to push the chair back in position, conscious of the need to maintain a parallel spacing to the chair on its left-hand side, alignment with the chair on the other side. He walked away and headed off for whatever it was she wanted him to do.

One of these days, I will strike back, he thought. He knew it would not be today.

***

An all-points had been issued for the car that had struck Rachel Winters' vehicle, not that anyone thought that anything would come of it, although if the damage were appreciable, then the other vehicle would be lodging an insurance claim. Clare, once she had left Salisbury Hospital, and after she had deposited Tremayne at Bemerton Road, struck out on her own for Avon Hill. 'I've got to go,' she said to Tremayne.

'Do you want me to go with you?' Tremayne offered.

'It's personal, I'll be alright.'

Tremayne wasn't so sure, but she was a grown woman, a seasoned police officer. He had no option but to comply. 'Give me a call if it becomes too much.'

'Two hours, and I'll be back.'

'I'll send out the troops to look for you if you don't return,' Tremayne said in an attempt at levity. He could see it was not well received.

Inside the station, the ominous presence of Superintendent Moulton. 'Have you wrapped up that case?' he said.

'I thought you were going to talk about the other matter.'

'Not every time. Sometimes I like to follow up on a case, check how my people are.'

'I'm fine. Yarwood went out to visit Harry Holchester's grave.'

'Will she be alright?'

'She'll be fine. No doubt she won't be too cheerful when she returns, but under the circumstances she's handled Salisbury better than I expected. I never thought she'd come back.'

'Any leads on who killed Alan Winters?'

'There are some with motives, but so far not an arrest. His funeral's this weekend. I'll be attending, along with Yarwood.'

'As representatives of the police?'

'Not me. I've known the family for a long time.'

'You'll be keeping an eye out?'

'Never off duty, you know that. There's some tension behind the scenes. Whether it's enough to murder the man with the money is to be seen.'

'Keep me posted.'

Tremayne phoned Jim Hughes, the crime scene examiner, a friend. 'The two who carried Winters' body from the road up to Stonehenge, male or female?'

'Either. Adidas trainers, nothing special. You can purchase them in a dozen shops in Salisbury alone.'

'Size?'

'It's in my report.'

'I'm sounding you out. Yarwood's not here.'

'You're feeling lonely, is that it?'

'Not you as well. I get enough from Yarwood. She's becoming good at the smart comment.'

'She's had a good teacher. Anyway, Adidas trainers. The grass was wet up there, muddy in places, so the sizing is not precise. But female is a definite possibility. It'd still require a certain amount of strength. Don't go looking for a couple of weaklings.'

'Thanks. Any more on the weapon?'

'In my report. Nothing special, just a very sharp kitchen knife. We've got one at home that could cut a throat. I nearly sliced the top of my finger off with it the other day.'

Tremayne opened his laptop, saw a few emails, a reminder of overdue reports. He checked the emails, one or two needed answering; the others included the usual reminders. Also, there was to be a change in administrative procedures. Not again, he thought. Another email to let all staff know that entry to the building would be by fingerprint recognition instead of a magnetic security card, with a transition period of fourteen days. If it was as good as the fingerprint recognition on his laptop, Tremayne thought, then it was going to be a disaster. He had been content when there was a key to the building, a person in reception, a book to sign in and out.

Two hours to the minute, Clare walked back into the office. Tremayne felt as if he wanted to put his arm around her, give her a reassuring hug, but did not. 'I'm fine,' she said. 'It was a nice day down there. I put some flowers, said some words and came back here.'

'I'm glad that you're back. We've got to put the lid on this case, or Moulton will be after me again.'

'He's been here?'

'Remarkably pleasant.'

'I've told you that he's a decent man.'

'I know that. It's just that he keeps going on about my retirement.'

'What does Jean want you to do?'

'If we get together again, she'll want to take trips here and there, but apart from that, she'll not be demanding. We're past the young and silly stage.'

'And I'm not?'

'You're not the cloistered nun type. You need to find yourself another man.'

'They're not so easy to find. Most of them want to buy you a meal and then back to their place.'

'That's not your style.'

'Harry was my style, and that didn't turn out too good.'

'It's like riding a bike; you've got to get back on it again.'

'I will. Anyway, my love life is not what we're here for, is it?'

Both of the police officers helped themselves to coffee.

'Jim Hughes reckons it could possibly have been two females up at Stonehenge,' Tremayne said.

'Polly Bennett and Liz Maybury?'

'What do we know about them?'

'I would have thought we knew plenty,' Clare said.

'List them.'

'Promiscuous, competent businesswomen, ambitious, not afraid of hard work, probably bisexual.'

'Is that it?'

'But why kill Alan Winters?'

'Maybe he was about to dispense with them, get some others.'

'The man was making up for lost time. All his life he had been poor, unable to get a woman, except for Mavis,' Clare said.

'She was a good catch when she was younger.'

'I didn't mean that. She's still a good catch. If it doesn't work out with Jean…'

'Don't go there, Yarwood. Stay focussed on the murder. Alan Winters dies on a slab of stone at Stonehenge. Who would benefit?'

'I just don't see how the two women would benefit unless they had an agreement with Mavis in place.'

'Or Gerry?'

'But why Gerry? The man's got no money, and there's no way that he'd convince Mavis to part with a share of hers.'

'Why? He reckoned he was entitled to a half-share, and that it was Alan who was refusing due to Mavis. What if Alan would have reconsidered without Mavis?'

'Then why didn't they kill Mavis? She'd be the easier solution, and then, if she weren't around, Alan would have been looking for a shoulder to cry on.'

'Or two shoulders?'

'It's a complicated plan. It could have backfired.'

'If Liz Maybury had not hit that wall, then the two women would have ended up with nothing, and Gerry's no closer to the money.'

'I don't like it. Too many uncertainties; too easy to fail.'

'I'll leave it to you, woman to woman, maybe find out where they're having a drink of an evening. See if you can slip under their guard.'

'What about Dean and Barbara Winters?' Clare said.

'Now there's a woman that's easy to read.'

'What do you mean?'

'How do you sum her up?'

'Aggressive, biased, a snob, a nagger, and someone who detests the Winters, even her husband probably.'

'Then why marry him?'

'She wanted her ideal husband. She knew she wouldn't find anyone the normal way, so she decided to create her own.'

'She's done a good job.'

'Not totally. There's still some bite in the man.'

'More a gnawing. He's just about worn down.'

***

Clare had to admit that her initial impression of Stan Winters had been wrong, and that, apart from his being a criminal, he was agreeable. The same could not be said for Fred, the oldest of Betty Winters' seven children.

'Tremayne, what do you want? Haven't you caused enough trouble?' Fred Winters said on entering the interview room at the prison. Clare could tell from his bearing that he was a man who intimidated, a man who had a history of violence.

Tremayne had warned her that the reception from Fred, closer in age to him than the other Winters' children, would not be good. Fred Winters, taller than average, though not as tall as Clare, not as tall as Tremayne, bore the marks of prison life: the tattooed knuckles on both hands – love, hate – as well as tattoos on his arms. His sleeves were rolled up, indicative of the warmth in the room.

'Fred, you know the drill,' Tremayne said. 'Your brother's been murdered. It's up to us to conduct interviews, investigate, arrest the person or persons responsible.'

'Alan, he may have been my brother, but he was a fool.'

'Why?'

'Look here, Tremayne, you were a pain in the rear end when you lived near to us, and you still are.'

'Still smarting over that hiding I gave you, is that it?'

Clare looked over at Tremayne, not sure what he meant.

'I caught Fred vandalising a car once. I laid him flat on his back, gave him a black eye and a sore head.'

'You wouldn't do it again. From what I can see, you're past it.'

'I may be, but I didn't arrest you back then, did I?'

'Okay, Tremayne. We'll declare a truce. I don't forget people who've wronged me, but you treated us fair. We were troublemakers, still are, especially Alan. That man could upset people.'

'What do you mean?'

'He had a mouth as a youth, always shouting off, accusing someone of being gay, queer back then.'

'Kept his distance when he was hurling insults,' Tremayne said.

'His only defence. He wasn't the toughest kid, although he tried to pretend he was. He got a few smacks from me.'

'You were violent back then, still are.'

'I make no bones about it. I'm a hard case, always will be, and in here, no one gives me aggravation.'

'This is Sergeant Yarwood, by the way.'

'Pleased to meet you. Gerry said you were a looker. He wasn't wrong.'

'Yarwood is a serving police officer,' Tremayne reminded him.

'No disrespect, Sergeant. It's not often I get to see a woman these days. I just said it as it is.'

'No offence was taken,' Clare said.

'Gerry has been here?' Tremayne said.

'And Mavis.'

'Is that unusual?'

'Not really. Gerry sometimes comes, and Mavis occasionally. She's a good woman, better than Alan deserved.'

'What did they speak about?'

'Alan's death initially. It came as a shock to all of us, or his murder did. Alan was always an idiot. If he had died at the wheel of a car, then I would have taken it in my stride, but murder, and up at Stonehenge, I can't go for that.'

'What do you mean?'

'It makes no sense. I know that he was showing off, and supposedly he was messing around with a couple of tarts.'

'We know who they are.'

'If it had been you who had won the lottery?' Clare said.

'No tarts, just one woman. And as for showing off, it doesn't interest me.'

'You'd not follow in your brother's footsteps?'

'I'd have kept the win secret, and if I couldn't, I'd have bought myself a place in the country, settled down, even farmed the land.'

'I never knew that about you,' Tremayne said.

'Nor did I. In here they have a farm, or at least a few acres. There are chickens, a few pigs, a chance to grow vegetables.'

'And you're there?'

'Every day. There wasn't much chance where we grew up, although in Salisbury we were never far from the countryside. Now, all I want is the chance to farm.'

'If you had money?'

'That's why Mavis was here. She's worried that I'm going to cause trouble when I get out.'

'Are you?'

'A lousy one hundred thousand. Of course I am. The Winters' family, or the children, look out for each other, always have, always will. Mavis's idea of money is not mine. Alan would have given each of us a couple of million. He'd have still had plenty left.'

'Is that what you want?'

'I've thought it through. I want two million, plus another three as a loan. I've done the sums, I know it's viable. I'm not looking for charity, I only want what is mine.'

'Is it?'

'Alan would have eventually agreed. Mavis is reluctant.'

'Do you blame her?'

'No, but she came from a decent family, we didn't.'

'Your father, any idea where he is? He'd have to be in his eighties.'

'Dead I hope.'

'And your mother?'

'Dead are far as I'm concerned.'

'We've met Margie, interviewed your mother.'

'My mother can go to hell, Margie is important.'

'She's not in a good way,' Clare said.

'That's what I've been told. Mavis, I know, makes sure she is safe, and that she has food and medicine.'

'You have a lot of respect for Mavis?'

'A lot, apart from her wanting to hang on to the money. She'll look after the family better than Alan ever did. He was a brainless fool, Mavis isn't, you know that.'

'I do.'

'She was keen on you once,' Fred Winters said, 'before you became old and grey.'

'Still good enough to give you a hiding,' Tremayne said.

Clare could see a grudging respect between the two men: one a criminal, the other an officer of the law. There was a history between them that the years had not destroyed.

'Your brother's funeral, will you be attending?' Clare said.

'I would have liked to, but they'll not let me out.'

'Any reason, anything I can do? Tremayne said.

'I lost my temper with another prisoner, a lifer. He walked on my vegetable patch, thought he was smart, although he probably fancied a few days in the prison hospital.'

'What happened?'

'I gave him his few days.'

'Any increase in sentence, restrictions placed on you?'

'None. The warden, he's not a bad man, he knew what had happened, and besides, some of the vegetables were for him. Anyway, they'll not let me out, classified as violent.'

'Are you?' Clare said.

'I defend my own. But yes, I'm violent. Not drunken violent, but if anyone gets in my way, I'll push through or punch. Not many can stop me. Only Tremayne when he was younger. Now he looks as if he'll struggle to get out of his chair.'

'You're not looking so great,' Tremayne replied.

'Whatever you do, look out for Margie. There's not much hope for her, but we all try.'

'Mavis will do the right thing,' Clare said.

'You like the woman?' Fred said.

'Yes, I do. Very much, actually.'

'I know she's worried about when I get out, they all are, but it'll be fine. With Alan gone, we'll come to an agreement.'

'Your brother Dean?'

'You've met his wife?'

'Unfortunately.'

'If she had the money, nobody would get anything.'

'She portrays herself as charitable.'

'Her, she's a bitch. She hates us, we hate her. It's mutual. Watch out for her. If there's an opportunity, she'll take it.'

'And your brother?'

'Poor Dean, the smartest in the family, now under her control. I doubt if he can go to the toilet without her permission. I nearly said that in the vernacular.'

'What stopped you?' Tremayne said.

'Lady present.'

'I've heard it all, no doubt said it myself occasionally,' Clare said.

'Still, I must show some respect. Next time you can come on your own, don't bring Tremayne. I've seen his ugly face enough times,' Fred Winters said, a grin on his face.

Chapter 13

Clare had not been to many funerals: just her grandmother's and a school friend who had died in a car accident. Tremayne had been to too many.

Neither expected the horse-drawn hearse, the funeral director and his assistant dressed in top hat and tails. In the street the police had erected barriers. It wasn't often that the county's wealthiest inhabitant was buried, having been murdered.

Tremayne knew that it would be magazine fodder within a week. The life story of an unremarkable man who by chance had become wealthy beyond belief, dead before his time, the victim of murder by persons unknown. He knew of the speculation: some wild and crazy, some logical.

Inside the church, Mavis sat at the front with her two children: Rachel, a bandage still on her arm, and Bertie, neatly-dressed, clean-shaven, and in a suit. Further back, Gerry and Cyril Winters. Alan Winters' mother sat next to Mavis at the front, the two women pretending to be united in sorrow, but Clare noticed the space, small though it was, that separated them. In the same pew, Stan Winters and Margie, his arm around her. And in that church she seemed at ease, although her look was vacant and she did not appear to want to speak, only nodded her head if someone talked to her. In another pew, Dean Winters and his wife. Clare had noticed him speaking to his family on arrival, saw that his wife had ignored them.

'Thanks, Tremayne,' Stan Winters had said on his arrival at the church. The man had reason to be thankful. Tremayne had received special authority to take responsibility for the convicted felon during the funeral and afterwards at the wake. A prison officer, outside and in plain clothes, would wait in his car to ensure that procedures were followed. After the evening had concluded, he would drive Stan back to prison.

'If you stuff up, it's my head.'

'I won't. You've done right by me, I'll do right by you,' Winters said. He was wearing a suit as well, new by the look of it, supplied by Mavis.

At the appropriate time, the coffin was brought into the church. Six men supported it on their shoulders: Bertie as the deceased's son at the front, as well as Cyril, Gerry, Stan and Dean. The funeral director completed the six, maintaining equilibrium as the other five men swayed under the weight of the coffin.

Clare could see the tears in Mavis's eyes, even had them in hers and she had never met the man. Alan Winters' mother held a handkerchief too, as did Margie. Barbara Winters looked impassively forward in silent prayer. Clare knew that she wanted her to be the guilty person in the murder, not because she thought she was, but because she did not like her.

She imagined the funeral was similar to Harry's although she did not know. His relatives had offered to send her some photos, but she had declined.

The coffin arrived at the front of the church and was placed on a trestle, sombre music echoing throughout the church. The men resumed their seats. A few words from Barbara Winters to her husband; derisory, Clare assumed.

Clare turned around, could see that Polly Bennett and Liz Maybury had slipped in by a side door, their presence unobtrusive. She had known they would be present, a special dispensation from Mavis Winters. 'They wanted to come. It shows some decency on their part,' Mavis had said when Clare had asked her why.

Rachel gave a reading from the Bible, Stan said a few words, as did the other men in turn. Mavis did not move from her seat. She kept looking at Margie, checking she was alright. Alan Winters' mother did not acknowledge anyone other than Mavis. She continued to look forward or at the coffin. At the conclusion of the ceremony, the coffin left, the entourage following, the Bentley at the front, the other cars, three Rolls Royces, following behind. Tremayne drove with Stan, Clare stayed back at the church.

Tremayne, not immediate family, would not enter the crematorium, where a few more words would be said before the coffin passed through some curtains on its way to the cremation of the body. Tremayne had only joined the entourage as part of the requirement to keep Stan Winters in his sight at all times.

Once free of the crematorium, Tremayne drove back to the Winters' house.

'Thanks, Tremayne. I'll not let you down,' Stan Winters said yet again.

'That's why you're here.'

At the house, there was security at the front gate. Tremayne drove straight through. A catering company's van was parked to one side of the driveway; the other cars parked one behind the other. Clare, Tremayne could see, had arrived and was talking to the prison officer assigned to look after Stan Winters.

'Prison Officer Dennis Marshall,' he said. Not that the introduction was necessary as Tremayne and the officer had signed the papers earlier in the day at Bemerton Road agreeing to Tremayne accepting responsibility.

'We'll make sure to get you some food and drink,' Tremayne said.

'Thanks. I'll be back within an hour.'

'Don't worry about me,' Stan said. 'I'll do nothing wrong.'

'Just following orders, you know that.'

'So is Tremayne. I've known the man since my teens, a family friend. If you don't mind driving someone who's drunk some alcohol back to Pentonville.'

'That's fine, not that I'll be drinking.'

Dennis Marshall got into his car and drove off down the road. 'He's got an aunt who lives not far from here. He's gone to see her,' Clare said.

'He seemed a decent man.'

'He is. It appears that he and Stan Winters get on well enough in Pentonville. That was why he volunteered to bring him down here today.'

Stan Winters left the two police officers and went inside.

'Any observations?' Tremayne said.

'Nothing especially. The two women were at the church.'

'Are they here?'

'No. Mavis wouldn't allow them, and besides, I doubt if they'd want to come.'

'They know the house well enough.'

'Barbara Winters?'

'She briefly hugged Mavis, more out of obligation than anything else.'

'And Margie?'

'Vague, staring into space. Apart from that, nothing to say. She's been cleaned up for the occasion.'

'She'll be the next funeral,' Tremayne said.

'That'll be a lot sadder than this one. I doubt there'll be a wake for her.'

'There will be, only it won't be a time for getting drunk and remembering the deceased with humour.'

'Not much humour from Barbara Winters, nor Alan's mother.'

'They're both a pair of miseries.'

Tremayne and Clare left the front porch of the house and went inside. Clare felt a little out of it, knowing full well that she was not a family friend, although she had become friendly with Mavis since her husband's death. Dean Winters sat in one corner, a glass of wine in his hand, his wife keeping a close watch on him. Clare could see that he wanted to join in.

Tremayne, a man who would have drunk more than his fair share but cognisant of his responsibilities, kept to the one beer. 'Damn nuisance,' he said to Gerry Winters. 'I can't drink.'

'Stan will do nothing. We'll not let him. Have a drink, more than what you're drinking now.'

'You're right, but he's my responsibility. Once he's on his way to prison, I'll be into it.'

'I'll join you if I'm still sober.'

'The way you're hitting it, I don't think so.'

'It's a good send-off for Alan. Did you see Polly and Liz at the church?'

'Are you still getting around to their place?'

'Occasionally. They know that I've been putting in a good word for them with Mavis.'

'They're using you, you know that. If it's not you, it'll be another man.'

'I'm using them. Polly and Liz are a lot of fun.'

'Mavis has clipped your wings; any animosity?'

'At the time, but she's easier to deal with now. I'll soon have the Bentley.'

'You were there when Mavis indicated that she'd pay off Fred. What did you think?'

'We've had a family meeting. At least, Mavis, Cyril, and me.'

'What was decided?'

'Fred wants two million, so do we.'

'Mavis?'

'Now she's got control of the money, she'll be agreeable. You've met Fred?'

'We have.'

'What did you think, be honest?'

'He'll cause trouble.'

'With two million?'

'He's a bully, even if he was polite to Yarwood. He'll aim to take control of Mavis, of your family.'

'We'll stop him.'

'How? Murder?'

'Mavis has a smart lawyer.'

'Fred won't listen to lawyers, nor police officers, you know that,' Tremayne said.

'Stan's fine. We're grateful for what you did.'

'He was eligible to come. I just added my weight to his application.'

'You did more than that. You acted like a friend. The Winters family will not forget.'

'They may. One of you is a murderer. It can only be people close to him.'

'I don't see it. What about Polly and Liz?'

'Where's the motive?'

'I don't know, but it can't be his own flesh and blood.'

***

A banging of a metal tray, a hushing of the hubbub in the house. 'Ladies and gentlemen, thank you for coming,' Bertie Winters said. He was standing on a chair, a glass of champagne in his hand. 'As sad as this occasion is, my father would want us to be here and to have a few drinks on his behalf. My mother, Mavis and my sister, Rachel, thank you for coming. Please enjoy yourselves. There is plenty of food and drink for everyone.'

Tremayne could see the caterers in the large kitchen. He joined the queue, as did Gerry, two people behind him. He was talking to Clare. In front of Tremayne stood Dean Winters. 'Your wife, she's not eating?'

'My wife is here under duress, you know that.'

'Where is she?'

'Outside in the car.'

'A tough woman.'

'She came here out of an obligation, to pay her respects to the dead. Apart from that, she wants nothing to do with this family.'

Tremayne could see that the man had a stiff drink in his hand, and he was on his way to being drunk, the reason for his loose tongue. 'Why do you let her control your life?' Tremayne said.

'You've only seen her bad side,' Dean Winters said.

Tremayne knew after years of policing that people such as Barbara Winters only have the one side. Dean Winters' life was a living hell. He knew that later on, when they drove back to Southampton, Dean would be on the receiving end of a severe ear-bashing and that he'd be in the dog house for weeks. And every time there was an argument, his behaviour at the Winters' home that day, his family of criminals, his mother, would be brought up.

Tremayne took his plate, full to overflowing. He knew he couldn't drink, but he could eat. 'Ten o'clock,' he said as he passed Stan.

'Don't worry about me, Tremayne. I'll be there.'

'Sober?'

'What do you reckon?'

'Not a chance. We need to make sure Prison Officer Marshall gets fed.'

'Don't worry. I'll take it out for him. He's decent, that is for a screw.'

'Margie?'

'We're trying to look after her. She seems better for being here. We're hopeful of getting her to move in.'

'Would that be okay with Mavis?'

'There's a small cottage at the end of the garden. Mavis will fix it up for her.'

'Will she come?'

'We remain optimistic.'

Tremayne walked through the group of people, stopping to converse as he went. He saw Yarwood sitting down, eating her meal. 'Barbara Winters is outside in her car. Once you've finished, go out and see if you can get her to talk.'

'She's missing out on this food?'

'As far as she's concerned, it was prepared by the devil.'

'Instead of a catering company.'

'You know that someone here is probably a murderer?'

'It's a shame. The Winters may be rough around the edges, but I like them, even Fred.'

'He's trouble. Stan's been a fool, getting involved in crime, but he'll probably go straight after his release. Fred won't.'

***

A tap on the car window, a reluctant opening. 'Mrs Winters, do you have a minute?' Clare said. She could see Barbara Winters in the driver's seat, dressed in black. Her hair, as always, immaculate, her makeup perfect, her mouth pinched and unsmiling.

'If you must.' The door lock was released. Clare got in and sat in the front passenger seat.

'The food is excellent,' she said as a way of opening the conversation. It was not a formal interview, more a way of getting to know the woman better, to see if there was anything remotely agreeable about her.

'I'll eat at home.'

'You're unable to be in their presence for more than a few minutes?'

'I honoured the Lord at his place. I care about him, not these people.'

'It's not mushy peas and soggy chips.'

'I've no doubt. They don't have to worry about the cost.'

'Your husband was offered a substantial amount of money.'

'He refused. Money derived from gambling is a sin. If you've read your Bible, you'd know that.'

'And now your husband is drinking alcohol.'

'He has defied me, defied God.'

'The priest who conducted the ceremony, he's here having a drink of beer.'

'He is not a true disciple of the God that I serve.'

'Then what is he?'

'He is a blasphemer, the same as those others. He will pay for his sins in the fires of hell.'

Clare shivered in the woman's presence. To her, God was meant to be a benevolent, forgiving entity; to Barbara Winters, he was vengeful, looking for retribution, punishing those who did not maintain his ideals.

'What will you do with your husband after tonight?'

'He will pay for his sins, offer up prayers for forgiveness.'

'Maybe he'll stand up to you and refuse.'

'He will not. The Lord will give me the strength to deal with him.'

'Tell me, when you had heard that Alan Winters had died, what did you think?'

'I praised the Lord that there was one less sinner in this world.'

'No sadness for your husband that his brother had died.'

'Why should there be? Dean is better off without him.'

'And when you were told that he had been murdered?'

'It does not concern me how he died.'

'But you must have had some feelings.'

'All those who have benefited from the money will die. That is the Lord's will.'

'He's told you this?'

'Yes, in the Bible: "for what will it profit a man if he gains the whole world, and loses his own soul?"'

'Their souls are lost?'

'The Lord will reclaim them in their repentance. Otherwise, they will burn in the fires of hell.'

'And your husband.'

'There is still time to save him.'

'After a few drinks?'

'Constant vigilance, constant praise of the Lord, constant piety.'

'Mrs Winters, could you kill a sinner?'

'If the Lord commanded it.'

'In the Bible?'

'Yes. It is the word of God written down for us to obey.'

Clare wondered what planet the woman came from. She made her excuses and retreated back to the sanctity of regular people.

Chapter 14

Back in the house, Clare found Tremayne in conversation with Mavis Winters. She saw Bertie, the son of the household, sitting on his own, orange juice in his hand. 'Can I sit here?' she said.

'Sure. Why not? Have you found out who killed him yet?'

'We're continuing our investigations. How about you?'

'After time in prison?'

'A centre to deal with your addiction.'

Clare could see that the man's initial respectable appearance at the church was waning. His suit jacket was flung to one side, his tie loosened, the top shirt button undone, and the shirt hanging out of his trousers. It was clear that the young man preferred to be a slob.

'I'm only sticking it out at Mum's insistence.'

'You'd prefer to be on drugs?'

'Life's for living. What's the point of worrying if you've got plenty of money?'

'Your mother has.'

'It's mine as well. He was my father.'

'Your father never worried about life, did he?'

'Not at all. Rich or poor, he was always the same. He'd still have time for a drink, and with me he was generous.'

'But he wouldn't let you have the car you wanted.'

'That was my mother. She was always in his ear.'

'If you had it, what would have happened?'

'I'd have pranged it, but so what? There's plenty more where it came from.'

'And if you were dead?'

'At least I would have had some fun, pulled some women.'

'You're aware of your father's mistresses?'

'Polly and Liz?'

'Yes.'

'I'd have to listen to them sometimes in the room down the hall.'

'With your father?'

'Yes.'

'How did you feel about that? Your father with other women, your mother in the same house.'

'Horny.'

'Nothing more?'

'Why? Should I? Should I care about my mother when she's controlling the money? She knew he was playing around, did nothing to stop him. Not that I blame him. That Polly's a bit of hot stuff, so are you, come to think of it.'

'Don't try it, Bertie. I'm a police officer. I'll break your arm if you come near.'

'I'm even sober, and I can turn you off.'

'You're the indulged son of a wealthy family, one of the idle rich.'

'It's better than being one of the idle poor. That's what my father was and what did it get him?'

'A lottery ticket,' Clare said.

'That's justice for you, and the man knew how to enjoy it. Those two women were classy.'

'If you had the money?'

'What he was doing, a better class of women.'

'And dead up at Stonehenge?'

'Not me. I'm smarter than that.'

'How?'

'I just am.'

'Do you know something. Something that you should tell me.'

'Not really. I'm just making conversation.'

Clare left the man with his orange juice, sure that he'd be back into drugs once he returned to the house on a permanent basis. She felt unclean when she left him. She found Rachel, the sister, talking to her mother.

'How are you?' Clare asked. The mother moved away.

'It's a good send-off for my father,' Rachel said. There was still some slight bruising on her forehead, but apart from that she looked fine.

'Yes, it's good. Are you pleased to see your family here?'

'I'm pleased to see Uncle Stan.'

'He's a favourite?'

'He always was. He always remembered my birthday, always bought me something silly. Inspector Tremayne helped to get him here?'

'Your uncle was eligible to attend the church with a prison officer, but not the wake, and certainly not to be here drinking. DI Tremayne organised that.'

'I'll thank him later. He was a friend of my mum's once.'

'What do you know?'

'My mum told me last night. It was just the two of us; one of those reminiscing about life, over Dad, mum and daughter things.'

'How much did she tell you?'

'She told me she was young, the same as him. There was a party, they'd both had a few drinks.'

'And?'

'The two of them in another room.'

'What did you think?'

'I laughed, we both did. My mum and the police officer. They'd make a good pair, even now.'

'It was a long time ago,' Clare said.

'Mum needs someone to help her. I know Uncle Gerry would like to be with her, but I can't see it. With Inspector Tremayne, he'd deal with them all, including Uncle Fred.'

'We've met him.'

'None of us wants to see him.'

'He's coming back.'

'We know. If Inspector Tremayne were with Mum, there'd be no trouble. He's probably the only man who could handle him.'

'That's up to Tremayne and your mother.'

'She'd be interested. I can't think of anyone she respects more.'

'He's a curmudgeon, can be cantankerous.'

'Mum can be awkward. See what you can do. We'd all welcome him into the family.'

'Not after we arrest one of you,' Clare said.

'We'd understand. If someone is capable of murdering my father, then they'd be capable of murdering Mum, and then Bertie and me.'

'That's true. We've always thought that the money was the motive. What if it isn't?'

'It must be. What else? My father was inoffensive. He could get drunk, cause a ruckus at the pub, but apart from that he wouldn't harm a fly.'

***

Tremayne and Clare continued to move around the house; the atmosphere was very congenial. Everyone was singing the praises of Alan Winters, the good fortune that he had had, the fact that he had struggled for years, barely making enough to live on. It didn't move Tremayne.

Relegated to one beer and then orange juice, at least until Stan Winters was off his hands and back in the care of the prison officer, he and Clare, apart from Barbara Winters who was outside in her car, were the only totally sober individuals in the house.

Tremayne knew that in spite of the accolades accorded the recently deceased, he was a lazy individual of little worth, which was surprising considering that Mavis, his widow, Tremayne's one-time lover, was full of energy. It was strange how two people so dissimilar in many ways could have forged a successful marriage, brought up two children, one smart, the other impacted by drug abuse.

Margie Winters had withered under drug abuse, apparently the result of her childhood experiences, but Tremayne wasn't sure. He was convinced of the maltreatment, but maybe the woman had an addictive personality, was susceptible to drugs, the same as Bertie Winters, an inherited trait that passed some, affected others. Tremayne knew that he had tried to give up cigarettes many times, never succeeded, whereas his brother, younger than him, had never smoked. Not that it had helped him as he had keeled over in his early forties with heart disease.

Tremayne found Mavis Winters sitting on her own in another room. 'I'll miss him,' she said as he sat down beside her. 'He wasn't much use, good at nothing, yet he was like an unruly dog. Good to have around but a damn nuisance.'

'He was good at purchasing lottery tickets.'

'We're not happier for all the money. It's just another responsibility. I remember the carefree nights at the pub, a singalong, everyone getting drunk. It was alright for Alan, he didn't care, but now, if I go anywhere, they always look for me to pay, and then the shops want to show me the most expensive items. And as for the begging letters…'

'Tough?'

'Some of the letters break your heart, not that you'd know if they were genuine or not.'

'You helped some?'

'At first, but then the word got out that I was an easy touch. Once it was revealed, even though those we helped had signed a non-disclosure agreement, on the advice of our solicitor, there was a flood of letters.'

'What did you do?'

'Alan wanted to continue to give; I said no. They'd approach him down the pub, he'd give them five hundred pounds to go away, but with me, I'm not willing to give our money away that easy. You know the saying: a fool and his money are easily parted. Alan was the fool, I was the bastard who wouldn't help. There were times when I wouldn't go out of the door for fear of being hassled.'

'But you do now.'

'I couldn't solve everyone's problems, nor could Alan. He was burning more than a million pounds every three months. Can you imagine it, a million pounds? When we were young, we were lucky to have a pound to buy an ice cream, and there was Alan throwing it away.'

'You've solved the problem now?'

'Only because he died.'

'What do you mean?'

'We can't help everyone. I've funded a cancer unit at Salisbury Hospital, a piece of equipment somewhere else. Not that it stopped Alan wasting the money, but he was under some sort of control.'

'What sort?'

'I was checking the finances.'

'It didn't stop him buying the furniture store for Polly and Liz.'

'I know, and that still annoys me.'

'But you'll let them continue?'

'For the time being. I've not forgiven them, nor Alan, and if I pull the plug, then that's more money lost.'

'You seem to understand finance.'

'Understand, maybe, but I never expected to be dealing with this, and now I've got to pay out to the brothers.'

'Two million each?'

'And how long before they exhaust that? Cyril's stupid enough to manage, but he'll probably be evicted from the council house, and then he'll want another place, and you've seen the price of property.'

'I've seen it,' Tremayne said. 'My place is worth three hundred thousand, and it's not much.'

'And if Cyril is evicted, do you think he'll want to buy a place the same as yours? Look at this house, beautiful, isn't it?'

'Yes.'

'That's the problem. Even I look at this and think I'd like somewhere bigger, better, maybe with some history. Once we were happy with a ten-year-old Ford, now it's a Bentley. There's no end to desire, and Fred will cause trouble. He thinks he's into farming, and two million pounds represents a compromise. That's not Fred. If he sees something, he wants it, and if he can't afford it, then he would steal it, but now, I'm the bank.'

'You don't want the responsibility?'

'Quite frankly, others may call me stupid, but I'd go back to the life we had, difficult as it was. This wake, how much?'

'Ten thousand pounds,' Tremayne said.

'And some. What with the funeral and the catering, there'll not be much change from forty thousand pounds, and what do we have to show for it?'

'It was a good send-off.'

'For Alan? He wasn't worth it. The family at the crematorium, a few drinks at the pub afterwards would have sufficed. It just never ends. Even with all this money, I'll need to make compromises.'

'It's not a problem that has ever worried me,' Tremayne said.

'We're very similar in many ways, you know.'

'Maybe we are,' Tremayne said, not certain where the conversation was heading. It was the woman's husband's funeral, and Mavis Winters was intimating something more. He was feeling uncomfortable, not sure what to say or do.

Tremayne looked at his watch. 'It's close to 10 p.m.' he said thankfully.

'Stan?'

'It's time for me to hand him over.'

Tremayne walked out to the other room, Mavis holding his arm. 'Stan, are you ready?'

It was clear that the prisoner was not sober. 'Ready when you are,' he said.

'Clare, give me a hand,' Tremayne said.

With that, the two police officers escorted Stan Winters back to Prison Officer Marshall's car and strapped him in, Stan attempting to give Clare a slobbery kiss, her avoiding it.

The others made their farewells, Tremayne signed off his responsibility, and wished Marshall well. 'Don't worry, he'll soon be back safe and sound. He wasn't meant to drink. I'm not sure how I'll square it with the warden,' Marshall said.

'Don't worry about it. I'll deal with it if it's an issue.'

Stan Winters left, Tremayne headed back inside for a beer. If Gerry were still sober, he'd find him; if he weren't, it would not make any difference. The detective inspector intended to enjoy the remainder of the evening. 'What have you found out, Yarwood?' Tremayne said to Clare who was sitting in one corner. The wake was coming to a conclusion, the caterers were packing up.

'Bertie fancies his chances, Rachel's a good person, the most likeable of them all, and Barbara Winters belongs on another planet,' Clare said.

'Stan?'

'He's okay, but he's not the murderer.'

'What about Dean?'

'Judging by the condition he was in when he left, he'll be doing penance for some time.'

'Self-flagellation?'

'Either he'll be whipping himself, or she'll be doing it for him.'

'The man's life must be miserable.'

'He chose which bed to lie in. Not really our concern, unless it's relevant to the investigation.'

'Yarwood, I'll make a detective out of you yet,' Tremayne said. He looked around the room, saw those who remained, Cyril and Gerry were close to comatose, their eyes closed. Rachel was helping her mother, and Bertie had taken off with his friends into town. Tremayne knew that would represent trouble, and he was only on temporary leave from the place that was treating him for his drug addiction. Margie sat outside in the garden, even though it was cold. Tremayne could see that she was shivering. He and Clare walked out through the French doors and put a coat around her shoulders. The woman gave no sign of recognition.

'Are you okay, Margie?' Clare asked. A feeble nod of the head.

'She needs medical treatment,' Tremayne said.

'She needs heroin,' Clare said.

'That's what I meant. I can agree with a doctor, the same as you. Neither of us can prescribe an illegal drug.'

'I want to go home,' Margie said. Apart from a few words at the church, they were the only other words she said that night.

'Mavis will have a room,' Clare said.

'I want my home, my cats.'

Tremayne knew that what she really wanted was her stash of drugs. Clare walked back inside, found no one able to drive her. She returned. 'I'll take her,' Clare said.

'I'll leave the same time as you.'

'Not drinking?'

'Not on my own, I'm not.'

Tremayne made his farewells, as did Clare. Mavis and Rachel gave Tremayne a big hug. Clare received a hug and a kiss as well. Margie was already in Clare's car, her seat belt buckled. Mavis held her for a long time as she sat there. Fifteen minutes later, Margie was back with her cats, twenty minutes later her shivering had stopped.

Clare phoned Tremayne. 'I've dropped her off.'

'She'll not last long, neither will Bertie.'

Chapter 15

Tremayne had barely had time to climb into his bed at his house in Wilton when the phone rang. It was Mavis. 'It's Alan's mother.'

'What about her?'

'She's dead, upstairs.'

'I'll be right over,' Tremayne said. He pulled himself up, rubbed his eyes to wake up and walked to the bathroom. For someone who had only drunk two beers, he was not feeling good. He looked for a toothbrush and toothpaste, took a quick shower, and left the house. The night had turned colder. He called Clare.

Upon arrival at the Winters' house, Tremayne found an ambulance and Yarwood's car.

'You were quick,' Tremayne said.

'I had just arrived home, not even opened the front door when you phoned.'

'Not like me.'

'I can see that. I suggest you button your shirt.'

'Thanks, Yarwood.'

Rachel Winters came outside. 'It's grandmother, she's dead.'

'Where?'

'Upstairs, her old room,' Rachel said. Tremayne and Clare hurried up the stairs; they knew the way, having interviewed the woman there once before. In the room was a medic, and Mavis, sitting to one side, looking at the body.

'If only I hadn't sent her to live with Cyril,' Mavis said.

'Who found her?' Tremayne said.

'I did. I was going to get Gerry to take her home, not that's he in a fit condition to drive. I may have let her stay here for the one night.'

'Any idea how she died?'

'Old age, grief. I don't know. I found her on the bed, the same as you can see her now.'

The medic stood nearby. 'Heart failure probably, but it's not for me to say,' the medic said.

'Pathology will tell us,' Tremayne said. He could see the woman, thought she looked peaceful, even saintly. Her arms were folded across her chest as if she knew her end was near. Clare found a clean sheet in a cupboard and placed it over her, only leaving her face showing. Rachel came into the room, kissed the dead woman's forehead.

Clare could see that the young woman had been crying. Even she could feel a lump in her throat.

'Don't say too much,' Mavis said. 'None of us liked her.'

'Please, mother, not now.'

Tremayne understood where Mavis was coming from; Rachel and Clare, younger and less cynical, less world-weary, did not. Tremayne had known about the Winters' mother back from his days when he lived nearby, the gossip about what went on in their house all too prevalent. He'd not heard about Margie. If he had, he was sure he would have taken some action, and now Margie had to be told that her mother had died. He'd leave that to Yarwood.

Jim Hughes arrived. The death of the old woman did not seem suspicious, but she had been the mother of a murdered man. Hughes was not pleased to be disturbed close to midnight. He set himself up near the bed, pulled back the sheet, took some photos. Another crime scene investigator checked the room, looking for anything suspicious. Mavis waited downstairs with Clare and Rachel. Cyril slept on a sofa in the living room; Gerry staggered around drinking black coffee, trying to sober up.

In the dead woman's room were Hughes, another CSI and Tremayne. 'You're not going to start asking me questions before I've finished, are you, Tremayne?'

'What do you think?'

'You're going to be a nuisance until I've given you something.'

'That's it.'

'Okay, a woman in her late seventies.'

'She was seventy-nine,' Tremayne said.

'Average height, marginally underweight, in apparently reasonable health for her age.'

'What makes you say that?'

'No immediate signs of injury to the body, a broken arm when she was younger. The body still retains some elasticity. Dead for two hours.'

'Conclusive?'

'Nothing's conclusive until I've finished and the pathologist's conducted his examination, you know that.'

'Is the death suspicious?'

'At seventy-nine, the funeral of her son? I'm not sure, but there's no sign of drugs in the room, no sign of injury to the body. Unless my examination and the pathologist reveal anything unusual, I'd say the woman died of natural causes. Nice house, by the way.'

'With their money, you'd expect it to be.'

'They can keep it. Too many hassles for me.'

'And for me,' Tremayne said.

'You know my next sentence?'

'Clear off and leave you to it.'

'Something like that.'

'Okay, I'll be downstairs.'

'Give me two to three hours, and we'll transport the body to Pathology. You can talk to the pathologist after that.'

'Thanks for coming.'

'It's better than having you on my back. Anyway, this soon after the death is always preferred.'

***

Downstairs, the mood was sombre. 'Poor granny,' Rachel said. Her mother sat to one side of her, her arm draped around her daughter.

'It was her time.'

Tremayne moved over close to Yarwood. 'How are they taking it?'

'Rachel's upset. The others are making all the right sounds.'

'A good woman, it's a shame, so young…?'

'Sort of. Cyril's still asleep; he's not been told yet.'

'Dean?'

'Mavis phoned him.' Clare said.

'And Stan?'

'He's been told, but he's still heading back to Pentonville. He'll need to apply for compassionate leave again.'

'I'll organise it,' Tremayne said.

'Someone will need to tell Fred, as well as Margie.'

'You'll not get much sense out of her tonight. You can visit her in the morning,' Tremayne said.

Tremayne walked over to Gerry, offered his condolences 'It's strange,' Gerry said. 'None of us liked her, but now she's dead, we feel sad. Why is that?'

'Don't ask me. Part of the grieving process, I assume.'

'I should get over and see Margie. She needs to know.'

'Will she be upset?'

'With Margie, who knows? We always thought she'd be the first to go, never considered that our mother would die, too mean-spirited to consider leaving us in peace. Cyril will not be upset. He had her back in his house, and she was giving him hell.'

'Dean?'

'He's got enough to deal with as it is. You saw his wife, the holier than thou bitch,' Gerry said.

'Yarwood had a talk with her.'

'Not in here.'

'Out in her car. She was not complimentary of your family.'

'A truly awful woman, even worse than our mother. Our mother only cared about herself, didn't aim to change us; we could have all gone to hell as far as she was concerned.'

'Why was she like that?' Tremayne said.

'Maybe it was something to do with our father; maybe that was her nature. We never knew, but then we were children. We survived, looked out for each other.'

'Except for Margie.'

'When she goes, there'll be a lot of sorrow.'

'For your mother?'

'Not much.'

Tremayne walked back upstairs, standing to one side as a stretcher was brought into the house. Jim Hughes came down the stairs. 'Pathology,' he said.

'Anything more?'

'Nothing else to report, if that's what you want. I could do with a cup of tea.'

'In the kitchen. You'll find the family, but they're fine.'

At 2 a.m. Clare and Tremayne left the house, along with Jim Hughes. Cyril was staying the night, Dean was coming up in the morning. Clare wondered if his bruises would be showing. Tremayne didn't care either way; he had a bottle of whisky at home, he'd have a couple of drinks before he went to bed. It had been a long day, a long night. He missed Jean.

***

To the south of Salisbury, a house, the same as all the others in the street. Inside a warring couple.

'She's my mother,' Dean Winters protested. His head still throbbed, it was three in the morning, and the woman was still going on about his condition when he had left his sister-in-law's house.

'I don't care. You're not going back there. You've got a job here, responsibilities, a wife.'

'What kind of a wife are you, sleeping in a single bed, denying me?'

'We're too old for that,' Barbara Winters said.

'Alan was older than me, and he never had any problem.'

'With that Mavis Winters, his tarts? What do you expect? The man was debased, not cognisant of his responsibilities to his religion, to his family. There's that whore of a sister, I saw her there, the needle marks in her arms. Your nephew, that Bertie, what a disreputable individual he was, and as for your niece…'

'Don't say a word about Rachel. She's holding down a steady job, and she was polite to you.'

'I could see through her. It was only an act. No doubt she's screwing whoever she fancies.'

'Just because you were too pure to have children, not wanting to soil your hands changing their nappies, feeding them, don't insult my family, don't insult Mavis or Rachel.'

'If you like them so much, why don't you go and live in that big house with all their money?'

'It'd be better than here. I'm afraid to sit down in case I crease the fabric, and as for you…'

Barbara Winters came forward; she hit her husband across the face. Dean, inflamed, for once in his life hit her back, and hard. 'You bastard, how dare you?'

'Shut up and sit down, will you.'

'I will not. I'm off to bed.'

Dean Winters sat down after she had left, not caring if the chair was out of symmetry with the others. He felt good. He picked up the keys of the car, even though he was still sobering up, and left for Salisbury.

***

Polly Bennett and Liz Maybury, both fast asleep, both in the same bed, did not expect a knock on their door. It was past two in the morning, and they had to be at the shop by eight.

'It's Gerry,' a voice through the door.

Polly opened the door. 'What is it?'

'My mother died.'

'The same day as Alan's funeral?'

'Yes. I saw you and Liz there.'

'He did right by us, the same as you. You'd better come in.'

Gerry entered the flat, saw Liz sitting up in bed. 'Sorry, I just wanted to see a friendly face.'

'Stay here tonight,' Liz said. 'There's room for three.'

Polly brought a coffee: black and strong. She also turned on the shower. 'You stink of alcohol. You'll need a shower if you want to be with us.' Gerry took off his clothes and opened the shower door. He was pleased to be welcome.

In the morning, he would remember their kindness, attempt to put in a word with Mavis about how well the shop was going. That night, he would enjoy the distraction of Polly and Liz.

***

Clare slept for a few hours, waking up at six in the morning. She fed the cats and left her cottage. By six forty-five she was outside Margie's place. She thought it was too early, but decided to knock on the door anyway. After ten minutes Margie opened the door.

'My mother's dead,' Margie said.

'You've been told?'
'Cyril phoned me.'
'Has he been here?'
'No one comes here.'
'How are you?' Clare asked.
'I'm not sure what I feel,' Margie said. Clare realised that it was the first time that the woman had spoken other than in monosyllables.
'Are you high on drugs?'
'I was last night, not now.'
'Can I come in?' Clare said. Standing outside on the doorstep discussing a dead mother did not seem right to her.
Clare thought the woman to be much improved from the previous times she had met with her.
'She's was my mother, but I hated her. Is that wrong?'
'It's unfortunate.'
'Do you love your mother?' Margie said.
'She drives me mad sometimes, but yes, I do.'
'I never loved mine. Did they tell you?'
'Your brothers are all concerned, so is Mavis.'
'I like Mavis and Rachel.'
'So do I,' Clare said, 'Very much. Do you want to be with them?'
'Today, I would. Will you take me to their house?'
It was a remarkably verbose conversation with a woman who had barely uttered a word before. Clare was pleased that she had come so early.
At the Winters' house in Quidhampton, a warm welcome. Mavis thanked Clare, pleased that Margie was in the house, hopeful that she would stay. Clare knew that was unlikely. Bertie was still not home, and Mavis was worried.
'He was meant to report back for his treatment,' Mavis said.
'If I see him, I'll send him back,' Clare said, although the man was in his twenties, and there wasn't much she could do. Rachel, diligent as always, was back at work.
Margie thanked Clare as she left, even gave her a kiss on the cheek, demonstrative for a woman who had been lacking any emotion before the death of her mother, even before her brother's

death, although Clare thought that the mother's death had brought memories flooding back, memories long suppressed.

***

Clare had never imagined that she would ever re-enter the Deer's Head, Harry's former pub, but Tremayne had been adamant. He'd had a tip-off that Bertie Winters was to be found there.

'Sorry about this, Yarwood. It was bound to happen at some time,' Tremayne had said.

Clare knew that he was right. She couldn't be a police officer in a city as compact as Salisbury and avoid places because they upset her. Inside, she found the pub had changed little, apart from a touch up of some flaking paint. The pub had been there for centuries, and it was the old-world charm that people wanted, not a modernised square with a poker machine in one corner, a bar in the other, a charmless landlord. The new publican, Clare had to admit, was not charmless; quite the opposite. 'Evan Bassett,' he said on introducing himself. 'First time in here for you,' he said to the two police officers.

'We've been before, often in fact,' Tremayne said.

'Apologies, I was insensitive.'

'You know?' Clare said.

'Not in detail, although I've heard the stories, and some of the regulars used to come in here before.'

'You've got Bertie Winters here,' Clare said, changing the subject. She looked around the bar, noticed the steps down to the cellar where she and Harry had almost made love, the stairs leading up to the small bedroom where they had. The table in the corner where Tremayne had usually sat was occupied. At least she was pleased that her senior, a man of habit, wouldn't have the chance to resume his usual place in the bar.

'Over there, sleeping it off.'

'Thanks. You know who he is?'

'I came from up north, never heard of the Winters family before I came here. One of the locals told me who he was. For someone with so much money, he doesn't look anything special.'

'He's not,' Clare said. 'One ticket and you could have what his family's got.'

'Not me. I'll keep to the occasional bet on the horses.'
'What do you reckon for the 2.30 at Newmarket?' Tremayne said.
'Sonny Boy.'
'I fancy Flash Comet.' Clare sighed; another horse racing aficionado. She could see the Deer's Head becoming Tremayne's favourite pub again. She was there as part of her job, she did not want to linger.
'Let's get Bertie Winters and get out of here,' Clare said.
'Excuse us, Evan. We need to take the young man back to his family.'
'I read that his father had been murdered.'
'We've not apprehended his murderer yet.'
'It must be hard coming in here, unpleasant memories,' Evan Bassett said to Clare.
'It is. Excuse me if we grab Bertie Winters and leave.'
'I understand.'
Tremayne and Clare grabbed Bertie by the collar and walked him out of the pub. The man was semi-conscious. Tremayne, Clare knew, wanted to stay and discuss horse racing. She knew that he would have to come back on his own. She had entered the pub once, she did not intend to enter it again.
Once they were back in Quidhampton, Mavis called for a doctor. Tremayne thought it a waste of money, as all the man needed was a good sleep and solid food.
Tremayne and Clare were surprised to see Dean Winters eating a steak with gusto, a newly-hired cook preparing food for the family. 'Too long on salads,' Winters said.
'Your wife?'
'Not here. She's back in Southampton.'
'You've got a black eye,' Clare said.
'She hit me fair and square.'
'It took you long enough to stand up to her,' Mavis said.
'Either she'll come around, or it's over.'
'What do you reckon?' Clare said.
'You've spent time with her. What do you think?'
'She has some very firm views on certain subjects.'
'The Winters family,' Mavis said.
'It was biased.'

'Her father was an unpleasant man, constantly haranguing his staff, paying them a pittance,' Dean said.

'Then why did you marry her?' Mavis asked.

'The same reason any man gets tied up with a woman when they're young and in love: rose-coloured glasses.'

Tremayne did not need to be told why. He had married Jean for the same reason, although she had been an agreeable woman, still was. They had broken up because of his policing, but he was about to reunite with her, not out of a youthful reason, more out of a need for companionship.

Gerry Winters walked in the door. 'You've been with them,' Mavis said. 'I hope they're making a good job of my business.'

'They are.'

Tremayne and Clare left for Bemerton Road. The Winters family was united in the one house, except for Stan and Fred. Tremayne phoned up both of their respective prisons, spoke to both men. Fred was derogatory about the woman who had died; Stan was more conciliatory. 'No chance before the funeral,' Tremayne said to Stan's immediate request for compassionate leave.

'Do your best,' Stan said. 'I'll miss Alan, not her, or not as much as I should.'

Chapter 16

Neither Tremayne nor Clare was in the best of moods. There was still a murder to solve, and emotional involvement with the primary suspects did not help.

Clare left the office early, an appointment to meet up with Polly and Liz at a pub. It had been Tremayne's suggestion to meet them where their guard would be down, to see if there were hidden depths to the women, a reason for them to want Alan Winters dead and Gerry Winters in their bed. It was clear that they did not need to be with Gerry, and there was no great love affair there, so why were they bedding him? His smile as he had entered the Winters' house earlier indicated that it had been full on with them. Even Mavis had smiled at the cheek of the man.

Tremayne remained in the office; there wasn't much for him at home. Superintendent Moulton paid another visit, the usual, but he was not pushing hard for a retirement. Tremayne thought the man may be suffering from his problem, so much time policing that it had taken over his life at the expense of family.

'Your reports are late again,' Moulton said. For once he had taken a seat in Tremayne's office, seemed content to stay.

'We're struggling with a breakthrough in the Winters' murder,' Tremayne admitted. 'We've suspects, but so far we've not been able to tie them together.'

'Do you need additional manpower?'

'Not really. It's a case of finding the significance of Stonehenge, and why the wealthiest man in the area had to die. It's not as if he wasn't generous, he certainly was to those he liked. His widow is not going to be such an easy touch; she'll want legal guarantees for any money given, payment schedules for money lent, and she's not about to throw it away on young lovers.'

'Alan Winters, he was into women?'

'It was in one of my reports.'

'I know that. I'm making conversation, just going through the case with you,' Moulton said. 'I know you see me as a pen pusher, but I was a regular policeman once.'

'On the beat, sir?'

'The same as you, the same as all of us. Sometimes I miss dealing with the criminals, being out on the street.'

'I thought you were a procedures man, enjoyed being in the office.'

'That's true, but it's no different from running a large business. The concern over budgets and KPIs. And then there's the constant battle about staffing levels.'

'And retirements?' Tremayne said.

'It's not you in particular. The modern police force is run along business lines. We're expected to be financially viable, and obtaining the necessary money to run this place, a yearly headache, is not easy.'

Tremayne realised that it was the first time that he and Moulton had sat down for a conversation. In the past, it had always been a letter on his desk, a discussion about retirement, a quick chat about the latest case.

'We think there's another element to this case,' Tremayne said.

'There are some crazy people out there with crazy ideas.'

'We've got one of those.'

'Any possibility there? You dealt with the paganists in Avon Hill, and they were rational people under normal circumstances.'

'This one's not,' Tremayne said. 'The woman breathes flames; her husband's life must be hell, although he walked out yesterday.'

'For how long?'

'Not for long. Some men want to be told what to do.'

'Not you, Tremayne.'

'Nobody's going to push me around.'

'Not even me.'

'Not even you, sir. I'll retire when I'm ready.'

'That's how I see it. Outside of this place, you're not sure what you'd do.'

'That's true enough. I only go home to sleep, watch the sports channel. I rarely eat there, maybe the occasional frozen pizza in the microwave, but nothing else.'

'Yarwood, how is she?'

'A good police officer; she should be an inspector.'

'She will be, but that wasn't the question.'

'I know that. She's bought a cottage in Stratford sub Castle; she's even been into Harry Holchester's pub. She'll pull through.'

'No man in her life?'

'Not yet.'

'Let me know what you need,' Moulton said. 'I'll not talk about your retirement for a couple of months.'

'Why's that?'

'The quotas have been met. Until there's another push, I'll leave you alone.'

Moulton left. Tremayne sat in his chair, somewhat stunned after his visit. He looked out of his office door and into the department beyond. Apart from a cleaner, the place looked depressing. He knew he needed company. He needed to discuss horse racing over a couple of beers.

The Deer's Head, the one place that Yarwood had not wanted to enter, although she had in the line of duty, and the one place he had never thought he would either, was welcoming.

'What'll it be?' the publican, Evan Bassett, said on his arrival. Tremayne remembered to duck his head as he entered. The pub had been built when people were a lot shorter, and the lintel above the door would have hit him in the centre of his forehead.

'The usual,' Tremayne said, forgetting that it wasn't Harry behind the bar but another man.

'And what's that?'

'A pint of your best. Any food?'

'Chicken pie.'

'I'll have one of those.' Tremayne instinctively made for his favourite seat. It was unoccupied. He took a drink of beer, opened up his newspaper, took out a pen. He felt at home.

'How did Sonny Boy go in the 2.30 at Newmarket?' the publican asked, remembering their earlier conversation when Tremayne and Clare had rescued Bertie Winters.

'Which horse did you choose?'

'Flash Comet, it romped home, 10 to 1.'

'Your skills are better than mine. Yarwood, that's the police officer that I came in with before, she reckons I'm wasting my time.'

'Do you ever get out to the Salisbury Races?'

'Whenever I can.'

'Next time you go, give me a call. We could make a day of it, have a few beers, a few bets.'

'What about the pub?'

'I'm not wedded to the place. I can always call in help, and my wife will serve behind the bar.'

'She's not here?'

'She is when it's necessary. Tell me about the former publican,' Evan said.

'Yarwood was engaged to the man. Harry Holchester was his name. I liked him.'

'He turned out bad?'

'Not according to Yarwood, but yes. He was one of those up at Avon Hill. Have you ever been out there?'

'Not yet. We're new to the area.'

'A pretty place. Most of the stone to build the cathedral came from a quarry nearby.'

'I didn't know that.'

'Most people don't. It's not the same as when we were there. Back then Avon Hill was a foreboding place where you hardly saw anyone. The last time I was there with Yarwood to put flowers on Harry's grave, it was more agreeable, children in the street.'

'Yarwood, will she come in here again?'

'It's unlikely. She'd not be pleased with my being here.'

A call from the bar for service and Evan left.

Tremayne ate his pie and drank his beer. After ninety minutes he left the pub; it just didn't feel right, almost disloyal to Yarwood.

***

Clare drank her wine. Polly Bennett and Liz Maybury were downing vodkas. Clare enjoyed their company, even though she knew their story, their willingness to use their bodies to gain what they wanted. She realised that ambition is achieved in many ways; she wanted to do it through competent policing, the two women, Polly clearly the more intelligent of the two, would use whatever was at their disposal.

'Why are we here?' Polly said. 'We're an open book, you know all about us, we know nothing about you.'

'What's to tell,' Clare said.

'Everyone's got a story.'

The three women were sitting in the Ox Row Inn. All of them had ordered. Clare knew she would be paying.

'You know about us,' Liz said. 'I don't think you approve either. Am I right?'

'I couldn't do what you have.'

'Alan?'

'And Gerry.'

'It was good to be chauffeured around in a Bentley. And Alan set us up in business.'

'That's what I don't get. Why, if you can seduce the man, do you bother with running a business?'

'Clare, we want our independence. Alan was fun, so is Gerry, no doubt another man will be, but we want each other, not them.'

'We've assumed you were.'

'Involved?'

'Does it worry you?'

'No. But why the men?'

'We swing both ways. It's not a big deal for us. We're not ashamed of using men if it achieves what we want. Alan was generous, and Gerry, well, he's a lot of fun.'

'Humorous?' Clare said.

'In bed,' Polly said. Both she and Liz laughed at Clare's apparent naivety.

'Clare, what's your story? You at least owe us that.'

'There's not much to say. I met a man, we were engaged, preparing to get married. And then he was killed.'

'We know more than that,' Liz said.

'If you don't want to talk about it,' Polly said, 'we'd understand.'

'No, you're right. I owe you the truth. I came here from Norfolk. We were involved in a series of murders, Tremayne and me, not all of them pleasant. We became aware of a group of pagans conducting ceremonies.'

'What sort of ceremonies?' Liz asked.

'Human sacrifice.'

'In Salisbury?'

'I've told you the story,' Polly said. 'I know all about it, Clare. You don't need to say anymore.'

'It's fine. It's good to talk. You're local, Liz isn't. Harry, he was the publican of the Deer's Head. We were in love, moving in together. And then DI Tremayne and myself are trapped out at Avon Hill, along with some others, and they're coming for us.'

'Who?' Liz said.

'Let Clare talk,' Polly said.

'Some of the others go for help, some try to make a run for it across the fields. Not all of them made it.'

'And then what?' Liz said. Clare could see that she enjoyed the macabre.

'We make a run for it. We take one of the police cars, there are four of us. We make it up the hill, no more than a mile, they catch us, tie us up.'

'And?'

'The chief elder invokes his gods, the others become desperate for a sacrifice. They decide I'm the first. They prepare to come for me, then some of them decide that it's gone too far. They start fighting amongst themselves. Some are killed, those left come for me. Harry, I didn't know he was one of the elders, releases me, tells me to get out of there with DI Tremayne and two uniforms. Harry then kills the elder, and they dissipate. Most are in jail now for murder.'

Liz had wanted to hear the ghoulish details, did not expect to be moved by the story. 'How sad,' she said.

'You must have read about it,' Clare said. 'It was the headline story on the television for a few days.'

'I remember it, but you were there. You were a witness.'

'I was meant to be dead.'

'And Harry?' Liz said.

'I don't know why I'm telling you this. It brings back painful memories.'

'You can't bottle them up forever,' Polly said. 'Maybe you see us as uninvolved. It's not something you can tell your parents, probably not even talk to the others who were there.'

'We have the same problem,' Liz said.

'What do you mean?'

'We want to tell our parents about us.'

'It may be best to sit them down and tell them the truth. It's never as bad as you imagine. I wanted to ask you about Alan's death,' Clare said.

'A few drinks and we'll talk, confess to the crime,' Polly said.

'I don't think you two did it, but you've been close to certain members of the family. You've been around to Alan and Mavis's house. The smallest piece of information helps in the final analysis. Something obscure may bring his murder to a conclusion.'

'We didn't kill him, although we slept with him. I suppose you see us as promiscuous.'

'Promiscuous is a term I would use.'

'You've been honest. We'll not hold it against you.'

The three women ordered more drinks.

'You never finished your story,' Liz said.

'We're safe, the four of us. Harry's still in the wood; he's killed the chief elder. Tremayne doesn't want me to go back, but I have to. I find him sitting down. He's guilty of murder, I can't ignore the fact, and he would be arrested. Before that can happen, a branch falls from a tree, hits him, and hurls him away from me. I saw him die.'

'It must have been awful,' Liz said.

Polly said nothing initially, overcome with emotion. 'I read about it. It seemed unreal then, but with you being there, your fiancé,' she said.

'It feels better for telling you. You two are the first people I've told the story to, probably the last. Now tell me about Alan and Mavis Winters.'

'There's not much to tell,' Polly said. 'We had a good time with the man. He looked after us, we looked after him.'

'Did he have other women?'

'He may have, but not that we're aware of in Salisbury. It's unlikely, though.'

'Why's that?' Clare said.

'Clare, don't be naive. One man in his late forties, two women. We were always available. He's unlikely to have had the energy for any others.'

'His relationship with his wife?'

'He was fond of her, even loved her. You can't blame the man, he was only human.'

'Why do you say that?'

'We're there and willing. What man could resist, especially if he had that much money?'

'Not all men are like that,' Clare said.

'They're all like that,' Polly said. 'It's part of the human condition; man, the hunter, woman, the mother of his children. Alan was just fortunate that he could indulge his fantasy.'

'Mavis Winters?'

'She saw us at the house once. Alan thought she wasn't there.'

'What happened?'

'She was upset. We were as well.'

'What about Alan?'

'He seemed to enjoy the spectacle, made up some story about she had another man.'

'Did you believe him?'

'Not really. We assumed it was Gerry, but we don't think it was.'

'Why's that?'

'He's been around to our place a few times. After a few drinks and us, he likes to talk. We know all about his family, the mother, the brothers, even Dean.'

'And Alan's children?'

'We asked Gerry why he'd never married.'

'What did he say?'

'After his childhood, his parents, he had never wanted to form a lasting relationship.'

'But he slept with you two.'

'He likes women. He was more active than Alan, but then he was a few years younger. Maybe that was the reason. He liked Alan's daughter, not so much his son.'

'You know his son?'

'We've seen him around. Spaced out, the same as his aunt.'

'You know her?'

'Not really. We know of her; Alan told us.'

'What did he tell you?'

'That she was in a terrible state, and not even he with all his money could save her.'

'Any more?'

'Not about his sister. We knew Cyril; he'd sometimes be with us.'

'Drinking?'

'We didn't sleep with Cyril. He didn't seem interested in us anyway.'

'What did Alan say about Dean?'

'He couldn't understand why he had married his wife; said she was a dragon.'

'Did you know her?'

'We saw her at the funeral, but apart from that, we'd never seen her, nor Dean and his other brother, the one in jail.'

'Stan.'

'If you say. We only went to the funeral. After that we came home.'

Chapter 17

Tremayne met up with Clare at Bemerton Road Police Station the next morning, 6 a.m. sharp. Clare realised that she had drunk more than she should have the previous night, even willing to admit that she had enjoyed herself. Tremayne had drunk a couple of beers at the Deer's Head and gone home. For once, he was looking the better of the two.

'Any further insights?' Tremayne said.

'No secrets revealed. The women are honest about why they were with Alan Winters, honest about their relationship and their plans for the future. Polly's the smarter of the two, but they're both well educated. I liked them.'

'That's the trouble with you, Yarwood, you like people. They could have been playing you for a fool.'

'I've not said they were not involved in the murder, have I?'

'No. Were they?'

'There's no reason. We'll need to look further afield for an answer.'

A phone call; Tremayne answered. 'Mavis Winters' house,' he said to Clare. A short drive and they were in Quidhampton, Tremayne having driven for once.

'It's Dean,' Mavis said.

'What's up? Tremayne asked.

'She came up, angry, out of her mind.'

'His wife?'

'Who else?'

'Where is she? Where is Dean?'

Clare had already moved into the house. Inside, lying on the floor of the kitchen, was Dean Winters. 'She went mad, she had a knife,' Rachel Winters said.

'From where?'

'From here. We've a drawerful.'

'Your uncle?'

'She stabbed him in the arm. She was aiming to kill him, but I pulled her away. She nicked me with the blade, but it's only a minor wound. Uncle Dean needs to be in the hospital.' Outside, the sound of an ambulance.

'Where's the patient?' the medic said.

'Over here,' the faint voice of Dean Winters said.

'Put out an all-points for Barbara Winters,' Tremayne said to Clare.

'Right away.' Clare made a phone call to instigate the process, opened her laptop and sent a photo and a description.

She returned to the kitchen to find Dean Winters sitting on a chair. 'It hurts like hell, but I'll survive.'

'Are you up to making a statement?' Tremayne asked.

'It was Barbara, not used to me standing up to her. It's the same with her family. They're all aggressive.'

'Why did you marry her?' Mavis said.

'I didn't know what her family was like.'

'Until they'd trapped you in their web.'

'Maybe I was, but it was good for a few years.'

'Not that we ever saw you.'

Clare looked around the kitchen. Apart from the blood on the tiled floor and the upturned chair, there was not much to see. 'Where is your wife?' she asked.

'Back in Southampton, I assume.'

'Mr Winters will need a few stitches.'

'We'll take him,' Mavis said. 'Unless he wants to go in the ambulance.'

'That's fine. I'll go with you,' Dean said.

'We'll need to take statements from everyone here,' Tremayne said.

The violence from Barbara Winters had not been expected by Tremayne and Clare. The woman's invective, her views on the Winters family, were well known, but a knife attack represented a new development. It was the second knife attack in the current investigation; the first one, fatal, the second, almost. Tremayne thought it was circumstantial, Clare was not so sure.

'We need to find Barbara Winters,' Tremayne said. 'I've phoned her local police station. They've been round to her house; she's not arrived yet.'

'We need her today,' Clare said. 'We need to know if her husband's stabbing is pre-meditated or an act of violence in the heat of the moment.'

'The latter, almost certainly, as the woman did not arrive with a knife, only found one in a kitchen drawer.'

'What do we know about this woman?'

'Enough to know that she's not pleasant.'

'Capable of murder?'

'Dean Winters would have been dead if Rachel hadn't interceded.'

The injured man left with Mavis and Rachel in the Bentley; Tremayne and Clare returned to Bemerton Road. At the station, the two police officers discussed the case. Clare was all for driving to Southampton; Tremayne was more circumspect.

'If she's not at the house, what then?' Tremayne said.

'We can check out her family.'

'What do we have? Have we interviewed them before?'

'She has a brother, two years older than her. Her father is retired, living in a home, dementia. We've just compiled the standard report on her, the same as the others in the investigation.'

'The father, any chance that he'll know where she is?'

'According to the report, he'll not be able to help. The brother is not far from Southampton.'

'Have you phoned him?'

'Not yet.'

'Then I suggest you do it right now.'

Clare dialled the number, no answer. She tried two more times, no success.

'Suspicious?' Tremayne said.

'Not really. He's a pilot. He may be out of the country.'

'Can we get the local police around to check him out?'

'It's only twenty minutes from here,' Clare said.

'Why didn't you say so?'

'You weren't listening.'

'You're driving. If she's not there, then we come back. When's the mother's funeral?'

'One week, maybe.'

'They've not set a date yet?'

'They need a death certificate. Her body is in Pathology.'

'Okay, first the brother's house and then Pathology.'

'Yes, guv.'

***

Clare took the A36 out of Salisbury, heading in the direction of Southampton. Ten miles from the centre of the city, she turned off to the right, and took the B3079 to the village of Landford, twenty-two minutes' driving time. The brother's house was not difficult to find. It was neat and tidy, the same as all the other houses in the village. In the driveway and on the road there was no sign of the car that Barbara Winters had used when she had driven to Salisbury. 'Wasted trip,' Tremayne said.

'We'll wait for twenty minutes. I'll park the car out of sight, and then have a look in the windows.'

'I'll stay in the car, in case she arrives. If she parks in the driveway, I can block her exit.'

Clare parked the car, made sure that the brother's house was visible. The owners of the house on the other side of the road, fifty feet away, expressed concern about a strange vehicle in their driveway. Tremayne flashed his ID, gave the lady a brief synopsis of the situation. 'They're a strange family. Arrest the lot of them for all we care,' she said. 'He's not sociable. If one of the children kicks a football over the fence, it comes back slashed with a knife, and if someone's dog defecates on the footpath outside, you'd think it was a criminal offence.'

'Have you seen his sister?'

'She comes here sometimes, doesn't speak to any of us. What's she done?'

'Have you seen her today?'

'Not today. She was here the other day, but not for long.'

'Do you know why?'

'Not me. I don't become involved. I'm only interested so I can keep my children away.'

'That bad?'

'They'll scream at the children if they go too near.'

'Is the brother married?' Tremayne knew the answer to the question, just wanted to check what else he could find out.

'There was a woman there once. She used to chat, but then she disappeared. One day she's there, the next she's gone. It was very suspicious; he was seen digging in the garden that night, as well.'

Tremayne noted what the woman said, but did not place too much credence on Barbara Winters' brother slaying a woman and burying her in the garden. It was too melodramatic for him, and a small village was a good place for gossip. However, he'd have it checked out.

Clare walked around the house. The back garden was the same as the front, neat and tidy with no flowers. The edges of the lawn were precise, the gravel paths freshly raked. She could see the family trait: the symmetry, everything in its place. Inside the house, there was no sign of movement. Clare heard a sound on the driveway. She peered around from where she was standing.

Tremayne moved over into the driver's seat of Clare's car. The neighbour was excited that she was there as the action unfolded. The local pub would be buzzing that night with the story of how the police had come to the village and arrested the woman.

Clare moved away from her hiding place; Barbara Winters got out of her car. 'Mrs Winters, we've a few questions for you.'

The woman, panicking, got back in her car, started the engine and reversed, stopping abruptly on seeing Tremayne blocking the driveway with Clare's car.

'I didn't mean to do it,' Barbara Winters said on getting out of her car for the second time.

Tremayne handcuffed her and put her in the back of the police car. Clare sat to one side of her, as Tremayne was driving. The woman could not be left free. On the other side of the road, the neighbour busily talking to another woman, taking in the scene, talking on her phone at the same time.

At Bemerton Road Police Station, Barbara Winters was taken into the interview room. Her legal representative was on his way, expected within five minutes. Outside, Dean Winters waited with Mavis. 'I want to see her,' he said to Tremayne.

'We'll need to interview your wife first.'

'For what?'

'It's a crime to stab someone with a knife; manslaughter if you had died.'

'But I haven't. Can't we forget about what happened?'

'Dean, shape up. She may be your wife, but if you keep whimpering around, she'll continue to make your life a living hell,' Mavis Winters said.

'But I love her; I need her. Without her I'm nobody.'

'You should have thought of that earlier before you stood up to her,' Tremayne said.

Barbara Winters' legal representative, Graham Davies, arrived.

In the interview room, Tremayne went through the procedure, informed Barbara Winters of her rights, asked everyone to state who they were and the time of commencement.

'Mrs Winters, you went to the house of Alan and Mavis Winters. Once there, you stabbed your husband, Dean, with a knife that you had found in the kitchen.'

'It was unintentional. I love my husband.'

'Are the facts correct?'

'Yes,' Barbara Winters said after conferring with Davies.

'This is a criminal offence. If your husband had died, you would have been charged with manslaughter, probably involuntary, and the punishment for such a crime would be custodial. Were you aware of this when you visited the house?'

'Not at all. I was angry. He had shamed me in front of his family.'

'A family you hate.'

'I do not like them, that is true.'

'Why?'

'They are common people, unbelievers. They are not my kind of people.'

'Your husband is one of them.'

'With me, he was not. At home, before his brother died, we were close.'

'And your husband defied you by drinking alcohol, by talking to one of his brothers, a criminal serving time in prison.'

'I do not want him associating with unworthy people.'

'But he is one of them. You were aware of the bond that exists between the children of Betty Winters.'

'Children of the devil, that's what they are. It is my duty to save Dean from them, to make him a better person.'

'Why do you feel that you can separate a person from his blood relatives? You are aware of the abuse that they suffered as children?'

'You knew them, and you were a police officer. Why didn't you do something?' Barbara Winters said.

'I'm asking the questions here, Mrs Winters. You have stabbed your husband, that is a crime that needs to be addressed. I put it to you that you came up to Salisbury fired up with anger after a night without your husband. You were angry; you wanted him dead. You approached him in that kitchen hoping that he would acquiesce and come back to you, the lost sheep that he was. And when he would not, you took the only action open to you. You stabbed him, you wanted him dead.'

'I was hurt, angry, but I did not want him dead.'

'This is intimidation,' Davies said. 'It is not within your right to conduct the interview in this manner.'

'I apologise,' Tremayne said. 'Alan Winters has been murdered, a knife in his heart; his brother Dean has also been stabbed. The crimes are similar.'

'I did not kill his brother,' Barbara Winters said. Clare could tell the woman wanted to get across the table and scratch out Tremayne's eyes. Davies had his hand firmly on his client's arm.

'Mrs Winters, Alan Winters was killed at Stonehenge. It has all the signs of a spiritual death, an offering to a god of a worthless man, an act of atonement.'

'He was worthless. All that money, not through toil and hard work but through a weakness of people to waste what they have earned. It was the devil's money, not his, and not ours.'

'That is why you refused the hundred thousand pounds?'

'Dean refused, not me. He understood the true way, the way of purity, the way of the Lord, until his brother with all his money tried to corrupt him.'

'Mavis Winters has offered all of the children of Betty Winters two million pounds. Your husband is going to accept. Did you know this? Did he phone you up to gloat? Is this when you decided to kill him?'

'He would have refused it if he had been with me.'

'Mrs Winters, I'm charging you with attempted involuntary manslaughter. You will be held in custody pending a trial. Is there anything that you want to say?'

'I did not mean to kill him. I swear on the Bible that it's the truth.'

'My client will defend herself against this charge,' Davies said.

'That is her right,' Tremayne said.

Chapter 18

Tremayne had to agree with Clare that Barbara Winters was a strange woman, with her attitude, her contradictory comments during her interview at Bemerton Road. On the one hand she was crediting her husband with refusing the hundred thousand pounds from Alan Winters, and on the other she was taking credit for her ability to convince him of right from wrong. Tremayne could not see evil in the occasional bet on the horses. And Yarwood, he knew, would regularly buy a lottery ticket, not in the belief that she would win sixty-eight million pounds but more as a diversion from the routine of life, a chance to joke if only I had, not believing that it would ever occur. It had for Alan Winters, one of the most undeserving. Tremayne had to agree with Barbara Winters on that score, but not much else. He had remained impartial during the woman's interview, so had Yarwood, and then her husband was pleading for her to be released.

Tremayne couldn't remember Dean Winters from his childhood; he would have only been ten when Mavis was sixteen, just twelve when Tremayne had finally moved away from there and rented a flat above a shop in Fisherton Street. After that one night when Mavis had turned sixteen, he had not made love to the woman since, nor had he wanted to. Tremayne had hoped at the time that no one would find out.

Mavis had been over the age of consent, but only just. She was still in school uniform during the week and looked like a child. It had been up to Constable Tremayne to set an example, to uphold the law, to be a beacon of decency, and there he had been, seducing a young woman barely past puberty. The department's superintendent, not his inspector, would have hauled him over the coals, given him a severe dressing down, probably a written warning, and if Mavis's father had found out, he could have found himself back behind the counter of his father's shop.

He'd had a nervous few days after Mavis had seduced him; not a defence, but the truth. He had had more than his fair share of beers mixed with a few shorts. All of the young policemen drank too much, although they knew how to handle their alcohol back then, not like it was now. Five pints of a night was Tremayne's maximum, and even that would give him a thick head in the morning. He knew that a woman like Barbara Winters would have driven him mad, and he'd have ended up wanting to throttle her, not that he would have. He wasn't a Dean Winters, never had been, never would be, and with Jean, they had always been equals. He wondered why it was that two people who had been so close could have drifted apart; why being a member of the police force was so important. He knew that Yarwood was falling into the same trap of the balance between the life of a police officer and that of a regular member of the public, the ability to just enjoy other people's company without trying to analyse, to figure out their backgrounds.

He knew he wasn't a Sherlock Holmes, he didn't have that attention to detail, but he had developed an ability to observe. He had studied Barbara Winters in the interview room, also at Alan Winters' funeral and wake. She was not a bad looking woman, dressed sensibly, although not unfashionably, probably appreciated the occasional humour, the usual amount of affection, yet she held views which others would have regarded as extreme. He wondered how she could go through life with such hostility towards others. Life was about getting along with your fellow citizens, not acting as if they were enemies. And then that woman, the gossip in Landford where they had arrested Barbara Winters. What was it that she said? If the local children kicked a football into her brother's garden, it would come back with a knife through it. What sort of people would do that, he thought.

Back at his house in Wilton, the local children had no fear of him. One of them had broken the window at the rear of his house with a cricket ball, almost hit him fair and square as it whizzed past him, but what had he done? Nothing. He'd given them their ball back. Even had a bowl and a few hits after one of the young children had bowled at him, pretending to let the ball get through and knock over the stumps, or in their case a few sticks propped up between two wooden boxes. The offender's parent had apologised, offered to pay for the broken window. In the end, he and the parent had gone halves on the repair, not that it cost much, and here was Barbara Winters' brother slashing footballs. For what reason? The man was probably as much as zealot as her; he needed to be interviewed.

***

Clare observed her senior in his office, mulling over the case, his eyes closed. She thought that he looked like a cuddly teddy bear, not that he would have appreciated being told so. But there he was, arms folded, leaning back, running through the case, weighing up all that they had. Even she had found benefit in the ability to sit quietly and evaluate her life, inside and out of the police force. She knew she was lonely, missing the touch of a man. She was young, and at an age when a woman thinks of children, yet she had no one, not slept with another man since Harry had died, and she wanted to, though she couldn't be a Polly or a Liz. For them, sex and love were detached. Clare knew that the women regarded the act of procreation as a means to an end. They were both attractive, yet they slept with a man, not their age, not in good condition, purely because he was wealthy and willing to spend money on them. And then there was the brother they were sleeping with as well, supposedly because he could help them. Clare would admit that Gerry, a man who could be violent, was not unattractive: muscular, a firm handshake, a pleasant manner, and willing to take her out if she agreed, not that she ever would. Harry had been her ideal man; Gerry Winters would never be. And besides, she could admit to liking Mavis and Rachel, but their DNA was not pure Winters, whereas Gerry's was.

A date with a fellow officer had been agreeable enough. He had treated her well, held the chair back at the restaurant for her to sit down, even insisted on paying, not going halves. Yet, no spark. He had attempted to kiss her at the end of the evening, went through the accepted seduction routine as if a decent meal and a bottle of wine automatically concluded with two people naked and in bed. The man who she saw on a daily basis had taken her negative response with grace, accepted a kiss on the cheek as payment for a pleasant night.

Clare had cried that night for the man she couldn't have. She wanted to forget, to get on with her life, yet Harry remained firmly implanted, almost as a ghost from the past.

'Yarwood, are you going to sit there all day?' The voice of reality, the sound of her senior, arisen from his chair.

'Waiting for you, guv.'

'There's plenty for you to be getting on with. You don't need me to hold your hand every minute, do you?'

'I didn't want to disturb you. You looked so peaceful.'

'Thinking, that's what I was doing. You thought I was asleep?'

'It crossed my mind.'

'You're becoming too quick with your comments, you know that?'

'Yes, guv.'

They both knew the routine, the harmless rubbing each other up the wrong way. To an outsider, it would have appeared disrespectful to her, abusive by him; it was neither.

'I thought we were visiting Pathology, checking on Betty Winters.'

'The mother of the family.'

'Did you know her from before?'

'Vaguely.'

'Mavis's parents?'

'Her mother was a pleasant woman, similar to the daughter. Her father, respectable, working-class, drove an old Vauxhall. He didn't say much, but he'd acknowledge you. He always seemed sad.'

'Any reason why?'

'Just an observation on my part. He wasn't a drinker, and most weekends he'd be washing the car, or out in his garden, not that he had much success. I can remember it being cold back then. Maybe it wasn't, but that's what I remember. We even had a white Christmas.'

'I'm driving?'

'What do you reckon, Yarwood?'

'I'll get the keys.'

Pathology was not far away. Stuart Collins, the pathologist, took one look at Tremayne as he walked in the door and sighed. 'Tremayne, the bane of my life. What do you want?'

'Purely social,' Tremayne's reply.

'What is it with this man, Sergeant? Every time I'm busy, he's here.'

'He's a taskmaster, you know that.'

'What is it?' Collins asked. The man appreciated the chance to indulge in some banter, a chance to remove himself from the gruesome task of examining dead bodies, though it didn't worry him anymore, impervious as he was to the whole process.

'Betty Winters.'

'Seventy-nine. No medical condition other than ageing. She had taken a few sleeping tablets, not enough to kill a younger person. I can't see suicide, definitely not murder. Her death will be recorded as natural. Is that sufficient?'

'Yes. We'll need a medical certificate, a release of the body.'

'You'll have the certificate today, the body tomorrow. Is that all?'

'It is.'

'Sergeant, get him out of here, will you?'

'My pleasure,' Clare said.

***

Two days passed. Clare had found out from Barbara Winters the details of her brother. He had been flying between England and Australia. Clare had sent out a request to his airline to pass on a message to him. The man presented himself at Bemerton Road Police Station at eight in the evening. Both Tremayne and Clare were in the office.

Clare went downstairs, met the man and escorted him upstairs. She had to admit to being impressed. Barbara Winters' brother, Archie Garrett, was tall with jet black hair. He was dressed in his pilot's uniform, British Airways. 'I've just arrived back. I came here straight from Heathrow. I'd like to see my sister.'

'That will be arranged. We'll need fifteen minutes to deal with the paperwork.'

'What paperwork? She's my sister, I'm entitled to see her.'

Clare sensed the change in the man's attitude.

'Where's that fool of a husband?'

'He's been here every day. We've not restricted his access.'

'And good to hear. The man's a snivelling imbecile, but Barbara seems to like him.'

Tremayne met the brother, had a brief discussion. Barbara Winters was brought to a visitor's room. The brother and sister were allowed to embrace, to sit next to each other, a police officer in one corner of the room, far enough away not to hear their conversation. Neither of the two was regarded as antagonistic to each other, hence the restrictions were relatively few.

'What happened?' Archie asked.

'It's that family. They've turned Dean.'

'You were warned about allowing tainted blood into our family.'

'What was I to do? You may be able to embrace a life of celibacy, I cannot.'

'The man was poor material.'

'He was pliable. I had controlled him for so long. If his brother had not won all that money, he would still be with me.'

'And you tried to kill him?'

'No, I didn't. I was angry. I wanted to make him pay for leaving me and joining with them again. He rejected the one true path, embraced depravity and ignorance and the way of the devil,' Barbara said.

'We have suffered for our beliefs. What hope was there for Dean? He has brothers in jail, a sister prostituting herself. And as for Alan Winters' wife, what a bitch. How I would like to deal with her. The anguish she would feel, the pain, the suffering. As for your Dean, if you are ever free of here, we will deal with him. He will not stray again.'

'How?'

'We will destroy his will to resist. Now, what do we need to do to get you out of here?'

'We need to convince them that my actions towards Dean were out of anger, not out of a desire to harm him.'

'But how?'

***

Betty Winters was not accorded the same degree of reverence that was shown to her son. This time just her coffin at the crematorium, the immediate family, a priest that Mavis knew to say a few words. Tremayne and Clare had been invited. Tremayne declined, Clare accepted as a special favour to Mavis.

The open casket, the woman's children filing past. Stan was allowed to attend, but not to drink, not that he wanted to. There had been trouble when he had arrived back at Pentonville the previous time. It had taken Tremayne a couple of phone calls to deal with the warden and to ensure that Prison Officer Marshall did not receive a warning.

Tremayne had put in a special request for Fred Winters to attend. It had been granted, although Fred would have to stay with a prison officer at all times. The man was listed as violent, whereas Stan was not. None of the other members of the Winters family was pleased to see him when he arrived.

'The man's trouble,' Mavis confided to Clare.

Stan Winters had spoken to his brother on his arrival, as had the others. Rachel Winters had given the man a kiss on the cheek and a hug. Bertie, her brother, had shaken his hand.

Dean Winters, dressed in a suit, sat on the front row of the chairs. There was a small pulpit to the right of the casket, now closed after everyone had filed in. Rachel stood up, took her place in the pulpit and said a few words in honour of the dead woman. Clare could hear the sincerity in her voice, the only one that day. Fred, although the eldest child, declined to say a few words, but Stan was willing to stand up. He chose to read the Bible. Clare asked Fred later why he had not followed on from Rachel. 'I couldn't, that's all.'

Dean Winters said a few words, read them straight from a piece of paper, never once looking up at the people in the small chapel. His words sounded insincere to Clare. She noticed that his wounds had healed. Bertie Winters fidgeted in his chair, a clear sign that Mavis Winters had wasted her money on trying to get the man off drugs.

Gerry and Cyril sat quietly throughout the service: some emotion on Cyril's face, none on Gerry's. Margie Winters sat impassively, the previous ability to communicate, temporary as it had been, gone. She did not utter a word, only nodded her head, not even wiping her eyes. Clare went up to her afterwards as everyone stood around drinking tea, eating cakes, attempting to talk about the dead woman who was now on her way to being prepared for cremation. Margie responded warmly when Clare put her arm around her, snuggled in close. The woman was skin and bones, in need of nourishment, but she was not even willing to eat cake. 'I hated her,' she said, the first words she had said that day.

'Today's not the day to talk ill of the dead,' Clare said.

After the ceremony, it was back to the Winters' house, now host to Dean as well. He was making the occasional trips to Southampton, but apart from that he was staying close to Barbara. Her brother had brought in their lawyer; he had argued his case for her to be released on bail. Tremayne would oppose it, but it would be up to a court hearing. The woman was unstable as far as Tremayne could see, and there remained a possibility that she would strike out at her husband or another member of the Winters family. He thought that she would get bail, as the lawyer was competent.

Tremayne went to Betty Winters' wake, had a terse but polite conversation with Fred. The man was a habitual criminal, and Tremayne represented the law, even though he had helped the family when he lived nearby. 'It's nothing personal, Tremayne, you know that.'

'Fred, leave well alone. Take the money and move away when you get out,' Tremayne said, knowing full well that he was wasting his time.

'I only wish I could, but I'm committed to farming. I've got a few ideas. I've been in the prison library, learning what I need to know.'

'Mavis has done well by your family.'

'I know that. A fine woman, better than Alan deserved. I wouldn't mind her alongside me.'

Tremayne knew that trouble was coming, but it was sometime in the future. He moved away, found Stan drinking a beer. 'I thought you weren't allowed.'

'Only the one. It's a miserable atmosphere in here. I've got to do something.'

'Give me one,' Tremayne said.

'You're a good man, you know that.'

'Don't tell the criminals, will you? And don't tell my sergeant.'

'Why? What will she do?'

'A smart comment.'

'But you don't mind?'

'Don't let her know, that's all.'

'How is she? After Holchester's death?'

'She's bearing up, the same as all of us.'

'Aye, that's true. All the money in the world, and it doesn't solve anything. Life's a bitch sometimes. Look at me, all those years in jail, never married, nothing.'

'That was your decision.'

'I know that, but it's a waste.'

'You're not that old.'

'As rich as any family could be, but what do you see? A room full of long faces, and outside in the driveway, Mavis's Bentley. What for? What does it do that an old bomb doesn't? I'll tell you, nothing. I'll take my two million, buy myself a small house and invest the rest. Maybe I'll take up a hobby.'

'Not robbing banks?'

'I'm not Fred. Maybe golf, maybe fishing.'

'You'd be bored.'

'Not me. I'm not an ambitious man, the need to chase young women doesn't interest me, well, not much anyway. I'm an emotional vacuum; it must be our mother that did that. We're all emotionally stunted. That one woman destroyed our lives.'

'What about those men who abused Margie and the others?' Tremayne asked.

Stan Winters took a seat. 'It was a long time ago. Do you want to bring up the past? Think of Margie. She's had a rough time, unpleasant memories. You'll only make it worse for her.'

'What happened to them?'

'We beat them up, put them on a train, one way, that's all.'

Tremayne knew it was not the truth; he decided to say no more on the subject. As Stan had said, it was a long time ago, the men's names lost in time, the chance of proving murder or otherwise was long gone.

'Fred will cause trouble,' Tremayne said.

'I'll be around. I can control him.'

'Can you?'

'I'm the only one who has a chance. We've a lot of history between us.'

Tremayne walked over to Clare. 'I'm taking Margie home,' she said.

'How is she?'

'Not good, but she'll talk to me, not the others. Her emotions are raw. She should be in a hospital, but she'll not go.'

'Her family could get a court order.'

'They'll not do that. For all their faults, they all love her, and she won't be around for much longer.'

'Are you sure?'

'No. But the woman doesn't look after herself. She's addicted, probably not selling herself, not too often that is, but the men she'd go around with wouldn't treat her too well.'

'I'll stay for a while. I'll see what the other brothers have to say, also Mavis and her children.'

'Don't expect much from Bertie.'

'I won't.'

Chapter 19

Tremayne left the wake. It was ten in the evening, and he was sober. He phoned Clare, she was back home in her cottage. 'Margie?' he asked.

'I sat her down, made sure she had some tomato soup.'

'It's hardly a meal.'

'It was the best I could do. How about you?' Clare asked. One of her cats sat on her lap; it was purring. The television was on, and she turned down the sound.

'Fred went back to prison, so did Stan. As for the others, Dean was upstairs by the time I left, so was Bertie. Gerry and Cyril were there, didn't have much to say, only that Cyril was glad to have his house to himself again. Gerry, I think he phoned up the two women.'

'Polly and Liz.'

'What about them? They're easy with their favours, especially with Gerry.'

'What do you make of Gerry?' Clare said.

'He makes sure that Mavis is safe. I believe the man is genuinely fond of her.'

'Yet she prefers you.'

'Yarwood, don't go down that road. Don't try to be the matchmaker, and besides, I've got Jean.'

'Have you?'

'I think so. We get on well. She's not coming to live with me; I'm not going to live with her. We'll meet every few weeks, have a weekend away. Mavis realises that I could keep Fred under control, but I'm not going to babysit the family. There are enough men there as it is.'

'Dean won't be much help.'

'Not at all, and his wife's bail hearing is coming up.'

'What do you reckon?'

'She'll get bail,' Tremayne said.

'And then what?'

'She'll be quiet for a few days, so will her brother.'

'He's as devout as her.'

'Possibly worse. A few days and Dean will be in their line of fire again.'

'Violence?'

'Coercion more like. I think Barbara Winters blew it down in Quidhampton. She's held the man in check for years, and then all of a sudden, he's with his family. They're in the background egging him on, telling him to stand up for his rights.'

'He'll not continue to stand up to her.'

'Not him. He likes to be told what to do. We've always assumed that all seven have the same father.'

'The differences in their characters, is that what you mean?'

'Dean is not like Fred, although Cyril is like Alan. There are similarities between Gerry, Fred, and Stan.'

'Margie?' Clare asked, as the woman concerned her more.

'She's similar to Dean, weak personality. Another woman may have eventually shrugged off what happened to her, but she's susceptible to drugs, same as Bertie. I'd say that Alan, Cyril, and Margie, probably Dean, had the same father, although there's an age difference of eight years between Alan and Margie.'

'Is it relevant?'

'Probably not. The father or fathers are not around.'

'They're not important,' Clare said.

***

Dean Winters visited his wife, found her in an ebullient mood. 'My hearing's coming up soon. I'll make it up to you, I promise,' she said. 'It'll be like it used to be, just you and me.'

'I'm sorry,' Dean said. He knew he wanted Barbara back and if that came with her funny ways, then he would accept them, even embrace them if it was required. He remembered the early years, the early nights, the passion. Back then, she had been firm in her beliefs, had told him about her father and how he had pushed her and her brother. How he had made them stand for hours on end reciting passages from the Bible. And then, the standing on street corners, a banner in one hand, a Bible in the other, attempting to waylay the pedestrians as they walked past, most taking a wide berth, others coming in too close, only to be caught. Even in winter, they'd be there at the weekend. How her school friends had ridiculed her, not invited her to their parties, not that she would have been allowed to attend. Her father would have seen to that, and now the man did not even recognise his children.

Dean knew he had been a lonely man, lacking in confidence, even a slight stutter at the first signs of nervousness, but with Barbara he had been articulate, with her always there building him up. The change in their relationship, imperceptible at first, dramatic afterwards, had occurred the day after Alan had won the money. There he was, outside Dean's house, in a red Ferrari. He had gone out to see Alan, even driven it at one stage, and inside the house, Barbara, unwilling to come out, was condemning his brother.

Up until then, he had not seen Alan for many years. He couldn't admit to missing his family that much, apart from Margie.

Apart from his isolation from his family, the relationship with Barbara had been great and the saying of prayers at meal times, the two visits to the church on a Sunday were only minor encumbrances. Yet with the Winters' wealth, his brother's insistence on him taking some for himself, his wife had changed.

No more was she dismissive of his family, not talking about them. Instead, she would bring up the subject at every opportunity, criticising them: the lazy, the incompetent, the criminal, the prostitute. He had reacted as any man would; he had fought back. With words at first, then with threats, and then by walking out on her, but not before hitting her. Not that she didn't deserve it as she'd beaten him enough times, and he had stood there and taken it. As he sat with her in that small room, he knew that the good outweighed the bad and by a large margin. He wanted to be with her, and if that meant that all the cutlery, all the plates and cups and saucers had to be in line, the food cans as well, then it was a small price to pay. And now, she was promising to go back to what she had been before.

'What about this two million pounds that Mavis has offered? he said.

'We will accept it. We will use it for charitable purposes. At least the evil will be of some good,' Barbara said. The two of them shared a warm embrace, the policewoman in the corner of the room saying nothing, only smiling. She was a sucker for a romance book, and here, in the room, there was true love, a happy ever after. She did not see the look in Barbara Winters' eye, nor did her husband.

***

Bertie Winters had been seen around Salisbury of a night time on a few occasions, invariably minding his own business, getting drunk or drugged, although the latter was unproven. What was clear to Tremayne was the man was too sullen when sober, too vocal when drunk, not that anything could be done about it, and the fact that the subject of his vexation was his mother did not bode well for family relationships. Tremayne, sitting in the Pheasant Inn one night, had taken the man to task, attempted to tell him that he should be grateful that his mother was making an effort to look after the family's interests. All Tremayne received in reply was a comment to mind his own business. Tremayne wondered why he had become involved; Clare, when Tremayne had told her, reckoned it was a guilty conscience, in that he had seduced the man's mother when he was younger. Tremayne told her she was talking nonsense.

Barbara Winters' hearing had been a formality, with her husband having made an impassioned plea for the love of his life to be released. He'd also given an account of the dangers of infinite and immediate wealth and how it impacted otherwise decent people, his wife included.

Clare had attempted another date with the police officer that she had been out with before. The same routine: the meal, the wine, the attempt at luring her back to his place. The same result, a goodnight kiss. She had wanted to invite him in, the need for a man to make love to her, but he had not been Harry, never would be. It worried her that she was heading down the Tremayne road of relationships.

Whatever the future held, it was certain that for now it was her and her two cats, though one of them was starting to age, struggling on its back legs.

Tremayne caught up with Mavis Winters after her sister-in-law's bail hearing. 'What do you reckon?' she had asked.

'I'm against it,' Tremayne said. 'The woman and her brother have some strange ideas.'

Mavis had been surprised at his appearance: a new white shirt, a freshly-pressed suit. She made no mention of it. 'Dean's gone back to Southampton with her,' she said.

'Let's hope he's okay.'

'For a few days, but she'll have him standing to attention soon enough.'

'What is it with Dean? The other brothers stand up for themselves.'

'No idea. He was the closest in age to Margie when they were growing up. He probably saw more of what was going on in that house than anyone else, no doubt some of his mother's men were abusing him, violently probably. One thing's for sure, he rarely talks about it.'

'The two million pounds?'

'I've signed it over to Dean. The other brothers will get theirs soon enough. With Fred, I'll want some further safeguards.'

'Such as?'

'I'm not sure. That's up to the solicitor. Fred has to take the money on his release on the condition that he does not ask for more.'

'He'll agree, take no notice.'

'Then he won't get the money.'

'That's a dangerous game.'

'I know it is, but what else can I do? Believe me, this money's a curse. So far, I've a son who's out of it and a dead husband.'

Tremayne did not want to get into a conversation about having too much money. It wasn't a condition he had ever suffered from, nor would he have wanted it. He preferred the uncomplicated life, and money only complicates. The solution for the Winters was straightforward, although none of them would ever take it. It had come up in the bail hearing that one of the brothers and his wife were going to devote themselves to charitable causes, how they were going to use the money for good.

Tremayne noticed that at the hearing Barbara Winters never mentioned that the money came from evil. She was careful to keep her extremist views in check. The woman was intelligent, in that she was capable of portraying the loving housewife, the friend of little children and animals. Tremayne knew there'd be trouble, and with instant millionaire status, how long before the woman cracked? Everyone has a price; he'd heard that before, not sure if he did, but what would have happened if he had had a run of wins on the horses, the money multiplying up into the thousands, possibly hundreds of thousands? Would he have looked at his house disparagingly, sought to buy a better one?

He thought he wouldn't, but now there was a woman with two million pounds. He was sure they had not heard the last of her.

'What about Gerry? He's still with Polly and Liz,' Tremayne said. Mavis had picked him up from Bemerton Road in the Bentley. He had to admit the car was magnificent, but it wouldn't have fitted in the garage at his house. Mavis had let him drive it, although he hadn't wanted to. He never let on, but his eyes weren't as sharp as they used to be, and at night he was finding it hard to focus on the road, especially if it had been raining, and the headlights of the other cars would sometimes dazzle him. They had settled themselves at a restaurant in Harnham, not far from where Alan used to go with Polly and Liz. As he drove, more like cruised, past Alan's favourite pub, the woman in the passenger's seat had not commented. Tremayne made no mention of it either.

If Gerry's got the money, they'll be friendly to him.'

'What's your feeling towards them?'

'Ambivalent. I was angry at first, but now I maintain a cordial relationship with Polly. I also needed to ensure my investments are sound. Alan won sixty-eight million pounds. If I cashed in now, sold the house, the furniture store, the car, and put it together with the money in the various banks, I'd be down to forty-two million, and now there are six children, including Margie, that's twelve off the total. That still leaves thirty million. It sounds a lot to us. I used to think that if I had a hundred pound in my pocket, I was rich, and now I talk in millions.'

'It is a lot,' Tremayne said.

'There's always someone hassling for a handout. You can't believe how popular you are when you give it; how despised when you refuse to give more, or none at all.'

'Some problems?'

'Alan gave a million to a charity in Africa. The man who came to the house gave a spiel about schooling the children in Liberia, though I hadn't heard of the place.'

'It's in West Africa,' Tremayne said.

'Anyway, we gave him the money, a bank transfer. I'd checked it out, it seemed above board.'

'What happened?'

'The next we heard, the man's driving around in a Jaguar, having built a few tin huts in a couple of villages. He was possibly well-intentioned, the same as us, but once the money hit the charity's account, greed took over.'

'After that?'

'I learnt my lesson, Alan didn't. Polly and Liz are a prime example.'

'They're hard workers.'

'They are, but there were other women before them. Not that I ever knew who they were. He used to go up to London with Gerry, extended visits, spend the night there, have a few drinks, watch a show.'

'Alan, a show?'

'As long as the women were scantily clad.'

The two friends laughed at Mavis's comment. Tremayne had to admit that he enjoyed her company. If she had been older, if he had been more mature all those years ago, they may have made a go of it, but now he felt comfortable with Jean, and besides, playing two women, not that he ever did, was for a younger man, not someone in his late fifties.

'Gerry, you never answered about him, not fully.'

'He's not a total fool, and he's devoted to the family. I've no interest in him either, if that's what you're asking.'

Tremayne hoped he hadn't walked into a trap.

'It was inferred that you had someone with you when Polly and Liz came visiting.'

'Not me. All I had was a hot water bottle and a rogue of a husband.'

'Why didn't you object?'

'Alan had the money. It was all in his name, the house, the cars, the bank accounts.'

'But you had money.'

'I always had plenty; he wasn't tight with me, but not total access. There was one bank account in my name, a few million pounds, but the bulk was in his name.'

'Why?'

'His solicitor, someone he'd known from his schooldays. He told him to do it.'

'Good advice?'

'I wasn't going to cheat Alan. No, it wasn't good advice, but then, this fair-weather friend charged him close to two hundred thousand to set it all up.'

'How much were they worth, his services?'

'Fifteen to twenty thousand. You see, that's what happens. Everyone wants to bleed you dry, assuming it's a pot of gold with no bottom.'

Mavis ordered fish, Tremayne ordered a steak, well done. A bottle of wine between the two of them. The place was expensive, and regardless of how much money Mavis had, he was paying. He was not going to be one of those who took advantage.

'What about you, Tremayne?' Mavis asked. It was only Jean who called him Keith.

'I'll keep working.'

'Happy?'

'Content would be a better word. I don't have your wealth, but then, what use is it to me? I can afford to buy what I want.'

'What do you want to buy?'

'Nothing.'

'That's what I thought. What about Clare?'

'You like her?'

'She's sad. I sometimes see it in her eyes, but yes, I like her very much.'

'You know her story?'

'I've always known, never mentioned it to her. Time heals, they say.'

'A lot of time in her case.'

'She needs to find someone else, move on.'

'She will, in time.'

'And you?'

'I've got Jean.'

'Serious?'

'We get on well. We meet up occasionally, glad of each other's company.'

'She's got herself a good man with you.'

'I've mellowed in my dotage,' Tremayne said.

'Dotage? You're still a difficult man. How does Clare deal with you?'

'Don't tell her, but I'm fond of her. Never let her know.'

'I won't. Now, what do you fancy for dessert, and not me. I'm off the menu.'

'I never presumed, besides…'

'No besides, you're not my type. Too old for me. I'll find myself a toy boy.'

'You can afford one,' Tremayne said, realising that Mavis was joking with him.

Chapter 20

Dean Winters sat in the corner of the kitchen. The chairs were lined up. He was sitting upright, shoulders back. 'We'll be alright,' Barbara said. Her brother stood next to her, both looking at the man who was waiting for instructions.

Dean realised that he had made a mistake in returning to Southampton.

'You will sign over the money to Archie, is that understood?'

'I thought we were going to use it for good?'

'We are, but Archie will take control. You will do what you are told. Is that understood?'

'But…'

'*Is that understood?*'

'Yes, it is understood.'

'Why did you marry this imbecile?' Archie said. He was no longer in his airline pilot's uniform but casually dressed in a tee-shirt and jeans. The brother and sister had the man where they wanted him.

'He does what he's told.'

'But he is still one of them.'

'That is why I have never bred with him, my dear brother.'

Dean looked at the pair standing next to the kitchen sink, knew what they were, knew that there was no escape. He had been happy in Salisbury in Mavis and Alan's home, he had even got drunk on a couple of occasions, and nobody had complained. But here, in this house of horrors, subjected to physical and mental abuse, there'd be no respite.

He knew about Barbara and Archie's childhood. The father who would lock them in a cupboard for days on end for the merest infraction, who'd beat them with a leather belt, who'd make them stand for hours at attention, all the while spouting fire and brimstone at them, eternal damnation for their being alive when their mother was not. Dean had sympathised with his wife, understood the pain she felt after the hold of the father had lessened. Back then, when they had met, she had been kind and gentle, at least with him, not his family, but she had changed. The father confined to a nursing home, the son taking on the mantle, subjecting his sister to abuse if she deviated from the one true course, blaming her for choosing love over righteousness, for seeking the pleasures of the flesh over abstinence.

Dean knew that he needed out and to be back in Salisbury, although if he made an attempt to move, they would restrain him, lock him in the cellar, while they sat upstairs and decided what to do with the money.

Dean knew that whatever it was, it would not be for the benefit of the deserving.

They had arrived back from Salisbury the day before. On the trip down, Barbara had spoken about a new beginning and how she was going to devote her life to her husband. Once at home, they had retreated upstairs and made love. For that night and the morning after, they had been as newly-weds, until Archie arrived at the front door with two large suitcases. He did not bother to knock, he had a key. He found the two of them embracing.

'I've taken three months' leave,' Archie had said.

'This is my house. Get out,' Dean had shouted, but to no avail. He had received a punch in the face for his impertinence.

'You're a miserable little worm. You will learn obedience. You will learn that total obedience to the Lord, to me, is the only way. I will guide you on your journey.'

'You're an evil bastard,' Dean had said, only to be thrust into a cupboard for a few hours to cool down. On his release he had found his wife and her brother in deep thought, deciding on their future, not his.

They had spoken about following the path of righteousness, of helping others, but he had not been swayed by the desire to do good. He knew that they intended to help themselves the way their father had, a businessman who had no issue about preaching goodness while doing anything and everything to increase his wealth. And now the family that they both abhorred had given them the easy way.

***

There were always two certainties in the Winters family: one, that the mother, Betty, would not die, and two, that Margie would.

The first certainty had proved to be incorrect, the second had not.

Clare was the first in the office to receive the news. Gerry phoned her. 'It's Margie.'

Clare phoned Tremayne who phoned Jim Hughes. Clare was the first at Margie's place. Upstairs, a medic as well as Mavis, Gerry, and Cyril. Rachel was on her way. Sprawled across the bed was the lifeless body of Margie Winters. Gerry and Cyril had tears on their faces, Mavis was resolute and in control. 'We just came to check on her. We hadn't heard from her for a couple of days.'

'We'll need our people to check out the room, conduct an autopsy,' Clare said, a lump in her throat. The woman had been doomed for most of her life; her death should not have come as a surprise, yet it hit home hard.

'We had always hoped,' Gerry said, 'that somehow she'd come back to us, and now, she's lying there.' Clare put her arms around him. He seemed better for her sympathy.

'Why?' Cyril asked. He was no better than Gerry, as he held a handkerchief to his eyes.

'We'll find out,' Clare said.

Tremayne entered the room, looked at the dead woman, put one of his arms around Mavis's shoulder. 'It was bound to happen one day,' he said.

'I know,' Mavis said.

Tremayne spoke to the medic. 'What's the diagnosis?'

'It's a possible drug overdose.'

'Intentional?'

'That's not for me to say.'

'Thanks,' Tremayne said. He realised that the medic would be non-committal. It was not the man's function to say what had happened; that belonged to Jim Hughes and his crime scene team, as well as Stuart Collins, the pathologist.

'It would be best if we leave the room,' Tremayne said.

At his suggestion, everyone moved to the hallway outside. Jim Hughes arrived, kitted himself up and entered the room, accompanied by Tremayne, who had also put on protective gear. 'What's the situation?' Hughes asked.

'Margie Winters, forty, drug-addict, a prostitute.'

'Is the death suspicious?'

'Not in itself but her brother was murdered. We'll need to see if this is related.'

'I'd hazard a guess that she's overdosed.'

'Any reason?'

'Don't hold me to it. There are no apparent signs of a struggle, even though the room's a mess. The woman was clearly not healthy, probably under-nourished.'

'How long do you need?'

'A few hours. My team will check it out, see who else was here. Was she actively prostituting herself?'

'We don't think so. She was looked after by her family, the best they could.'

'Not very well by the look of this place.'

'That was her decision. There was a firm offer for her to move into the Winters' home in Quidhampton, all the medical help she could ever want.'

'And?'

'She refused it all.'

'Okay. We'll do our job and then send the body to Pathology. You'll have a verbal report later today, a written one tomorrow. After that, you can check with Pathology.'

Outside, Tremayne spoke to the assembled family. Rachel had just arrived. 'Margie will be transported to Pathology in the next few hours. It appears not to be suspicious, although we'll confirm later. We'll need to take statements from those who were here. Rachel, you've arrived later, so we don't need your statement. Yarwood, can you go back to Quidhampton and deal with it?'

'Yes, DI.'

'I'll phone Stan and Fred,' Mavis said.

'I'll contact Dean,' Gerry said.

***

Tremayne sat in his car outside of Margie Winters' flat, realising that the Winters family were part of his life story. Even though there had been years when he had not seen them, he had occasionally bumped into one or another of them, always guaranteed a warm welcome, and now Margie was dead.

He had seen it before: one murder and then a string of deaths, some violent, some not. Betty Winters, the mother, dead from old age, Margie, the youngest of the seven children, died because of her mother. Tremayne hoped that no one else would die.

He turned the ignition in the car, prepared to return to the police station. His phone rang. 'Tremayne,' he answered.

'Stan Winters here. Mavis just phoned me. I want to be with the family.'

'I'll see what I can do. I'm not sure it's possible.'

'I trust you, Tremayne. If you can't, I'll understand.'

'How are you?'

'You know the answer to that question.'

'Let me see what I can do for you. No promises.'

'That's understood.'

'I'll not be able to get Fred out, not until the funeral.'

'He'll know that.'

Tremayne prepared to leave for the second time, the phone rang again. Tremayne recognised the number. 'Gerry,' he said.

'Mavis has phoned Fred. He took it bad. He'll be looking for you to arrange for him to come to the funeral.'

'I can do that. I'll try and get Stan out before. He's already phoned me.'

'We'll not forget what you've done for us.'

'I must admit to feeling upset over Margie.'

'Your sergeant's here with Mavis and Rachel. All three are in tears, especially your sergeant.'

'That's fine. She'll take the statements in due course.'

'One other thing. We can't contact Dean. I'm driving down there.'

'I'll come with you,' Tremayne said. 'I'll meet you in Guildhall Square, ten minutes. We'll use my car.' Tremayne knew that something was amiss. There was no evidence, no reason, but he felt a sense of foreboding. Whatever it was, he needed to be in Southampton at Dean and Barbara Winters' house.

Ten minutes later, Gerry arrived in Guildhall Square. He was driving the Bentley. If it were purely social, Tremayne would have gone with him, but it was not. 'We'll use my car,' he said.

Gerry parked the car, phoned for Cyril to come and pick it up. It didn't pay to leave an expensive motor car standing idle for too long. The hooligans, the envious, would see it as a target for vandalism.

'Not much of a car,' Gerry complained as they drove down to Southampton.

'We may need it.'

'You've got your suspicions?'

'About Dean's wife and her brother, yes.'

'And Dean is there. As children, he was a damn nuisance. If it were Cowboys and Indians, he'd be the Indian tied to the post.'

Tremayne phoned Yarwood. 'What's the mood there?'

'Sombre. We've not seen Bertie. Supposedly he's coming to the house.'

'Get some uniforms from Bemerton Road to find him.'

'I've already done that.'

'Mavis and Rachel?'

'Rachel's taking it badly. What about Jim Hughes?'

'It's a possible OD, probably unintentional. If it's not, I'll talk to Stuart Collins to say it was.'

'The family will understand. If it's suicide, then declare it.'

'Okay. We're nearly at Dean Winters' house. I've got a bad feeling about this.'

'The sixth sense?'

'Whatever it is, it just doesn't feel right.'

***

Tremayne drew up outside Dean and Barbara Winters' house. In the driveway, a Mercedes. 'I've not seen that car before,' Gerry said.

'Spending the money already,' Tremayne said.

The two men walked up the driveway, passed the car. Tremayne rang the doorbell, the chimes audible inside the house. No answer. He rang again. Still no response. The two men walked around to the back of the house; the lights were on, indicating that someone was at home. Tremayne knocked on the kitchen window, and then the back door. The sound of a car at the front. He rushed around the house to see the Mercedes reversing at speed from the driveway, clipping his vehicle as it went, breaking a tail light. In the driver's seat was Archie Garrett. His sister was in the passenger seat. Tremayne, realising the urgency of the situation at the house, dialled Yarwood. 'Mercedes SL350, YA16 UMS, late model, one or two years old, dark green. Put out an all-points, use Dean and Barbara Winters house as the reference. Instruct them to stop and detain two occupants: Barbara Winters and Archie Garrett.'

'What else.'

'Just do it, Yarwood. We're busy.'

Tremayne pushed up against the front door of the house with no success. Gerry assisted, the lock broke, and the two men entered the house. Inside, everything was spick and span. 'Dean,' Gerry shouted. No response. Tremayne headed for the rear of the house, Gerry ran up the stairs.

'He's down here, Gerry,' Tremayne shouted.

In the corner of the kitchen lay Dean Winters, black and blue from a severe beating. He was naked and unconscious. Tremayne dialled the emergency services.

'Dean, Dean,' Gerry said, sitting his brother up. Tremayne found a sheet in the utility room next to the kitchen and covered the man.

'What kind of bastards are these people?' Gerry said to Tremayne, as his brother slowly came around.

Six minutes later, there was an ambulance siren and a medic came into the house. 'What's happened,' the woman asked.

'The man's taken a severe beating. Severe lacerations across his back.'

A police car from the local station arrived. Tremayne showed his badge; they held back although it was in their jurisdiction and they would need to file a report.

'Is this what you've suffered all these years?' Gerry asked his brother.

'No, not like this,' Dean said. He was weak but conscious, the medic applying ointment to the exposed wounds, administering a painkiller.

'He'll need to go to the hospital,' she said. 'No broken bones from what I can see, but he'll need to be observed for a few days.'

'Before, Archie left us alone, but with the money he became inflamed. It corrupts, it always has. It's killed Alan. And now it's almost killed me.'

'You'll be alright, Dean. We've put out an all-points for them.'

Tremayne looked at Gerry; he understood. Margie's death would be kept secret from Dean for the time being.

Chapter 21

Dean Winters' injuries were not life-threatening, although he would be in Southampton hospital for several days, and then convalescing for a few weeks. As expected, Mavis came to the rescue with the best medical care, the counselling required after such a traumatic occurrence. Also, a room was being prepared for him at the house in Quidhampton.

As for the man himself, Dean was profoundly ashamed to admit the level of abuse that he had suffered over the years, mainly mental, sometimes physical.

'What can you tell us, Dean?' Tremayne asked him. Clare was with him, having driven down from Salisbury. Outside, waiting to visit him, were Mavis, Rachel, Gerry, and Cyril. Tremayne had briefly let them in to see Dean, or at least, Mavis, the undisputed matriarch of the family now. It was a police investigation, the two absconders not seen since they had reversed out of their driveway. The car was found abandoned less than five miles away.

The two of them had vanished. Tremayne was worried. Two people with no criminal records, apart from Barbara's pending trial, had clearly flipped, and he knew that people in their state of mind were no longer responsible for their actions. Caged animals facing imminent starvation will attack another and eat it; trapped humans will react in a similar manner. They had to be regarded as very dangerous, to be approached with caution.

'It was always Archie. You don't know what their childhood was like,' Dean said.

'That's not an excuse,' Tremayne said.

'Barbara's innocent.'

Clare could see that the man, no matter what was said or done, would continue to support his wife.

'What happened?' Tremayne asked. He had been forewarned by a trauma counsellor at the hospital that asking the patient too many questions could have a deleterious effect on his well-being, not that Tremayne needed to be told. He had encountered people during his career who had been subjected to severe mental and physical abuse, some who had nearly died at the hands of another.

'I had to be disciplined, don't you see? I had sinned.'

Clare stood to one side of the bed, wondering what it was with people who felt the need to harm others, to harm themselves, to believe that life was a set of rules: break them and it was eternal damnation or the need to self-punish.

'Did they kill Alan?' Tremayne asked.

'Not Barbara. She only did what Archie told her to do.'

'Have you been beaten like this before?'

'No. It's the first time. Barbara would hit me sometimes, lock me in the cupboard for my own good, but nothing more. It's Archie, I'm telling you. He's the one who controls.'

'But why?'

'Don't you understand. Their father controlled them, blamed them for the death of their mother.'

'Why?'

'I don't know. The man was always pleasant to me, but Barbara told me things; things that no child should endure.'

'Such as?'

'Physical disciplining, psychological conditioning, a house without entertainment where all three would sit around the table reciting biblical passages. And then Barbara was not allowed to socialise: straight to school, straight home. It's a wonder she survived.'

'It doesn't sound as if she did,' Clare said.

'I was working for her father; he deemed me suitable. Sometime afterwards, Barbara and I married.'

'Deemed?'

'Oh, yes. I had to ask his permission. But I knew I wanted Barbara, still do.' Dean moved in his bed, attempting to ease the pressure on the bandages wrapped around his upper body. His face was swollen, the first signs of bruising starting to show.

'We need to find your wife and her brother. Any ideas?'

'None.'

'Do they have any money?'

'I withdrew eighty thousand pounds for them.'

'Why?'

'For their charitable work.'
'And you believed this?'
'Barbara would not lie to me.'
'But you say she's controlled by Archie. Why, Dean, why? You've had a good education, better than anyone else in your family, yet you defend your wife's actions. Didn't you enjoy your time away with Mavis? The chance to do what you want? The chance to get drunk and overeat?'
'It was sinful. I see it all so clearly.'
'Barbara will be arrested, you know that?'
'I'll not testify against her.'
'That's your right. What about her brother?'
'He was right to do what he did. I understand.'

Tremayne and Clare left the man in his private room at the hospital. Outside, Tremayne spoke to Mavis. 'He still believes in her.'

'After all he's been through?'
'Stockholm Syndrome,' Clare said.
'What's that?' Mavis asked.
'It's conditioning whereby the hostage develops a psychological allegiance to their captor. That's what has happened with Dean. They've done this to him, and he still sides with them.'
'Is it permanent?'
'Probably not, but it will take time. He can't have any association with his wife.'
'Did they kill Alan?' Mavis asked.
'It seems possible, although why?'
'Maybe they realised that Alan would never give his brothers any more money? Maybe they assumed that I would be more generous?'
'It's possible. Devious, but a risk on their part,' Tremayne said.
'Am I in danger?' Mavis asked.
'We don't know. Until we find them, we're all in danger. This pair is desperate; their actions will not be rational.'

***

Tremayne and Clare returned to Salisbury. The local police in Southampton had a full description of the missing pair, as had their counterparts in Salisbury. The possibility remained that they had killed Alan Winters. The case file for his murder would now have the name of Samuel Garrett's two children on it.

Archie Garrett, well respected, bachelor, a senior captain for British Airways, remained an enigma. The man was highly regarded for his skills, and not once, not even after psychological tests had been conducted at British Airways, had he shown anything other than a man with moderate views, calm under pressure.

Tremayne knew that he was a dangerous individual. A weak man, such as Dean Winters, would be panicking, but not Garrett. He'd been calm, ensuring that he and his sister remained hidden, planning the next move.

Superintendent Moulton, briefly in Tremayne's office on his return, was excited that another murder was about to be solved.

'A change in the man,' Clare said.

'He blows hot and cold. Not to worry; he'll be back to form soon enough. What do you reckon, Yarwood? Do we have Alan Winters' murderers?'

'I'm not ready to concede that yet.'

'The right answer,' Tremayne said. 'Granted that they would have hated Alan Winters, but it's not conclusive.'

'The plan, if it is that, is full of too many variables. How would they have known that Mavis would give the money to the brothers, and why did they refuse the first offer?'

***

After three days there was still no sign of Archie Garrett and Barbara Winters. Dean, able to be moved from his hospital bed, had relocated to Salisbury, a nurse hired to look after him. Clare met up with him after one day back, noted that he seemed fine. It was early, and he was eating a full English breakfast. Mavis was busying herself arranging Margie's funeral, Dean having been told of her death.

The pathologist had issued a report that the woman's death had been as the result of a heroin addiction and her general poor health.

Clare sat down next to Dean, the cook serving her a full English breakfast as well. She had been trying to cut back, as a few extra pounds were creeping on, but she would not refuse. 'How are you?' Clare asked. She could see that the swelling on the man's face was going down in places, still black and blue in others.

'It's impossible to say. I loved my wife, but now it's over. Whatever happens, we could never be the same again.'

Clare could sympathise. After all, she had loved Harry Holchester, and he was dead. It was difficult, always would be, but life moves on. She was, she knew, a strong personality, and that she would rise above it. Dean Winters was not; the man would suffer.

'Margie?' Clare asked, not sure if the man was up to the question.

'It's probably better for her.'

Clare thought his answer was rational. She finished her breakfast and went and spoke to Mavis. 'Barbara Winters and her brother, Alan's murderers?' Mavis said.

'Did you see what they did to Dean?'

'Sadly, yes.'

'It doesn't make sense. How did they know the money would come to them eventually?' Clare said.

'What do you mean?'

'Did you give any indication that you would be more generous to the family if Alan weren't around?'

'I suppose I may have. Alan had never experienced money, assumed it would never run out, but there were enough rogues out there wanting to take it.'

'The charity in Liberia,' Clare reminded her.

'You don't need to go to Africa to find rogues. There are plenty here. We gave fifty thousand to a committee in another village to organise food for the aged.'

'What happened?'

'They went on a fact-finding tour overseas.'

'And the aged?'

'Still hungry.'

'And with Alan alive, there'd be no attempt to deal with these people?'

'He'd get angry, but that was all. And, besides, he was occupied.'

'Polly and Liz?'

'He also needed to help out the local publicans.'

'Violent when riled?'

'Not with me.'

'And Dean? What are you going to do with him?'

'He'll not change. I've become the mother now.'

'You'll do a better job than she ever did.'

'I'll do it, but it's not a job I want. Bertie's enough for me, and now there's Dean, and Cyril will need help.'

'Why?'

'The same old problem. Before, his financial situation kept him in check, but now he's got money, and he doesn't know what to do with it.'

'The same as Alan?'

'No doubt, but I had to give the brothers a reasonable amount, otherwise if I showed favouritism to one over the other, there'd be jealousy, and me having to listen to them. If Cyril spends his share, then I'll ensure he has somewhere to live.'

'What are you going to do about Bertie?'

'I hope he'll grow out of it.'

'Will he?'

'I hope so, but I'm not optimistic.'

***

Archie Garrett knew that he had been foolish. He thought of the father, the man who had destroyed their lives. The savagery of the man who had beaten his children for the slightest infraction. And now that man was dead to the world, locked in his own mind, not conscious of those around him. And still Archie could find no sympathy in his heart, only a feeling of hatred for him and for those who had impacted his life.

He had loved his sister, the only person who knew what went on in their childhood home. He had loved her until she had tired of him and had wanted another. He remembered the first time that she had introduced Dean Winters to him. Their meeting had been uncomfortable. He had been polite but resented the man who had usurped his sister's affection, distorted her, and there they were, exchanging smiles, knowing smiles, holding hands. He knew then that she had given herself to him, the one person that he had wanted. He remembered the day their mother died. It had been cold that day, ice on the path at the rear of the house. He and Barbara, wrapped up against the cold, only ten and eight respectively. Their mother, loving as always, shouting from the kitchen to keep themselves warm, not to catch a cold.

As their mother watched, he remembered Barbara calling for her to come outside and to help them to make a tree house, although it was only two feet off the ground. And then their mother coming out of the back door, slipping on the path, cracking her head on the concrete as she fell, the blood oozing.

It had been him, the more sensible of the two children, who had rushed next door to summon help. He remembered the ambulance and then the time in the hospital waiting for news, only to be told that their mother had died.

The two of them had attended the funeral, a hundred people there, a sign of how much she had been loved. And then the grieving process, the decline in their father's stability, his need to express his anger in violence, his extreme belief in the Bible, the Old Testament in particular. In time Archie understood that their mother's death had driven the man to despair, not that anyone outside the house would notice, not from him or from his children. They were too scared to tell anyone, too young to stand up to his bullying.

And in time he understood his father, his sister's inability to give herself entirely to her father's beliefs, her need to dress in the latest fashion, the need to have friends. He had not wanted friends since then, and whereas the pretence was complete, with the hearty bravado of a night out with the boys, even the occasional woman, he did not want any of them on a permanent basis. For him, he would prefer to spend his evenings with the good book, reading it page by page, memorising it, trying to learn from it.

As he and his sister sat in a room in a hotel in Portsmouth, not far from Southampton, not far from where Charles Dickens had lived, he knew that the future would need to be an affirmation of their father's teachings, a need to show that the Garretts were a pious and honourable people. Dean Winters came from a family of sinners, even before they had won the devil's money. Archie Garrett looked over at his sister, saw that she was desperately sad. He considered their options.

Chapter 22

For two weeks there was no sign of Archie Garrett and Barbara Winters, but time enough to conduct Margie's funeral. Not this time the horse-drawn hearse, the floral bouquets; instead, a funeral held in the chapel at the crematorium. Tremayne and Clare attended, on this occasion as friends of the family. Clare was glad to be invited, sorry that it was to commemorate the life of one of the fallen. Apart from the immediate family and the two police officers, there was no one else. Mavis read from the Bible, Dean, improved but still not fully recovered, gave a eulogy, long on the good parts of her life, short on the degradation that she had experienced in later life. Even Tremayne, at the request of the family, had agreed to read a short passage from the Bible. Clare was grateful that she had not been asked. There had been too many sad moments over the last year; she was overcome with emotion, so much so that it was Mavis, the stalwart, who had comforted her.

Rachel Winters also rose and spoke about her aunt, as did Stan and Fred Winters. Stan had been released from prison three days before the funeral on strict conditions: no visiting the local pubs, no causing trouble. He adhered to them, not venturing from Mavis's house in Quidhampton other than to deal with Margie's funeral. Fred arrived ten minutes before the funeral service started, a prison officer at his side. Once the ceremony was over, he would be going back to prison. Tremayne had spoken to him on his arrival, found out that he wasn't happy about the restrictions but pleased that he was present.

At Betty Winters' funeral there had been little sadness; at Margie's it was excessive. Once the funeral had concluded, the assembled group returned to the house in Quidhampton, everyone saying their farewells to Fred, including Tremayne and Clare.

'Thanks for getting me here,' Fred said. It had been Tremayne who had supported his request to be allowed to attend.

Back at the house, the mood, sombre initially, became increasingly lively afterwards. Bertie Winters sat in another room drinking a can of beer. Clare thought that his condition had worsened. She went and sat by his side. 'Bertie, you're not joining in.'

'Not me. I don't feel like it. They're out there pretending to care, but did they?'

Clare sensed the negativity, knew that the young man was incorrect. 'What do you mean?'

'They didn't stop her, did they?'

'They tried. She was welcome in this house. There was always the best medical assistance available.'

'That's easy. Just throw enough money around, ease the conscience.'

Clare left and went back to the other room. Bertie was obviously blaming his increasing addiction to drugs on others, not himself, his negativity being directed at others as if they were responsible. It was clear that the best medical treatment would not solve his problems. Margie had had an abusive childhood; Bertie had not. It would make no difference, his genetics were inclined to addiction, his sister, Rachel's, were not.

Back in the other room, Clare helped herself to another glass of wine, spoke to Stan. She knew that he would like to take her out, knew that she would decline. Stan was not her kind of man, although he had proved to be kind, and had helped Mavis in the days leading up to the funeral, not once deviating from his task. Fred, on the occasions that Clare had spoken to him, even at the church, was a different kind of man; he'd cause trouble whatever happened. Tremayne, free of policing responsibilities for once, was indulging in two of his favourite pastimes, beer and cigarettes, having found a willing partner in Stan. In spite of his previous release from prison when Stan had violated the conditions and had got drunk, Tremayne had managed to organise an extra day for him. Tomorrow when both he and Tremayne were sober, Tremayne would drive him back.

Dean was not drinking. Clare went over to talk to him. 'How are you?' she asked.

'I'm fine,' the man said. It was clear that he was still suffering trauma. He was dressed in a dark suit, the bruising on his face barely visible.

'We're still looking.'

'We were happy in those early years. What went wrong?'

Clare could see that Bertie was not the only one in a bad mood. 'That's life,' she said. A flippant remark, she thought. The only one she could think of.

'It was her father. With us, it was our mother. Why is it that the people who should love you end up destroying your lives?'

She spent a few minutes with Dean, and then went and spoke to Rachel. This time, the reception was more positive. 'It was a good send-off,' Rachel said. Of all those in the family, Rachel was the most balanced, Clare could see that. She had inherited her mother's good sense, her positive outlook on life, her father's good looks. Mavis, Clare had to admit, was not the most attractive of women. She was pleasant to look at, but the symmetry of the face and her complexion were not ideal, whereas with Rachel they were.

'No boyfriend here?' Clare asked.

'I'm not sure about him. How about you?'

'Not at the present time.'

'But one day?' Rachel said, conscious of Clare's former relationship.

'In time, I hope so.' Clare was genuine in her comment. She had visited Harry's grave during the week, placed some flowers on it, said some words to him. For the first time, she had not cried, not even felt sad. She knew, standing at the grave, it was time to move on, her period of mourning was over.

Tremayne leant against a pillar in the sunroom to the rear of the house. Clare went out to talk to him, found him to be in a good mood; Stan, a kindred spirit was keeping him company.

'What is it, Yarwood?' he said, although with a slurring of his words. She was pleased that he was taking it easy. The last few weeks had been difficult for everyone. There was still no arrest for the murder of Alan Winters, and since then two more of the Winters' family had died, one beloved, the other not, as well as the savage beating of one of the brothers.

'It's remarkable how cheerful everyone is,' she said.

'It's a wake. It's not a time to be miserable. We can reflect on Margie, but we can't allow our lives to be brought down because of it.'

Clare had wanted to discuss the case; the fact that there were still two people who had not been found. Further research into the Garrett household and the children revealed some anomalies. The man's treatment of his children was not unknown, even at the time. One of the schools they had attended had registered a complaint to the authorities after Barbara Garrett had arrived at the school with a broken arm; her brother, on another occasion, with a black eye. At one stage, both of the children had been removed from their father and placed in care, only to be back with him within a month.

Clare hoped that the rules had tightened up since then and that no child would be suffering in the present day.

Mavis was busy ensuring that everyone was fed and had a drink, even though caterers had been brought in.

'How's Dean?' Clare asked.

'He still misses her,' Mavis said. The two women had sat down, the caterers taking over.

'After all that has happened to him?'

'I know we were always unkind to her, bitch that she was, but what had happened to her as a child must have twisted her.'

'It doesn't excuse her for what she has become.'

'I suppose so. Do you believe that she and her brother murdered Alan?'

'It seems the logical conclusion.'

'And no idea where they are?'

'None. We know they were in Portsmouth, but since then, nothing. They must be desperate by now. They had cash, but they're not using credit cards or withdrawing money from an ATM. It's only a matter of time before they reappear.'

'I keep telling Rachel and Bertie to be careful, to take security, but neither takes any notice.'

'Rachel's sensible,' Clare said.

'The car that rammed her up near the hospital? Any more news as to who and why?'

'None. We've assumed it was an accident, possibly someone who had drunk too much or didn't have a licence.'

'Rachel was sure it was deliberate.'

'We don't think it was Barbara or her brother.'

'Someone else?'

'We're not pursuing that line of enquiry at the present time. Our focus is on Barbara and her brother. They're both capable of violence.'

'So's Fred. Did you see him at the church?'

'I saw him. He was pleasant, at least to me.'

'Of all the Winters children, he's the only one I can't like,' Mavis said.

'Does he know about Dean and his problem?'

'Dean told him at the church.'

It was ten in the evening before Clare left, giving a drunken detective inspector a lift home, his vehicle left in Quidhampton. She knew that she'd be in the office the next morning bright and early; he wouldn't.

***

Archie Garrett and Barbara Winters sat in a small café not far from Salisbury. Archie had purchased a car in a private sale and had paid cash. He had not shaved since their rapid retreat from Barbara and Dean's house. Barbara had dyed her hair blonde, cut it short. They knew they would not be easily recognised, and apart from the police showing photos in the hotel in Portsmouth, the first day after they had left Dean unconscious, they had seen no police presence.

Archie had realised that beating Dean had been wrong, but that was what had happened to him. He knew that both he and his father had a sadistic side. In the garden at home, he had enjoyed pulling the wings off butterflies, watching them squirm before stamping on them. With his father, it was tormenting his children, hurling them across the room, not feeding them, locking them in a cupboard or in the cellar.

'What are we going to do?' Barbara said. Archie could see that she was becoming sadder. He knew that there was no hope for them. He had nurtured his career, not once having faltered in his duty. To British Airways, he was the exemplary pilot, the man who could be relied on, but outside, the uniform removed, another persona. His father had been the same. At the time he had hated him, but now he understood.

'We cannot go back,' Archie said. He looked at his sister, the one person he had loved, but she had not loved him; she had loved Dean. Maybe that was the reason he had beaten him. They had been in that house, attempting to convince him of his sins in Salisbury, attempting to bring him back the way he had been before. Barbara, he could see, had weakened during her husband's absence.

He assumed Dean's belligerent attitude, his insistence that Archie was not welcome, was because of his family. They had convinced him that he had to stand up for his rights, to take control of his wife. Archie knew that could not be allowed. His father had only consented to the marriage on condition that Dean would look after Barbara in the manner to which she was accustomed, and now he was not following that order. And when Dean had stood up to him, throwing his suitcases out onto the driveway, he had reacted and hit the man. The first time with gentle force, and then with more, taking out the belt that his father had beaten him and Barbara with. The two of the children, both naked, both cowering as the man had come at them, both holding each other, hoping for relief. Relief that never came, and now Dean was resisting him. He had literally ripped the man's clothes off him, hitting him with the belt, throwing the occasional fist. Barbara had been shouting for him to stop, not wanting to get too close, the sight of the belt frightening her, and then the doorbell rang, the sound of the police knocking on the kitchen window.

The two of them, he and Barbara, running for the front door, jumping into the Mercedes and taking off. Archie knew the situation was grim; Barbara was not able to make any decisions. He knew that if he were not there, she would weaken and offer herself to Dean, give evidence against him to the police.

Chapter 23

Clare was in the office by seven in the morning the day after the funeral. Tremayne came in forty-five minutes later. Clare had not expected him to be bright-eyed and bushy-tailed so was not surprised to see him bleary-eyed and with no tail at all.

'Aren't you taking Stan Winters back to the prison today?' Clare said.

'At 10 a.m. He'll be ready.'

'Will you?'

'If you get me a cup of tea, I will be,' Tremayne said.

'Just this once.'

The two sat in Tremayne's office. Clare was full of energy; her detective inspector was not. 'Maybe I should drive him back?' Clare said.

'Maybe you should.'

Clare spent her time dealing with paperwork, Tremayne started with it, put it to one side. He was troubled. There were two people on the loose who had been willing to indulge in violence, and so far there was no sign of them.

Although the Winters maintained some security, it was insufficient. The question lingered in Tremayne's mind as to how Archie Garrett – his sister was regarded as subservient in their relationship – managed to get Alan Winters from Polly and Liz's place up to Stonehenge. It was known that the Bentley was outside their flat and that Gerry was driving, yet his recollection of the evening had been vague. If Alan had been dropped at home, then why was he at Stonehenge? Had he gone out again and why? Still more unanswered questions.

Tremayne did not have long to dwell on the matter. Realising that he was not in the best condition from the night before, he took a walk around the police station. Superintendent Moulton was in the hallway.

'Tremayne, what's the latest?'

'We're following up on all possible lines of enquiry. It's only a matter of time.'

'That's as maybe, but these two have been on the loose for some time. Do you regard them as dangerous?'

'Not to the general public, only to the Winters.'

'It's amazing what all that money can do.'

'It is. Not that you and I will ever find out.'

'Not me,' Moulton said. 'A police pension is all I've got to look forward to.'

'The same for me.'

'Don't you ever feel like throwing in the towel?'

'Are we talking retirement here, sir?' Tremayne said.

'Not at all. All the negativity of a murder investigation, the sorrow, the anger, the senseless taking of life by another, that's all.'

'It gets to me sometimes, I'll admit to that, but I've become inured to it. The Winters are an exception in that I've known them a long time.'

Tremayne could see the subtle attempts to talk about his retirement; he had no intention of rising to the bait, and besides, he had one man to return to his prison, two suspect murderers to deal with, and Jean, his former wife, to phone. The first responsibility he saw as an obligation, the second as confusing, the third as pleasurable.

Tremayne returned to his office; Clare was waiting. 'Yarwood, time to go?'

'If you want to pick up Stan Winters at 10 a.m.'

The two walked to Clare's car. She could see the look on her senior's face. 'What is it?'

'How did they get Alan Winters to Stonehenge?'

'He was unconscious.'

'That's not what I mean. We know that he left Polly and Liz's place, with a car outside. Did he drive or did someone else? And where was Gerry?'

'Are you having doubts about the Garrett siblings?'

'Not in itself. They're both capable of violence, or at least, Archie is, but from what we know, his violence comes from anger.'

'And taking a man up to Stonehenge to kill him does not. It's a calculated act spread over a few hours.'

'Precisely. And there was no anger in Alan's murder.'

'We've been down this road before. We have a murdered man, two violent people. Do you need more?'

'It may be enough to ensure a conviction, especially if they can place the Garretts in the vicinity of Salisbury.'

'But how? According to Dean, Archie was overseas at the time.'

'We have proof that was the case, but it's not conclusive. He could have flown back using a different name, committed the murder and then left the country again.'

'It's not logical.'

'I know, but why kill the man? They despised him and what he represented, but why murder? And then, why accept the two million pounds, and reject the one hundred thousand? Archie Garrett is a logical man, firm in his beliefs, as is Barbara. Why did they change?'

'Seduced by the money?'

'Not them. I just don't believe it.'

'But the car in the driveway?'

'That's unclear. We know they had purchased a Mercedes. According to Dean, he had signed over sufficient money to Archie, and that he had bought the car.'

'Dean's word.'

'There's no proof that the car was the result of the Winters' money. Archie Garrett must be paid well. He may just have bought it for himself.'

'We'll need to talk to Dean and Gerry on our return.'

***

Neither Tremayne nor Stan Winters said much on the way up to Pentonville. The previous evening, the police inspector and the convicted felon had both drunk excessively. That morning, of the two, Tremayne seemed the better, although it was marginal. For the first fifty minutes of the trip, both of them slept soundly; the only noise in the vehicle was the snoring of the two men. Clare could see the humour in the situation. Her phone rang. 'There's been an incident,' Moulton said.

It was unusual for him to phone her. 'What kind of incident?'

'Rachel Winters is missing.' Clare woke Tremayne. She handed her phone over to him.

'The woman never reported for work. They phoned her mother to check. Apparently, Rachel Winters is known for her timekeeping. The mother went looking, found the daughter's car a mile from the hospital.'

'They knew our phone numbers. Why didn't they phone us?'

'They didn't think it was suspicious at the time.'

'But now?'

'They've received a phone call,' Moulton said. Tremayne looked at his phone, flat battery. 'Your phone didn't ring?' he asked Clare.

'Not mine. It's been with me all the time.'

'You'll need to come back. We've put out an all-points.'

'The phone call?'

'Ransom. One million pounds or else.'

'Understood. Archie Garrett?'

'That's for you to find out.'

'And Mavis Winters has told the police?'

'She's an astute woman. She knew that the best chance of her daughter being returned alive was to let us know.'

'I've got Stan Winters with me. He's due back in Pentonville.'

'I'll phone the relevant people. He's under your control. Just make sure he abides by the conditions of his release.'

'I trust Stan. He'll do the right thing.'

Clare turned the car around and headed back to Mavis Winters' house. Bemerton Road was not the best place, other than for setting up a search.

At the Winters' house, there was surprise at seeing Stan again, concern over Rachel's safety.

'What did this person say?' Tremayne said on seeing Mavis.

'It was a muffled voice. One million pounds, or else they'd return Rachel to us in a box.'

'Archie Garrett?' Tremayne asked.

'We don't know.'

'You've found the car,' Tremayne said. 'Any sign of violence?'

'Not that we could see. It appeared that she had pulled off the road.'

'Jim Hughes is checking the car for fingerprints,' Clare said.

'We'll assume they find nothing. Coming back to the phone call, Mavis. What else was said?'

'Only that we were to ensure the money was available by six this evening and to wait for further instructions.'

'You realise that you are not to pay this. If you do, they'll want more money.'

'They can have it all. I want Rachel back.'

'Very well. Why did you call the police, if you'll not take my advice?' Why didn't you phone us instead of Bemerton Road?'

'I was panicking. Your phone wasn't working, and I couldn't get through to Clare.'

'My phone was fine,' Clare said.

'I tried once or twice, and then I phoned the police station.'

'The person on the phone told you not to contact the police?'

'I didn't want to, but with Alan dead, I thought the person on the phone may be his killer as well. Do you think Rachel is dead?'

'We don't know,' Tremayne said. 'Next time they phone, let me talk to them.'

'With respect, guv. It would be better if I spoke to them,' Clare said.

'Are you sure about this?' Mavis said.

'If they intend to harm Rachel, they will, regardless of police involvement. They'll respond better to me than DI Tremayne.'

'You're right,' Tremayne conceded. He knew that Yarwood was more diplomatic than him, and she had a calming voice, not like his, the effect of too many cigarettes.

Jim Hughes phoned. 'We've checked the car, no fingerprints other than Rachel Winters'. We have hers on record. Also, three cars at the site. Rachel Winters' car, the Bentley, we know it from the tyres, and another vehicle. The tyres are worn.'

'Any idea as to the make of car?'

'From a tyre print? Not a chance. The best we can tell you is that it's not a new car, small in size.'

'How?'

'The size of the tyres, as well as some oil that it dripped. We're assuming the Bentley doesn't drip oil.'

'If there's no more you can tell us, thanks.'

***

The next phone call was scheduled for four in the afternoon, almost a three-hour wait. Neither of the police officers wanted to relocate back to the police station. The cook, an eager woman from a nearby village, prepared lunch for everyone. Stan was sitting in one corner of the main room, anxious for action, wanting to grab hold of the person or persons responsible. Gerry Winters was also agitated. Dean Winters was worried that his wife was involved.

Mavis Winters spent her time talking to Clare. Tremayne rested in a comfortable chair, picked up a newspaper, and started to read it. Clare could see that it was a pretence.

At six o'clock, Mavis's phone rang. Only three people remained in the room: Clare, Tremayne, and Mavis. It did not need outbursts of anger or glaring eyes if Mavis and Clare were to deal with the call.

'I want to talk to Rachel,' Mavis said.

'She's fine,' a muffled voice replied.

'Male or female?' Tremayne mouthed.

'Male,' Mavis mouthed back. The phone was on speaker. Tremayne had heard the voice as well, but he needed confirmation from the two women.

'Do you have the money?'

'I do.'

'Very well. We will phone again.'

'My daughter?'

The phone line went dead. 'What are we to do?' Mavis said.

'He'll phone back within an hour. Whoever he is, he's not very experienced,' Tremayne said.

'Why do you say that?'

'He's too quick to demand the money; you're too quick to agree.'

Fifty-eight minutes, another phone call. 'The price is now two million.' No more was said before the call cut off.

'See what I told you,' Tremayne said.

'What about Rachel? The money's not important,' Mavis said.

'Stall them this time, ask to talk to Rachel. Unless you have proof that she's fine and well, then no deal.'

Another phone call, another attempt at tracing the location. 'They're moving around,' Clare whispered to Tremayne.

Mavis looked at the two police officers to be quiet. On the other end of her phone, the voice spoke. 'Have you informed the police?'

Mavis did not answer the question. 'I want to talk to my daughter.'

'That's not possible.'

'If you've harmed her?'

'We have not. The price is two million.' Yet again the phone line went dead.

Clare briefly went into the other room where the other members of the family were waiting, Bertie included. Cyril had also arrived.

Tremayne, frustrated with the kidnapper's procrastination, walked around the room; Clare remained impassive, sitting alongside Mavis. Clare's phone rang; it was a Skype call. Clare answered; on the other end, a nervous woman. 'They know you're there,' Rachel said. 'Tell Mum that I'm fine. They've not harmed me.' Another voice took over. 'We told her mother not to contact the police. We cannot deal with dishonest people.' The Skype call ended.

'It was Rachel,' Clare said. 'They know we're here.' Tremayne came over close to her; Mavis put her face in her hands in relief.

'How?' Tremayne said.

'If it's Archie Garrett, he would have assumed that we'd be somewhere around.'

'That's unlikely.'

'It's either Dean, or they've driven past the house in the last few hours.'

Clare left the room, went and found Dean. He was sitting with the other brothers and Bertie. 'Has anyone made a phone call recently?' she said, not directing her comment at anyone in particular.

'No one in here, Gerry said.'

'Dean?'

'Not me. My phone's in the other room.'

'Whoever it is, knows I'm here with Tremayne.'

'Rachel?' Stan Winters asked.

'I've spoken to her briefly.'

'Is she fine?'

'It was brief, and she sounded nervous, but she was coherent, a good sign.'

Clare had no intention of indulging in idle conversation with those not directly involved. She returned to Mavis and Tremayne. The cook had prepared sandwiches. Clare brought them back to the negotiating team.

Superintendent Moulton phoned; Tremayne's phone was on silent. He excused himself and went out through the back door of the house, lighting a cigarette.

'Yarwood's spoken to Rachel Winters,' Tremayne said.

'Do you need assistance?' Moulton asked.

'We don't know what we're looking for. It appears that they are in the area and they may have driven past the Winters' house. Apart from that, we've no idea what car they are driving. Random searches are not going to help.'

'Is the woman in danger?'

'Not sure. We know that Archie Garrett, if he's not angry, is not violent. That's the hope. Yarwood is with the mother. They'll deal with the negotiating, and now it's two million pounds.'

'Do you have the money?'

'One million. The other one will be here soon.'

'Get the woman back. The money's expendable.'

'We know that.'

Tremayne returned to Clare and Mavis. 'Any more?'

'Not yet,' Mavis said. 'She's going to be fine, isn't she?'

Tremayne could see that the woman wanted reassurance. 'Yes, she'll be fine,' he said, knowing that statistically Rachel's well-being was far from certain.

All three ate the sandwiches, supplemented with freshly-brewed coffee. It wasn't Tremayne's first hostage situation. Last time it had been an angry father denied visitation rights to his children. He had barricaded himself in his former wife's house, along with their two children. It had ended badly.

Chapter 24

Rachel sat in the back room of the old farmhouse. It was cold, and she was shivering. Her hands were tied together in front of her and secured to a wooden beam by a length of rope. She knew she could not escape. She also knew that she should be frightened, yet she remained remarkably calm. Rachel assumed it was delayed shock, or maybe it was her training in hostile situations, the dealing with grief, part of her work at Salisbury Hospital.

She had met the man once before when she was a lot younger. It had been at the wedding of her Uncle Dean. She vaguely remembered that he had not spoken much. The woman with him she knew well. Barbara Winters had given her some food and drink. 'Sorry about this, Rachel,' she had said.

Rachel could tell that she was not sorry for her, only for herself. Rachel knew some of the stories about what had happened to her uncle, yet had not been able to accept it fully. Although now, in that farmhouse, the two people, the brother and the sister, had a look about them that concerned her. The situation seemed unreal, the sort of thing that happened in the movies, not in real life. She had stopped her car when she had seen Barbara waving from the side of the road. At the time Barbara had been apologetic about what her brother had done to Dean. A trusting soul, Rachel had got out of her car, walked around and on to the pavement by Barbara's car. Unbeknown to her, Archie had been hiding in it. He had appeared behind Rachel, thrust a hessian sack over her head and tossed her into the back of the car, securing her hands with a cable tie.

Once inside, as the vehicle hurtled down the road, almost turning over at one stage, Barbara had spoken to her. 'Sorry for my brother. We're desperate, and you are our only hope.'

At the time, the woman had been conciliatory, but Rachel saw afterwards that the brother and sister vacillated between caring and malevolent. They had hit her once, would again if she tried to reason with them.

Rachel could tell that the relationship between the couple was unnatural, almost as if they were husband and wife. Archie, the elder of the siblings, caring for his sister's well-being, promising her that things would be better, they could go overseas, start their lives anew, just the two of them.

'Once your mother pays we will let you go,' Barbara said.

Archie Garrett busied himself in another room, Rachel could hear him. Whenever he approached her, she was careful about what she said. The man was unstable, spouting about the Lord's work, and what the two million pounds would do for them.

During her time at Salisbury Hospital Rachel had experienced her fair share of frightening people, but the two who held her captive took the biscuit.

She knew she was in serious trouble. A police car had moved fast down the road not more than a hundred yards away, its siren sounding. She had felt a quickening of the pulse, assuming it to be coming to her rescue, but it had passed by.

Archie came into the room where Rachel was held. He knelt down close to her. 'They've agreed. You'll soon be going home,' he said.

Rachel did not trust him. The man's expression revealed insincerity. 'Good,' she said, not wanting to say more, not knowing his reaction. She had remembered that the family had wanted to love Uncle Dean's wife, but it had not been able to. Even though she had been young, she could remember the woman's manner, her disparaging comments about her mother, Mavis. And then the years when her uncle had kept away, although he was only a thirty-minute drive away, and then it was her father, newly rich, who had made contact, taken his Ferrari around to show off to his brother.

The meeting had been acrimonious from her aunt's side, friendly from her uncle's, and then within less than twenty-four hours the car was totalled, written off in an accident with a lamppost, and now the wife was trying to be agreeable, almost obsequious. Rachel wanted to ask her why the change of heart.

Rachel looked around the room. It lacked any charm, just a basic farm cottage; the only acknowledgement of the twenty-first century was a solitary light bulb hanging up high, suspended from the ceiling by its electrical cable. It was night outside; the stars could be seen high in the sky. The sound of cars was not far away, the rustling of trees. From the other room came the voices of two people talking. She wanted to listen, to know what they planned to do with her, whether they intended to free her. Or would the two of them kill her, the same as they had killed her father? Was she to be secured to a sacred stone somewhere, offered up in a ceremony? How would it feel to have a knife thrust into her? Would it be painful, or would there be a shock? She realised that the situation was getting to her. She thought of happy times: her mother and her, not so much of her father or her brother.

And then the door in the other room slammed, and she heard the sound of her captors outside the farmhouse. She knew she had to seize the opportunity. Grabbing hold of the rope tied to the beam she pulled hard, the first time with no success, but at the second attempt it fell free. She moved over to a drawer, pulled it open. Her hands were still tied, no longer with cable ties but with rope. In the drawer, a knife. She wedged it in the top of the drawer, its serrated blade pointing upwards. Using her body to push the drawer in to clamp the knife, she secured it firmly enough. She began a sawing action, listening for those outside. They were now distant from the farmhouse, she was sure.

The rope sufficiently cut through, it released its grip on her wrists. She was free; she knew she had to make a run for it.

Opening the door on the other side of the room, she was quickly out of the cottage. She was running, the cars in the distance, their lights blazing, getting closer. She reached the gate to the road; she was shouting for one of the vehicles to stop, they were ignoring her. As she opened the gate to rush out into the road, a voice came from behind. 'No, you don't.'

She remembered the man grabbing her in a bearlike grip and dragging her back to the cottage. The rope, doubled up, cutting into her wrists, restricting the circulation to her hands. Expecting the man to laugh, and then seeing the belt.

'Don't. She's our hostage. If she's harmed, they'll not pay,' Barbara said.

And then the man's voice. She remembered that before the pain started. The belt cut her hard across the face, and then her buttocks, her breasts, her legs.

It was some time before she regained consciousness. She was lying on a bed, her feet secured to the metal frame, her hands tied in front of her, this time with a cable tie. Not that it mattered. She was in agony, initially unable to move. Barbara sat on one side of the bed, with a bowl of warm water. There was the smell of disinfectant. 'You shouldn't have got him angry,' she said.

'Do you intend to kill me?' Rachel asked.

'Of course not, but Archie's under a lot of pressure,' Barbara said. Rachel, weakened as she was, unable to move other than with care, could tell that the woman had had a lifetime of abuse and brainwashing.

Managing to lift herself from her prostrate position, putting two pillows behind her, Rachel sat up. She could see that the room, in comparison to where she had been before, was pleasant. The sheets on her bed were clean, and there were flowers in a vase on the dresser close to the window.

'Has this been your life?'

'With our father, and then with Archie.'

'And Dean?'

'I loved him. He treated me well, and we were happy.'

'You hated my family.'

'I came from hate, yet I loved Dean.'

'Do you still hate me?'

'Not you, but you are different. Please, you cannot understand. If I could be back with Dean, I would treat him differently.'

'Would you?'

'I would try.'

Rachel could see a dim spark of humanity in the woman. The door to the bedroom swung open, the face of Archie Garrett appeared. 'Sorry,' he said. 'You should not have tried to escape. We will have the money soon, and you will be free. Barbara will stay with you and make sure that you heal.' The door closed and the man left.

'He is like my father. We hated him, but he has left his legacy. Archie could kill in his anger, remember that. Don't try to escape again.'

It was clear to Rachel that she would not be capable of escape for several days, maybe for weeks. She ran her hands over her legs and arms, pushed in on her body. There appeared to be no broken bones.

'I'll get you some soup,' Barbara said. She left the room; Rachel leant back and fell asleep.

***

There was only one concern for Tremayne and Clare: the safe return of Rachel Winters. It had been nine days of on-again, off-again negotiations with her captors. A voiceprint comparison of the muffled voice and Archie Garrett's voice messaging on his mobile had confirmed the two people to be one and the same.

The money was ready, an agreement had been struck. Clare had been nominated as the person to deal with the handover of the ransom, a retrieval location for Rachel not yet determined.

Tremayne sensed a hesitancy in Archie Garrett, who knew full well that once Rachel had been handed over, then the full weight of the police forces across southern England would be mobilised. Dean paced through the house in Quidhampton, his primary concern for his wife. Mavis thought that there was no hope for him. Gerry disagreed, as he had been spending time with the man. Cyril was staying in Quidhampton for the time being, although Stan had transferred back to prison the day after the kidnapping.

Superintendent Moulton had tried his best, Tremayne knew that, but Stan Winters was a prisoner serving a jail sentence, and his continued freedom did not assist in his niece's rescue. Tremayne agreed to keep him updated on a daily basis.

Analysis of the phone calls from Archie Garrett had picked up the sound of a road close by, but none of the noises associated with a city location. It was agreed that it was somewhere in the country, although the birds chirping in the background had revealed nothing significant.

Clare and Tremayne were now based at Mavis's house, a couple of bedrooms set up for them. A neighbour had agreed to look after Clare's cats. The primary contact was Mavis's phone and now Clare's, as she had taken the lead role in the negotiations. Moulton had wanted to bring in a trained negotiator from London; Tremayne had resisted. Clare had met Barbara Winters and Archie Garrett; a professional would not have.

Tremayne knew he was putting on weight, the difference between snatched pub meals and a cook on hand keeping everyone fed.

The Bentley was outside and ready. It had been agreed that Clare would drive the car to the retrieval point; the money was to be deposited elsewhere. Clare had been adamant that no money would be handed over until Rachel was confirmed to be free and was inside the car. Archie had not liked the idea, which took up another day of negotiations.

Clare's phone rang. She was in the kitchen. She moved to the other room with Tremayne and Mavis.

'Is it?' Mavis whispered. Clare nodded her head.

'Sergeant Yarwood, the money is to be deposited in cash at a location in Southampton. I suggest you leave now.'

'And Rachel?'

'We will discuss that later.'

Tremayne looked over at Clare, gave her a clear sign to follow instructions. Clare walked out of the front door of the house and settled herself into the Bentley, her phone on hands-free, a location device fitted inside the car. She pulled out of the driveway and headed towards Southampton. There was an explicit instruction to all police vehicles to report if they saw the car, but not to hinder its progress.

Clare arrived in Southampton. Her mind was focussed on handing over the money, expendable as far as all were concerned, and taking Rachel back to her mother.

She headed for the dock area, as per the instruction received. Her phone rang. 'You will leave there and drive to Southsea. You can use the car's GPS to find the way.'

'I know the way,' Clare said. 'Is this going to continue?'

'It will until I am satisfied that you are alone.'

'We want Rachel, not you.'

It was twenty miles; the traffic was heavy. She arrived in Southsea on the Hampshire coast. She parked the car near the South Parade Pier. Her phone rang. 'Proceed to the corner of Nightingale Road and Kent Road.'

Clare followed instructions, saw a police car not far away, its number plate recognition technology picking up the Bentley. Clare knew that her phone's location, as well as the car's position, would be confirmed as one and the same. She could only imagine the situation at Mavis's house, the assembled family waiting for news. She knew that Tremayne would be smoking more than usual.

'You will see in front of you a rubbish bin. You will place the money in there and leave.'

'Rachel?'

'Until you remove that police car from the other side of the road, she will not be freed.'

Clare phoned Tremayne. 'Please keep all vehicles away from the area,' she said.

One phone call and the police car left.

'Now, put the money in the bin and leave.'

'Rachel?'

'She is here with me.'

'I need to talk to her.'

'Clare, I'm fine. Do what he says,' Rachel said in the background.

With the money placed where instructed, Clare waited. Five minutes later, an open-bed truck pulled up alongside the bin. A man got out of the driver's seat, picked up the bin and put it in the back. The truck then drove off. Clare noted the number, although she did not inform anyone of it.

'Good, I can see that you're following instructions.'

'Rachel?'

'You will drive to Buckler's Hard on the Beaulieu River.'

'That will take me nearly two hours,' Clare said. 'You have reneged on our agreement.'

'Not at all. I will wait for the truck to come to me. Once I have the money, you will have Rachel.'

Clare phoned Tremayne, told him of the situation. 'You've no option,' Tremayne said.

'What about Rachel?' Mavis asked.

'I've spoken to her,' Clare said.

'And?'

'She said she was fine. Let me carry on with what I'm doing.'

'We trust you, Clare.'

'Thanks.'

It was over thirty miles to Buckler's Hard, now a tourist attraction. In the past, it had been a busy shipbuilding community that had built ships for Horatio Nelson, the great naval hero of Trafalgar.

After an hour and twenty minutes, another phone call. 'I have the money. I will need another three hours.'

'This is not the agreement.'

'It is the only agreement if you want the young woman returned.'

'Is she unharmed?'

'She is well.'

'That's not what I asked.'

'She will be returned in one piece. Be thankful for that. And do not phone Detective Inspector Tremayne again. If your phone rings, check it is my number.'

'Your number keeps changing.'

'To stop you tracing it.'

'Then how will I know it is you?'

'The last three digits will be 346.'

Clare arrived at Buckler's Hard. It was late in the day, and the tourists had left. She found a café open and ordered two sandwiches and coffee. She had to admit the village was attractive. Her phone rang, it was Tremayne. She cancelled the phone call and sent an SMS instead.

No more contact until Rachel is free. Garrett's instructions.

Tremayne understood; Mavis did not.

After two more hours, Clare's phone rang. She checked the last three digits: 346. She pressed the answer button.

'At the top of the village, there is a park bench. Can you see it?'

'Yes.'

'Underneath the left-hand leg there is an envelope with a key. Inside you will find an address. Rachel Winters is there.'

Clare walked up to the bench, felt underneath the leg, found an envelope. She opened it and then phoned Tremayne. 'It's a five-minute walk from where I am.'

'We'll get down there as soon as possible.'

'Don't. We've played this his way so far. Let me get Rachel first.'

The road up to the farmhouse was not in good condition; it was quicker to walk, although Clare ran. At the farmhouse, rundown but still with a rustic charm, she found the main door. She inserted the key; it opened. She moved quickly through the house, checking the downstairs, then upstairs. In a bedroom at the top, she found Rachel, restrained, her mouth covered with tape. She was conscious and alive. Clare quickly removed the ropes securing her, and the tape from her mouth.

'Clare, thank you, thank you.'

Rachel had her arms around Clare; both women were in tears. Clare called Tremayne, barely able to operate the phone. 'I've got her.'

Rachel spoke to her mother who was hugging Tremayne. After five minutes, while everyone calmed down, Clare was able to talk to Rachel. 'What happened?'

'They left this morning. Barbara treated me well, especially after…'

'After what?'

'I tried to escape. Archie went mad, beat me the same way he had beaten Uncle Dean.'

'How are you now?'

'With you here, I'm fine.'

A police car from the local police station pulled up outside, as well as an ambulance. Clare spoke to them, informed them of the situation. She was taking Rachel back to her family home.

Chapter 25

Archie Garrett boarded the plane at Heathrow. He had made contacts over the years; a false passport and the necessary documentation were his. He knew that where he was going, life would be excellent, although without Barbara it would not be the same. He had given her enough to survive, and she had been guilty of no other crime than kidnapping. He knew that it would be Dean Winters who would care for her, whether she was in prison or not. The man was weak, whereas he, Archie Garrett, was not. He would never fly for British Airways again, never see England, but the one thing he regretted most of all was that he would never see his beloved sister, the only person who could understand what had happened when they were children.

Once Archie's plane had left, Barbara Winters phoned Tremayne. She was arrested the day after Rachel had returned to the family home.

***

Tremayne had not expected to hear from Barbara Winters unless it was as a result of the search for the woman, and there she was, on his phone. 'Archie's gone.'

'Gone where?'

'He's left the country. I'm willing to hand myself in.'

Not willing to take the risk, Tremayne phoned a local police station in London close to the address that the woman had given as her location. Fifteen minutes later, she was in their custody. Three hours later, she was in the back seat of Clare's car. Clare was driving, with Tremayne in the back handcuffed to Barbara Winters. 'I'll not cause you any trouble,' she had said.

Upon arrival at Bemerton Road, Dean Winters was waiting. He rushed up to his wife, threw his arms around her and kissed her. She turned away. 'I'm guilty of kidnapping Rachel.'

'I'll wait,' Dean said. Clare could see romance in the scene; Tremayne thought the man a whimpering fool.

Superintendent Moulton was delighted; a murderer in custody, waiting to be charged. Tremayne felt that the man was premature. It was clear that Barbara Winters had crimes to answer to, but homicide was still far from certain.

The scene at the Quidhampton home the previous day, when Clare had driven in with Rachel, had been jubilant. Tremayne was there, proud of his sergeant, not willing to show it other than to offer his congratulations for good policing, although wanting to give her a hug.

No such reluctance to show emotion inhibited Rachel's mother. She grabbed hold of her daughter who winced from the pain, her mother easing off, not letting her go. Once the initial tender moment was over, Mavis embraced Clare, even lifting her off the ground. 'Thank you for bringing my daughter back to me,' she said. 'Anything you want, just say the word.'

Clare wanted to say give me the Bentley. She knew she'd be back to driving a police issue car, nothing compared to the elegance of the car she had just been driving. Inside the house, Gerry and Cyril were pleased to see Rachel back, Dean was apologetic for his wife, and Bertie struggled to say anything.

A doctor was on hand to check Rachel out. 'I need a bath first,' she said. Mavis almost bounded up the stairs to run the water, Rachel sat downstairs. Tremayne wanted to ask questions but decided that could wait.

Tremayne phoned Stan and Fred Winters to update them; both men were appreciative of the call. A police commendation was due for Clare, too, for the manner in which she had dealt with the woman's rescue, a satisfactory outcome for all concerned.

Once Clare had released Rachel from the cottage, the local police established a crime scene. Jim Hughes and his crime scene investigators were dispatched to check out the cottage, reporting nothing untoward other than that three people had been there, their fingerprints all on record. A local shopkeeper remembered Archie Garrett when she was shown a photo.

***

Barbara Winters, after being formally charged with the kidnapping of Rachel Winters, had been taken to the interview room. Dean had wanted to employ a lawyer; Barbara had declined. And besides, she had no intention of denying the charge.

Outside the interview room, Dean waited. Inside, Tremayne and Clare sat on one side of the table; on the other, the charged woman.

Tremayne followed the procedure, informed Barbara Winters of her rights. Once that was over, the questioning began. 'Mrs Winters, you have been charged with the kidnapping and holding for ransom of Rachel Winters. Is there anything you want to say in your defence?'

'I am offering no defence. I'm guilty as charged.'

'Your brother, Archie Garrett, is no longer in the country, is that true?'

'I have already told you this.'

'Do you know where he has gone?'

'I do not know.'

'But you could have gone?'

'Yes.'

Clare looked at the woman, could only see someone oblivious to the seriousness of her situation. If she had been on drugs, the police sergeant would have said she was high.

'Why didn't you go?' Clare asked.

'I could not agree with what he did to Rachel.'

'Why?'

'My father had treated me that way.'

'And you were reliving it?'

'I liked Rachel. She was my friend, and I allowed her to be hurt.'

'And your brother?'

'He has become what our father was. I no longer want to be with him. I want to be with Dean.'

'You will go to jail.'

'Dean will wait,' Barbara Winters said.

'We have contacted Interpol, the overseas police agencies, to keep a watch out for your brother. We will find him in due course,' Tremayne said.

'You will not. He knows his way around the world.'

Tremayne knew that the woman was probably telling the truth, although two million soon goes, or one million five hundred thousand, as he had given his sister half a million at Heathrow. Once the man had exhausted his money staying hidden he would eventually tire of exile and would return.

'We need to know about Stonehenge. How and why you and your brother killed Alan Winters.'

'We did not kill him.'

'But you hated the man and what he represented.'

'I hated his family and the money he had stolen.'

'Gambling is perfectly legal in this country.'

'Not to my brother and myself.'

'Yet you are willing to accept two million pounds for returning Rachel?'

'It was only the money that Dean had signed over to Archie before…'

'Before we broke up your little tête-à-tête. Your brother nearly beat Dean to death for that money, and you say it was illegal money. Why did you want it when you would not accept the hundred thousand? Were you holding out in the hope of a bigger payout? Did you murder Alan Winters because you couldn't control him, assuming his wife would be more generous? I put it to you that you contrived a plan to take him up to Stonehenge, to point the blame away from you and your brother.'

'It's not true. We're innocent of his murder. That would be against God's law.'

'Isn't kidnapping?'

'Yes, but…'

'But what? Mrs Winters, you and your brother murdered Alan Winters. Who did you think to place the blame on? His wife, his children, his brothers? Mrs Winters, you and your brother killed Alan Winters solely for the sake of getting two million pounds. How do you plead?'

Clare thought that her senior had gone too far, but said nothing.

'We did not kill Alan Winters.'

'Then who did? Your brother has the anger, the ability to inflict violence, and you both had a motive. Why have you handed yourself in? Are you hoping to make a plea bargain?'

'We are innocent.'

'Then why take the two million? And don't give me that baloney that you were going to use the money for good.'

'That is what it was for. We had great plans.'

'And what happened? You and your brother saw the money, decided it was better in your pockets than in those of a starving child in a refugee camp, is that it?'

'No, yes. I'm confused,' Barbara Winters said.

'I suggest a ten-minute break,' Clare said. Tremayne took the hint.

'You were tough in there, guv,' Clare said once the two of them were outside the interview room.

'I need to break through. I need to know the truth.'

'And she's not giving it?'

'Not yet.'

'She could be telling the truth.'

'If it's not them, then who else could have killed Alan Winters?'

'Polly Bennett and Liz Maybury?'

'But why? Alan was the sugar daddy, not Mavis.'

'They've still achieved their aim.'

'Okay, what about the brothers? Alan's given them a hundred thousand each; they want more.'

'Stonehenge?'

'Concentrate on the murderer, not the location.'

The interview recommenced. Barbara Winters looked composed. 'I wish to make a statement.'

'Very well,' Tremayne's reply.

'I am genuinely sorry for what was inflicted on Rachel Winters. My brother, Archie, as a result of what we both suffered as children, holds sway over my life. For many years, he was not around, or at least not on a regular basis, as he was based overseas. My marriage with Dean was troubled, although I still loved him, even if I could not like his family. Rachel, I realise in the time that I spent with her in that farmhouse, is not the same as the other Winters. She is a lovely woman, who I allowed to be beaten by Archie.

'Archie, who suffered more than me as a child, has become what our father was. A man who could be charming, yet held inside him dark secrets and dark thoughts. I instructed Dean to refuse the one hundred thousand pounds initially offered; I saw it as the proceeds of gambling. Dean agreed with me, and besides, we were financially sound. The money was not vital.

'Archie returned to our lives. He became aware of the two million. He said it would be used for good, but now I know that was not the case.

'After Rachel's release, I drove Archie to Heathrow. He boarded a plane and left. There was a ticket for me in a false name; I declined the offer. I am certain that I will not hear from him again. I spent several hours deliberating my future before phoning Detective Inspector Tremayne. My brother was overseas at the time of Alan Winters' death. Neither he nor I were involved, although it is clear that we are the most likely suspects. Regardless of that fact, we are innocent. I will admit my guilt in the kidnapping of Rachel Winters; that is my only crime.'

Clare could tell that the woman had told the truth. She looked at Tremayne.

'Mrs Winters, we will conclude this interview. You will be remanded in custody pending a trial,' Tremayne said.

Outside in the hallway, Dean Winters approached the two police officers. 'My wife?'

'She is in custody,' Clare said.

'Can I see her?'

'It will be arranged.'

Stepping out of the building while Tremayne lit a cigarette, Clare asked him for his evaluation. 'They did not kill Alan Winters,' he said.

'No evidence?'

'The woman is penitent. She told the truth.'

'The family?'

'Who else? The Winters family's problems are not over yet. Two of them are guilty, and the man's death has given them sufficient motive.'

'Who's the most likely?'

'Mavis.'

Chapter 26

Tremayne knew of one way to bring the investigation to a conclusion. He'd used it before; it was brutal and people's emotions would be laid raw. Before he arranged it, he needed to talk to Mavis. He knew she was the prime suspect now, in that she had received the lion's share of the money, and if she were guilty, she would have had an accomplice.

Tremayne phoned Jim Hughes, the CSE. 'Two people at Stonehenge?' he asked.

'Two to carry the body to the Altar Stone, one to inflict the fatal wound,' Hughes's reply.

'Any possibility of cult behaviour, ritual?'

'You've read my report.'

'I'm just running ideas past you. I need to raise the heat to wrap up this case.'

'Alan Winters' death has a sense of the macabre, nothing more.'

'Someone with a dark humour?'

'Maybe. The man was the golden goose, hardly a reason to kill him though.'

'Unless others gained from his death.'

'Did some?'

'They did, but they could not have been sure beforehand.'

'The two million for each of his brothers could have been known.'

Tremayne ended the phone call, sat back in his chair. It was early in the afternoon. Clare was busy typing up a report.

'Tremayne, is that all you've got to do?' Moulton said as he walked in the door.

'What do you think I'm doing?'

'Sleeping by the look of it.'

'I'm thinking through the case, trying to get an angle on who would gain from the man's death, and why.'

'I'll grant that you and your sergeant handled the kidnapping of Rachel Winters well enough, but this murder enquiry has dragged on too long. I need it wrapped up within five days.'

'Why the deadline?'

'The usual.'

'I'll fight you on that.'

'That's why I'm letting you know. I don't want a battle on my hands. If you wrap this up, I'll make sure you're not on the list.'

'Magnanimous of you, sir.'

'Not magnanimous, just being a realist. I've got a big enough fight arguing to secure enough money to make Bemerton Road viable. I just don't want you giving me aggravation as well.'

'It won't be the same, you not dropping in every five minutes with your latest retirement offer' Tremayne said.

'That's as maybe. Five days and then someone needs to be charged with the murder of Alan Winters.'

'We'll do our best,' Tremayne said as Moulton left.

Clare came into Tremayne's office. 'Friendly?' she said.

'We've got five days.'

'Mavis?'

'She's the only one who knew what would happen on her husband's death.'

'But you don't believe it was her?'

'I don't want to.'

'You can't let personal feelings interfere with this.'

'I'll do my duty, the same as you. You're friendly with the woman as well.'

'I admire her. She's a thoroughly decent human being. You could have done worse than her, guv.'

'Maybe,' Tremayne said.

***

Tremayne and Clare found Mavis at the house in Quidhampton. She was fussing over Rachel. Both of the women gave Clare a hug first and then Tremayne. He was a little embarrassed by the show of affection.

'How are you, Rachel?' Clare asked.

'I'm fine, thanks to you.'

'Any long-lasting effects?'

'Am I mentally scarred, is that what you are asking?'

'At least you can talk about it. And you're a strong-minded individual. Dean, unfortunately, is not,' Clare said.

'He's determined to make sure she has the best legal team on her side.'

'How do you feel about it?'

'I'm down nearly two million pounds as a result of her, what do you think?'

'I think you'll support Dean with whatever he wants.'

'You're right, I suppose.'

'Our visit is not social,' Tremayne said. He had taken a seat in the kitchen, the cook busy at the other end preparing the evening meal.

'You'll stay?' Mavis asked.

'You may not want us to,' Clare said.

'You'd better explain.'

Tremayne stood up, took the mug of coffee that the cook thrust into his hand. 'Archie Garrett and Barbara Winters did not murder Alan,' he said.

'Then who did?' Rachel asked.

'Someone in this family.'

'One of us?' Mavis said.

'There is no proof against Garrett and Dean's wife. Archie Garrett's alibi holds up, and Barbara could not have committed the murder on her own.'

'But she could have with Dean?'

'It's a possibility. Mavis, you've given two million pounds to each of the brothers?'

'That's been done, but you've known that for some time.'

'Did Alan's brothers know that you would do that if you had financial control.'

'Gerry did.'

'You had discussed the possibility with him?'

'Not in detail, but we spent a lot of time together. If I went anywhere, he'd invariably drive.'

'And you used to speak with him.'

'Just chatting mainly.'

'But he was concerned about the money that was being wasted?'

'He enjoyed spending the money, and he had no problems getting drunk with Alan, taking on his women.'

'Polly Bennett and Liz Maybury?'

'Yes.'

'Where is Bertie?'

'You don't suspect him? Mavis said. Clare could see the concern on the woman's face.

'Not entirely, but I need everyone here. We need to wrap this up.'

'It will destroy Mum,' Rachel said.

'It is not the victim who suffers in a murder, it is those who are left, and I must do my duty,' Tremayne said.

'That's why we liked you all those years ago,' Mavis said.

'You may not like me after tonight.'

'We will.'

'I want Polly and Liz here as well.'

'If it is required.'

'It is. And Bertie, what's his condition?'

'Asleep.'

'Drugs?'

'He'll be fine. When do you want everyone here?'

'One hour. That's Cyril, Gerry, and Dean as well.'

'They may not all come,' Rachel said. 'They may be busy.'

'They'll be here. I've already pre-warned Bemerton Road. Either we meet here or at the police station. We know where everyone is and they will all be picked up in a police car and brought here. Yarwood, make the phone call.'

***

It was closer to ninety minutes before everyone was in the house. Polly Bennet and Liz Maybury sat in one corner; Mavis had acknowledged their presence, a courtesy hello. On the other side of the main living room were Cyril, better dressed than usual, Gerry, surprised to see the two women in the house, and Dean, quiet, his head down.

Rachel, dressed for the occasion, instead of the dressing gown she had been wearing earlier, sat next to Clare. Mavis stood in one corner.

'Thanks for coming,' Tremayne said. 'Let me give you all a rundown of the investigation so far.'

'We know what happened,' Bertie said. Clare could see that he had been drinking.

'I need to remind everyone that this is a police investigation into the murder of Alan Winters. If I repeat myself, stating what is already known, then I will. Is that understood?' Tremayne said, directing his gaze at Bertie.

'I suppose so, but I've got to go out in thirty minutes.'

'No one is leaving this house until I've concluded. It's either here or down Bemerton Road Police Station.'

'We understand,' Mavis said.

'Very well. We know that Archie Garrett was not involved in Alan's murder. Not because he would not be capable, but his alibi is watertight. During the hours when the murder was committed, he was at thirty-five thousand feet.'

'Barbara?' Dean said.

'Not on her own, which would mean that you were involved. Were you?'

'I'd not kill my own brother.'

'But one of his brothers did.'

Cyril stood up. 'Not me, not my own brother.' Gerry felt the need to press his innocence as well.

'Don't look at me,' Bertie said.

Tremayne ignored the previous comment. 'The motive is money; the significance of Stonehenge is unclear.'

'Get to the point,' Gerry Winters said. He was trying to avoid looking at Polly and Liz, not successfully.

'Alan, for all his generosity, did not know how to handle the sixty-eight million pounds that he had won. It's not unusual for people with no experience of vast amounts of money to lose it within a short period of time. If Alan had continued the way he was, the money would have all gone in five to ten years. At that time, the Winters family would be back living in a council house and scratching by on a meagre wage. Some of you would be concerned about that; others would not.'

'We'd all be upset if there was no money,' Cyril said.

'The issue is not whether you would be concerned in five to ten years. The issue is whether you understood the situation and were willing to do something about it before that time.'

'What do you mean?'

'Mavis is clearly more financially competent than Alan. With her, the family fortune is safe. All of you would recognise that fact. Since she has gained control of the money, she has given each of the brothers two million pounds, something that Alan had not. The most he had given was one hundred thousand each, on Mavis's urging. As far as Alan was concerned, he'd won the money fair and square; it was up to him who he gave it to.'

'Why are we here?' Polly Bennett asked.

'I'm coming to that,' Tremayne said. 'Mavis had told Gerry that she would give a substantial amount of money to each of the brothers. He probably told Cyril, possibly Stan. Stan, as we know, is in prison so he could not have been involved in the murder, as is the case with Fred. Cyril is too laid back, similar to Alan. He'd wait until the money ran out before complaining, and he was quite happy to live in his council house as long as he had sufficient money to live on. Dean was in Southampton under Barbara's control. Which means there are two possibilities. It was either Dean and Barbara who killed Alan, or else it was Gerry and one other.'

Dean was quick to protest his innocence; Gerry was not.

'Which of you two killed Alan Winters?' Tremayne asked.

'I didn't,' Dean said. 'Barbara may have had her faults, but murder was not one of them.'

'Yet she allowed her brother to beat you, almost killed you, and then there is what happened to Rachel.'

'The woman was kind,' Rachel said.

'Maybe she was, but she does what her brother tells her. Maybe Dean knew about the possibility of the two million, told his wife, who then told her brother. Archie could have been the driving force up at Stonehenge, Dean doing what he was told, but there's another complication.'

'And what is it?' Mavis asked.

'The reason Polly and Liz are here,' Tremayne said.

'What have we got to do with this?' Liz Maybury said.

'You were screwing him, you and Polly,' Mavis said. Up till then, she had been polite to the women. Tremayne was pleased. Everyone was starting to get a little tense.

Tremayne continued. 'On the night of the murder, Alan was with Polly and Liz. Outside, according to the two women, was the Bentley. Who was in that car? It would normally be Gerry.'

'Not that night. Alan was driving the car.'

'That's the first time that anyone's admitted to that, and why didn't Alan tell the women that he was driving? And how did the three get to their place?'

'I drove them, and then I left the car and took a taxi home.'

'And now you are sleeping with Polly and Liz?'

'You know that, and so what?'

'The two women had not been responsive to you when you had no money, but once Alan was dead, you were in their bed. Is that correct?'

'Not for some time.'

'Not until you told them about the two million. And even before you had the money, they were sleeping with you. Let me evaluate Polly and Liz.'

Clare looked over at the two women. 'DI Tremayne will not be diplomatic. Please say nothing,' she said.

'Thanks, Yarwood. Polly Bennett and Liz Maybury are ambitious women. They are not afraid of hard work, as can be seen by the furniture store that they convinced Alan to buy for them. He did not, however, give them a clear title. They knew this, and it's possible he was tired of them. Both of the women are bisexual by their own admission. They are willing to use their bodies to get what they want, and Alan was the vessel through which they channelled their efforts. They are also intelligent and able to formulate the way forward. They could see that Alan was a hopeless cause, whereas Gerry was not, and if he had two million, then they would have had no trouble transferring their affections to him. Also, he was able to convince Mavis, or she had figured it out, that the furniture store remained a significant asset, and that it would be better to let the two women stay there until the business could be sold. After the altercation between Liz and Mavis, the relationship between Mavis and the two women has been tenuous but workable.'

'It's purely business,' Mavis said.

'Cyril, I'm discounting you from our enquiry,' Tremayne said.

'Thank you.'

'Don't thank me. It's only because you have no drive and no ambition. It's hardly a ringing endorsement. Dean, you were not involved. Not because Archie would not have been capable, but he wasn't there, and his violence comes from anger. It needed a clear head to take Alan up to Stonehenge, someone with the ability to think ahead. Stonehenge was a diversion in that it would shift the blame onto other individuals who had been wronged by Alan, who had failed to give them money when they had asked. It needed Polly and Liz to set it up.'

'We did not kill him,' Liz said. She was on her feet and ready to come forward at Tremayne. Clare interceded and put her back in her seat, roughly pushing on the woman's shoulder.

'Gerry Winters,' Tremayne said, 'you'll be taken to Bemerton Road Police Station for further questioning, as will Polly Bennett and Liz Maybury. We will find a case against you and the two women for the murder of Alan Winters, your brother.'

'It was Polly's idea,' Liz said.

'You bitch,' Polly said. 'You thought it up, but it was me with Gerry at Stonehenge. And I'm not taking the blame for killing him, that was Gerry.'

'Will you sign a statement to that effect.'

'Yes.'

'You two bitches,' Gerry said. 'If only you had kept quiet. Couldn't you see what Tremayne was trying to do? He had no proof.'

'Gerry, why?' Mavis asked.

'You don't get it, do you? I saw how he treated you; the money he wasted. Someone needed to do something, and you would not have killed him. It was up to me to save the family.'

'At what cost?'

Clare went and sat down next to Rachel, who was in tears. She put her arm around the young woman. Cyril sat still, stunned by the revelation; Dean looked down at the floor. Polly Bennett and Liz Maybury said nothing, both sitting apart.

'Yarwood, ask the two uniforms to come in,' Tremayne said.

Gerry attempted to make a run for it; he had the keys to the Bentley. Outside, the driveway was blocked by a police car. A brief tussle, the handcuffs applied, and he was driven to Bemerton Road. Polly Bennett and Liz Maybury, handcuffed by the two uniforms who had come into the house, were led away.

'I'm sorry about this, Mavis,' Tremayne said.

'It's not your fault. It's the damn money.'

'Maybe Alan wasn't so lucky after all.'

'There was no luck there. It cursed our life, I know that now.'

The End.

Printed in Great Britain
by Amazon